THE COMEDIES OF ARISTOPHANES: VOL. 11

WEALTH

edited with translation and commentary by

ALAN H. SOMMERSTEIN

Aris & Phillips Ltd – Warminster – England

ISBNs
085668 738 3   clothbound
085668 739 1   limpbound

British Library Cataloguing-in-Publication Data
A catalogue record of this book is available from the British Library

Printed and published in England by Aris & Phillips Ltd, Warminster, Wiltshire BA12 8PQ

To the memory of my father

Theophil Sommerstein

1909–1990

Contents

Preface

It had been intended that this should be the final volume of *The Comedies of Aristophanes*, but the consolidated indexes, which it was to have included, have proved to be so extensive that it has been thought better to reserve them for an additional index volume, which is expected to appear in 2002. The present volume does, however, contain Addenda and Corrigenda to the ten previous volumes, including bibliographical updates; full bibliographies are provided for *Acharnians, Knights, Clouds* and *Wasps*, since none appeared in the original volumes. It has not been possible to take systematic account of material appearing later than September 2000, owing mainly to the determination of what is misleadingly called the Department *for* Education and Employment that the scholars and scientists of the United Kingdom shall spend most of their working hours demonstrating to the Department's agents, with massive documentation, how well they are doing their job, regardless of how little time this leaves them for actually doing it.

Eighteen years ago, in a review of my *Knights* volume, the late David Lewis was kind enough to write that "our blessings go with S[ommerstein] on the long road to *Wealth*". Having reached the end of that road (even if the car is not yet quite parked), I must again express my heartfelt thanks to the many who have helped me on my journey, and above all, as I did at the outset, to the five without whom it would never have begun – David Barrett, Betty Radice, George Goold, Eric Handley and John Aris – three of whom, alas, are not here to see the end, to Adrian Phillips who has produced volume after volume with remarkable celerity, increasing sophistication, and unfailing solicitude, and to my family, especially my wife Rebecca, for their patience, understanding and love over so many years.

But there are also two others who must not be forgotten: two men who both lived through tragic times and both constantly contrived to see, and help others to see, the mirthful side of a situation whenever that was humanly possible. To Aristophanes himself, of course, these volumes owe everything. To my father, whose life was a model of principle and selflessness but also of understanding, sympathy and humour, I owe more than I can put into words, but in particular that taste for the comic in life and language that drew me to the appreciation and the study of Aristophanes in the first place. Let this volume, which completes my exegesis of the surviving work of the one, be my tribute to the memory of the other.

ALAN H. SOMMERSTEIN
Nottingham, April 2001

References and Abbreviations

(A) Collections of Fragments

All citations of fragments of Greek authors (other than comic dramatists) made in this volume either are from one of the collections in the following list or else are accompanied by the abbreviated title of the edition cited or by the name(s) or initial(s) of the editor(s); fuller particulars will be found in list (C) below if there might otherwise be difficulty in identifying the edition. If no editor or edition is designated and the author is not listed here, it may be assumed that the author is an Attic comic dramatist and the citation is from *PCG* (see (C) below).

Aelian	R. Hercher, *Claudii Aeliani De Natura Animalium Libri XVII, Varia Historia, Epistulae, Fragmenta* [etc.] (Leipzig, 1864-6).
Aeschylus	S.L. Radt, *TrGF* iii (Göttingen, 1985).
Alcaeus	D.A. Campbell, *Greek Lyric I* (Cambridge MA, 1982).
Antiphon	T. Thalheim, *Antiphon: Orationes et Fragmenta* (Leipzig, 1914).
Archilochus	M.L. West, *Iambi et Elegi Graeci*[2] i (Oxford, 1989).
Astydamas, Chaeremon, Critias	B. Snell, *TrGF* i (Göttingen, 1971).
Dicaearchus	F. Wehrli, *Die Schule des Aristoteles* i (Basle, 1944).
Epicharmus	G. Kaibel, *Comicorum Graecorum Fragmenta* i.1: *Doriensium comoedia, mimi, phlyaces* (Berlin, 1899).
Euripides	A. Nauck, *Tragicorum Graecorum Fragmenta*[2] (Leipzig, 1889).
Hesiod	R. Merkelbach and M.L. West, *Fragmenta Hesiodea* (Oxford, 1967).
Hipponax	M.L. West, *Iambi et Elegi Graeci*[2] i (Oxford, 1989).
Hypereides	F.G. Kenyon, *Hyperidis Orationes et Fragmenta* (Oxford, 1906).
Lysias	T. Thalheim, *Lysiae Orationes* (Leipzig, 1901).
Orphica	O. Kern ed. *Orphicorum Fragmenta* (Berlin, 1922).
Sappho	D.A. Campbell, *Greek Lyric I* (Cambridge MA, 1982).
Semonides, Solon	M.L. West, *Iambi et Elegi Graeci*[2] ii (Oxford, 1992).
Sophocles	S.L. Radt, *TrGF* iv[2] (Göttingen, 1999).
Tyrtaeus	M.L. West, *Iambi et Elegi Graeci*[2] ii (Oxford, 1992).

(B) Abbreviations: Ancient Authors and Works

Ach.	*Acharnians.*
Aen.	*Aeneid* (Virgil).
Aen.Tact.	Aeneas Tacticus.

Aesch.	Aeschylus.
Ag.	*Agamemnon* (Aeschylus).
Airs	*Airs, Waters, Places* (Hippocratic treatise).
Aj.	*Ajax* (Sophocles).
Alc.	*Alcestis* (Euripides) or *Alcibiades* (Plutarch).
Alc. I	*Alcibiades I* (Plato).
Alex.	*Alexipharmaca* (Nicander) or *Alexander* (Lucian).
Amph.	*Amphitruo* (Plautus).
Anab.	*Anabasis* (Xenophon or Arrian).
Andoc.	Andocides.
Andr.	*Andromache* (Euripides).
Anecd.Bachm.	*Anecdota Graeca e codd. manuscriptis bibliothecae regiae Parisinae* ed. L. Bachmann (Leipzig, 1828-9).
Anecd.Bekk.	*Anecdota Graeca* ed. I. Bekker (Berlin, 1814-21).
Anecd.Oxon.	*Anecdota Graeca e codd. manuscriptis bibliothecarum Oxoniensium* ed. J.A. Cramer (Oxford, 1835-7).
Ant.	Antiphon.
Ant.	*Antigone* (Sophocles).
AP	*Ars Poetica* (Horace) or *Anthologia Palatina*..
ap.	*apud* (= in the text of).
Apol.	*Apology* (Plato).
Apoll.	Apollodorus.
Ap.Rh.	Apollonius Rhodius.
Ar.	Aristophanes.
Archil.	Archilochus.
Arist.	Aristotle.
Arist.	*Aristeides* (Plutarch).
Arr.	Arrian.
Asin.	*Asinaria* (Plautus).
Ath.	Athenaeus.
Ath.	*Against Athenogenes* (Hypereides).
Ath.Pol.	*Athenaion Politeia* (pseudo-Xenophon or Aristotle).
Ba.	*Bacchae* (Euripides).
Bibl.	*Bibliotheca* (pseudo-Apollodorus).
Catast.	*Catasterismi* (ascribed to Eratosthenes).
Char.	*Characters* (Theophrastus).
Charm.	*Charmides* (Plato).
Cho.	*Choephoroi* (Aeschylus).
Cic.	Cicero.
Clem.Alex.	Clement of Alexandria.
com.	comic dramatist.
com.adesp.	*comica adespota* (anonymous fragments of comedy, cited from *PCG* viii).
Crat.	*Cratylus* (Plato).
Cycl.	*Cyclops* (Euripides).
Cyr.	*Cyropaedia* (Xenophon).

Dein.	Deinarchus.
Dem.	Demosthenes.
Dem.	*Demosthenes* (Plutarch).
Demetr.	*Demetrius* (Plutarch).
D.H.	Dionysius of Halicarnassus.
Diosc.	Dioscorides.
D.L.	Diogenes Laertius.
D.S.	Diodorus Siculus.
Dysk.	*Dyskolos* (Menander).
Eccl.	*Ecclesiazusae.*
El.	*Electra* (Sophocles or Euripides).
EN	*Ethica Nicomachea* (Aristotle).
Ep.	*Epistulae* (Alciphron).
Epich.	Epicharmus.
Epid.	*Epidemiae* (Hippocratic treatise).
Epitr.	*Epitrepontes* (Menander).
Et.Mag.	*Etymologicum Magnum.*
Eum.	*Eumenides* (Aeschylus).
Eur.	Euripides.
Fab.	*Fabulae* (Hyginus).
fr(r).	fragment(s).
fr. dub.	fragment doubtfully ascribed.
Gorg.	*Gorgias* (Plato).
Greg. Cypr.	Gregory of Cyprus (in *CPG*).
HA	*Historia Animalium* (Aristotle).
Harpocr.	Harpocration.
Hdt.	Herodotus.
Hec.	*Hecuba* (Euripides).
Hel.	*Helen* (Euripides).
Hell.	*Hellenica* (Xenophon).
Hell.Oxy.	*Hellenica Oxyrhynchia.*
Heracl.	*Heracleidae* (Euripides).
Hes.	Hesiod.
HF	*Hercules Furens (The Madness of Heracles)* (Euripides).
h.Hom.	*Homeric Hymn.*
Ap.	... *to Apollo.*
Dem.	... *to Demeter.*
Herm.	... *to Hermes.*
Hipp.	*Hippolytus* (Euripides).
HP	*Historia Plantarum* (Theophrastus).
HT	*Heauton Timorumenos* (Terence).
Hippocr.	Hippocratic treatises.
Hyp.	Hypereides.
IA	*Iphigeneia at Aulis* (Euripides).

Imag.	*Imagines* (Philostratus[1]).
Inc.An.	*De Incessu Animalium* (Aristotle).
Isoc.	Isocrates.
Isthm.	*Isthmians* (Pindar).
IT	*Iphigeneia in Tauris* (Euripides).
Jul.	*Divus Iulius* (Suetonius).
Lex.Vind.	*Lexicon Vindobonense.*
Luc.	Lucian.
Lyc.	Lycurgus.
Lyc.	*For Lycophron* (Hypereides).
Lyr. Alex. Adesp.	*Lyrica Alexandrina Adespota.*
Lys.	Lysias.
Lys.	*Lysistrata* (Aristophanes) or *Lysis* (Plato) or *Lysias* (Dionysius of Halicarnassus) or *Lysander* (Plutarch).
Med.	*Medea* (Euripides).
Mem.	*Memorabilia* (Xenophon).
Men.	Menander[2].
Menex.	*Menexenus* (Plato).
Met.	*Metaphysics* (Aristotle) or *Metamorphoses* (Ovid).
Mir.	*Mirabilia* (ascribed to Aristotle).
Mis.	*Misoumenos* (Menander).
Mor.	*Moralia* (Plutarch).
Mul.	*Women's Conditions (Muliebria / Gynaikeia)* (Hippocratic treatise).
NA	*De Natura Animalium* (Aelian).
Nem.	*Nemeans* (Pindar).
NH	*Naturalis Historia* (Pliny the Elder).
Nic.	Nicander.
Nic.	*Nicias* (Plutarch).
OC	*Oedipus at Colonus* (Sophocles).
Oec.	*Oeconomicus* (Xenophon).
Olymp.	*Olympians* (Pindar).
Or.	*Orestes* (Euripides) or *Orationes* (Libanius).
OT	*Oedipus Tyrannus* (Sophocles).
Ov.	Ovid.
Paus.	Pausanias.
Per.	*Pericles* (Plutarch).
Perik.	*Perikeiromene* (Menander).
Pers.	*Persians* (Aeschylus).
Phd.	*Phaedo* (Plato).

---

1   There exist two works of this title, ascribed to two authors named Philostratus; unless otherwise specified, references are to the *elder* Philostratus.

2   Where a fragment of a named play of Menander is cited in the form "Men. *Thph.* F 1.15", the citation is from F.H. Sandbach, *Menandri Reliquiae Selectae*[2] (Oxford, 1990), unless otherwise stated.

Phdr.	*Phaedrus* (Plato).
Pherecr.	Pherecrates.
Phil.	*Philoctetes* (Sophocles).
Phoen.	*Phoenician Maidens* (Euripides).
Phryn.	Phrynichus.
Pind.	Pindar.
Pl.	Plato.
Plaut.	Plautus.
Plin.	Pliny the Elder.
Plut.	Plutarch.
Poet.	*Poetics* (Aristotle).
Pol.	*Politics* (Aristotle).
Polit.	*Politicus* (Plato).
Probl.	*Problems* (ascribed to Aristotle).
Prom.	*Prometheus Bound* (ascribed to Aeschylus).
Prot.	*Protagoras* (Plato).
Protr.	*Protrepticus* (Clement of Alexandria).
Pyth.	*Pythians* (Pindar).
Rep.	*Republic* (Plato).
Rh.	*Rhesus* (ascribed to Euripides).
Rhet.	*Rhetoric* (Aristotle).
Sam.	*Samia* (Menander).
schol.	scholium or scholia (ancient and medieval commentaries).
SHA	*Scriptores Historiae Augustae.*
Sik.	*Sikyonios (-oi)* (Menander).
Sol.	*Solon* (Plutarch).
Soph.	Sophocles.
Suet.	Suetonius.
Supp.	*Suppliants* (Aeschylus or Euripides).
Symp.	*Symposium* (Plato or Xenophon).
TD	*Tusculanae Disputationes* (Cicero).
Ter.	Terence.
test.	testimonium.
Theaet.	*Theaetetus* (Plato).
Theocr.	Theocritus.
Thes.	*Theseus* (Plutarch).
Thesm.	*Thesmophoriazusae.*
Thg.	*Theogony* (Hesiod).
Thph.	*Theophoroumene* (Menander).
Thphr.	Theophrastus.
Thom. *Ecl.*	Thomas Magister, *Eclogae.*
Thuc.	Thucydides.
Tim.	*Timaeus* (Plato) or *Timotheus* (Cornelius Nepos).
Top.	*Topica* (Aristotle).
Trach.	*Trachiniae* (Sophocles).

trag. adesp.	*tragica adespota* (anonymous fragments of tragedy, cited from *TrGF* ii).
Tro.	*Troades* (Euripides).
VH	*Varia Historia* (Aelian).
Virg.	Virgil.
Works	*Works and Days* (Hesiod).
Xen.	Xenophon.
[*author*]	(used to designate works traditionally but wrongly ascribed to the author)

(C) Abbreviations: Modern Authors and Publications

AA	*Archäologischer Anzeiger.*
AAH	*Acta Antiqua Academiae Scientiarum Hungaricae*
ABSA	*Annual of the British School at Athens.*
AC	*L'Antiquité Classique.*
AD	*Arkhaiologikon Deltion.*
AE	*Arkhaiologike Ephemeris.*
Agora xv	B.D. Meritt and J.S. Traill, *The Athenian Agora xv: The Athenian Councillors* (Princeton, 1974).
Agora xvi	A.G. Woodhead, *The Athenian Agora xvi: Inscriptions: The Decrees* (Princeton, 1997).
AION	*Annali dell'Istituto Universitario Orientale di Napoli.*
AJA	*American Journal of Archaeology.*
AJAH	*American Journal of Ancient History.*
AJP	*American Journal of Philology.*
APF	*Archiv für Papyrusforschung und verwandte Gebiete.*
Arnott	W.G. Arnott, *Menander* (Cambridge MA / London, 1979-2000).
ARV^2	J.D. Beazley, *Attic Red-Figure Vase-Painters*^{2} (Oxford, 1963).
Austin	C.F.L. Austin, *Nova Fragmenta Euripidea in Papyris Reperta* (Berlin, 1968).
BCH	*Bulletin de Correspondance Hellénique.*
Bernabé	A. Bernabé, *Poetarum Epicorum Graecorum Testimonia et Fragmenta. Pars I* (Leipzig, 1987).
BICS	*Bulletin of the Institute of Classical Studies, University of London.*
BMCR	*Bryn Mawr Classical Review.*
Burkert	W. Burkert, *Greek Religion: Archaic and Classical* tr. J. Raffan (Oxford, 1985).
CA	*Classical Antiquity.*
CAH	*Cambridge Ancient History.*
CCL	C. Collard, M. Cropp and K.H. Lee, *Euripides: Selected Fragmentary Plays I* (Warminster, 1995).
CFC(:egi)	*Cuadernos de Filología Clásica(: estudios griegos y indoeuropeos).*
CGITA	*Cahiers du Groupe Interdisciplinaire du Théâtre Antique.*

CIL	*Corpus Inscriptionum Latinarum.*
CJ	*Classical Journal.*
C&M	*Classica et Mediaevalia.*
CP	*Classical Philology.*
CPG	E.L. von Leutsch and F.G. Schneidewin, *Corpus Paroemiographorum Graecorum* (Göttingen, 1839-51).
CQ	*Classical Quarterly.*
CR	*Classical Review.*
Csapo & Slater	E.G. Csapo and W.J. Slater, *The Context of Ancient Drama* (Ann Arbor, 1994).
Davidson	J.N. Davidson, *Courtesans and Fishcakes: The Consuming Passions of Classical Athens* (London, 1997).
Davies	M. Davies, *Epicorum Graecorum Fragmenta* (Göttingen, 1988) .
Defix.	R. Wuensch, *Defixionum Tabellae in Attica regione repertae* = *IG* iii, *pars iii* (Berlin, 1897).
Denniston	J.D. Denniston, *The Greek Particles*[2] (Oxford, 1954).
Deubner	L. Deubner, *Attische Feste* (Berlin, 1932).
D-K	H. Diels, *Die Fragmente der Vorsokratiker* (rev. W. Kranz) (Berlin, 1951-2).
Dover *AC*	K.J. Dover, *Aristophanic Comedy* (Berkeley, 1972).
Dover *GPM*	K.J. Dover, *Greek Popular Morality in the Time of Plato and Aristotle* (Oxford, 1974).
E&E	E.J. and L. Edelstein, *Asclepius* (Baltimore, 1945).
EH	*Entretiens sur l'antiquité classique* (Fondation Hardt, Geneva).
EMC	*Échos du Monde Classique / Classical Views.*
EMI	L.R. LiDonnici, *The Epidaurian Miracle Inscriptions* (Atlanta, 1995).
FGrH	F. Jacoby et al., *Die Fragmente der griechischen Historiker* (Berlin/Leiden, 1923-).
GDI	H. Collitz et al., *Sammlung der griechischen Dialekt-Inschriften* (Göttingen, 1884-1915).
Gentili-Prato	B. Gentili and C. Prato, *Poetarum Elegiacorum Testimonia et Fragmenta* (Leipzig, 1979-85).
GFF	*Giornale Filologico Ferrarese.*
G&R	*Greece and Rome.*
GRBS	*Greek, Roman and Byzantine Studies.*
Halliwell	S. Halliwell, *Aristophanes: Birds, Lysistrata, Assembly-Women, Wealth* (Oxford, 1997).
Heberlein	F. Heberlein, *Pluthygieia: Zur Gegenwelt bei Aristophanes* (Frankfurt, 1980).
Henderson[2]	J.J. Henderson, *The Maculate Muse*[2] (New York, 1991).
Henderson (LCL)	J.J. Henderson, *Aristophanes* (Cambridge MA/London, 1998-).
HSCP	*Harvard Studies in Classical Philology.*
HTR	*Harvard Theological Review.*
IC	*Inscriptiones Creticae* ed. M. Guarducci (Rome, 1935-50).

ICS	*Illinois Classical Studies.*
IG	*Inscriptiones Graecae.*
" i³	*Voluminis I editio tertia: Inscriptiones Atticae Euclidis anno anteriores* ed. D.M. Lewis and L. Jeffery (Berlin, 1981-94).
" ii²	*Voluminis II et III editio minor: Inscriptiones Atticae Euclidis anno posteriores* ed. J. Kirchner (Berlin, 1913-40).
" iv²	*Voluminis IV editio minor: Inscriptiones Argolidis (Fasc. I: Inscriptiones Epidauri)* ed. F. Hiller von Gaertringen (Berlin, 1929).
" xii[1]	*Voluminis XII fasciculus 1: Inscriptiones Rhodi, Chalces, Carpathi cum Saro, Casi* ed. F. Hiller von Gaertringen (Berlin, 1895).
" xii[9]	*Voluminis XII fasciculus 9: Inscriptiones Euboeae insulae* ed. E. Ziebarth (Berlin, 1915).
IGSK	*Inschriften griechischer Städte aus Kleinasien* (Bonn, 1972-).
IGUR	*Inscriptiones Graecae Urbis Romae* ed. L. Moretti (Rome, 1968-).
Inschr.Priene	*Inschriften von Priene* ed. F. Hiller von Gaertringen (Berlin, 1906).
Inscr.Magn.	*Die Inschriften von Magnesia am Maeander* ed. O. Kern (Berlin, 1900).
JHS	*Journal of Hellenic Studies.*
JRS	*Journal of Roman Studies.*
K-A	= *PCG* (q.v.)
Kassel & Austin	= *PCG* (q.v.)
Kugelmeier	C. Kugelmeier, *Reflexe früher und zeitgenössischer Lyrik in der alten attischen Komödie* (Stuttgart, 1996).
LCM	*Liverpool Classical Monthly.*
LGPN	*A Lexicon of Greek Personal Names* (Oxford, 1987-)³.
LIMC	*Lexicon Iconographicum Mythologiae Classicae* (Zürich, 1981-97).
MacDowell	D.M. MacDowell, *Aristophanes and Athens* (Oxford, 1995).
MCr	*Museum Criticum.*
MDAI(A)	*Mitteilungen des Deutschen Archäologischen Instituts (Athenische Abteilung).*
MH	*Museum Helveticum.*
MEFRA	*Mélanges d'archéologie et d'histoire de l'École française de Rome.*
NCLS	*Nottingham Classical Literature Studies.*
Nesselrath	H.G. Nesselrath, *Die attische Mittlere Komödie* (Berlin, 1990).
Norvin	W. Norvin, *Olympiodori Philosophi in Platonis Phaedonem Commentaria* (Leipzig, 1913).

---

3   A reference such as "*LGPN* 3", in relation to a person, means that this person is the 3rd of that name listed in volume 2 (Attica) of the *Lexicon*.

PA	J. Kirchner, *Prosopographia Attica* (Berlin, 1901-3).
Parke	H.W. Parke, *Festivals of the Athenians* (London, 1977).
Parker *Songs*	L.P.E. Parker, *The Songs of Aristophanes* (Oxford, 1997).
PCG	R. Kassel and C. Austin, *Poetae Comici Graeci* (Berlin, 1983-).
PCPS	*Proceedings of the Cambridge Philological Society.*
Perusino	F. Perusino, *Platonio: La commedia greca* (Urbino, 1989).
PGM	K. Preisendanz, *Papyri Graecae Magicae* (Leipzig/ Berlin, 1928-31).
P.Heid.	*Veröffentlichungen aus der Heidelberger Papyrussammlung* (Heidelberg, 1905-).
P.Lit.Lond.	H.J.M. Milne, *Catalogue of the Literary Papyri in the British Museum* (London, 1927).
PLLS	*Papers of the Leeds International Latin Seminar.*
PMG	D.L. Page, *Poetae Melici Graeci* (Oxford, 1962).
Powell	J.U. Powell, *Collectanea Alexandrina* (Oxford, 1925).
POxy	*The Oxyrhynchus Papyri* (London, 1898-); citations are by serial number of papyrus.
Proleg.	W.J.W. Koster, *Prolegomena de Comoedia = Scholia* IA.
QSt	*Quaderni di Storia.*
QUCC	*Quaderni Urbinati di Cultura Classica.*
RA	*Revue Archéologique.*
Rau	P. Rau, *Paratragodia: Untersuchung einer komischen Form des Aristophanes* (Munich, 1967).
RE	*Paulys Realencyclopädie der klassischen Altertums-wissenschaft.*
REG	*Revue des Études Grecques.*
RFIC	*Rivista di Filologia e d'Istruzione Classica.*
RhM	*Rheinisches Museum für Philologie.*
RIL	*Rendiconti del Reale Istituto Lombardo di Scienze e Lettere: Classe di lettere e scienze morali e storiche.*
RPh	*Revue de Philologie.*
Scholia	*Scholia in Aristophanem* (see Bibliography).
SEG	*Supplementum Epigraphicum Graecum.*
SH	H. Lloyd-Jones and P.J. Parsons ed. *Supplementum Hellenisticum* (Berlin, 1983).
SIFC	*Studi Italiani di Filologia Classica.*
SIG[3]	W. Dittenberger, *Sylloge Inscriptionum Graecarum*[3] (Leipzig, 1915-24).
SRCG	*Seminari Romani di Cultura Greca.*
Stone	L.M. Stone, *Costume in Aristophanic Comedy* (New York, 1981).
Strauss	B.S. Strauss, *Athens after the Peloponnesian War* (London, 1986).
Taillardat	J. Taillardat, *Les images d'Aristophane*[2] (Paris, 1965).

REFERENCES & ABBREVIATIONS

TAPA	*Transactions (and Proceedings) of the American Philological Association.*
Thiercy	P. Thiercy, *Aristophane: Théâtre complet* (Paris, 1997).
Threatte	L. Threatte, *The Grammar of Attic Inscriptions* (Berlin, 1980-96).
Tod	M.N. Tod, *A Selection of Greek Historical Inscriptions* (Oxford, 1946-8).
Travlos	J. Travlos, *Pictorial Dictionary of Ancient Athens* (London, 1971).
TrGF	*Tragicorum Graecorum Fragmenta* (Göttingen, 1971-)[4].
WJA	*Würzburger Jahrbücher für die Altertumswissenschaft.*
West	M.L. West, *Iambi et Elegi Graeci*[2] (Oxford, 1989-92).
YCS	*Yale Classical Studies.*
Zimmermann	B. Zimmermann, *Untersuchungen zur Form und dramatischen Technik der aristophanischen Komödien* (Königstein/Frankfurt, 1984-7).
ZPE	*Zeitschrift für Papyrologie und Epigraphik.*

(D) Metrical Symbols

− a heavy (long) syllable
∪ a light (short) syllable
× a position that may be occupied by a syllable of either kind ("anceps")
OO the "aeolic base": two syllables, at least one of which is heavy

---

4 A reference such as "*TrGF* 57", applied to a person, means that that person is the 57th of the minor tragic dramatists for whom testimonia (and fragments, if any) are included in *TrGF* i.

Introduction

1. Occasion and Background

Wealth (Plutus) was produced in 388 BC[1]; we do not know at which of the two dramatic festivals it was staged, nor with what success, though we do know the authors and titles of the four plays that competed against it. It is a notable sign of changing fashions in comedy that three of the four had characters and plots derived from myth — *Admetus* by Aristomenes[2], *Adonis* by Nicophon, and *Pasiphaë* by Alcaeus; the fourth was *The Laconians* by Nicochares, son of Aristophanes' old collaborator Philonides[3]. *Wealth* was the last play Aristophanes was to produce in his own name; the two plays he wrote subsequently, *Cocalus* and *Aeolosicon* — both of which were themselves mythical burlesques — were produced by his son Araros[4].

The so-called Corinthian War, fought against Sparta by an alliance whose leading members were Athens, Thebes, Argos and Corinth with the aim of ending the *de facto* hegemony of Greece that Sparta had exercised since the end of the Peloponnesian War, was now in its seventh year. In its early stages the allies had received vital assistance, both financial and naval, from Persia, whose fleet under the Athenian admiral Conon had gained control of the Aegean, while the Spartans had been driven from most of northern and central Greece and the Isthmus of Corinth fortified against them; but Persian support ended as a result of developments in 392/1, including the arrest of Conon by the satrap Tiribazus and the failure of two Spartan peace initiatives, and the war entered a phase of near-stalemate. A spectacular success by the Athenian Iphicrates in 390, when with light-armed

1 For the information in this paragraph, cf. Hypothesis III Coulon = III Chantry. On Ar.'s earlier play of the same name, produced in 408, see section 8 below.

2 Aristomenes was easily the senior comic dramatist still active, having competed as early as 439 (*IGUR* 216.13 = Aristomenes test. 5 K-A) though never very highly regarded either in his own time or subsequently.

3 Suda v407 = Nicochares test. 1 K-A. Philonides had produced *The Preview* (422), *Amphiaraus* (414), *Frogs* (405), and possibly *Wasps* (422) and other plays, on Ar.'s behalf, as well as being a comic dramatist on his own account.

4 Araros won first prize with one of these plays at the City Dionysia of 387 (*IG* ii² 2318.196 = Araros test. 3 K-A). The ancient *Life of Aristophanes* (Ar. test. 1.56) says that *Wealth* itself was produced by Araros, and the Hypothesis seems to be uncertain on the matter, saying both that this was the last play Ar. produced in his own name and that he "wanted to introduce his son Araros to the spectators through it". The conflict of evidence can be resolved in various ways, of which the simplest is to delete *di' autou* "through it" as an interpolation in the Hypothesis (which will then be saying that Ar. "introduce[d] his son ... to the spectators" by having him produce the two *later* plays) and suppose that the statement in the *Life* is a deduction from the already corrupted text of the Hypothesis.

mercenary troops[5] he destroyed a battalion (*mora*) of 600 Spartan hoplites and with it the general Greek belief that the Spartan hoplite was invincible[6], was heavily exploited in allied propaganda[7] but had little practical effect on the course of the war. In the same year, for the first time since the Peloponnesian War, Athens sent out a naval expedition financed entirely from its own resources, under Thrasybulus (see on 550), with the aim of re-establishing Athenian influence in the northern and eastern Aegean (Xen. *Hell.* 4.8.25-30); but it is significant evidence of the state of Athenian public finances that this expedition comprised no more than forty ships, that in order to mount it the Athenians had been forced to suspend work on the refortification of the Peiraeus[8] as well as imposing a special property tax (*eisphorā*) (Lys. 28.3, 28.4, 29.9), that even so it had taken over a year before the fleet was ready to sail, that it had largely to pay its own way by exactions and plundering (one episode of which resulted in Thrasybulus' death), and that though it achieved fair success in military and diplomatic terms, it brought home so little money that Thrasybulus and his associates were accused of embezzlement and at least one of them, Ergocles, condemned and executed (Lys. 28 and 29)[9]. In 389 an expedition sent under Pamphilus (see on 174 and 385) to besiege Aegina, from which the Spartans had begun to make regular sea-raids on Athenian territory, had ended up

---

5   This is the "mercenary force at Corinth" referred to in *Wealth* 173.

6   Xen. *Hell.* 4.5.11-18; cf. D.S. 14.91.2 (misdated).

7   Iphicrates and his allies, principally the Argives and their Corinthian supporters, followed up their victory by recapturing three fortresses to the north-east of the Isthmus, two of which had been held by the Spartans for two years, while the third, Oenoe, had been taken recently by the very *mora* that Iphicrates had just destroyed (Xen. *Hell.* 4.5.19, cf. 4.5.5). The recapture of Oenoe seems to have been commemorated (Paus. 10.10.4) by the Argives with a dedication at Delphi (crediting the victory to themselves and *epikouroi* [= both "allies" and "mercenaries"] provided by the Athenians) and by the Athenians with a painting in the Stoa Poikile at Athens which implied that this victory was comparable in importance with that gained over the Persians at Marathon exactly a hundred years previously (and whose inscription spoke of Oenoe as being "in Argive territory", since at this time Argos and Corinth officially formed one state whose name was Argos [Xen. *Hell.* 4.4.6, 4.5.1]). See J.G. Taylor, *AJP* 119 (1998) 223-243, esp. 239-241, who shows that the Argive-Athenian victory at Oenoe, usually supposed to have occurred in the early 450s, is more likely to belong to the early fourth century, but does not attempt to identify it (and who takes a different view of the Stoa Poikile painting from that adopted here).

8   This project had been begun soon after the outbreak of war (*IG* ii² 1656 = Tod 107); in 393, when Conon brought his fleet to the Peiraeus, he also brought Persian money to help finance the refortification, which progressed apace (Xen. *Hell.* 4.8.9-10). The last of the series of inscriptions recording expenditure on the project (*IG* ii² 1658-64) relates to 392/1, the year during which Athens lost its Persian funding, and work seems then to have been suspended indefinitely: in 378 the Peiraeus had still not been provided with defensible gates (Xen. *Hell.* 5.4.20, 34).

9   His trial may have taken place not long before the production of *Wealth*: see on 381 and 567-570.

being virtually besieged itself, and a further large force had to be mounted merely to evacuate the original force (Xen. *Hell.* 5.1.1-5); Aegina, on Athens' very doorstep, again became an important raiding base for the Spartans, under their enterprising commander Gorgopas, until he was killed in 388 (Xen. *Hell.* 5.1.5-13).

The Spartans as much as their enemies were waging war on a shoestring[10], and for both sides a vital consideration was relations with possible allies and sources of funding beyond the bounds of Greece and the Aegean. Apart from Dionysius I of Syracuse (see on 550) and the Thracian kings Amedocus and Seuthes whom Thrasybulus had brought on to the Athenian side (Xen. *Hell.* 4.8.26), most of these were to the east — Artaxerxes II of Persia, his satraps, and one or two rulers in rebellion against him. In regard to these, Athens had two possible policies. One was to take advantage of the King's hostility to the Spartans, who had supported his brother Cyrus against him at the start of his reign, campaigned in Asia Minor from 399 to 394, and invaded his territory again in 391 soon after they had offered to recognize his overlordship over all the Greek cities on the Asian mainland (Xen. *Hell.* 4.8.17-22, 31-33, cf. 4.8.14): Struthas, the satrap in charge of Greek affairs[11], was pro-Athenian, and Pharnabazus, the long-serving satrap of the Hellespontine region, had worked closely with Conon and in 389 was encouraging the Greek states in his area to support Athens (Xen. *Hell.* 4.8.31). The other was for Athens to ally herself with two rulers seeking, with some success, to make themselves independent of Persia: Euagoras of Cyprus, who had been made an Athenian citizen many years before and awarded further honours for his share in Conon's victory at Cnidus in 394[12], and Acoris of Egypt (see on 178). Faced with the choice between these alternatives, the Athenians chose both; otherwise put, they assumed that Artaxerxes would never be prepared to become the ally of Sparta and that therefore they could with safety support his other enemies. They were wrong. By the time *Wealth* was produced, Artaxerxes had perhaps already given one indication of a change of policy by dismissing Struthas and reappointing his predecessor, Tiribazus, the man who in 392 had arrested Conon, secretly passed funds to the Spartans, and advised the King to endorse Sparta's terms for peace (Xen. *Hell.* 5.1.6, cf. 4.8.12-16); soon afterwards he also recalled Pharnabazus and replaced him with Ariobarzanes, who like Tiribazus was a friend of the Spartan admiral Antalcidas (Xen. *Hell.* 5.1.28). In 387 Antalcidas secured a promise of full Persian support if Sparta's Greek enemies would not accept such peace terms as the King might decree, and proceeded to block

---

10   Cf. Xen. *Hell.* 5.1.6 (Nicolochus, on the way to Abydos, ravages the territory of Tenedos to force the Tenedians to contribute money), 5.1.13-14 (crews refuse to fight for Eteonicus because they are not being paid; Teleutias, sent to succeed him, brings no money with him).

11   He is called "satrap of Ionia" in Tod 113.42, and his predecessor and successor, Tiribazus, is called "general for Ionia" in Xen. *Hell.* 4.8.12 and 5.1.28.

12   *IG* i³ 113 (ca. 410 BC); *SEG* xxix 86 (see D.M. Lewis and R.S. Stroud, *Hesperia* 48 [1979] 180-193); Isoc. 9.54-57, 68; [Dem.] 12.10; Paus. 1.3.2.

Athens' vital corn route at the Hellespont with a fleet of 80-90 ships, most of them supplied by Tiribazus, Ariobarzanes, or Dionysius; and when soon afterwards, at a conference at Sardis, Tiribazus announced the King's ruling – all Greek states on the Asian mainland, plus Clazomenae and (crucially) Cyprus, to belong to the King; all others to be independent except that Athens could keep the islands of Lemnos, Imbros and Scyros – Athens accepted the terms forthwith, though Thebes, Corinth and Argos had to be persuaded by a show of force[13] (Xen. *Hell.* 5.1.30-34).

The war makes singularly little impact on our play; indeed there are perhaps only two lines (172-3) that can be said to refer to it directly. This is probably because, at any rate after 392/1, the fighting impinged little on the consciousness of most Athenians, except when commanders were put on trial for their failures[14]. Attica was secure from invasion, for the Isthmus barrier held right to the end of the war – and it was held almost entirely by Corinthians, Argives, and mercenaries, not Athenian citizen soldiers; the raids from Aegina affected only the coastal villages; at no time during the war had there been heavy Athenian casualties[15]. Not war, but poverty, is seen as the evil that most needs to be combated. And poverty, in this play, does not merely mean, as its eponymous goddess claims, "liv[ing] economically and keep[ing] at one's work, not having any surplus but not having a shortfall either" (553-4); it means, as we are frequently and specifically reminded, living with the constant possibility of finding that one is unable to feed oneself and one's family[16] or afford clothing and fuel to keep them warm[17]. *Wealth* makes no sense unless there was a widespread perception in 389/8 that many Athenians were at serious risk of falling into such want as that. Whether that perception was justified is quite another matter[18]: no one was collecting statistics on the subject or knew how to do so, but (for example) anyone visiting the public bath-houses (as most men did from time to time) could see whether it was the case that in winter there were more people than there had once been crowding round the stoves to get a

---

13   This was because the independence clause meant that the union of Argos and Corinth would be dissolved, and that Thebes would lose its hegemony over Boeotia.

14   See on 174, 381, 385, 550, and 567-570.

15   The costliest battle in the war, in terms of Athenian lives, had been that at Nemea in 394. The Athenians who fought there numbered 6,600, about a quarter of the whole allied force (Xen. *Hell.* 4.2.17); of their ten tribal regiments, six suffered particularly heavily while the other four were almost unscathed (*ibid.* 4.2.19-21). Since the allies lost in all 2,800 killed (D.S. 14.83.2), the Athenian dead perhaps numbered some 800. At Coronea two months later the allies, though defeated, had lost only 600 dead all told (D.S. 14.84.2); since then there had been no major land battle.

16   219, 253, 283, 504, 536, 539, 543-4, 562, 595, 627-8, 763. After Wealth regains his sight, contrariwise, it is the wicked who go hungry (873, 892).

17   263, 535, 540, 842-7; here too the tables are later turned upon the wicked (896, 952-3). The play's presupposition of widespread, serious poverty in Athens is highlighted by E. Lévy, *Ktèma* 22 (1997) 202-4.

18   There are useful discussions of living standards in early fourth-century Athens by V.N. Andreyev, *Eirene* 12 (1974) 5-46, and A. French, *G&R* 38 (1991) 24-40.

bit of warmth (535, 952-3), and anyone walking the streets of Athens could see whether the number of beggars had increased[19]. Poverty had already been seen as a serious social problem three years before, in *Ecclesiazusae* (408-426, 592); in *Wealth* this theme is developed far more fully, and given an ethical dimension, lacking in the earlier play, with the complaint, made first by Chremylus (28-31), assented to by every other character until the arrival of the Informer, and not denied even by Poverty herself, that in the present state of the world the only way to become rich is to be a criminal. It is not quite true to say that this is the injustice that Chremylus sets out to remedy, because what he originally set out to do was ask Apollo whether, given that this was the way the world was, he should bring up his son to lead a criminal life (36-38). Apollo's response results in Chremylus being brought into contact with the god of Wealth, and Wealth's explanation of his blindness (87-92) inspires Chremylus to the Great Idea[20] of having him healed.

2. The god Wealth[21]

Wealth (*Ploutos*) was a god who had, in a sense, two identities, if not three. In one of them he was the son of Demeter and her mortal lover Iasius or Iasion (Hes. *Thg.* 969-973, *PMG* 885), conceived "in a thrice-turned fallow field" in Crete (Hes. loc. cit., cf. *Odyssey* 5.125-8). This Wealth was primarily the god of agricultural plenty (cf. Hesychius ε7077), an agent of the bounty of Demeter and her daughter Persephone-Kore (cf. Hes. loc.cit., *h.Hom.Dem.* 486-9) and is usually represented in art as a boy holding a cornucopia from which corn is sprouting[22]; he is never blind. In almost all his appearances, whether in art or in literature, he is closely associated with Demeter and her cult, especially the Eleusinian Mysteries; in the prayer that opens the women's assembly held in the Thesmophorium in Aristophanes' *Thesmophoriazusae* he is named (*Thesm.* 299) directly after Demeter and Kore. It is widely believed that Wealth was the child whose birth or epiphany formed part of the *drōmena* enacted before those undergoing initiation at Eleusis (cf. *PMG* 862)[23]; at a more popular level he figures in an Athenian drinking song (*skolion*) that is also a prayer to his mother and his sister:

---

19 Particularly since, as in modern cities, they would tend to concentrate in the most frequented areas (especially, doubtless, the Agora) and the impression would thus be created that they were much more numerous than they actually were.

20 See my introduction to *Acharnians* (this series, 1980), pp.11-13.

21 On Wealth as an allegorical figure see especially H.J. Newiger, *Metapher und Allegorie* (Munich, 1957) 165-178 and G. Hertel, *Die Allegorie von Reichtum und Armut* (Nuremberg, 1969) 7-41.

22 See N.J. Richardson, *The Homeric Hymn to Demeter* (Oxford, 1974), on v.489; K. Clinton, *Myth and Cult: The Iconography of the Eleusinian Mysteries* (Stockholm, 1992) 49-59, 82-83, 91-95, 96; E.J. Stafford in L. Foxhall and J.B. Salmon ed. *Thinking Men* (London, 1998) 47-49.

23 See Richardson *loc.cit.* (also *op.cit.* 26-28); Clinton *op.cit.* 91-95.

I sing of the Olympian mother of Wealth,
Demeter, in the season when garlands are worn,
and of thee, Persephone, daughter of Zeus:
greeting to you both, and take good care of this city (*PMG* 885).

Secondly, Cratinus in or about 429 wrote a play which appears from its major surviving fragment (Cratinus fr. 171) to have been, at least in part, a parody on the Aeschylean *Prometheus Unbound*[24]. As in *Prometheus Unbound*, the chorus consisted of Titans (fr. 171.11), the brethren of Cronus, now released from their imprisonment (cf. fr. 171.20, 21) and coming to visit their brother Prometheus; but here they add that "we were called *Ploutoi* when [Cronus ruled]" (fr. 171.12), and *Ploutoi* was the title of Cratinus' play. This play was one, probably the first, of a long series of comedies (many of which are named, and extracts from them quoted, in Athenaeus 6.267e-270a) describing the life of fantastic ease enjoyed by men either in a past or in a future Golden Age, when all the good things of life come to men "of their own accord" (fr. 172) without having to be laboured for; in *Ploutoi* we hear, for example, of men using loaves of bread as dice (fr. 176, cf. *Wealth* 816-7) and of sausages being hung on the walls of public buildings "for old men to bite off with their teeth" (fr. 175). We do not hear of plural *Ploutoi* elsewhere[25], and it is possible that this designation for the Titans was invented by Cratinus in order to portray them as benefactors of humanity, a role not normally associated with Titans even though "the age of Cronus" was proverbially a utopian era[26].

The Wealth of our play is a different being again, who exists (so far as we can tell) not in cult but only in poetic and popular imagination. Already in the time of the iambic poet Hipponax (mid sixth century) it was taken for granted that this Wealth was blind, and that this was why many humans who deserved to be rich were in fact poor and vice versa:

Wealth — for he is all too blind —
has never come to my house and said
"Hipponax, I'm giving you thirty minae of silver
and many other things too"; for he's got a wretched mentality
(Hipponax fr. 36)[27].

---

24 This tragedy, together with *Prometheus Bound* to which it was a sequel, was probably written by Aeschylus' son Euphorion and presented by him as a posthumous work of his father, possibly as late as 431 when Euphorion defeated both Sophocles and Euripides. See M.L. West, *Studies in Aeschylus* (Stuttgart, 1990) 51-72; R. Bees, *Zur Datierung des Prometheus Desmotes* (Stuttgart, 1993); and my *Aeschylean Tragedy* (Bari, 1996) 321-7.

25 Kassel & Austin iv 204 identify them with the "good spirits, averters of evil, guardians of mortal men, *bringers of wealth*" mentioned by Hes. *Works* 122-6; these, however, are not the Titans but the "golden race" of *mortals* who lived in Cronus' time, endowed after their death with semi-divine powers.

26 Cf. Hes. *Works* 109-119; *Alcmeonis* fr. 7 Davies; Arist. *Ath.Pol.* 16.7; Plut. *Arist.* 24.3.

27 So, though less selfishly, a character in Amphis' comedy *The Lady's Maid (Kouris)* says that Wealth must be blind because he does not come to "this woman" [the title

A drinking song (*skolion*) by Timocreon of Rhodes (early fifth century), popular enough in the 420s for Aristophanes to be able to expect a parody of it to be instantly recognizable[28], goes so far as to assert that Wealth is the root of all evil in the world:

> If only, blind Wealth,
> you had never appeared
> on land or on sea or on the continent[29],
> but had dwelt in Tartarus
> and Acheron; for it is because of you
> that men have all evils always[30] (Timocreon *PMG* 731)

We do not know whether this was the whole of the song, or whether it went on to explain more fully the nature of Wealth's responsibility for evil. Since, however, the singer wishes not that Wealth *could see*, but that Wealth *did not exist*, the point, whether it was expressed or understood, is probably that humans cause misery to other humans by committing crimes, waging wars, etc., through *desire* for wealth: the same point made with great clarity and pithiness by the fourth-century comic dramatist Antiphanes (fr. 259):

> Wealth is just like a bad oculist:
> he takes us sighted and makes us all blind[31].

The first known comedy that *may* have featured a singular Wealth-god was Epicharmus' *Hope or Wealth*, of which we know only that it included a full-scale portrayal of what later became the stock comic type of the parasite[32]. Next, so far as we know, came Aristophanes' own first *Wealth*, produced in 408 (see §8); we do not know how the theme was treated[33], or even which of the *personae* of Wealth was represented in the play — indeed we cannot be certain that the god was a character in it at all[34]. Probably a few years later[35] Archippus produced a play of the same name;

---

character?] but spends all his time with famous *hetairai* like Sinope, Lyca and Nannion (Amphis fr. 23).

28   *Ach.* 532-4.

29   The apparent tautology may be due to Timocreon's having composed the song in the first instance for a Rhodian milieu in which "land" meant primarily Rhodes and "the mainland" the Asian continent facing it (ruled by the immensely wealthy Persian king).

30   Chremylus says the opposite at *Wealth* 144-5.

31   Cf. Men. fr. 74 "Wealth is blind, and he makes everyone blind who looks at him"; similarly already Eur. fr. 776 = *Phaethon* 164-7 Diggle "It is strange, but the rich are just innately stupid; what's the cause of it? is it that they are mentally blind because blind Wealth (*Olbos*) overclouds them?" For blind Wealth cf. also Pl. *Laws* 631c, Theocr. 10.19.

32   Epich. fr. 34-35 come from a speech by this character, and fr. 37 is addressed to him.

33   Although Ar. fr. 459 (discussed in §8) suggests that, as in the surviving play, someone tried to argue, no doubt unsuccessfully, that it was better (for the individual) to be poor than to be rich.

34   Any more than we can be sure whether Old Age (*Gēras*) was a character in Ar.'s play of that name, or Peace in his second *Peace*.

its central character may have been an old man embittered by the wickedness he saw all around him (fr. 37), who became rich during the course of the play (fr. 39) and whom someone then tried to cheat (fr. 38), but our evidence again gives no clue as to what role, if any, was played by the god Wealth. By 388 there was thus a fairly well-established tradition of comedies in which the contrast between wealth and poverty was a central issue, but there is no definite evidence that a singular Wealth-god was a character in any of them, still less that any of them had featured the *healing* of a *blind* Wealth-god[36].

Before 388, so far as our evidence goes, all references to Wealth-the-blind had been in a context of complaint. If Wealth the cornucopia-holding son of Demeter was a dispenser of blessings, Wealth-the-blind was a dispenser of curses, whether he was seen as encouraging human wickedness or as denying his favour to those who deserved it. Aristophanes' innovation may thus have been to enable the latter Wealth to play the role of the former. He did this by the simple device of inventing a myth to account for Wealth's blindness as a misfortune, deeply felt by him, for which the blame lies on a malicious Zeus: if Wealth favours the wicked only because he cannot see to know better, then he has only to be healed and he will favour the virtuous instead. And if one wants to heal the blind, to whom should one go if not to Asclepius?

3.   Asclepius[37]

Asclepius, the healing god, was a latecomer to the Greek pantheon. In Homer he is merely a hero, an "excellent physician" (*Iliad* 4.194) and the father of Podaleirius and Machaon, medical experts to the Greek army before Troy; the home of the family is at Tricca in Thessaly (*Iliad* 2.729). His mortality, though also his marvellous power of healing, is emphasized by the well established story[38] of how

---

35   G. Kaibel, *Hermes* 24 (1889) 55, argued that Archippus' play was an imitation of Ar.'s surviving *Wealth*; but the evidence of the fragments does not compel this conclusion, and it is not likely that Archippus was still active in the 380s (of his five other known plays, the two that are datable, *The Fishes* and *Rhinon*, both belong to the first few years after the restoration of democracy in 403).

36   There is one reference to a later play called *Wealth*: the title appears in the Suda's list of the comedies of the fourth-century dramatist Nicostratus (a son of Ar. according to Apollodorus *FGrH* 244 F 75). No quotations from it survive.

37   See generally E.J. and L. Edelstein, *Asclepius* (Baltimore, 1945); the second edition (1998) contains a valuable introduction by G.B. Ferngren reviewing the scholarship of the intervening half-century, to which may be added M.P.J. Dillon, "The didactic nature of the Epidaurian iamata", *ZPE* 101 (1994) 239-260; R. Parker, *Athenian Religion: A History* (Oxford, 1996) 175-185; and S.R.F. Price, *Religions of Ancient Greece* (Cambridge, 1999) 109-112.

38   Hes. frr. 51-52; *Naupactia* fr. 10a-c Davies; Stesichorus *PMG* 194; Acusilaus *FGrH* 2 F 18; Panyassis fr. 19a-e Davies; Pherecydes *FGrH* 3 F 35; Pind. *Pyth.* 3.55-58; Aesch. *Ag.* 1022-4; Eur. *Alc.* 3-4, 122-9. Scarcely any two authors, in this period or later, can agree on who it was that Asclepius raised.

Zeus slew him with a thunderbolt for taking the art of healing beyond its ordained bounds by raising, or attempting to raise, the dead; but beyond this and the story of his birth (usually to Apollo and Coronis[39]) and education by Cheiron the Centaur[40] he has virtually no mythology — and unlike most heroes (but like another who became a god, Heracles) he did not even, so far as our evidence goes, have a cult at a recognized tomb. He seems, however, from an early date to have been specially venerated by the medical profession, whose practitioners regarded themselves as his spiritual descendants[41]; since doctors tended to be semi-itinerant, establishing their practices where the best income was to be had (cf. on 408), this helps to account for the lack of early fixed, independent cult-sites for Asclepius.

Asclepius was, however, sometimes worshipped alongside his father Apollo, and this may well be the route by which he himself rose to divine status. In particular, he was associated at more than one place with Apollo Maleatas, whom we can safely assume to have been a healing god. His original dependence on Apollo was so close that Isyllus of Epidaurus (ca. 300 BC) could write that "even in Thessalian Tricca" (and *a fortiori* elsewhere) one would not seek healing from Asclepius "unless one first sacrificed on the holy altar of Apollo Maleatas" (*IG* iv² 1.128.29-31); and the great miracle inscription at Epidaurus is headed "Cures of Apollo and Asclepius"[42].

It was from Epidaurus, almost certainly, that Asclepius came to be venerated as a god all over the Greek world, as a result of two developments that seem to have taken place in the late sixth or early fifth century[43]. One was that the sanctuary of Apollo and Asclepius there became a centre to which pilgrims came from far and wide in quest of healing; the other was that Asclepius, as it were, kicked his father upstairs. Apollo was an ambivalent god. He could cure diseases, but he could also cause them. His oracles always told the truth, but they often told it in a form almost impossible to interpret correctly. And he could be a cruel avenger, as witness, to look no further, the story of Asclepius' own birth, snatched from the burning body of

---

39 Most fully told in Pind. *Pyth.* 3.8-44; the story of Apollo, Coronis and her mortal lover Ischys goes back to the Hesiodic *Catalogue of Women* (Hes. fr. 59-60), but in the *Catalogue* the mother of Asclepius is not Coronis but Arsinoe, daughter of Leucippus (Hes. fr. 50, cf. fr. 52 which states that the killing of the Cyclopes by Apollo, in revenge for Zeus' slaying of Asclepius, was narrated "in the catalogue of the daughters of Leucippus").

40 Already in Homer (*Iliad* 4.219).

41 Cf. Theognis 432; Pl. *Prot.* 311b, *Symp.* 186d, *Rep.* 405d, *Phdr.* 270c. Some medical families, such as that from which Aristotle came (D.L. 5.1), claimed to be literally descended from Asclepius through Podaleirius or Machaon. At Athens there came to be a twice-yearly sacrifice to Asclepius by the public physicians (*IG* ii² 772 [third century BC]).

42 As late as AD 224 a healed patient made a dedication "to Apollo Maleatas and the Saviour Asclepius" (*IG* iv² 1.127.2-4) — but the inscription goes on to speak of Asclepius simply as "the god", as though Apollo were irrelevant.

43 See R.A. Tomlinson, *Epidauros* (London, 1969) 15, 22-24.

Coronis on her funeral pyre, after she had been slain by Artemis' arrows at Apollo's bidding[44] for having slept with Ischys while pregnant by the god. Asclepius was a healer, and a healer only. He might refuse to heal, and no doubt often did; he might even inflict punishment on villains or scoffers[45], though ready to forgive and cure them if they repented[46]; but, like the good physicians whose patron he remained, he never did wanton or spiteful harm, and the fate of Neocleides in our play (716-725) was something that could have happened only in comedy[47]. At any rate Apollo's role soon became a mere (though an essential) formality, hardly more important than that of other recipients of preliminary sacrifice like Hermes and the mysterious Hounds and Hunters (see on 660); the inscription whose heading reads "Cures of Apollo and Asclepius" never mentions Apollo again, and regularly speaks of Asclepius simply as "the god".

At Athens the first signs of interest in Asclepius' cult come in the 420s[48]. At that time Epidaurus was an enemy state, and Athenians seeking healing therefore had to go to one of the daughter-sanctuaries that were beginning to be established elsewhere. The most conveniently situated of these was on the island of Aegina (Paus. 2.30.1), then an Athenian possession[49], and the earliest evidence for Athenian participation in the healing cult comes from Aristophanes' *Wasps*, produced in 422. Bdelycleon has been trying to cure his father Philocleon of his mania for jury-service, and has tried persuasion and ritual (bathing, purification, Corybantic music-therapy) without effect:

> So then as he was doing no good to him ... he sailed across to Aegina,
> took the old man with him, and bedded him down for the night in the
> sanctuary of Asclepius (*Wasps* 121-3)

But the old man gave Asclepius no chance to heal him: "before daybreak he'd made his appearance at the bar of the court" back in Athens. The story is, of course,

---

44 Pind. *Pyth.* 3.8-44; later accounts omit the pyre and have Apollo deliver the baby by a post-mortem Caesarean section (implicit in Virg. *Aen.* 10.315-6 and made explicit by Servius *ad loc.*)

45 Cf. *EMI* 7 (a notably mild punishment, which shames the offender but does no harm to his health).

46 Cf. *EMI* 11, 22, 36. Sometimes he did not wait for repentance, but cured even a scoffer immediately: cf. *EMI* 3, 4.

47 And even the harm done to Neocleides is done for the benefit of Athenians generally (723-6).

48 It has been often, and plausibly, suggested that this was at least in part a reaction to the great plague of 430-427; it is striking that a Athenian expedition sent out soon after the plague first struck made not for Laconia, as the previous year, but for Epidaurus (Thuc. 2.56.4) – "sacred Epidaurus", as Plutarch (*Per.* 35.3) calls it in referring to the event – and came close to capturing the city. Cf. Tomlinson *op.cit.* 24; A. Burford, *The Greek Temple Builders at Epidauros* (Liverpool, 1969) 20-21; J.D. Mikalson in A.L. Boegehold et al. ed. *Studies Presented to Sterling Dow* (Durham NC, 1984) 220.

49 Hence this sanctuary must have been established before the outbreak of war in 431. This would make it the oldest known Asclepieum outside the Peloponnese.

fictitious, but it implies that a visit to an Asclepieum had by now become an option available for consideration when there seemed no other prospect of curing a serious malady.

The obvious next step was to establish an Asclepieum in Athens itself; but this could not be done while the war continued, presumably because an authentic Asclepieum could only be founded from Epidaurus. This was done soon after peace was made in 421, when one Telemachus, possibly an Epidaurian[50] or an Athenian with Epidaurian connections, brought Asclepius to Athens and founded two sanctuaries, one in the Peiraeus and one in the city, probably in that sequence, the latter being established at the time of the Great Mysteries in the autumn of 420[51]. This was surely done with the agreement, and quite possibly at the invitation, of the Athenian state; and it also had an extremely prominent and respected individual patron — the tragic dramatist Sophocles. The exact nature of Sophocles' connection with the introduction of the cult is disputed[52]; but the ancient tradition that he *did* have some connection with it is strong, and an inscription of the third century AD from the city Asclepieum[53] preserves part of what it calls "Sophocles' paean" in honour of the god and of his parents Coronis and Apollo. At an uncertain date Sophocles gave Asclepius a prominent role in one of his two plays about the blind seer Phineus, where he was represented as restoring Phineus' sight[54]; and in

---

50   Two Epidaurians of this name are known (*LGPN* IIIa Τηλέμαχος 2, 3), but the name is also common at Athens where 12 bearers of it are attested, most of them in the fifth and fourth centuries.

51   *IG* ii² 4960+4961 = *SEG* xxv 226; cf. *IG* ii² 4355. The Peiraeus sanctuary is not epigraphically attested until the second quarter of the fourth century, and R. Parker, *Athenian Religion: A History* (Oxford, 1996) 181-2 has argued that it was only founded at that time; but (i) the reference to the sea in *Wealth* 656-8 indicates that it is to the Peiraeus that Wealth is taken (see further on 411); (ii) Parker himself cites Plato com. fr. 188.16 as probably parodying the Peiraeus sacrificial regulations of *IG* ii² 4962 — but this fragment comes from a play produced in 391; (iii) it would be pointless to mention that Asclepius (or even, as Parker prefers, Telemachus) had "come up from Zea" to the city (*SEG* xxv 226.9) unless the little harbour at Zea already had some special association with the cult. Cf. S.B. Aleshire, *The Athenian Asklepieion* (Amsterdam, 1989) 13; F. Graf in *EH* 37 (1992) 177-8.

52   The ancient evidence is collected in *TrGF* iv 57-58; for sceptical analyses of it, see M.R. Lefkowitz, *The Lives of the Greek Poets* (London, 1981) 84, and A. Connolly, *JHS* 118 (1998) 1-21.

53   *SEG* xxviii 225, left side (part of the so-called "Sarapion monument") = *PMG* 737(b); see J.H. Oliver, *Hesperia* 5 (1936) 91-122, and Aleshire, *Asklepios at Athens* 49-74. The paean is also referred to by Philostratus, *Life of Apollonius* 3.17; Philostratus junior, *Imagines* 13; [Lucian], *Encomium of Demosthenes* 27.

54   Soph. fr. 710 (cf. *Wealth* 634-6). In another version of the story (Phylarchus, *FGrH* 81 F 18) Asclepius healed the *sons* of Phineus; but the fragment refers to the healing of one person, not two. It is not clear whether Asclepius in this play was presented as a hero or a god: a mortal Asclepius could have met and healed Phineus during the voyage of the Argonauts (cf. Clem. Alex. *Strom.* 1.21.105).

Philoctetes, produced in 409, he seems to go out of his way to give Asclepius the credit for healing Philoctetes' festering leg wound[55].

After this time evidence of Asclepius' popularity in Athens steadily increases. Dedications to him become frequent[56], and children begin to bear names like Asclepiodorus, at first perhaps given by parents who believed they had the god to thank for the child's birth[57]. The comic dramatist Theopompus (active ca.410-370) dedicated a marble relief to the god for having cured him of consumption (Aelian fr. 99 = E&E T456); a generation later he was the central figure in comedies by Philetaerus and Antiphanes both of which, like *Wealth*, included narratives of healings[58]. About the turn of the century it had still been possible for his name to be included in a comic catalogue of "foreign" gods (Apollophanes fr. 6), but that must have been almost the last occasion when he could credibly have been mentioned in such company. The last words of Socrates, condemned to death in 399 on the charge (of which he insisted he was innocent) of "not believing in the gods whom the city recognizes, but in other strange divinities", were "We owe a cock to Asclepius; pay the debt and do not neglect it"[59].

The usual procedure for seeking healing from Asclepius was "incubation"[60]: the patient visited a sanctuary of the god and, after specified preliminary rituals[61],

---

55   After Neoptolemus has told Philoctetes, on the authority of the seer Helenus, that he can be cured of his malady only by coming voluntarily to Troy where he will "meet the sons of Asclepius [i.e. Podaleirius and Machaon] whom we have with us, and be relieved of this affliction" (1333-4), Heracles, appearing a little later as *deus ex machina*, says he will "send Asclepius [himself] to Ilium to put an end to your malady" (1437-8). This is the only known passage in fifth-century tragedy that clearly treats Asclepius as a god.

56   See F.T. van Straten in H.S. Versnel ed. *Faith, Hope and Worship* (Leiden, 1981) 105-113, 120; Aleshire, *The Athenian Asklepieion* 37-51, 103-369.

57   Cf. *EMI* 2, 31, 34, 39, 42. Probably the earliest known is a man whose son Philagrus died some time before 350 (*IG* ii² 12888) and who may himself therefore have been born not long after Asclepius first came to Athens; cf. also *IG* ii² 276; 2346.23; 4619; 7879.

58   Philetaerus fr. 1; Antiphanes fr. 47. Philetaerus' play, in which the orator Hypereides was mentioned (fr. 2), probably belongs to the 340s. In that decade or later, Alexis wrote a comedy called *Asclepiocleides*, but we know nothing of its plot or characters (except that one of them was a typically boastful cook: Alexis fr. 24).

59   Pl. *Phd.* 118a. Whatever may be the extent to which Plato has fictionalized the death-scene, these words (which nothing else in the dialogue serves to explain to his readers) are likely to be authentic; if so, it is probably vain to inquire what boon conferred by the god caused the debt to be incurred, since that will have been known only to Socrates himself and perhaps his immediate family. Plato also makes Socrates take the divine status of Asclepius for granted at *Ion* 530a.

60   The evidence relating to the procedure is analysed by E&E pp. 145-154, though they exaggerate the "singular ... lack of complicated ritualistic rules" (149 n.16): for example, pilgrims had to be dressed all in white (see on 625), and at the Peiraeus shrine they had to offer no less than twenty-four cakelets as preliminary sacrifices to eight different recipients, besides whatever offering was made to Asclepius himself. See also M.P.J. Dillon, *Pilgrims and Pilgrimage in Ancient Greece* (London, 1997) 73-80.

slept a night in the *adyton*, in the hope that the god would come to him[62], normally in a dream, and by words, drugs, applications, surgery, or otherwise, heal the sickness so that when day came, in the phrase repeatedly used in the Epidaurian cure narratives, the patient would "walk out whole". Carion's narrative of Wealth's incubation is much the fullest surviving account, and there is no reason to doubt that it represents with fair fidelity the course of an incubation up to the point where the lights are extinguished and the patients bidden to close their eyes and keep silent (668-671); beyond that point Carion is describing things which no dutiful worshipper could have seen, but everything we hear of Asclepius[63] tends to increase his glory, not to diminish or debunk him, and the actual healing of Wealth involves procedures known from other Asclepian narratives[64], so we may safely suppose that in broad terms Carion's narrative represents what was commonly imagined as happening when Asclepius effected a cure.

4. Chremylus' plan and its fulfilment

When Chremylus learns that the reason why the wicked are wealthy and the virtuous poor is that Wealth is blind, and that Wealth's blindness was inflicted by Zeus precisely because Zeus did not want the virtuous to prosper (87-92), he resolves to remedy this iniquitous state of affairs by restoring Wealth's sight[65]. To what effect? In most places where he or others anticipate, describe or discuss the results of his success, it is said that the virtuous are to become, or have become, wealthy and the wicked poor[66]. Sometimes, however, it is assumed that in the new order of things *everybody* will be, or is, wealthy, and that poverty is (to be) totally abolished[67]. Superficially these two ideas appear to contradict each other, and some recent critics

---

61   See on 658 and 660.

62   Or her; about a quarter of the Epidaurian miracle narratives relate to women.

63   Including his "clever, patriotic" (726) maltreatment of Neocleides, and probably also his failure to show disgust at Carion's fart (705: doctors often had to deal with patients suffering from foul discharges, and they could not be squeamish about such things if they were to do their job properly).

64   Cf. on 710, 733-4; also *EMI* 6 for the use of a cloth.

65   That this involves defying and defeating Zeus is nothing new in Ar.; the heroes of *Peace* and *Birds* do likewise, each time with the assistance of other gods (respectively Hermes and Prometheus; similarly Chremylus is aided by Apollo, without whose oracle he would never have met Wealth).

66   95-97, 218-221, 386-8, 475, 490-6, 502-6, 627-630, 751-6, 774-781, 823-958, 1026-30; cf. 969-972.

67   430, 434, 463-5, 510 (where it is assumed that wealth will be *equally* distributed), 519-520, 523-4, 1178.   At 864-5 the Informer complains that Wealth has broken his promise to "make us all rich straight away"; but then he regards himself as virtuous (cf. 900), so that we cannot automatically count 864-5 as an instance of the "universal wealth" theme.

have drawn subtle and far-reaching inferences from this apparent incongruity[68]. Yet no character in the play, whether among Chremylus' supporters or among his opponents, ever takes the least notice of it. On the contrary, they all persistently treat the enrichment of the virtuous and the total abolition of poverty as if they were *equivalent* to one another[69]. And as Rogers saw, Ar. has spelt out quite explicitly how this can be so[70]. When Chremylus outlines his programme at the start of the *agōn*, this is what he says:

> I think this much can be plainly recognized by everyone alike – that it's right and just that the virtuous among mankind should have prosperity, and the wicked and the godless, of course, the reverse of that. Desiring to achieve that, we have found a way to do it, so that a scheme has come into existence which is noble, admirable, and beneficial in every way. It is that if Wealth now regains his sight and no longer wanders around blind, he will direct his steps to the good among mankind and never forsake them, and will shun the wicked and the godless; *and consequently he will bring it about that everyone is virtuous – and rich, of course –* and reveres the power of the gods (489-497).

If Aristophanes had wanted even the acutest intellects among his audience to suppose that Chremylus' scheme contained a fundamental internal incoherence as to who were to be the beneficiaries of Wealth's healing, he would not have written this passage. In the early part of the play, to be sure, Chremylus speaks only of making the virtuous rich and the wicked poor. Then, at 430, Poverty accuses him of planning to expel her from Greece, or even from the world, entirely. At that stage he makes no reply, because he does not yet know (nor do the audience) who the speaker is; but after she has identified herself (437), far from denying the charge he proudly asserts, unprompted, that expelling Poverty from Greece is precisely what

---

68   This approach particularly characterizes the important articles by D. Konstan and M.J. Dillon (*AJP* 102 [1981] 371-394, revised in D. Konstan, *Greek Comedy and Ideology* [New York, 1995] 75-90) and by S.D. Olson (*HSCP* 93 [1990] 223-242); even J. McGlew, *AJP* 118 (1997) 44-45, whose general position is much closer to that taken here, still speaks of an "apparent narrative incongruity".

69   This is already noticeable in the initial argument between Chremylus, Blepsidemus and Poverty (415-486). Poverty condemns the two men for trying to "drive me out of every land" or "make me disappear from these parts" (430, 434) – and presently Chremylus confirms that that is precisely what he wants to do (463); then Poverty tells Chremylus this will be a great mistake (464-5), but shortly afterwards she tell him that he will be making a great mistake if he intends to "make honest men wealthy" (475) without his having given any indication meanwhile that his aims have changed.

70   Rogers wrote (on 430) that this insight "seems to have escaped the notice of every Scholiast and Commentator"; but it was in fact perceived by the medieval commentator Thomas Magister, who comments thus on 497: "For when the wicked see that because of this [sc. the healing of Wealth] the virtuous are faring well, they will wish to abandon their previous life and change to better ways, in order to benefit thereby."

he wants to do (463). And in 489-497 he explains how this will be done. Wealth, his sight recovered, will make the virtuous rich and the wicked poor; and "consequently he will bring it about that everyone is virtuous"[71] — because whereas previously there had been a strong material incentive to vice (cf. 28-50), there will now be an equally strong material incentive to virtue. And if everyone is virtuous, then everyone will be rich.

Is this what actually happens? After the triumphal return of Wealth from the sanctuary of Asclepius, the consequences of his recovery of sight are presented in five scenes.

(1)   *The household of Chremylus* (802-822) become rich immediately. That Chremylus describes himself as a virtuous man (28) is of course not evidence that he actually is one; but if a man is not virtuous who has the god of Wealth in his home and, rather than keep him to himself, enables and encourages him to spread his bounty over all virtuous people and ultimately over all humanity, then virtue must be a rare thing indeed!

(2)   *The Honest Man and the Informer* (823-958) provide a clear case of the reversal of fortunes that has taken place as between the virtuous and the wicked — for here, as everywhere else in comedy and other Athenian literature (see on 31), it is assumed by everyone that informers (*sūkophantai*) are wicked: by everyone, that is, except informers themselves. The Informer is unrepentant to the end of the scene, because he still believes he will be able to turn the tables on his enemies (944-950); but the fact that he speaks of this as "mak[ing] this mighty god pay the penalty of his crimes" (946-7) demonstrates the futility of his hopes. Whether he *ultimately* repents and reforms is a matter of much ethical but no comic interest, and the play follows his fortunes no further.

(3)   *The Old Woman and the Young Man* (959-1096). This scene has sometimes been seen as more problematic for the validity of Chremylus' programme. To our way of thinking, the Young Man, who unashamedly extracts as much money as possible from his rich mistress[72] and then deserts her the instant he

---

71   I do not doubt that Ar. and most of his audience would agree that it is a mark of excellence beyond the ordinary to benefit one's fellow human beings *without* the incentive of reward for doing so or punishment for not doing so. Their society, however, like our own, was built on the assumption that even those who do good without the promise of a reward will do more good with it; and as we can see from much that Athenians were prepared to say in court, they were less hypocritical than we often are about acknowledging this. There is accordingly no reason to believe that any significant proportion of Ar.'s audience would have supposed that behaviour beneficial to society lost all its merit if it was motivated by desire for material gain, and no need to see irony in a statement that "everyone [will be] virtuous" if virtuous behaviour is made a necessary and sufficient condition for material prosperity. See K.J. Dover, *Greek Popular Morality in the Time of Plato and Aristotle* (Oxford, 1974) 223-242.

72   Logically we would expect the Old Woman to be wicked, since she was comfortably off before Wealth was healed; but she indignantly denies suggestions that she might be a

no longer needs her support, might well seem a heartless villain; Chremylus too regards him (1071-85) as having a duty to continue a relationship that has brought him so many benefits, a duty in which he has failed; and yet the Young Man is enriched when Wealth recovers his sight. The explanation is probably (see on 1003) that women who "worked with their bodies" were at least tacitly assumed not to be full members of the moral community, so that while it might be laudable to behave considerately towards them, it was not necessarily blameworthy to treat them with ingratitude or injustice[73]. The Old Woman herself naturally does not see things that way (cf. 1030), and in the end the issue becomes moot as Chremylus apparently succeeds[74] in persuading the Young Man to return to her (1201). How he succeeds we are not told; what matters is that he does — which means that the Young Man's fault, such as it was, is fully purged.

(4-5)   *Hermes and the Priest of Zeus* (1097-1196). Both Hermes and the Priest complain that men have ceased to sacrifice to the (Olympian) gods (1113-6, 1177-84), and the latter makes it explicit that this is because "they're all rich" (1178). We have thus, in these final scenes, passed tacitly to the final stage of Chremylus' plan. Nothing is explicitly said about the fulfilment of the precondition mentioned previously, that everyone should become virtuous; but it is at any rate striking that of the two persons of bad or questionable character whom we have seen, one (the Young Man) proves to have undergone a change of heart, however induced, at some point between 1096 and 1201. However, given that Chremylus had earlier spoken of "the wicked *and the godless*" (491) and predicted that in his new world everyone would be virtuous and rich and *revere the power of the gods* (497), it might well seem paradoxical that the main effect of universal wealth — indeed the only effect actually mentioned — is that sacrifices have ceased and temples are being used as

---

wrongdoer (970-3), and she at no point complains of having lost her wealth (indeed, if anything, she is better off materially than before, since her resources are no longer being milked by her lover).

73   In the same way, while an Athenian might possibly be commended if he did not beat his slaves, he certainly would not be condemned if he did.

74   One might be tempted to argue that we do not know for certain that Chremylus is telling the truth at 1201: is he just making the Old Woman a promise in order to get her out of his house? The Old Woman, however, suspects this herself, and demands a solemn pledge (1202-3), which she presumably receives; and to dishonour such a pledge is a serious matter, however humble the person to whom it is given. Cf. Lys. 1.18-20, where Euphiletus gives his maidservant a pledge that she will "suffer no harm", whereupon she tells him the whole story of his wife's affair with Eratosthenes; the pledge is probably mentioned to explain why Euphiletus, who is now on trial for murdering Eratosthenes and is pleading that what he did was the lawful killing of an adulterer, has refused a challenge to surrender the maid for questioning under torture (see C. Carey, *Lysias: Selected Speeches* [Cambridge, 1989] 63). If Euphiletus (wants his judges to believe that he) thinks it vital to keep a solemn pledge even at the risk of his life, it is unimaginable that Chremylus would give such a pledge to escape a minor nuisance unless he was sure he would be able to fulfil it.

public conveniences (1184). The explanation of the apparent paradox lies in a basic principle of ancient religion: that reverence towards, worship of, and sacrifice to the gods was obligatory not because the gods were good, but because they were powerful. If a god, or a group of gods, lost their power – as some had done, over the course of cosmic (pre)history – they also lost their entitlement to reverence, worship and sacrifice: accordingly the cult of Cronus and his brethren was scanty[75] and that of Uranus non-existent, although both had once been rulers of the universe. In myth there were tales of prophecies foretelling that under certain circumstances Zeus too would fall from power; but Zeus always came to know of these prophecies and always frustrated them[76]. In the fantasy of Old Comedy, the fall of Zeus becomes possible, and a man may say to Zeus' messenger that "birds are men's gods now, and to them men must sacrifice – and not to Zeus, by Zeus!" (*Birds* 1236-7). Socrates and Strepsiades, to be sure, suffer in *Clouds* for denying the power of Zeus and refusing to worship him; but Socrates' error there was to assert, and Strepsiades' to believe, that Zeus had been overthrown, or had been destroyed, or had never existed in the first place (cf. *Clouds* 365-381) *when this was not in fact the case*. In *Wealth* Chremylus tells Wealth that he, Wealth, would be far more powerful than Zeus if only he recovered his sight (124-9), and so indeed it proves to be, to the extent that Zeus himself joins his supplanter's camp (1189-90). The Olympians have treated mortals scurvily in the past (1116-7) and cannot expect mortals to treat them any better once they have lost the power to compel obedience. The only god who matters now is Wealth, and to "revere the power of the gods" means in effect to revere *his* power – so that it is appropriate that the play should end with a procession in his honour.

But although Chremylus has thus triumphed, it remains true that before he even began to put his plan into operation, questions had been raised about it which he did not so much answer as ignore or override[77]. This was done by Poverty in the *agōn*. Chremylus had earlier argued that all human toil and endeavour is engaged in because of (i.e. in order to acquire) wealth (144-168); now Poverty[78], putting exactly

---

75   His Athenian festival, the Cronia, was so little regarded that in the mid fourth century it was possible to hold a session of the legislative commission (the *nomothetai*) on the same day (Dem. 24.26-31) to enact a law that had nothing to do with the festival.

76   Though sometimes only by the skin of his teeth. In the *Prometheus Unbound* ascribed to Aeschylus, Zeus may have been literally in hot amorous pursuit of Thetis when Prometheus told him that any son Thetis bore would be mightier than his father (cf. schol. [Aesch.] *Prom.* 167; see my *Aeschylean Tragedy* [Bari, 1996] 315, 317-8); Metis was already pregnant when Uranus and Gaea told Zeus that if she gave birth to Athena she would also bear a new ruler for the universe, whereupon Zeus swallowed her and "gave birth" to Athena himself (Hes. *Thg.* 886-900, cf. 924).

77   I now think that in my article "Aristophanes and the demon Poverty" (*CQ* 34 [1984] 314-333) I tried too hard to explain away this aspect of *Wealth*, and concluded too readily that the play would be seen as offering a practicable remedy for Athens' ills.

78   Who significantly is not the first to speak in the debate; see on 487-618.

the same proposition in different words, says (507-534) that all human activity is performed because of (i.e. in order to avoid or reduce) poverty, so that if poverty is abolished no one will work, no goods or services will be produced, and the result will be greater universal misery than ever — a *reductio ad absurdum* of Chremylus' whole project, unless some flaw can be demonstrated in Poverty's logic or assumptions.

It would not have been difficult for the dramatist, if he had wished, to let Chremylus point out such a flaw. His project is based on the principle that Wealth will enrich *the virtuous* and that this will result in everyone becoming *virtuous* and thereby rich. Now in *Wealth*, to be virtuous is normally, *inter alia*, to work for one's living: the Informer's claim to be "virtuous and patriotic" (901) is unmasked when he admits that he is neither a farmer nor a merchant nor a craftsman (903-5) but one who does nothing (906). Chremylus could thus have said to Poverty that anyone who took advantage of Wealth's bounty to live in idleness was thereby proving himself not to be virtuous and would therefore be deprived by the god of the wealth he had shown he did not deserve. Alternatively he could have relied frankly on the miraculous power of the Wealth-god, arguing (truly, as will appear in 802-822) that he will supply the virtuous not just with money[79] but with all the necessities and comforts of life. He does neither; instead he launches into a tear-jerking tirade on the wretched existence of the very poor, which has great emotive power but in no way refutes Poverty's argument.

Were this an academic debate, Poverty would point this out and ask again how a policy of automatic (monetary) enrichment would actually ensure that these people were provided with the necessities they now lack. To maintain audience interest, however, it is preferable that she should strike out in a fresh direction; accordingly she first complains that Chremylus is confusing "poverty" (defined as having just enough to live on, 553-4) with "destitution", when in truth they differ as much from each other as Dionysius does from Thrasybulus (550), and then argues that poor men (so defined) are superior to rich men both in physical fitness and in moral character (558-570)[80]. Chremylus admits that she is right (571) but despite this he still insists, in a manner that Poverty finds childish (576-8), that it is better to be rich than poor. The debate then loses itself in imponderable arguments as to whether Zeus, who gives worthless prizes to the victors at his Olympic festival, is poor or merely mean (581-591) and a final reminder from Chremylus of the destitute who snatch the food left out for Hecate (594-7). Neither side has convinced the other, and there is not, as

---

79 Poverty's argument assumes, though she never makes this explicit, that Wealth's bounty will be dispensed in the form of money alone — which is useless if there is nothing it can buy.

80 The example she chooses to illustrate this point — the politician who has become rich "from the public purse" (569) — actually refutes it, since a man who becomes rich by embezzling public money must have resolved to commit that crime while he was still poor; but once again, Chremylus is not permitted to draw attention to this illogicality.

there often is in earlier plays, a third party who can pronounce judgement; that is a task left for the audience, who are, however, given a strong hint in the words given to Chremylus at this point (598-600):

> Now get out of here, blast you, and don't utter another sound! *You won't persuade us, not even if you persuade us!*

In other words: no amount of reasoned argument, however cogent, will move us from our instinctive certainty that it is better (for us) to be rich than poor. That is not what one says if one believes that one has won the argument on evidence and logic. In effect, Chremylus acknowledges he has lost it — and carries on regardless. And, as we have seen, he is successful — though at the very end, when Wealth is led off in procession to be installed in the *opisthodomos* on the Acropolis, the installation sacrifice is the cheapest possible, pots of boiled vegetables (see on 1197).

How will the *agōn* affect our response to the rest of the play? There are some fundamental assumptions on which the action is premised, which Poverty has not refuted and has not tried to refute. She may have drawn a careful distinction between "poverty" and "destitution", but she has not denied that many hard-working people are in real want of necessities[81]; nor has she denied — indeed she has asserted — that the poor are generally virtuous and the rich wicked. What she has proved, at least against such counter-arguments as Chremylus has been allowed to adduce, is that a redistribution of wealth, either on a basis of equality or according to desert, would not, in the real world, remedy this state of affairs. Such a redistribution was certainly imaginable, at least as regards land; it was recommended by the political philosopher Phaleas of Calchedon (Arist. *Pol.* 1266a37-1267b13) and put into effect in some fourth-century democracies (Arist. *Ath.Pol.* 40.3, cf. Pl. *Rep.* 566a)[82], and Athenian jurors may have been required to swear not to permit it (Dem. 24.149)[83].

---

81 Lest anyone should forget this, Chremylus interrupts her encomium on the poor man's wiry physique with a reference to hunger (562).

82 Cf. also Solon fr. 34.8-9; Pl. *Laws* 684d-e; Arist. *Pol.* 1305a3-7, 1309a14-20, *Ath.Pol.* 11.2.

83 Dem. 24.149-151 preserves what purports to be the text of the juror's oath as a document inserted in the speech. Such documents are sometimes manifest forgeries (e.g. all those found in Dem. 18), but many show every sign of being genuine (e.g. those in Andoc. 1). This particular text reads as though an original simple oath (to judge according to law, not to take bribes, to give both sides a fair hearing, and to vote strictly on the question at issue) had been expanded at various times by the insertion into its midst of lengthy new sections on matters that happened to be of special concern at some particular moment. Such a structure is unlikely to have occurred to a forger; on the other hand at least one clause known to have been part of the actual juror's oath is missing from the document. The clause "I will not vote for the cancellation of private debts, or for the redistribution of the land or houses of the Athenians", is not inappropriate for fourth-century jurors: the panels of *nomothetai* who considered proposals for new laws were chosen from those who had sworn the juror's oath (Dem.

If Chremylus recognizes that in real-world terms Poverty is right, and yet still proceeds with his plan, it is because he is not operating in the real world but in the world of comedy, in which nothing is impossible or impracticable that could make life easier or more enjoyable[84]. The effect of the *agōn* – and perhaps likewise of the appearance of those pots of vegetables at 1197 – will thus be to remind us that this *is* a comic fantasy and should not be taken as a prescription for actual legislation.

But as usual in Aristophanes, though the remedy may be fantastic, the evil which it aims to cure is real enough. It can hardly be said that the play even suggests any remedy for this evil that *could* possibly be effective in the real world, apart from the unmasking and punishment of "crooked politicians, informers and all sorts of villains" (30-31): Poverty may reject Chremylus' solution, but has none of her own to offer except to assure the poor that deprivation is good for their souls. The play offers its audience a dream of easy affluence, but as regards the prospects of any actual amelioration of their lot its implications are as bleak and pessimistic as those of any play that its author had written[85].

5. *"Wealth" and "Ecclesiazusae"*

Wealth exhibits strikingly close resemblances, though also notable contrasts, with *Ecclesiazusae*, produced three years earlier[86]. In both plays the evil to be combated is, or is closely connected with, the problem of widespread poverty in the Athenian community (cf. *Eccl.* 408-426, 566-7, 590-606); in both the solution adopted is a radical redistribution of wealth – in the later play it is allotted according to desert, in the earlier all property is surrendered into the hands of the state and used to support and supply the population on a communal basis. The parallels extend to details far from essential to the themes of the plays. In *Ecclesiazusae* there are two older male characters who are named, *Blep*yrus and *Chrem*es; in *Wealth* there are two older

---

24.21, 27), and jurors might also find themselves voting on such issues in ordinary court trials on charges of proposing an "illegal decree" or an "inappropriate law".

84   P. Sfyroeras (*GRBS* 36 [1995] 231-261) and J. McGlew (*AJP* 118 [1997] 35-53), approaching the subject from very different angles, have both recently emphasized how fully the triumph of Chremylus' scheme accords with the norms and spirit of Aristophanic comedy.

85   This sentence has been designedly phrased to leave open the issue whether *Wealth* is more or less pessimistic than *Knights*, in which it is assumed that the conditions under which Athenian politics operates are such that a vicious demagogue like Cleon can only be defeated by an even more vicious demagogue; or *Lysistrata*, in which, even as the women's fantasy scheme succeeds in bringing an end to the war, the chorus take it for granted (1055) that in reality peace is an exceedingly remote prospect; or *Frogs*, in which, at an attention-drawing moment (the end of the parabasis), Athenians are invited (736-7) to consider it a blessing if posterity thinks Athens has met its end "on a respectable tree".

86   For the date of *Eccl.* (391, more likely City Dionysia than Lenaea) see my edition of *Eccl.* in this series (1998), pp.5-7.

male characters who are named, *Chremylus* and *Blep*sidemus. In the second half of each play, after the socioeconomic revolution has been effected, the principal scenes show first a supporter of the new order (*not* its creator) arguing with an opponent presented as selfish and anti-social (the Neighbour with the Dissident, *Eccl.* 730-876; the Honest Man with the Informer, *Wealth* 823-958), and then one or more lustful old women pursuing, eventually with success, a young man who is desperately endeavouring to escape (*Eccl.* 877-1111, *Wealth* 959-1096 + 1197-1203): no scene resembling either of these is found in any of Aristophanes' extant fifth-century plays. In these two plays, again, alone of the surviving corpus, the spouse of the hero(ine) has a speaking part[87]. Even the ophthalmological problems of the politician Neocleides (see on 665) figure in both plays, and though the passing of three years has made them considerably more severe, he is each time prescribed virtually the same "treatment" (*Eccl.* 404-7, *Wealth* 716-722) which is guaranteed to leave his last state worse than his first.

An obvious point of contrast between the two plays is that in *Ecclesiazusae* salvation is effected by a woman aided by other women, acting through the institutions of the male civic community, whereas in *Wealth* it is effected by a man aided by other men, acting quite independently of those institutions[88]. More subtle, but perhaps even more important — and perhaps interrelated — are two other contrasts. The deep pessimism which, as noted above (p. 20), is implicit in *Wealth* has no parallel in *Ecclesiazusae*, where Athens' ills are ascribed in large part to the prevalence of selfishness among the citizenry[89], an evil to whose remedy it is in the power of every individual to make a contribution. It is thus appropriate that in *Ecclesiazusae* the remedy that is applied is in fact devised and implemented entirely by human intelligence and human effort, without divine assistance of any kind, in one of the two most "secular" of all Aristophanes' comedies[90]. In *Wealth*, on the other hand, gods are everywhere. The hero consults the Delphic oracle and is instructed by Apollo to follow the first person he meets on coming out of Apollo's temple. This person proves to be the god Wealth, blinded long ago by Zeus, whom the hero persuades to allow himself to be healed. Despite the warnings of the goddess Poverty, he takes Wealth to the sanctuary of Asclepius, who comes with his

---

87 The wife of Dicaeopolis appears briefly in *Acharnians* (262) but does not speak; the wife of Strepsiades (whose extravagant habits, through her influence on her son, have been the main cause of her husband's financial distress) is much talked about in *Clouds* (46-74, 438, 800, 1443-6) but is never seen. The spouses of other hero(in)es are mentioned only briefly (*Wasps* 610-2; *Lys.* 510-520; *Thesm.* 1021, 1206).

88 As the Informer complains (948-950). Even the final procession, which is to install Wealth in a state temple, is organized by Chremylus on his own initiative and on his own authority, though the presence of the Priest of Zeus gives it a veneer of official endorsement.

89 *Eccl.* 186-8, 197-8, 202-3, 207-8, 282-4, 289-310, 376-393, 412-3, 547-8, and the entire part of the Dissident (746-876); see my edition of *Eccl.*, pp. 18-22.

90 See my edition of *Eccl.*, pp. 27-28.

divine daughters Iaso and Panacea (701-2) and restores Wealth's sight. Wealth then declares that he will in future dispense his blessings in accordance with justice (771-781) and enters the hero's house; presently we find that the hero is making a lavish sacrifice, presumably to him (819-820), and other beneficiaries of the new order come to make dedications to him (840-9, 1088-9). Meanwhile the Olympian gods and their priests are starving for want of offerings, and first Hermes and then Zeus himself (1189-90) join Wealth's camp; and the play ends with a procession to install Wealth in the *opisthodomos* of one of Athena's temples on the Acropolis[91]. Chremylus is more completely dependent on divine assistance than any other Aristophanic hero. He achieves what he does only thanks to the positive cooperation of three gods (Apollo, Wealth and Asclepius) at three separate moments: without the last-named his plan would have failed, without either of the other two it could never even have been begun[92]. The restoration of justice is effected through supernatural aid and could not have been effected without it. In the world of comedy, where it is virtually always possible for a hero(ine) to find a kindly (or at least a corruptible) god who will permit the fulfilment of the Great Idea even when Zeus is opposed to it[93], such things can happen; but something that can only happen with the help of *three* kindly gods must surely be even more thoroughly impossible than Old Comic fantasies normally are. In 391, it seems, Athens had a chance of saving herself by her exertions. In 388 it will take a miracle.

---

91   The exact identification of the *opisthodomos* is controversial (see on 1193), but in any case there would be no offence to Athena, since the *opisthodomos* of a temple was by definition a separate room from that containing the cult-statue. In any case it was common for a deity to dwell as a co-resident (*sunnāos*) in the temple of another deity: thus Erechtheus had always shared the temple of Athena Polias on the Acropolis, and even Asclepius at Epidaurus was technically a *sunnāos* of Apollo Maleatas (see p. 9 above).

92   Most other successful Aristophanic heroes, to be sure, receive signs of the favour of the gods, but only rarely do they *depend* crucially on divine assistance for their success. The occasions in question are: the divine messenger whom Dicaeopolis sends to make peace between his family and Sparta (*Ach.* 129-132, 175-203); Trygaeus persuading, or rather bribing, Hermes not to tell Zeus of his plan to rescue Peace (*Peace* 362-425); Prometheus advising Peisetaerus that in his peace negotiations with the gods he must demand not only the sceptre of cosmic kingship but also the hand of the maiden Basileia ("Princess") (*Birds* 1531-45). *Wealth* is the only play whose hero benefits crucially from *multiple* divine assistances in the course of the action.

93   This is usually made possible by the assumption that Zeus can be successfully hoodwinked. In *Peace* (376ff) Zeus will not know what Trygaeus is doing if Hermes can be persuaded not to inform on him; in *Birds* he will not know about Prometheus' meeting with Peisetaerus if they talk quietly (1504-5) and conceal themselves under a parasol. (In serious poetry Zeus can be deceived only temporarily, and the deceiver is always discovered and punished: cf. *Iliad* 15.4-219, 19.91-133, Hes. *Thg.* 521-616.) In *Wealth* nothing is said about Zeus being deceived: the question of why he does not intervene to prevent the restoration of Wealth's sight, or afterwards blind him anew, is simply not raised.

6.   *Structure and style*

The plot structure, or story pattern, of *Wealth* in all essentials maintains the format to be found, with minor variations, in all other Aristophanic comedies[94].   A character (here Chremylus) perceives that (s)he, or Athens, or the whole Greek world, is in a serious predicament, and conceives a plan (the "Great Idea"), normally of a fantastic nature, to put things right. The plan meets opposition, at first sometimes violent but usually culminating in a verbal contest in which the opponents of the Idea are defeated; in *Wealth* the opposition comes mainly from Poverty but also from the scepticism of Blepsidemus. It is then carried into effect, and the remainder of the play (beginning in *Wealth* at line 771 or 802 according to taste) presents the consequences of its implementation, usually ending, as here, with a triumphal procession or revel-rout. If we possessed only a synopsis of *Wealth* it would probably have been impossible to show convincingly that it was written towards the end of Aristophanes' career[95].

In its formal structure, however, *Wealth* carries considerably further certain changes in the form of comedy already evident in *Ecclesiazusae*. In particular, the choral and lyrical element is still further atrophied. After the entrance-sequence or *parodos* (253-321), which includes a lyric dialogue[96] (290-321) between Carion and the chorus, the surviving script includes only two further lyric utterances, the cries of joy and praise in dochmiacs (636, 639-640) when the chorus first learn of the healing of Wealth; and *Wealth* is the only surviving Aristophanic play in which no *actor* has anything to sing after the *parodos*. On the other hand, there are six points[97] where there is good evidence that ancient texts of the play contained the annotation *khorou* "<song> of the chorus" (or, at 770/1, *kommation khorou* "short stanza by the chorus"), and we know that at least one of these songs must have been relevant to the action, for Wealth's first words when he enters at 771 seem to be uttered in response to what the chorus have been singing. It appears therefore that the text of the majority of choral songs were omitted from the scripts that went into circulation, not because the songs were necessarily irrelevant to the play or not composed by its author (though this may in fact have been true of some of them),

---

94   Expounded briefly in the General Introduction prefixed to my edition of *Acharnians* (1980) in this series (pp. 11-13) and more fully by G.M. Sifakis, *JHS* 112 (1992) 123-142; see also the important earlier analysis by K.D. Koch, *Kritische Idee und komisches Thema* (Bremen, 1965).

95   It is instructive to compare the synopses of all the surviving Aristophanic plays printed in tabular form by Sifakis *op.cit.* 140-2. *Wealth* has all the features that Sifakis regards as typical except for "persuasion exercised [sc. successfully] in debate".

96   Though technically lyric, the verse of 290-321 actually differs very little from the chanted iambic tetrameters of 253-289; it consists, in fact, entirely of sequences of iambic *metra* with catalexis, eleven of which are in fact tetrameters while the other seven range in length from six *metra* to twelve (317-321).

97   321/2, 626/7, 770/1, 801/2, 958/9, 1096/7; see commentary at all these places.

but because a convention was growing up among those who read drama that they were not fully part of the play[98]. If so, the evidence of *Wealth* (as of *Aeolosicon*, cf. note 98) suggests that Aristophanes' practice was not yet, and perhaps never came to be, in conformity with the assumptions underlying this convention.

The structure of the formal debate (*agōn*), already considerably simplified in *Ecclesiazusae*, is now simplified further by the omission of the introductory choral song[99]; the chorus now merely introduce the debate with a couplet (*katakeleusmos*) encouraging the contestant they support (Chremylus, with his ally Blepsidemus) and incidentally setting the metre for the whole debate. This metre is the anapaestic tetrameter (with a continuous anapaestic run or *pnīgos* at the end); the rest of the script, with the exception of the *parodos*, the two choral cries previously mentioned, and two concluding anapaestic tetrameters from the chorus, is entirely in spoken iambic trimeters.

One of the innovations of *Ecclesiazusae* is not persisted with. In that play, the principal character, Praxagora, had left the scene little more than half-way through (727) and had never returned, with the result that there was no clear thread of continuity binding the subsequent scenes[100]. In the second half of *Wealth*, by contrast, Chremylus and his family are a constant presence: he takes the leading role in three of the six scenes (782-801, 965-1096, 1172-end), his slave Carion in the other three (627-770, 802-958, 1097-1170), in strict alternation[101]. Carion is the most prominent slave character in all Aristophanic comedy, being present for well over half the length of the play, speaking about a quarter of its lines, and supplying much of such comic power as the play ever shows, in contrast with the earnest rectitude usually displayed by his master. Like Xanthias in *Frogs*, but to an even greater extent, he foreshadows the slave characters who guide the action of some of the comedies of Menander and Plautus[102]. Aristophanes gives some signs of being

---

98 . This convention was apparently powerful enough to remove the choral songs from many copies of Ar.'s later play *Aeolosicon* (cf. Platonius, *On the Different Kinds of Comedy* 27-28 Perusino; see also note 113 below), even though fragments of them that survive from the fuller version of the text (Ar. frr. 9-10, possibly also fr. 8) suggest that they may have been highly entertaining, including e.g. an extensive catalogue of women's sexual misdeeds. The surviving fragments of *Cocalus* include some anapaests (Ar. frr. 364-5; common in Middle Comedy, cf. H.G. Nesselrath, *Die attische Mittlere Komödie* [Berlin, 1990] 267-280) but no lyrics.

99 Cf. *Eccl.* 571-580. There is no evidence that *khorou* or the like ever stood at *Wealth* 486/7.

100 This applied especially to the scene 877-1111, none of whose five characters appeared elsewhere in the play, and during which Praxagora was never even mentioned (contrast 835, 870, 1113, 1126, 1137).

101 Carion is also probably present in 782-801 and 1196-end, but does not speak.

102 For these see E. Fraenkel, *Elementi plautini in Plauto* tr. F. Munari (Florence, 1960) 223-241, 428-431. The clearest Menandrian example (not known of when Fraenkel wrote) is Daos in *Aspis*, but *Dyskolos* 183-4, where Sostratos describes his father's slave Getas as "a ball of fire, experienced in all sorts of matters" — which is not at all what

conscious that he is doing something new with Carion, since he takes some pains to establish him as one who had become a slave relatively late in life and retained much of the mental outlook of a free man[103].

As comedy, it has to be said, *Wealth* is of uneven quality. There are substantial passages, especially in the first half of the play, which it is hard to imagine arousing much laughter from an audience accustomed to plays like *Ecclesiazusae*, to say nothing of Aristophanes' earlier works. Except in certain sections (notably the lyric number 290-321) there is little of the typically Aristophanic verbal wit that juggles effortlessly with multiple meanings and elaborate puns, and even less of slapstick or obscenity. It is unlikely that Aristophanes was adapting himself in these respects to changes in public taste, for what we know of *Aeolosicon* suggests that even after 388 he could sometimes let imaginative fantasy run riot in his old way[104]; more probably he was now, at the age of sixty or thereabouts[105], able to do so only intermittently, and concentrated his most intense efforts on selected passages that could be expected to make a strong impact on the audience. It may have been as much to spare his own physical and mental resources for the task of writing as "to introduce his son ... to the spectators" that he entrusted to Araros the theatrical realization of the only two plays he was to compose subsequently.

7. *Staging*

The theatrical requirements of *Wealth* are very simple: the entire action takes place before the house of Chremylus[106], no other dwelling is represented on stage at any time, and there is no indication that any special-effects devices (*ekkuklēma* or *mēchanē*) are used. All entrances and exits are made either into or out of this house, or else by one of the two side-passages. It is possible to establish with fair

---

Getas proves to be like when he actually comes on the scene — suggests that the type was already well established when *Dyskolos* was produced in 316.

103   See on 6 and 147-8.

104   The title character was probably a cook (like the Sicon mentioned by the third-century dramatist Sosipater [fr. 1.14] as the father of the culinary art) who was simultaneously an Aeolus — and Euripides' *Aeolus*, which Ar. was parodying (Platonius op.cit. 34-35 Perusino), notoriously had as its main theme the incestuous relations between Aeolus' son(s) and daughter(s). Certainly at one point in the play Aeolosicon was organizing some highly unusual domestic arrangements for his daughters ("one bedroom and one bathtub will be enough for them all", fr. 6) and at another there was extensive discussion of women's sexual irregularities (cf. note 98 above).

105   He was probably born in the early 440s; see my edition of *Acharnians* (1980) in this series, p.24 n.2. He had had, or at least claimed to have had, a serious illness, lasting several months, in the winter preceding the production of the second *Thesmophoriazusae* (Ar. fr. 346), perhaps in 408/7 or 407/6.

106   Though it is some time before we are made aware that it *is* the house of Chremylus: see on 53-54.

confidence, on almost every occasion, which side-passage was used for any particular entrance or exit. The arguments are as follows.

(1)   Both the sanctuary of Asclepius to which Wealth is taken (see §3 above) and the temple of Zeus the Saviour (see on 1175) were in the Peiraeus, the road to which ran south-westwards from the vicinity of the Theatre of Dionysus. Accordingly all movements to or from these sanctuaries should be via the western passage (stage-left)[107], viz. the exit of Chremylus and party at 626, the return of Carion at 627, his exit at 770, and the entrance of the Priest at 1171.

(2)   When Chremylus returns from the Asclepieum at 782, he has come by way of the Agora (cf. 787); so too then, presumably, has Wealth who entered at 771. Since Carion went out westwards to meet them (770), they must enter at this side too. It follows that the western passage is to be regarded, not only as the route to the Peiraeus, but also as that to the Agora, and all movements to or from the Agora must be via this passage. This requires us to assign the following further movements to the west (left) side: the entrance of Blepsidemus at 335 (cf. 338: only in the Agora would there be several barbers' shops in close proximity); the entrance of the Informer at 850 and his exit at 950 (cf. 874); and probably also the flight of his witness at 929.

(3)   The final procession has the Acropolis as its destination (see on 1193), and therefore must also make its exit to the west, since the Acropolis, just behind and above the theatre, is only accessible at its west end.

(4)   There is good evidence, dating back to the fifth century (Cratinus fr. 229), that when a dramatic chorus entered in formation, it always entered from the left, with the result that the left file of the marching body was nearest the audience and the best performers were placed in this file[108]. There is no reason to doubt that this convention was followed in Wealth. Carion's exit at 229, where he is sent to fetch the farmers who form the chorus, will thus also be to the left.

(5)   So many movements have thus to be assigned to the left side (thirteen in all) that there is every reason to assign as many of the others as possible to the right, and in some cases there are positive arguments for doing so. At the beginning of the play, the group arriving from Delphi should enter from the opposite direction to that in which Carion will be sent at 229; the direction in which Poverty leaves at 618 should not be that by which Wealth is taken to be healed only eight lines later, but should be the same as the direction from which she enters at 415, since having failed in her mission she should be seen to return whence she came; and the Honest Man and the Informer, diametrically opposed characters, should appear from

---

107   In my stage-directions, and in the Commentary, I consistently use "right" and "left" in the modern theatrical sense, which defines these directions from the *performers'* point of view: hence in the Theatre of Dionysus, where the *skēnē* was on the south side and the performers faced north, "right" means east and "left" west. Much modern writing on the ancient theatre, contrariwise, defines right and left from the *spectators'* viewpoint.

108   Cf. Aristides 3.154 with scholia; see Csapo & Slater 353.

opposite directions. So should the Old Woman and the Young Man, who has been trying to keep as far away from her as possible; there is no direct evidence as to who enters from which side, but I have allotted their entries in such a way that throughout the last third of the play (823-end) entrances are alternately from right and left[109].

Wealth, like most of Aristophanes' other plays, was probably written to be performed by four speaking actors[110]. The first two no doubt played Chremylus and Carion throughout: the part of Chremylus is slightly the longer, but that of Carion demands a livelier and more versatile comedian, and it may well have been given to the protagonist. A possible assignment of parts is thus:

> *First actor:* Carion, Poverty
> *Second actor:* Chremylus
> *Third actor:* Wealth, Honest Man, Old Woman, Hermes
> *Fourth actor:* Blepsidemus, Wife, Informer, Youth, Priest[111]

Little attempt is made in *Wealth* to make imaginative use of properties, masks and costumes; even the comic phallus has attention drawn to it only once (see on 295). For one character, however, mask and costume are of vital importance: this is Wealth, who at first is a blind old man in rags, then is seen wearing the white raiment appropriate to a pilgrim seeking a cure from Asclepius (see on 625), and on his third appearance has the same white costume but a rejuvenated, bright-eyed face (see on 770/1). After he goes into Chremylus' house at 253, Wealth is present on stage for less than fifty of the remaining 956 lines of the play[112], and speaks only

---

109 Over the play as a whole, if the assignments here proposed are correct, entrances are made on 8 occasions from the left, on 5 from the right, and on 10 from the house; exits are made on 6 occasions to the left, on 8 to the house, and on just one occasion to the right (the odd character out who departs in this unfavoured direction is, appropriately, Poverty, the only character who has no chance whatever of sharing in the universal prosperity with which the play ends).

110 See D.M. MacDowell, *CQ* 44 (1994) 325-335. In theory the play could be performed by three actors if there was a choral song between 1170 and 1171, but there is no evidence that there was one (see on 1170/1). In the final scene there may, from 1197, be five characters present who had at one time or another had a speaking part (see on 1194-1209), but only three of them speak, so the others may be represented by supernumeraries (so too Carion and Wealth in their brief appearance at 626, and Carion in 782-801).

111 In my introduction to *Ecclesiazusae* (this series, 1998), p.31 n.122, I suggested that the scene-by-scene alternation between Chremylus and Carion in the latter part of *Wealth* was designed in part to give the leading actors opportunities to rest when they might otherwise be tiring; accordingly I have assigned all minor parts in the last third of the play to the third and fourth actors, who would have had relatively little to do in the first 800 lines and would be comparatively fresh.

112 626 (very briefly), 771-801, 1197-1209; on the first and third occasions he does not speak.

nineteen or twenty of them; yet his appearance alone shows him as both the cause and the embodiment of the transformation that has taken place in the nature and government of the universe.

8.   The first and the second "Wealth"

Several scholia on *Wealth* (all of which will be quoted below), by referring to the play of 388 as "the second", indicate that Aristophanes had written another play of the same title[113], and one of them, on 179, indicates that that play was produced in the archonship of Diocles (409/<u>8</u>). There survive eight fragments (Ar. fr. 458-465) which are ascribed by the writers who quote them to Aristophanes' *Wealth* (in one case specifically to "the first *Wealth*") and which are not found in the text of our play as transmitted. One of these may well be misattributed[114], two are single words which may derive not from a lost play but from scholiasts' explanations of related words in the surviving play[115], and one is a variant version of a line from our play[116]; but there is nothing in the remaining four to suggest why they might have been falsely attributed to *Wealth*, and they should be regarded as genuine fragments of the lost play. They tell us nothing about its plot or subject[117], but the rhythm of one of them (fr. 459) suggests that it is the end of an long iambic run (*pnīgos*) such as commonly follows a speech in iambic tetrameters in a formal debate (*agōn*), and its content suggests that this speech may have been to some extent parallel to the

---

113   Or, to be precise, that on two occasions, separated by an interval of years, he had produced a play called *Wealth*. References to a "first" and a "second" play of the same title do not by themselves tell us whether we are dealing with two quite distinct compositions (as in the case of the two plays called *Peace* or the two called *Thesmophoriazusae*) or with the original and the revised versions of what was essentially the same play (as in the case of *Clouds* and perhaps *Aeolosicon* – though the "first" and "second" versions of *Aeolosicon* may well in fact have been scripts of precisely the same play differing only in that in the "first" version the choral songs were written out in full whereas in the "second", as in our text of *Wealth*, there were only indications of the places where these songs were to stand; see my forthcoming paper in J.A. López Férez ed. *Estudios actuales sobre textos griegos: Comedia* [Madrid]); and in fact this is currently a disputed question in the case of *Wealth* (see below, pp. 31–33).

114   Fr. 460 (*anapēriā* "deformity") is ascribed by one of the four sources that cite it (Pollux 2.61) to "Cratinus' *Wealth*" (Cratinus fr. 179); Cratinus did not write a play called *Wealth (Ploutos)*, but he did write a play called *The Wealth-gods (Ploutoi)*, and it is possible that the word was used in that play and the attribution to Ar. is mistaken.

115   Fr. 461 *graïzein* "remove skim" (cf. *Wealth* 1206 *graus* "skim"); fr. 462 *epikrousasthai* "rebuke, criticize" (cf. *Wealth* 548 *epekrousō* "you have condemned").

116   Fr. 458, which I believe to be Ar.'s revised, and (somewhat) improved, version of *Wealth* 115 (see *ad loc.*)

117   Though fr. 465 suggests that there was at least one character who spoke a non-Attic dialect.

speech of Poverty in the *agōn* of our play, arguing (as in *Wealth* 558-570) that poor men are physically and morally better than rich men[118].

That Aristophanes should have written, twenty years apart, two plays with the same title and at least partly parallel content is in no way surprising. What *is* surprising is that at least one of the ancient commentators on our play clearly thought that he was commentating on the play of 408. There are six scholia, scattered through the play, that betray this confusion[119]; they are translated below.

> *115:* He uses *ophthalmiā*, which properly means a disease of the eyes <rather than actual blindness>; for which reason it has been altered in the second <*Wealth*> to read "release you from this affliction that has you in its grip".
>
> *119:* This also has been altered in the second <*Wealth*>.
>
> *173:* "The mercenary force at Corinth": because the Corinthians always had some mercenary force, not with special reference to the current situation. This is clear because it is found in the second <*Wealth*>, which was the author's last production twenty years later. Unless, as is likely, it has been transferred <to this place> from the second; for there it is appropriate, because the Corinthian war had already begun three or four years[120] before the archonship of Antipater in which <the second *Wealth*> was produced.
>
> *179:* "Laïs[121] loves Philonides": Note that what Aristophanes says does not fit the chronology; for they say that she was captured in Sicily at the age of seven when a small town was taken by Nicias ... . If one grants that this happened in the archonship of Charias [415/4], when the Athenians were doing well in Sicily, there are <only> fourteen years <from her birth> to the archonship of Diocles, so that it would be absurd to praise her by name. Plato <the comic dramatist> refers to her in *Phaōn*, which was produced seventeen years later in the archonship of Philocles [392/1], as "no

---

118 The fragment speaks of something (we do not know what, except that the Greek word for it was singular and feminine) that is "the cause of many slaps for the stragglers in the torch-race"; this recalls *Frogs* 1089-98 (at the end of an *agōn*!) where Dionysus recalls how he once saw, during the Panathenaic torch-race, a "slow fellow ... pale-faced and fat" (cf. *Wealth* 560: rich men are "pot-bellied and thick-calved and obscenely fat") being slapped on all parts of his body as he passed the Dipylon Gate (apparently a traditional method of "encouraging" the slowest runners on such occasions).

119 In the translations of these scholia, words in angled brackets have been added by me for ease of understanding.

120 The *war* had begun seven years before; the mercenary force itself had been in existence for about four and a half years.

121 All mss. and scholia call the woman Laïs, though external evidence suggests that the name Ar. wrote was Naïs; see commentary *ad loc.*

longer existing", though it is possible that this might be said even while she was alive.

> *972:* As a matter of fact they also sat in the Council in this way <viz. in groups distinguished by letters of the alphabet>, beginning in the year before this; for Philochorus says: "In the archonship of Glaucippus [410/9] the Council too for the first time sat by letter."
>
> *1146:* But this <viz. the occupation of Phyle by Thrasybulus> had not yet taken place, nor had the events of the time of the Thirty yet occurred; as Philochorus says, they happened five years later ... . Therefore someone has apparently transferred this from the second *Wealth*, ignoring the illogicality, or else the poet himself inserted it later.

It will be seen that the commentator in question was so certain that he was correct in hypothesizing the play before him to be the play of 408 that when he found passages in the text that were clearly incompatible with so early a date, rather than abandon the hypothesis he preferred to assume that these passages were interpolated from the second *Wealth*. How did this extraordinary error arise?

It is clear from the above scholia that our commentator was acquainted with two, and only two, versions of the text of *Wealth*: the version we have, which he called the "first *Wealth*", and another which he identified as the second. These two, moreover, were not the scripts of two different plays, but alternative versions, differing only in particular passages or scenes, of one and the same play: this is evident, not only from the implication in the scholia to 173 and 1146 that these lines were present in the "second *Wealth*", but also from the fact that 115 and 119 are specifically said to have been "altered" in that version, which implies that most of their context was retained unaltered. And both versions contained passages that could not have been written so early as 409/8. From this it follows that the actual text of the *Wealth* of 408 was not available to this commentator, just as the text of the second *Peace* was not available to Eratosthenes[122] (librarian at Alexandria ca. 245-195 BC). Probably the Alexandrian library did not have a copy of the real *Wealth I*[123]; the scanty surviving quotations from it may well derive, as in the case of *Peace II*[124], from scholars like Crates (early second century BC) working at the rival library of Pergamum.

Our commentator, then, who thought he was looking at the *Wealth* of 408 and the *Wealth* of 388, must actually have been looking at two alternative versions of the script of the latter play. They no doubt differed at more than the two points (115 and 119) about which we happen to be informed, but we have no evidence that the differences were more extensive than the minor updates and stylistic revisions that

---

122 Hypothesis II (Olson, Holwerda) to *Peace*.
123 Cf. W. Kraus, *Testimonia Aristophanea cum scholiorum lectionibus* (Vienna, 1931) 55.
124 *Ibid.* These two plays are the worst attested of all the undisputedly genuine lost plays of Ar.; *The Phoenician Maidens* comes next with seven citations.

appear to have been made in *Frogs* between its original production early in 405 and
its restaging (by special decree of the Athenian Assembly) a year later[125]. *Wealth*
too, then, it seems, was revised for a second production, in this case presumably not
at the Lenaea or City Dionysia but at one or more local celebrations of the Country
Dionysia, nine to eleven months after the original performance[126]. In the one case
where we possess both versions of the text (115; see commentary *ad loc.*) the
revision seems to have been made merely to remove a stylistic infelicity.

Our knowledge of the *Wealth* of 408 is thus limited to what can be inferred
from the few surviving quotations (see above) — unless, that is, we can accept a
recent, radical suggestion by MacDowell (324-7). Noting that "about half" of all the
topical allusions in our play are concentrated in one passage of eleven lines (170-
180)[127] and that several others either are not essential to their context or (like the
reference to Pauson at 602) would or might also have been topical in 408,
MacDowell has argued that the *Wealth* of 388 was not a new play but a revised
version of the play produced twenty years earlier. On this view, Ar. had deleted all
outdated topical allusions, almost all the original lyrics, and the parabasis if any, and
had inserted one highly concentrated passage of current topicalities and a few others
at scattered points, as well as one new song (290-321)[128], but may well have left
most of the rest of the play largely unchanged. This proposal is, however, open to a
number of serious objections, of which I summarize the most important here:

(a)   MacDowell holds that the commentator whose work we have been
considering had both the 408 and the 388 text available to him, at least at one stage
of his work, and mistook each for the other[129]. Since no one could have made such
an error had he actually read through the two texts, MacDowell is forced to suppose

---

125   See my notes on *Frogs* 1251-60, 1431a-b, 1435-66, and 1512.

126   A surviving inscription (*IG* i^3 970 = ii^2 3090) appears to commemorate a victory by Ar.
      in such a contest at Eleusis. The explanation here adopted of the scholiast's error is due
      to B.B. Rogers, *The Plutus of Aristophanes* (London, 1907) vii-xiii, which remains by
      far the best discussion of this problem. Kraus *loc.cit.* finds the revised text of 115 so
      insipid that he supposes the revision to have been the work of a producer reviving the
      play later in the fourth century; but there are enough other insipid lines in the play to
      make such an inference decidedly unsafe.

127   Though one is hardly justified in saying that "this looks very much like a package which
      has been thrust in at a convenient point" (MacDowell 325), given that there is a very
      similar "package" of concentrated topicality in *Ecclesiazusae* (193-203).

128   This song contains a reference (302-5) to the liaison between Naïs/Laïs and Philonides
      (cf. the scholium on 179 cited above); moreover, the dithyramb of which it is a parody,
      the *Cyclops* of Philoxenus of Cythera, was believed in antiquity to have been written
      during or after Philoxenus' residence at the court of Dionysius of Syracuse who first
      came to power in 405.

129   This is never explicitly stated in MacDowell's discussion, which, however, speaks
      throughout of "the two versions" of the play, refers to the text of 408 as "the first
      version", and claims that the scholium on 115 "shows that [the scholiast] had both
      versions in front of him when he was writing his note".

that whereas at 115 and 119 this commentator "had both versions in front of him" and compared them in detail, by the time he wrote his notes on 173 and 1146 "he did not bother to check the other version to see whether these lines were in it too, or perhaps ... the other version was no longer available to him"[130]. This supposition, however, is in conflict with the text of the scholium on 173, which argues for a particular interpretation of that line *on the ground that it is present* in the "second" *Wealth*.

(b)   It is true, as MacDowell claims, that neither the reference to Thrasybulus and Dionysius in 550, nor that to the amnesty of 403 BC in 1146, is "essential to the passage in which it occurs", in the sense that both passages are *intelligible* if the lines in question are omitted. In both cases, however, their omission would damage the *run of the dialogue*. Poverty's retort to 549 is far more effective rhetorically with 550 than without it; and Carion's abandonment at 1148 of his previous attitude of dismissive contempt towards Hermes, which otherwise would seem entirely unmotivated, finds an explanation in Hermes' appeal at 1146 to the principle of clemency to the defeated.

(c)   Both in 408 and in 388 Athens was at war with Sparta, so that it would not have been necessary, in revision, to delete all references to the war and the Spartans; yet the text we have contains no mention whatever of the Spartans, and its only references to war come in a passage (172-3) which cannot have been part of the 408 text.

(d)   Every surviving fifth-century play by Ar. contains at least one mention by name of Sophocles and/or Euripides. Such references would not have become dated in 388, since Sophocles and Euripides continued to be regarded as the greatest of tragic dramatists and their works remained popular (indeed, official restagings of "old" tragedies at the City Dionysia began only two years later[131]); but none appear in the surviving text of *Wealth*.

(e)   The one substantial fragment that is explicitly attributed to *Wealth I* (Ar. fr. 459, discussed above), coming as it probably does from the end of a speech in the *agōn*, shows that that speech was in iambic tetrameters[132]; the whole *agōn* of the surviving play is in anapaestic rhythm. Hence *either* the metre of the *agōn* as a whole was changed in the revision of the play, *or* the debate in *Wealth I*, unlike that in *Wealth II*, had the complex, bipartite structure found in all Ar.'s other fifth-century plays that have an *agōn* at all, and his revision involved the complete suppression of one of its two halves and the expansion of the other. Either of these alternatives would imply a complete rewriting of this part of the play.

---

130   Alternatively, and perhaps more plausibly, it could be supposed that our commentator's information about the text of the "second" version in 115 and 119 was second-hand information obtained from the work of an earlier scholar, which was itself perhaps available to him only through excerpts preserved in another commentary.

131   *IG* ii² 2318.201-3.

132   Cf. *Knights* 841-940, *Clouds* 1034-84, 1351-90, 1397-1451, *Frogs* 905-991.

(f)   The surviving script contains, in addition to the 252-line "prologue" preceding the entry of the chorus, three continuous passages, respectively of 165, 157 and 138 iambic trimeters (322-486, 802-958, 959-1096), unbroken by any passage in any other metre or any indication of a choral interlude. The longest such stretch of trimeters, outside the prologue, in any of Ar.'s surviving fifth-century plays is 132 lines (*Frogs* 1119-1250), and none of these plays contains more than one such stretch extending beyond 105 lines; whereas his one other surviving fourth-century play, *Ecclesiazusae*, has three of 177, 147 and 178[133] lines respectively (311-477, 730-876, 976-1153).

(g)   *Wealth* contains the only three Aristophanic passages (29, 695, 822) in which metre guarantees that the first person singular imperfect tense of the verb "to be" has the later Attic form *ēn* instead of the earlier *ē*.

(h)   Personal names based on the roots *Chrem-* and *Blep-* occur both in *Ecclesiazusae* and in *Wealth*, and also in later comedy, but not in any fifth-century comic text[134].

(i)   There are doubtless many things in the script we have that could have been said equally well in 408; but there is nothing that fits *better* in 408 than in 388, and that would be very surprising in a revised text whose author, according to MacDowell, "lacked the energy and will to do much new writing": it takes very careful revision indeed to remove from a text, after twenty years, *everything* that has become even mildly out of date.

I conclude that MacDowell's proposal is unacceptable and that *Wealth* as we have it must be regarded as a play composed *de novo* for production in 388, as is anyway suggested by its strong affinity of theme with *Ecclesiazusae* and its tendency to carry further trends already evident in that play (see §§5 and 6 above).

---

133   Or 136 if there was a choral interlude after *Eccl.* 1111.

134   See on 22 and 332. Compare section 5 above for other close parallels between *Wealth* and *Ecclesiazusae* — though a determined advocate of the revision theory might in principle argue that some of these could result from Ar.'s having modelled *Eccl.* on the *Wealth* of 408.

NOTE ON THE TEXT

Fragments of 200-250 lines of *Wealth* are preserved in seven papyri; the oldest of these, published only in 1999, makes a vital contribution to the long-standing debate about choral interludes in this play (see on 321/2 and 958/9) and also provides evidence of a hitherto unsuspected extra line (whether genuine or spurious) before or after 968. In the Middle Ages (and long thereafter) *Wealth* was the most popular of Aristophanes' plays, and the surviving medieval manuscripts number more than 150. As in the other plays most intensively studied (*Clouds* and *Frogs*), the tradition is "open" — which means that those who owned or copied texts often had, and often took advantage of, the opportunity to correct them from sources other than the exemplars from which they had originally been copied — and virtually any reading found in one or more mss. not substantially affected by the editorial work of the early fourteenth-century scholars Thomas Magister and Demetrius Triclinius *may* in principle have come down from antiquity[1] (though the great majority of such readings are scribal errors, or good or bad attempted emendations). Accordingly no attempt has been made in the apparatus of this edition to specify the precise source(s) of readings reported from medieval mss., except for the two oldest, R and V; later mss. in the pre-Thoman tradition are denoted collectively by *n* (or *n'* where two or more readings are reported from mss. of this class), Thoman emendations by Th., Triclinian emendations by Tricl., and emendations apparently originating from unknown scholars of the later fourteenth and fifteenth centuries by *x*.

SIGLA[2]
Manuscripts etc.

Century

Fragments of ancient manuscripts

Π18	Oxyrhynchus Papyrus 1617 (contains fragments of 1-56)	5th
Π19	Berlin Papyrus 13231A+21202 (contains 134-8, 140-4, 171-3, 289-293, 311-9, 326-330, 347-355)	5th/6th
Π21	Antinoopolis Papyrus III 180 (contains 466-7, 476-7, 499-501, 510-1, 806-8, 842-5)	5th/6th
Π63	Laurentian Papyrus III 319 (contains 1135-9)	5th/6th
Π81	Oxyrhynchus Papyrus 4519 (contains 1-16)	3rd
Π82	Oxyrhynchus Papyrus 4520 (contains 635-679, 698-738)	5th
Π83	Oxyrhynchus Papyrus 4521 (contains 687-705, 726-731, 957-970)	2nd

---

1   See K.J. Dover, "Explorations in the history of the text of Aristophanes", in *The Greeks and their Legacy: Collected Papers, Vol. II* (Oxford, 1989) 223-265. There is still no adequate detailed study of the textual tradition of *Wealth* to match Chantry's of the scholia (see Bibliography).

2   Not all the mss. listed here are actually cited in the apparatus.

Middle Byzantine manuscripts

R	Ravennas 429	10th
V	Venetus Marcianus 474	11th/12th

Late Byzantine manuscripts unaffected by Thomas' and Triclinius' editorial work[3]

A	Parisinus Regius 2712	13th/14th
E	Estensis gr. 127 (= α.U.5.10)	late 14th
K	Ambrosianus C222 inf.	13th/14th
M	Ambrosianus L39 sup.	early 14th
Md1	Matritensis 4683 (older portion contains 1-528 only)	13th/14th
Np1	Neapolitanus II F 22	14th
P22	Parisinus gr. supp. 655	14th
Vb3	Vaticanus Barberinianus gr. 126	14th
Vs1	Vaticanus Reginae Suecorum gr. 147	14th
Θ	Laurentianus *conv. soppr.* 140	14th
Φ	Laurentianus *conv. soppr.* 66	late 13th

n'	one or more of the above mss.
n	the tradition represented by the above mss.

Manuscripts reflecting the recension of Thomas Magister (c.1300)

Cr	Cremonensis 171 (older portion contains 253-366, 423-1097, 1127-82)	late 14th
P25	Parisinus Regius 2820 (older portion contains 354-615, 769-941)	early 14th
V2	Venetus Marcianus 472	early 14th
Vv2	Vaticanus gr. 57 (lacks 805-914)	14th
Th.	emendations first appearing in Thomas' recension	

Manuscripts reflecting the recensions of Demetrius Triclinius (c.1315-30)

P20	Parisinus suppl. gr. 463 (extensively annotated in Triclinius' hand)	early 14th
L	(Oxoniensis Bodleianus) Holkhamensis 88	early 15th
Vv5	Vaticanus gr. 1294	14th
Tricl.	emendations first appearing in Triclinius' recension	

x	emendations first appearing in later recensions based on those of Triclinius
Ald.	the Aldine *editio princeps* (Venice, 1498)

---

3   In some of these mss., notably Θ, some Triclinian readings have been inserted by later correctors.

codd. = RV*n*

Other Symbols

Σ	scholion
Σ(i), Σ(ii), ...	separate scholia on the same passage in the same ms(s).
λ	lemma (words from the text quoted as the heading of a scholion)
γρ	reading noted in ms. or scholia as a variant
i	implied by or inferable from
ac	before correction
pc	after correction
s	above the line
mg	in the margin
vel sim.	or the like; with unimportant or irrelevant variations
R^1 (et sim.)	the hand of the original copyist
R^2 (et sim.)	any later hand
αρ (et sim.)	these letters cannot be identified with certainty from the visible traces
[ ]	denotes portions of the text of a papyrus that are lost
< >	denotes tentative editorial supplements[4]
† †	denotes corrupt readings that have not been satisfactorily emended
Suda^A	the ms. A of the Suda lexicon
Suda^r	all significant mss. of the Suda except those cited for a different reading

---

4   Or, in the Commentary, words added to clarify the sense of elliptical expressions.

Select Bibliography

Aristophanes

Editions of the complete plays. The best complete modern edition is still that of V. Coulon (Collection Budé: Paris, 1923-30), with French translation, introductions, and brief notes by H. van Daele. A critical edition of the eleven comedies will form volume III.1 of *Poetae Comici Graeci* (see next paragraph). The edition of F.W. Hall and W.M. Geldart (Oxford Classical Texts: 2nd ed., Oxford, 1906-7) provides neither a reliable text nor a systematic apparatus. Of importance for their commentaries are the editions of J. van Leeuwen (Leiden, 1896-1909) and B.B. Rogers (London, 1902-15); Rogers' text and translation formed the basis of the very inadequate Loeb Classical Library edition (London/Cambridge MA, 1924), now being replaced by a new Loeb edition by J.J. Henderson (1998-). Two series of editions with commentary, by various editors, are currently in progress (Oxford, 1965- , 7 vols. so far published; Milan, 1985- , with Italian translation by D. Del Corno, 4 vols. so far published).

Fragments of lost plays. R. Kassel and C. Austin, *Poetae Comici Graeci* (Berlin, 1983-), is superseding, as its publication progresses, all previous collections of comic fragments; the fragments of Aristophanes are in volume III.2 (1984).

Scholia (ancient and medieval commentaries). The edition of all the *Scholia in Aristophanem* under the direction of W.J.W. Koster and D. Holwerda (Groningen, 1960-) is now complete for nine of the eleven plays. The scholia to *Wealth* are contained in Pars III, Fasc. IVa (older scholia; ed. M. Chantry, 1994); Pars III, Fasc. IVb (later scholia; ed. M. Chantry, 1996); and Pars IV, Fasc. I (commentary of Ioannes Tzetzes; ed. L. Massa Positano, 1960). The edition by W.G. Rutherford (London, 1896) is of the scholia in the ms. R only.

There is an *index verborum* to Aristophanes by O.J. Todd (Cambridge MA, 1932).

Bibliographies. Reports on research on, and literature about, Aristophanes appeared in *(Bursians) Jahresbericht über die Fortschritte der klassischen Altertumswissenschaft* every few years from 1877 to 1939. Subsequent surveys (those asterisked also cover other writers of Old Comedy) include those by K.J. Dover, *Lustrum* 2 (1957) 52-112 (for 1938-55); W. Kraus, *Anzeiger für die Altertumswissenschaft* 24 (1971) 161-180 (for 1949-70);*H.J. Newiger, *Aristophanes und die alte Komödie* (Darmstadt, 1975) 487-510 (for 1955-73); *I.C. Storey, *EMC* 6 (1987) 1-46 (for 1975-84) and *Antichthon* 26 (1992) 1-29 (for 1982-91); and B. Zimmermann, *Anzeiger für die Altertumswissenschaft* 45 (1992) 161-184 and 47 (1994) 1-18 (for 1971-92).

General studies

W. Schmid, *Geschichte der griechischen Literatur* I.iv (Munich, 1946) 174-440.

A. Lesky, *A History of Greek Literature* (tr. J. Willis and C. de Heer) (London, 1966) 417-452.

T. Gelzer, "Aristophanes (12)", in *RE* Supplementband XII cols. 1391-1570; also published separately as *Aristophanes der Komiker* (Stuttgart, 1971).

E.W. Handley, "Comedy", in P.E. Easterling and B.M.W. Knox ed. *The Cambridge History of Classical Literature* i (Cambridge, 1985) 355-425 = *Greek Drama* (Cambridge, 1989) 103-173 (for bibliography, by M. Drury, see pp.773-9 = 189-195).

H.J. Newiger ed. *Aristophanes und die alte Komödie* (Darmstadt, 1975). An anthology of twentieth-century articles.

E. Segal ed. *Oxford Readings in Aristophanes* (Oxford, 1996). Another anthology.

K.J. Dover, *Aristophanic Comedy* (London, 1972).

A. Solomos, *The Living Aristophanes* (tr. A. Solomos and M. Felheim) (Ann Arbor, 1974).

K.J. Reckford, *Aristophanes' Old-and-New Comedy I: Six Essays in Perspective* (Chapel Hill NC, 1987).

J.M. Bremer and E.W. Handley ed. *Aristophane* (*Entretiens sur l'antiquité classique* 38) (Geneva, 1993).

A.M. Bowie, *Aristophanes: Myth, Ritual and Comedy* (Cambridge, 1993).

L.K. Taaffe, *Aristophanes and Women* (London, 1993).

G. Mastromarco, *Introduzione a Aristofane* (Bari, 1994).

D.M. MacDowell, *Aristophanes and Athens: An Introduction to the Plays* (Oxford, 1995).

G.W. Dobrov ed. *Beyond Aristophanes: Transition and Diversity in Greek Comedy* (Atlanta, 1995).

P. Thiercy and M. Menu ed. *Aristophane: la langue, la scène, la cité* (Bari, 1996).

S. Halliwell, *Aristophanes: Birds, Lysistrata, Assembly-Women, Wealth* (Oxford, 1997) ix-lxxix.

G.W. Dobrov ed. *The City as Comedy: Society and Representation in Athenian Drama* (Chapel Hill, 1997).

B. Zimmermann, *Die griechische Komödie* (Düsseldorf/Zürich, 1998) 9-188.

P. Thiercy, *Aristophane et l'Ancienne Comédie* (Paris, 1999).

M.S. Silk, *Aristophanes and the Definition of Comedy* (Oxford, 2000).

Dramatic technique

T. Zielinski, *Die Gliederung der altattischen Komödie* (Leipzig, 1885).

P. Mazon, *Essai sur la composition des comédies d'Aristophane* (Paris, 1904).

H.J. Newiger, *Metapher und Allegorie: Studien zu Aristophanes* (Munich, 1957).

T. Gelzer, *Der epirrhematische Agon bei Aristophanes* (Munich, 1960).

C.H. Whitman, *Aristophanes and the Comic Hero* (Cambridge MA, 1964).

K.D. Koch, *Kritische Idee und komisches Thema* (Bremen, 1965).

P. Rau, *Paratragodia: Untersuchungen einer komischen Form des Aristophanes* (Munich, 1967).

G.M. Sifakis, *Parabasis and Animal Choruses* (London, 1971).

M. Landfester, *Handlungsverlauf und Komik in den frühen Komödien des Aristophanes* (Berlin, 1977).

K. McLeish, *The Theatre of Aristophanes* (London, 1980).

B. Zimmermann, "The parodoi of the Aristophanic comedies", *SIFC* (3rd ser.) 2 (1984) 13-24; reprinted with revisions in Segal ed. *Oxford Readings in Aristophanes* 182-193.

P. Thiercy, *Aristophane: fiction et dramaturgie* (Paris, 1986).

N.J. Lowe, "Greek stagecraft and Aristophanes", in J. Redmond ed. *Themes in Drama 10: Farce* (Cambridge, 1988) 33-52.

T.K. Hubbard, *The Mask of Comedy: Aristophanes and the Intertextual Parabasis* (Ithaca NY, 1991).

G.M. Sifakis, "The structure of Aristophanic comedy", *JHS* 112 (1992) 123-142.

W.G. Arnott, "Comic openings", *Drama* 2 (1993) 14-32, with response by N. Felson-Rubin (33-38).

P. von Möllendorff, *Grundlagen einer Ästhetik der Alten Komödie* (Tübingen, 1995).

G. Mastromarco, "La commedia antica fra tradizione e innovazione", in J.A. López Férez ed. *La comedia griega y su influencia en la literatura española* (Madrid, 1998) 23-42.

B. Zimmermann, "Innovation und Tradition in den Komödien des Aristophanes", *SRCG* 1 (1998) 275-287.

J.P. Poe, "Entrances, exits, and the structure of Aristophanic comedy", *Hermes* 127 (1999) 189-207.

N.W. Slater, "Making the Aristophanic audience", *AJP* 120 (1999) 351-368.

P. Totaro, *Le seconde parabasi di Aristofane* (Stuttgart, 1999).

M. Treu, *Undici cori comici: aggressività, derisione e tecniche drammatiche in Aristofane* (Genoa, 1999).

Language and style

J. Taillardat, *Les images d'Aristophane*[2] (Paris, 1965).

E.S. Spyropoulos, *L'accumulation verbale chez Aristophane* (Thessaloniki, 1974).

K.J. Dover, "The style of Aristophanes", in *Greek and the Greeks* (Oxford, 1987) 224-236.

K.J. Dover, "Language and character in Aristophanes", *ibid.* 237-248[5].

---

5   These two articles are revised versions of papers originally published in Italian in 1970 and 1976 respectively.

J.J. Henderson, *The Maculate Muse: Obscene Language in Attic Comedy*[2] (Oxford, 1991).

S.D. Olson, "Names and naming in Aristophanic comedy", *CQ* 42 (1992) 304-319.

A. López Eire, *La lengua coloquial de la comedia aristofánica* (Murcia, 1996).

A. López Eire, "Lengua y política en la comedia aristofánica", in A. López Eire ed. *Sociedad, política y literatura: comedia griega antigua* (Salamanca, 1997) 45-80.

A.H. Sommerstein, "The anatomy of euphemism in Aristophanic comedy", in F. De Martino and A.H. Sommerstein ed. *Studi sull'eufemismo* (Bari, 1999) 181-217.

S. Colvin, *Dialect in Aristophanes* (Oxford, 1999).

L. McClure, *Spoken like a Woman: Speech and Gender in Athenian Drama* (Princeton, 1999), esp. ch. 2 and 6.

Metre

J.W. White, *The Verse of Greek Comedy* (London, 1912). Still valuable on the spoken and chanted (as distinct from lyric) metres.

A.M. Dale, *The Lyric Metres of Greek Drama*[2] (Cambridge, 1968).

B. Zimmermann, *Untersuchungen zur Form und dramatischen Technik der aristophanischen Komödien* (3 vols., Königstein/Frankfurt, 1984-7).

L.P.E. Parker, *The Songs of Aristophanes* (Oxford, 1996).

Production

T.B.L. Webster, *Monuments Illustrating Old and Middle Comedy*[3] (rev. J.R. Green) (*BICS* Suppl. 39, 1978).

C.W. Dearden, *The Stage of Aristophanes* (London, 1976).

H.J. Newiger, "Drama und Theater", in G.A. Seeck ed. *Das griechische Drama* (Darmstadt, 1979) 434-503.

L.M. Stone, *Costume in Aristophanic Comedy* (New York, 1981).

A.W. Pickard-Cambridge, *The Dramatic Festivals of Athens*[3] (rev. J. Gould and D.M. Lewis) (Oxford, 1988).

J.R. Green, "On seeing and depicting the theatre in classical Athens", *GRBS* 32 (1991) 15-50.

O.P. Taplin, *Comic Angels and Other Approaches to Greek Drama through Vase-Paintings* (Oxford, 1993).

C.F. Russo, *Aristophanes: An Author for the Stage* (London, 1994).

Comedy and society

G.E.M. de Ste Croix, *The Origins of the Peloponnesian War* (London, 1972), Appendix XXIX.

J.J. Winkler and F.I. Zeitlin ed. *Nothing to Do with Dionysos?* (Princeton, 1990), esp. chapters by Goldhill, Ober & Strauss, and Henderson.

S. Halliwell, "Comic satire and freedom of speech in classical Athens", *JHS* 111 (1991) 48-70.

A.H. Sommerstein, "Old Comedians on Old Comedy", *Drama* 1 (1992) 14-33.

A.H. Sommerstein et al. ed. *Tragedy, Comedy and the Polis* (Bari, 1993), esp. chapters by Henderson, Halliwell, Mastromarco and Handley.

A.T. Edwards, "Historicizing the popular grotesque: Bakhtin's *Rabelais* and Attic Old Comedy", in R.S. Scodel ed. *Theater and Society in the Classical World* (Ann Arbor, 1993).

C. Carey, "Comic ridicule and democracy", in R.G. Osborne and S. Hornblower ed. *Ritual, Finance, Politics: Athenian Democratic Accounts Presented to David Lewis* (Oxford, 1994) 69-83.

E.G. Csapo and W.J. Slater, *The Context of Ancient Drama* (Ann Arbor, 1994); a sourcebook of texts and images on all aspects of the theatrical and social environment of drama.

P.A. Cartledge, *Aristophanes and his Theatre of the Absurd* (3rd ed., Bristol, 1995).

J.R. Green, *Theatre in Ancient Greek Society* (London, 1995).

A.H. Sommerstein, "How to avoid being a *komodoumenos*", *CQ* 46 (1996) 327-356.

M. Heath, "Aristophanes and the discourse of politics", in Dobrov ed. *The City as Comedy* (Chapel Hill, 1997; see above) 230-249.

A.H. Sommerstein, "The theatre audience and the Demos", in J.A. López Férez ed. *La comedia griega y su influencia en la literatura española* (Madrid, 1998) 43-62.

I.C. Storey, "Poets, politicians and perverts: personal humour in Aristophanes", *Classics Ireland* 5 (1998) 85-134.

J.J. Henderson, "Attic Old Comedy, frank speech, and democracy", in D. Boedeker and K.A. Raaflaub ed. *Democracy, Empire and the Arts in Fifth-century Athens* (Cambridge MA, 1998) 255-273.

M.M. Mactoux, "Esclaves-femmes dans le Corpus d'Aristophane", in F. Reduzzi Merola and A. Storchi Marino ed. *Femmes-esclaves: modèles d'interprétation anthropologique, économique, juridique* (Naples, 1999) 21-46.

C.B.R. Pelling, *Literary Texts and the Greek Historian* (London, 2000) 123-163.

Miscellaneous

E. Fraenkel, *Beobachtungen zu Aristophanes* (Rome, 1962).

V. Ehrenberg, *The People of Aristophanes: A Sociology of Old Attic Comedy*[3] (New York, 1962).

W. Süss, *Aristophanes und die Nachwelt* (Leipzig, 1911).

G.A.H. van Steen, *Venom in Verse: Aristophanes in Modern Greece* (Princeton, 2000).

Wealth

Editions. The only twentieth-century editions with commentary of *Wealth* were two which formed part of complete Aristophanes series, those by J. van Leeuwen (Leiden, 1904) and B.B. Rogers (London, 1907). There is also a posthumously published commentary by K. von Holzinger (Vienna, 1940; reprinted New York, 1979), which concentrates on questions of text and linguistic interpretation; unfortunately Holzinger's recension of the text, which he had assumed would be available to users of the commentary, was never published. Valuable annotations accompany the Italian translation (with facing text) by G. Paduano (Milan, 1988).

Books and articles

T.B.L. Webster, *Studies in Later Greek Comedy* (Manchester, 1953; 2nd ed. 1970) 10-36.

H. Flashar, "Zur Eigenart des aristophanischen Spätwerkes", *Poetica* 1 (1967) 154-175; reprinted in H.J. Newiger ed. *Aristophanes und die alte Komödie* (Darmstadt, 1975) 405-434, and translated as "The originality of Aristophanes' last plays" in Segal ed. *Oxford Readings in Aristophanes* 314-328.

G. Hertel, *Die Allegorie von Reichtum und Armut* (Nuremberg, 1969).

F. Heberlein, *Pluthygieia: Zur Gegenwelt bei Aristophanes* (Frankfurt, 1980).

F. Heberlein, "Zur Ironie im 'Plutus' des Aristophanes", *WJA* 7 (1981) 27-49.

D. Konstan and M.J. Dillon, "The ideology of Aristophanes' *Wealth*", *AJP* 102 (1981) 371-394; revised version in D. Konstan, *Greek Comedy and Ideology* (New York, 1995) 75-90.

M.J. Dillon, *Aristophanes' Ploutos: Comedy in Transition* (Diss. Yale 1984)

E. David, *Aristophanes and Athenian Society of the Early Fourth Century B.C.* (Leiden, 1984).

A.H. Sommerstein, "Aristophanes and the demon Poverty", *CQ* 34 (1984) 314-333; reprinted in Segal ed. *Oxford Readings in Aristophanes* 252-281.

M.J. Dillon, "Topicality in Aristophanes' *Ploutos*", *CA* 6 (1987) 155-183.

S.D. Olson, "Cario and the new world of Aristophanes' *Plutus*", *TAPA* 119 (1989) 193-9.

S.D. Olson, "Economics and ideology in Aristophanes' *Wealth*", *HSCP* 93 (1990) 223-242.

A.H. Groton, "Wreaths and rags in Aristophanes' *Plutus*", *CJ* 86 (1990/1) 16-22.

P. Sfyroeras, "What wealth has to do with Dionysus: from economy to poetics in Aristophanes' *Plutus*", *GRBS* 36 (1995) 231-261.

J. McGlew, "After irony: Aristophanes' *Wealth* and its modern interpreters", *AJP* 118 (1997) 35-53.

E. Lévy, "Richesse et pauvreté dans le *Ploutos*", *Ktèma* 22 (1997) 201-212.

ΠΛΟΥΤΟΣ

WEALTH

ΤΑ ΤΟΥ ΔΡΑΜΑΤΟΣ ΠΡΟΣΩΠΑ

ΠΛΟΥΤΟΣ.
ΧΡΕΜΥΛΟΣ, γέρων.
ΚΑΡΙΩΝ, οἰκέτης Χρεμύλου.
ΧΟΡΟΣ γερόντων γεωργῶν, δημοτῶν Χρεμύλου.
ΒΛΕΨΙΔΗΜΟΣ, φίλος Χρεμύλου.
ΠΕΝΙΑ.
ΓΥΝΗ Χρεμύλου.
ΑΝΗΡ ΔΙΚΑΙΟΣ.
ΣΥΚΟΦΑΝΤΗΣ.
ΓΡΑΥΣ ἑταίρα.
ΜΕΙΡΑΚΙΟΝ, οὗ ἐρᾷ ἡ γραῦς.
ΕΡΜΗΣ.
ΙΕΡΕΥΣ Διὸς σωτῆρος.

Κωφὰ πρόσωπα

ΠΑΙΣ, θεράπων τοῦ δικαίου ἀνδρός.
ΜΑΡΤΥΣ τοῦ συκοφάντου.
ΘΕΡΑΠΑΙΝΑ τῆς γραός.
ΟΙΚΕΤΑΙ Χρεμύλου.

CHARACTERS OF THE PLAY

WEALTH.
CHREMYLUS, *an old man.*
CARION, *his servant.*
CHORUS *of elderly peasants, fellow-demesmen of Chremylus.*
BLEPSIDEMUS, *a friend of Chremylus.*
POVERTY.
WIFE *of Chremylus.*
AN HONEST MAN.
AN INFORMER.
AN OLD WOMAN *(a courtesan).*
A YOUNG MAN, *loved by the old woman.*
HERMES.
PRIEST *of Zeus the Saviour.*

Silent Characters

BOY, *servant to the Honest Man.*
WITNESS *brought by the Informer.*
MAIDSERVANT *of the Old Woman.*
SERVANTS *of Chremylus.*

ΚΑΡΙΩΝ

Ὡς ἀργαλέον πρᾶγμ' ἐστίν, ὦ Ζεῦ καὶ θεοί,
δοῦλον γενέσθαι παραφρονοῦντος δεσπότου.
ἢν γὰρ τὰ βέλτισθ' ὁ θεράπων λέξας τύχῃ,
δόξῃ δὲ μὴ δρᾶν ταῦτα τῷ κεκτημένῳ,
μετέχειν ἀνάγκη τὸν θεράποντα τῶν κακῶν.   5
τοῦ σώματος γὰρ οὐκ ἐᾷ τὸν κύριον
κρατεῖν ὁ δαίμων, ἀλλὰ τὸν ἐωνημένον.
καὶ ταῦτα μὲν δὴ ταῦτα· τῷ δὲ Λοξίᾳ,
ὃς θεσπιῳδεῖ τρίποδος ἐκ χρυσηλάτου,
μέμψιν δικαίαν μέμφομαι ταύτην, ὅτι   10
ἰατρὸς ὢν καὶ μάντις, ὥς φασιν, σοφὸς
μελαγχολῶντ' ἀπέπεμψέ μου τὸν δεσπότην,
ὅστις ἀκολουθεῖ κατόπιν ἀνθρώπου τυφλοῦ,
τοὐναντίον δρῶν ἢ προσῆκ' αὐτῷ ποιεῖν.
οἱ γὰρ βλέποντες τοῖς τυφλοῖς ἡγούμεθα·   15
οὗτος δ' ἀκολουθεῖ, κἀμὲ προσβιάζεται,
καὶ ταῦτ' ἀποκρινόμενός τὸ παράπαν οὐδὲ γρῦ.
ἐγὼ μὲν οὖν οὐκ ἔσθ' ὅπως σιγήσομαι,
ἢν μὴ φράσῃς ὅ τι τῷδ' ἀκολουθοῦμέν ποτε,
ὦ δέσποτ', ἀλλά σοι παρέξω πράγματα.   20
οὐ γάρ με τυπτήσεις στέφανον ἔχοντά γε.

ΧΡΕΜΥΛΟΣ

μὰ Δί', ἀλλ' ἀφελὼν τὸν στέφανον, ἢν λυπῇς τί με,
ἵνα μᾶλλον ἀλγῇς.

Κα.   λῆρος· οὐ γὰρ παύσομαι
πρὶν ἂν φράσῃς μοι τίς ποτ' ἐστὶν οὑτοσί.
εὔνους γὰρ ὢν σοι πυνθάνομαι πάνυ σφόδρα.   25

Χρ. ἀλλ' οὔ σε κρύψω· τῶν ἐμῶν γὰρ οἰκετῶν
πιστότατον ἡγοῦμαί σε καὶ κλεπτίστατον.
ἐγὼ θεοσεβὴς καὶ δίκαιος ὢν ἀνὴρ
κακῶς ἔπραττον καὶ πένης ἦν.

Κα.   οἶδά τοι.
Χρ. ἕτεροι δ' ἐπλούτουν ἱερόσυλοι ῥήτορες   30
καὶ συκοφάνται καὶ πονηροί.

---

17   ἀποκρινόμενος Bentley: ἀποκρινομένου Π18 Vn Σ^VMdl Suda: ἀποκρινομένῳ R.

[Scene: in front of a house in Athens. Enter, right, a blind old man, filthy and in rags, walking slowly and hesitantly with the aid of his stick; behind him, keeping pace, there follows an elderly citizen (Chremylus), poorly but respectably dressed, accompanied by his slave Carion, both of them wearing laurel garlands, Carion carrying luggage as if they have been on a long journey. Carion has been gesturing inquisitively to his master, but Chremylus is concentrating all his attention on the blind man. Eventually, exasperated, Carion turns to the audience and speaks.]

CARION: Zeus and all you gods, what a ghastly thing it is to be the slave of a master who's out of his mind! It may happen that the servant is the one who makes the best recommendation, but if his owner decides not to

5   follow it, then the servant's forced to take the evil consequences together with him: the deity won't let a man be in charge of his own body, but puts it in the power of his purchaser. Well, so much for that. But it's Loxias "who

10   chants his oracles from his golden tripod" — it's Loxias I blame, with every right, and for this reason: that, expert healer and prophet as he's said to be, he's sent my master home insane — my master who's now following in the footsteps of a blind man, doing the opposite of what by rights he ought to be

15   doing. Normally we who can see *lead* the blind, but this guy's *following*, and forcing me to do the same — and what's more, never answering me so much as a grunt! *[Confronting Chremylus]* Now then, there's no way I'm

19-20 going to keep quiet if you don't tell me, master, why on earth we're following after this man; no, I'll make myself a thorough nuisance. You won't dare hit me, when I've got a garland on.

CHREMYLUS: No, by Zeus, I won't — if you annoy me at all, I'll take off the garland and *then* hit you, so it'll hurt you more!

CARION: Phooey! I'm not going to leave off until you've told me

25   who the deuce this man is. You're being asked by someone who's very, very loyal to you.

CHREMYLUS: Well, I won't keep it a secret from you, because I regard you as the most faithful and thievish of all my servants. I've been a pious and honest man, and I've done badly in life and been poor.

CARION: I know that, I can assure you.

30   CHREMYLUS: While other people were rich — crooked politicians, informers and all sorts of villains.

Κα.   πείθομαι.

Χρ. ἐπερησόμενος οὖν ᾠχόμην ὡς τὸν θεόν,
τὸν ἐμὸν μὲν αὐτοῦ τοῦ ταλαιπώρου σχεδὸν
ἤδη νομίζων ἐκτετοξεῦσθαι βίον,
τὸν δ᾽ υἱόν, ὅσπερ ὢν μόνος μοι τυγχάνει,   35
πευσόμενος εἰ χρὴ μεταβαλόντα τοὺς τρόπους
εἶναι πανοῦργον, ἄδικον, ὑγιὲς μηδὲ ἕν,
ὡς τῷ βίῳ τοῦτ᾽ αὐτὸ νομίσας ξυμφέρειν.

Κα. τί δῆτα Φοῖβος ἔλακεν ἐκ τῶν στεμμάτων;

Χρ. πεύσει. σαφῶς γὰρ ὁ θεὸς εἶπέ μοι ταδί·   40
ὅτῳ ξυναντήσαιμι πρῶτον ἐξιών,
ἐκέλευε τούτου μὴ μεθίεσθαί μ᾽ ἔτι,
πείθειν δ᾽ ἐμαυτῷ ξυνακολουθεῖν ἐνθάδε.

Κα. καὶ τῷ ξυναντᾷς δῆτα πρώτῳ;

Χρ.   τουτῳί.

Κα. εἶτ᾽ οὐ ξυνιεῖς τὴν ἐπίνοιαν τοῦ θεοῦ   45
φράζουσαν, ὦ σκαιότατε, σοι σαφέστατα
ἀσκεῖν τὸν υἱὸν τὸν ἐπιχώριον τρόπον;

Χρ. τῷ τοῦτο κρίνεις;

Κα.   δῆλον ὁτιὴ καὶ τυφλῷ
γνῶναι δοκεῖ τοῦθ᾽, ὡς σφόδρ᾽ ἐστὶ συμφέρον
τὸ μηδὲν ἀσκεῖν ὑγιὲς ἐν τῷ νῦν γένει.   50

Χρ. οὐκ ἔσθ᾽ ὅπως ὁ χρησμὸς εἰς τοῦτο ῥέπει,
ἀλλ᾽ εἰς ἕτερόν τι μεῖζον. ἢν δ᾽ ἡμῖν φράσῃ
ὅστις ποτ᾽ ἐστὶν οὑτοσὶ καὶ τοῦ χάριν
καὶ τοῦ δεόμενος ἦλθε μετὰ νῷν ἐνθαδί,
πυθοίμεθ᾽ ἂν τὸν χρησμὸν ἡμῶν ὅ τι νοεῖ.   55

Κα. ἄγε δὴ σὺ πότερον σαυτὸν ὅστις εἶ φράσεις,
ἢ τἀπὶ τούτοις δρῶ; λέγειν χρὴ ταχὺ πάνυ.

ΠΛΟΥΤΟΣ
    ἐγὼ μὲν οἰμώζειν λέγω σοι.

Κα.   μανθάνεις
ὅς φησιν εἶναι;

Χρ.   σοὶ λέγει τοῦτ᾽, οὐκ ἐμοί·

---

50 γένει ᵞᵖV: cf. Critias fr. trag. 21, Men. *Thph.* F 1.15: ἔτει V: χρόνῳ Π18 *n* ᵞᵖV: βίῳ R.

55 ἡμῶν P18ˢ codd.: om. Π18ᵃᶜ: ἡμῖν Bergk.

56 πότερον Rᵃᶜ: πρότερον RᵖᶜV*n*.

CARION: I believe you.

CHREMYLUS: So I went to visit the god and ask him a question. I
reckoned that my own miserable life had already pretty well shot its bolt, but
I wanted to ask about my son, the one and only son I have: ought he to
change his ways and become a villain, a criminal, an absolute no-good?
Because I reckoned that that was just what gives one the best chance in life.

CARION: Well, what did Phoebus cry forth from among his sacred
fillets?

CHREMYLUS: You'll hear. The god said this to me, in plain words:
whoever I first met on coming out of the temple, he told me never to let that
person go again, but to persuade him to accompany me home.

CARION: And who *was* the first person you met, then?

CHREMYLUS [*pointing to the blind man*]: This one.

CARION: And you don't understand the god's meaning? You were
being told, you stupid fool, in the plainest of terms, to train your son in the
way that's regular in these parts .

CHREMYLUS: How do you come to that interpretation?

CARION: Because what looks so obvious that even a *blind man* can
perceive it, is that in the present state of the world it very much pays to
behave like a no-good!

CHREMYLUS: It's simply not possible that that's what the oracle is
driving at; it's pointing to something else, something bigger. Now if this
man will tell us who he might be, and why he's come here with us, and what
he wants, then we might discover the meaning of this oracle of ours.

[*At this, Carion runs up to the blind man and addresses him in rough
tones.*]

CARION: Look here, you, are you going to say who you are, or
[*shaking his fist*] shall I go on to the next stage? You'd better answer good
and quick.

THE BLIND MAN: I say to you, go to blazes!

CARION [*to Chremylus, who is now standing near him*]: Do you hear
who he says he is?

CHREMYLUS: He's saying that to you, not to me; it's because you're

σκαιῶς γὰρ αὐτοῦ καὶ χαλεπῶς ἐκπυνθάνει.   60
ἀλλ' εἴ τι χαίρεις ἀνδρὸς εὐόρκου τρόποις,
ἐμοὶ φράσον.
Πλ.   κλάειν ἔγωγέ σοι λέγω.
Κα. δέχου τὸν ἄνδρα καὶ τὸν ὄρνιν τοῦ θεοῦ.
Χρ. οὗτοι μὰ τὴν Δήμητρα χαιρήσεις ἔτι.
εἰ μὴ φράσεις γάρ—
Κα.   ἀπό σ' ὀλῶ κακὸν κακῶς.   65
Πλ. ὦ τᾶν, ἀπαλλάχθητον ἀπ' ἐμοῦ.
Χρ.   πώμαλα.
Κα. καὶ μὴν ὃ λέγω βέλτιστόν ἐστ', ὦ δέσποτα·
ἀπολῶ τὸν ἄνθρωπον κάκιστα τουτονί.
ἀναθεὶς γὰρ ἐπὶ κρημνόν τιν' αὐτὸν καταλιπὼν
ἄπειμ', ἵν' ἐκεῖθεν ἐκτραχηλισθῇ πεσών.   70
Χρ. ἀλλ' αἶρε ταχέως.
Πλ.   μηδαμῶς.
Χρ.   οὔκουν ἐρεῖς;
Πλ. ἀλλ' ἢν πύθησθέ μ' ὅστις εἴμ', εὖ οἶδ' ὅτι
κακόν τί μ' ἐργάσεσθε κοὐκ ἀφήσετον.
Χρ. νὴ τοὺς θεοὺς ἡμεῖς γ', ἐὰν βούλῃ γε σύ.
Πλ. μέθεσθέ νύν μου πρῶτον.
Χρ.   ἤν, μεθίεμεν.   75
Πλ. ἀκούετον δή· δεῖ γάρ, ὡς ἔοικέ, με
λέγειν ἃ κρύπτειν ἦν παρεσκευασμένος.
ἐγὼ γάρ εἰμι Πλοῦτος.
Κα.   ὦ μιαρώτατε
ἀνδρῶν ἀπάντων, εἶτ' ἐσίγας Πλοῦτος ὤν;
Χρ. σὺ Πλοῦτος, οὕτως ἀθλίως διακείμενος;   80
ὦ Φοῖβ' Ἄπολλον καὶ θεοὶ καὶ δαίμονες
καὶ Ζεῦ, τί φής; ἐκεῖνος ὄντως εἶ σύ;
Πλ.   ναί.
Χρ. ἐκεῖνος αὐτός;
Πλ.   αὐτότατος.
Χρ.   πόθεν οὖν, φράσον,
αὐχμῶν βαδίζεις;

questioning him in a rude, unpleasant way. [*To the blind man*] If you take any pleasure in the character of a man who keeps his sworn word, tell it to me.

THE BLIND MAN: I say, blast and curse you!

CARION [*to Chremylus, sarcastically*]: Take the man in, and take the god's omen with him!

[*Chremylus angrily seizes hold of the blind man, and Carion follows suit.*]

CHREMYLUS [*to the blind man*]: By Demeter, you won't be pleased you said that! If you're not going to answer—

CARION [*interrupting*]: I'll put a miserable end to your miserable existence!

THE BLIND MAN: Get away from me, my good man, both of you.

CHREMYLUS: No way!

CARION: No, master, the best thing to do is what I said: I'll put a thoroughly miserable end to this person. I'll set him on top of some cliff, leave him there and go away, so he can fall down and break his neck.

CHREMYLUS [*to Carion*]: Right, off the ground with him, quick!

THE BLIND MAN [*desperately, as Carion is about to take him by the legs*]: No, no!

CHREMYLUS: Well, speak, then, won't you?

THE BLIND MAN: But if you learn who I am, I know very well that you'll do me an injury and won't let me go.

CHREMYLUS: No, we will, by the gods, if that's what you want.

THE BLIND MAN: Very well, first of all, let go of me.

CHREMYLUS [*as he and Carion release their hold on him*]: There, we're doing so.

THE BLIND MAN: Listen, then, both of you. It looks as though I've got to tell you what I was set on keeping secret. I am Wealth.

CARION: You're the filthiest villain in the world! You're Wealth, are you, and you kept quiet about it?

CHREMYLUS [*amazed*]: *You?* Wealth? In such a wretched condition? Phoebus Apollo and all you gods and spirits, and Zeus too — what are you saying? You're really *him?*

WEALTH: Yes.

CHREMYLUS: Wealth himself?

WEALTH: His very self.

CHREMYLUS: Then tell me, how come you're walking around in such a filthy state?

Πλ.   ἐκ Πατροκλέους ἔρχομαι,
ὃς οὐκ ἐλούσατ' ἐξ ὅτουπερ ἐγένετο.   85
Χρ.   τουτὶ δὲ τὸ κακὸν πῶς ἔπαθες; κάτειπέ μοι.
Πλ.   ὁ Ζεύς με ταῦτ' ἔδρασεν ἀνθρώποις φθονῶν.
ἐγὼ γὰρ ὢν μειράκιον ἠπείλησ' ὅτι
ὡς τοὺς δικαίους καὶ σοφοὺς καὶ κοσμίους
μόνους βαδιοίμην· ὁ δέ μ' ἐποίησεν τυφλόν,   90
ἵνα μὴ διαγιγνώσκοιμι τούτων μηδένα.
οὕτως ἐκεῖνος τοῖσι χρηστοῖσι φθονεῖ.
Χρ.   καὶ μὴν διὰ τοὺς χρηστούς γε τιμᾶται μόνους
καὶ τοὺς δικαίους.
Πλ.   ὁμολογῶ σοι.
Χρ.   φέρε, τί οὖν;
εἰ πάλιν ἀναβλέψειας ὥσπερ καὶ πρὸ τοῦ,   95
φεύγοις ἂν ἤδη τοὺς πονηρούς;
Πλ.   φήμ' ἐγώ.
Χρ.   ὡς τοὺς δικαίους δ' ἂν βαδίζοις;
Πλ.   πάνυ μὲν οὖν·
πολλοῦ γὰρ αὐτοὺς οὐχ ἑόρακά πω χρόνου.
Κα.   καὶ θαυμά γ' οὐδέν· οὐδ' ἐγὼ γὰρ ὁ βλέπων.
Πλ.   ἄφετόν μέ νυν· ἴστον γὰρ ἤδη τἀπ' ἐμοῦ.   100
Χρ.   μὰ Δί', ἀλλὰ πολλῷ μᾶλλον ἑξόμεσθά σου.
Πλ.   οὐκ ἠγόρευον ὅτι παρέξειν πράγματα
ἐμέλλετόν μοι;
Χρ.   καὶ σύ γ', ἀντιβολῶ, πιθοῦ,
καὶ μή μ' ἀπολίπης· οὐ γὰρ εὑρήσεις ἐμοῦ
ζητῶν ἔτ' ἄνδρα τοὺς τρόπους βελτίονα.   105
Κα.   μὰ τὸν Δί'· οὐ γάρ ἐστιν ἄλλος πλὴν ἐγώ.
Πλ.   ταυτὶ λέγουσι πάντες· ἡνίκ' ἂν δέ μου
τύχωσ' ἀληθῶς καὶ γένωνται πλούσιοι,
ἀτεχνῶς ὑπερβάλλουσι τῇ μοχθηρίᾳ.
Χρ.   ἔχει μὲν οὕτως, εἰσὶ δ' οὐ πάντες κακοί.   110
Πλ.   μὰ Δί', ἀλλ' ἀπαξάπαντες.
Κα.   οἰμώξει μακρά.

---

98   ἑόρακά ¦Anecd.Oxon. i 445.24 (καὶ διὰ τοῦ ο λέγεται), Tyrwhitt: ἑώρακά vel
sim. codd., Anecd.Oxon. in citation.

WEALTH: I've just come from Patrocles' place; he's not had a bath since the day he was born.

CHREMYLUS [*with a gesture towards Wealth's blind eyes*]: And tell me, how did you come to suffer this affliction?

WEALTH: Zeus did this to me, out of ill-will to mankind. Once, when I was a lad, I vowed that I would only go to the honest, the wise, the decent; and so he struck me blind, so I wouldn't be able to recognize any of them. That's how ill-willed he is towards virtuous people.

CHREMYLUS: And yet it's only thanks to the virtuous and the honest that he gets any worship.

WEALTH: I quite agree with you.

CHREMYLUS: Well, tell me then, if you were to regain your sight like in the old days, would you keep away from the wicked in future?

WEALTH: Yes, I would.

CHREMYLUS: And go to the honest folk?

WEALTH: Absolutely; I've not seen them now in a very long time.

CARION [*aside*]: And no wonder; I've got my eyes, and I haven't seen them either.

WEALTH: Let me go away now; you know all that I've got to tell you.

CHREMYLUS [*stopping him*]: Certainly not; we're going to hold on to you all the more—

WEALTH: Didn't I *say* that you two were going to give me trouble?

CHREMYLUS [*ignoring his interruption*]: And for your part, I beg you, do what I ask and don't abandon me. Because these days, search as you like, you won't find a man with a better character than me.

CARION [*aside*]: No, by Zeus, because there aren't any — except for me.

WEALTH [*dismissively*]: That's what they all say; but when they actually get possession of me and become rich, they show wickedness absolutely beyond measure.

CHREMYLUS: There's truth in that, but not *everyone* is wicked.

WEALTH: No, everyone, without exception!

CARION [*aside*]: You'll really catch it for that!

Χρ. σὺ δ' ὡς ἂν εἰδῇς ὅσα, παρ' ἡμῖν ἦν μένῃς,
γενήσετ' ἀγαθά, πρόσεχε τὸν νοῦν, ἵνα πύθῃ.
οἶμαι γάρ, οἶμαι – ξὺν θεῷ δ' εἰρήσεται –
τῆς συμφορᾶς ταύτης σε παύσειν ἤ σ' ἔχει,   115
βλέψαι ποιήσας.

Πλ.   μηδαμῶς τοῦτ' ἐργάσῃ·
οὐ βούλομαι γὰρ πάλιν ἀναβλέψαι.

Χρ.   τί φῄς;

Κα. ἄνθρωπος οὗτός ἐστιν ἄθλιος φύσει.

Πλ. ὁ Ζεὺς μὲν οὖν οἶδ' ὡς ἂν ἐπιτρίψειέ μ' εἰ
πύθοιτο τοῦτ'.

Χρ.   ὦ μῶρε, νῦν δ' οὐ τοῦτο δρᾷ,   120
ὅστις σε προσπταίοντα περινοστεῖν ἐᾷ;

Πλ. οὐκ οἶδ'· ἐγὼ δ' ἐκεῖνον ὀρρωδῶ πάνυ.

Χρ. ἄληθες, ὦ δειλότατε πάντων δαιμόνων;
οἴει γὰρ εἶναι τὴν Διὸς τυραννίδα
καὶ τοὺς κεραυνοὺς ἀξίους τριωβόλου,   125
ἐὰν ἀναβλέψῃς σὺ κἂν μικρὸν χρόνον;

Πλ. ἆ, μὴ λέγ', ὦ πόνηρε, ταῦτ'.

Χρ.   ἔχ' ἥσυχος·
ἐγὼ γὰρ ἀποδείξω σε τοῦ Διὸς πολὺ
μεῖζον δυνάμενον.

Πλ.   ἐμὲ σύ;

Χρ.   νὴ τὸν οὐρανόν.
αὐτίκα γὰρ ἄρχει διὰ τί ὁ Ζεὺς τῶν θεῶν;   130

Κα. διὰ τἀργύριον· πλεῖστον γάρ ἐστ' αὐτῷ.

Χρ.   φέρε,
τίς οὖν ὁ παρέχων ἐστὶν αὐτῷ τοῦθ';

Κα.   ὁδί.

Χρ. θύουσι δ' αὐτῷ διὰ τίν'; οὐ διὰ τουτονί;

---

112   σὺ RVn: σοὶ x.

115   τῆς συμφορᾶς ταύτης σε (γε V) παύσειν ἤ σ' ἔχει (Valckenaer: ἧς ἔχεις
RVE) ˠᵖΣᴿⱽᴱ (saying this is "an alteration made in the second <version of the play>"):
ταύτης ἀπαλλάξειν σε τῆς ὀφθαλμίας codd. Suda, Lex.Vind. 132.14-15.

119   οἶδ' ὡς x: εἰδὼς RVn.

119-120   ἂν ἐπιτρίψειέ μ' εἰ πύθοιτο τοῦτ'. (Χρ.) ὦ μῶρε, νῦν ... Badham: τὰ
τούτων μῶρ' ἔμ' εἰ (μῶρ' ἔπη or μῶρ' ἔπη εἰ or μῶρ' ἐπεὶ n') πύθοιτ' ἂν
(om. V) ἐπιτρίψειε (με add. n'). (Χρ.) νῦν ... codd.

130   τί x: τίν' RVn, Lex.Vind. 14.2.

CHREMYLUS: Now if you want to know what a lot of good it'll do you to stay with us, listen carefully and you'll learn. I believe, I believe —
15 and, asking god's blessing, I'll say it — that I can release you from this affliction that has you in its grip, by giving you back your sight.

WEALTH [*alarmed*]: Don't do that on any account! I don't *want* to have my sight back.

CHREMYLUS [*amazed*]: What are you saying?

CARION: This man's a real born saddo!

WEALTH: No, the thing is, I know for sure that Zeus would utterly
20 crush me if he found out about this.

CHREMYLUS: You idiot, isn't he doing that anyway as it is, letting you wander stumbling around like this?

WEALTH: I don't know about that, but I am very afraid of him.

CHREMYLUS: What a thing to say! You're the most cowardly
25 divinity in the world. Do you think that the sovereignty of Zeus or his thunderbolts will be worth three obols, if you regain your sight even for a short time ?

WEALTH [*alarmed again*]: Oh, you poor fool, don't talk like that!

CHREMYLUS; Keep calm, now. I'm going to prove that you've got far greater power than Zeus has.

WEALTH: *Me,* you say?

30 CHREMYLUS: Yes, by heaven! For a start, — [*addressing himself to Carion, but speaking for Wealth to hear*] what enables Zeus to rule over the gods?

CARION: Money does; he's the one who's got most of it.

CHREMYLUS: Well then, who provides him with it?

CARION [*pointing to Wealth*]: *He* does.

CHREMYLUS: And who's the cause of people sacrificing to Zeus? Isn't it him?

Κα. καὶ νὴ Δί᾽ εὔχονταί γε πλουτεῖν ἄντικρυς.

Χρ. οὔκουν ὅδ᾽ ἐστὶν αἴτιος καὶ ῥᾳδίως   135
    παύσειεν, εἰ βούλοιτο, ταῦτ᾽ ἄν;

Πλ.   ὅτι τί δή;

Χρ. ὅτι οὐδ᾽ ἂν εἷς θύσειεν ἀνθρώπων ἔτι,
    οὐ βοῦν ἄν, οὐχὶ ψαιστόν, οὐκ ἀλλ᾽ οὐδὲ ἕν,
    μὴ βουλομένου σοῦ.

Πλ.   πῶς;

Χρ.   ὅπως; οὐκ ἔσθ᾽ ὅπως
    ὠνήσεται δήπουθεν, ἢν σὺ μὴ παρὼν   140
    αὐτὸς διδῷς τἀργύριον· ὥστε τοῦ Διὸς
    τὴν δύναμιν, ἢν λυπῇ τι, καταλύσεις μόνος.

Πλ. τί λέγεις; δι᾽ ἐμὲ θύουσιν αὐτῷ;

Χρ.   φήμ᾽ ἐγώ.
    καὶ νὴ Δί᾽ εἴ τί γ᾽ ἐστὶ λαμπρὸν καὶ καλὸν
    ἢ χαρίεν ἀνθρώποισι, διὰ σὲ γίγνεται.
    ἅπαντα τῷ πλουτεῖν γάρ ἐσθ᾽ ὑπήκοα.   145

Κα. ἔγωγέ τοι διὰ μικρὸν ἀργυρίδιον
    δοῦλος γεγένημαι, πρότερον ὢν ἐλεύθερος.

Χρ. καὶ τάς γ᾽ ἑταίρας φασὶ τὰς Κορινθίας,
    ὅταν μὲν αὐτάς τις πένης πειρῶν τύχῃ,   150
    οὐδὲ προσέχειν τὸν νοῦν, ἐὰν δὲ πλούσιος,
    τὸν πρωκτὸν αὐτὰς εὐθὺς ὡς τοῦτον τρέπειν.

Κα. καὶ τούς γε παῖδάς φασι ταὐτὸ τοῦτο δρᾶν,
    οὐ τῶν ἐραστῶν ἀλλὰ τἀργυρίου χάριν.

Χρ. οὐ τούς γε χρηστούς, ἀλλὰ τοὺς πόρνους· ἐπεὶ   155
    αἰτοῦσιν οὐκ ἀργύριον οἱ χρηστοί.

Κα.   τί δαί;

Χρ. ὁ μὲν ἵππον ἀγαθόν, ὁ δὲ κύνας θηρευτικάς.

Κα. αἰσχυνόμενοι γὰρ ἀργύριον αἰτεῖν ἴσως
    ὀνόματι περιπέττουσι τὴν μοχθηρίαν.

Χρ. τέχναι δὲ πᾶσαι διὰ σὲ καὶ σοφίσματα   160
    ἐν τοῖσιν ἀνθρώποισίν ἐσθ᾽ ηὑρημένα.
    ὁ μὲν γὰρ αὐτῶν σκυτοτομεῖ καθήμενος,

---

148   πρότερον ὢν ἐλεύθερος R^mg: διὰ τὸ μὴ πλουτεῖν ἴσως RVn.
161   αὐτῶν n: om. R: ἡμῶν V.

CARION: Yes, and indeed they pray in so many words to become rich.

CHREMYLUS: So isn't he the cause of it all, and couldn't he easily stop it if he wanted to?

WEALTH: Why do you say that?

CHREMYLUS: Because not a single person could offer sacrifices any more — not an ox, not a ground-cake, not anything at all — if you didn't want them to.

WEALTH: How come?

CHREMYLUS: How come? There's no way they can *buy* the things, of course, unless you yourself are with them and give them the money. So if you're aggrieved at all with Zeus, you can overthrow his power all by yourself.

WEALTH [*who has been too much struck with amazement to follow the argument fully*]: What are you saying? That I make them sacrifice to him?

CHREMYLUS: That's right. And what's more, whatever there is that's splendid and noble, or that's pleasant and charming, in human life, happens because of you. Everything is subordinate to being wealthy.

CARION [*aside*]: I certainly became a slave because of a petty little sum of money, having previously been free.

CHREMYLUS: And they say, too, about the courtesans in Corinth, that when the man who's propositioning them happens to be poor, they don't take the least notice of him, but when he's rich, they turn their backside at him instantly.

CARION: And people say that when the young lads do the same thing, it's not for the sake of their lovers but for the sake of money.

CHREMYLUS: The young *gentlemen* don't do that, it's only the young *professionals*. Decent lads don't ask for *money*.

CARION: Oh, what *do* they ask for?

CHREMYLUS: One wants a top-class horse, another wants some hunting dogs ...

CARION: I suppose they're ashamed to ask for money, so they cover up their immorality by a verbal trick.

[*Throughout the following dialogue, Chremylus addresses himself to Wealth, while Carion speaks to Chremylus but for Wealth's ears.*]

CHREMYLUS: And all crafts and skills that exist among mankind have been invented because of you. One of them sits indoors making shoes,

ἕτερος δὲ χαλκεύει τις, ὁ δὲ τεκταίνεται,
ὁ δὲ χρυσοχοεῖ γε, χρυσίον παρὰ σοῦ λαβών–
Κα. ὁ δὲ λωποδυτεῖ γε, νὴ Δι', ὁ δὲ τοιχωρυχεῖ–   165
Χρ. ὁ δὲ γναφεύει γ'–
Κα.   ὁ δέ γε πλύνει κῴδια–
Χρ. ὁ δὲ βυρσοδεψεῖ γ'–
Κα.   ὁ δέ γε πωλεῖ κρόμμυα–
Χρ. ὁ δ' ἁλούς γε μοιχὸς διὰ σέ που παρατίλλεται.
Πλ. οἴμοι τάλας, ταυτί μ' ἐλάνθανεν πάλαι.
Κα. μέγας δὲ βασιλεὺς οὐχὶ διὰ τοῦτον κομᾷ;   170
    ἡκκλησία δ' οὐχὶ διὰ τοῦτον γίγνεται;
Χρ. τί δέ; τὰς τριήρεις οὐ σὺ πληροῖς; εἰπέ μοι.
Κα. τὸ δ' ἐν Κορίνθῳ ξενικὸν οὐχ οὗτος τρέφει;
    ὁ Πάμφιλος δ' οὐχὶ διὰ τοῦτον κλαύσεται;
Χρ. ὁ βελονοπώλης δ' οὐχὶ μετὰ τοῦ Παμφίλου;   175
Κα. Ἀγύρριος δ' οὐχὶ διὰ τοῦτον πέρδεται;
Χρ. Φιλέψιος δ' οὐχ ἕνεκα σοῦ μύθους λέγει;
    ἡ ξυμμαχία δ' οὐ διὰ σὲ τοῖς Αἰγυπτίοις;
    ἐρᾷ δὲ Ναῒς οὐ διὰ σὲ Φιλωνίδου;
Κα. ὁ Τιμοθέου δὲ πύργος–
Χρ.   ἐμπέσοι γέ σοι.   180
    τὰ δὲ πράγματ' οὐχὶ διὰ σὲ πάντα πράττεται;
    μονώτατος γὰρ εἶ σὺ πάντων αἴτιος,
    καὶ τῶν κακῶν καὶ τῶν ἀγαθῶν, εὖ ἴσθ' ὅτι.
Κα. κρατοῦσι γοῦν κἂν τοῖς πολέμοις ἑκάστοτε,
    ἐφ' οἷς ἂν οὗτος ἐπικαθέζηται μόνον.   185
Πλ. ἐγὼ τοσαῦτα δυνατός εἴμ' εἷς ὢν ποιεῖν;
Χρ. καὶ ναὶ μὰ Δία τούτων γε πολλῷ πλείονα·
    ὥστ' οὐδὲ μεστός σου γέγον' οὐδεὶς πώποτε.
    τῶν μὲν γὰρ ἄλλων ἐστὶ πάντων πλησμονή,
    ἔρωτος–
Κα.   ἄρτων–

---

168 που (or ποῦ) codd. Suda: γ' οὐ Bentley.
171 ἡκκλησία Brunck: ἐκκλησία codd. Suda, Zonaras.
172 δέ; τὰς n': δαί; τὰς n' Suda: δαί RV.
179 Ναῒς Athenaeus 13.592d, Harpocration ν1, Suda^G ν16; cf. Lys. fr. 82: Λαῒς codd.
     Suda.
185 μόνον R: μόνος Vn Suda.

another is a blacksmith, another a carpenter, another is a goldsmith — and he gets his gold from you——

65   CARION: And another is a footpad, by Zeus, and another a burglar——

CHREMYLUS: Another is a fuller——

CARION: And another washes fleeces——

CHREMYLUS: Another is a tanner——

CARION: And another sells onions——

CHREMYLUS: And when an adulterer is caught in the act, it's down to you that he gets ... a token plucking.

WEALTH: My god, I never realized that!

70   CARION: And doesn't the Great King plume himself because of him? Doesn't the Assembly get held because of him?

CHREMYLUS: Another thing, tell me, don't you get our warships manned?

CARION: Doesn't he maintain the mercenary force at Corinth? Isn't it because of him that Pamphilus ... will cop it?

75   CHREMYLUS: And that needle-seller as well along with Pamphilus?

CARION: Isn't it because of him that Agyrrhius is in clover?

CHREMYLUS: Isn't it for your sake that Philepsius tells stories? Isn't it because of you that we've an alliance with the Egyptians? Isn't it because of you that Nais loves Philonides?

80   CARION: And Timotheus' tower——

CHREMYLUS [*rounding on him*]: I wish it would fall on your head! [*To Wealth*] Isn't it true that *everything* is done because of you? You, by yourself, alone, are the cause of everything, both good and bad, I assure you.

CARION: Certainly that's what always happens in war too:
85   whichever side he so much as perches on, they're victorious.

WEALTH: Do I, all on my own, have the power to do all that?

CHREMYLUS: And much more than that, by Zeus! So much so that no one has ever felt surfeited with you. With everything else there comes a
90   time when you've had your fill, whether it's love——

CARION: Or bread——

Χρ.   μουσικῆς–
Κα.   τραγημάτων–   190
Χρ. τιμῆς–
Κα.   πλακούντων–
Χρ.   ἀνδραγαθίας–
Κα.   ἰσχάδων–
Χρ. φιλοτιμίας–
Κα.   μάζης–
Χρ.   στρατηγίας–
Κα.   φακῆς–
Χρ. σοῦ δ' ἐγένετ' οὐδεὶς μεστὸς οὐδεπώποτε.
    ἀλλ' ἦν τάλαντά τις λάβῃ τριακαίδεκα,
    πολὺ μᾶλλον ἐπιθυμεῖ λαβεῖν ἑκκαίδεκα·   195
    κἂν ταῦθ' ἀνύσηται, τετταράκοντα βούλεται,
    ἤ φησιν οὐκ εἶναι βιωτὸν τὸν βίον.
Πλ. εὖ τοι λέγειν ἔμοιγε φαίνεσθον πάνυ·
    πλὴν ἓν μόνον δέδοικα.
Χρ.   φράζε, τοῦ πέρι;
Πλ. ὅπως ἐγὼ τὴν δύναμιν, ἣν ὑμεῖς φατε   200
    ἔχειν με, ταύτης δεσπότης γενήσομαι.
Χρ. νὴ τὸν Δί' ἀλλὰ καὶ λέγουσι πάντες ὡς
    δειλότατόν ἐσθ' ὁ πλοῦτος.
Πλ.   ἥκιστ', ἀλλά με
    τοιχωρύχος τις διέβαλ'. εἰσδὺς γάρ ποτε
    οὐκ εἶχεν εἰς τὴν οἰκίαν οὐδὲν λαβεῖν,   205
    εὑρὼν ἁπαξάπαντα κατακεκλημένα·
    εἶτ' ὠνόμασέν μου τὴν πρόνοιαν δειλίαν.
Χρ. μή νυν μελέτω σοι μηδέν· ὡς ἐὰν γένῃ
    ἀνὴρ πρόθυμος αὐτὸς εἰς τὰ πράγματα,
    βλέποντ' ἀποδείξω σ' ὀξύτερον τοῦ Λυγκέως.   210
Πλ. πῶς οὖν δυνήσει τοῦτο δρᾶσαι θνητὸς ὤν;
Χρ. ἔχω τιν' ἀγαθὴν ἐλπίδ' ἐξ ὧν εἶπέ μοι

---

196   ἀνύσηται (ἁ-) Dawes: ἀνύσῃ codd., Olympiodorus *in Pl. Alc. I* p.50.22 Creuzer:
     ἀνύσῃ τις Reisig.
197   οὐκ εἶναι βιωτὸν Tricl.: οὐκ εἶναι βιωτὸν αὐτῷ RV*n*' (... αὐτῷ ⁱΣ^(RVb¹):
     ἀβίωτον αὐτῷ *n*': εἶν' ἀβίωτον αὐτῷ Hall & Geldart.
203   δειλότατον V*n*'^(λΣEVs1): δειλότατος R*n*' *Lex.Vind.* 26.10.
205   εἰς τὴν οἰκίαν codd.: ἐκ τῆς οἰκίας Bothe.

CHREMYLUS: Or culture—

CARION: Or sweetmeats—

CHREMYLUS: Or honour—

CARION: Or flat-cakes—

CHREMYLUS: Or valour—

CARION: Or dried figs—

CHREMYLUS: Or ambition—

CARION: Or barley-cake—

CHREMYLUS: Or high command—

CARION: Or lentil soup—

CHREMYLUS: But no one's ever had their fill of *you*! What happens is that if someone comes into possession of thirteen talents, it only makes him all the more eager to get sixteen; and if he succeeds in that, he wants forty, or else (he says) life isn't worth living.

WEALTH: I think, you know, that what the two of you are saying is quite right; but there's just one thing that makes me afraid.

CHREMYLUS: What's it about, tell me?

WEALTH: This power that you say I have – *how* am I going to become master of it?

CHREMYLUS [*scornfully*]: Why, isn't that just what they all say – that wealth is the most cowardly thing on earth!

WEALTH: That's not true at all; it's a slanderous lie made up by some burglar. He dug his way into my house one time, and found he had nothing to steal because absolutely everything was locked up; and because of that he called my foresight cowardice.

CHREMYLUS: Well, don't you worry about anything; because if you for your part throw yourself whole-heartedly into the plan, I'm going to make sure you have better eyesight than Lynceus!

WEALTH: So how are you, mortal that you are, going to be able to do that?

CHREMYLUS: I have high hopes of it, because of what Phoebus

195

200

205

210

ὁ Φοῖβος αὐτὸς Πυθικὴν σείσας δάφνην.
Πλ. κἀκεῖνος οὖν ξύνοιδε ταῦτα;
Χρ.   φήμ' ἐγώ.
Πλ. ὁρᾶτε–
Χρ.   μὴ φρόντιζε μηδέν, ὦγαθέ·   215
ἐγὼ γάρ, εὖ τοῦτ' ἴσθι, κἂν δῇ μ' ἀποθανεῖν,
αὐτὸς διαπράξω ταῦτα.
Κα.   κἂν βούλῃ γ', ἐγώ.
Χρ. πολλοὶ δ' ἔσονται χἄτεροι νῷν ξύμμαχοι,
ὅσοις δικαίοις οὖσιν οὐκ ἦν ἄλφιτα.
Πλ. παπαῖ, πονηρούς γ' εἶπας ἡμῖν ξυμμάχους.   220
Χρ. οὔκ, ἤν γε πλουτήσωσιν ἐξ ἀρχῆς πάλιν.
ἀλλ' ἴθι σὺ μὲν ταχέως δραμών–
Κα.   τί δρῶ; λέγε.
Χρ. τοὺς ξυγγεώργους κάλεσον–εὑρήσεις δ' ἴσως
ἐν τοῖς ἀγροῖς αὐτοὺς ταλαιπωρουμένους–
ὅπως ἂν ἴσον ἕκαστος ἐνταυθοῖ παρὼν   225
ἡμῖν μετάσχῃ τοῦδε τοῦ Πλούτου μέρος.
Κα. καὶ δὴ βαδίζω· τουτοδὶ τὸ κρεάδιον
τῶν ἔνδοθεν τις εἰσενεγκάτω λαβών.
Χρ. ἐμοὶ μελήσει τοῦτό γ'· ἀλλ' ἀνύσας τρέχε.
σὺ δ', ὦ κράτιστε Πλοῦτε πάντων δαιμόνων,   230
εἴσω μετ' ἐμοῦ δεῦρ' εἴσιθ'· ἡ γὰρ οἰκία
αὕτη 'στὶν ἣν δεῖ χρημάτων σε τήμερον
μεστὴν ποιῆσαι καὶ δικαίως κἀδίκως.
Πλ. ἀλλ' ἄχθομαι μὲν εἰσιών, νὴ τοὺς θεούς,
εἰς οἰκίαν ἑκάστοτ' ἀλλοτρίαν πάνυ·   235
ἀγαθὸν γὰρ ἀπέλαυσ' οὐδὲν αὐτοῦ πώποτε.
ἢν μὲν γὰρ ὡς φειδωλὸν εἰσελθὼν τύχω,
εὐθὺς κατώρυξέν με κατὰ τῆς γῆς κάτω·
κἄν τις προσέλθῃ χρηστὸς ἄνθρωπος φίλος
αἰτῶν λαβεῖν τι μικρὸν ἀργυρίδιον,   240
ἔξαρνός ἐστι μηδ' ἰδεῖν με πώποτε.

---

216   κἂν δῇ Neobari: κἂν δέῃ Lex.Vind. 45.5: κἂν δεῖ vel sim. R²Vn': κεἰ δεῖ n': R¹
       omits 215-7.
227   τουτοδὶ Dobree: τουτοδὴ or τοῦτο δὴ RVn': τοῦτο δὲ n'.
231   ἐμοῦ Vn: ἐμέ R.
237   ὡς x: εἰς RVn.

himself, "rustling the Pythian laurel", said to me.

    WEALTH: You mean *he* knows about all this?

    CHREMYLUS: That's right.

215   WEALTH [*alarmed*]: Take care——

    CHREMYLUS: Don't be worried in the least, my good friend. I myself will get this done, I assure you of that, even if I have to give my life for it .

    CARION: And so will I, if you want.

    CHREMYLUS: And the two of us will have many others as well to support us — all the honest men who have not been getting their daily bread.

220   WEALTH: Heavens, they sound a pretty poor set of allies for us!

    CHREMYLUS: Not if they become rich once again. [*To Carion*] Now come on, you, run quickly and——

    CARION: Do what, please?

    CHREMYLUS: Summon my fellow-peasants here — you'll probably

225   find them toiling in the fields — so that every one of them can come and join us in getting his fair share of our Wealth here.

    CARION: I'm on my way. But [*taking a pot out of the luggage bundle, and calling into the stage-house*] will someone in there please take this bit of meat inside?

    CHREMYLUS [*taking the pot from him*]: I'll see to that; just run and

230   get on with it. [*Exit Carion, left. Chremylus moves towards the door.*] And now, Wealth, most powerful of all divinities, come inside here with me; because this is the house which today, by fair means or foul, you've got to fill full of good things.

235   WEALTH [*hesitating*]: Well, I'm always very reluctant, by the gods, to go into anyone else's house, because I've never yet had any good come to me from doing so. If I happen to have entered the home of a miserly man, he straight away buries me down under ground; and then if a decent person,

240   a friend of his, comes to him asking to borrow some small little sum of

ἢν δ' ὡς παραπλῆγ' ἄνθρωπον εἰσελθὼν τύχω,
πόρναισι καὶ κύβοισι παραβεβλημένος
γυμνὸς θύραζ' ἐξέπεσον ἐν ἀκαρεῖ χρόνῳ.

Χρ. μετρίου γὰρ ἀνδρὸς οὐκ ἐπέτυχες πώποτε.   245
ἐγὼ δὲ τούτου τοῦ τρόπου πώς εἰμ' ἀεί·
χαίρω τε γὰρ φειδόμενος ὡς οὐδεὶς ἀνὴρ
πάλιν τ' ἀναλῶν, ἡνίκ' ἂν τούτου δέῃ.
ἀλλ' εἰσίωμεν, ὡς ἰδεῖν σε βούλομαι
καὶ τὴν γυναῖκα καὶ τὸν υἱὸν τὸν μόνον,   250
ὃν ἐγὼ φιλῶ μάλιστα μετὰ σέ.

Πλ.   πείθομαι.
Χρ. τί γὰρ ἄν τις οὐχὶ πρὸς σὲ τἀληθῆ λέγοι;

Κα. ὦ πολλὰ δὴ τῷ δεσπότῃ ταὐτὸν θύμον φαγόντες,
ἄνδρες φίλοι καὶ δημόται καὶ τοῦ πονεῖν ἐρασταί,
ἴτ', ἐγκονεῖτε, σπεύδεθ'· ὡς ὁ καιρὸς οὐχὶ μέλλειν, 255
ἀλλ' ἔστ' ἐπ' αὐτῆς τῆς ἀκμῆς, ᾗ δεῖ παρόντ' ἀμύνειν.

ΧΟΡΟΣ

οὔκουν ὁρᾷς ὁρμωμένους ἡμᾶς πάλαι προθύμως,
ὡς εἰκός ἐστιν ἀσθενεῖς γέροντας ἄνδρας ἤδη;
σὺ δ' ἀξιοῖς ἴσως με θεῖν, πρὶν ταῦτα καὶ φράσαι μοι,
ὅτου χάριν μ' ὁ δεσπότης ὁ σὸς κέκληκε δεῦρο.   260
Κα. οὔκουν πάλαι δήπου λέγω, σὺ δ' αὐτὸς οὐκ ἀκούεις;
ὁ δεσπότης γάρ φησιν ὑμᾶς ἡδέως ἅπαντας
ψυχροῦ βίου καὶ δυσκόλου ζήσειν ἀπαλλαγέντας.
Χο. ἔστιν δὲ δὴ τί καὶ πόθεν τὸ πρᾶγμα τοῦθ', ὅ φησιν;
Κα. ἔχων ἀφῖκται δεῦρο πρεσβύτην τιν', ὦ πόνηροι, 265
ῥυπῶντα, κυφόν, ἄθλιον, ῥυσόν, μαδῶντα, νωδόν·
οἶμαι δὲ νὴ τὸν οὐρανὸν καὶ ψωλὸν αὐτὸν εἶναι.
Χο. ὦ χρυσὸν ἀγγείλας ἐπῶν, πῶς φής; πάλιν φράσον μοι.
δηλοῖς γὰρ αὐτὸν σωρὸν ἥκειν χρημάτων ἔχοντα.

---

255 μέλλειν codd. Suda: μέλλει Meineke.

money, he denies ever having seen me in his life. Or if I happen to have entered the home of a mad profligate, I get thrown around on whoring and dicing till in next to no time I'm cast naked out of doors.

CHREMYLUS: That's because you've never come across a reasonable middle-of-the-road person. And that's always been more or less the way I am: I enjoy being economical like no one on earth, and I also enjoy spending when that's the right thing to do. But let's go inside; I want you to meet my wife and my only son, whom I love more than anyone — next to you.

WEALTH: I believe you there!

CHREMYLUS [as he leads Wealth inside]: After all, why shouldn't one tell you the truth?

[Re-enter Carion, left, calling back to the Chorus who have not yet appeared.]

CARION: You who have so often eaten thyme together with my master — his friends, his fellow-demesmen, lovers of hard work — come on, get moving, hurry up; because this is no time for delay — no, we're right at the critical moment, and you've got to be there to help!

[Enter the Chorus of elderly peasants, hurrying as fast as they can but still not very fast.]

CHORUS-LEADER: Why, can't you see that we've been hurrying all the time with all our might, as much as you can expect from weak old men as we now are? I suppose [sarcastically] you think I ought to run, before you've even told me this: what's the reason why your master has called us here?

CARION: I told you long ago, of course, didn't I, and you just haven't been listening. My master says that you, all of you, are going to live happily from now on, freed from the cold, disagreeable life that you've had.

CHORUS-LEADER: And what exactly is this thing he says has happened, and where has it come from?

CARION: He's come here, you poor fools, with an old man who's filthy and bent and wretched and shrivelled and bald and toothless; and I dare say, by heaven, that he's minus his foreskin too!

CHORUS-LEADER [immensely excited]: What a golden tale you've told! What did you say? Tell me again! It's obvious from what you say that he's come here with a heap of money!

Κα. πρεσβυτικῶν μὲν οὖν κακῶν ἔγωγ' ἔχοντα σωρόν.   270
Χο. μῶν ἀξιοῖς φενακίσας ἔπειτ' ἀπαλλαγῆναι
ἀζήμιος, καὶ ταῦτ' ἐμοῦ βακτηρίαν ἔχοντος;
Κα. πάντως γὰρ ἄνθρωπον φύσει τοιοῦτον εἰς τὰ πάντα
ἡγεῖσθέ μ' εἶναι κοὐδὲν ἂν νομίζεθ' ὑγιὲς εἰπεῖν;
Χο. ὡς σεμνὸς οὑπίτριπτος· αἱ κνῆμαι δέ σου βοῶσιν   275
"ἰοὺ ἰού", τὰς χοίνικας καὶ τὰς πέδας ποθοῦσαι.
Κα. ἐν τῇ σορῷ νυνὶ λαχὸν τὸ γράμμα σου δικάζει,
σὺ δ' οὐ βαδίζεις; ὁ δὲ Χάρων τὸ ξύμβολον δίδωσιν.
Χο. διαρραγείης· ὡς μόθων εἶ καὶ φύσει κόβαλος,
ὅστις φενακίζεις, φράσαι δ' οὔπω τέτληκας ἡμῖν,   280
οἳ πολλὰ μοχθήσαντες, οὐκ οὔσης σχολῆς, προθύμως   282
δεῦρ' ἤλθομεν, πολλῶν θύμων ῥίζας διεκπερῶντες.
Κα. ἀλλ' οὐκέτ' ἂν κρύψαιμι. τὸν Πλοῦτον γάρ, ὦνδρες, ἥκει
ἄγων ὁ δεσπότης, ὃς ὑμᾶς πλουσίους ποιήσει.   285
Χο. ὄντως γάρ ἐστι πλουσίοις ἡμῖν ἅπασιν εἶναι;
Κα. νὴ τοὺς θεοὺς Μίδαις μὲν οὖν, ἢν ὦτ' ὄνου λάβητε.
Χο. ὡς ἥδομαι καὶ τέρπομαι καὶ βούλομαι χορεῦσαι
ὑφ' ἡδονῆς, εἴπερ λέγεις ὄντως σὺ ταῦτ' ἀληθῆ.   289

Κα. καὶ μὴν ἐγὼ βουλήσομαι — θρεττανελο — τὸν Κύκλωπα (στρ.
μιμούμενος καὶ τοῖν ποδοῖν ὡδὶ παρενσαλεύων
ὑμᾶς ἄγειν. ἀλλ' εἶα, τέκεα, θαμίν' ἐπαναβοῶντες
βληχωμένων τε προβατίων
αἰγῶν τε κιναβρώντων μέλη
ἕπεσθ' ἀπεψωλημένοι· τράγοι δ' ἀκρατιεῖσθε.   295

---

271   ἔπειτ' Bergk: ἡμᾶς ἔπειτ' V: ἡμᾶς Rn Suda.
277   δικάζει Rᴾᶜ: δικάδει Rᵃᶜ: δικάζειν Vn.
[281] ὅτου χάριν μ' ὁ δεσπότης ὁ σὸς κέκληκε δεῦρο (= 260) vel sim. n, Lex.Vind.
       46.6-7: om. RV, del. Bergk.
285   ὑμᾶς Vn': ἡμᾶς Rn'.
287   Μίδαις Küster: Μίδας codd.
293   βληχωμένων Bergk: βληχώντων Thom.Ecl. 311.7: βληχώμενοί codd. Suda.

CARION: With a heap of the miseries of old age, more like, I'd say!

CHORUS-LEADER [*brandishing his walking-stick*]: You don't expect, do you, to make fools of us and get off scot-free with it, and when I've a stick, too?

CARION: Why, do you think I'm born and bound to be that kind of person whatever I'm doing? Do you suppose I'd never talk anything but nonsense?

CHORUS-LEADER: Getting above himself, this damned rogue! Your legs are crying out in distress — they're just *yearning* for their old shackles and fetters!

CARION: Your letter's been allotted to the Court of the Coffin, and it's judging there now. Aren't you going there? Charon's already handing out the tickets!

CHORUS-LEADER: Blast you to pieces! You're such a born cheeky imp. You go on playing games with us, and you still haven't condescended to explain! And we've come here, with great difficulty, when we're short of time, and we've passed right through field after field full of thyme roots!

CARION: Well, I won't keep you in the dark any longer. My master, gentlemen, has come home bringing with him Wealth, who is going to make you rich men.

CHORUS-LEADER: You mean we're really all now able to be wealthy?

CARION: As rich as Midas, by the gods, if you get yourselves asses' ears [*putting his hands to the sides of his head and waving them about*]!

CHORUS-LEADER: Oh, I'm so happy and delighted! I want to dance for joy, if what you've told me is really true!

[*The following song is accompanied by appropriate mimetic dancing.*]
CARION:
All right then, what I'll want to do — tra la la!
[*strumming an imaginary lyre*]
— is play the Cyclops and lead you, with swaying steps,
like this. Hey then, little ones, raise up cry on cry
with the song of bleating sheep
and of stinking goats
and follow me, cocks skinned; you'll have a billygoat's breakfast!
[*He raises his phallus to his lips.*]

Χο. ἡμεῖς δέ γ' αὖ ζητήσομεν — θρεττανελο — τὸν Κύκλωπα   (ἀντ.
βληχώμενοι, σὲ τουτονί, πεινῶντα καταλαβόντες,
πήραν ἔχοντα λάχανά τ' ἄγρια δροσερά, κραιπαλῶντα,
ἡγούμενον τοῖς προβατίοις,
εἰκῇ δὲ καταδαρθόντα που,   300
μέγαν λαβόντες ἡμμένον σφηκίσκον ἐκτυφλῶσαι.

Κα. ἐγὼ δὲ τὴν Κίρκην γε, τὴν τὰ φάρμακ' ἀνακυκῶσαν,   (στρ.
ἢ τοὺς ἑταίρους τοῦ Φιλωνίδου ποτ' ἐν Κορίνθῳ
ἔπεισεν ὡς ὄντας κάπρους
μεμαγμένον σκῶρ ἐσθίειν, αὐτὴ δ' ἔματτεν αὐτοῖς,   305
μιμήσομαι πάντας τρόπους·
ὑμεῖς δὲ γρυλίζοντες ὑπὸ φιληδίας
ἕπεσθε μητρί, χοῖροι.

Χο. οὐκοῦν σὲ τὴν Κίρκην γε, τήν τὰ φάρμακ' ἀνακυκῶσαν   (ἀντ.
καὶ μαγγανεύουσαν μολύνουσάν τε τοὺς ἑταίρους,   310
λαβόντες ὑπὸ φιληδίας
τὸν Λαρτίου μιμούμενοι τῶν ὄρχεων κρεμῶμεν,
μινθώσομέν θ' ὥσπερ τράγου
τὴν ῥῖνα· σὺ δ' Ἀρίστυλλος ὑποχάσκων ἐρεῖς
"ἕπεσθε μητρί, χοῖροι".   315

Κα. ἄγ' εἶά νυν τῶν σκωμμάτων ἀπαλλαγέντες ἤδη   (ἐπ.
ὑμεῖς ἐπ' ἄλλ' εἶδος τρέπεσθ',
ἐγὼ δ' ἰὼν ἤδη λάθρα
βουλήσομαι τοῦ δεσπότου
λαβών τιν' ἄρτον καὶ κρέας   320
μασώμενος τὸ λοιπὸν ἤ-
δη τῷ κόπῳ ξυνεῖναι.

ΧΟΡΟΥ

Χρ. "χαίρειν" μὲν ὑμᾶς ἐστιν, ὦνδρες δημόται,
ἀρχαῖον ἤδη προσαγορεύειν καὶ σαπρόν·

---

297 πεινῶντα RVn: πινῶντα x.
300 καταδαρθόντα Porson: καταδαρθέντα (-δραθ- R²) codd.
316 ἄγ' Vn'Σᴷ (cf. Frogs 394): om. Rn': ἀλλ' n' (cf. Thesm. 985).
after 321 χοροῦ Vn': om. Rn'.

CHORUS:
And *we* will be trying, while we bleat — tra la la!
— to catch the Cyclops (that means *you*) when he's hungry,
with a beggar's bag and some damp wild greens in it — and a hangover —
leading his flocks,
and then when he's casually fallen asleep somewhere
to take a big pointed stake, set light to it, and blind him!

CARION:
Now I'll be Circe, the woman who stirred up potions,
who once in Corinth got the companions of Philonides
to behave like pigs
and eat kneaded shit — *she* did their kneading for them.
I'll play her role in all its varieties;
and as for you, why, follow your mummy, little piggies,
squealing with delight!

CHORUS:
Then we'll take you, Circe, the woman who stirred up potions
and bewitched and befouled our companions —
take you, with delight,
in the role of Laertes' son, and — hang you up by the balls
and rub your nose in shit like a billygoat's;
and you'll be like Aristyllus and be saying [*mimicking him*] "follow
          your mummy, little piggies"
with your mouth half open!

CARION:
Come on now, hey, you leave off this joking now
and turn to another style,
and I'll want to go now
and without my master knowing
take some bread and meat,
and still be chewing it when I get back to the hard slog afterwards!

[*Carion goes inside. The chorus continue to dance, singing a song whose words have not survived. Then Chremylus comes out of the house.*]

CHREMYLUS: To greet you with "good day", my fellow-demesmen,

ἀσπάζομαι δ', ὁτιὴ προθύμως ἥκετε
καὶ συντεταμένως κοὺ κατεβλακευμένως.   325
ὅπως δέ μοι καὶ τἄλλα συμπαραστάται
ἔσεσθε καὶ σωτῆρες ὄντως τοῦ θεοῦ.

Χο. θάρρει· βλέπειν γὰρ ἄντικρυς δόξεις μ' Ἄρη.
δεινὸν γὰρ εἰ τριωβόλου μὲν οὔνεκα
ὠστιζόμεσθ' ἑκάστοτ' ἐν τἠκκλησίᾳ,   330
αὐτὸν δὲ τὸν Πλοῦτον παρείην τῳ λαβεῖν.

Χρ. καὶ μὴν ὁρῶ καὶ Βλεψίδημον τουτονὶ
προσιόντα· δῆλος δ' ἐστὶν ὅτι τοῦ πράγματος
ἀκήκοέν τι τῇ βαδίσει καὶ τῷ τάχει.

ΒΛΕΨΙΔΗΜΟΣ
τίς ἂν οὖν τὸ πρᾶγμ' εἴη; πόθεν καὶ τίνι τρόπῳ   335
Χρεμύλος πεπλούτηκ' ἐξαπίνης; οὐ πείθομαι.
καίτοι λόγος γ' ἦν, νὴ τὸν Ἡρακλέα, πολὺς
ἐπὶ τοῖσι κουρείοισι τῶν καθημένων,
ὡς ἐξαπίνης ἀνὴρ γεγένηται πλούσιος.
ἔστιν δέ μοι τοῦτ' αὐτὸ θαυμάσιον, ὅπως   340
χρηστόν τι πράττων τοὺς φίλους μεταπέμπεται.
οὔκουν ἐπιχώριόν γε πρᾶγμ' ἐργάζεται.

Χρ. ἀλλ' οὐδὲν ἀποκρύψας ἐρῶ, μὰ τοὺς θεούς.
ὦ Βλεψίδημ', ἄμεινον ἢ χθὲς πράττομεν,
ὥστε μετέχειν ἔξεστιν· εἶ γὰρ τῶν φίλων.   345

Βλ. γέγονας δ' ἀληθῶς, ὡς λέγουσι, πλούσιος;

Χρ. ἔσομαι μὲν οὖν αὐτίκα μάλ', ἢν θεὸς θέλῃ·
ἔνι γάρ τις, ἔνι κίνδυνος ἐν τῷ πράγματι.

Βλ. ποῖός τις;

Χρ.   οἷος–

Βλ.   λέγ' ἀνύσας ὅ τι φῄς ποτε.

Χρ. ἢν μὲν κατορθώσωμεν, εὖ πράττειν ἀεί·   350
ἢν δὲ σφαλῶμεν, ἐπιτετρῖφθαι τὸ παράπαν.

Βλ. τουτὶ πονηρὸν φαίνεται τὸ φορτίον,
καί μ' οὐκ ἀρέσκει. τό τε γὰρ ἐξαίφνης ἄγαν
οὕτως ὑπερπλουτεῖν τό τ' αὖ δεδοικέναι
πρὸς ἀνδρὸς οὐδὲν ὑγιές ἐστ' εἰργασμένου.   355

---

335   πόθεν n', Tricl.:   καὶ πόθεν RVn'.
343   μὰ n: νὴ RV.
345   ἔξεστιν RVn: σ' ἔξεστιν x: σοὔξεστιν Blaydes.

is old-fashioned and past it now. So, a warm welcome to you for having
come so eagerly, so energetically and so unslothfully. Now be sure to stand
loyally by my side to do what remains, and become in the full sense the
saviours of the god.

CHORUS-LEADER: Don't worry; you'll reckon I've got the real look
of war in my eyes. It would be appalling, when we jostle with each other all
the time in the Assembly for the sake of three obols, if I were to let go of
Wealth himself for someone else to take.

CHREMYLUS [*looking off, left*]: And look, here I see Blepsidemus
coming too. It's obvious from the way and the speed he's walking that he's
heard something of what's happened.

[*Enter Blepsidemus, preoccupied, musing to himself, and not at first
noticing the others.*]

BLEPSIDEMUS: So what *can* this business be all about? Where and
how has Chremylus got these riches all of a sudden? I don't believe it. And
yet, by Heracles, there was all this talk among the people sitting at the
barbers' shops, that the man had suddenly become wealthy. But that's
exactly what I find amazing — that he's having it lucky, so he sends for his
friends. Certainly it's not a customary thing to do in these parts.

CHREMYLUS [*aside*]: No, I won't try any concealment, by the gods,
I'll say it out. [*To Blepsidemus*] Blepsidemus, we're doing better than we
were yesterday, so there's an opportunity to share in it, because you're one of
my friends.

BLEPSIDEMUS: Have you really become wealthy, as they say you
have?

CHREMYLUS: No, but I shall be very soon, god willing — because
there is, there is, some danger in the business.

BLEPSIDEMUS: What sort of danger?

CHREMYLUS: One that means— [*He hesitates.*]

BLEPSIDEMUS: Well, get on and say what you're on about.

CHREMYLUS: That if we succeed, we'll be happy ever after; but if
we fail, we're totally ruined.

BLEPSIDEMUS: Sounds like shady goods, this; I don't like it. To be
hyper-rich like this, altogether too suddenly, and also on the other hand to be
frightened — it's the behaviour of a man who's done something dirty.

Χρ.   πῶς οὐδὲν ὑγιές;

Βλ.   εἴ τι κεκλοφὼς νὴ Δία
      ἐκεῖθεν ἥκεις ἀργύριον ἢ χρυσίον
      παρὰ τοῦ θεοῦ, κᾆπειτ' ἴσως σοι μεταμέλει.

Χρ.   Ἄπολλον ἀποτρόπαιε· μὰ Δί' ἐγὼ μὲν οὔ.

Βλ.   παῦσαι φλυαρῶν, ὦγάθ'· οἶδα γὰρ σαφῶς.   360

Χρ.   σὺ μηδὲν εἰς ἔμ' ὑπονόει τοιοῦτο.

Βλ.   φεῦ·
      ὡς οὐδὲν ἀτεχνῶς ὑγιές ἐστιν οὐδενός,
      ἀλλ' εἰσὶ τοῦ κέρδους ἅπαντες ἥττονες.

Χρ.   οὗτοι μὰ τὴν Δήμητρ' ὑγιαίνειν μοι δοκεῖς.

Βλ.   ὡς πολὺ μεθέστηχ' ὧν πρότερον εἶχεν τρόπων.   365

Χρ.   μελαγχολᾷς, ὦνθρωπε, νὴ τὸν οὐρανόν.

Βλ.   ἀλλ' οὐδὲ τὸ βλέμμ' αὐτὸ κατὰ χώραν ἔχει,
      ἀλλ' ἔστιν ἐπίδηλόν τι πεπανουργηκότος.

Χρ.   σὺ μὲν οἶδ' ὃ κρώζεις· ὡς ἐμοῦ τι κεκλοφότος
      ζητεῖς μεταλαβεῖν.

Βλ.   μεταλαβεῖν ζητῶ; τίνος;   370

Χρ.   τὸ δ' ἐστὶν οὐ τοιοῦτον, ἀλλ' ἑτέρως ἔχον.

Βλ.   μῶν οὐ κέκλοφας, ἀλλ' ἥρπακας;

Χρ.   κακοδαιμονᾷς.

Βλ.   ἀλλ' οὐδὲ μὴν ἀπεστέρηκάς γ' οὐδένα;

Χρ.   οὐ δῆτ' ἔγωγ'.

Βλ.   ὦ Ἡράκλεις, φέρε, ποῖ τις ἂν
      τράποιτο; τἀληθὲς γὰρ οὐκ ἐθέλεις φράσαι.   375

Χρ.   κατηγορεῖς γὰρ πρὶν μαθεῖν τὸ πρᾶγμά μου.

Βλ.   ὦ τᾶν, ἐγώ σοι τοῦτ' ἀπὸ σμικροῦ πάνυ
      ἐθέλω διαπρᾶξαι πρὶν πυθέσθαι τὴν πόλιν,
      τὸ στόμ' ἐπιβύσας κέρμασιν τῶν ῥητόρων.

Χρ.   καὶ μὴν φίλως γ' ἄν μοι δοκεῖς, νὴ τοὺς θεούς,   380
      τρεῖς μνᾶς ἀναλώσας λογίσασθαι δώδεκα.

Βλ.   ὁρῶ τιν' ἐπὶ τοῦ βήματος καθεδούμενον
      ἱκετηρίαν ἔχοντα μετὰ τῶν παιδίων
      καὶ τῆς γυναικός, κοὐ διοίσοντ' ἄντικρυς

---

368   πεπανουργηκότος Valckenaer: πεπανουργηκότι (-γευκ-R) codd.
374   ἂν Küster: οὖν codd.
375   ἐθέλεις RVn': ἐθέλει n'.
380   δοκεῖς n'Σᴷ: δοκῇς RVn': δοκοῖς n'.

CHREMYLUS [*indignantly*]: What do you mean, dirty?

BLEPSIDEMUS: If perhaps, by Zeus, you've come from where you've been with some silver or gold stolen from the god, and now maybe you're regretting it.

CHREMYLUS: Apollo preserve us! By Zeus, I have *not*.

360 BLEPSIDEMUS: Stop talking rubbish. I know the truth very well.

CHREMYLUS: Don't you dare suspect me of anything of the sort!

BLEPSIDEMUS [*to himself*]: Ah, how true it is that there's no pure honesty in anyone! All alike are the slaves of gain!

CHREMYLUS: By Demeter, I think you're just not in your right mind.

365 BLEPSIDEMUS [*as before*]: How much he's changed from the character he once had!

CHREMYLUS: You've gone potty, man, by heaven.

BLEPSIDEMUS [*as before*]: Even the very look in his eyes has gone shifty; it's plainly the look of a man who's committed some villainy.

CHREMYLUS: I know what *you're* driving at. You think I've stolen
370 something, and you're after a share.

BLEPSIDEMUS: Me after a share? What of?

CHREMYLUS: Well, it's not like that. It's something quite different.

BLEPSIDEMUS: You don't mean to say that it wasn't a *theft* but a *robbery*?

CHREMYLUS: You must be possessed!

BLEPSIDEMUS: Or again, you haven't been defrauding anyone, have you?

375 CHREMYLUS: No, I have not.

BLEPSIDEMUS [*despairingly*]: Heracles! Where is one supposed to go from here? You're just not prepared to tell the truth!

CHREMYLUS: You think that because you're accusing me without having heard from me what this is all about.

BLEPSIDEMUS [*ignoring this*]: Look, old chap, I'm willing to sort this out for you at very small expense, before the public get to know of it, by stopping the politicians' mouths with little bits of silver.

380 CHREMYLUS [*sarcastically*]: Oh yes, by the gods, I'm sure you'd treat me like a real friend — spend three minas and claim twelve!

BLEPSIDEMUS: I see a man who's going to be sitting on the speaker's platform, holding a suppliant-branch, with his wife and his

τῶν Ἡρακλειδῶν οὐδ' ὁτιοῦν τῶν Παμφίλου. 385

Χρ. οὔκ, ὦ κακόδαιμον, ἀλλὰ τοὺς χρηστοὺς μόνους
ἔγωγε καὶ τοὺς δεξιοὺς καὶ σώφρονας
ἀπαρτὶ πλουτῆσαι ποιήσω.

Βλ. τί σὺ λέγεις;
οὕτω πάνυ πολλὰ κέκλοφας;

Χρ. οἴμοι τῶν κακῶν,
ἀπολεῖς.

Βλ. σὺ μὲν οὖν σεαυτόν, ὥς γ' ἐμοὶ δοκεῖς. 390

Χρ. οὐ δῆτ', ἐπειδὴ Πλοῦτον, ὦ μόχθηρε σύ,
ἔχω.

Βλ. σὺ πλοῦτον; ποῖον;

Χρ. αὐτὸν τὸν θεόν.

Βλ. καὶ ποῦ 'στιν;

Χρ. ἔνδον.

Βλ. ποῦ;

Χρ. παρ' ἐμοί.

Βλ. παρὰ σοί;

Χρ. πάνυ.

Βλ. οὐκ ἐς κόρακας; Πλοῦτος παρὰ σοί;

Χρ. νὴ τοὺς θεούς.

Βλ. λέγεις ἀληθῆ;

Χρ. φημί.

Βλ. πρὸς τῆς Ἑστίας; 395

Χρ. νὴ τὸν Ποσειδῶ.

Βλ. τὸν θαλάττιον λέγεις;

Χρ. εἰ δ' ἐστὶν ἕτερός τις Ποσειδῶν, τὸν ἕτερον.

Βλ. εἶτ' οὐ διαπέμπεις καὶ πρὸς ἡμᾶς τοὺς φίλους;

Χρ. οὐκ ἔστι πω τὰ πράγματ' ἐν τούτῳ.

Βλ. τί φής;
οὐ τῷ μεταδοῦναι;

Χρ. μὰ Δία· δεῖ γὰρ πρῶτα-

Βλ. τί; 400

Χρ. -βλέψαι ποιῆσαι νὼ-

Βλ. τίνα βλέψαι; φράσον.

Χρ. -τὸν Πλοῦτον, ὥσπερ πρότερον, ἑνί γέ τῳ τρόπῳ.

---

391 ἐπειδὴ Blaydes: ἐπειδὴ τὸν RVᵖᶜn': ἐπεὶ τὸν Vᵃᶜn'.

85   children, and looking absolutely no different at all from Pamphilus' *Children of Heracles*!

CHREMYLUS: No, you wretched fool. What I'm going to do is to make the virtuous and the wise and the decent, just them alone, to make them be rich.

BLEPSIDEMUS: What are you saying? Have you stolen *that* much?!

90   CHREMYLUS: Dash it all, you'll be the death of me!

BLEPSIDEMUS: You'll be your own, as far as I can see.

CHREMYLUS: No, because I've got Wealth, you idiot.

BLEPSIDEMUS: You've got wealth? What wealth?

CHREMYLUS: The god himself.

BLEPSIDEMUS: And where is he?

CHREMYLUS: Inside.

BLEPSIDEMUS: Inside where?

CHREMYLUS: In my house.

BLEPSIDEMUS: In your house?

CHREMYLUS: Exactly.

BLEPSIDEMUS: To hell with you! Wealth is in your house?

CHREMYLUS: Yes, by the gods, he is.

395   BLEPSIDEMUS: Are you telling me the truth?

CHREMYLUS: Yes, I am.

BLEPSIDEMUS: In the name of Hestia, do you mean it?

CHREMYLUS: Yes, by Poseidon, I do.

BLEPSIDEMUS [*suspiciously*]: You do mean the sea-god?

CHREMYLUS: If there's any other Poseidon, then I mean the other too.

BLEPSIDEMUS: And yet you're not sending him round to us, your friends?

CHREMYLUS: Things aren't at that stage yet.

400   BLEPSIDEMUS [*again suspicious*]: What do you mean? Not at the stage of sharing?

CHREMYLUS: No, they're not. First of all we need—

BLEPSIDEMUS: Need to do what?

CHREMYLUS: —the two of us, to give back sight—

BLEPSIDEMUS: Give who back sight? Go on.

CHREMYLUS: ——to Wealth, like he used to have, by hook or by crook.

Βλ. τυφλὸς γὰρ ὄντως ἐστί;

Χρ.   νὴ τὸν οὐρανόν.

Βλ. οὐκ ἐτὸς ἄρ’ ὡς ἔμ’ ἦλθεν οὐδεπώποτε.

Χρ. ἀλλ’ ἢν θεοὶ θέλωσι, νῦν ἀφίξεται.   405

Βλ. οὔκουν ἰατρὸν εἰσάγειν ἐχρῆν τινα;

Χρ. τίς δῆτ’ ἰατρός ἐστι νῦν ἐν τῇ πόλει;
     οὔτε γὰρ ὁ μισθὸς οὐδέν ἔστ’ οὔθ’ ἡ τέχνη.

Βλ. σκοπῶμεν.

Χρ.   ἀλλ’ οὐκ ἔστιν.

Βλ.   οὐδ’ ἐμοὶ δοκεῖ.

Χρ. μὰ Δί’, ἀλλ’ ὅπερ πάλαι παρεσκευαζόμην   410
     ἐγώ, κατακλίνειν αὐτὸν εἰς Ἀσκληπιοῦ
     κράτιστόν ἐστι.

Βλ.   πολὺ μὲν οὖν, νὴ τοὺς θεούς.
     μή νυν διάτριβ’, ἀλλ’ ἄνυτε πράττων ἕν γέ τι.

Χρ. καὶ δὴ βαδίζω.

Βλ.   σπεῦδέ νυν.

Χρ.   τοῦτ’ αὐτὸ δρῶ.

ΠΕΝΙΑ
     ὦ θερμὸν ἔργον κἀνόσιον καὶ παράνομον   415
     τολμῶντε δρᾶν ἀνθρωπαρίω κακοδαίμονε–
     ποῖ, ποῖ; τί φεύγετον; οὐ μενεῖτον;

Βλ.   Ἡράκλεις.

Πε. ἐγὼ γὰρ ὑμᾶς ἐξολῶ κακοὺς κακῶς·
     τόλμημα γὰρ τολμᾶτον οὐκ ἀνασχετόν,
     ἀλλ’ οἷον οὐδεὶς ἄλλος οὐδεπώποτε   420
     οὔτε θεὸς οὔτ’ ἄνθρωπος· ὥστ’ ἀπολώλατον.

Χρ. σὺ δ’ εἶ τίς; ὠχρὰ μὲν γὰρ εἶναί μοι δοκεῖς.

Βλ. ἴσως Ἐρινύς ἐστιν ἐκ τραγῳδίας·
     βλέπει γέ τοι μανικόν τι καὶ τραγῳδικόν.

Χρ. ἀλλ’ οὐκ ἔχει γὰρ δᾷδας.

BLEPSIDEMUS: You mean he really is blind?

CHREMYLUS: Yes, he is, by heaven.

BLEPSIDEMUS: No wonder he never came to me!

405   CHREMYLUS: Well, if the gods are willing, he'll come now.

BLEPSIDEMUS: Well, shouldn't we be calling in a doctor?

CHREMYLUS: Why, what doctors are there now in Athens? The pay's not there, so the profession's not there either.

BLEPSIDEMUS: Let's have a look. [*They survey the audience.*]

CHREMYLUS: There aren't any.

BLEPSIDEMUS: I agree, there aren't.

410   CHREMYLUS: No, the best thing is what I was already getting ready to do, to have him spend the night in the sanctuary of Asclepius.

BLEPSIDEMUS: Just the thing, by the gods! So don't waste time, get on and *do* something!

CHREMYLUS [*moving towards the house*]: Look, I'm on my way.

BLEPSIDEMUS: Hurry, then!

CHREMYLUS [*half running*]: That's what I'm *doing*.

[*Just as Chremylus is about to go inside to fetch Wealth, there suddenly enters, right, a withered old woman of hideous appearance, who at once begins to bawl at him and Blepsidemus at the top of her voice.*]

415   THE OLD WOMAN: You miserable little pair of humans, who have the audacity to do so reckless, so impious, so lawless a deed— [*By now both men have taken to their heels.*] Where, where are you off to? Why are you running away? Stop, won't you? [*The two men stop running, but stay cowering at a safe distance.*]

BLEPSIDEMUS [*in terrified appeal*]: Heracles!

THE OLD WOMAN: I shall put a miserable end to your miserable
420   existence! You are venturing a venture that is not to be tolerated, a thing such as no god and no man has ever dared to do before! For that, you are both dead men!

CHREMYLUS [*edging back towards her*]: And who are you? You certainly look very pale to me!

BLEPSIDEMUS [*still keeping his distance*]: Perhaps she's a Fury out of some tragedy; at any rate she has that crazy tragic look about her.

425   CHREMYLUS: She can't be, she hasn't got any torches.

Βλ.   οὐκοῦν κλαύσεται.   425
Πε. οἴεσθε δ' εἶναι τίνα με;
Χρ.   πανδοκεύτριαν
ἢ λεκιθόπωλιν.   οὐ γὰρ ἂν τοσουτονὶ
ἐνέκραγες ἡμῖν οὐδὲν ἠδικημένη.
Πε. ἄληθες; οὐ γὰρ δεινότατα δεδράκατον
ζητοῦντες ἐκ πάσης με χώρας ἐκβαλεῖν;   430
Χρ. οὔκουν ὑπόλοιπον τὸ βάραθρόν σοι γίγνεται;
ἀλλ' ἥτις εἶ λέγειν σ' ἐχρῆν αὐτίκα μάλα.
Πε. ἢ σφὼ ποιήσω τήμερον δοῦναι δίκην
ἀνθ' ὧν ἐμὲ ζητεῖτον ἐνθένδ' ἀφανίσαι.
Βλ. ἆρ' ἐστὶν ἡ καπηλὶς ἡ 'κ τῶν γειτόνων,   435
ἢ ταῖς κοτύλαις ἀεί με διαλυμαίνεται;
Πε. Πενία μὲν οὖν, ἢ σφῷν ξυνοικῶ πόλλ' ἔτη.
Βλ. ἄναξ Ἄπολλον καὶ θεοί, ποῖ τις φύγῃ;
Χρ. οὗτος, τί δρᾷς; ὦ δειλότατον σὺ θηρίον,
οὐ παραμενεῖς;
Βλ.   ἥκιστα πάντων.
Χρ.   οὐ μενεῖς;   440
ἀλλ' ἄνδρε δύο γυναῖκα φεύγομεν μίαν;
Βλ. Πενία γάρ ἐστιν, ὦ πόνηρ', ἧς οὐδαμοῦ
οὐδὲν πέφυκε ζῷον ἐξωλέστερον.
Χρ. στῆθ', ἀντιβολῶ σε, στῆθι.
Βλ.   μὰ Δί' ἐγὼ μὲν οὔ.
Χρ. καὶ μὴν λέγω, δειλότατον ἔργον παρὰ πολὺ   445
ἔργων ἁπάντων ἐργασόμεθ', εἰ τὸν θεὸν
ἔρημον ἀπολιπόντέ ποι φευξούμεθα
τηνδὶ δεδιότε, μηδὲ διαμαχούμεθα.
Βλ. ποίοισιν ὅπλοις ἢ δυνάμει πεποιθότες;
ποῖον γὰρ οὐ θώρακα, ποίαν δ' ἀσπίδα   450
οὐκ ἐνέχυρον τίθησιν ἡ μιαρωτάτη;
Χρ. θάρρει· μόνος γὰρ ὁ θεὸς οὗτος οἶδ' ὅτι
τροπαῖον ἂν στήσαιτο τῶν ταύτης τρόπων.

---

445 δειλότατον x: δεινότατον RVn Suda.

BLEPSIDEMUS [*emboldened; rejoining Chremylus, and shaking his fist at the old woman*]: Then she's going to howl!

THE OLD WOMAN [*ignoring these exchanges*]: Who do you *think* I am?

CHREMYLUS: Oh, an innkeeper or a porridge-vendor. Otherwise you wouldn't have bawled so loud at us when we'd done you no harm.

THE OLD WOMAN: No harm? Have you two not done a most
430 appalling wrong to me, by seeking to drive me out of every land?

CHREMYLUS: Well, you'll still have the Barathron left to go to, won't you? But you ought to be telling us who you are — right away.

THE OLD WOMAN: One who will see that you get your just deserts, this very day, for your attempt to make me disappear from these parts.

435 BLEPSIDEMUS: Is she the tavern-keeper from round the corner, who always gives me short measure in my half-pints?

THE OLD WOMAN: No, I am Poverty, Poverty who has dwelt with you both these many years.

BLEPSIDEMUS [*in terror*]: Lord Apollo and all you gods, where can one run to? [*He beats a rapid retreat.*]

CHREMYLUS [*calling after him*]: Hey, what are you doing? You
440 cowardly, cowardly creature, won't you stay with me?

BLEPSIDEMUS [*not stopping*]: No way!

CHREMYLUS: Stay here, won't you? What's this — us two men running away from one woman?

BLEPSIDEMUS [*not stopping*]: She's Poverty, you idiot, the most deadly creature in the natural world.

CHREMYLUS: Stop, I beg you, *stop*!

BLEPSIDEMUS [*who has now almost reached the right-hand exit*]: No, I will not!

445 CHREMYLUS [*desperately*]: Look — I say — we'll be guilty of by far the most cowardly action ever committed, if we leave the god in the lurch and run off somewhere because we're afraid of *her*, without fighting it out.

BLEPSIDEMUS [*stopping and turning, but staying well away from
450 Poverty*]: "What weapons or what allies can we trust?" What cuirass, what shield is there that this filthy female hasn't forced us to pawn?

CHREMYLUS: Have courage. That god [*gesturing towards his house*], I'm certain, all on his own, can triumph over her and her trying ways.

[*Blepsidemus comes a little way back towards him, but from now on remains largely a spectator.*]

Πε. γρύζειν δὲ καὶ τολμᾶτον, ὦ καθάρματε,
ἐπ' αὐτοφώρῳ δεινὰ δρῶντ' εἰλημμένω; 455
Χρ. σὺ δ', ὦ κακῶς ἀπολουμένη, τί λοιδορεῖ
ἡμῖν προσελθοῦσ' οὐδ' ὁτιοῦν ἀδικουμένη;
Πε. οὐδὲν γάρ, ὦ πρὸς τῶν θεῶν, νομίζετε
ἀδικεῖν με, τὸν Πλοῦτον ποιεῖν πειρωμένω
βλέψαι πάλιν;
Χρ.   τί οὖν ἀδικοῦμεν τοῦτό σε, 460
εἰ πᾶσιν ἀνθρώποισιν ἐκπορίζομεν
ἀγαθόν;
Πε.   τί δ' ἂν ὑμεῖς ἀγαθὸν ἐξεύροιθ';
Χρ.   ὅ τι;
σὲ πρῶτον ἐκβαλόντες ἐκ τῆς Ἑλλάδος.
Πε. ἔμ' ἐκβαλόντες; καὶ τί ἂν νομίζετον
κακὸν ἐργάσασθαι μεῖζον ἀνθρώποις;
Χρ.   ὅ τι; 465
εἰ τοῦτο δρᾶν μέλλοντες ἐπιλαθοίμεθα.
Πε. καὶ μὴν περὶ τούτου σφῷν ἐθέλω δοῦναι λόγον
τὸ πρῶτον αὐτοῦ· κἂν μὲν ἀποφήνω μόνην
ἀγαθῶν ἁπάντων οὖσαν αἰτίαν ἐμὲ
ὑμῖν δι' ἐμέ τε ζῶντας ὑμᾶς— · εἰ δὲ μή, 470
ποιεῖτον ἤδη τοῦθ' ὅ τι ἂν ὑμῖν δοκῇ.
Χρ. ταυτὶ σὺ τολμᾷς, ὦ μιαρωτάτη, λέγειν;
Πε. καὶ σύ γε διδάσκου· πάνυ γὰρ οἶμαι ῥᾳδίως
ἅπανθ' ἁμαρτάνοντά σ' ἀποδείξειν ἐγώ,
εἰ τοὺς δικαίους φῂς ποιήσειν πλουσίους. 475
Χρ. ὦ τύπανα καὶ κύφωνες, οὐκ ἀρήξετε;
Πε. οὐ δεῖ σχετλιάζειν καὶ βοᾶν, πρὶν ἂν μάθῃς.
Χρ. καὶ τίς δύναιτ' ἂν μὴ βοᾶν "ἰοὺ ἰού"
τοιαῦτ' ἀκούων;
Πε.   ὅστις ἐστὶν εὖ φρονῶν.
Χρ. τί δῆτά σοι τίμημ' ἐπιγράψω τῇ δίκῃ, 480
ἐὰν ἁλῷς;
Πε.   ὅ τι σοι δοκεῖ.
Χρ.   καλῶς λέγεις.
Πε. τὸ γὰρ αὔτ', ἐὰν ἡττᾶσθε, καὶ σφὼ δεῖ παθεῖν.

---

476   τύπανα Bentley, cf. Aesch. fr. 57.10, Eur. *Hel.* 1347, *Ba.* 59, Arist. *Ath.Pol.* 45.1, and
      alphabetical order in Suda[AFV] τ1174: τύμπανα codd. Suda (τ1174 and κ2800).

POVERTY: How dare you open your mouths, you scum, when you
455 have been caught red-handed committing an appalling crime?

CHREMYLUS: And you, damn and blast you, why do you come here
and revile us, when we haven't done you the least injury?

POVERTY: In the gods' name, do you think you've done me *no*
460 *injury*, when you're trying to give Wealth back his sight?

CHREMYLUS: So how's that injuring you, if we provide a benefit
for all mankind?

POVERTY: And what benefit could *you* find to confer?

CHREMYLUS: What benefit? Turfing *you* out of Greece, for a start.

465 POVERTY: Turfing me out? And what greater *harm* do you think
you could do mankind than that?

CHREMYLUS: What greater harm? If we were meaning to do that
and then forgot to.

POVERTY: Very well, I am prepared, before that, to render my
account, here and now, to the two of you. And if I prove that I alone am the
470 cause of all the good things you have, and that it is thanks to me that you are
even alive— ; but if I fail, then you can do whatever you like to me.

CHREMYLUS: You dare to assert that, you filthy creature?

POVERTY: And you should be ready to learn that it's true. I expect
475 to prove very easily that you are making a total mistake if you mean to make
honest men wealthy.

CHREMYLUS: Pillories and execution-boards, come to our aid!

POVERTY: You shouldn't scream and go all indignant before you've
learned the facts.

CHREMYLUS: And who could *keep* from screaming with rage at
hearing such a thing?

POVERTY: Anyone with good sense.

480 CHREMYLUS: All right, what penalty shall I enter on my
indictment, should you be convicted?

POVERTY: Whatever you like.

CHREMYLUS: Very good.

POVERTY: Meaning, of course, that if you lose, the same penalty
must apply to the two of you.

Χρ. ἱκανοὺς νομίζεις δῆτα θανάτους εἴκοσιν;
Βλ. ταύτῃ γε· νῶν δὲ δύ' ἀποχρήσουσιν μόνω.
Πε. οὐκ ἂν φθάνοιτε τοῦτο πράττοντες· τί γὰρ   485
     ἔχοι τις ἂν δίκαιον ἀντειπεῖν ἔτι;
Χο. ἀλλ' ἤδη χρῆν τι λέγειν ὑμᾶς σοφόν, ᾧ νικήσετε τηνδὶ
     ἐν τοῖσι λόγοις ἀντιλέγοντες· μαλακὸν δ' ἐνδώσετε μηδέν.
Χρ. φανερὸν μὲν ἔγωγ' οἶμαι γνῶναι τοῦτ' εἶναι πᾶσιν ὁμοίως,   489
     ὅτι τοὺς χρηστοὺς τῶν ἀνθρώπων εὖ πράττειν ἐστὶ δίκαιον,
     τοὺς δὲ πονηροὺς καὶ τοὺς ἀθέους τούτων τἀναντία δήπου.
     τοῦτ' οὖν ἡμεῖς ἐπιθυμοῦντες μόλις ηὕρομεν, ὥστε γενέσθαι
     βούλευμα καλὸν καὶ γενναῖον καὶ χρήσιμον εἰς ἅπαν ἔργον.
     ἢν γὰρ ὁ Πλοῦτος νυνὶ βλέψῃ καὶ μὴ τυφλὸς ὢν περινοστῇ,
     ὡς τοὺς ἀγαθοὺς τῶν ἀνθρώπων βαδιεῖται κοὐκ ἀπολείψει,   495
     τοὺς δὲ πονηροὺς καὶ τοὺς ἀθέους φευξεῖται· κᾆτα ποιήσει
     πάντας χρηστούς – καὶ πλουτοῦντας δήπου – τά τε θεῖα
                                                  σέβοντας.
     καίτοι τούτου τοῖς ἀνθρώποις τίς ἂν ἐξεύροι ποτ' ἄμεινον;
Βλ. οὐδείς· τούτου μάρτυς ἐγώ σοι· μηδὲν ταύτην γ' ἀνερώτα.
Χρ. ὡς μὲν γὰρ νῦν ἡμῖν ὁ βίος τοῖς ἀνθρώποις διάκειται,   500
     τίς ἂν οὐχ ἡγοῖτ' εἶναι μανίαν κακοδαιμονίαν τ' ἔτι μᾶλλον;
     πολλοὶ μὲν γὰρ τῶν ἀνθρώπων ὄντες πλουτοῦσι πονηροί,
     ἀδίκως αὐτὰ ξυλλεξάμενοι· πολλοὶ δ' ὄντες πάνυ χρηστοὶ
     πράττουσι κακῶς καὶ πεινῶσιν μετὰ σοῦ τε τὰ πλεῖστα
                                                  σύνεισιν.
     οὔκουν εἶναί φημ', εἰ παύσει ταυτὶ βλέψας ποθ' ὁ Πλοῦτος,
     ὁδὸν ἥντιν' ἰὼν τοῖς ἀνθρώποις ἀγάθ' ἂν μείζω πορίσειεν. 506
Πε. ἀλλ', ὦ πάντων ῥᾷστ' ἀνθρώπων ἀναπεισθέντ' οὐχ ὑγιαίνειν
     δύο πρεσβύτα, ξυνθιασῶτα τοῦ ληρεῖν καὶ παραπαίειν,
     εἰ τοῦτο γένοιθ' ὃ ποθεῖθ' ὑμεῖς, οὔ φημ' ἂν λυσιτελεῖν σφῶν.
     εἰ γὰρ ὁ Πλοῦτος βλέψειε πάλιν διανείμειέν τ' ἴσον αὐτόν, 510
     οὔτε τέχνην ἂν τῶν ἀνθρώπων οὔτ' ἂν σοφίαν μελετῴη

---

485   τί γὰρ n': εἴ τι γὰρ R^{ac}V: ἢ τί γὰρ R^{pc}: ἢ τί γ' ἂν n'.
493   βούλευμα x: βούλημα RVn Suda.
499   τούτου μάρτυς ἐγώ σοι Hall & Geldart: τ<u>ο</u>ύτου μ[Π21: ἐγώ σοι τούτου
      μάρτυς vel sim. RVn: τούτου σοι (σοὶ) μάρτυς ἐγώ Fraenkel.
505   ταυτὶ βλέψας Meineke: ταύτην βλέψας R 'Σ(i)^{RVEΘVb3}: ταύτην βλάψας
      'Σ(ii)^{REMΘVb3}: ταύτ' ἢν βλέψῃ vel sim. Vn 'Σ(iii)^{VEMΘMdlVb3}.

CHREMYLUS [*to Blepsidemus*]: What about it? Do you think that twenty deaths will be enough?

BLEPSIDEMUS: For *her*, yes. For *us*, just two will do perfectly well.

485 POVERTY: You might just as well do that straight away; because what is there left that anyone could rightly say to oppose my case?

CHORUS-LEADER [*to Chremylus and Blepsidemus*]: Now it's time for you to say something clever, so you can defeat this adversary in a debate of opposing arguments; you mustn't yield or soften an inch.

CHREMYLUS: Well, I think this much can be plainly recognized by 490 everyone alike — that it's right and just that the virtuous among mankind should have prosperity, and the wicked and the godless, of course, the reverse of that. Desiring to achieve that, we have found a way to do it, so that a scheme has come into existence which is noble, admirable, and beneficial in every way. It is that if Wealth now regains his sight and no 495 longer wanders around blind, he will direct his steps to the good among mankind and never forsake them, and will shun the wicked and the godless; and consequently he will bring it about that everyone is virtuous — and rich, of course — and reveres the power of the gods. And who could ever find anything better for mankind than that?

BLEPSIDEMUS: Nobody. I'm your witness to that. Don't bother asking *her*!

500 CHREMYLUS: Because the way life is arranged at present for us humans, who would not regard it as sheer insanity and, even more, sheer wretchedness? Many men are wealthy who are wicked, having amassed it by crime; and many who are very virtuous are in a bad way, and starve, and 505 live most of their lives in your company. So I say that if Wealth at last recovers his sight and puts a stop to this situation, there is no road he could take that would confer greater benefits on mankind.

POVERTY: You two old men are the easiest in the world to persuade out of your wits! You are comrades of the order of balderdash and lunacy! If what you desire were actually to happen, I tell you it would not be to your 510 advantage at all. If Wealth were to regain his sight and distribute himself on an equal basis, no person on earth would practise any craft or any skill; and

οὐδείς· ἀμφοῖν δ' ὑμῖν τούτοιν ἀφανισθέντοιν ἐθελήσει
τίς χαλκεύειν ἢ ναυπηγεῖν ἢ ῥάπτειν ἢ τροχοποιεῖν
ἢ σκυτοτομεῖν ἢ πλινθουργεῖν ἢ πλύνειν ἢ σκυλοδεψεῖν
ἢ γῆς ἀρότροις ῥήξας δάπεδον καρπὸν Δηοῦς θερίσασθαι, 515
ἢν ἐξῇ ζῆν ἀργοῖς ὑμῖν τούτων πάντων ἀμελοῦσιν;

Χρ.   λῆρον ληρεῖς· ταῦτα γὰρ ἡμῖν πάνθ', ὅσα νυνδὴ κατέλεξας,
οἱ θεράποντες μοχθήσουσιν.

Πε.   πόθεν οὖν ἕξεις θεράποντας;

Χρ.   ὠνησόμεθ' ἀργυρίου δήπου.

Πε.   τίς δ' ἔσται πρῶτον ὁ πωλῶν,
ὅταν ἀργύριον κἀκεῖνος ἔχῃ;

Χρ.   κερδαίνειν βουλόμενός τις   520
ἔμπορος ἥκων ἐκ Θετταλίας παρὰ πλείστων ἀνδραποδιστῶν.

Πε.   ἀλλ' οὐδ' ἔσται πρῶτον ἁπάντων οὐδεὶς οὐδ' ἀνδραποδιστὴς
κατὰ τὸν λόγον ὃν σὺ λέγεις δήπου. τίς γὰρ πλουτῶν ἐθελήσει
κινδυνεύειν περὶ τῆς ψυχῆς τῆς αὑτοῦ τοῦτο ποιήσας;
ὥστ' αὐτὸς ἀροῦν ἐπαναγκασθεὶς καὶ σκάπτειν τἄλλα τε μοχθεῖν
ὀδυνηρότερον τρίψεις βίοτον πολὺ τοῦ νῦν.

Χρ.   εἰς κεφαλήν σοί. 526

Πε.   ἔτι δ' οὐχ ἕξεις οὔτ' ἐν κλίνῃ καταδαρθεῖν – οὐ γὰρ ἔσονται –
οὔτ' ἐν δαπίσιν – τίς γὰρ ὑφαίνειν ἐθελήσει, χρυσίου ὄντος; –
οὔτε μύροισιν μυρίσαι στακτοῖς, ὁπόταν νύμφην ἀγάγησθον,
οὔθ' ἱματίων βαπτῶν δαπάναις κοσμῆσαι ποικιλομόρφων. 530
καίτοι τί πλέον πλουτεῖν ἐστιν τούτων πάντων ἀποροῦντας;
παρ' ἐμοῦ δ' ἐστὶν ταῦτ' εὔπορα πάνθ' ὑμῖν ὧν δεῖσθον· ἐγὼ γὰρ
τὸν χειροτέχνην ὥσπερ δέσποιν' ἐπαναγκάζουσα κάθημαι
διὰ τὴν χρείαν καὶ τὴν πενίαν ζητεῖν ὁπόθεν βίον ἕξει.

Χρ.   σὺ γὰρ ἂν πορίσαι τι δύναι' ἀγαθόν, πλὴν φῴδων ἐκ βαλανείου
καὶ παιδαρίων ὑποπεινώντων καὶ γραϊδίων κολοσυρτόν; 536
φθειρῶν δ' ἀριθμὸν καὶ κωνώπων καὶ ψυλλῶν οὐδὲ λέγω σοι
ὑπὸ τοῦ πλήθους, αἳ βομβοῦσαι περὶ τὴν κεφαλὴν ἀνιῶσιν,
ἐπεγείρουσαι καὶ φράζουσαι "πεινήσεις· ἀλλ' ἐπανίστω".

---

514   σκυλοδεψεῖν Bentley: σκυτοδεψεῖν R*n*: βυρσοδεψεῖν V.
524   κινδυνεύειν R: κινδυνεύων V*n*.
524   ποιήσας Blaydes: ποιῆσαι codd.
531   ἀποροῦντας V*n*': ἀποροῦντα R*n*'.
537   δ' Küster: τ' codd.

if you have both of these disappear, who will be willing to be a smith or a shipwright or a stitcher or a wheelwright or a cobbler or a brickmaker or a launderer or a tanner, or "to break the surface of the ground with ploughs and reap the fruits of Deo", if you're able to live in idleness without bothering about all that?

CHREMYLUS: You're just blabbering nonsense. All those laborious jobs you've just listed, the slaves will do them for us.

POVERTY: So where are you going to get slaves from?

CHREMYLUS: We'll buy them with money, of course.

POVERTY: But who's there going to be to sell them in the first place, when he's got money too?

CHREMYLUS: Oh, some trader wanting to make a profit, coming from Thessaly where all the kidnappers are.

POVERTY: But surely on the case *you're* putting there just won't *be* any kidnappers at all to start with. Who, if he's rich, will want to risk his own life doing that? The result will be, you'll be forced to do your ploughing yourself, and your digging yourself, and all the other hard labour, and you'll be spending a much more distressful life than you do now.

CHREMYLUS: May those words be on *your* head!

POVERTY: Again, you won't be able to sleep on a bed (because there won't be any), nor under blankets (because who's going to want to weave them, when he's flush with gold?); nor, when you bring a bride home, to anoint her with distilled unguents, nor to adorn her with costly garments in variegated colours. And really, what's the good of being rich when you're lacking all these things? From me, on the other hand, all these things that you want are available in ample supply, because I sit over the craftsman as a mistress sits over her slaves, compelling him through need and penury to seek a means of getting a livelihood.

CHREMYLUS: *What?* Is there any good thing *you'd* be capable of supplying — except for blisters from the bath-house and crying gaggles of half-starved little kids and old grannies? I won't even mention the numbers of lice and gnats and fleas — there are just too many — that buzz maddeningly around your head, waking you up and warning "You'll starve; up you get!"

πρὸς δέ γε τούτοις ἀνθ' ἱματίου μὲν ἔχειν ῥάκος· ἀντὶ δὲ
                                        κλίνης
στιβάδα σχοίνων κόρεων μεστήν, ἣ τοὺς εὕδοντας ἐγείρει· 541
καὶ φορμὸν ἔχειν ἀντὶ τάπητος σαπρόν· ἀντὶ δὲ προσκεφαλαίου
λίθον εὐμεγεθῆ πρὸς τῇ κεφλῇ· σιτεῖσθαι δ' ἀντὶ μὲν ἄρτων
μαλάχης πτόρθους, ἀντὶ δὲ μάζης φυλλεῖ' ἰσχνῶν ῥαφανίδων·
ἀντὶ δὲ θράνου στάμνου κεφαλὴν κατεαγότος, ἀντὶ δὲ μάκτρας
φιδάκνης πλευρὰν ἐρρωγυῖαν καὶ ταύτην. ἆρά γε πολλῶν 546
ἀγαθῶν πᾶσιν τοῖς ἀνθρώποις ἀποφαίνω σ' αἴτιον οὖσαν;
Πε. σὺ μὲν οὐ τὸν ἐμὸν βίον εἴρηκας, τὸν τῶν πτωχῶν δ' ἐπεκρούσω.
Χρ. οὔκουν δήπου τῆς Πτωχείας Πενίαν φαμὲν εἶναι ἀδελφήν;
Πε. ὑμεῖς γ', οἵπερ καὶ Θρασυβούλῳ Διονύσιον εἶναι ὅμοιον.   550
ἀλλ' οὐχ οὑμὸς τοῦτο πέπονθεν βίος οὐ μὰ Δί', οὐδέ γε μέλλει.
πτωχοῦ μὲν γὰρ βίος, ὃν σὺ λέγεις, ζῆν ἐστιν μηδὲν ἔχοντα·
τοῦ δὲ πένητος ζῆν φειδόμενον καὶ τοῖς ἔργοις προσέχοντα,
περιγίγνεσθαι δ' αὐτῷ μηδέν, μὴ μέντοι μηδ' ἐπιλείπειν.
Χρ. ὡς μακαρίτην, ὦ Δάματερ, τὸν βίον αὐτοῦ κατέλεξας,   555
εἰ φεισάμενος καὶ μοχθήσας καταλείψει μηδὲ ταφῆναι.
Πε. σκώπτειν πειρᾷ καὶ κωμῳδεῖν τοῦ σπουδάζειν ἀμελήσας,
οὐ γιγνώσκων ὅτι τοῦ Πλούτου παρέχω βελτίονας ἄνδρας
καὶ τὴν γνώμην καὶ τὴν ἰδέαν. παρὰ τῷ μὲν γὰρ ποδαγρῶντες
καὶ γαστρώδεις καὶ παχύκνημοι καὶ πίονές εἰσιν ἀσελγῶς, 560
παρ' ἐμοὶ δ' ἰσχνοὶ καὶ σφηκώδεις καὶ τοῖς ἐχθροῖς ἀνιαροί.
Χρ. ἀπὸ τοῦ λιμοῦ γὰρ ἴσως αὐτοῖς τὸ σφηκῶδες σὺ πορίζεις.
Πε. περὶ σωφροσύνης ἤδη τοίνυν περανῶ σφῶν, κἀναδιδάξω
ὅτι κοσμιότης οἰκεῖ μετ' ἐμοῦ, τοῦ Πλούτου δ' ἐστὶν ὑβρίζειν.
Χρ. πάνυ γοῦν κλέπτειν κόσμιόν ἐστιν καὶ τοὺς τοίχους διορύττειν.
                                                      565

544   φυλλεῖ' ᵛΣᴿ: φύλλ' codd. Σᴱᴳ Ach. 469.
544   ἰσχνῶν codd. ᵛΣᴿᴱᴹᶿ Σᴱᴳ Ach. 469: ἰσχνὰ Velsen.
545   θράνου Pollux 10.48: θράνους codd. Suda.
546   φιδάκνης Velsen: πιθάκνης codd. Suda, Pollux 10.48.
547   αἴτιον Bentley: αἰτίαν codd.
548   ἐπεκρούσω ᶦPollux 9.139: ὑπεκρούσω codd. Suda.
550   εἶναι n' Suda π966 Sudaᴬⱽ π3052: φάτ' εἶναι vel sim. RVn' Sudaᴳᴹ π3052.
[566] (Βλ.) νὴ τὸν Δί' (νὴ τὸν Δία γ' n': om. Suda) εἴ γε (εἰ R) δεῖ λαθεῖν αὐτὸν
      (λαθεῖν αὐτὸν δεῖ Vn' Suda) πῶς οὐχὶ (πῶς οὐ n' Suda: om. V) κόσμιόν ἐστι(ν)
      codd. Suda: del. Bentley.

And on top of all that, to have rags for clothing; instead of a bedstead, a bed of rushes, teeming with bugs, that can wake the soundest sleeper; instead of a blanket, to have a worn-out piece of matting; instead of a pillow, a good-sized stone at one's head; and to feed on mallow shoots instead of bread, on withered radish leaves instead of barley-cake; instead of a stool, the top of a broken wine-jar; instead of a kneading-trough, one side of a storage-jar, and cracked at that. [*With heavy sarcasm*] *Am* I demonstrating that you are the cause of *many* blessings to the *whole* of humanity?

POVERTY: You haven't been talking about *my* way of life at all; you've been inveighing against the lot of the *destitute*.

CHREMYLUS: Well, we do say, don't we, that Poverty is the sister of Destitution?

POVERTY: Yes, you do, and you also say that Dionysius is no different from Thrasybulus! *My* kind of life doesn't involve that sort of thing, by Zeus, and it never could. The life of the destitute, which is what you're talking about, is to have to live on nothing. The life of a *poor* man is to live economically and keep at one's work, not having any surplus but not having a shortfall either.

CHREMYLUS: Damater! what a *blessed* life you've described for him, if after toiling and scrimping he won't even leave enough behind him to pay for his funeral!

POVERTY: You are trying to mock and make jokes, with no concern for serious discussion, and refusing to recognize that I produce better men than Wealth does — better men both mentally and physically. With him, they are gouty and pot-bellied and thick-calved and obscenely fat; with me they're lean and wasp-like and sting their enemies hard.

CHREMYLUS: I supppose you use starvation to give them that wasp shape!

POVERTY: I shall now, then, go on to tell you about morality, and explain to you that with me is where decent behaviour dwells, whereas what goes with Wealth is wanton insolence.

CHREMYLUS: Oh, yes, it's *very* decent behaviour to steal or dig through walls!

Πε. σκέψαι τοίνυν ἐν ταῖς πόλεσιν τοὺς ῥήτορας, ὡς ὁπόταν μὲν
567
ὦσι πένητες, περὶ τὸν δῆμον καὶ τὴν πόλιν εἰσὶ δίκαιοι,
πλουτήσαντες δ' ἀπὸ τῶν κοινῶν παραχρῆμ' ἄδικοι γεγένηται
ἐπιβουλεύουσί τε τῷ πλήθει καὶ τῷ δήμῳ πολεμοῦσιν. 570
Χρ. ἀλλ' οὐ ψεύδει τούτων γ' οὐδέν, καίτοι σφόδρα βάσκανος οὖσα.
ἀτὰρ οὐχ ἧττόν γ' οὐδὲν κλαύσει – μηδὲν ταύτῃ γε κομήσῃς –
ὁτιὴ ζητεῖς τοῦτ' ἀναπείσειν ἡμᾶς, ὡς ἔστιν ἄμεινον
πενία πλούτου.
Πε.   καὶ σύ γ' ἐλέγξαι μ' οὔπω δύνασαι περὶ τούτου,
ἀλλὰ φλυαρεῖς καὶ πτερυγίζεις.
Χρ.   καὶ πῶς φεύγουσί σ' ἅπαντες; 575
Πε. ὅτι βελτίους αὐτοὺς ποιῶ. σκέψασθαι δ' ἐστὶ μάλιστα
ἀπὸ τῶν παίδων· τοὺς γὰρ πατέρας φεύγουσι φρονοῦντας ἄριστα
αὐτοῖς. οὕτω διαγιγνώσκειν χαλεπὸν πρᾶγμ' ἐστὶ †δίκαιον†.
Χρ. τὸν Δία φήσεις ἆρ' οὐκ ὀρθῶς διαγιγνώσκειν τὸ κράτιστον·
κἀκεῖνος γὰρ τὸν Πλοῦτον ἔχει.
Βλ.   ταύτην δ' ἡμῖν ἀποπέμπει. 580
Πε. ἀλλ', ὦ Κρονικαῖς λήμαις ὄντως λημῶντες τὰς φρένας ἄμφω,
ὁ Ζεὺς δήπου πένεται, καὶ τοῦτ' ἤδη φανερῶς σε διδάξω.
εἰ γὰρ ἐπλούτει, πῶς ἂν ποιῶν τὸν Ὀλυμπικὸν αὐτὸς ἀγῶνα,
ἵνα τοὺς Ἕλληνας ἅπαντας ἀεὶ δι' ἔτους πέμπτου ξυναγείρει,
ἀνεκήρυττεν τῶν ἀσκητῶν τοὺς νικῶντας στεφανώσας 585
κοτίνου στεφάνῳ; καίτοι χρυσῷ μᾶλλον ἐχρῆν, εἴπερ ἐπλούτει.
Χρ. οὔκουν τούτῳ δήπου δηλοῖ τιμῶν τὸν Πλοῦτον ἐκεῖνος;
φειδόμενος γὰρ καὶ βουλόμενος τούτου μηδὲν δαπανᾶσθαι
λήροις ἀναδῶν τοὺς νικῶντας τὸν Πλοῦτον ἐᾷ παρ' ἑαυτῷ.
Πε. πολὺ τῆς πενίας πρᾶγμ' αἴσχιον ζητεῖς αὐτῷ περιάψαι, 590
εἰ πλούσιος ὢν ἀνελεύθερός ἐσθ' οὑτωσὶ καὶ φιλοκερδής.
Χρ. ἀλλὰ σέ γ' ὁ Ζεὺς ἐξολέσειεν κοτίνου στεφάνῳ στεφανώσας.
Πε. τὸ γὰρ ἀντιλέγειν τολμᾶν ὑμᾶς ὡς οὐ πάντ' ἔστ' ἀγάθ' ὑμῖν
διὰ τὴν Πενίαν.
Χρ.   παρὰ τῆς Ἑκάτης ἔξεστιν τοῦτο πυθέσθαι,

---

573   ὁτιὴ n': ὅτι n': ὅτι γε RVn'.
578   †δίκαιον† RVn': τὸ δίκαιον n': τὸ κρεῖττον Dindorf: τὸ λῷστον Blaydes.
583   τὸν Ὀλυμπικὸν αὐτὸς x: τὸν Ὀλυμπιακὸν αὐτὸς n': αὐτὸς τὸν Ὀλυμπικὸν
       RV: αὐτὸς τὸν Ὀλυμπιακὸν n'.
592   σέ γ' n': σε or σ' RVn'.

567   POVERTY: Then look at the politicians in the different states. As long as they're poor, they act honestly towards the state and the people; but when they've enriched themselves from the public purse they at once
570   become crooks, plot against the masses and make war on the people.

CHREMYLUS: Well, *that's* certainly no lie you've told, malignant witch though you are! But don't get cocky about it — you're going to howl none the less, for trying to persuade us that being poor is a better thing than being rich.

POVERTY: Well, *you* haven't been able to refute me on that yet;
575   you're just wittering and flailing the air.

CHREMYLUS: All right, how come everyone tries to escape from you?

POVERTY: Because I make them better people. You can see it most easily from what children do: their fathers have their best interests at heart, but the children run away from them. That's how hard a thing it is to recognize what's best for you.

CHREMYLUS: In that case you'll be saying that Zeus doesn't
580   properly recognize what's best for him. *He* has Wealth too.

BLEPSIDEMUS [*to Chremylus*]: And sends *her* off to plague *us*!

POVERTY: The truly prehistoric purblindness of your intellects, the pair of you! Why, Zeus is *poor*, of course, and I'll now demonstrate that to you very clearly. If he were rich, can you imagine that when he himself holds the Olympic festival, where he gathers all the Greeks together every
585   four years, when proclaiming the victors in the athletic events he would crown them with a crown of *wild olive*? Surely, if he was rich, a gold crown would be more appropriate!

CHREMYLUS: Doesn't he make it obvious, just by that very fact, that he sets the greatest value on Wealth? He's a penny-pincher, anxious not to let any of it get spent, so he gives worthless garlands to the victors and keeps his Wealth safe at home!

590   POVERTY: You're trying to pin something on him that's much more shameful than poverty, if you're saying that he's rich and yet so very mean and grasping.

CHREMYLUS [*whose patience is fast running out*]: Oh, may Zeus crown *you* with wild olive, and then crush you!

POVERTY: The very idea that you should dare contradict me, and deny that all good things come to you thanks to Poverty!
595   CHREMYLUS: You can get the answer from Hecate as to whether

εἴτε τὸ πλουτεῖν εἴτε τὸ πεινῆν βέλτιον. φησὶ γὰρ αὐτῇ 595
τοὺς μὲν ἔχοντας καὶ πλουτοῦντας δεῖπνον προσάγειν κατὰ μῆνα,
τοὺς δὲ πένητας τῶν ἀνθρώπων ἁρπάζειν πρὶν καταθεῖναι.
ἀλλὰ φθείρου καὶ μὴ γρύξῃς
ἔτι μηδ' ὁτιοῦν.
οὐ γὰρ πείσεις, οὐδ' ἢν πείσῃς.   600

Πε. ὦ πόλις "Αργους, κλύεθ' οἷα λέγει.
Χρ. Παύσωνα κάλει τὸν ξύσσιτον.
Πε. τί πάθω τλήμων;
Χρ. ἔρρ' ἐς κόρακας θᾶττον ἀφ' ἡμῶν.
Πε. εἶμι δὲ ποῖ γῆς;   605
Χρ. εἰς τὸν κύφων'. ἀλλ' οὐ μέλλειν
     χρή σ', ἀλλ' ἀνύτειν.
Πε. ἦ μὴν ὑμεῖς ἔτι μ' ἐνταυθοῖ
     μεταπέμψεσθον.
Χρ. τότε νοστήσεις· νῦν δὲ φθείρου.   610
     κρεῖττον γάρ μοι πλουτεῖν ἐστιν,
     σὲ δ' ἐᾶν κλάειν μακρὰ τὴν κεφαλήν.
Βλ. νὴ Δί' ἐγὼ γοῦν ἐθέλω πλουτῶν
     εὐωχεῖσθαι μετὰ τῶν παίδων
     τῆς τε γυναικός, καὶ λουσάμενος   615
     λιπαρὸς χωρῶν ἐκ βαλανείου
     τῶν χειροτεχνῶν
     καὶ τῆς Πενίας καταπαρδεῖν.

Χρ. αὕτη μὲν ἡμῖν ἠπίτριπτος οἴχεται·
     ἐγὼ δὲ καὶ σύ γ' ὡς τάχιστα τὸν θεὸν
     ἐγκατακλινοῦντ' ἄγωμεν εἰς 'Ασκληπιοῦ.   620
Βλ. καὶ μὴ διατρίβωμέν γε, μὴ πάλιν τις αὖ
     ἐλθὼν διακωλύσῃ τι τῶν προὔργου ποιεῖν.
Χρ. παῖ Καρίων, τὰ στρώματ' ἐκφέρειν ἐχρῆν
     αὐτόν τ' ἄγειν τὸν Πλοῦτον, ὡς νομίζεται,
     καὶ τἄλλ' ὅσ' ἐστὶν ἔνδον ηὐτρεπισμένα.   625

---

595 αὐτῇ (αὑτῇ) R: αὕτη Vn Suda.
596 προσάγειν κατὰ μῆνα Tyrwhitt: κατὰ μῆνα προσάγειν Rn' ʸᵖV: κατὰ μῆνα
     προσπέμπειν n': κατὰ μήν' ἀποπέμπειν Vn' Suda.
598 γρύξῃς Brunck: γρύζῃς Rn: γρύζεις V.
607 χρή Rn' Σ^VEMΘVb3Vsl: χρῆν V.

it's better to be rich or to be hungry. She says that the "haves", the rich, offer her a dinner every month, but poor people snatch it away before it's even been set down! [*Advancing on Poverty and confronting her as if to force her towards the exit-passage*] Now get out of here, blast you, and don't utter another sound! You won't persuade us, not even if you persuade us!

POVERTY [*indignant*]: "City of Argos, hark at what he says!"

CHREMYLUS [*unmoved*]: Call for your messmate Pauson to help you.

POVERTY [*with tragic intensity*]: What will become of me, wretched that I am?

CHREMYLUS: Get the hell out of our sight, fastish!

POVERTY: And where on earth shall I go?

CHREMYLUS: To the pillory. And stop hanging around – get a move on!

POVERTY [*reluctantly turning to go*]: I swear that you will one day send for me to come back here!

CHREMYLUS [*calling after her as she departs, right*]: When we do, you can come back. Till then, get out, and to blazes with you! It's better for me to be rich and let *you* go and boil your head!

BLEPSIDEMUS [*rejoining his friend now that Poverty is safely gone*]: Yes, by Zeus, *I* certainly want to be rich, and to celebrate with my wife and children, and when I've bathed and I'm coming, sleek and gleaming, from the bath-house, I want to fart in the face of the craftsmen and Poverty!

CHREMYLUS: Well, we've got rid of *her*, the damnable creature. Now let's you and I take the god, as quickly as possible, to lie him down in the sanctuary of Asclepius.

BLEPSIDEMUS: Yes, and let's not dawdle about it, either; we don't want someone new coming along and stopping us doing any of what needs doing.

CHREMYLUS [*calling into his house*]: Boy! Carion! You should be bringing out our bedding, and also bringing Wealth himself in the customary garb, and all the other things that have been got ready in there.

[*Carion comes out of the house, carrying bedding and other requisites for the trip, and accompanied by Wealth dressed all in white; and the whole party go off, left.*]

ΧΟΡΟΥ

Κα. ὦ πλεῖστα Θησείοις μεμυστιλημένοι
γέροντες ἄνδρες ἐπ' ὀλιγίστοις ἀλφίτοις,
ὡς εὐτυχεῖθ', ὡς μακαρίως πεπράγατε,
ἄλλοι θ' ὅσοις μέτεστι τοῦ χρηστοῦ τρόπου.   630

Χρ. τί δ' ἐστίν, ὦ βέλτιστε τῶν σαυτοῦ φίλων;
φαίνει γὰρ ἥκειν ἄγγελος χρηστοῦ τινος.

Κα. ὁ δεσπότης πέπραγεν εὐτυχέστατα,
μᾶλλον δ' ὁ Πλοῦτος αὐτός· ἀντὶ γὰρ τυφλοῦ
ἐξωμμάτωται καὶ λελάμπρυνται κόρας,   635
Ἀσκληπιοῦ παιῶνος εὐμενοῦς τυχών.

Χο. λέγεις μοι χάραν, λέγεις μοι βοᾶν.

Κα. πάρεστι χαίρειν, ἤν τε βούλησθ' ἤν τε μή.

Χο. ἀναβοάσομαι τὸν εὔπαιδα καὶ
μέγα βροτοῖσι φέγγος Ἀσκληπιόν.   640

ΓΥΝΗ

τίς ἡ βοή ποτ' ἐστίν ἆρ' ἀγγέλλεται
χρηστόν τι; τοῦτο γὰρ ποθοῦσ' ἐγὼ πάλαι
ἔνδον κάθημαι περιμένουσα τουτονί.

Κα. ταχέως ταχέως φέρ' οἶνον, ὦ δέσποιν', ἵνα
καὐτὴ πίῃς – φιλεῖς δὲ δρῶσ' αὐτὸ σφόδρα –   645
ὡς ἀγαθὰ συλλήβδην ἅπαντά σοι φέρω.

Γυ. καὶ ποῦ 'στιν;

Κα.   ἐν τοῖς λεγομένοις· εἴσει τάχα.

Γυ. πέραινε τοίνυν ὅ τι λέγεις ἀνύσας ποτέ.

Κα. ἄκουε τοίνυν, ὡς ἐγὼ τὰ πράγματα
ἐκ τῶν ποδῶν εἰς τὴν κεφαλήν σοι πάντ' ἐρῶ.   650

Γυ. μὴ δῆτ' ἔμοιγ' εἰς τὴν κεφαλήν.

Κα.   μὴ τἀγαθὰ
ἃ νῦν γεγένηται;

Γυ.   μὴ μὲν οὖν τὰ πράγματα.

Κα. ὡς γὰρ τάχιστ' ἀφικόμεθα πρὸς τὸν θεὸν
ἄγοντες ἄνδρα τότε μὲν ἀθλιώτατον,
νῦν δ' εἴ τιν' ἄλλον μακάριον κεὐδαίμονα,   655

after 626 χοροῦ Vn': om. Rn'.
632 ἥκειν codd.: perh. ἥκων, cf. Σ^{MVs1}.
641 ἆρ' ἀγγέλλεται Porson: ἀρά γ' ἀγγέλλεται R: ἀρά γ' ἀγγελεῖ Vn': ἆρ'
ἀγγελεῖ n': ἀρά γ' ἀγγελεῖται n': αρα πραττε[τε?] Π82^{pc}: αρ επραττε[τε]
Π82^{ac}.

[*Enter, left, Carion.*]

CARION [*to the chorus*]: You old men who have so often, at the Thesea festival, feasted on bread dunked in broth to go with very short rations of groats — what good fortune you have had, what bliss you have
630   attained, you and all others who possess a virtuous character!

CHORUS-LEADER: What's happened, you most splendid of your kind? You seem to have come with some good news.

CARION: My master has had the greatest of good fortune — or rather Wealth himself has:

            having been blind till now
635   He has the bright orbs of his eyes restored,
            Finding a friend and healer in Asclepius!

CHORUS [*breaking into song*]:
            Your words give me joy, your words make me cry aloud!

CARION: It's a time to rejoice, whether you want to or whether you don't !

CHORUS [*singing at the tops of their voices*]:
            I shall shout forth the name of that father of fine children,
640   Asclepius, a great light to humanity!

[*The noise brings Chremylus' wife to the house door.*]

WIFE: What on earth is this noise? Is there some good news? That's what I've been yearning for this long time, sitting in there waiting for this boy to come.
645   CARION: Quick, quick, mistress, bring wine, so that you can drink too — you do so love doing that — because I'm bringing you all the good things in the world in one bundle!

WIFE [*bewildered*]: Why, where are they?

CARION: In what I'm going to tell you. You'll learn very soon.

WIFE: Well, hurry up and get on with what you've got to say.
649-50   CARION: Listen, then, because I'm going to give you an exhaustive exposé of the whole business.

WIFE [*misunderstanding him*]: Don't you expose *me*!

CARION: What, you don't want all the good things that we can now have?

WIFE: Not that — I don't want the exhausting business.

CARION: Well then, as soon as we arrived on our visit to the god,
655   bringing a man who was then in great wretchedness but now is blest and

πρῶτον μὲν αὐτὸν ἐπὶ θάλατταν ἤγομεν,
ἔπειτ᾽ ἐλοῦμεν.

Γυ.   νὴ Δί᾽ εὐδαίμων ἄρ᾽ ἦν
ἀνὴρ γέρων ψυχρᾷ θαλάττῃ λούμενος.

Κα. ἔπειτα πρὸς τὸ τέμενος ᾖμεν τοῦ θεοῦ.
ἐπεὶ δὲ βωμῷ πόπανα καὶ προθύματα   660
καθωσιώθη πελανὸς Ἡφαίστου φλογί,
κατεκλίναμεν τὸν Πλοῦτον, ὥσπερ εἰκὸς ἦν·
ἡμῶν δ᾽ ἕκαστος στιβάδα παρεκαττύετο.

Γυ. ἦσαν δέ τινες κἄλλοι δεόμενοι τοῦ θεοῦ;
Κα. εἷς μέν γε Νεοκλείδης, ὅς ἐστι μὲν τυφλός,   665
κλέπτων δὲ τοὺς βλέποντας ὑπερηκόντικεν,
ἕτεροί τε πολλοὶ παντοδαπὰ νοσήματα
ἔχοντες. ὡς δὲ τοὺς λύχνους ἀποσβέσας
ἡμῖν παρήγγειλεν καθεύδειν τοῦ θεοῦ
ὁ πρόπολος, εἰπών, ἤν τις αἴσθηται ψόφου,   670
σιγᾶν, ἅπαντες κοσμίως κατεκείμεθα.
κἀγὼ καθεύδειν οὐκ ἐδυνάμην, ἀλλά με
ἀθάρης χύτρα τις ἐξέπληττε κειμένη
ὀλίγον ἄπωθεν τῆς κεφαλῆς τοῦ γρᾳδίου,
ἐφ᾽ ἣν ἐπεθύμουν δαιμονίως ἐφερπύσαι.   675
ἔπειτ᾽ ἀναβλέψας ὁρῶ τὸν ἱερέα
τοὺς φθοῖς ὑφαρπάζοντα καὶ τὰς ἰσχάδας
ἀπὸ τῆς τραπέζης τῆς ἱερᾶς· μετὰ τοῦτο δὲ
περιῆλθε τοὺς βωμοὺς ἅπαντας ἐν κύκλῳ,
εἴ που πόπανον εἴη τι καταλελειμμένον·   680
ἔπειτα ταῦθ᾽ ἥγιζεν εἰς σάκταν τινά.
κἀγὼ νομίσας πολλὴν ὁσίαν τοῦ πράγματος
ἐπὶ τὴν χύτραν τὴν τῆς ἀθάρης ἀνίσταμαι.

Γυ. τάλαντατ᾽ ἀνδρῶν, οὐκ ἐδεδοίκεις τὸν θεόν;
Κα. νὴ τοὺς θεοὺς ἔγωγε, μὴ φθάσειέ με   685
ἐπὶ τὴν χύτραν ἐλθὼν ἔχων τὰ στέμματα·
ὁ γὰρ ἱερεὺς αὐτοῦ με προυδιδάξατο.
τὸ γρᾴδιον δ᾽, ὡς ᾔσθετο δή μου τὸν ψόφον,

---

660   προθύματα codd.: θυλήματα ᵞᵖΣ⁰ᵛᵇ³: θηλύματα ᵞᵖΣᴺᵖ¹.
677   ὑφαρπάζοντα Blaydes: ἀφαρπάζοντα codd.

happy beyond all others, we first took him down to the sea, and then we bathed him.

WIFE: That *must* have made him happy — an old man being bathed in cold sea water!

660 CARION: Then we went to the sanctuary of the god; and when the preliminary sacrifice of cakelets had been consecrated on the altar as "a sop for Hephaestus' flame", we made Wealth lie down, naturally, and each of us cobbled together a rough bed to lie on.

WIFE: Were there any others there seeking the god's aid?

665 CARION: Well, Neocleides for one — he's blind, but at thieving he's got the sighted folk beaten by a distance — and many others with all kinds of
668-70 illnesses. When the god's minister extinguished the lamps and gave the word for us to go to sleep, warning that anyone who heard a noise should keep silent, we all dutifully lay down. But I couldn't get to sleep; I was very stricken with a pot of broth that was standing a little way from the head of one old woman, and I had an incredible urge to creep up on it. Then I look
675 up, and I see the priest nicking the cheesecakes and dried figs from the holy table; and after that he went right round all the altars to see if there might be
680 any cakelets left on any of them, and then consecrated them into a sack he had. So I reckoned that this sort of thing must be thoroughly lawful, and accordingly I got up to go to the pot of broth.

WIFE: You wretched, wretched man, weren't you afraid of the god?

CARION: By heaven, yes, I was — afraid he would come, wearing his
685 headtire, and get to the pot before I did! I'd just had a lesson in that from his priest. Well, the old woman, when she happened to hear the sound of me

τὴν χεῖρ' ὑφείρει· κᾆτα συρίξας ἐγὼ
ὀδὰξ ἐλαβόμην ὡς παρείας ὢν ὄφις.   690
ἡ δ' εὐθέως τὴν χεῖρα πάλιν ἀνέσπασεν,
κατέκειτο δ' αὐτὴν ἐντυλίξασ' ἡσυχῇ,
ὑπὸ τοῦ δέους βδέουσα δριμύτερον γαλῆς.
κἀγὼ τότ' ἤδη τῆς ἀθάρης πολλὴν ἔφλων·
ἔπειτ', ἐπειδὴ μεστὸς ἦν, ἀνεπαυόμην.   695
Γυ. ὁ δὲ θεὸς ὑμῖν οὐ προσῄειν;
Κα.   οὐδέπω,
μετὰ τοῦτο δ' ἤδη. καὶ γελοῖον δῆτά τι
ἐποίησα· προσιόντος γὰρ αὐτοῦ μέγα πάνυ
ἀπέπαρδον· ἡ γαστὴρ γὰρ ἐπεφύσητό μου.
Γυ. ἦ πού σε διὰ τοῦτ' εὐθὺς ἐβδελύττετο.   700
Κα. οὔκ, ἀλλ' Ἰασὼ μέν γ' ἐπακολουθοῦσ' ἅμα
ὑπηρυθρίασε, χἠ Πανάκει' ἀπεστράφη
τὴν ῥῖν' ἐπιλαβοῦσ'· οὐ λιβανωτὸν γὰρ βδέω.
Γυ. αὐτὸς δ' ἐκεῖνος;
Κα.   οὐ μὰ Δί' οὐδ' ἐφρόντισεν.
Γυ. λέγεις ἄγροικον ἄρα σύ γ' εἶναι τὸν θεόν.   705
Κα. μὰ Δι' οὐκ ἔγωγ', ἀλλὰ σκατοφάγον.
Γυ.   αἴ, τάλαν.
Κα. μετὰ ταῦτ' ἐγὼ μὲν εὐθὺς ἐνεκαλυψάμην
δείσας, ἐκεῖνος δ' ἐν κύκλῳ τὰ νοσήματα
σκοπῶν περιῄει πάντα κοσμίως πάνυ.
ἔπειτα παῖς αὐτῷ λίθινον θυείδιον   710
παρέθηκε καὶ δοίδυκα καὶ κιβώτιον.
Γυ. λίθινον;
Κα.   μὰ Δί' οὐ δῆτ', οὐχὶ τό γε κιβώτιον.
Γυ. σὺ δὲ πῶς ἑώρας, ὦ κάκιστ' ἀπολούμενε,
ὃς ἐγκεκαλύφθαι φῄς;
Κα.   διὰ τοῦ τριβωνίου·
ὀπὰς γὰρ εἶχεν οὐκ ὀλίγας, μὰ τὸν Δία.   715
πρῶτον δὲ πάντων τῷ Νεοκλείδῃ φάρμακον
καταπλαστὸν ἐνεχείρησε τρίβειν, ἐμβαλὼν
σκορόδων κεφαλὰς τρεῖς Τηνίων· ἔπειτ' ἔφλα

---

689   ὑφείρει x, Chantry: cf. ἐξείραντες Men. fr. 908.6 (cited by Σ^v): ὑφή(ι)ρει RVn
λΣᵣRVEMΘVb3

701   μέν γ' ἐπακ- Reisig: μέν γε τις ἀκ- R: μέν γε ἀκ- V: μέν τις ἀκ- n.

approaching, she stuck out her hand from under her cover; so then I hissed
and grabbed it in my teeth, pretending to be a sacred snake. She instantly
drew her hand back again, wrapped herself tight and lay there still, farting
with terror with a worse pong than a ferret. So that was my chance to guzzle
a good helping of the broth, and then, when I was full, I rested again.

WIFE: And didn't the god come to you?

CARION: He hadn't yet, but he did straight afterwards. And I did do
something very amusing: as he was approaching, I let off an enormous great
fart — my tummy had got bloated, you see.

WIFE: I suppose that made him sick of you right away.

CARION: No, but Iaso, who was following behind him, at once came
out in a blush, and Panacea held her nose and turned away — my farts aren't
frankincense!

WIFE: And what about the god himself?

CARION: Why, by Zeus, he didn't even notice it.

WIFE: A boorish sort of a god you're calling him!

CARION: No, I'm not; I'm calling him a shit-eater!

WIFE: Oh, you wretched fellow!

CARION: After that I got frightened, and covered myself up straight
away; and he went right round, looking very carefully at all the patients'
afflictions. Then a boy set beside him a stone mortar, pestle, and medicine-
chest.

WIFE: A *stone* one?

CARION: Of course not, not the medicine-chest.

WIFE: And how did you see all this, you blasted liar, when you say
you were covered up?

CARION: Through my cloak; it had plenty of holes in it, by Zeus
[*displaying some of them*]! First of all he set to work to pound a medicinal
plaster for Neocleides. He threw three heads of Tenos garlic into the mortar

ἐν τῇ θυείᾳ συμπαραμειγνύων ὀπὸν
καὶ σχῖνον· εἶτ' ὄξει διέμενος Σφηττίῳ   720
κατέπλασεν αὐτοῦ τὰ βλέφαρ' ἐκτρέψας, ἵνα
ὀδυνῷτο μᾶλλον. ὁ δὲ κεκραγὼς καὶ βοῶν
ἔφευγ' ἀνάξας· ὁ δὲ θεὸς γελάσας ἔφη·
"ἐνταῦθά νυν κάθησο καταπεπλασμένος,
ἵν' ὑπομνύμενον παύσω σε τὰς ἐκκλησίας."   725

Γυ. ὡς φιλόπολίς τίς ἐσθ' ὁ δαίμων καὶ σοφός.
Κα. μετὰ ταῦτα τῷ Πλούτωνι παρεκαθέζετο.
   καὶ πρῶτα μὲν δὴ τῆς κεφαλῆς ἐφήψατο,
   ἔπειτα καθαρὸν ἡμιτύβιον λαβὼν
   τὰ βλέφαρα περιέψησεν· ἡ Πανάκεια δὲ   730
   κατεπέτασ' αὐτοῦ τὴν κεφαλὴν φοινικίδι
   καὶ πᾶν τὸ πρόσωπον· εἶθ' ὁ θεὸς ἐπόππυσεν.
   ἐξῃξάτην οὖν δύο δράκοντ' ἐκ τοῦ νεὼ
   ὑπερφυεῖς τὸ μέγεθος.
Γυ.   ὦ φίλοι θεοί.
Κα. τούτω δ' ὑπὸ τὴν φοινικίδ' ὑποδύνθ' ἡσυχῇ   735
   τὰ βλέφαρα περιέλειχον, ὥς γ' ἐμοὶ δοκεῖ·
   καὶ πρίν σε κοτύλας ἐκπιεῖν οἴνου δέκα,
   ὁ Πλοῦτος, ὦ δέσποιν', ἀνειστήκει βλέπων.
   ἐγὼ δὲ τὼ χεῖρ' ἀνεκρότησ' ὑφ' ἡδονῆς
   τὸν δεσπότην τ' ἤγειρον. ὁ θεὸς δ' εὐθέως   740
   ἠφάνισεν αὑτὸν οἵ τ' ὄφεις εἰς τὸν νεών.
   οἱ δ' ἐγκατακείμενοι παρ' αὐτῷ πῶς δοκεῖς
   τὸν Πλοῦτον ἠσπάζοντο καὶ τὴν νύχθ' ὅλην
   ἐγρηγόρεσαν, ἕως διέλαμψεν ἡμέρα.
   ἐγὼ δ' ἐπῄνουν τὸν θεὸν πάνυ σφόδρα,   745
   ὅτι βλέπειν ἐποίησε τὸν Πλοῦτον ταχύ,
   τὸν δὲ Νεοκλείδην μᾶλλον ἐποίησεν τυφλόν.
Γυ. ὅσην ἔχεις τὴν δύναμιν, ὦναξ δέσποτα.
   ἀτὰρ φράσον μοι, ποῦ 'σθ' ὁ Πλοῦτος;
Κα.   ἔρχεται.

---

721   ἐκτρέψας RV: ἐκστρέψας n: εκ[Π82.
725   ὑπομνύμενον ἰΣ^EΘNp1Vb3Vv2, Girard: ἐπομνύμενον codd. λΣ^EMΘNp1Vb3Vv2
725   τὰς RVn': τα[Π82: τῆς n'.
727   ταῦτα V:]α Π83: τοῦτο Rn.

and crushed them, mixing in fig-juice and mastic with them, and then he
soaked the lot with Sphettus vinegar and plastered his eyes with it — turning
his eyelids out, so that it would hurt him more. The man jumped up and ran
off, shouting and yelling, and the god laughed and said, "Now sit there with
that plaster on, so I can stop you disrupting Assembly meetings with sworn
objections!"

WIFE: What a very clever, patriotic fellow that god is!

CARION: After that he sat down beside Wealth. First he gently
touched his head, then he took a clean napkin and wiped all round his eyes.
Next, Panacea spread a crimson cloth over his head and the whole of his
face; then the god clicked his tongue, and two enormous serpents darted out
of the temple.

WIFE: Dear gods!

CARION: They dived under the crimson cloth, making no sound, and
licked all round his eyes, or so I suppose; and before you could drink off five
pints of wine, mistress, Wealth was standing up, and he could see! I clapped
my hands above my head for joy, and tried to wake up master. The god at
once vanished back into the temple, and so did the serpents. And the people
who were lying there with him — you can just imagine how they
congratulated Wealth, and stayed awake all night till break of day. And I
was praising the god very highly indeed, because he had given Wealth his
sight so quickly, and had made Neocleides more blind than before!

WIFE [*stretching out her hands*]: O Lord and Master, what great
power thou hast! [*To Carion*] But tell me, where's Wealth?

ἀλλ' ἦν περὶ αὐτὸν ὄχλος ὑπερφυὴς ὅσος. 750
οἱ γὰρ δίκαιοι πρότερον ὄντες καὶ βίον
ἔχοντες ὀλίγον αὐτὸν ἠσπάζοντο καὶ
ἐδεξιοῦνθ' ἅπαντες ὑπὸ τῆς ἡδονῆς·
ὅσοι δ' ἐπλούτουν οὐσίαν τ' εἶχον συχνήν,
οὐκ ἐκ δικαίου τὸν βίον κεκτημένοι, 755
ὀφρῦς συνῆγον ἐσκυθρώπαζόν θ' ἅμα.
οἱ δ' ἠκολούθουν κατόπιν ἐστεφανωμένοι,
γελῶντες, εὐφημοῦντες· ἐκτυπεῖτο δὲ
ἐμβὰς γερόντων εὐρύθμοις προβήμασιν.
ἀλλ' εἶ', ἁπαξάπαντες ἐξ ἑνὸς λόγου 760
ὀρχεῖσθε καὶ σκιρτᾶτε καὶ χορεύετε·
οὐδεὶς γὰρ ὑμῖν εἰσιοῦσιν ἀγγελεῖ
ὡς ἄλφιτ' οὐκ ἔνεστιν ἐν τῷ θυλάκῳ.
Γυ. νὴ τὴν Ἑκάτην, κἀγὼ δ' ἀναδῆσαι βούλομαι
εὐαγγέλιά σε κριβανωτῶν ὁρμαθῷ 765
τοιαῦτ' ἀπαγγείλαντα.
Κα.	μή νυν μέλλ' ἔτι,
ὡς ἄνδρες ἐγγύς εἰσιν ἤδη τῶν θυρῶν.
Γυ. φέρε νυν ἰοῦσ' εἴσω κομίσω καταχύσματα
ὥσπερ νεωνήτοισιν ὀφθαλμοῖς ἐγώ.
Κα. ἐγὼ δ' ἀπαντῆσαί γ' ἐκείνοις βούλομαι. 770

KOMMATION XOPOY

Πλ. καὶ προσκυνῶ γε πρῶτα μὲν τὸν ἥλιον,
ἔπειτα σεμνῆς Παλλάδος κλεινὸν πέδον
χώραν τε πᾶσαν Κέκροπος, ἥ μ' ἐδέξατο.
αἰσχύνομαι δὲ τὰς ἐμαυτοῦ συμφοράς,
οἵοις ἄρ' ἀνθρώποις ξυνὼν ἐλάνθανον, 775
τοὺς ἀξίους δὲ τῆς ἐμῆς ὁμιλίας
ἔφευγον, εἰδὼς οὐδέν. ὦ τλήμων ἐγώ,
ὡς οὔτ' ἐκεῖν' ἄρ' οὔτε ταῦτ' ὀρθῶς ἔδρων.
ἀλλ' αὐτὰ πάντα πάλιν ἀναστρέψας ἐγὼ
δείξω τὸ λοιπὸν πᾶσιν ἀνθρώποις ὅτι 780
ἄκων ἐμαυτὸν τοῖς πονηροῖς ἐνεδίδουν.
Χρ. βάλλ' ἐς κόρακας· ὡς χαλεπόν εἰσιν οἱ φίλοι

---

after 770 κομμάτιον χοροῦ RVn': om. n'.

CARION: He's on his way. But there was such an immense crowd surrounding him! Those who had always been honest, and had had a meagre livelihood, all welcomed him joyfully and gave him their right hands; at the same time those who were rich and had ample fortunes, having gained their wealth by less than honest means, knitted their brows and put on sour faces. But the good folk followed on behind him, garlanded, laughing, shouting in triumph, "and old men's shoes with rhythmic tread resounded". [*To the chorus*] But hey now, every single one of you with one accord, dance and leap and caper — because no one's ever going to be telling you again, when you come home, that there's no groats in the sack!

WIFE: And, by Hecate, I also want to garland you, in honour of your good tidings, with a string of oven-baked loaves, for bringing news like this!

CARION: Well, don't wait any longer, because they're already near our door.

WIFE: Very well, I'll go inside and bring out sweetmeats to shower, as it were, on a newly-bought pair of eyes. [*She goes inside.*]

CARION: And *I* want to go and meet them. [*He goes out, left.*]

[*The chorus sing and dance. During their song, whose words have not survived, Wealth enters alone, left, rejuvenated and with his sight restored; the chorus welcome him and bid him address the gods in thanksgiving.*]

WEALTH: More than that, I make obeisance to the Sun [*doing so*], and [*turning to face the Acropolis and the audience*] to the glorious precinct of august Pallas and the whole land of Cecrops which has taken me in. I am ashamed of my past circumstances — the kinds of men with whom I now perceive I consorted unawares, while in utter ignorance I shunned those who were worthy of my company. Ah, wretch that I am, how wrong I was both in the one case and in the other! But I now mean to reverse all that completely, and for the future to show all humanity that it was not of my free will that I surrendered myself to the wicked.

[*Chremylus enters, left, pausing once or twice to massage his apparently sore arms and shins; he is accompanied by Carion carrying the luggage.*]

CHREMYLUS: Damn and blast, the nuisance they are, these

οἱ φαινόμενοι παραχρῆμ᾽, ὅταν πράττῃ τις εὖ.
νύττουσι γὰρ καὶ φλῶσι τἀντικνήμια,
ἐνδεικνύμενος ἕκαστος εὔνοιάν τινα.   785
ἐμὲ γὰρ τίς οὐ προσεῖπε; ποῖος οὐκ ὄχλος
περιεστεφάνωσεν ἐν ἀγορᾷ πρεσβυτικός;
Γυ.   ὦ φίλτατ᾽ ἀνδρῶν, καὶ σὺ καὶ σὺ χαίρετε.
φέρε νυν, νόμος γάρ ἐστι, τὰ καταχύσματα
ταυτὶ καταχέω σου λαβοῦσα.
Πλ.   μηδαμῶς.   790
ἐμοῦ γὰρ εἰσιόντος εἰς τὴν οἰκίαν
πρώτιστ᾽ ἀναβλέψαντος οὐδὲν ἐκφέρειν
πρεπῶδές ἐστιν, ἀλλὰ μᾶλλον εἰσφέρειν.
Γυ.   εἶτ᾽ οὐχὶ δέξει δῆτα τὰ καταχύσματα;
Πλ.   ἔνδον γε παρὰ τὴν ἑστίαν, ὥσπερ νόμος.   795
ἔπειτα καὶ τὸν φόρτον ἐκφύγοιμεν ἄν·
οὐ γὰρ πρεπῶδές ἐστι τῷ διδασκάλῳ
ἰσχάδια καὶ τρωγάλια τοῖς θεωμένοις
προβαλόντ᾽ ἐπὶ τούτοις εἶτ᾽ ἀναγκάζειν γελᾶν.
Γυ.   εὖ πάνυ λέγεις· ὡς Δεξίνικός γ᾽ οὑτοσὶ   800
ἀνίσταθ᾽ ὡς ἁρπασόμενος τὰς ἰσχάδας.

ΧΟΡΟΥ

Κα.   ὡς ἡδὺ πράττειν, ὦνδρές, ἐστ᾽ εὐδαιμόνως,
καὶ ταῦτα μηδὲν ἐξενεγκόντ᾽ οἴκοθεν.
ἡμῖν γὰρ ἀγαθῶν σωρὸς εἰς τὴν οἰκίαν
ἐπεισπέπαικεν οὐδὲν ἠδικηκόσιν.   805
ἡ μὲν σιπύη μεστή ᾽στι λευκῶν ἀλφίτων,
οἱ δ᾽ ἀμφορῆς οἴνου μέλανος ἀνθοσμίου·
ἅπαντα δ᾽ ἡμῖν ἀργυρίου καὶ χρυσίου
τὰ σκευάρια πλήρη ᾽στιν, ὥστε θαυμάσαι·
τὸ φρέαρ δ᾽ ἐλαίου μεστόν· αἱ δὲ λήκυθοι   810
μύρου γέμουσι, τὸ δ᾽ ὑπερῷον ἰσχάδων·
ὀξὶς δὲ πᾶσα καὶ λοπάδιον καὶ χύτρα

---

792   πρώτιστ᾽ ἀναβλέψαντος van Leeuwen: πρώτιστα καὶ βλέψαντος codd.
801   τὰς ἰσχάδας codd.: τῶν ἰσχάδων Suda.
after 801   χοροῦ RVn': om. n'.
[805a] οὕτω τὸ πλουτεῖν ἐστιν ἡδὺ πρᾶγμα δή (που n: τι Th.) codd.: del. Bentley.

"friends" who appear out of nowhere when you're doing well! They elbow
you and crush your shins, each one wanting to make some display of
goodwill to you. Who was there that didn't greet me? Who wasn't in that
mob of old men who ringed me round in the Agora?

[*Chremylus' wife comes to the door, carrying a basket containing
sweetmeats, nuts, etc.*]

WIFE: My dearest husband, welcome, both of you! [*To Wealth*]
Come, now, let me take these sweetmeats and throw them over you as the
custom is.

WEALTH: No, I beg you. When *I* am entering the house, having just
regained my sight, it is not proper for anything to be taken out of the house,
but rather *into* it.

WIFE: You mean you really won't accept the showering?

WEALTH: Yes, but inside, by the hearth, according to custom. That
way we can also avoid vulgarity; it doesn't befit our producer to throw dried
figs and nibbles to his audience and then make them feel obliged to laugh on
account of that.

WIFE: That's very well said; because [*pointing into the audience*]
there's Dexinicus standing up there, meaning to grab the figs. [*She goes
back inside; Wealth, Chremylus and Carion follow.*]

CHORAL INTERLUDE

[*Carion comes out of the house. For a moment he is shielding his eyes
and coughing, until he has closed the door. He is wearing new, expensive-
looking clothes.*]

CARION: What a delightful thing it is, gentlemen, to enjoy
abundance, and that without having any outgoings! A vast horde of good
things has stormed into our house, although we're totally innocent of any
wrongdoing! Our meal-tub is full of white barley groats, our jars full of dark
wine with a beautiful bouquet. Every container is miraculously filled with
gold and silver coin. Our well is full of olive oil; our flasks are overflowing
with perfume, our upstairs room with dried figs. Every vinegar-cruet and

χαλκῆ γέγονε· τοὺς δὲ πινακίσκους τοὺς σαπροὺς
τοὺς ἰχθυηροὺς ἀργυροῦς πάρεσθ' ὁρᾶν·
ὁ δ' ἵπνος γέγον' ἡμῖν ἐξαπίνης ἐλεφάντινος·   815
στατῆρσι δ' οἱ θεράποντες ἀρτιάζομεν
χρυσοῖς· ἀποψώμεσθα δ' οὐ λίθοις ἔτι,
ἀλλὰ σκοροδίοις ὑπὸ τρυφῆς ἑκάστοτε.
καὶ νῦν ὁ δεσπότης μὲν ἔνδον βουθυτεῖ
ὗν καὶ τράγον καὶ κριὸν ἐστεφανωμένος·   820
ἐμὲ δ' ἐξέπεμψεν ὁ καπνός. οὐχ οἷός τε γὰρ
ἔνδον μένειν ἦν· ἔδακνε γὰρ τὰ βλέφαρά μου.

ΑΝΗΡ ΔΙΚΑΙΟΣ
        ἕπου μετ' ἐμοῦ, παιδάριον, ἵνα πρὸς τὸν θεὸν
        ἴωμεν.
Κα.   ἔα· τίς ἐσθ' ὁ προσιὼν οὑτοσί;
Δι.   ἀνὴρ πρότερον μὲν ἄθλιος, νῦν δ' εὐτυχής.   825
Κα.   δῆλον ὅτι τῶν χρηστῶν τις, ὡς ἔοικας, εἶ.
Δι.   μάλιστ'.
Κα.   ἔπειτα τοῦ δέει;
Δι.   πρὸς τὸν θεὸν
        ἥκω· μεγάλων γάρ μοὐστὶν ἀγαθῶν αἴτιος.
        ἐγὼ γὰρ ἱκανὴν οὐσίαν παρὰ τοῦ πατρὸς
        λαβὼν ἐπήρκουν τοῖς δεομένοις τῶν φίλων,   830
        εἶναι νομίζων χρήσιμον πρὸς τὸν βίον.
Κα.   ἦ πού σε ταχέως ἐπέλιπεν τὰ χρήματα.
Δι.   κομιδῇ μὲν οὖν.
Κα.   οὐκοῦν μετὰ ταῦτ' ἦσθ' ἄθλιος.
Δι.   κομιδῇ μὲν οὖν. κἀγὼ μὲν ᾤμην, οὓς τέως
        ηὐεργέτησα δεομένους, ἕξειν φίλους   835
        ὄντως βεβαίους, εἰ δεηθείην ποτέ·
        οἱ δ' ἐξετρέποντο κοὐκ ἐδόκουν ὁρᾶν μ' ἔτι.
Κα.   καὶ κατεγέλων γ', εὖ οἶδ' ὅτι.
Δι.   κομιδῇ μὲν οὖν·
        αὐχμὸς γὰρ ὢν τῶν σκευαρίων μ' ἀπώλεσεν.
        ἀλλ' οὐχὶ νῦν· ἀνθ' ὧν ἐγὼ πρὸς τὸν θεόν   840
        προσευξόμενος ἥκω δικαίως ἐνθάδε.
Κα.   τὸ τριβώνιον δὲ τί δύναται, πρὸς τῶν θεῶν,

---

834   τέως Rn: τότε V ᵞᵖΣᴿ: ποτε ᵞᵖΣᴿ.
838   γ' Vn': ομ. n': δ' R.

bowl and pot has turned to bronze; those rotten cleaning-boards that stank of
815   fish, you can see they're all silver; and all of a sudden we've got an ivory
kitchen! We servants are playing odd-and-even with golden staters; and we
don't even wipe our bottoms with stones any more — we're so spoilt, we now
always use garlic cloves! And now master, inside, with a garland on his
820   head, is making a great sacrifice of a boar, a he-goat and a ram; but I've been
forced outside by the smoke. I couldn't stay in there; it was stinging my
eyes.

[*Enter, right, a middle-aged, well-dressed man ("the Honest Man"),
followed by a boy slave who is carrying a ragged cloak and a much-worn
pair of shoes.*]

HONEST MAN [*calling over his shoulder*]: Come along with me,
boy, so that we can get to where the god is.

CARION [*noticing them*]: Hey, who's this coming to us?

825   HONEST MAN: A man who used to be wretched, but who's now
prospering.

CARION: You seem plainly to be one of the good sort.

HONEST MAN: Quite right.

CARION: Then what do you want of us?

HONEST MAN: I'm coming to the god, because he has been the
829-30 cause of such great blessings to me. I inherited a reasonable amount of
property from my father, and I used to give assistance to my friends when
they were in need, believing that that would be to my advantage in life.

CARION: And your property rapidly failed you, I dare say.

HONEST MAN: Exactly so.

CARION: And so after that you were in distress.

HONEST MAN: Exactly so. And I thought that those that I'd
835   previously helped in time of need, that I'd have them as really steadfast
friends if *I* should ever be in need; but they turned me away and pretended
they couldn't see me any more.

CARION: And made mock of you too, I'm sure.

HONEST MAN: Exactly so; there was a drought in my stores, and it
840   ruined me. But not any more; and for that reason, as is only right, I've come
here to the god, to address my prayers to him.

CARION: But tell me, in the name of the gods, what's the meaning of

ὃ φέρει μετὰ σοῦ τὸ παιδάριον τουτί; φράσον.

Δι. καὶ τοῦτ᾽ ἀναθήσων ἔρχομαι πρὸς τὸν θεόν.

Κα. μῶν ἐνεμυήθης δῆτ᾽ ἐν αὐτῷ τὰ μεγάλα;   845

Δι. οὔκ, ἀλλ᾽ ἐνερρίγωσ᾽ ἔτη τριακαίδεκα.

Κα. τὰ δ᾽ ἐμβάδια;

Δι.   καὶ ταῦτα συνεχειμάζετο.

Κα. καὶ ταῦτ᾽ ἀναθήσων ἔφερες οὖν;

Δι.   νὴ τὸν Δία.

Κα. χαρίεντά γ᾽ ἥκεις δῶρα τῷ θεῷ φέρων.

ΣΥΚΟΦΑΝΤΗΣ

οἴμοι κακοδαίμων, ὡς ἀπόλωλα δείλαιος,   850
καὶ τρισκακοδαίμων καὶ τετράκις καὶ πεντάκις
καὶ δωδεκάκις καὶ μυριάκις· ἰοὺ ἰού,
οὕτω πολυφόρῳ συγκέκραμαι δαίμονι.

Κα. Ἄπολλον ἀποτρόπαιε καὶ θεοὶ φίλοι,
τί ποτ᾽ ἐστὶν ὅ τι πέπονθεν ἄνθρωπος κακόν;   855

Συ. οὐ γὰρ σχέτλια πέπονθα νυνὶ πράγματα,
ἀπολωλεκὼς ἅπαντα τἀκ τῆς οἰκίας
διὰ τὸν θεὸν τοῦτον, τὸν ἐσόμενον τυφλὸν
πάλιν αὖθις, ἤνπερ μὴ 'πιλίπωσιν αἱ δίκαι;

Δι. ἐγὼ σχεδὸν τὸ πρᾶγμα γιγνώσκειν δοκῶ.   860
προσέρχεται γάρ τις κακῶς πράττων ἀνήρ·
ἔοικε δ᾽ εἶναι τοῦ πονηροῦ κόμματος.

Κα. νὴ Δία, καλῶς τοίνυν ποιῶν ἀπόλλυται.

Συ. ποῦ ποῦ 'σθ᾽ ὁ μόνος ἅπαντας ἡμᾶς πλουσίους
ὑποσχόμενος οὗτος ποιήσειν εὐθέως,   865
εἰ πάλιν ἀναβλέψειεν ἐξ ἀρχῆς; ὁ δὲ
πολὺ μᾶλλον ἐνίους ἐστὶν ἐξολωλεκώς.

Κα. καὶ τίνα δέδρακε δῆτα τοῦτ';

Συ.   ἐμὲ τουτονί.

Κα. ἦ τῶν πονηρῶν ἦσθα καὶ τοιχωρύχων;

Συ. μὰ Δί᾽ οὐ μὲν οὖν ἐσθ᾽ ὑγιὲς ὑμῶν οὐδὲ ἕν,   870
κοὐκ ἔσθ᾽ ὅπως οὐκ ἔχετέ μου τὰ χρήματα.

Κα. ὡς σοβαρός, ὦ Δάματερ, εἰσελήλυθεν

---

845 ἐνεμυήθης R ᴸΣᴿ: ἐμυήθης V ᴸΣᴱᴹᴺᵖ¹: οὖν ἐμυήθης ν ᴸΣᶿ:]ης Π21.

852 ἰοὺ ἰού Tricl.: καὶ ἰοὺ ἰού RVn.

859 'πιλίπωσιν Hemsterhuys: λίπωσιν Rn: λείπωσιν V.

870 ὑμῶν οὐδὲ ἕν Scaliger: ὑμῶν οὐδενός vel sim. Rn: οὐδενὸς ὑμῶν V.

this old cloak, which this young boy with you is carrying?

HONEST MAN: I've also come to dedicate that to the god.

CARION: It's not, is it, the one you wore for your initiation in the Greater Mysteries?

HONEST MAN: No, it's the one that I got frozen in for the last thirteen years.

CARION: And the shoes?

HONEST MAN: They endured those winters with me too.

CARION: So you've come to dedicate them as well?

HONEST MAN: Yes, indeed.

CARION: A nice set of presents you've come with for the god!

[*Enter, left, an Informer. He is wearing a thin and shabby cloak, though not as thin and shabby as the one the Honest Man's slave is carrying. He is accompanied by a friend, who can act as witness should one be needed. As he walks slowly towards the house, he at first does not notice Carion and the Honest Man.*]

INFORMER [*to himself*]: Wretched, wretched me, I'm accursed and ruined — thrice wretched, four times, five times, twelve times, ten thousand times! Ah, ah, what a voracious fate has swallowed me!

CARION: Apollo and all you dear gods preserve us, what *can* be the trouble this fellow's got into?

INFORMER [*as before*]: What I've suffered now is truly outrageous! I have lost everything that was in my house, thanks to this god — who is going to be blind once again, if my lawsuits don't fail me!

HONEST MAN [*to Carion*]: I think I know pretty much what's going on. The man who's coming this way has fallen on hard times; looks like he's a piece of bad coinage.

CARION: So much the better, then, by Zeus, if he's ruined!

INFORMER [*seeing Carion*]: Where is he, where is he, the one who promised that he'd make us all rich straight away, all by himself, if only he could recover his sight once again? What he'd *done* is much more like totally *ruin* some of us!

CARION: And who has he actually done that to?

INFORMER [*pointing to himself*]: This man here!

CARION: Oh, were you one of the crooks and villains?

INFORMER: On the contrary, *you* are a thoroughly depraved lot, and I'm quite positive that you're in possession of my property!

CARION [*mockingly*]: Damater, this informer has certainly blown in

ὁ συκοφάντης. δῆλον ὅτι βουλιμιᾳ.

Συ. σὺ μὲν εἰς ἀγορὰν ἰὼν ταχέως οὐκ ἂν φθάνοις·
ἐπὶ τοῦ τροχοῦ γὰρ δεῖ σ' ἐκεῖ στρεβλούμενον 875
εἰπεῖν ἃ πεπανούργηκας.

Κα. οἰμώξᾳρα σύ.

Δι. νὴ τὸν Δία τὸν σωτῆρα, πολλοῦ γ' ἄξιος
ἅπασι τοῖς Ἕλλησιν ὁ θεὸς οὗτος, εἰ
τοὺς συκοφάντας ἐξολεῖ κακοὺς κακῶς.

Συ. οἴμοι τάλας, μῶν καὶ σὺ μετέχων καταγελᾷς; 880
ἐπεὶ πόθεν θοἰμάτιον εἴληφας τοδί;
ἐχθὲς δ' ἔχοντ' εἶδόν σ' ἐγὼ τριβώνιον.

Δι. οὐδὲν προτιμῶ σου· φορῶ γὰρ πριάμενος
τὸν δακτύλιον τονδὶ παρ' Εὐδάμου δραχμῆς.

Κα. ἀλλ' οὐκ ἔνεστι "συκοφάντου δήγματος". 885

Συ. ἆρ' οὐχ ὕβρις ταῦτ' ἐστὶ πολλή; σκώπτετον,
ὅ τι δὲ ποιεῖτον ἐνθάδ' οὐκ εἰρήκατον·
οὐκ ἐπ' ἀγαθῷ γὰρ ἐνθάδ' ἐστὸν οὐδενί.

Κα. μὰ τὸν Δί' οὔκουν τῷ γε σῷ, σάφ' ἴσθ' ὅτι.

Συ. ἀπὸ τῶν ἐμῶν γὰρ ναὶ μὰ Δία δειπνήσετον. 890

Δι. ὡς δὴ 'π' ἀληθείᾳ σὺ μετὰ τοῦ μάρτυρος
διαρραγείης—

Κα.   μηδενός γ' ἐμπλήμενος.

Συ. ἀρνεῖσθον; ἔνδον ἐστίν, ὦ μιαρωτάτω,
πολὺ χρῆμα τεμαχῶν καὶ κρεῶν ὠπτημένων.
ὑῦ ὑῦ ὑῦ ὑῦ ὑῦ ὑῦ. 895

Κα. κακόδαιμον, ὀσφραίνει τι;

Δι.   τοῦ ψύχους γ' ἴσως,
ἐπεὶ τοιοῦτον γ' ἀμπέχεται τριβώνιον.

Συ. ταῦτ' οὖν ἀνασχέτ' ἐστίν, ὦ Ζεῦ καὶ θεοί,
τούτους ὑβρίζειν εἰς ἔμ'; οἴμ', ὡς ἄχθομαι,
ὅτι χρηστὸς ὢν καὶ φιλόπολις πάσχω κακῶς. 900

Δι. σὺ φιλόπολις καὶ χρηστός;

Συ.   ὡς οὐδείς γ' ἀνήρ.

Δι. καὶ μὴν ἐπερωτηθεὶς ἀπόκριναί μοι—

Συ.   τὸ τί;

---

878   οὗτος, εἰ x: ἔσθ' οὗτος, εἰ n': ἔσθ' οὑτοσί, [879] εἰ Rn': ἔσθ', ὅτι Vn'.
897   line deleted by Rutherford.

like a full gale! It's plain he's ravenous!

INFORMER: Well, *you*, for one, can be off to the Agora, fast — you
875 can't be there too soon; because there you'll be racked on the wheel until you
confess your villainies.

CARION [*with spirit*]: You'll howl if you try!

HONEST MAN: By Zeus the Saviour, this god will really be doing
an invaluable service to the whole Greek people, if he brings evil destruction
to these evil informers!

880 INFORMER: Heaven help me, *you're* not in on it as well, are you,
making fun of me like this? Come to think of it, where did you get that
cloak from? Only yesterday I saw you in an old homespun thing!

HONEST MAN [*displaying a ring on his finger*]: I'm not concerned
about you, because I'm wearing this ring which I bought from Eudamus for a
drachma.

885 CARION [*looking at the ring; in mock alarm*] But it doesn't say on it
"For informer-bites"!

INFORMER: This is utterly, blatantly outrageous! You're making
game of me, the two of you, but you haven't said what you're doing here.
You're certainly up to no good being here.

CARION: No good of *yours*, by Zeus, I can tell you that!

890 INFORMER: Indeed not, by Zeus, because you're about to dine on
my money!

HONEST MAN [*infuriated by this accusation*]: May you, and your
witness too, really and truly burst apart——

CARION: From being stuffed full of nothing!

INFORMER: You deny it, do you? There's any amount of sliced fish
895 and roast meat there, you filthy villains! [*Sniffing the aroma of the food*]
Hnf-hnf, hnf-hnf, hnf-hnf, hnf-hnf, hnf-hnf, hnf-hnf!

CARION [*in mock sympathy*]: Poor thing! can you smell something?

HONEST MAN: The cold, perhaps, what with that wretched cloak
he's got on.

INFORMER: Zeus and all you gods! is this endurable, the way these
900 people are insulting me? I'm fed up to the teeth with being ill-used like this
— a virtuous, patriotic man like me!

HONEST MAN: *You*, patriotic and virtuous?

INFORMER: More so than any man alive.

HONEST MAN: Well then, would you answer if I ask you——

INFORMER: What?

Δι. γεωργὸς εἶ;

Συ.   μελαγχολᾶν μ' οὕτως οἴει;

Δι. ἀλλ' ἔμπορος;

Συ.   ναί, σκήπτομαί γ', ὅταν τύχω.

Δι. τί δαί; τέχνην τιν' ἔμαθες;

Συ.   οὐ μὰ τὸν Δία.   905

Δι. πῶς οὖν διέζης ἢ πόθεν, μηδὲν ποιῶν;

Συ. τῶν τῆς πόλεώς εἰμ' ἐπιμελητὴς πραγμάτων
    καὶ τῶν ἰδίων πάντων.

Δι.   σύ; τί μαθών;

Συ.   βούλομαι.

Δι. πῶς οὖν ἂν εἴης χρηστός, ὦ τοιχωρύχε,
    εἰ, σοὶ προσῆκον μηδέν, εἶτ' ἀπεχθάνει;   910

Συ. οὐ γὰρ προσήκει τὴν ἐμαυτοῦ μοι πόλιν
    εὐεργετεῖν, ὦ κέπφε, καθ' ὅσον ἂν σθένω;

Δι. εὐεργετεῖν οὖν ἐστι τὸ πολυπραγμονεῖν;

Συ. τὸ μὲν οὖν βοηθεῖν τοῖς νόμοις τοῖς κειμένοις
    καὶ μὴ 'πιτρέπειν, ἐάν τις ἐξαμαρτάνῃ.   915

Δι. οὔκουν δικαστὰς ἐξεπίτηδες ἡ πόλις
    ἀρχὴν καθίστησιν;

Συ.   κατηγορεῖ δὲ τίς;

Δι. ὁ βουλόμενος.

Συ.   οὔκουν ἐκεῖνός εἰμ' ἐγώ;
    ὥστ' εἰς ἔμ' ἥκει τῆς πόλεως τὰ πράγματα.

Δι. νὴ Δία, πονηρόν γ' ἆρα προστάτην ἔχει.   920
    ἐκεῖνο δ' οὐ βούλοι' ἄν, ἡσυχίαν ἔχων
    ζῆν ἀργός;

Συ.   ἀλλὰ προβατίου βίον λέγεις,
    εἰ μὴ φανεῖται διατριβή τις τῷ βίῳ.

Δι. οὐδ' ἂν μεταμάθοις;

Συ.   οὐδ' ἂν εἰ δοίης γέ μοι
    τὸν Πλοῦτον αὐτὸν καὶ τὸ Βάττου σίλφιον.   925

Κα. κατάθου ταχέως θοἰμάτιον—

Δι.   οὗτος, σοὶ λέγει.

Κα. ἔπειθ' ὑπόλυσαι.

---

917   ἀρχὴν Meineke: ἄρχειν codd. Suda.

HONEST MAN: Do you work on the land?

INFORMER: Do you think I'm as barmy as that?

HONEST MAN: Then are you a merchant?

INFORMER: Yes — at least I claim to be one, when occasion arises.

905   HONEST MAN: What then? Have you learned a trade?

INFORMER: Certainly not.

HONEST MAN: Then how and where did you get a living, if you didn't do anything?

INFORMER: I am the supervisor of all public and private business in Athens.

HONEST MAN: *You*? What makes you think that?

INFORMER: I am a *wisher*.

HONEST MAN: Then how can you call yourself virtuous, you rogue
910   — making enemies for yourself, over things that are none of your business?

INFORMER: Isn't it my business, you booby, to work for the good of my own community to the best of my ability ?

HONEST MAN: Oh, it's working for the good of the community, is it, to poke your nose into other people's affairs?

INFORMER: No, to go to the aid of the established laws, and not to
915   stand idly by if someone commits a crime.

HONEST MAN: Doesn't the city establish an authority, namely the juries, for precisely that purpose?

INFORMER: But who's to bring prosecutions before them?

HONEST MAN: Anyone who wishes.

INFORMER: Well, that's me, innit? So all the affairs of the city depend on me.

HONEST MAN: Pretty miserable champion it's got, then, by Zeus!
920   Wouldn't you like instead to just keep quiet and live in idleness?

INFORMER: You're expecting me to live like a sheep, if I'm not going to see any activity in my life.

HONEST MAN: Or wouldn't you learn another trade?

INFORMER: Not if you gave me Wealth himself, and all the
925   silphium of Battus too!

CARION [*losing patience*]: Drop your cloak, right away, — [*The Informer takes no notice.*]

HONEST MAN: Hey, you, he's talking to *you*!

CARION: — and then take off your shoes. [*The Informer still takes no notice.*]

HONEST MAN: He's saying all this to *you*!

Δι.   πάντα ταῦτα σοὶ λέγει.
Συ.   καὶ μὴν προσελθέτω πρὸς ἔμ' ὑμῶν ἐνθαδὶ
      ὁ βουλόμενος.
Κα.   οὔκουν ἐκεῖνός εἰμ' ἐγώ;
Συ.   οἴμοι τάλας, ἀποδύομαι μεθ' ἡμέραν.   930
Κα.   σὺ γὰρ ἀξιοῖς τἀλλότρια πράττων ἐσθίειν.
Συ.   ὁρᾷς ἃ ποιεῖς; ταῦτ' ἐγὼ μαρτύρομαι.
Κα.   ἀλλ' οἴχεται φεύγων ὃν εἶχες μάρτυρα.
Συ.   οἴμοι, περιείλημμαι μόνος.
Κα.   νυνὶ βοᾷς;
Συ.   οἴμοι μάλ' αὖθις.
Κα.   δὸς σύ μοι τὸ τριβώνιον,   935
      ἵν' ἀμφιέσω τὸν συκοφάντην τουτονί.
Δι.   μὴ δῆθ'· ἱερὸν γάρ ἐστι τοῦ Πλούτου πάλαι.
Κα.   ἔπειτα ποῦ κάλλιον ἀνατεθήσεται
      ἢ περὶ πονηρὸν ἄνδρα καὶ τοιχωρύχον;
      Πλοῦτον δὲ κοσμεῖν ἱματίοις σεμνοῖς πρέπει.   940
Δι.   τοῖς δ' ἐμβαδίοις τί χρήσεταί τις; εἰπέ μοι.
Κα.   καὶ ταῦτα πρὸς τὸ μέτωπον αὐτίκα δὴ μάλα,
      ὥσπερ κοτίνῳ, προσπατταλεύσω τουτῳί.
Συ.   ἄπειμι· γιγνώσκω γὰρ ἥττων ὢν πολὺ
      ὑμῶν. ἐὰν δὲ σύζυγον λάβω τινὰ   945
      κἂν σύκινον, τοῦτον τὸν ἰσχυρὸν θεὸν
      ἐγὼ ποιήσω τήμερον δοῦναι δίκην,
      ὁτιὴ καταλύει περιφανῶς εἷς ὢν μόνος
      τὴν δημοκρατίαν, οὔτε τὴν βουλὴν πιθὼν
      τὴν τῶν πολιτῶν οὔτε τὴν ἐκκλησίαν.   950

---

932   ποιεῖς codd.: ποιεῖ Budaeus.
933   εἶχες Rn': ἦγες Vn'.
946   κἂν Hemsterhuys: καὶ codd.

INFORMER [*showing himself ready to fight*]: Very well, let one of you come at me, right here, any one who wishes—

CARION: Well, that's me, innit?! [*He sets upon the Informer, trying to strip off his cloak, and is joined by the Honest Man. The witness takes to his heels.*]

30   INFORMER: Help, help! I'm being stripped in broad daylight!

CARION: Well, *you're* the one who sees fit to get his bread by minding other people's business.

INFORMER: Are you aware what you're doing? [*He is answered only by punches and kicks.*] Witness this, everyone!

CARION: No good – the witness you had has run off and gone.

INFORMER [*defending himself desperately*]: Help, I'm surrounded – alone!

CARION: Shrieking now, are you?

INFORMER [*reeling under a powerful blow*]: "Ah, yet another!"

35   [*He falls to the ground, and Carion and the Honest Man quickly strip him of his cloak and shoes.*]

CARION [*to the Honest Man's slave*]: You give me that old cloak, so I can throw it round this informer.

HONEST MAN: No, don't; it's already sacred, the property of Wealth.

CARION: Then where better to have it lie as a dedication than around a rogue and villain of a man? Wealth ought to be adorned with *stately*

40   garments. [*He takes the old cloak and drapes it roughly round the Informer's shoulders.*]

HONEST MAN: And what are we going to do with the shoes, tell me?

CARION: He can have those too; I'll nail them to his forehead, right away, like a dedication nailed to a wild olive tree! [*He thrusts a nail through the forehead of the Informer's mask, and ties the Honest Man's old shoes to it by their straps, completing the task just as the Informer recovers his senses.*]

INFORMER [*rising to his feet*]: I'm off. I can see that you're much

45   stronger than I am. But if I can find an ally, even a frail one, I am going to make this mighty god pay the penalty of his crimes this very day, because he is manifestly guilty of attempting to subvert our democracy, acting entirely on his own sole authority, without obtaining the approval of the citizens'

50   Council or of the Assembly either. [*He goes out, left.*]

Δι. καὶ μήν, ἐπειδὴ τὴν πανοπλίαν τὴν ἐμὴν
ἔχων βαδίζεις, εἰς τὸ βαλανεῖον τρέχε·
ἔπειτ' ἐκεῖ κορυφαῖος ἑστηκὼς θέρου.
κἀγὼ γὰρ εἶχον τὴν στάσιν ταύτην ποτέ.

Κα. ἀλλ' ὁ βαλανεὺς ἕλξει θύραζ' αὐτὸν λαβὼν   955
τῶν ὀρχιπέδων· ἰδὼν γὰρ αὐτὸν γνώσεται
ὅτι ἔστ' ἐκείνου τοῦ πονηροῦ κόμματος.
νὼ δ' εἰσίωμεν, ἵνα προσεύξῃ τὸν θεόν.

ΧΟΡΟΥ

ΓΡΑΥΣ
ἆρ', ὦ φίλοι γέροντες, ἐπὶ τὴν οἰκίαν
ἀφίγμεθ' ὄντως τοῦ νέου τούτου θεοῦ;   960
ἢ τῆς ὁδοῦ τὸ παράπαν ἡμαρτήκαμεν;
Χο. ἀλλ' ἴσθ' ἐπ' αὐτὰς τὰς θύρας ἀφιγμένη,
ὦ μειρακίσκη· πυνθάνει γὰρ ὡρικῶς.
Γρ. φέρε νυν ἐγὼ τῶν ἔνδοθεν καλέσω τινά.
Χρ. μὴ δῆτ'· ἐγὼ γὰρ αὐτὸς ἐξελήλυθα.   965
ἀλλ' ὅ τι μάλιστ' ἐλήλυθας λέγειν ἐχρῆν.
Γρ. πέπονθα δεινὰ καὶ παράνομ', ὦ φίλτατε.
ἀφ' οὗ γὰρ ὁ θεὸς οὗτος ἤρξατο βλέπειν,
ἀβίωτον εἶναί μοι πεποίηκε τὸν βίον.
Χρ. τί δ' ἐστίν; ἢ που καὶ σὺ συκοφάντρια   970
ἐν ταῖς γυναιξὶν ἦσθα;
Γρ.   μὰ Δί' ἐγὼ μὲν οὔ.
Χρ. ἀλλ' οὐ λαχοῦσ' ἔπινες ἐν τῷ γράμματι;
Γρ. σκώπτεις· ἐγὼ δὲ κατακέκνησμαι δειλάκρα.
Χρ. οὔκουν ἐρεῖς ἀνύσασα τὸν κνησμὸν τίνα;
Γρ. ἄκουέ νυν. ἦν μοί τι μειράκιον φίλον,   975
πενιχρὸν μέν, ἄλλως δ' εὐπρόσωπον καὶ καλὸν

---

after 958 Π83 shows a gap of one line, in which χοροῦ probably stood (in this passage only
the ends of lines survive); χοροῦ was also inserted by Triclinius (om. RVn).

966   ἐχρῆν Π83 Vn': cf. Birds 1201: σ' ἐχρῆν Rn': σε χρῆν n'.

967-9 Π83 had two verses (none of whose text can now be read) between 967 and 969; it is
impossible to tell whether the extra verse preceded or followed 968.

973   κατακέκνησμαι n': κατακέκνισμαι RVn' Suda: cf. on 974.

974   κνησμὸν Vᵃᶜn' Σᵛᶿᴺᵖ¹ᵛᵇ³ ᴢᶿᴺᵖⁱ: κνισμὸν RVᵖᶜn' Σᴱᴹᴾ²² ᴬᴢᴱᴹ.

HONEST MAN [*calling after him*]: Oh, and since you're going about with my panoply on you, why not run off to the bath-house, and stand there in pole position to warm yourself? Because that was a privilege that I used to have!

955   CARION: No good; the bathman will take him by the balls and drag him outside — as soon as he sees him, he'll know he's one of those "pieces of bad coinage". Now let's both go inside, so that you can pray to the god. [*They go into the house, followed by the slave-boy, who takes the Informer's cloak and shoes with him.*]

CHORAL INTERLUDE

[*Enter, right, an old woman, brightly dressed and heavily made-up with white lead, accompanied by a girl slave who is carrying a tray of cakes and sweetmeats.*]

960   OLD WOMAN [*trying exaggeratedly to sound youthful*]: My dear old friends, have we really arrived at the home of this new god? Or have we completely mistaken the way?

CHORUS-LEADER: I assure you, you've come right to his door, young lady — because you do speak in a youthful kind of way.

OLD WOMAN: All right, let me call someone from inside.

[*As she is speaking, the door opens and Chremylus comes out.*]

965   CHREMYLUS: No need; I've come out myself anyway. But you ought to say what exactly you've come here about.

OLD WOMAN: I've been treated disgracefully and criminally, darling. Since this god began to see again, he's made my life be not worth living!

970   CHREMYLUS: What's it all about? Were you too, perhaps, an informeress among the women?

OLD WOMAN: I most certainly was not!

CHREMYLUS: Or were you in the habit of ... drinking with your letter-class when you hadn't been drawn for a place?

OLD WOMAN: You're making fun of me. I've been put right through the mincer, wretched me!

CHREMYLUS: Well, won't you hurry up and tell us how this mincing happened?

975   OLD WOMAN: Listen, then. I had a young boyfriend, a poor lad, but handsome and good-looking all the same, and very decent too: if ever I

καὶ χρηστόν· εἰ γάρ του δεηθείην ἐγώ,
ἅπαντ' ἐποίει κοσμίως μοι καὶ καλῶς·
ἐγὼ δ' ἐκείνῳ πάντ' ἂν ἀνθυπηρέτουν.

Χρ. τί δ' ἦν ὅ τι σου μάλιστ' ἐδεῖθ' ἑκάστοτε;   980

Γρ. οὐ πολλά· καὶ γὰρ ἐκνομίως μ' ᾐσχύνετο.
ἀλλ' ἀργυρίου δραχμὰς ἂν ᾔτησ' εἴκοσιν
εἰς ἱμάτιον, ὀκτὼ δ' ἂν εἰς ὑποδήματα·
καὶ ταῖς ἀδελφαῖς ἀγοράσαι χιτώνιον
ἐκέλευσεν ἂν τῇ μητρί θ' ἱματίδιον,   985
πυρῶν τ' ἂν ἐδεήθη μεδίμνων τεττάρων.

Χρ. οὐ πολλὰ τοίνυν, μὰ τὸν Ἀπόλλω, ταῦτά γε
εἴρηκας, ἀλλὰ δῆλον ὅτι σ' ᾐσχύνετο.

Γρ. καὶ ταῦτα τοίνυν οὐχ ἕνεκεν μισητίας
αἰτεῖν μ' ἔφασκεν, ἀλλὰ φιλίας οὕνεκα,   990
ἵνα τοὐμὸν ἱμάτιον φορῶν μεμνῇτό μου.

Χρ. λέγεις ἐρῶντ' ἄνθρωπον ἐκνομιώτατα.

Γρ. ἀλλ' οὐχὶ νῦν ὁ βδελυρὸς ἔτι τὸν νοῦν ἔχει
τὸν αὐτόν, ἀλλὰ πολὺ μεθέστηκεν πάνυ.
ἐμοῦ γὰρ αὐτῷ τὸν πλακοῦντα τουτονὶ   995
καὶ τἄλλα τἀπὶ τοῦ πίνακος τραγήματα
ἐπόντα πεμψάσης ὑπειπούσης θ' ὅτι
εἰς ἑσπέραν ἥξοιμι—

Χρ.   τί σ' ἔδρασ'; εἰπέ μοι.

Γρ. ἄμητα προσαπέπεμψεν ἡμῖν τουτονί,
ἐφ' ᾧτ' ἐκεῖσε μηδέποτέ μ' ἐλθεῖν ἔτι,   1000
καὶ πρὸς ἐπὶ τούτοις εἶπεν ἀπόπεμπων ὅτι
"πάλαι ποτ' ἦσαν ἄλκιμοι Μιλήσιοι".

Χρ. δῆλον ὅτι τοὺς τρόπους τις οὐ μοχθηρὸς ἦν·
ἔπειτα πλουτῶν οὐκέθ' ἥδεται φακῇ,
πρὸ τοῦ δ' ὑπὸ τῆς πενίας ἅπανθ' ὑπήσθιεν.   1005

Γρ. καὶ μὴν πρὸ τοῦ γ' ὁσημέραι, νὴ τὼ θεώ,
ἐπὶ τὴν θύραν ἐβάδιζεν ἀεὶ τὴν ἐμήν.

---

979 πάντ' ἂν ἀνθυπηρέτουν Porson (ἀνθυπηρέτουν Σ^M): πάντα ταῦτ' (Vn': πάντα
τ' αὖτ' n': ταῦτα πάντ' Rn') ὑπηρέτουν codd.: πάντα γ' ἀνθυπηρέτουν
Hemsterhuys.

998 σ' RV: om. n.

1005 (ἅπαν)θ' ὑπήσθιεν R: τ' ἐπήσθιεν Ath. 4.170d (-ον Ath.^{AC}), Greg. Cypr. 1.100: -
τα γ' ἤσθιεν V Suda (γ' om. Suda^A)· τα κατήσθιεν n.

wanted anything, he did everything for me so nicely and dutifully! And in return I was ready to do any service for him.

CHREMYLUS: And what exactly did he regularly ask you to do?

OLD WOMAN: Not a lot; he was extraordinarily respectful towards me. But he might request twenty drachmas in cash for a cloak, or eight for shoes; and again, he'd ask me to buy an underdress for his sisters or a nice little cloak for his mother, and he'd also want some wheat, say four bushels.

CHREMYLUS [*ironically*]: That's certainly not a lot, by Apollo, that you say he asked for! It's obvious that he did respect you!

OLD WOMAN: Yes, and he used to say that he wasn't asking me for these things out of greed, but out of affection, so that he would be reminded of me by wearing my cloak.

CHREMYLUS: As you describe the man, he was most desperately in love .

OLD WOMAN: But *now* he's not thinking that way at all any more, the loathsome fellow; he's just totally altered. When I sent him this flat-cake [*pointing to it*] and the other sweetmeats that are on the tray, and added that I'd be coming to him this evening— [*She pauses.*]

CHREMYLUS: What did he do to you? Go on.

OLD WOMAN: He sent them back to me, and he added this milk-cake — on condition that I never went there again; and on top of that he sent back with them the message that "the Milesians were brave men — once upon a time"!

CHREMYLUS: He obviously wasn't a bad sort, character-wise; and accordingly now, having become rich, he doesn't like lentil soup any more, whereas previously he was so poor, he'd lick up anything!

OLD WOMAN: And yet until now, by the Two Goddesses, he used to come to my door every day.

Χρ. ἐπ' ἐκφοράν;
Γρ.   μὰ Δί', ἀλλὰ τῆς φωνῆς μόνον
ἐρῶν ἀκοῦσαι.
Χρ.   τοῦ λαβεῖν μὲν οὖν χάριν.
Γρ. καὶ νὴ Δί' εἰ λυπουμένην αἴσθοιτό με,   1010
νηττάριον ἂν καὶ φάττιον ὑπεκορίζετο.
Χρ. ἔπειτ' ἴσως ᾔτησ' ἂν εἰς ὑποδήματα.
Γρ. μυστηρίοις δὲ τοῖς μεγάλοις ὀχουμένην
ἐπὶ τὴν ἄμαξαν ὅτι προσέβλεψέν μέ τις,
ἐτυπτόμην διὰ τοῦθ' ὅλην τὴν ἡμέραν·   1015
οὕτω σφόδρα ζηλότυπος ὁ νεανίσκος ἦν.
Χρ. μόνος γὰρ ᾔδεθ', ὡς ἔοικεν, ἐσθίων.
Γρ. καὶ τάς γε χεῖρας παγκάλας ἔχειν μ' ἔφη,–
Χρ. ὁπότε προτείνοιέν γε δραχμὰς εἴκοσιν.
Γρ. ὄζειν τε τῆς χροιᾶς ἔφασκεν ἡδύ μου,–   1020
Χρ. εἰ Θάσιον ἐνέχεις, εἰκότως γε νὴ Δία.
Γρ. τὸ βλέμμα θ' ὡς ἔχοιμι μαλακὸν καὶ καλόν.
Χρ. οὐ σκαιὸς ἦν ἄνθρωπος, ἀλλ' ἠπίστατο
γραὸς καπρώσης τἀφόδια κατεσθίειν.
Γρ. ταῦτ' οὖν ὁ θεός, ὦ φίλ' ἄνερ, οὐκ ὀρθῶς ποιεῖ,   1025
φάσκων βοηθεῖν τοῖς ἀδικουμένοις ἀεί.
Χρ. τί γὰρ ποιήσῃ; φράζε, καὶ πεπράξεται.
Γρ. ἀναγκάσαι δίκαιόν ἐστι, νὴ Δία,
τὸν εὖ παθόνθ' ὑπ' ἐμοῦ πάλιν μ' ἀντευποιεῖν·
ἢ μηδ' ὁτιοῦν ἀγαθὸν δίκαιός ἐστ' ἔχειν.   1030
Χρ. οὔκουν καθ' ἑκάστην ἀπεδίδου τὴν νύκτα σοι;
Γρ. ἀλλ' οὐδέποτέ με ζῶσαν ἀπολείψειν ἔφη.
Χρ. ὀρθῶς γε· νῦν δέ γ' οὐκέτι ζῆν σ' οἴεται.
Γρ. ὑπὸ τοῦ γὰρ ἄλγους κατατέτηκ', ὦ φίλτατε.
Χρ. οὔκ, ἀλλὰ κατασέσηπας, ὥς γ' ἐμοὶ δοκεῖς.   1035

1011 νηττάριον Th.: νιτ(τ)άριον RV*n* Suda, Thom. *Ecl.* 366.2.
1011 φάττιον Bentley: βάττιον *n'* Suda^{GM} Thom. *Ecl.* 366.2: βάτιον RV*n'*: βιτάριον Suda^{AFV}.
1013 μεγάλοις ὀχουμένην R*n*: μεγάλοισι νὴ Δία V.
1027 ποιήσῃ Bekker: ποι(ι)ήσει codd.
1029 μ' Tricl.: om. RV*n*.
1030 ἀγαθὸν δίκαιός Brunck: ἀγαθὸν δίκαιόν R: δίκαιον ἀγαθόν vel sim. V*n*.

CHREMYLUS: To join your funeral procession?

OLD WOMAN: Of course not! He just longed to hear the sound of my voice.

CHREMYLUS: You mean he wanted to get something out of you!

10 OLD WOMAN: And if he sensed that I was upset, by Zeus, he'd call me pet names like "my little duck" and "my little dove".

CHREMYLUS: And then, I suppose, he'd ask for the price of a pair of shoes!

15 OLD WOMAN: And at the Great Mysteries, because someone had so much as looked at me when I was riding in my carriage, for that I'd get a beating that lasted all day. That's how awfully jealous the young man was.

CHREMYLUS: He enjoyed being alone at table, apparently.

OLD WOMAN: *And* he used to say that my hands were supremely beautiful—

CHREMYLUS: When they were holding out twenty drachmas to him, yes!

20 OLD WOMAN: And he'd say that my skin smelled sweet—

CHREMYLUS: Very likely, by Zeus, if you were pouring out Thasian wine at the time!

OLD WOMAN: And that I had a lovely tender look on my face.

CHREMYLUS: The fellow was no fool: he knew very well how to eat up a randy old woman's life savings!

25 OLD WOMAN: Well, my dear man, it's not right that the god should be doing this, when he claims to always help the victims of wrongdoing.

CHREMYLUS: What is he to do, then? Say, and it shall be done.

OLD WOMAN: Why, by rights he should force this man that I've 30 treated well to treat me well in return; otherwise, the man has no right to have any of life's good things at all!

CHREMYLUS: Why, didn't he repay you already, every night?

OLD WOMAN: But he said he'd never leave me as long as I lived!

CHREMYLUS: And he meant it; only now he doesn't think you *are* alive any more.

OLD WOMAN: Because I've wasted away from grief, darling!

35 CHREMYLUS: *Rotted* away, more like, if you ask me!

Γρ. διὰ δακτυλίου μὲν οὖν ἐμέ γ' ἂν διελκύσαις.
Χρ. εἰ τυγχάνοι γ' ὁ δακτύλιος ὢν τηλίας.
Γρ. καὶ μὴν τὸ μειράκιον τοδὶ προσέρχεται,
οὗπερ πάλαι κατηγοροῦσα τυγχάνω·
ἔοικε δ' ἐπὶ κῶμον βαδίζειν.
Χρ.   φαίνεται·   1040
στεφάνους γέ τοι καὶ δᾷδ' ἔχων πορεύεται.
ΜΕΙΡΑΚΙΟΝ
    ἀσπάζομαί σε.
Γρ.   τί φησιν;
Με.   ἀρχαία φίλη,
πολιὰ γεγένησαι ταχύ γε, νὴ τὸν οὐρανόν.
Γρ. τάλαιν' ἐγὼ τῆς ὕβρεος ἧς ὑβρίζομαι.
Χρ. ἔοικε διὰ πολλοῦ χρόνου σ' ἑορακέναι.   1045
Γρ. ποίου χρόνου, ταλάνταθ', ὃς παρ' ἐμοὶ χθὲς ἦν;
Χρ. τοὐναντίον πέπονθε τοῖς ἄλλοις ἄρα·
μεθύων γάρ, ὡς ἔοικεν, ὀξύτερον βλέπει.
Γρ. οὔκ, ἀλλ' ἀκόλαστός ἐστιν ἀεὶ τοὺς τρόπους.
Με. ὦ Ποντοπόσειδον καὶ θεοὶ πρεσβυτικοί,   1050
ἐν τῷ προσώπῳ τῶν ῥυτίδων ὅσας ἔχει.
Γρ. ἆ ἆ,
τὴν δᾷδα μή μοι πρόσφερ'.
Χρ.   εὖ μέντοι λέγει·
ἐὰν γὰρ αὐτὴν εἷς μόνος σπινθὴρ λάβῃ,
ὥσπερ παλαιὰν εἰρεσιώνην καύσεται.
Με. βούλει διὰ χρόνου πρός με παῖσαι;
Γρ.
Με.   ποῖ, τάλαν;   1055
Με. αὐτοῦ, λαβοῦσα κάρυα.
Γρ.   παιδιὰν τίνα;
Με. πόσους ἔχεις ὀδόντας.
Χρ.   ἀλλὰ γνώσομαι
κἄγωγ'· ἔχει γὰρ τρεῖς ἴσως ἢ τέτταρας.

1037 τηλίας R: τηλία Vn Suda: Σ^RVENp1Vb3θ have notes interpreting both readings.
1041 στεφάνους R: στέφανον Vn.
1042 σε.– τί n': σε R: – τί Vn'.
1044 ὕβρεος Tricl.: cf. Eubulus fr. 67.9, 93.7: ὕβρεως codd.
1047 ἄλλοις V Σ^EMNp1θ. πολλοῖς R.
1053 λάβῃ RVn' Suda: λάβοι n': βάλῃ Wakefield.

OLD WOMAN: No, really, you could pass me through a ring [*taking a ring from her finger to emphasize her point*].

CHREMYLUS: Yes, if the ring happened to be attached to a bread-seller's tray [*moving both hands in semicircular paths from a position behind his neck to one in front of his stomach*].

OLD WOMAN [*looking off, right*]: But now here comes the young
1040 man, the one I've been complaining about all this time. It looks as if he's going on the revel.

CHREMYLUS: It looks like it. At any rate he's coming with garlands and a torch.

[*Enter, left, a young man, rather drunk. He is wearing two or three garlands at different angles, and carrying a lighted torch.*]

YOUNG MAN [*to Chremylus; rather indistinctly*] Greeting to you!

OLD WOMAN [*to Chremylus*]: What's he saying?

YOUNG MAN [*noticing her*]: My ancient friend, your hair's gone white very quickly, by heaven !

OLD WOMAN [*almost in tears*]: Poor me, the insults I have to endure!

1045 CHREMYLUS: Looks as though he hasn't seen you for a long time.

OLD WOMAN: What do you mean, you wretched man, a long time? He was at my place yesterday!

CHREMYLUS: Then his system works the opposite way to other people's; apparently he sees more clearly when he's drunk!

OLD WOMAN: No, it's the effrontery in his character that he's always had.

1050 YOUNG MAN [*looking closely at her face, and holding the torch dangerously near it*]: Oh, Poseidon of the Sea! O ye gods of old age! What a quantity of wrinkles she has on that face!

OLD WOMAN [*in alarm*]: Ah, ah, don't wave that torch near me!

CHREMYLUS [*to Young Man*]: She's quite right. If just one spark catches hold of her, it'll send her up in flames like an old harvest wreath!

1055 YOUNG MAN [*to Old Woman*]: Would you like to play with me? It's been quite a time since you did!

OLD WOMAN [*coyly*]: Where could we go, my dear?

YOUNG MAN [*producing some nuts*]: Right here. Just take some nuts.

OLD WOMAN [*disappointed, but trying not to show it*]: What game?

YOUNG MAN: "How many have you got" — how many *teeth*.

CHREMYLUS: I'll guess too. I think she's got three or four.

Με. ἀπότεισον· ἕνα γὰρ γομφίον μόνον φορεῖ.
Γρ. ταλάντατ' ἀνδρῶν, οὐχ ὑγιαίνειν μοι δοκεῖς,   1060
πλύνον με ποιῶν ἐν τοσούτοις ἀνδράσιν.
Με. ὄναιο μέντἄν, εἴ τις ἐκπλύνειέ σε.
Χρ. οὐ δῆτ', ἐπεὶ νῦν μὲν καπηλικῶς ἔχει,
εἰ δ' ἐκπλυνεῖται τοῦτο τὸ ψιμύθιον,
ὄψει κατάδηλα τοῦ προσώπου τὰ ῥάκη.   1065
Γρ. γέρων ἀνὴρ ὢν οὐχ ὑγιαίνειν μοι δοκεῖς.
Με. πειρᾷ μὲν οὖν ἴσως σε, καὶ τῶν τιτθίων
ἐφάπτεταί σου λανθάνειν δοκῶν ἐμέ.
Γρ. μὰ τὴν Ἀφροδίτην, οὐκ ἐμοῦ γ', ὦ βδελυρὲ σύ.
Χρ. μὰ τὴν Ἑκάτην οὐ δῆτα· μαινοίμην γὰρ ἄν.   1070
ἀλλ', ὦ νεανίσκ', οὐκ ἐῶ τὴν μείρακα
μισεῖν σε ταύτην.
Με.   ἀλλ' ἔγωγ' ὑπερφιλῶ.
Χρ. καὶ μὴν κατηγορεῖ γέ σου.
Με.   τί κατηγορεῖ;
Χρ. εἶναί σ' ὑβριστήν φησι καὶ λέγειν ὅτι
"πάλαι ποτ' ἦσαν ἄλκιμοι Μιλήσιοι".   1075
Με. ἐγὼ περὶ ταύτης οὐ μαχοῦμαί σοι—
Χρ.   τὸ τί;
Με. — αἰσχυνόμενος τὴν ἡλικίαν τὴν σήν, ἐπεὶ
οὐκ ἄν ποτ' ἄλλῳ τοῦτ' ἐπέτρεπον ἂν ποιεῖν·
νῦν δ' ἄπιθι χαίρων συλλαβὼν τὴν μείρακα.
Χρ. οἶδ', οἶδα τὸν νοῦν· οὐκέτ' ἀξιοῖς ἴσως   1080
εἶναι μετ' αὐτῆς.
Με.   ὁ δ' ἐπιτρέψων ἐστὶ τίς;
οὐκ ἂν διαλεχθείην διεσπλεκωμένη
ὑπὸ μυρίων ἐτῶν γε καὶ τρισχιλίων.
Χρ. ὅμως δ', ἐπειδὴ καὶ τὸν οἶνον ἠξίους
πίνειν, συνεκποτέ' ἐστί σοι καὶ τὴν τρύγα.   1085
Με. ἀλλ' ἔστι κομιδῇ τρὺξ παλαιὰ καὶ σαπρά.
Χρ. οὔκουν τρύγοιπος ταῦτα πάντ' ἰάσεται;
ἀλλ' εἴσιθ' εἴσω.

1078 ἐπέτρεπον ἂν Bamberg: ἐπέτρεπον Rn': ἐπέτρεψ' ἐγὼ Vn'.
1081 ἐπιτρέψων n Σᴱᴺᵖ¹ⱽᵇ³ᵛ+λ: ἐπιστρέψων R: ἐπιτρέπων V ᵛΣᴿ: ἐπιτάξων van
Leeuwen.
1083 ἐτῶν γε codd.: ἐτῶν τε Suda: γε τῶνδε Rutherford: τε τῶνδε Willems.

YOUNG MAN: Pay up! She's got one back tooth and that's all.

OLD WOMAN: You wretched, wretched man, I do think you're out
of your mind, treating me like dirty washing in front of all these men
[*indicating the audience*]!

YOUNG MAN: Well, it would certainly do you good if someone did
give you a thorough wash.

CHREMYLUS: No, it wouldn't, because at present she's dolled
herself up for sale; if that white lead gets washed off, you'll see the wreckage
of her face in all its nakedness!

OLD WOMAN [*to Chremylus*]: At your age, I do think you're out of
your mind!

YOUNG MAN: No, I think he's trying to make a move on you —
fingering your boobs and fancying I won't notice.

OLD WOMAN [*indignantly*]: He is *not*, by Aphrodite, you loathsome
man!

CHREMYLUS: No, indeed, by Hecate — I *would* be barmy to! But
now, my lad, I'm not having you hate this young lady.

YOUNG MAN: Hate her? I love her passionately!

CHREMYLUS: Well, she's certainly complaining about you.

YOUNG MAN: What's her complaint?

CHREMYLUS: She says you've been insolent towards her and told
her that "the Milesians were brave men — once upon a time".

YOUNG MAN: I'm not going to fight with you over her—

CHREMYLUS: What do you mean?

YOUNG MAN: — out of respect for your age — because I'd never
have let anyone else get away with this; but you take the girl and go, and
good luck to you.

CHREMYLUS: I know what you're up to, I know what you're up to!
I gather you don't choose to be with her any more.

YOUNG MAN [*belligerently*]: And who's going to tell me to? I'm
not having anything to do with a woman who's been shagged to pieces by
thirteen thousand ... years.

CHREMYLUS: All the same, you did choose to drink the wine, and
that being so, you've got to drink off the dregs as well along with it.

YOUNG MAN: But they're such very old, rancid dregs!

CHREMYLUS: Well, won't a filter-cloth put that all to rights?
Anyway, come inside.

Με.   τῷ θεῷ γοῦν βούλομαι
ἐλθὼν ἀναθεῖναι τοὺς στεφάνους τούσδ' ὡς ἔχω.

Γρ. ἐγὼ δέ γ' αὐτῷ καὶ φράσαι τι βούλομαι.   1090

Με. ἐγὼ δέ γ' οὐκ εἴσειμι.

Χρ.   θάρρει, μὴ φοβοῦ·
οὐ γὰρ βιάσεται.

Με.   πάνυ καλῶς τοίνυν λέγεις·
ἱκανὸν γὰρ αὐτὴν πρότερον ὑπεπίττουν χρόνον.

Γρ. βάδιζ'· ἐγὼ γάρ σου κατόπιν εἰσέρχομαι.

Χρ. ὡς ἐντόνως, ὦ Ζεῦ βασιλεῦ, τὸ γρᾴδιον   1095
ὥσπερ λέπας τῷ μειρακίῳ προσείχετο.

ΧΟΡΟΥ

Κα. τίς ἐσθ' ὁ κόπτων τὴν θύραν; τουτὶ τί ἦν;
οὐδείς, ἔοικεν· ἀλλὰ δῆτα τὸ θύριον
φθεγγόμενον ἄλλως κλαυσιᾷ.

ΕΡΜΗΣ   σέ τοι λέγω,
ὁ Καρίων, ἀνάμεινον.

Κα.   οὗτος, εἰπέ μοι,   1100
σὺ τὴν θύραν ἔκοπτες οὑτωσὶ σφόδρα;

Ερ. μὰ Δί', ἀλλ' ἔμελλον· εἶτ' ἀνέῳξάς με φθάσας.
ἀλλ' ἐκκάλει τὸν δεσπότην τρέχων ταχύ,
ἔπειτα τὴν γυναῖκα καὶ τὰ παιδία,
ἔπειτα τοὺς θεράποντας, εἶτα τὴν κύνα,   1105
ἔπειτα σαυτόν, εἶτα τὴν ὗν.

Κα.   εἰπέ μοι,
τί δ' ἐστίν;

Ερ.   ὁ Ζεύς, ὦ πόνηρε, βούλεται

1088 γοῦν V: γ' οὖν R: γὰρ n: all these give ἀλλ' εἴσιθ' εἴσω to the Young Man.

1089 ὡς R: οὓς Vn.

1093 ὑπ- RV: προσ- ᵍΣᴿ: om. n Suda ᵍΣᴱᴹᶿ, Zonaras, Et.Mag. 656.8.

1093 (-)επίττουν n', ⁱΣ(i)ᴿⱽᴱᴹᶿⱽᵇ³, Zonaras: (-)έπιττον RVn' Suda ᵍΣᴿᴱᴹᶿ ⁱΣ(ii)ⱽ: ἐπίττων n', Et.Mag.: (ὑπ)επείρων ʸᵖΣᴿⱽ.

1095 ἐντόνως Meineke: εὐτόνως codd.

1096 προσείχετο RV: προσίσχεται n.

after 1096 χοροῦ n': om. RVn'.

1100 ὁ n': om. n': ὦ RV.

YOUNG MAN: Well, yes, I do certainly want to come right away and dedicate these garlands to the god. [*He begins to move towards the door, together with Chremylus.*]

1090 OLD WOMAN [*making to follow them*]: And *I* want to *say* something to him.

YOUNG MAN [*stopping in his tracks*]: Then *I'm* not going inside.

CHREMYLUS: Take courage, don't be frightened. She won't rape you.

YOUNG MAN: That's fine, then. I've spent quite enough time before now working on the underside of that old boat! [*He continues towards the door.*]

OLD WOMAN [*moving up close behind him*]: Go on, then, but I'm coming in right behind you. [*Both go inside, the Old Woman almost treading on the Young Man's heels; the slave-girl follows.*]

1095 CHREMYLUS: King Zeus! how determined that old bag was! She was clinging to the lad like a limpet! [*He too goes inside*]

CHORAL INTERLUDE

[*Enter, right, the god Hermes. He comes to Chremylus' door, knocks, and then hides himself out of sight.*]

CARION [*within*]: Who's that knocking at the door? [*He opens the door. He is carrying some offals in one hand, and a chamber-pot in the other. He is taken aback to find no one waiting outside.*] What's all this? There's no one, apparently. Well, if the door must make a noise for no reason, it's asking for a thump! [*He kicks the door, and turns to go back inside.*]

HERMES [*suddenly coming out of concealment*]: Hey, you – you, I
1100 say, Carion – wait there a moment!

CARION [*turning again to address him*]: Here, you, tell me, was it you that was knocking so hard on the door just now?

HERMES: No, I didn't; I was going to, but you opened the door first.
1105 Now run quickly and call out your master, then his wife and children, then the servants, then the dog, then yourself, and then the pig.

CARION [*puzzled*]: What's all this about, may I ask?

HERMES: It is the will of Zeus, you wretched villain, to hash you all

εἰς ταὐτὸν ὑμᾶς συγκυκήσας τρύβλιον
ἀπαξάπαντας εἰς τὸ βάραθρον ἐμβαλεῖν.

Κα. ἡ γλῶττα τῷ κήρυκι τούτῳ τέμνεται.   1110
    ἀτὰρ διὰ τί δὴ ταῦτ' ἐπιβουλεύει ποιεῖν
    ἡμᾶς;

Ερ.   ὁτιὴ δεινότατα πάντων πραγμάτων
    εἴργασθ'. ἀφ' οὗ γὰρ ἤρξατ' ἐξ ἀρχῆς βλέπειν
    ὁ Πλοῦτος, οὐδεὶς οὐ λιβανωτόν, οὐ δάφνην,
    οὐ ψαιστόν, οὐχ ἱερεῖον, οὐκ ἀλλ' οὐδὲ ἕν   1115
    ἡμῖν ἔτι θύει τοῖς θεοῖς.

Κα.   μὰ Δί' οὐδέ γε
    θύσει· κακῶς γὰρ ἐπεμελεῖσθ' ἡμῶν τότε.

Ερ. καὶ τῶν μὲν ἄλλων μοι θεῶν ἧττον μέλει·
    ἐγὼ δ' ἀπόλωλα κἀπιτέτριμμαι.

Κα.   σωφρονεῖς.

Ερ. πρότερον γὰρ εἶχον ἂν παρὰ ταῖς καπηλίσιν   1120
    πάντ' ἀγάθ' ἕωθεν εὐθύς, οἰνοῦτταν, μέλι,
    ἰσχάδας, ὅσ' εἰκός ἐστιν Ἑρμῆν ἐσθίειν·
    νυνὶ δὲ πεινῶν ἀναβάδην ἀναπαύομαι.

Κα. οὔκουν δικαίως, ὅστις ἐποίεις ζημίαν
    ἐνίοτε τοιαῦτ' ἀγάθ' ἔχων;

Ερ.   οἴμοι τάλας,   1125
    οἴμοι πλακοῦντος τοῦ 'ν τετράδι πεπεμμένου.

Κα. ποθεῖς τὸν οὐ παρόντα καὶ μάτην καλεῖς.

Ερ. οἴμοι δὲ κωλῆς, ἣν ἐγὼ κατήσθιον.

Κα. ἀσκωλίαζ' ἐνταῦθα πρὸς τὴν αἰθρίαν.

Ερ. σπλάγχνων τε θερμῶν, ὧν ἐγὼ κατήσθιον.   1130

Κα. ὀδύνη σε περὶ τὰ σπλάγχν' ἔοικέ τις στρέφειν.

Ερ. οἴμοι δὲ κύλικος ἴσον ἴσῳ κεκραμένης.

Κα. ταύτην ἐπιπιὼν ἀποτρέχων οὐκ ἂν φθάνοις.

Ερ. ἆρ' ὠφελήσαις ἄν τι τὸν σαυτοῦ φίλον;

Κα. εἴ του δέει γ' ὧν δυνατός εἰμί σ' ὠφελεῖν.   1135

Ερ. εἴ μοι πορίσας ἄρτον τιν' εὖ πεπεμμένον
    δοίης καταφαγεῖν καὶ κρέας νεανικὸν
    ὧν θύεθ' ὑμεῖς ἔνδον.

1110 τούτῳ (or τούτω) n': τούτων RVn' Suda, Eustathius 1471.13.
1120 εἶχον ἂν Dobree: εἶχον RVn': ἔγωγ' εἶχον n': εἶχον μὲν Tricl.
1131 ἔοικέ τις στρ- n': ἔοικέ τι στρ- RV: ἔοικ' ἐπιστρ- vel sim. n'.

up in a bowl together and then throw the whole lot of you into the Barathron!

1110   CARION: This herald needs a tongue cutting out! — But why is he planning to do this to us?

HERMES: Because you have done the most monstrous of deeds!
1114-6 Since Wealth began to be able to see once again, no one sacrifices any more to us gods — no incense, no laurel, no ground-cakes, no animals, no nothing!

CARION: And they *won't* sacrifice any more, by Zeus, because you took such bad care of us in the old days.

HERMES: Now I'm not so much concerned about the *other* gods — but *I'm* completely ruined and done for!

CARION [*ironically*]: Very thoughtful of you.

1120   HERMES: Until now, I used to get all kinds of goodies, first thing in the morning, from the women tavern-keepers — wine-cakes, honey, dried figs — all the things that you'd expect Hermes to eat; but now I just rest with my feet up and starve.

1124-5   CARION: And doesn't it serve you right, when you used to get those goodies from them and then sometimes do them damage?

HERMES [*in mock-tragic woe*]: Ah me, alas! Ah me, the flat-cakes baked on the fourth of the month!

CARION: "You yearn for one that is no longer here
                   And call in vain. "

HERMES: Ah me, the legs of pork that once I guzzled!

CARION: Up on *one* leg with you, here in the open air, and hop it!

1130   HERMES: And the hot innards, too, that once I guzzled!

CARION: I think there's a sharp pain doubling you up around the innards!

HERMES: Ah me, the cup of fifty-fifty blend!

CARION [*thrusting the chamber-pot at him*]: Drink *this* with your meal, and then run off, the sooner the better!

HERMES [*wheedling*]: Can you give some assistance to your dear old friend?

1135   CARION: Yes, if you need something that I'm *able* to help you with.

HERMES: If you could rustle up a well-baked loaf and give it me to eat, and a healthy-sized piece of meat from the sacrifice you're making in there?

Κα.   ἀλλ' οὐκ ἐκφορά.

Ερ. καὶ μὴν ὁπότε τι σκευάριον τοῦ δεσπότου
      ὑφέλοι', ἐγώ σ' ἂν λανθάνειν ἐποίουν ἀεί.   1140

Κα. ἐφ' ᾧ γε μετέχειν καὐτός, ὦ τοιχωρύχε·
      ἧκεν γὰρ ἄν σοι ναστὸς εὖ πεπεμμένος.

Ερ. ἔπειτα τοῦτόν γ' αὐτὸς ἂν κατήσθιες.

Κα. οὐ γὰρ μετεῖχες τὰς ἴσας πληγὰς ἐμοί,
      ὁπότε τι ληφθείην πανουργήσας ἐγώ.   1145

Ερ. μὴ μνησικακήσῃς, εἰ σὺ Φυλὴν κατέλαβες.
      ἀλλὰ ξύνοικον πρὸς θεῶν δέξασθέ με.

Κα. ἔπειτ' ἀπολιπὼν τοὺς θεοὺς ἐνθάδε μενεῖς;

Ερ. τὰ γὰρ παρ' ὑμῶν ἐστι βελτίω πολύ.

Κα. τί δέ; ταὐτομολεῖν ἀστεῖον εἶναί σοι δοκεῖ;   1150

Ερ. πατρὶς γὰρ ἐστι πᾶσ', ἵν' ἂν πράττῃ τις εὖ.

Κα. τί δῆτ' ἂν εἴης ὄφελος ἡμῖν ἐνθάδ' ὤν;

Ερ. παρὰ τὴν θύραν στροφαῖον ἱδρύσασθέ με.

Κα. στροφαῖον; ἀλλ' οὐκ ἔργον ἔστ' οὐδὲν στροφῶν.

Ερ. ἀλλ' ἐμπολαῖον.

Κα.   ἀλλὰ πλουτοῦμεν· τί οὖν   1155
      Ἑρμῆν παλιγκάπηλον ἡμᾶς δεῖ τρέφειν;

Ερ. ἀλλὰ δόλιον τοίνυν.

Κα.   δόλιον; ἥκιστά γε·
      οὐ γὰρ δόλου νῦν ἔργον, ἀλλ' ἁπλῶν τρόπων.

Ερ. ἀλλ' ἡγεμόνιον.

Κα.   ἀλλ' ὁ θεὸς ἤδη βλέπει,
      ὥσθ' ἡγεμόνος οὐδὲν δεησόμεσθ' ἔτι.   1160

Ερ. ἐναγώνιος τοίνυν ἔσομαι. καὶ τί ἔτ' ἐρεῖς;
      Πλούτῳ γάρ ἐστι τοῦτο συμφορώτατον,
      ποιεῖν ἀγῶνας μουσικοὺς καὶ γυμνικούς.

Κα. ὡς ἀγαθόν ἐστ' ἐπωνυμίας πολλὰς ἔχειν·
      οὗτος γὰρ ἐξηύρηκεν αὑτῷ βιότιον.   1165
      οὐκ ἐτὸς ἅπαντες οἱ δικάζοντες θαμὰ
      σπεύδουσιν ἐν πολλοῖς γεγράφθαι γράμμασιν.

Ερ. οὐκοῦν ἐπὶ τούτοις εἰσίω;

Κα.   καὶ πλῦνέ γε
      αὐτὸς προσελθὼν πρὸς τὸ φρέαρ τὰς κοιλίας,
      ἵν' εὐθέως διακονικὸς εἶναι δοκῇς.   1170

1170 εἶναι Bentley: εἶναί μοι vel sim. codd.

CARION: Sorry, it's "not to be taken out".

HERMES: Just think of the times when you nicked some little thing of your master's, and I'd always make sure that you weren't discovered!

CARION: On the understanding that you'd get a share yourself, you crook! A well-baked stuffed loaf would be sure to come your way.

HERMES: Yes, and then you'd eat that up yourself.

CARION: Well, you didn't get hit the number of times I did, when I'd done some villainy and happened to get caught.

HERMES: Now you've seized Phyle, it's time to forget old grudges. In the gods' name, take me in as a member of your household.

CARION: You mean you're going to abandon the gods and stay here?

HERMES: Yes, because things are much better with you.

CARION: What, you think it's a clever thing to defect to the enemy?

HERMES: "My homeland's any land where I can prosper."

CARION: Well, what good would you be to us, if you stayed here?

HERMES: Install me by the door as Hermes Strophaios, the god of the turning hinge.

CARION: God of the turning hinge? There's no need of turners and twisters now .

HERMES: Then as Hermes Empolaios, the god of commerce.

CARION: But we're rich, so why should we keep a huckster of a Hermes?

HERMES: Then as Hermes Dolios, the god of deceit.

CARION: Deceit? Most certainly not! There's no place for deceit now, only for honest behaviour.

HERMES: Then as Hermes Hegemonios, the divine Guide.

CARION: But Wealth can see now, so we won't need a guide any more.

HERMES: All right, I'll be Hermes Enagonios, the god of competitions. *Now* what can you say? Nothing more appropriate for Wealth than that, holding competitions in the arts and athletics.

CARION [*to the audience*]: What a good thing it is to have lots of titles! This fellow's used his to find himself a nice little living. No wonder all the jurors are constantly doing all they can to get themselves registered under several letters.

HERMES: So may I come in on those terms?

CARION: Yes — and *you* can go to the well and wash these offals [*handing them to him*], so as to appear right away in the role of Hermes Diakonikos, the divine Dogsbody!

ΙΕΡΕΥΣ

　　τίς ἂν φράσειε ποῦ 'στι Χρεμύλος μοι σαφῶς;
Χρ.　τί δ' ἐστίν, ὦ βέλτιστε;
Ιε.　　　　　　　　τί γὰρ ἄλλ' ἢ κακῶς;
　　ἀφ' οὗ γὰρ ὁ θεὸς οὗτος ἤρξατο βλέπειν,
　　ἀπόλωλ' ὑπὸ λιμοῦ· καταφαγεῖν γὰρ οὐκ ἔχω,
　　καὶ ταῦτα τοῦ σωτῆρος ἱερεὺς ὢν Διός.　　　　　1175
Χρ.　ἡ δ' αἰτία τίς ἐστιν, ὦ πρὸς τῶν θεῶν;
Ιε.　θύειν ἔτ' οὐδεὶς ἀξιοῖ.
Χρ.　　　　　　　τίνος οὕνεκα;
Ιε.　ὅτι πάντες εἰσὶ πλούσιοι· καίτοι τότε,
　　ὅτ' εἶχον οὐδέν, ὁ μὲν ἂν ἥκων ἔμπορος
　　ἔθυσεν ἱερεῖόν τι σωθείς, ὁ δέ τις ἂν　　　　　　1180
　　δίκην ἀποφυγών, ὁ δ' ἂν ἐκαλλιερεῖτό τις
　　κἀμέ γ' ἐκάλει τὸν ἱερέα. νῦν δ' οὐδὲ εἷς
　　θύει τὸ παράπαν οὐδὲν οὐδ' εἰσέρχεται,
　　πλὴν ἀποπατησόμενοί γε πλεῖν ἢ μύριοι.
Χρ.　οὔκουν τὰ νομιζόμενα σὺ τούτων λαμβάνεις;　　1185
Ιε.　τὸν οὖν Δία τὸν σωτῆρα καὐτός μοι δοκῶ
　　χαίρειν ἐάσας ἐνθάδ' αὐτοῦ καταμένειν.
Χρ.　θάρρει· καλῶς ἔσται γάρ, ἢν θεὸς θέλῃ.
　　ὁ Ζεὺς ὁ σωτὴρ γὰρ πάρεστιν ἐνθάδε,
　　αὐτόματος ἥκων.
Ιε.　　　　　πάντ' ἀγαθὰ τοίνυν λέγεις.　　　1190
Χρ.　ἱδρυσόμεθ' οὖν αὐτίκα μάλ'– ἀλλὰ περίμενε –
　　τὸν Πλοῦτον, οὗπερ πρότερον ἦν ἱδρυμένος
　　τὸν ὀπισθόδομον ἀεὶ φυλάττων τῆς θεοῦ.
　　ἀλλ' ἐκδότω τις δεῦρο δᾷδας ἡμμένας,
　　ἵν' ἔχων προηγῇ δεῦρο τῷ θεῷ σύ.
Ιε.　　　　　　　πάνυ μὲν οὖν　　　1195
　　δρᾶν ταῦτα χρή.
Χρ.　　　　τὸν Πλοῦτον ἔξω τις κάλει.
Γρ.　ἐγὼ δὲ τί ποιῶ;

1173 θεὸς Elmsley: Πλοῦτος codd.

[*They both go inside. Enter, left, the Priest of Zeus the Saviour.*]

PRIEST [*to the chorus*]:   Can anyone tell me exactly where Chremylus is?

[*Before he has finished speaking, Chremylus comes out of the house.*]

CHREMYLUS: What's your problem, my good sir?

PRIEST: A very bad one, that's what! Since this god began to see
175 again, I've found myself starving to death! I've nothing to eat, and that when I'm the priest of Zeus the Saviour.

CHREMYLUS: And what's the reason, in the gods' name?

PRIEST: No one chooses to make sacrifices any more.

CHREMYLUS: Why not?

PRIEST: Because they're all rich! Now in the old days, when they
180 had nothing, a merchant might sacrifice a victim when he'd come safe home, another man when he'd successfully defended a lawsuit, another might be seeking favourable omens for a journey and would also invite me, the priest. But *now* no one sacrifices anything at all; they don't even come into the sanctuary − except that there's thousands on thousands who come in to have a crap!

185 CHREMYLUS: Well then, you get your customary portions of *their* offerings, don't you?

PRIEST [*a little hesitantly*]: Well, anyway, I also think I want to say farewell to Zeus the Saviour and stay right here with you.

CHREMYLUS: Don't worry. It'll all be fine, god willing; because
190 Zeus the Saviour has come of his own accord and is with us here.

PRIEST: Then there's no problem.

CHREMYLUS: So we're going to install Wealth right away−− [*The Priest rushes towards the house.*] Wait a moment! [*The Priest comes back.*] In the place where he used to reside before, ever watching over the inner chamber of the Goddess. [*Calling into the house*] Someone bring out
195 lighted torches! − [*to the Priest*] so that you can hold one and lead the god in the procession.

PRIEST: Certainly that's what we should do. [*Carion brings out two torches, giving one to Chremylus and the other to the Priest.*]

CHREMYLUS: Call Wealth out, someone!

[*Carion puts his head in at the door, and a moment later Wealth comes out, followed immediately by the Old Woman and two slaves carrying pots of boiled vegetables.*]

OLD WOMAN [*to Chremylus*]: And what am I supposed to do?

Χρ.   τὰς χύτρας, αἷς τὸν θεὸν
ἱδρυσόμεθα, λαβοῦσ' ἐπὶ τῆς κεφαλῆς φέρε
σεμνῶς· ἔχουσα δ' ἦλθες αὐτὴ ποικίλα.
Γρ.   ὧν δ' οὕνεκ' ἦλθον;
Χρ.   πάντα σοι πεπράξεται·   1200
ἥξει γὰρ ὁ νεανίσκος ὥς σ' εἰς ἑσπέραν.
Γρ. ἀλλ' εἴ γε μέντοι νὴ Δί' ἐγγυᾷ σύ μοι
ἥξειν ἐκεῖνον ὡς ἔμ', οἴσω τὰς χύτρας.
Χρ. καὶ μὴν πολὺ τῶν ἄλλων χυτρῶν τἀναντία
αὗται ποιοῦσι· ταῖς μὲν ἄλλαις γὰρ χύτραις   1205
ἡ γραῦς ἔπεστ' ἀνωτάτω, ταύτης δὲ νῦν
τῆς γραὸς ἐπιπολῆς ἔπεισιν αἱ χύτραι.
Χο. οὐκέτι τοίνυν εἰκὸς μέλλειν οὐδ' ἡμᾶς, ἀλλ' ἀναχωρεῖν
εἰς τοὔπισθεν· δεῖ γὰρ κατόπιν τούτων ᾄδοντας ἔπεσθαι.

1205 μὲν ἄλλαις γὰρ n': μὲν ἄλλαις γε V: μὲν γὰρ ἄλλαις Rn': γὰρ ἄλλαις μὲν
n'.

CHREMYLUS: Take the pots, which are going to be the god's installation-offering, and carry them on your head in the proper dignified fashion; you've come richly dressed anyway.

OLD WOMAN: But what about what I came *for*?

CHREMYLUS: It'll all be seen to for you. The young man will come to you tonight.

OLD WOMAN: Well, yes, all right, *if* you *pledge* to me that he *will* come to me, then I'll carry the pots. [*Chremylus gives her his right hand to confirm the promise; whereupon the Old Woman takes the pots on her head, supporting one with each hand.*]

CHREMYLUS [*to the audience*]: Look how these pots are completely the opposite of all other pots! In all other boiled pots there's a wrinkly skin on the top, but *this* time the pots are on top and the wrinkly skin is underneath!

CHORUS-LEADER: Well, we shouldn't be waiting any longer either, but move back a bit, because we ought to follow behind them, singing.

[*The chorus retire a little way to the right, so as to be out of the way of the procession; then, as it moves off, left, led by the Priest, they form up again behind it, and depart, singing.*]

Commentary

1 **CARION:** the slave's name will not be known to the audience until line 624; it indicates that he is a native of Caria in south-western Asia Minor. "Carian" and "slave" were sometimes treated as virtually synonymous (cf. *Birds* 764, Cratinus fr. 18, Pl. *Laches* 187b), and in the records of property confiscated from those convicted of sacrilege in 415 (*IG* i³ 421-430) "Carian", a

long with "Thracian", is the most frequent ethnic designation for male slaves. The name of one of these slaves (*IG* i³ 427.8) is given as Carion; in the second half of the fourth century (*IG* ii² 1672.59, 67; 1673.22) several men of this name, presumably freedmen, are found as contractors supplying labour and materials for building projects. In comedy, correspondingly, the name was borne both by slaves (cf. Aeschines 2.157) and, later, by cooks (e.g. Euphron fr. 9, Men. *Epitr.*); a fourth-century comedy by Eubulus bore the name *Sphingokariōn* "Carion as the Sphinx".

6-7 **won't let a man be in charge of his own body:** lit. "doesn't let the [sc. body's] owner [*kūrios*] control the body". Since *kūrios* can mean "master of a slave" (e.g. Ant. 2.4.7), the expression is paradoxical and implies a principled critique of slavery as an institution, along the lines that the right and proper person (another meaning of *kūrios*) to control a man's body is the man himself whereas slavery gives that control to another. The earliest explicit evidence for such a critique comes from the 370s or 360s (Alcidamas ap. schol. Arist. *Rhet.* 1373b18: "God has set all free; nature has made no one a slave"; cf. Arist. *Pol.* 1253b20-22); but our passage indicates that someone, probably a sophist, had advanced similar arguments before 388. See E. Lévy in *Actes du colloque 1972 sur l'esclavage = Annales littéraires de l'Univ. de Besançon* 163 (Paris, 1974) 44-45. Carion is fairly consistently characterized as a man born and brought up in freedom (cf. 147-8) who has never fully adjusted to the constraints of a slave's life, and who frequently addresses free men, including his own master, almost as if he were their equal (e.g. 18-25, 45-47, 56-60, 253-309, 872-6).

8 **Loxias:** a mainly poetic name for Apollo, especially though not exclusively in his role as giver of oracles.

9 **"who chants his oracles from his golden tripod":** the language is tragic, but the source is unknown (indeed it is not clear whether the line is quotation or pastiche). The "golden tripod" is the seat in the inner chamber of the temple at Delphi where the Pythia sat when she delivered Apollo's responses (cf. Aesch. *Eum.* 18, 29; Eur. *Ion* 91-93, *IT* 1252-7); it appears e.g. on a fourth-century Paestan bell-krater showing Orestes as a suppliant at Delphi (London BM 1917.12-10.1; see J.R. Green and E.W. Handley, *Images of the Greek Theatre* [London, 1995], frontispiece and pl.24).

10 **I blame, with every right, and for this reason:** lit. "I blame with this just(ified) blaming".

11 **expert healer and prophet:** these two traditional functions of Apollo (for which cf. Lucian, *Dialogues of the Gods* 3.1, 18.1, and contrast the words of the god Death in *trag. adesp.* 405) are blended at Aesch. *Eum.* 62 into the single word *iātromantis* "healer-seer". The epithet *sophos* "expert, wise" is also traditionally associated with Apollo, and sometimes used, as here, to point up criticism of actions or utterances by Apollo that strike the speaker as very *un*wise (e.g. Eur. *Andr.* 1165, *El.* 971-2, 1246, 1302).

12 **insane:** Greek *melankholōn* , lit. "suffering from black bile". Contemporary medical theory seems to have recognized a specific syndrome of bodily and mental disturbances which it ascribed to a morbid darkening of the bile (cf. Hippocr. *Airs* 10, *Epid.* 3.17.2); but in popular usage "black-biled" merely meant "utterly insane" (cf. 366, 903; *Birds* 14; *Eccl.* 251; Pl. *Phdr.* 268e; Dem. 48.56; Men. *Dysk.* 89). See generally H. Flashar, *Melancholie und Melancholiker in den medizinischen Theorien der Antike* (Berlin, 1966).

17 **never answering me:** on either of the two readings offered by the manuscripts, it is the blind man who is being said not to answer. Bentley's emendation (substituting a nominative case for a genitive or dative) makes the non-answerer Chremylus, and his arguments are cogent: (i) when the blind man is eventually questioned (52ff) there is not the slightest indication that this is not the first attempt that has been made to question him; (ii) immediately after the present passage (18-25) Carion importunately demands an answer, not from the blind man, but from Chremylus. The line should be understood in close connection with the words that directly precede it: Carion resents being treated like a mindless automaton (cf. on 6-7) and thinks he has the right to know why his master is behaving so oddly.

17 **a grunt:** Greek *grū*, the orthographic representation of a non-verbal vocalization, possibly comparable to that represented in English as *grr*: for the use of the vowel *u* in writing to help represent vowelless noises cf. 895 (*hū* = a sniff), *Knights* 10 (*mū* = humming). *Grū* is found not only in comedy (e.g. Men. fr. 412) but even in lawcourt oratory (Dem. 19.39).

21 **when I've got a garland on:** those who consulted the Delphic oracle wore garlands of Apollo's laurel (cf. Livy 23.11.5), and if the response was favourable they would travel home still wearing it (cf. Soph. *OT* 82-83), since to wear a garland was also a sign that the wearer brought good news (cf. Aesch. *Ag.* 493-4, Soph. *Trach.* 178, Chaeremon fr. 6). One who wore a sacred garland was himself in a measure sacred (cf. Aeschines 1.19), and it was impious to strike him (cf. Dem. 21.33); see R. Parker, *Miasma* (Oxford, 1983) 153.

22 **CHREMYLUS:** this character is first named in the text at 336. The name, from a root meaning "to clear one's throat", is a variant of "Chremes", a name often given to old men in comedy (e.g. Antiphanes fr. 189.22; Terence, *Andria* 166; Hor. *AP* 94; Alciphron 4.2.5) which Ar. had used in *Ecclesiazusae* (477); similarly the only other named Athenian in our play, Blepsidemus, bears a name reminiscent of another character in *Eccl.*, Blepyrus. No actual Athenian named Chremylus is known, but the name is found in the fifth and fourth centuries on the nearby island of Euboea (*IG* xii[9] 56.437-8 and 245B.174).

23 **Phooey!:** Greek *lēros* "nonsense".

26-27 **the most faithful and thievish of all my servants:** the superlatives show that, poor though he claims to be, Chremylus owns at least three slaves. The comically wry insertion of "thieving" insinuates (correctly, cf. 317-321) that Carion takes advantage of the trust in which he is held to commit petty thefts (mainly no doubt of food and drink); comedy regularly assumes that slaves can be expected to steal (cf. *Ach.* 272-3, *Knights* 95ff, *Wasps* 449, *Peace* 14).

29 **I can assure you** represents the Greek particle *toi*, which draws the addressee's special attention to what is being said and therefore suggests that Carion is "hinting at something" (so the scholia): probably his implied point is that he has had good reason to know that his master is poor because *his own* conditions of life have been so bad.

30 **crooked politicians:** lit. "temple-robbing politicians"; *hierosūlos* "temple-robber" became in the course of the fourth century a generalized term of abuse which could be

applied to any person (Men. *Dysk.* 640; *Epitr.* 952, 1064, 1100; *Perik.* 366) or even object (Eubulus fr. 6.4) that the speaker disliked; this development seems to have begun by 399 when a client of Lysias (30.21) calls his opponent a *hierosūlos* in the course of arguing that by ordaining new sacrifices he has caused traditional ones to be omitted for lack of funds – a serious religious offence, no doubt, if true, but hardly qualifying as the crime of *hierosūliā* which ranked equal with treason and for which the penalty was death with prohibition of burial in Attica (Xen. *Hell.* 1.7.22). Most editors have treated these words as denoting two separate classes of malefactors, viz. temple-robbers and politicians (on the standard comic assumption that all or virtually all politicians are criminals); but it is more likely that they form a single phrase referring to a single group, since (i) whereas the sequence "crooked politicians *and* informers *and* other villains" is a normal form of enumeration in Greek, the sequence "temple-robbers, politicians, *and* informers *and* other villains", with conjunctions between the second, third and fourth items but none between the first two, is not, and (ii) among the many colourful accusations of criminality in which Old Comedy abounds, that of temple-robbery is elsewhere conspicuous by its absence.

31   **informers:** Greek *sūkophantai* "improperly motivated prosecutors" such as the man who appears in 850-957. The enforcement of many Athenian laws, particularly those regarding crimes committed against the state rather than against individual victims, depended on the willingness of private citizens to initiate prosecutions under laws which permitted "whoever wishes" (*ho boulomenos*, cf. on 908) to do so. Such a volunteer prosecutor would normally claim to be acting out of concern for the public good (cf. on 910 and 914) and/or because he or his family had themselves been wronged by the accused on other occasions (e.g. [Dem.] 58.1-2, 59.1-14, Aeschines 1.1-2); the defendant, contrariwise, would assert that the prosecutor was a *sūkophantēs* actuated by desire for material gain (by receiving a share of property taken in fines or confiscations, or by inducing a defendant to bribe him to withdraw the charge) and/or by an unhealthy delight in meddling in other people's business (cf. 910, 913, 931). R.G. Osborne and F.D. Harvey, in P.A. Cartledge et al. *Nomos* (Cambridge, 1990) 83-102 and 103-121 respectively, present contrasting assessments of the role and perception of the *sūkophantēs* in Athenian democracy (see also now M.R. Christ, *The Litigious Athenian* [Baltimore, 1998]); it is at any rate certain that the *word* is always a term of abuse, and no Athenian would ever speak of himself as a *sūkophantēs* – though a character in *Birds* (1423, 1452) calls himself one (cf. perhaps Ar. fr. 228), by the same comic technique whereby characters representing Cleon in *Knights* and *Wasps* speak of themselves as thieves (e.g. *Knights* 296, *Wasps* 928).

33-34   **had pretty well shot its bolt:** lit. "had almost been shot empty of arrows", life being imaged as a quiver. There may be an implicit pun on *bíos* "life" and the poetic word *biós* "bow"; cf. Soph. *Phil.* 931-3 "By taking my bow (*toxa*) you have robbed me of my life (*bíos*). ... Don't take my life away from me!", Heracleitus fr. 48 D-K, and see D.B. Robinson, *CQ* 19 (1969) 43-44.

35   **my son:** mentioned again only at 250-1. As in *Birds*, the hero has an inspiration (here, that of having Wealth healed) which superseded his original concerns and plans, and the son as an individual becomes dramatically irrelevant; note the contrast between 249-250 ("I want you to meet my wife and *my only son*") and 1103-4 ("call out your master, then his wife and *his children*").

39   **what did Phoebus cry forth from among his sacred fillets?:** again (cf. 9) this is tragic quotation or pastiche, as the poetic verb *elaken* "cried forth" indicates; this verb is frequently used in tragedy in relation to oracular and prophetic utterances (e.g. Eur. *IT* 976, *Or.* 162, 329; Soph. *Trach.* 824, *Ant.* 1094). The "sacred fillets" (*stemmata*) are

bands of wool, hung on various sacred objects in the oracular chamber (*adyton*), which Aesch. *Eum.* 39 (cf. also Eur. *Ion* 1309-10) therefore calls the "many-filleted inner shrine" (*polystephēs mykhos*): on fourth-century Italian vase-paintings showing Orestes at Delphi (e.g. *LIMC* s.v. Orestes 23 = Leto 70; Erinys 46, 51, 64) they festoon now the navel-stone (*omphalos*), now the sacred laurel-tree.   On the meaning of *stemma* (wrongly glossed "wreath, garland, chaplet" in LSJ) see J. Servais, *AC* 36 (1967) 415-453.

41-43 For this response cf. Eur. *Ion* 534-6 where Apollo tells Xuthus (falsely) that the first person he meets on coming out of the temple will prove to be his son; also *Epigonoi* fr. 3 Davies (Manto to marry the first man she meets); Arist. fr. 504 Rose (Cephalus to have intercourse with the first female he meets – which turns out to be a female bear, and becomes the great-grandmother of Odysseus); *Inscr.Magn.* 17.36-41 ("the first man you meet on leaving my temple will guide you to a mainland territory rich in wheat").

44 **who *was* the first person you met?:** we may think that the answer is obvious (to the audience as well as Carion), but this is a "marking-time" question giving Carion a breathing space to recover from his amazement.

45-46 **... the god's meaning? You were being told ...:** lit. "the god's meaning, which was telling you ...".

46 **you stupid fool:** the only other slave in Ar. who uses so disrespectful a form of address in speaking to his owner is Dionysus' slave Xanthias in *Frogs* (480, 486) – and then only after his master has collapsed in terror; but cf. Men. *Sam.* 69 where the slave Parmenon calls his young master Moschion "girlie" (*androgyne*) for not having the courage to face the consequences of his action in getting Plangon pregnant.

47 **in the way that's regular in these parts:** i.e. as a criminal – very likely spoken with a glance round the audience. For such generalized abuse of the Athenian public (effective and safe because each individual spectator assumes that it does not apply to *him*) cf. *Clouds* 1096-9, *Thesm.*814-829, *Frogs* 274-6, 783, 807-8, *Eccl.* 436-440.

48-50 The "logic" of this very far-fetched interpretation is: Apollo told you to follow a blind man; but (even) a blind man can perceive that it pays to be a criminal; therefore you should follow his perception and make your son a criminal. Cf. *Knights* 1067-77 where an oracle warning Athenians to "beware of the fox-dog" is interpreted by the Sausage-seller to mean "don't support Paphlagon-Cleon's proposals to send out squadrons of warships with troops to collect revenue" (dog = warship, because both move fast; fox = soldier, because soldiers steal food from enemy farms).

50 **in the present state of the world:** lit. "in the present race (*genos*)", i.e. in this last and worst of the five Hesiodic ages of the world with their five different human races (gold, silver, bronze, heroic, iron: *Works and Days* 109-201), the fifth of which is developing towards a state in which "there will be no gratitude for a man who keeps his oath [cf. 61 below] or for a good or honest man, but rather they will honour a man who does outrageous evil; the only justice will be violence, and there will be no shame" (*ibid.* 190-3). Cf. Critias fr. trag. 21 "there is no justice in the present *genos*", Men. *Thph.*F 1.14-15 "If a man is good, well-born, really noble, it's no help to him in the present *genos*". The true reading *genei* (dative case of *genos*) is preserved only as a marginal variant in V; it seems to have been early corrupted into the nonsensical *etei* "year" (V in text), of which *khronōi* "time" (most mss., and a fifth-century papyrus) and *biōi* "life" (R) are attempted corrections. R's reading (for which cf. Men. *Kolax* 1) gives good sense, but does not help to explain how the other readings arose.

53-54 **why he's come here with us:** in fact, of course, *they* have come here with (or after) *him*; but the fact of which Chremylus desires an explanation is that this blind man has led him and Carion *to their own home*. It is odd, though, that while Chremylus and

Carion of course know that they are now in front of their home, the audience, to judge from the script so far, do not – and Chremylus' words here, even if accompanied by gesture, would not enlighten them; the location is not even indirectly identified for the audience until 63 (assuming that the words "take the man in" there were aided by a gesture). Ar. could easily have avoided puzzling the audience here by writing *oikade* "home" instead of *enthadi* "here", but there is no evidence that he did. Either, then, he forgot that a fact known to him and his characters was not known to his audience, or he expected that in the absence of indications to the contrary they would take it for granted that when a traveller, returning from a journey abroad, stopped outside a house, the house was his home.

55   **the meaning of this oracle of ours:** or, with Bergk, "what this oracle means for us (is trying to say to us)".

57   **go on to the next stage** (lit. "do what comes after that"): i.e. use violence; cf. Xen. *Hell.* 2.3.55 "We hand over to you this man Theramenes, condemned according to law; now you, the Eleven, are to take him to the proper place and do what follows from that", i.e. put him to death.

58   **go to blazes:** lit. "say *oimoi*", i.e. "cry in pain". Wealth as yet knows nothing to these men's discredit, but like Cnemon in Menander's *Dyskolos* (718-721) he has come by experience to believe that all men are wicked and selfish (97-111, 234-245) and wants to have nothing to do with any of them.

58-59 **do you hear who he says he is?:** viz. someone who hates us.

61   **a man who keeps his sworn word:** it is not obvious from the context why Chremylus should here highlight this particular virtue; most likely the explanation is that the line is a tragic quotation (this hypothesis is supported by the poetic omission of the definite article before *tropois* "habits, character") and that the keeping of oaths was significant in its original tragic context.

63   **take the man ... the god's omen with him:** i.e. Apollo has warned you, through the man's ill-omened words, that he will bring you bad luck if you take him into your home.

64   That both men here seize hold of Wealth is shown by his words in 65 and 75; see S.D. Olson, *TAPA* 119 (1989) 194 n.7. Chremylus' sudden change from sweet reasonableness to anger and threats neatly subverts his superior, didactic attitude a moment before towards Carion.

64   **you won't be pleased you said that:** lit. "you won't rejoice any more", implying a threat as in *Knights* 235, 828, *Wasps* 186, *Thesm.* 1094, *Frogs* 843.

65   **If you're not going to answer ... your miserable existence!:** the mss. continue this whole line to Chremylus; Hemsterhuys gave it all to Carion; W.G. Rutherford, *CR* 10 (1896) 98-99, divided it as shown here. The threat to kill the blind man must come from Carion, as 67-68 shows; it perhaps comes in most effectively if, as here assumed, Carion (in his usual insubordinate manner) interrupts his master with it, possibly when Chremylus is momentarily hesitating as to how he should make more specific the vague threat of 64.

69-70 **leave him there and go away:** unlike Heracles when he killed Iphitus and Lichas (Soph. *Trach.* 270-3, 777-782), or Neoptolemus throwing Astyanax to his death from the walls of Troy (*Little Iliad* fr. 20.3-5 Davies), or the Athenian executioner when he cast criminals down to the *barathron* (see on 431), Carion would not need to push or throw his victim from the cliff and would not therefore incur blood-pollution through his death.

71   **off the ground with him:** Chremylus pretends to accept Carion's suggestion, in order to intimidate the blind man into revealing his identity.

74   we will: sc. let you go (I have added "no" in the translation to make this clear). Out of context; the Greek could be taken to mean "we will <do you an injury>", but Wealth's response shows that he understands the words as friendly, not hostile; this must have been conveyed by tone of voice (for Wealth's benefit) and by gesture (for the audience's).

74   if that's what you want: Chremylus, while promising not to detain the blind man by force, thus reserves the right to detain him by persuasion if he can.

78-79 You're the filthiest villain in the world: lit. "O most filthy/villainous (*miaros*) of all men, ...". Several times in Ar. (*Birds* 1638; *Frogs* 1160, 1472) an angry or emotionally wrought speaker is made to address a god as "man", as Carion in effect does here; in *Birds* 1638 this is done primarily to raise a laugh at the stupidity of the (divine) speaker (in a scene where the human hero thoroughly outsmarts three gods; cf. also 118 below), but in the other passages, including this one, it seems to serve mainly to highlight his emotional state.

80   In such a wretched condition?: for one would naturally expect Wealth to be rich, as one would expect War to be violent (as he is in *Peace* 236-288), Old Age to be old (see *LIMC* s.v. Geras), etc. See E. Stafford, *Worshipping Virtues: Personification and the Divine in Ancient Greece* [London/Swansea, 2000].

83   his very self: Greek *autotatos*, a comic superlative form of *autos* "(him)self"; it was probably not coined for this passage, since a comparative form, *autoteros*, is known to have been used by Epicharmus (fr. 5).

84   Patrocles: we can say nothing about this man except that he was rich (as our passage implies) and had the reputation of a miser (so the scholia, referring to Ar.'s *Storks* [fr. 455]). The scholia also say that he was a tragic poet (*PA* 11692; *LGPN* 4; *TrGF* 57), but there is no other reference to an Athenian tragic poet of this name, and they are probably confusing our man with the tragic poet Patrocles of Thurii (*TrGF* 58; cf. Clem.Alex. *Protr.* 2.30.4). We know of several men of the name in the late fifth and early fourth centuries; our man might be any or none of them.

85   he's not had a bath since the day he was born: the point may be (i) that Patrocles grudged the expense of heating water for a bath and/or (ii) that he never gave or attended parties (as a corrupt scholium seems to say, probably on the evidence of *Storks* or another comedy; for the association between bathing and parties cf. *Birds* 130-2, *Lys.* 1065-7, Pl. *Symp.* 174a).

87   out of ill-will to mankind: an idea familiar from the Prometheus-Pandora myth (Hes. *Thg.* 551-612, *Works* 42-105) but here given a twist that makes it even more discreditable to Zeus: he acts in such a way as to harm, not humanity as a whole, but *virtuous humans only.*

93-94 it's only thanks to ... gets any worship: thus Zeus is guilty of ingratitude and of violating the fundamental Greek ethical rule that one should treat well those by whom one has been well treated (cf. 1028-9, Aesch. *Eum.* 725, 868; see C. Gill et al. ed. *Reciprocity in Ancient Greece* [Oxford, 1998], especially the chapter on religion by R. Parker [105-125]).

95   if you were to regain your sight ... : here Chremylus has the inspiration on which the play's main action will be based; comparable moments in other plays include *Ach.* 128 and *Birds* 162.

99   and no wonder ... seen them either: the mss. give this to Chremylus, but its cynicism is inconsistent with his words at 110; see V. Tammaro, *Museum Criticum* 18 (1983) 133-4.

111   you'll really catch it for that!: lit. "you'll howl long", sc. for implicitly including Carion himself in his denunciation of the whole human race.

112 **what ... good it'll do you to stay with us:** this is the first time Chremylus has actually asked Wealth to take up residence in his house. This will, of course, make Chremylus wealthy, but nothing is said of this, even indirectly, until 226.

114 **and, asking god's blessing, I'll say it:** lit. "and, with god, it will be said": the phrase "with god" (*xyn theōi*) was often added to an assertion that might otherwise seem overbold, as a precaution against incurring divine resentment. Cf. Eur. *Med.* 625 (verbally identical with our passage); Pl. *Prot.* 317b, *Theaet.* 151b.

115 **release you from this affliction that has you in its grip:** the mss. have a quite different wording ("free you from this eye-disease"), on which the scholia comment: "He uses *ophthalmiā* 'eye-disease' peculiarly to mean blindness of the eyes; for which reason it has been rewritten in the second <version of the play to read> 'release you from this affliction ...'". Here as in several other places (see Introduction §8) the scholia are derived from a commentary whose author (i) thought that the text in front of him was Ar.'s earlier *Wealth* of 408, and (ii) also possessed another version of the text, differing (so far as we can tell) only in detail, which he took to be that of the play produced in 388. In fact he was probably dealing with copies derived, respectively, from the 388 script before and after it had undergone some minor revisions, and there is no reason to disagree with his diagnosis that 115 was revised in order to get rid of the abnormal use of the word *ophthalmiā*. The new version of the line is still not very inspired stylistically, but the same is true of much else in the play, and at least it gives a correct sense; since Ar. is known to have made much more far-reaching revisions to *Clouds* after its first production, and seems to have made smaller but not insignificant changes to *Frogs* as well (see my notes on *Frogs* 1251-60, 1431a-b, 1435-66, and 1512), the balance of probability is that he was responsible for this modification too, and I have accordingly incorporated it in the text.

118 **This man's a real born saddo!:** unlike Carion's remarks at 99, 106 and 111, this is not an aside, since Wealth's next words are spoken in response to it (note *men oun* "no", "on the contrary"). As at 78-79, Carion forgets that he is speaking about a god; Wealth's abject acquiescence in his own suffering and humiliation makes this hardly surprising. I have used the current slang term "saddo" (= a pitiful, passive wretch devoid of self-respect) to render Greek *āthlios*, which usually means no more than "miserable, ill-starred" but here seems to denote a person who is perversely *content* to live in misery: cf. Dem. 21.191 "I would certainly be *āthlios* if, after what I have suffered and am suffering, I neglected to prepare properly for my speech before you".

119-120 **I know for sure ... isn't he doing that anyway:** the transmitted text can be construed (just) as meaning "Zeus, knowing the follies of these men, would utterly crush me if he found out" with Chremylus replying "Isn't he doing that anyway ...?"; but (i) its word-order is bizarre even by the standards of this play, (ii) "knowing" and "if he found out" overlap, and (iii) if Zeus crushes Wealth, it will not be for "the follies of *these men*" (Chremylus and Carion) but for *Wealth's own* defiance of his authority in agreeing to cooperate with them. I therefore adopt Badham's brilliant emendation, which is based on the assumption that two blocks of letters in successive lines (αυεπιτριψει and τουτωμμωρ) have accidentally changed places. The corruption probably originated in a misunderstood authorial correction, for the scholia report that this line too (cf. on 115) "has been rewritten in the second <version>".

123 **the most cowardly divinity in the world:** cf. on 202-3.

124 **sovereignty:** Greek *turannis*. In prose, and in comedy when referring to the rulers of human communities, this was by now always a pejorative term; in tragedy, however, *turannos* and *turannis* often merely meant "monarch" and "monarchy" without any evaluative overtones. When speaking of the rulership of the supreme god, there seems

to have been some tendency to use these words in contexts relating, as here, to the possible overthrow of Zeus: cf. *Birds* 1605, 1643, [Aesch.] *Prom.* 756, 909, 996, and possibly Cratinus fr. 171.22.

130-197 In this demonstration that virtually everything done in the world is done "because of" (*dia*) Wealth, Chremylus and Carion alternate freely and unsystematically between two quite different senses in which wealth can be said to be a cause of actions or situations: as a *prerequisite* (of Zeus' power or that of the Great King, of being able to offer sacrifices, of Agyrrhius' immunity from prosecution, etc.) and as an *object* (of prayer, of labour, etc.). Sometimes wealth is *both* prerequisite *and* object, as in the case of the goldsmith (164) who needs wealth to acquire his raw material and then, like other craftsmen, works on it in order to acquire more wealth; sometimes in a two-sided transaction it is a prerequisite for one party and an object for the other, as in mercenary sexual relationships (149-159, 179) or in the case of warships (172), *for* manning which the state *needs* money, and *by* manning which the oarsmen *earn* money. Since the aim of the demonstration is to show Wealth that he is more powerful than Zeus, the insistent repetition of *dia* may well be designed to recall Hesiod's assertion (*Works* 3) that men are famous or obscure because of (*dia*) Zeus (accusative case *Dia*); similarly the chorus of Aeschylus' *Agamemnon* (1482-8) reflected that the disasters afflicting the house of Atreus must have come "because of Zeus (*diai Dios*) the cause of all, the doer of all".

131 **he's the one who's got most of it:** no evidence is provided for this statement, and none is taken to be needed; it is simply assumed, as the scholia see, that since on earth a monarch is always the richest man in his kingdom, the same must be true in heaven. Similarly later (580-592), when Poverty argues that Zeus is in fact *poor*, Chremylus can only show that the evidence she brings does not prove him to be poor; he does not offer any positive evidence that Zeus is rich.

132 *he* **does:** for this statement, too, no evidence is offered – because it is true by definition.

134 **they pray ... to become rich:** the reference will be primarily, but need not be exclusively, to prayers accompanying sacrifices. At the end of *Peace* (1320-8), the peasants returning to the countryside pray (i) for wealth, (ii) for ample food crops, (iii) for offspring, and (iv) for no more war; wealth similarly holds a prominent place among the petitions addressed to Apollo by Clytaemestra in Soph. *El.* 648-654.

138 **a ground-cake:** Greek *psaiston*, a cake made from wheat or barley meal soaked in honey and oil (cf. *Anecd. Bachm.* 419.24, *Anecd.Bekk.* i 317.26-27). It was almost the cheapest possible sacrifice (cf. Antiphanes fr. 204.3, *com.adesp.* 820), as an ox was the most expensive.

147 **because of a petty little sum of money:** i.e., probably, for a small debt. Carion treats wealth and money as synonymous (cf. 131, 194-7); hence to be enslaved because of a sum of money is to be enslaved because of wealth/Wealth. Debt-slavery and debt-bondage had famously been abolished at Athens by Solon, at least for citizens (Arist. *Ath.Pol.* 6.1, 9.1), but they were common elsewhere (cf. D.S. 1.79.5): Lysias (12.98) claimed that had the Thirty not been overthrown in 403, the children of exiled Athenian democrats abroad "would have become slaves on account of small debts", and the Plataean speaker of Isocrates 14 (§48) says that the same fate had actually befallen the children of his fellow-citizens after the destruction of their city in 373. Since in both cases it is *children* who are assumed to be particularly liable to fall into slavery in this way, it is perhaps likely that this was the most common situation, a man pledging his children (rather than himself) as security for a loan when he had nothing else to pledge (cf. the Megarian in *Ach.* 729-835, who sells his children in exchange for food). We know, however, that at Gortyn in Crete it was common for a man to pledge himself for a debt (see R.F. Willetts, *The Law Code of Gortyn* [Berlin, 1967] 14; cf. the Code at col. X 25-29, and *IC* iv 41 V-VI), as it had apparently been at Athens before Solon (Arist. *Ath.Pol.* 2.2 "both they [the debtors] and their children could be seized"); so we cannot tell whether Carion is to be imagined as having become a slave in childhood for his father's debts, or in adulthood for his own.

148   having previously been free: this reading is preserved in the margin of R, having been ousted in the text of all the mss. (including R itself) by the feeble phrase "perhaps because of not being rich", in origin an (erroneous) annotation on 147 which was later mistaken for a textual variant.

149   the courtesans in Corinth: Corinth was the capital of commercial sex in mainland Greece, and home to more famous and expensive courtesans than any other city; "Corinthian girls" (such as Nais, cf. 179) were as much a byword for luxury as "Syracusan tables" (Pl. *Rep.* 404d), and a proverb doubtfully ascribed to Ar. (fr. dub. 928) said that "not every man can afford to travel to Corinth". When the Corinthian slave-courtesan Neaera was given her freedom on condition that she did not practise her trade in Corinth, she found it impossible to earn elsewhere an income sufficient to maintain her accustomed lifestyle ([Dem.] 59.32, 36). Cf. also Ar. fr. 370 (for a verb *korinthiazesthai* "to be a prostitute" or "to be a pimp"), Strattis fr. 27, Anaxandrides fr. 9, Eriphus fr. 6, Eubulus fr. 53, Alexis fr. 255, Strabo 8.6.20, and see J.B. Salmon, *Wealthy Corinth* (Oxford, 1984) 398-400.

152   they turn their backside at him: sc. for intercourse *a tergo* (the position called "standing on all fours" in *Peace* 896a and "lioness on a cheese-grater" in *Lys.* 231; cf. also *Thesm.* 489). In late archaic and early classical art this position for heterosexual penetration is shown more often than any other (see M.F. Kilmer, *Greek Erotica on Attic Red-figure Vases 520-460 BC* 33-43), but some of these images suggest that even women who were professional sex-workers could be imagined as requiring at least a show of force before they would submit to this form of penetration (see Kilmer in E.M. Craik ed. *"Owls to Athens": Essays on Classical Subjects for Sir Kenneth Dover* [Oxford, 1990] 270-2), and a high-class courtesan might regard it as an insult even to be asked to do so (cf. Machon 327-332 Gow) – but it could be another matter if the reward was big enough (cf. Machon 226-230 Gow).

153   do the same thing: i.e. submit to anal penetration – which, though freely talked about in comedy (e.g. *Ach.* 716, *Knights* 874-7, *Clouds* 1084-1104, *Wasps* 1070, *Peace* 11-12, *Thesm.* 59-62, 200, 1124), was considered so degrading to a male that it was only rarely depicted in homoerotic vase paintings, and never when the participants were of widely different ages (see K.J. Dover, *Greek Homosexuality* [London, 1978] 99; Kilmer, *Greek Erotica* 22-25).

155   the young *gentlemen* ... the young*professionals*: lit. "the virtuous ... the male whores (*pornoi*)". The distinction made briefly here is more fully expounded by Aeschines (1.137) when prosecuting Timarchus for taking part in politics when disqualified for having once been a male prostitute: defending himself from a possible charge of hypocrisy in that he was himself notoriously an assiduous pursuer of handsome young males, he argues that "to be loved without corruption is honourable, but to be induced by payment to prostitute oneself (*peporneusthai*) is disgraceful". Socrates is made to take a very similar line in Xen. *Mem.* 1.6.13. In practice the distinction was inevitably blurred: it may have been the act of a *pornos* to *demand* money from a lover as the price of submission, but, as some vase-paintings show, a respectable youth might sometimes *accept* a money present (see G. Koch-Harnack, *Knabenliebe und Tiergeschenke* [Berlin, 1983] 161-4); normally, though, when love-gifts to youths are shown in art they are presents in kind, especially animals and birds (cf. *Birds* 705-7; see Dover *op.cit.* 92).

157   **a top-class horse ... some hunting dogs:** extremely expensive presents: in *Clouds* 21-23 and 1224-5 a horse for racing costs 1200 drachmas (cf. Lys. 8.10, Xen. *Anab.* 7.8.6), a sum which could buy (for example) seven or eight adult slaves (cf. *IG* i³ 421.34-49). Chremylus does not mean that such lavish gifts are *typically* demanded (in art the biggest gift normally depicted is a single dog), but that a youth *could* demand them without ceasing to be considered "virtuous".

159   **by a verbal trick:** lit. "by a name".

160-8   Most mss. give the whole of this passage to Chremylus; but the alternation, in its middle section, between recognized crafts and activities which are criminal (165) or require no skill (166b, 167b) makes it likely that the latter are introduced by Carion, who certainly takes an active part in the preceding and following passages.

162   **one of them:** V has "one of us"; both readings make sense, but *n*'s is slightly preferable because it makes Chremylus draw an implicit distinction between practitioners of specialized crafts (*tekhnai*) and peasants like himself (cf. 223 "my *fellow*-peasants"), a distinction that is strongly emphasized at 617-8 where the supreme joy that wealth brings is that of being able to "fart in the face of the craftsmen". Fourth-century lawcourt orators regularly assume that the juries they address consist preponderantly of peasants, or at least of men with a peasant's view of society (cf. S.C. Todd, *JHS* 110 [1990] 158-169), and almost throughout Old Comedy the normal pattern is that characters with whom the audience are expected to sympathize are country dwellers, and vice versa (so too sometimes in tragedy: contrast the peasant orator in Eur. *Or.* 917-930, who "rarely darkened the town or the Agora with his presence" and whose speech "seemed good to the virtuous", with the "man-about-town, expert in speech" of Eur. *Ba.* 717-721 who disastrously encourages the impressionable herdsmen to attack the maenads on Mount Cithaeron).

162   **sits indoors:** "indoors" is not explicit in the Greek, but it is clearly implied: not all the occupations to be named are sedentary, but all those mentioned by Chremylus are indoor. This was one of the reasons why peasants (who had to labour in the sun) despised craftsmen – and especially shoemakers, whose faces were proverbially so pale (cf. schol. *Peace* 1310) that (at least in comedy) they could be confused with women (*Eccl.* 385-7, 432).

165   **a footpad:** Greek *lōpodutēs* means strictly "one who robs people of their clothes" either by attacking them in the street or on a journey, or by taking away clothes which the victim had laid aside in order to bathe or exercise.

166   **washes fleeces:** the first stage in the preparation of wool (cf. *Lys.* 574-5), and a particularly menial activity because it involved removing the dung clinging to the fleece (*ibid.*); it is antithetical to the work of the fuller, a relatively respectable tradesman but also one who cleans wool (after it has been made into garments).

167   **sells onions:** is there again (cf. previous note) an association of ideas here, inasmuch as both the tanner and the onion-seller work among strong smells (cf. *Knights* 891-3)?

168   **when an adulterer ... a token plucking:** a man who caught a seducer *in flagrante delicto* with his wife (or sister, daughter, etc.) could deal with him in various ways: (i) kill him out of hand, as the speaker of Lysias 1 did; (ii) imprison him until he was ransomed (cf. [Dem.] 59.41, 64-66); (iii) prosecute him in the courts (Arist. *Ath.Pol* 59.3, Hyp. *For Lycophron* 10); (iv) subject him to whatever bodily degradation he wished (cf. Lys. 1.49, Xen. *Mem.* 2.1.5) – those traditionally used included thrusting a large-rooted radish up his anus (*Clouds* 1083-4; Lucian, *On the Death of Peregrinus* 9) and sprinkling his pubic area with hot ash to facilitate the (extremely painful) plucking of its hair (*Clouds* loc.cit., cf. *Thesm.* 537-543; see J.F. Gannon, *Thesmophoriazusae Restitutae* [Diss. Yale 1982] 267-272). The scepticism of D. Cohen, *Zeitschrift der Savigny-Stiftung* 102 (1985) 385-7, and of J. Roy, *LCM* 16 (1991) 73-76, as to whether alternative (iv) had any existence outside comedy, has been refuted by C. Carey, *LCM* 18 (1993) 53-55. But what precisely does it mean to say that because of Wealth the captured adulterer *paratilletai* (lit. "is plucked")?

   (a) It could mean that he is plucked (and, by implication, suffers the other penalties detailed under (iv) above) because he *lacks* the wealth which would have bought him safety: this is one of two interpretations offered in the scholia, the other being (c) below. But in this quick-fire dialogue (162-180) "because of you (Wealth)" always elsewhere means either "with the motive of acquiring wealth" (162-7, 177) or "by reason of possessing sufficient wealth" (170, 176) or is ambivalent between the two (see on 130-197), and in the very short time available a hearer might well fail to understand the phrase here in the sense "by reason of *not* possessing sufficient wealth".

   (b) It could mean (so Rogers) that if the adulterer is rich, he is plucked (and otherwise maltreated) *rather than being killed*; but it is hardly a very impressive demonstration of the power of Wealth (as Wealth himself apparently takes it to be, cf. 169) that an adulterer can use it to escape with his life at the cost of being subjected to humiliations, deliberately designed to assimilate him to a woman (cf. Dover *op.cit.* 106), which could not even be kept secret in a society where public male nudity (at the gymnasium and the baths) was the norm, and which would therefore disgrace him before the whole community.

   (c) A widely accepted interpretation (van Leeuwen, van Daele, Halliwell) is that the focus is less on the adulterer than on the master of the house, who plucks (and otherwise maltreats) him *in order to extract a ransom from him* (or force him to give sureties, cf. [Dem.] 59.65) on the understanding that the maltreatment will then cease. One would have thought, however, that with the adulterer completely at his captor's mercy, the mere *threat* of such maltreatment would almost always be sufficient to secure a promise of payment.

   (d) Bentley, finding no interpretation of the transmitted text satisfactory, proposed a simple emendation (ΓΟΥ for ΠΟΥ) that would give the sense "it's down to you that he *doesn't* get plucked": by paying a ransom, that is, the adulterer avoids all physical punishment. This may be right, but the transmitted text may not in fact be beyond reasonable interpretation.

   (e) The interpretation I wish to suggest begins from the fact that in passages where plucking with the aid of hot ash is mentioned (*Clouds* 1083, *Thesm.* 537-543) the verb used is *tillein*, whereas here it is *paratillein*. Now *tillein* (or, when the action is performed on oneself, *tillesthai*) means to tear out hair (or feathers) wholesale, as a distraught person may do (e.g. Priam in *Iliad* 22.78; cf. *Frogs* 424) or as one may pluck a fowl (Ephippus fr. 3.8); *paratillein* (-*esthai*) is to pluck hairs out one at a time, as one may do out of boredom (e.g. *Ach.* 31) or, usually, for cosmetic purposes (e.g. *Lys.* 89, 151, *Frogs* 516, Plato com. fr. 188.14). I suggest that it was customary, when an adulterer acknowledged his guilt and offered a ransom, for acceptance to be conditional on the token satisfaction of the wronged man's honour by the extraction by hand, presumably before witnesses, of a single pubic hair: the pain would be minimal and momentary, the shame no greater than was inevitable in any case. Alternatively, with Holzinger (who does not, however, take note of the distinction between the two verbs), one might suppose that the idea is that if verbal threats of maltreatment fail to elicit a promise of payment, the captor begins plucking out hairs by hand to show that he is in earnest and ready to proceed to severer measures if payment is not offered. The ransoms demanded in such circumstances could be very large: Epaenetus had to give sureties for 3000 drachmas before Stephanus would release him ([Dem.] 59.65), and the very rich Callias was alleged to have paid 18,000 drachmas when taken in adultery with the wife of one Phocus (Cratinus fr. 81).

170-9   Here (contrast 160-8) the mss. all have both Chremylus and Carion speaking, though they do not agree on where to place the speaker-changes. That both do speak is clear (i) from Chremylus' annoyance at 180b, which indicates that 180a is not Carion's first recent interruption, and (ii) from the way in which Wealth is sometimes addressed in the second person (172, 177, 178, 179) and sometimes spoken of in the third (170, 171, 173, 174, 176) on no apparent principle. Certainty as to the distribution of lines is impossible, but one can at least account for (ii) by assuming, with Coulon, Thiercy and Halliwell, that lines addressed to Wealth are spoken by Chremylus (cf. 160) and those that refer to him in the third person are spoken by Carion. This provides an assignment for every line except 175, which as a corrective addendum to 174 (note that it is introduced by the adversative particle *de*, not the purely additive *te* or *kai*) is best given to the character who did *not* speak 174. It need occasion no surprise that the slave Carion is knowledgeable about politics and politicians: so are Sosias and Xanthias in the prologue of *Wasps* (esp. 31-51) and another slave in Plato com. fr. 182.

170   **the Great King:** the King of Persia, whose immense wealth was proverbial, and who had largely determined the course of the Corinthian War by first providing, and later denying, financial and naval aid to Sparta's opponents.

171   **doesn't the Assembly get held because of him?:** the reference is to the fee of three obols paid to (probably) the first 6,000 citizens to arrive for each Assembly meeting (cf. 329-330); before this fee had been introduced (by Agyrrhius, cf. on 176) in the 390s it had sometimes been impossible to deal with certain Assembly business owing to the lack of a quorum (*Eccl.* 183-4, Arist. *Ath.Pol.* 41.3). Hence, if (as was the case later in the century) pay was provided for forty meetings a year (Arist. *Ath.Pol.* 62.2 with 43.4-6), the state needed to have 40 x 3 x 6,000 = 720,000 obols = 120,000 drachmas = 20 talents available for this purpose annually, if quorate Assemblies were to be regularly held.

172   **don't you get our warships manned?:** sc. by providing money to pay the crews. Even at the low rate of three obols a day (regular in the last years of the Peloponnesian War, cf. Plut. *Alc.* 35.5, Xen. *Hell.* 1.5.7-8) it cost half a talent per month per ship in pay alone to keep a fleet of triremes in the water; in the later stages of the Corinthian War, sufficient funds often were not available, and in 390 Thrasybulus' men had been paid largely by compulsory contributions from the cities at which his fleet put in (Xen. *Hell.* 4.8.30).

173   **the mercenary force at Corinth:** this force had been created by Conon when he put in at the Isthmus with the Persian fleet in 393, and put under the command of Iphicrates (Xen. *Hell.* 4.8.8, Harpocr. ξ2), who had sensationally used it to destroy a Spartan battalion (*mora*) at Lechaeum in 390 (Xen. *Hell.* 4.5). Probably in 389 (cf. *IG* ii² 21.2, 21, 22) he was succeeded in this command by Chabrias (D.S. 14.92.2, Dem. 4.24).

174   **Pamphilus** of the deme Ceiriadae (*PA* 11545, *LGPN* 52) was a politician and general. He was a cavalry commander in 395 (Lys. 15.5), and in 389 was sent to besiege Aegina (Xen. *Hell.* 5.1.2) but soon lost his naval squadron and found himself besieged by the Spartans, until in the end a fleet had to be sent from home to evacuate him (*ibid.* 5.1.5). He was afterwards prosecuted for embezzlement (so the scholia here, citing Plato com. fr. 14) and fined so heavily that even after the confiscation of all his property a balance of five talents remained unpaid (Dem. 40.22). He may well have been awaiting trial when *Wealth* was produced; hence the prediction that as a result of his (allegedly ill-gotten) wealth he "will cop it" (Greek *klausetai*, lit. "will howl"; a surprise substitute for another verb connoting happiness or luxury).

175 **the needle-seller:** the scholia name this man as Aristoxenus (not in *PA* or *LGPN*) and say that he was a hanger-on of Pamphilus, that he was condemned together with him, and that he was a vain boaster (*alazōn*); the first and second assertions could be no more than deductions from Ar.'s text, but the third, together with the name, must be derived from some other comic reference to the man. He is one of a long series of politicians who were ridiculed in comedy by reference to the trades from which they or their families had allegedly made their money, among them Cleon "the tanner", Hyperbolus "the lamp-maker" (*Clouds* 1065, *Peace* 690), Cephalus "the potter" (*Eccl.* 248-253), and Margaret Thatcher "the grocer's daughter from Grantham".

176 **Agyrrhius,** of the deme Collytus (*PA* 179; *LGPN* 1), was one of the most prominent political leaders of the 390s and early 380s. He is not known to have been politically active before 404 (unless schol. *Frogs* 367 is right in associating him with measures to reduce festival expenditures in 406/5), but immediately after the restoration of democracy in 403 he appears as secretary to the Council (*IG* ii² 1.41); in 402/1 he was head of a tax-farming syndicate (Andoc. 1.133), and in 400 he took part in the prosecution of Andocides (*ibid.*) In the 390s he proposed the introduction of Assembly pay, and later increased the fee to three obols (Arist. *Ath.Pol.* 41.3). Possibly helped by an alliance with Conon (see Strauss 137-8), he was a powerful figure by 394/3, when his friends included the wealthy freedman banker Pasion and the son of the chief minister to the king of corn-rich Bosporus (Crimea) (Isoc. 17.31-32). In 392, when Conon led the Athenian delegation at the Sardis peace conference, his colleague Callimedon (Xen. *Hell.* 4.8.13) may have been a relative and agent of Agyrrhius (cf. below), but after the failure of the conference and Conon's arrest by the Persians Agyrrhius seems to have turned against peace negotiations, and his nephew Callistratus prosecuted the Athenian delegates to the subsequent conference at Sparta (one of them Agyrrhius' old enemy Andocides). In 389 he reached the peak of his career when he was elected a general (for the first time so far as is known) and succeeded Thrasybulus (see on 550) in command of the Athenian fleet then off southern Asia Minor (cf. Plato com. fr. 201); he may have been a general again in 388/7, since there is a reference in schol. *Eccl.* 102 to his holding a command at Lemnos. Later, probably after the unsatisfactory peace of 387/6, he was prosecuted for embezzlement (as Pamphilus had been) and, being unable to pay his fine, was imprisoned for many years (Dem. 24.135). Eventually, however, his fine was paid off (very likely by Callistratus, who by the mid 370s was the most powerful man in Athens) and he returned to public life; in 374/3 he proposed and carried a new law concerning the corn tax (see R.S. Stroud, *The Athenian Grain-Tax Law of 374/3 B.C.* [Princeton, 1998], especially pp.16-25 which is the fullest discussion of Agyrrhius' career). A pun in *Eccl.* 186 (see Stroud *op.cit.* 21) strongly suggests that he may have been nicknamed *Argyrios* "Mr Money", and our passage shows that in 388 he certainly had plenty of it. He was almost certainly the grandfather of Callimedon "the Crayfish", a politician of the later fourth century who was mentioned in comedy (mainly for his gastronomic rather than his political tastes) more often than any other man of his time (we know of fourteen references; see e.g. Eubulus fr. 8, Alexis fr. 57, Menander fr. 224.14).

176 **is in clover:** lit. "farts", i.e. "hasn't a care in the world" (cf. Dover on *Clouds* 9; similarly *Peace* 335, *Eccl.* 464).

177 Philepsius of the deme Lamptrae (*PA* 14256, *LGPN* 1) was yet another politician who was afterwards prosecuted for embezzlement and imprisoned (Dem. 24.134). Harpocration φ16 says he was satirized in comedy for "telling stories (or fables; Greek *mūthoi*) during his public speeches"; the scholia here add, citing Plato com. fr. 238, that he was satirized for being deformed and glib-tongued (they also say he was poor, but no authority is cited for this and it may be merely an inference from Ar.'s text). Chremylus' point is that Philepsius tells stories in order to gain popular favour, hence to gain political power, hence to gain money through bribery and peculation. Cf. *Wasps* 566-7 (defendants telling *mūthoi* and making jokes in court to gain the jurors' favour).

178 an alliance with the Egyptians: this passage, and its scholia, are our sole source for the making of such an alliance at this time. Egypt was at this time *de facto* independent of Persia, but Artaxerxes II was anxious to bring it back into his empire and considered himself to be at war with the Egyptian king Acoris (D.S. 15.2.3). Athens, already allied to the anti-Persian rebel Euagoras of Cyprus (Xen. *Hell*. 4.8.24), took the logical (but very dangerous) step of making an alliance with Acoris as well, probably in 389. In what sense this alliance is being said to have been made "because of Wealth" is not clear; the scholia say that the Egyptians sent Athens a large gift of corn, but their inability to distinguish between the fourth century and the sixth (they name the Egyptian king Amasis or Psammetichus, and in in one place the Persian king is identified as Cambyses) does not inspire confidence here, and elsewhere (schol. *Wasps* 718) the same gift is recorded, on the authority of Philochorus *FGrH* 328 F 119, as having been made by a different Egyptian ruler in 445/4! Possibly the point is indeed that Athens made the alliance in the hope of getting free or cheap corn from Egypt, thereby both freeing financial resources for the war effort (i.e. effectively increasing the state's wealth) and reducing their dependence on the vulnerable Bosporus-Hellespont corridor for their food supply; alternatively or additionally, there may be a suggestion that the politicians who recommended the alliance had been bribed to do so. The individual spectator's interpretation of this line may thus have depended on whether he was a supporter or an opponent of the alliance.

179 Nais loves Philonides: Philonides, probably son of Onetor (or, as the wags said, of a donkey [*onos*]; cf. Plato com. fr. 65.5-6, Theopompus com. fr. 5), of the deme Melite (*PA* 14907, *LGPN* 52) was a lumbering, ugly, uncultured man (Nicochares fr. 4, Philyllius fr. 22) – but a rich one, well able to meet the monetary demands of "the courtesans in Corinth" (149, cf. 303) however unattractive he might seem in all other respects. The mss. and scholia name his mistress as Lais, a courtesan of great fame, born in Sicily about 422, taken captive by the invading Athenians at the age of seven (Plut. *Nic*. 15.4; Paus. 2.2.5; Timaeus *FGrH* 566 F 24), trafficked as a slave to Corinth where she soon became renowned (Strattis fr. 27), and still practising her profession there in sadly degenerate old age in the 360s or thereabouts (Epicrates fr. 3, cf. Philetaerus fr. 9.4), whatever a character in a play of 391 (Plato com. fr. 196) may have meant by saying she "is no more". However, Athenaeus (13.592c-d) and Harpocration (ν1) cite a passage from Lysias' lost speech *Against Philonides* (Lys. fr. 82) in which it is stated that Philonides "says he is in love" with a courtesan named *Nais*, who is also known from Ar. fr. 179 and Philetaerus fr. 9.7, and of whom the rhetorician Alcidamas wrote an encomium; and it is easier to suppose that NAIΣ was early corrupted into ΛΑΙΣ in Ar.'s text than to suppose that Philonides successively courted the only two top-class *hetairai* in Corinth who had almost identical names! Since Nais was mentioned in Ar.'s *Gerytades*, produced in or about 408, she must have been a few years older than Lais, whom, however, she outlived (Philetaerus *loc.cit.*).

180   Timotheus' tower: Timotheus (*PA* 13679, *LGPN* 32), son of the famous admiral Conon, of the deme Anaphlystus, had inherited an estate of 17 talents (Lys. 19.40) on his father's death in 392 or 391, and had evidently used some of the money to build himself a splendid mansion, marked out from others by its tall tower. Ten years later he was elected a general (D.S. 15.29.7) and went on to become perhaps the most distinguished military man in fourth-century Athens until failure in the Social War of 357-355 led to his trial and exile (Nepos *Tim.* 3.5); he died soon afterwards, and in 354/3 his friend and teacher Isocrates included in his *Antidosis* (Isoc. 15.101-139) a splendid eulogy of his abilities and achievements.

180   I wish it would fall on your head: Carion would no doubt have finished his sentence with something like "... was built thanks to him".

185   whichever side he ... perches on: Ar. transfers to Wealth language more appropriate to Victory (Nike), who in two famous sculptures by Pheidias was shown perching on the hand of Athena in the Parthenon (Paus. 1.24.7; Plin. *NH* 36.19; *LIMC* s.v. Athena 214, 216, 217, 220) and of Zeus at Olympia (Paus. 5.11.1-2). It is true that the image thus conjured up of a youthful, winged Wealth is very different from the old, blind god we see on stage, but that fits well with the paradox that informs Chremylus and Carion's whole argument – that he who seems to be among the most powerless of beings is in reality the most omnipotent. At the time of production Athens was all too conscious of the importance of money to a state at war (cf. on 172).

188-9   no one has ever ... you've had your fill: inspired on the one hand by *Iliad* 13.636-9 ("In all things satiety comes, in sleep and lovemaking and sweet song and elegant dance ... but the Trojans never have their fill of battle"), on the other by Solon fr. 13.71-73 ("There is no limit plainly set to wealth for men; those of us who now have the most resources are eager to have twice as much; who could glut them all?"). This peculiarity of money (that is, of any commodity that is used as a general medium of exchange) – that however much of it one has, it is always to one's advantage to acquire more – is discussed analytically (and disapprovingly) by Arist. *Pol.* 1256b26-1258a14.

190-2   Chremylus draws his examples of the good things of life from the upper-class world of politics, art and the symposium (not that this was the world actually inhabited by poor farmers like himself, but lawcourt speeches sufficiently show that those who served on juries could be expected to understand and appreciate its values; see S.C. Todd, *JHS* 110 [1990] 146-173, esp. 158-167); Carion draws his exclusively from food.

190   love (Greek *erōs*) means here, unusually (but cf. Soph. *Aj.* 1205), not merely amorous desire (which, if unsatisfied, is not one of the good things of life) but the whole complex of desire + pursuit + fulfilment.

190   culture: Greek *mousikē*, which as part of a Greek boy's education comprised poetry, song, dance, and instrumental music (cf. Pl. *Alc. I* 108c-d, *Prot.* 325e-326b).

192   ambition: it is possible that Greek *philotīmiā* ηere denotes rather the *goal* of ambition ("success, high repute"), a sense first found in Eur. *IA* 342, 385 and common from the 360s onwards (e.g. Xen. *Hiero* 1.27, Dem. 24.210). On the various shades of meaning possessed by *philotīmiā* and its cognates, see K.J. Dover, *Greek Popular Morality in the Time of Plato and Aristotle* (Oxford, 1974) 230-6.

195   thirteen talents: a very substantial fortune (cf. on 180), three or four times the amount which would render a man liable to be required to undertake compulsory public services ("liturgies") such as equipping a warship (trierarchy) or funding a festival chorus (choregia); see J.K. Davies, *Athenian Propertied Families 600-300 B.C.* (Oxford, 1971) xxiii-xxiv. For comparison, the total of all taxable wealth in private hands in Attica was estimated on two separate occasions in the fourth century (in 378/7 and in 354) to be approximately 6,000 talents (Polybius 2.62.6-7, cf. Dem. 22.44; Dem. 14.19, cf. Philochorus *FGrH* 328 F 46).

196 forty: this was the approximate total value of the estate left by Conon at his death (Lys. 19.40).

203 wealth is the most cowardly thing on earth: a reapplication, in a new sense, of an established proverb (cf. Eur. *Phoen.* 597; Eur. fr. 235). The proverb asserted, in effect, that *rich men* were cowards: Chremylus is using the same words to accuse *the god of wealth* of cowardice. The original point of the proverb may have been either (i) that to be rich is to be afraid of thieves and swindlers (cf. *com. adesp.* 852, D.L. 6.51) or (ii) that the rich are reluctant to go to war because they have most to lose by it (cf. [Xen.] *Ath.Pol.* 2.14) or (iii) that wealth leads to soft, luxurious living which enervates a man's martial qualities (cf. Pl. *Rep.* 590b); the god's reply here suggests that (i) was the usual interpretation.

204 burglar: Greek *toikhōrukhos* "one who digs through walls", the housebreaker's traditional mode of entry. House walls were usually made of mud-brick; see J.E. Jones in H. Mussche et al. ed. *Thorikos and the Laurion in Archaic and Classical Times* (Ghent, 1975) 63-136, and W. Hoepfner and E.L. Schwandner, *Haus und Stadt im klassischen Griechenland* (Munich, 1994) 312-324.

206 locked up: in chests, cupboards or store-rooms.

208-9 throw yourself whole-heartedly into the plan: lit. "become a zealous man for the business". For *anēr* "man" used in addressing a god cf. on 78-79; here it may carry the suggestion that Wealth needs to think and behave in a more manly, courageous (Greek *andreios*) fashion than he has so far given evidence of doing.

210 Lynceus, son of Aphareus, was involved, together with his brother Idas, in a celebrated conflict with the Dioscuri (Castor and Polydeuces). The Dioscuri hid in a hollow oak, but Lynceus, whose eyes, "the sharpest of anyone on earth" (Pind. *Nem.* 10.63, cf. Ap.Rh. 1.153-5), could scan the whole extent of the Peloponnese and see through solid objects, saw them there, enabling Idas to kill Castor with a spear thrust through the tree; Polydeuces, left alone, nevertheless succeeded in killing both brothers, in some versions with the assistance of a thunderbolt from his father Zeus to dispose of Idas. See *Cypria* frr. 13-14 Davies (and Proclus' summary of the poem), and Pind. *Nem.* 10.60-72 with scholia.

213 "rustling the Pythian laurel": probably a tragic quotation (*trag. adesp.* 61c). There seems to have been a laurel-bush growing within the temple at Delphi (cf. Eur. *Andr.* 1115), and it was said to tremble when the god approached or spoke (cf. Callim. *Hymn to Apollo* 1; Aristonous *Paean* 10-11; Virg. *Aen.* 3.90-91 [Delos]; Ov. *Met.* 15.634-5); hence Apollo could be spoken of as "responding from the laurel-bush" (*h.Hom.Ap.* 395-6).

215 take care—: addressed to both Chremylus and Carion (the Greek verb is plural). Wealth apparently assumes (wrongly, but understandably) that Chremylus had already formed the plan to heal him before he went to Delphi, and fears that Apollo, knowing of this plan, may inform his father Zeus with catastrophic consequences.

217 and so will I, if you want: Carion sees himself as an honest man (cf. 106) who has become a slave through (his or his father's) debt (see on 147-8), and has therefore almost as much reason as Chremylus to desire the restoration of Wealth's ability to reward the honest; this spontaneous utterance, breaking his longest silence in the entire scene, suggests that he also has the courage (more than would normally be expected of a slave) to face the dangers that the plan may entail. Cf. on 6-7.

219 **their daily bread:** Greek *alphita* "barley groats", out of which was made the kneaded, uncooked cake (*maza*) that was the staple fare of the poor; for *alphita* meaning in effect "basic food" cf. *Knights* 1359, *Clouds* 106, 648, *Peace* 477, 636.

221 **if they become rich once again:** this does not refer to the current generation of honest people (for there is nothing to indicate that Chremylus, for example, had ever himself been anything but poor), but to honest people as a species (so to speak), whom Wealth had favoured before he was blinded (cf. 88-98).

223 **summon my fellow-peasants:** even before Chremylus has actually become rich, he invites his friends to share his good fortune, a singular demonstration of his honesty and generosity which Blepsidemus will find almost incredible (340-2). We have not previously been told that Chremylus is a peasant; but we have probably been expected to deduce it from his dress (see Stone 273-4), and moreover Aristophanes' elderly male heroes usually are peasants – Dicaeopolis, Strepsiades, Trygaeus (cf. *Peace* 190), Peisetaerus (cf. *Birds* 111).

224 **toiling in the fields:** or, taking Greek *autous* in its emphatic sense, "toiling in the fields themselves", implying that they do not have enough slaves to be able to avoid the hardest labour themselves even though, as we shall see, they are "weak old men" (258). Poverty will later warn Chremylus that if everyone becomes rich the supply of slaves will dry up and men like him will be forced "to plough and dig and do all the other hard jobs [him]self" (518-526).

226 **our Wealth here:** lit. "this Wealth/wealth", with a gesture towards the god who is both the patron and the embodiment of riches.

227 **this bit of meat:** except where the rules of a particular cult or festival forbade it (cf. on 1138), it was usual for those taking part in a sacrifice anywhere other than their home to bring some of the meat home to their families. At Delphi each inquirer had theoretically to offer a sheep as a consultation-sacrifice (*khrēstērion*) before entering the temple (cf. Eur. *Andr.* 1100ff, *Ion* 228-9); in practice a single sacrifice was offered on behalf of all before the consultation session began (cf. Eur. *Ion* 419-420).

229 **I'll see to that:** Chremylus wants to assemble his friends without delay.

233 **by fair means or foul:** this need not be taken to imply that Chremylus puts wealth ahead of justice; indeed he has given clear evidence to the contrary only a few moments ago (see on 223), and in any case he is well aware that Wealth desires always to act in accordance with justice (otherwise it would not have been necessary for Zeus to blind him) and, being a god, will be able to enrich him miraculously without wronging anyone else. The phrase should therefore be understood as a polar expression used loosely, as is the Greek way with such expressions (see Wilamowitz on Eur. *HF* 1106), to emphasize the importance of the task; similar expressions are frequently used today, and their users would be amazed if they were understood *au pied de la lettre* as authorizing or condoning criminal acts.

237-244 Wealth's double aspect, as person and as personification, is particularly in evidence here. It is money that is buried by the miser (238) or squandered by the profligate (243), but it is an anthropomorphic being that is "cast naked out of doors" (244).

240 **asking to borrow some small little sum:** it was considered a duty to lend money (free of interest) to a friend in difficulties, if able to do so; cf. *Clouds* 1214-9, Lys. 19.25-26, and see P.C. Millett, *Lending and Borrowing in Ancient Athens* (Cambridge, 1991), esp. 127-159.

245 **a reasonable middle-of-the-road person:** the Greek adjective is *metrios* "moderate". The ethical principle, best known from Aristotle (*EN* 1106a14-1109b26), that "virtue is ... a mean between two vices, one of excess, the other of deficiency" (1106b36-1107a3;

so generosity is the mean between profligacy and meanness, 1107b8-14, cf. 1119b22-1122a17), goes back to archaic times; cf. Theognis 335, Phocylides fr. 12 Gentili-Prato, Aesch. *Eum.* 529-530.

249   to meet: Greek *idein* (lit. "to see") often means "to converse with" (cf. Thuc. 4.125.1, Xen. *Anab.* 2.4.15, and the semantic development of English *interview*), and its literal sense can sometimes be totally forgotten, as at Men. *Dysk.* 234-6 "you ought immediately, Daos, to have seen (*idein*) the man who was approaching the girl" (in the literal sense Daos *had* in fact seen him immediately, but he had not spoken to him and had let him depart unchallenged) or Men. *Perik.* 159-162. Hence we need not, merely on account of Wealth's blindness, assume that he cannot be the subject of this verb (though syntactically speaking the words are perfectly capable of being construed with him as object, "I want my wife and son to see you").

251   whom I love more than anyone – next to you: this statement does not indicate that Chremylus is avaricious, only that he is frank (cf. 252); he has already made clear his view that *every* human being has an insatiable desire to be wealthy (188-197), and he does not pretend that he himself is an exception. Moreover, there is no question of Chremylus sacrificing his son's well-being to his own material interests; on the contrary, if he becomes wealthy, his son will benefit both in the short term and (as his heir) in the long.

253-321, together with the song that followed (see on 321/2), constitute the entrance-number (*parodos*) of the chorus (see Zimmermann i 57-64). The first part (253-289) is in iambic tetrameters, a metre also used in the *parodoi* of *Wasps* (230-248) and *Lysistrata* (254-5, 266-270, 281-5, 306-318), both times by old men trying to hurry but (as their words show) making relatively slow progress, and briefly in that of *Ecclesiazusae* (285-8) by women disguised as old men (they have been told to sing "an old men's song", *Eccl.* 277-8).

253   thyme: to eat thyme for sustenance, rather than for seasoning, was proverbially a mark of extreme poverty: cf. Aristophon fr. 10.3, Antiphanes fr. 166.8, 225.7, Hippolochus ap. Ath. 4.130d.

254   his fellow-demesmen: membership of the 139 demes (local districts) into which Attica was divided was hereditary, depending on the place of residence of one's paternal ancestor when the system was established in the late sixth century, but in the fourth century most members of rural demes still lived in their ancestral villages (cf. Dem. 57.10). In Ar. the words "friend" (*philos*) and "fellow-demesman" (*dēmotēs*) tend to go together (*Knights* 320, *Clouds* 1210, *Eccl.* 1023; similarly *dēmotēs* has associations with *geitōn* "neighbour" and *syngenēs* "relative", *Clouds* 1322, *Eccl.* 1115), and it is considered shameful to harm, or fail to help, a fellow-demesman (*Ach.* 333, 349, 675, *Clouds* 1219, 1322, *Lys.* 685).

255   this is no time for delay: or, adopting Meineke's conjecture, "the opportunity isn't waiting".

267   I dare say (Greek *oimai* "I think, I fancy"): because whereas the condition of Wealth's hair, teeth, skin, etc., is visible and can be reported as fact, the condition of his penis is a matter for conjecture. This is evidence that the actor playing Wealth did not wear a visible stage-phallus (cf. Stone 121 n.77 [*contra* Stone 91]); probably his garments (though presumably ragged) were long enough to conceal it.

267   minus his foreskin: Greek *psōlos* normally means "with *glans penis* uncovered", whether as a result of circumcision (e.g. *Birds* 507) or of sexual excitement (e.g. *Lys.* 979, 1136). The latter is obviously irrelevant here (when old men in Ar. have erections it is an outward and visible sign of rejuvenation), and though Greeks regarded circumcision as a ludicrous self-inflicted deformity (cf. *Ach.* 158-161, *Clouds* 538-9) they did not associate it with old age or poverty but with membership of particular barbarian peoples such as the Egyptians and Phoenicians. The suggestion is, rather, that Wealth is suffering from adhesion of the foreskin, whose Greek medical name *lipodermiā* (cf. ps.-Galen 19.445 Kühn, Diosc. 2.82.2) indicates that it was thought of as tantamount to lack of a functioning foreskin (cf. Diosc. *loc.cit.* "those who are *lipodermoi* otherwise than by circumcision"). By making it impossible to clean under the foreskin, this condition would increase the risk of painful and dangerous urinary tract infections, and would end any possibility of sexual activity.

269 it's obvious ... that he's come with a heap of money: it has several times been suggested that the chorus-leader, being old and hard of hearing (cf. *Ach.* 681, *Knights* 42-43), is supposed to have misheard a word or two of what Carion has said (e.g. mistaking *rhūson* "shrivelled" for *khrūson* "gold" and/or *psō lon* "minus his foreskin" for *sōron* "heap"). The chorus, however, give no other indication of hearing problems, and "it's obvious from what you say that ..." (lit. "you make it obvious that ...", Greek *dē lois*) suggests that they are not *repeating* what they think they have heard, but *making an inference from* what they have heard: cf. 587-9 where Chremylus says that the (cheap) crowns of wild olive given to Olympic victors "make it obvious" (*dēloi*) that Zeus is a stingy hoarder of wealth. If so, the inference will be that if Chremylus regards the arrival at his house of so ugly and wretched-looking a man as good news, it can only be because the man is very rich (and can be expected to die soon, enabling Chremylus to possess himself of his wealth).

273-4 born and bound to be that kind of person: lit. "a person of that kind in all circumstances by birth". Carion thinks the chorus-leader is taking it for granted that a slave will never tell the truth: it was, indeed, proverbial that "there's no trusting servants" (Lys. 7.35), and the crafty, scheming, deceiving slave was to become a stock figure of New Comedy.

275-6 crying out in distress: lit. "shouting 'iou, iou'".

276 they're just *yearning* for their old shackles and fetters: i.e. your behaviour is so impudent that anyone would think you positively *wanted* to be punished by shackling (for this punishment cf. *Wasps* 435, Men. *Heros* 2-3, Herodas 3.95-97, 5.59-62, Dem. 18.129) despite your previous experience of it. That Carion has suffered shackling before, i.e. has a history of serious misbehaviour, is half implied by *pothousai* "yearning for" (which often, though not always, implies a longing for something *which one has lost*), half implied by the following phrase (lit. "the shackles and the fetters", i.e. either "the shackles/fetters <in which miscreant slaves are customarily confined>" or "the shackles/fetters <with which you used to be familiar>"), and rather strongly implied by the combination of the two.

277-8 If the chorus-leader can taunt Carion with his inferiority of status, Carion can retaliate by taunting him with his age and feebleness. Carion's own physical vigour is evidenced by the order given to him at 71 to lift Wealth off the ground (which must be credible if it is to be effective in forcing the victim to reveal his identity); it will shortly be put to good theatrical use in the dancing at 290-321.

277 your letter: Carion is assuming that the chorus-leader is a juryman; any citizen over thirty could volunteer for jury service, and so many older men did so that in comedy "old man" and "juryman" were often virtually synonymous (cf. *Wasps* passim, *Ach.* 375-6, *Knights* 255, 977-9, *Peace* 349, *Birds* 109, *Lys.* 380, *Eccl.* 460). In the fourth century each juror had a permanent personal ticket (*pinakion*), inscribed with his name, his deme, and one of the ten letters from *alpha* to *kappa* (Arist. *Ath.Pol.* 63.4, cf. *Eccl.* 681-8; many such tickets have been found, usually buried with their owners, see J.H. Kroll, *Athenian Bronze Allotment Plates* [Cambridge MA, 1972]); letters were assigned to individuals randomly, presumably in the order in which they had originally registered for service. At the time when *Wealth* was performed, all jurors in a given letter-class (or perhaps all members of a given tribe in a given letter-class – see my note on *Eccl.* 683) were assigned together by lot, for a day at a time, to sit in a particular court (see D.M. MacDowell, *The Law in Classical Athens* [London, 1978] 36-38); Carion mockingly tells the chorus-leader that for today the destination assigned to *his* group is ... the coffin. This system, under which the same large group of jurors (several dozen strong on one assumption, several hundred on another) would find itself sitting together day after day, was replaced later in the century by a more complex system of allotment on an individual basis, described in Arist. *Ath.Pol.* 63-65, under which the probability of two members of one of today's juries serving together on one of tomorrow's was the same no matter which tribe or letter-class either belonged to.

277 **and it's judging there now:** or, with the mss. other than R, "to judge"; but this reading requires us to assume two pieces of abnormal (though not impossible) grammar (an accusative absolute construction with a non-impersonal participle, and a main clause linked back to a subordinate participial phrase by the connecting particle *de*), and is also inferior in sense. R's reading gives greater urgency to Carion's advice to hurry: not only has the allotment been completed, but the jurors are already in court, and if the addressee doesn't get there quickly he will miss getting his pay for the day (once a trial had begun, late-coming jurors were not admitted; cf. *Wasps* 891-2).

278 **Charon** was the ferryman who punted (or rowed) the souls of the dead across the Acherusian lake; cf. *Frogs* 137-140, 180-270, Eur. *Alc.* 252-5, and see C. Sourvinou-Inwood in *LIMC* iii 210-223 and *AION* 9 (1987) 145-158. A scholium ingeniously points out that his name *Kharōn* bears a close resemblance to *arkhōn*; the nine archons were the principal annual magistrates and presided over most of the jury-courts (Arist. *Ath.Pol.* 56.6, 57.2, 58.2-3, 59.2-6, 66.1), but in the "court" to which *this* "juror" is going Charon will take the archon's place.

278 **tickets:** the Greek word used here, *xumbolon* or *sumbolon*, appears twice in the account of the allotment and procedure of the jury courts in Arist. *Ath.Pol.* At 65.2 (cf. Dem. 18.210) it refers to a token handed to each juror as he enters the court in which he is to serve; the function of this is nowhere stated, but it has been suggested (A.L. Boegehold, *Hesperia* 29 [1960] 400-1) that it was used to assign jurors randomly to their seats. At 68.2 it refers to a different token stamped with the mark III (i.e. 3) which jurors received when they voted, and which they exchanged afterwards for their daily pay of three obols. The reference here is probably to the former token, for mention is required of a procedure relating to the *beginning* (not the end) of a trial: it would be pointless to urge a "juror" to hurry to "court" if the day's business was nearly over and he had no chance whatever of being allowed to serve. It is true that the *sumbolon* of *Ath.Pol.* 65.2 is distributed not by the archon who presided over the court (cf. previous note) but by a minor official; but this was inevitable in Aristotle's time, when the presiding officers were themselves assigned to courts by lot after the jurors had all taken their places (*Ath.Pol.* 66.1), and if in the 380s, as in the fifth century (cf. *Wasps* 1108), each archon still always sat in the same court, he probably entered before the jury (as *Wasps* 891, spoken by Bdelycleon acting the part of presiding officer, would seem to imply), and it would be he who issued (i.e. supervised and was responsible for the issue of) tokens to the jurors.

280 **you go on playing games with us:** Greek *phenākizeis* "you cheat <us>", the same verb translated as "make fools of us" in 271.

[281] After "condescended to explain" the mss. other than RV present a line identical with 260 ("what's the reason why your master has called us [lit. me] here"). This was probably added by an ancient or medieval reader to clarify (unnecessarily) what it was that Carion was expected to "explain"; similar interpolations seem to have occurred at *Ach.* 436 (= 384) and *Birds* 192 (= 1218). The repetition would not of itself prove the line spurious (cf. 138 ~ 1115, 968 ~ 1173); but it disrupts the syntax of the sentence, separating a relative pronoun at the beginning of 282 from its antecedent at the end of 280, and the singular pronoun *me*, appropriate in 260 after two first-person singular pronouns earlier in the sentence, does not fit the present speech in which all other pronouns of first-person reference are plural.

283   **field after field full of thyme roots:** lit. "many roots of thyme plants" which (it is implied) they would normally have stopped to pluck for food (cf. 253). The ellipsis ("passing through thyme roots" = passing through fields containing thyme roots) is similar to that whereby travellers or armies are said to pass through peoples when what is meant is that they passed through the territory of these peoples (e.g. Hdt. 7.113.1 "passing right through the Doberae and Paeoplae", 7.128.1 "he intended to take the upper route through the Macedonians who live in the highlands").

285   **to make you rich men:** many mss. read "to make us rich men", but "you" is rhetorically preferable: if Carion were to say "us", the sceptical chorus might very well take this to refer to Chremylus and his household (Wealth is, after all, now in his house) and react, not with amazement and delight, but with even greater anger.

287   **as rich as Midas:** there is no full account of the myth of Midas before Ovid (*Met.* 11.85-193 – though cf. Conon *FGrH* 26 F 1.1), but it was well known in the time of Herodotus (8.138.2-3), and a crucial episode, the capture of Silenus, appears in vase paintings from the mid sixth century onwards (see M.C. Miller in *LIMC* viii 846-851). Midas, possibly finding his wealth (proverbial as early as Tyrtaeus fr. 12.6) had not brought him true happiness, and wishing to acquire the profound knowledge which he believed Silenus to possess, took him prisoner (in what seems to have been the most common account) by putting wine in a fountain from which he drank (Theopompus *FGrH* 115 F 75a, cf. Xen. *Anab.* 1.2.13). After learning what Silenus had to teach him (accounts of its content vary, but Silenus' message is always basically pessimistic) Midas returned him to his master Dionysus, who asked him what reward he desired; Midas unwisely requested that everything he touched should turn to gold, and nearly starved to death as a result (our earliest source for this part of the story, Arist. *Pol.* 1257b14-17, seems to imply that he did perish). The historical Midas (Mita) was a king of Phrygia (and other parts of Asia Minor) in the late eighth century BC (see J.D. Hawkins in *CAH*[2] iii.1 417-420), who married a Greek wife (Arist. fr. 611.37 Rose) and dedicated a throne at Delphi (Hdt. 1.14.3); it is not clear whether he himself became a legendary figure among Greeks (as some other Asian rulers did, e.g. Semiramis, Sardanapallus, even to some extent the sixth-century figure of Croesus) or whether the mythical Midas was from the first thought of as his distant ancestor (like Archelaus son of Temenus, celebrated and possibly created by Euripides as the founder of the family of Archelaus, king of Macedon 413-399). On the development of the myth see L.E. Roller, *CA* 2 (1983) 299-313. It evidently does not occur to the chorus that Midas' wealth had unfortunate consequences for him; whether it will occur to the audience is not clear (see F. Heberlein, *WJA* 7 [1981] 45-46, for an argument that they are expected to think of this and reflect on its implications).

287   **ass's ears:** Midas has ass's ears in art from c.440 (see Miller *loc.cit.*); the scholia here give a variety of explanations of the story, some mythical (e.g. that he was punished for having spoken ill of Dionysus), others rationalizing (e.g. that he was said to have long ears because he employed many spies). In the later canonical version of the story, Midas was given ass's ears by Apollo because he had judged Apollo's music inferior to that of Pan (Ovid *Met.* 11.146-193, placing this episode *after* that of Silenus and the golden touch) or Marsyas (Hyginus, *Fab.* 191; Fulgentius, *Mitologiae* 3.9). It is likely, as Rogers suggests, that Carion at this point makes the insulting gesture referred to by Persius 1.59 ("a waving hand imitating [sc. an ass's] white ears"); if so, the chorus, so ready to take offence shortly before, are now so enchanted by the prospect of riches that they take no notice at all.

288-9 Oh, I'm so happy ... I want to dance for joy: compare the reaction of the chorus of *Peace* (301-345) to the news that they have the opportunity to rescue Peace from her prison. Trygaeus, the hero of that play, tries desperately to restrain them, fearful that War (310) or the deceased Cleon (313-9) may intervene to thwart his plans (in fact it is Hermes who does so, though he is soon won over); here there has been, and will be, no such apprehension on anyone's part, and the intervention of Poverty will come completely out of the blue.

290-321 The lyric part of the *parodos* is basically a short role-playing song-and-dance number, in which Carion impersonates first Polyphemus the Cyclops and then Circe, while the chorus represent, at some moments Odysseus and his companions, at other moments various animals. It is intertextually related, on the one hand to the ninth and tenth books of the *Odyssey*, on the other to a recent quasi-dramatic dithyramb by Philoxenus of Cythera (435/4-380/79), *The Cyclops* or *Galatea* (surviving fragments: *PMG* 815-824), which depicted the Cyclops as being in love with the Nereid sea-nymph Galatea; Odysseus, when imprisoned in the Cyclops' cave, apparently offered to help him win her (cf. *PMG* 818 = Synesius, *Letter* 121) and the poem concluded with the blinding of the Cyclops (so the scholia here) and probably the escape of Odysseus. There are many stories, mutually inconsistent and not particularly credible, of how Philoxenus came to compose the poem as a result of his experiences at the court of Dionysius I of Syracuse (some of them, e.g. Phaenias ap. Ath. 1.7a, say that his Cyclops was designed to be perceived as a caricature of Dionysius himself). The poem was much imitated in the fourth century (cf. Didymus on [Dem.] 11.22 [p.30 Diels-Schubart]), and was parodied by several comic dramatists – Nicochares in *Galatea* (produced probably not long after *Wealth*, cf. fr. 4), Antiphanes in *The Cyclops*, Alexis (probably in the 350s or 340s) in another *Galatea*. By calling Philoxenus' poem "quasi-dramatic" I do not wish to be taken as implying more than that, as e.g. in Bacchylides 18, all or most of its text consisted of words spoken in the persona of characters in the story (*PMG* 819, 821, 823 and probably 822 are spoken in the character of the Cyclops, 824 in that of Odysseus); some ancient statements imply a performance (contrary to the normal conventions of dithyramb) with individual actors, costumes and properties, but this may be guesswork. See D.F. Sutton, *QUCC* 13 (1983) 37-43; P. Mureddu, *AION* 4/5 (1982/3) 77-83; W.G. Arnott, *Alexis: The Fragments* (Cambridge, 1996) 139-141; G.W. Dobrov, *Drama* 5 (1997) 66-69; Kugelmeier 255-264; J.H. Hordern, *CQ* 49 (1999) 445-455. For evidence from this song that may help us to reconstruct Philoxenus' presentation of the Cyclops story, see on 297 below.

290-321 Metre: the rhythm is iambic throughout, mostly a mixture of dimeters and tetrameters.

290 tra la la: Greek *threttanelo*, "imitating the sound of a *kithara*" (scholia) as Philoxenus' Cyclops had done in attempting to woo Galatea (*PMG* 819). In *Frogs* 1285-96 the sound of a lyre is represented by *phlattothrattophlattothrat*.

292 and lead you: i.e. the chorus are to represent the Cyclops' flocks of sheep and goats (*Odyssey* 9.184).

292 hey then, little ones, raise up cry on cry: according to the scholia, these words are taken over directly from Philoxenus' poem (*PMG* 819); *tekea* "children, little ones" and *thamin(a)* "repeatedly" are words from a high poetic register which would not normally appear in comic lyrics.

293   with the song of bleating sheep: the mss. read "and bleat the song of sheep", but: (i) this is tautological since the "cry on cry" surely includes, rather than being separate from, the bleating; (ii) it would make the chorus "*bleat* ... the song of ... *goats*"; (iii) the sheep, who are more prominent than the goats in the Homeric account and in the following stanza, deserve an epithet at least as much as the goats do. *Prima facie* this passage and 307 imply that the chorus utter animal noises before or during their responding stanzas (so B. Zimmermann in *Primeras jornadas internacionales de teatro griego* [Valencia, 1995] 125, comparing Pl. *Rep.* 396b, 397a), but in comedy such vocalizations are regularly included in the script (cf. 895, *Ach.* 800-3, *Knights* 10, *Birds* 227ff, 737ff, *Frogs* 1285ff). Philoxenus' dithyramb may well itself have included animal imitations, but it appears that Ar., while reminding his audience of these, has decided against actually using them in his own adaptation/parody.

295   cocks skinned: lit. "made *psōloi*" (cf. on 267); in what sense and why, is clarified in the second half of the line.

295   you'll have a billygoat's breakfast: "after copulation," say the scholia, "male goats lick their genitals." In other words, the chorus (or the animals they represent) are going to perform *fellatio* on themselves (cf. *Eccl.* 470, also *Knights* 1010, Artemidorus 1.80, Catullus 88.8, *CIL* iv 2360.3, 8512) – an act for whose simulation the large comic phallus would be uniquely convenient. Combining as it did the opprobrious connotations of masturbation and of submission to oral penetration, self-fellation seems to have been thought so utterly gross an act that in the heyday of Attic erotic vase-painting, even satyrs were not depicted doing it; Catullus *loc.cit.* implies that it is the worst imaginable perversion (or was, before the days of Gellius!). Hence these words are the climax (but see on 305) to the series of insults which Carion has been directing at the chorus (277-8, 287) and they at him (275-6, 279-280); it is not surprising that in the following stanza they retaliate by rejecting the role of animals and instead becoming the companions of Odysseus so that they can put out Polyphemus-Carion's eye(s).

297   when he's hungry: this reading has often been regarded as suspect, since neither in Homer nor, it tends to be assumed, in Philoxenus was the Cyclops hungry when he fell into a drunken sleep and was blinded; and a few late mss. (possibly by accident) replace *peinōnta* "hungry" by *pinōnta* "dirty". The verb *pinān*, however, is nowhere securely attested, and "hungry" has a point. The chorus have now cast themselves as the companions of Odysseus, but they (and the audience) will certainly recall that the reason why the Homeric Cyclops had a full stomach when he fell asleep was that he had killed and eaten six of Odysseus' companions (*Odyssey* 9.288-293, 311, 344, 374), and this is not a scenario they wish to re-enact; hence they will make sure they catch and blind the Cyclops *before* he has had a chance to have that kind of meal. The scenario actually here envisaged seems to be as follows: the Cyclops, having drunk Odysseus' wine the previous evening (cf. 298) on an empty stomach, and fallen asleep without his dinner (which would have been a human one), has now been woken up (presumably by Odysseus) early in the morning (before his breakfast – cf. 295 – which would also have been a human one) and urged to go out at once with his flocks and gather flowers, branches, etc., to make into garlands for himself and Galatea (see next note); he goes (probably accompanied by Odysseus as his love-tutor), but he only gathers some unlovely wild herbs, which he takes to the seashore where he sings a love-song to Galatea (*PMG* 819, 822; cf. Theocr. 11.19-79) and then falls asleep – not because he is a despairing *exclusus amator* (cf. *Eccl.* 962, Pl. *Symp.* 183a, 203d, Theocr. 3.52-53) but because he is tired and sick with a hangover; whereupon Odysseus calls up his companions (the fuddled Cyclops having perhaps forgotten to close up his cave) who duly blind the giant. Since this story, so different from that of Homer, could hardly have been deduced rapidly by an audience from the words of this song alone, it may well be the story that Philoxenus' poem had told.

298   with a beggar's bag and some damp wild greens in it: in substance, though not necessarily in wording, this comes from Philoxenus' poem (*PMG* 820), in which, apparently, the Cyclops was said to carry with him a bag (*pērā*) of the kind that beggars used to keep the scraps they were given (cf. *Clouds* 923-4, *Odyssey* 13.437-8). In the *Odyssey* (9.219-249) the Cyclops lives (when human flesh is not available) on extremely ample supplies of milk and cheese from his flocks (in Euripides' *Cyclops* [122, 325] he also eats meat), and there is no apparent reason why Philoxenus or Ar. should have presented him living a life of wretched poverty and want (cf. 253, 283). Is it possible that, taking a hint from Synesius (see on 290-321), we should assume that the wild greens have been gathered to be made into garlands for the Cyclops' anticipated tryst with Galatea? It is true that in the story told by Synesius, the Cyclops saw through Odysseus' ploy and refused to let him leave the cave; but Synesius also adds that Odysseus, "because he was really being wronged, was destined eventually to profit from his cunning", and it is therefore reasonable to suppose that once he had got the Cyclops well on in liquor, Odysseus renewed his suggestion and this time the Cyclops agreed to it. The greens are "damp" (lit. dewy) either (i) because they are freshly gathered and it is early morning, or (ii) from sea-spray on the shore.

301   to take a big pointed stake ... and blind him: essentially as in *Odyssey* 9.319-333, 375-397.

302-315 This Circe sketch corresponds in rhythm and style to the preceding Cyclops sketch, but so far as we know it does not depend in the same way on any recent dithyrambic or other antecedent. Its satirical point, instead, is the relationship of Philonides and Nais (see on 179).

302   the woman who stirred up potions: cf. *Odyssey* 10.234-6 "she *stirred* cheese and barley groats and fresh honey into Pramnian wine for them, and with the food she mixed baleful *potions*".

303   in Corinth ... the companions of Philonides: we had expected "in Aeaea ... the companions of Odysseus"; now we perceive that this Circe is none other than Nais the Corinthian courtesan. The phrase "the companions of Philonides" should not be interpreted literally, since even a Philonides would not have brought a party of friends with him on his visits to his mistress. Possibly the things said about Circe-Nais' treatment of them are meant to be applied only to Philonides himself, the "companions" being imaginary and mentioned only (i) for the sake of the *Odyssey* parallel and (ii) so that they can be represented by the chorus; but it is perhaps more likely that by Philonides' "companions" we are to understand all those who had successively had the expensive and (according to this song) extremely degrading experience of being, like him, lovers of Nais.

304   to behave like pigs: as Circe had turned Odysseus' companions into swine.

305   eat kneaded shit: like the dung-beetle in *Peace* 1-49. "Shit-eater" (*skatophagos*) was a common term of abuse (cf. 706, *Peace* 48, Men. *Dysk.* 488), and if Carion can get the chorus to accept the role of Odysseus-Philonides' "companions" he will have succeeded in insulting them grossly again (cf. on 295); but this time he will turn the tables on him. Pigs were proverbially scatophagous: cf. Antiphanes fr. 124.4, Crobylus fr. 7.

305   *she did their kneading for them:* I am unable to determine from the words (or more usually silence) of earlier commentators whether they thought they knew what this meant, and equally unable to understand the interpretation offered by J.J. Henderson,

The Maculate Muse² (New York, 1991) 194, 200-1. The key to the joke, I believe, is that Circe-Nais is not said to have kneaded *excrement* for her visitors: she is only said to have *kneaded* for them – what she kneaded, is not stated. Now if "to knead (for) oneself" (*dephesthai* or, in *Clouds* 676, *anamattesthai*) can mean, as it can, "to masturbate", it follows that to "knead" (for) another person should be capable of meaning "to stimulate him manually to (orgasm or) erection", as a prostitute might have to do to an elderly client in order to enable him to penetrate her (*Ach.* 1149, *Wasps* 739-740, 1343-4). This therefore compounds the insult just perpetrated against the chorus: not only are they "shit-eaters", they are also semi-impotent.

306 **in all its varieties:** since Circe is also Nais, *tropoi* "ways, varieties, styles" is almost bound to carry a suggestion of its specialized sense "varieties of sexual activity" (cf. *Eccl.* 8, [Dem.] 59.114, and for a similar *double entendre*, though an inadvertent one on the speaker's part, *Thesm.* 152); see my discussion in F. De Martino and A.H. Sommerstein ed. *Studi sull'eufemismo* (Bari, 1999) 206, 216. Carion may well aid the interpretation of his words with some appropriately sensuous body movements.

307-8 **follow your mummy, little piggies:** the chorus are thus again conscripted into an animal role. According to the scholia "Follow your mummy, little piggies" was a popular catch-phrase, but they give two alternative accounts of it: (i) it is something that "children are accustomed to say" (presumably in a game); (ii) it is said "in reference to the uneducated" (presumably meaning, in effect, "you're stupid and so were your parents"; for "swinish" = "stupid" or "uncultured" cf. *Knights* 986, *Peace* 928, Cratinus fr. 77, Pherecrates fr. 271, Callias com. fr. 38, Pl. *Theaet.* 166c).

310 **our companions:** the chorus again reject the attempt to cast them as animals, but for the moment it is not clear whether they are identifying themselves with Philonides or with Odysseus.

312 **the son of Laertes** resolves this uncertainty. In the Greek, the name of Odysseus' father is given in the Attic form *Lārtios*, common in tragedy (e.g. Soph. *Aj.* 1, Eur. *Tro.* 421).

312 **hang you up by the balls** is a surprise. What Odysseus did to Circe (*Odyssey* 10.318-396) was to threaten her with his sword, accept her ensuing invitation to bed (having first made her swear not to harm him) and then, over a meal, ask her to release his comrades from her spell, which she did. But the chorus abruptly stop thinking of Carion as Circe or even as Nais, and see him merely as a saucy (male) slave who deserves severe punishment (cf. 275-6) for his insolence. For the "hanging up" of slaves (normally by wrists or feet) by way of punishment or torture, cf. *Clouds* 870, *Frogs* 619, Soph. *Ant.* 309, Herodas 4.78; for sadistic threats involving the testicles, cf. 955-6, *Knights* 772. Diogenes the Cynic is alleged (D.L. 6.51) to have said of a man named Didymon, who had been taken in adultery, that he "deserved to be hung up by his name" (*didymoi* "twins" could mean "testicles").

313 **like a billygoat's:** according to the scholia, it was the practice to smear goats' nostrils with dung to induce them to sneeze and so clear their air passages when blocked.

314-5 **like Aristyllus:** Aristyllus (*PA* 2126; *LGPN* 2) is also mentioned in *Eccl.* 646-8 and Ar. fr. 551; he is not known outside Ar. Both in this passage and in *Eccl.* his name conjures up the idea of a face smeared with dung, in both we find the Greek root *minth-*, and the scholia on both say that he was a sexual pervert (*aischropoios*); it is therefore likely that he was (alleged to be) a *minthōn* (Lucian, *Lexiphanes* 12; cf. Philodemus *On Vices* p.37 Jensen, Hesychius k2652), i.e. probably a coprophiliac (cf. *minthos* "excrement") who kissed or licked anuses (see J.F. Gannon, *Thesmophoriae Restitutae* [Diss. Yale 1982] 127 n.81).

314-5 with your mouth half open: the mouth is probably Carion's rather than Aristyllus'; he would be keeping his lips parted in a desperate attempt to avoid tasting the dung – and would therefore have serious trouble in enunciating the consonants *p, b, ph* and *m*, two of which unfortunately appear in the phrase *hepesthe mēri khoiroi* "follow your mummy, little piggies". Aristyllus, who presumably likes the taste of excrement, would have no such reason to keep his mouth open.

317   another style: sc. of entertainment.

318-320 without my master knowing take some bread and meat: cf. on 26-27.

321   and still be chewing it: being in a hurry to avoid detection, he would conceal the food as quickly as possible in the safest place, viz. his mouth, and some of it would still be there when he resumed work. Cf. *Wasps* 779-780 where Philocleon, told that in his new domestic lawcourt he can if he wishes eat during a long defence speech, objects that he will not be able to "decide cases properly ... if I'm still chewing my food" (because the speech may end, and Philocleon as sole "juror" be called on to vote, before he has finished eating).

321   the hard slog (Greek *kopos*, properly "fatigue", hence "exhausting toil") is taken by the scholia to refer to the task of healing Wealth; but at present neither Carion nor we have any idea how this will be done (Chremylus' plan is first revealed at 411) and there is no reason to suppose it will involve exhausting toil. Holzinger suggests that the toil meant is that of the ensuing choral performance (see next note); but for one thing Carion is not proposing to feed the chorus (only himself), and for another there is no evidence in the text that he is even present during the choral performance (if he exited into the house immediately after it, he would collide with Chremylus coming out; yet he cannot have remained on stage, since he is not provided with any subsequent opportunity to depart). More probably the reference here is merely to Carion's ordinary work as a slave, which he expects to have to resume now that the trip to Delphi is over; before doing so he might well feel the need of some sustenance, and of more than his master would be likely to provide for him. Such an exit-line for Carion gives the strong impression that we will not see him again as a significant character, and sure enough he does not return to the scene for over 300 lines, his place as Chremylus' associate being taken by Blepsidemus; but in the second half of the play Carion returns to take a leading role (he is on stage more than twice as long as anyone else, including Chremylus), and it is Blepsidemus who is forgotten as completely as if he had never existed.

321/2 Here V and some other mss. have the note *khorou*, an abbreviation of *khorou melos* "song of the chorus". This indication also appears in several mss. (including V and twice *R) at 626/7, *770/1 (*kommation khorou* "short stanza by the chorus") and *801/2, in K at 1096/7, in R at *Eccl.* 729/730 and 876/7, in RV at *Clouds* 888/9, and in many papyri of fourth-century and later drama, including those of Menander where it invariably marks the breaks between the five acts of which each play is composed. It is now generally accepted that in later drama these breaks were filled by choral performances of some kind whose words, if any, were not considered worth recording as part of the play-script; and if this was true of Menander and his contemporaries, it may be taken *a fortiori* that it was true of Aristophanes. It is still necessary, however, to consider the following questions:

(1) How far can we trust the manuscript evidence (whether positive or negative) as to the placement of these choral interludes? On the one hand there are two further points late in this play (958/9 and 1170/1) where the action pauses, the stage is empty, and a *khorou* marking *may* have been lost; indeed some late mss. actually insert *khorou* at 958/9, and it probably once stood there in Π83, the first papyrus of the play that includes any relevant passage. On the other hand we know from the later scholia (on 1,

252/3, 619, 626/7, 641, 771, 802, 850, 1042) that by the Middle Ages the meaning of *khorou* was not properly understood, and the word might therefore have been wrongly inserted. In the present passage we seem to have at 317 an actual instruction by Carion to the chorus to continue dancing and/or singing in his absence, and there can be little doubt that they do so. On 626/7, 770/1, 801/2, 958/9, 1096/7 and 1170/1, see notes *ad locc.*

(2) What was the nature of the choral performances? Song is positively attested where *melos* "lyric" or *kommation* "short stanza" is added to *khorou*, i.e. at 770/1, Astydamas fr. 1h.10, *trag.adesp.* 625.8/9, and probably *com.adesp.* 1056.12; moreover Arist.*Poet.* 1456a27-30 implies that tragic choruses still regularly sang in Aristotle's day (cf. *Probl.* 922b10-28, probably of even later date), and Men. fr. 130 probably indicates that New Comic choruses did too. Already in Aristophanes several plays, including *Wealth*, appear to end with choral exit-songs which are announced in the concluding words of the surviving text (1209, *Ach.* 1231-4, *Lys.* 1320-1) but whose own lyrics were apparently never included in the script. It may thus be taken as virtually certain that throughout the fourth century choral interludes regularly included song as well as dance, whether or not their words formed part of the texts that went into circulation.

(3) Why are some choral songs included in the script and others not? In *Wealth* the only choral lyrics that do appear in the text (the Cyclops-Circe song just concluded, and some short exclamations at 637-640) form part of dialogues which would make no sense without them, and this is certainly part of the reason why they have been retained (only part of the reason, for at 771 Wealth's opening words require there to have been a preceding choral song to which he is replying and yet this song is not in the script; see on 770/1). In addition, the association of 290-321 with the *entrance* of the chorus is probably also a relevant factor: even in Menander the first entrance of the chorus (at the end of Act I) is the one moment at which the characters invariably take notice of its existence.

See generally on this subject E.W. Handley, *CQ* 3 (1953) 55-61; W.J.W. Koster, *Autour d'un manuscrit d'Aristophane écrit par Démétrius Triclinius* (Groningen, 1957) 117-135; E. Pöhlmann, *WJA* 3 (1977) 69-81; R.L. Hunter, *ZPE* 36 (1979) 23-38; A.H. Sommerstein, *BICS* 31 (1984) 139-152; M.J. Dillon, *Aristophanes' Ploutos: Comedy in Transition* (Diss. Yale 1984) 122-141; F. Perusino, *Dalla commedia antica alla commedia di mezzo* (Urbino, 1987) 61-72; R. Hamilton, *CQ* 41 (1991) 346-355; and A.H. Sommerstein in J.A. López Férez ed. *Estudios actuales sobre textos griegos: Comedia* (Madrid, forthcoming).

322 **"good day":** Greek *khairein* (lit. "rejoice, be happy"), the normal word of greeting and farewell in Ar.'s earlier plays (used once in this play, at 788) and in classical Greek generally. Its alleged obsolescence must have been merely a short-lived fad; it remains frequent (at meeting, though not at parting) in Menander (e.g. *Georgos* 41, *Dis Exapaton* 103, *Epitr.* 860, *Leucadia* 3 Arnott).

324 **a warm welcome to you:** Greek *aspazomai*, a form of greeting that had long been in use (cf. *Clouds* 1145, *Birds* 1378) but which may have become more popular about this time (cf. 1042, and later Alexis fr. 172.5).

327 **in the full sense the saviours of the god** is an allusion to Orphic and/or Dionysiac myth and mystery-cult. This told of the killing and dismemberment of Dionysus by the Titans (*Orphica* frr. 205-220; see M.L. West, *The Orphic Poems* [Oxford, 1985] 140-174), and in at least one version of it his body was reconstituted by Apollo, who is accordingly described by Olympiodorus (*Commentary on Plato's Phaedo* p.111.14-19 Norvin, cf. p.43.15-17) as "in truth the saviour of Dionysus"; Olympiodorus derives from this story the title Dionysodotes ("giver of Dionysus") under which Apollo was worshipped in the mystery-cult at Phlya in Attica (Paus. 1.31.4), in a temple old enough to have been destroyed by the Persians and restored by Themistocles (Plut. *Them.* 1.4) and famous enough to have been mentioned in a poem of Simonides (*PMG* 627). In one of the rituals associated with this myth (described by Firmicus Maternus, *The Error of Profane Religions* 22; the relevance of this passage to *Wealth* was noted by P. Sfyroeras, *GRBS* 36 [1995] 237-8; it is not known whether it reflects the Phlya cult or another), an image was laid on a bier and mourned in darkness, then a light was brought in, all the worshippers were anointed, and the priest said: "Initiates, take courage (*tharreite*, cf. *tharrei* "don't worry" in 328), for the god has been saved, and we will have salvation from our troubles". The parallels between this myth and the plot of our play would be evident to any spectator who knew the myth and (any of) the cult(s): to the destruction of Dionysus by the Titans and his revival, in a burst of light, through the aid of Apollo corresponds the blinding of Wealth by Zeus and the restoration of light to his eyes through the aid of Apollo (who gave the oracle that set Chremylus' scheme in motion) – and was not Dionysus himself called Ploutodotes, "giver of wealth" (schol. *Frogs* 479 = *PMG* 879)?

328 **I've got the real look of war in my eyes:** lit. "I'm absolutely looking Ares [the god of war]"; this phrase (imitated by Timocles fr. 12.7 in reference to the orator Demosthenes) may have been coined by Ar. as a variant of a favourite locution of his whereby a mordant, irate facial expression is called "an X look", where X is the name of some acrid herb or fluid; cf. *Ach.* 254 (savory), *Knights* 631 (mustard), *Wasps* 455 (cress), *Peace* 1184 (fig-juice), *Frogs* 603 (marjoram), *Eccl.* 292, and for variants *Ach.* 566 (a lightning look), *Knights* 855 (an ostracism look), *Birds* 1169 (a war-dance look), 1671 (an assault-and-battery look), *Frogs* 562, also *com.adesp.* 633 (an unripe-grape look). See Taillardat 165, 216-8.

329-330 **we jostle ... for the sake of three obols:** cf. on 171. It is a repeated theme in the earlier part of *Ecclesiazusae* that the average citizen attends the Assembly only for the sake of this payment; see *Eccl.* 183-8, 206-8, 282-4, 289-310, 380-393, 547-8.

332 **Blepsidemus:** this name (lit. "he who looks/peers at the public") is interpreted by one medieval commentator (Ioannes Tzetzes? in Σ^KU) as reflecting the character or situation of its bearer (as many other Aristophanic names do, e.g. Dicaeopolis, Strepsiades, Peisetaerus, Praxagora) either as a poor man (who looks to the public for assistance) or as a strong democrat (who looks to promote the public interest). Given, however, that the names of the two old men in this play so closely echo the names of the two old men in *Ecclesiazusae*, Chremes and Blepyrus, it is likely that this name should be regarded merely as (a variant of) a ready-made typical name for an elderly man in comedy; another variant, Blepes, appears in Menander's *Sikyonios* (188), and an old man in Menander's *Encheiridion* (F 7 Arnott = Men. fr. 862 K-A) bears the name Dercippus (not Dersippus; see Arnott i 359) whose first element comes from *derkesthai*, a synonym of *blepein* "look". In names of comic old men, these verbs may have been understood to mean "look closely, peer", suggesting failing eyesight. Various names derived from *blepein* are known to have been borne by actual Athenians, but Blepsidemus is not at present among them.

335 For the entrance of Blepsidemus, wrapped up in his own thoughts, cf. the entrance of the sceptical citizen at *Eccl.* 746-752; in Ar.'s earlier comedies such musing monologues appear only at the very beginning of a play, but cf. Men. *Dysk.* 153-166, *Sam.* 641-657.

338 **at the barbers' shops:** these were great centres of male gossip; cf. *Birds* 1440-3; Eupolis fr. 194; Lys. 23.3; Men. *Sam.* 509-513; Plut. *Nic.* 30.1-2, and see S. Lewis in A. Powell ed. *The Greek World* (London, 1995) 432-441.

342 **it's not a customary thing to do in these parts:** similarly at 47 Carion had implied that criminality was "the way that's regular in these parts" (using the same Greek word, *epikhōrion*); and in *Eccl.* 777-9 the sceptical citizen says that it is "not our tradition" to surrender property, and when asked whether this means he thinks "we must only take" (sc. and not give), responds with a strong affirmative.

344 **we're doing better:** speakers in comedy, unlike those in tragedy, do not normally refer to themselves in the first person plural, so by "we" Chremylus must mean either his household or, more probably, himself and all his friends, including in particular the chorus who have already been told that they are going to share in his good fortune (225-6, 262-3, 285).

345 **because you're one of my friends:** on the principle *koina ta tōn philōn* "the property of friends is common property" (cf. Eur. *Andr.* 376-7, *Or.* 735; Pl. *Lys.* 207c, *Rep.* 424a, *Phdr.* 279c, *Laws* 739c; Arist. *EN* 1159b29-32; Men. fr. 13 ~ Terence, *Adelphoe* 803-4).

351 **if we fail, we're totally ruined:** sc. because Zeus can be expected to punish us for attempting to thwart his will – whereas if the plan succeeds, Zeus (so Chremylus believes) will be powerless (cf. 119-142).

352 **goods:** lit. "load, cargo": Blepsidemus' language here is that of a trader considering whether to buy (say) a shipload of imported corn, and dubious about its quality or about the validity of the seller's title to it.

357 **from where you've been:** lit. "from there", i.e. from Delphi. Either, as Rogers suggests, Chremylus is still wearing his laurel garland, or else Ar. expects it to be taken for granted that he had told his friends where he was going.

359 **Apollo preserve us!:** lit. "Apollo the Averter!" (sc. of evil), an exclamation uttered on seeing or hearing something frightening or horrifying (cf. 854, *Knights* 1307, *Wasps* 161, *Birds* 61); here prompted by the suggestion that Chremylus might have committed the heinous crime of temple-robbery (cf. on 30).

363 **all alike are the slaves of gain:** Chremylus himself has said something very similar (146, 181), but it is one thing to say that everyone desires wealth and another to say that everyone values material gain above all else; if the latter were true, Chremylus and his friends would have turned to a life of crime long ago.

366 **you've gone potty:** lit. "you're suffering from black bile" (see on 12).

367 **has gone shifty:** lit. "is not staying in one place".

368 **it's plainly the look of a man who's committed some villainy:** lit. (with possibly excessive, but intelligible, compression) "it's plain <being the look> of one having committed some villainy" (cf. *Eccl.* 661 "he is plain being a thief" = "he is plainly a thief"). The mss.' reading (*ti pepanourgēkoti* instead of *-otos*) gives the impossible sense "a plain thing to a man who's committed some villainy"; the corruption will have arisen when TI was omitted before the similar-looking letter Π, reinserted in the margin or above the line, and then mistaken for a correction to the ending of the following word.

369 **driving at:** lit. "croaking" like a crow (cf. *Birds* 2, 24), i.e. saying to my irritation (cf. *Lys.* 506).

370 **you're after a share:** sc. as your price for not denouncing me – the kind of demand that a *sūkophantēs* (see 850-958) would make; cf. *Knights* 439, 775, *Wasps* 914-6, 971-2, [*Lys.*] 20.7, Andoc. 1.101, Isoc. 18.9, and numerous other passages collected and discussed by F.D. Harvey in P.A. Cartledge et al. *Nomos: Essays in Athenian Law, Politics and Society* (Cambridge, 1990) 110-2.

372-3 In face of Chremylus' denial that he has "stolen" anything, Blepsidemus assumes that he is quibbling and has actually acquired ill-gotten gains in some other way.

373 defrauding: Greek *aposterein* strictly speaking denotes the crime of refusing to repay a loan (*Clouds* 1305, 1464) or to return goods or money with which one had been entrusted (Isoc. 17.9, Dem. 21.44), typically by denying that one had received it.

374-5 where is one supposed to go from here?: lit. "whither can one turn?"

375 you're just not prepared: many editors prefer "he's just not prepared" (cf. 365, 367-8), a reading that appears first in mss. of the late thirteenth and early fourteenth centuries and was favoured by medieval scholars; but there is no reason why Blepsidemus should not here appeal directly to his friend, particularly since after 369, though still convinced Chremylus is a criminal, he never otherwise reverts to speaking of him in the third person.

377-385 It should be noted that Blepsidemus assumes that Chremylus' impending tribulations will occur in the Assembly, not in a lawcourt: this is shown by his reference (379) to "the politicians" (Greek *rhētores* "speakers", normally meaning Assembly speakers) and to Chremylus making himself a suppliant at the *bēma*, the Assembly speakers' platform (382). The reason is that if Chremylus, as he supposes, has robbed the temple, or committed some other crime, during his visit to Delphi, he cannot be prosecuted at Athens; rather the Delphians must demand his extradition, and it will be for the Assembly to decide whether to agree. The most famous case of such a demand was that made by Alexander in 335 for the surrender by Athens of Demosthenes and other anti-Macedonian politicians, when the Assembly, rather than complying or refusing, sent an embassy to request, successfully, that the demand be withdrawn (Aeschines 3.161; Dem. 18.41, 322; Plut. *Dem.* 23.4-6; D.S. 17.15).

379 stopping the politicians' mouths with little bits of silver: the metaphor whereby buying a man's silence is called "stopping his mouth with money" also appears in *Peace* 645; it gains added point in Greek from the fact that it was common to carry small change in one's mouth (cf. *Wasps* 791-6, *Birds* 502-3, *Eccl.* 818). Of course, as Chremylus rightly assumes, it would require rather more than some "little bits of silver" (Greek *kermata* "small coins") for such an attempt to be effective.

381 three minas: equal to 300 drachmas or about the price of two adult slaves. This would not be high on the scale of political bribes (or rather, of the bribes which politicians were alleged by their enemies to have accepted): in a contemporary speech (Lys. 29.6, cf. 28.9) it is alleged that three talents (or 180 minas) had been deposited with a third party on behalf of the general Ergocles, to be paid "to the speakers [sc. in the Assembly], should they succeed in saving him [sc. from being put on trial for treason]", and that when Ergocles was indeed committed for trial (ultimately to be sentenced to death) this money was repaid to his associate Philocrates.

381 claim: lit. "enter in your accounts". The idea is that Chremylus will employ Blepsidemus as his agent, giving him authority to make what deals he thinks necessary in Chremylus' interests and bill him afterwards for his expenses. Ergocles (see previous note) was similarly alleged to have employed Philocrates as his bribery agent.

382 I see a man who's going to ... : the phraseology is that of a fortune-teller practising catoptromancy (mirror-gazing); cf. *Ach.* 1128-31 (where a bronze shield substitutes for the mirror), Paus. 7.21.12, *SHA Didius Julianus* 7.10, and see E.R. Dodds, *The Ancient Concept of Progress and Other Essays* (Oxford, 1973) 186-7.

382-3 sitting on the speaker's platform holding a suppliant-branch: the ritual of supplication (on which see J. Gould, *JHS* 93 [1973] 74-103) gave a petitioner a strong, religiously-sanctioned claim to have his plea heeded, and from time to time formal supplications were made to the Council or Assembly (for the latter cf. Aeschines 2.15, Dem. 24.12) which gave the suppliant's business (as being a matter with religious implications) priority over the Assembly's normal agenda. In the latter half of the fourth century such supplications came to be used as little more than a procedural device to secure this priority (*IG* ii^2 337.33-38 is a good example), and apparently disrupted the Assembly's business so much that they came to be allowed only at one of the four Assembly meetings in each prytany (Arist. *Ath.Pol.* 43.6). The formal act of supplication was the laying of a suppliant's branch (an olive branch wreathed with wool) on an altar, in this case the altar of Zeus Agoraios on the Pnyx (cf. schol. *Knights* 410) at which were offered the sacrifice and prayer that preceded an Assembly meeting (Aeschines 1.23; Dein. 2.14; schol. *Ach.* 44) and which must have been on or very close to the *bēma* (in the later fourth century it seems to have stood behind and above the *bēma*: see H.A. Thompson and R.L. Scranton, *Hesperia* 12 [1943] 299-300; H.A. Thompson, *Hesperia* 21 [1952] 92-93). But the supplication could be made more dramatic if the suppliant himself sat at the altar (cf. Andoc. 1.44, 2.15, Dem. 18.107), as the Spartan Pericleidas was said to have done when seeking Athenian aid for Sparta in the 460s (*Lys.* 1138-41), and more so still if he had his wife and children with him (as defendants so often did when appearing in court: cf. *Wasps* 568-9, 976-8, [Lys.] 20.34, Andoc. 1.148, Aeschines 2.152).

383 his children: referred to again in the plural at 1104. Chremylus has only one son (35, 250) but is assumed also to have one or more (young, unmarried) daughters.

385 Pamphilus' *Children of Heracles:* a painting showing Hyllus and the other children of Heracles, probably accompanied by their grandmother Alcmene and perhaps their cousin Iolaus, begging the Athenians for assistance against their father's old enemy Eurystheus – a story, dramatized in Euripides' play of the same name, which was regularly quoted as an example of Athens' pious, altruistic devotion to protecting the rights of the helpless (cf. Lys. 2.11-16, Pl. *Menex.* 239b, Isoc. 4.56-63, Dem. 60.8). There are two possible interpretations of the reference to Pamphilus.

(i)   Pamphilus of Amphipolis (later of Sicyon) was a famous fourth-century painter, the teacher of perhaps the greatest of all Greek painters, Apelles, and the first to propose making drawing part of children's education; see Plin. *NH* 35.75-77, 123. One scholium says that his *Children of Heracles* was painted in "the Portico (*stoā*) of the Athenians" (it is not clear to which of the several *stoai* in and around the Agora this refers); another, however, states that this painting "is said not to be by Pamphilus but by Apollodorus [late fifth century], and Pamphilus, it seems, was younger than Aristophanes". In principle a date not long before 388 for the painting is entirely compatible with our other evidence about Pamphilus, who might for example have been born c.425 and been Apelles' teacher in the 350s and early 340s before his pupil left him to win fame at the courts of Philip, Alexander and Ptolemy I. On the other hand, the second scholium cited above does tend to suggest that ancient commentators knew of no evidence outside this passage that he was responsible for the Athens *Children of Heracles*; and the Alexandrian scholars Callistratus and Euphronius (second century BC) were apparently so sure he could not have been that they preferred to suppose that the Pamphilus here meant was an (otherwise unattested) tragic dramatist, and his *Children of Heracles* not a painting but a play.

(ii)   Alternatively, as was suggested by Holzinger and again by M. Robertson *ap.* L.H. Jeffery, *ABSA* 60 (1965) 47, the reference may be to the contemporary general Pamphilus (see on 174) whose name is unexpectedly substituted for that of the painter of the mural (presumably Apollodorus, cf. above). In this case we would have to assume that after his return from the Aegina expedition he had made supplication before the Assembly together with his family. Were the Assembly perhaps about to consider a proposal to put him on trial for treason (which would almost certainly have ended in a sentence of death) by the procedure of *eisangelia* (on which see M.H. Hansen, *The*

Athenian Democracy in the Age of Demosthenes [Oxford, 1991] 212-8), as they did about this very time in the case of Ergocles (cf. on 381), and did Pamphilus' emotive supplication persuade them to drop the charge with the result that he was prosecuted only for embezzlement?

It is not possible to decide with certainty between (i) and (ii); but (ii) gives the passage greater comic and satirical force, and the evident reluctance of some well-informed ancient scholars to countenance the idea that Ar. was referring to Pamphilus the painter strongly suggests that they knew of good reasons to reject it.

It is worth noting that in Euripides' play (whose action is set not at Athens but at or near Marathon) Iolaus describes the family of Heracles as "suppliants of Zeus Agoraios" (Eur. *Heracl.* 70; see on 382-3); it is not likely that Ar.'s audience were expected to recall this brief reference, but Apollodorus' painting is likely to have been inspired, at least in part, by Euripides' play (it prominently featured Heracles' daughter, a character probably invented by Euripides), and it may have shown the suppliants at an altar recognizably modelled on that of Zeus Agoraios on the Pnyx.

390   **you'll be your own:** sc. by refusing the assistance I have offered, and thereby making it certain that you will be extradited to Delphi and in due course executed.

394   **to hell with you:** lit. "<will you> not <go> to the ravens?", a very common curse (in effect "may your corpse remain unburied to be eaten by scavenger birds"), here presumably provoked by what Blepsidemus takes to be a blatant lie.

396   **you do mean the sea-god?:** Blepsidemus is still so sceptical that he even suspects Chremylus' plainly stated oath may be a subterfuge: when Chremylus says "Poseidon", does he mean the great Olympian and brother of Zeus, or is he referring to some insignificant namesake with little or no power to punish an oath-breaker? For a similar (alleged) subterfuge cf. *Birds* 521 "Lampon swears 'by Goose' [*khēna* instead of *Zēna* "Zeus"] when he's trying to put one over on you".

397   **if there's any other Poseidon, then I mean the other too:** i.e. I should be taken as having sworn by *every* being named Poseidon, including therefore the great Olympian. This seems to convince Blepsidemus, who from this point expresses no further doubts about Wealth's being really present in Chremylus' house.

398   **sending him round to us, your friends:** Chremylus did in fact send for his friends at the first opportunity (as Blepsidemus himself had observed with surprise, 340-1), and he has assured them, and Blepsidemus (345), that they will have "an opportunity to share" in Chremylus' new-found prosperity; but he has not yet done anything to fulfil this promise.

401   **the two of us:** Chremylus never requests or invites Blepsidemus to become his partner in the task of restoring Wealth's sight; he simply assumes it, and Blepsidemus is made to accept the role without comment even though he has been told "there is some danger in the business" (348-351). Ar. wants to move the action on to its next stage without further wrangling between the pair, and is confident that if he makes the characters thus take it for granted that Blepsidemus has stepped into what was previously Carion's role (cf. on 321) the audience will do so too.

406   **shouldn't we be calling in a doctor?:** this suggestion is mainly designed to provide a feed for Chremylus' retort and the ensuing survey of the audience; we are given no opportunity to consider what chance a mortal practitioner would have of curing an affliction that had been imposed by Zeus. The line also, however, enables Ar. to have Blepsidemus be the first to propose practical action to get Wealth cured; he is represented as now being at least as eager as Chremylus to achieve this (cf. 413-4, 622-3), and this is not surprising – Chremylus already has Wealth in his home, whereas it is

assumed (398-402) that Wealth/wealth can go to other deserving houses once he has been cured but not before.

408 **the pay's not there, so the profession's not there:** further evidence of the power of Wealth (cf. 160-8). It is not to be supposed that Athens was devoid of medical practitioners (cf. *Eccl.* 363-4); the reference is to *public* physicians, outstanding members of the profession who were employed by states, at very high salaries (part of which went to pay a staff of assistants; cf. *Ach.* 1032), to give free treatment to all citizens (cf. Hdt. 3.131; Pl. *Gorg.* 514d-515b; Xen. *Mem.* 4.2.5; *IG* xii[1] 1032). In the 420s a certain Pittalus had held this position at Athens (*Ach.* 1030-2, 1222; *Wasps* 1432); now, it appears, the post was in abeyance through lack of funds to finance it.

409 **let's have a look:** for such surveys of the audience cf. *Clouds* 1096-1100, *Wasps* 72-85, *Peace* 543-9, *Frogs* 275-6, *Eccl.* 440. Ar. is of course perfectly safe in assuming that, whether or not any medical men are present in the theatre, none will stand up and offer to treat a "patient" who in the real world outside the dramatic fiction is not suffering from any complaint at all!

410-1 **what I was already getting ready to do:** designed to arouse the expectation of an almost immediate departure for the temple; the necessary preparations, we are encouraged to assume, had been ordered by Chremylus while he was indoors (between 252 and 322) and will have been completed by now. The intervention of Poverty results in delay, but as soon as she is got rid of at 618 the party leave for the temple without even going indoors (Carion and Wealth come out to join them, with all the requisites for the visit).

411 **to have him spend the night in the temple of Asclepius:** see Introduction §3. There were two sanctuaries of Asclepius in Attica, one on the south slope of the Acropolis, the other at Zea on the Peiraeus peninsula. Both were daughter-shrines of the great Asclepieum of Epidaurus and dated from the years 421-420, the Zea sanctuary being the senior (cf. *IG* ii² 4960 = *SEG* xxv 226); before then the nearest Asclepius sanctuary where Athenians could go for healing had been on Aegina (*Wasps* 122-3). The reference to the sea in 656-8 shows that in this play Wealth is taken to the Zea sanctuary, which appears from the inscriptional evidence to have been the more popular of the two in the early fourth century. See F. Robert, *RPh*³ 5 (1931) 132-3; R. Garland, *The Piraeus* (London, 1987) 115-7, 208-9, 230-1; S.B. Aleshire, *The Athenian Asklepieion* (Amsterdam, 1989) 13, 35.

417 **Heracles** is appealed to here as *alexikakos* "deliverer from evil" – a title that Ar. awards to himself at *Wasps* 1043, in a passage where he has cast himself in the role of Heracles (cf. 1030) fighting the fearsome monster Cleon; cf. also *Clouds* 1372, Hellanicus *FGrH* 4 F 109, Luc. *Alex.* 4. It cannot be established with complete certainty which of the two men utters the appeal, but a little later (438-453) Blepsidemus is clearly the more frightened of the two.

418 **I shall put a miserable end to your miserable existence:** the language is almost identical to that used by Carion to the as yet unrecognized Wealth at 65.

422 **you certainly look very pale to me:** probably implying that he thinks she may be a ghost or underworld demon: the spirits of the dead are pale because they are bloodless and/or because they never see the sun. The adjective *ōkhros* "pale yellow" is applied in *Clouds* (1016, 1112) to the faces of students of philosophy, one of whom, Chaerephon (yellow-complexioned at *Wasps* 1413), is described elsewhere as "half a corpse" (*Clouds* 504) and as a spirit flitting batlike up from Hades (*Birds* 1562-4); and at *Eccl.* 1073 an old woman with a whitened face is mistaken for "an old hag who's risen from the majority [i.e. from the dead]". See J. McGlew, *AJP* 119 (1997) 38-39.

423 **a Fury out of some tragedy:** not Aeschylus' seventy-year-old *Eumenides* (in which torches appeared only in the triumphant finale) but some more recent (probably contemporary) play in which Furies (Erinyes) had appeared. Furies became something of a cliché in fourth-century tragedy (cf. Aeschines 1.190). It has been suggested that this passage implies that the contest between Poverty and Chremylus should be seen as one between the spirit of tragedy and that of comedy, between hard reality and wish-fulfilment fantasy: see S.D. Olson, *HSCP* 93 (1990) 233-6 and P. Sfyroeras, *GRBS* 36 (1995) 242-8.

424 **that crazy tragic look:** Poverty's mask is evidently reminiscent of those worn in tragedy by women who have been driven half mad by their sufferings (among Euripidean characters, one might think of Hecuba and Agaue). The Furies are several times spoken of in tragedy as madwomen (*mainades, potniades, margoi*); cf. Aesch. *Eum.* 67, 500, Eur. *Or.* 318.

425 **she hasn't got any torches:** this is the earliest evidence of any kind that directly connects torches with Furies. The Aeschylean Furies, children of Night, certainly did not carry torches; torches are not mentioned in connection with Furies in later fifth-century tragedy (not even in Euripides' very influential *Orestes*); torch-bearing Furies do not appear in art until the 370s at the earliest (*LIMC* s.v. Erinys no. 45); yet from the mid fourth century onwards, torches were *the* typical attribute of a Fury in art or on stage (cf. Aeschines 1.190; Lucian, *Kataplous* 22), and our passage shows that as early as 388 it could be taken for granted that a Fury without torches (the plural suggests one in each hand) was no real Fury. Probably this association derives from a memorable recent tragic scene in which one or more torch-bearing Furies had appeared (cf. last note but one); the unidentifiable author of this play may well have been inspired by the scene in Euripides' *Trojan Women* (306-461) in which Cassandra appears in a state of madness, brandishing two torches (351) in a ghastly mockery of bridal celebrations, and speaks of herself, just before her final exit (457), as "one of the three Erinyes", destined as she is to take vengeance on Agamemnon for the dead of Troy.

426 **she's going to howl:** i.e. I am not afraid of her \<since she is merely human\> and am ready to beat her for her insulting behaviour.

426-7 **an innkeeper or a porridge-vendor:** free women who worked outside the domestic environment, especially those who sold goods in the market, were proverbially bellicose and foul-mouthed; cf. *Lys.* 456-461 where women of half a dozen trades, including the two mentioned here, are summoned to mount an attack in which insulting words and obscene gestures (460) feature almost as prominently as physical violence, and put their opponents to flight; also *Wasps* 493-9, 1388-1414, *Frogs* 857-8. See J.J. Henderson, *TAPA* 117 (1987) 121.

430 **out of every land:** most editors and translators take the meaning to be "out of the whole land" (i.e. Attica), but that would be not *ek pāses khōrās* but *ek pāses tēs khōrās*. Chremylus in the *agōn* repeatedly speaks as champion of the interests of the human race (490, 495, 498, 500, 502, 506, 547; cf. 461), and while he may well in practice be unconcerned about the welfare of non-Greeks (see on 461-3), his inability to answer Poverty's argument at 522-6 shows that he does intend his new ethico-economic order to include at least all free Greeks, not just Athenians. This complaint by Poverty is the first indication we have had that his ultimate aim is not merely to enrich the virtuous but to bring it about that *everyone* is (virtuous and) rich; see Introduction, §4.

431 **the Barathron:** a rocky gully a short distance outside Athens, near the Peiraeus road, into which condemned criminals were sometimes thrown: cf. 1109, *Knights* 1362, *Clouds* 1449, *Frogs* 574; Hdt. 7.133; Xen. *Hell.* 1.7.20; Pl. *Gorg.* 516d-e; for the location, Pl. *Rep.* 4.439e and W. Judeich, *Topographie von Athen* (Munich, 1931) 140.

434 from these parts: Greek *enthende* "from here" can, according to context, mean "from this spot" or "from this earth" (cf. Pl. *Apol.* 40c, *Phd.* 107e, and *enthade* "on this earth" at *Frogs* 82, 155) or anything in between; here, in view of 430, "from this earth" seems required.

435-6 the tavern-keeper ... who always gives me short measure: cf. 347-8 where a curse is pronounced on tavern-keepers (male or female) who do this; for women tavern-keepers cf. also 1120 and *IG* ii² 1553.16.

436 half-pints: Greek *kotulai*; the *kotulē* (lit. "cup") was a measure of about 270 millilitres (a UK pint is 568 millilitres).

437 Poverty, "the ugliest of divinities" (Eur. fr. 248), makes her first known appearance as a goddess in Alcaeus fr. 364 (cf. Hdt. 8.111.3). She has no cult, no presence in art and no authentic mythology, though she can figure in genealogies devised *ad hoc* for allegorical purposes (Alcaeus *loc.cit.*; Democritus fr. 24 D-K; Pl. *Symp.* 203a-d). See H.J. Newiger, *Metapher und Allegorie* (Munich, 1957) 155-164.

442-3 the most deadly creature in the natural world: lit. "than whom no more utterly destructive animal has been born anywhere".

445 the most cowardly action (Greek *deilotaton ergon*) is no more than a late medieval conjecture (or possibly error) for *deinotaton ergon* "the most terrible action"; of modern editors, only Rogers has adopted it. It is, however, likely to be what Ar. wrote. To be described as *deino(tato)n* an action, whether good or bad, must almost by definition be audacious (cf. 429, 455, 1112, *Ach.* 128, *Wasps* 908, *Peace* 403, *Birds* 1175), and a pathetic *failure* to act would be the last thing to be so called.

449 "what weapons or what allies can we trust?": probably adapted from an unknown tragedy, since the text as offered by the mss. (except R^ac) requires the first syllable of *hoplois* "weapons" to be scanned long, a scansion found in comedy only when quoting or imitating tragedy. The quotation cannot, however, be exact, since the line has an anapaest in the fourth foot (permissible in tragedy only to accommodate a proper name); probably *dunamei* "armed force" (here rendered "allies") has been substituted by Ar. for some other word (e.g. *kratei* "power") so as to create a line that mixes tragic with comic rhythmic patterns.

451 hasn't forced us to pawn: lit. "doesn't place in pawn".

453 can triumph over her and her trying ways: lit. "can set up a trophy over her ways", with a rather forced pun on *tropaion* "trophy" (an improvised monument set up on the site of a battle by the victorious army) and *tropoi* "ways, habits".

456 damn and blast you: lit. "you who will perish miserably".

461-3 all mankind ... out of Greece: an interesting piece of unconscious racism, Chremylus (and possibly Ar. too) implicitly assuming that non-Greeks are not (fully) human; there were many fifth- and fourth-century Greeks, among them (intermittently) Plato and Aristotle, who were prepared to assert that it was just or natural for all or most non-Greeks to be slaves (cf. Eur. *IA* 1400; Pl. *Rep.* 469b-c; Arist. *Pol.* 1252b5-9, 1255a21-35) – and Chremylus, like Praxagora (*Eccl.* 651), takes it for granted (517-521) that slaves will not benefit at all from his new world-order (nor does Poverty question this: her counter-argument, 518-526, is not, as one might expect, that slaves will become rich like everyone else and so will be able to buy their freedom and stop working, but that the kidnappers and dealers on whom the supply of slaves depends will no longer have any economic motive to ply their trade).

468 before that: lit. "firstly", i.e. before you expel me.

468-470 and if I prove ... — : the consequence of this alternative is left to be understood, since it is obvious (the two men will, in their own and everyone else's interest, desist from their attempt to restore Wealth's sight). Cf. *Thesm.* 536, Plato com. fr. 23, Men. fr. 659, Soph. fr. 458, *Iliad* 1.135-9.

472 to assert that: referring back to Poverty's claim that she is "the cause of all ... good things".

476 pillories and execution-boards: Greek *kūphōnes* and *tu(m)pana*, respectively. The *tu(m)panon* (lit. "drum", i.e. stretching-frame) was the instrument with which was inflicted the form of execution called *apotu(m)panismos*. It was a large board to which were fixed an iron collar (which could be tightened or loosened by adjusting a nail) and clamps for wrists and ankles; when the criminal had been clamped to the board, it was stood up in a vertical position, leaving him stretched out with feet off the ground, degradingly and agonizingly exposed, probably until sunset (cf. Arist. *Rhet.* 1385a9-13) when, if still alive, he would be garrotted by tightening the collar: see *Thesm.* 930ff (where Euripides' in-law is subjected to this punishment for sacrilege, but eventually rescued); L. Gernet, *REG* 37 (1924) 261-293 = *The Anthropology of Ancient Greece* tr. J. Hamilton and B. Nagy (Baltimore, 1981) 252-276; R.J. Bonner and G. Smith, *The Administration of Justice from Homer to Aristotle* (Chicago, 1930-8) ii 279-287. Our evidence is consistent with the hypothesis that this was the standard form of execution for all crimes for which the death penalty was mandatory rather than discretionary. The *kūphōn* (lit. "stooper") was a frame in which lesser criminals (especially, according to Pollux 10.177, those guilty of offences against market laws) were made to stand or sit with their necks clamped (cf. 606, Cratinus fr. 123, Arist. *Pol.* 1306b2, and perhaps *Clouds* 592 and *Lys.* 680-1); we also hear of a "five-holed frame" (*Knights* 1049) which had holes for wrists and ankes as well as neck, and it is not clear whether these were different instruments of punishment or the same instrument used in different ways.

478 screaming with rage: lit. "shouting 'iou, iou'" (cf. 276, 852).

480 what penalty shall I enter on my indictment: for some types of prosecution the penalty was fixed by law; for others it was determined by the jury, who had to choose between the prosecutor's and the defendant's proposal. The prosecutor stated at the end of his indictment what penalty he intended to propose (cf. *Wasps* 897); the defendant did not have to make his counter-proposal until after he had been found guilty. See A.R.W. Harrison, *The Law of Athens* (Oxford, 1968-71) ii 166; S.C. Todd, *The Shape of Athenian Law* (Oxford, 1993) 133-5.

482 if you lose, the same penalty must apply to ... you: unlike in a real trial, where an unsuccessful prosecutor could be punished only by a fine and disqualification from prosecuting, only in certain classes of case, and only if he failed to gain one-fifth of the jury's votes (see Harrison *op.cit.* ii 83; D.M. MacDowell, *The Law in Classical Athens* [London, 1978] 64-65).

483 twenty deaths: at the trial of Ergocles, about this time, one prosecutor said (Lys. 28.1) that in his opinion Ergocles would not be sufficiently punished "even if he were put to death several times for every one of his actions"; cf. also Dem. 21.21 "I shall show that he deserves many deaths, not one", Men. *Dysk.* 291-3.

484 just two: i.e. one each.

485 do that: i.e. die (because you are certain to lose).

485-6 what is there left that anyone could ...?: lit. "what could anyone still ... ?", implying that Chremylus has already said all that anyone could validly say against her (viz. nothing).

487-618 This passage, in anapaestic tetrameters ending (from 598) with a *pnīgos*, corresponds to the formal debate (*agōn*) which appears in most of Ar.'s earlier plays; but the traditional double structure of the comic *agōn*, with two speeches each introduced by a song from the chorus and a couplet (*katakeleusmos*) by the chorus-leader, has been reduced (as in *Eccl.* 571-709) to a single structure, from which in *Wealth* the choral song has also been dropped, leaving the *katakeleusmos* (487-8) as the chorus's sole contribution. The debate itself is more loosely structured than any of its predecessors: it begins with a 17-line speech by Chremylus broken only by a reinforcing remark from Blepsidemus, but thereafter the two antagonists interrupt each other freely (sometimes with questions or brief remarks, sometimes with what develop into fresh speeches) and the impression is less that of a formal debate than of a running argument. Its equivocal outcome, in which Poverty is forcibly driven off when it is far from obvious that she has been beaten in the argument, is to some extent paralleled in the second *agōn* of *Clouds* (1345-1451): there Strepsiades seems at one moment to have accepted defeat (1437-9), but when Pheidippides, misguidedly hoping to conciliate his father, offers to beat up his mother, the old man is so revolted by the suggestion that he tells Pheidippides he can "throw yourself into the Barathron along with Socrates" (1448-51; cf. *Wealth* 431) and on that note the *agōn* ends. Here, as there, a case is cleverly argued for a proposition that almost everyone would regard as contrary to right reason (that it is not wrong to strike one's father; that it is better to be poor than to be rich), and the representative of traditional thinking, after striving without success to refute this case, in the end resolves simply to ignore it. These are the only two Aristophanic *agōnes* in which the second speaker is not the clear winner; in both of them it is the champion of the unorthodox cause who is the second speaker.

497 that everyone is virtuous – and rich, of course: this is the only explicit statement in the play of the mechanism whereby the distribution of wealth according to desert will ultimately result in everyone being wealthy; see Introduction §4.

505 puts a stop to this situation: most editors read, with R, "puts a stop to her" (i.e. Poverty/poverty); but while Chremylus sometimes refers to Poverty by her name (549, 574, 590) – as indeed she herself can do (594) – he never refers to her by a third-person pronoun (except in 445-453 when he is desperately trying to prevent Blepsidemus from abandoning him), and such a pronoun would be particularly jarring here when Poverty had been addressed in the second person in the previous line. R's reading would be acceptable only if 505-6 were given (as by van Leeuwen) to Blepsidemus (cf. 484, 499, 580); but Chremylus cannot be deprived of these lines, without which his speech would end on a negative note, describing the unjust present instead of the happy future. It is evident from the scholia – where in several mss. three different interpretations are offered, each based on a different version of the text – that in this passage variant readings already existed well back in antiquity.

507-8 you two old men are ... balderdash and lunacy: in the Greek these are not separate sentences but form an elaborate vocative phrase ("you two old men who are the easiest ... , who are comrades of ...") introducing the sentence that follows ("if what you desire ... no advantage at all").

508 order: Greek *thiasos* "religious association, guild". A *thiasos* normally bore the name of the god or hero whom it collectively worshipped: Chremylus and Blepsidemus are thus, in Poverty's eyes, among those who worship at the altar of Balderdash and Lunacy: cf. *Knights* 221, 634-6 (where the Sausage-seller is invited to make libation to Imbecility, and later prays to the Swindlers, the Tricksters and similar divinities) and 255 (where Paphlagon-Cleon addresses his allies, the jurymen, as "members of the phratry [another kind of religious guild] of the Three Obols").

510-6 Chremylus and Carion had told Wealth (160-7) that all crafts and skills were practised because of him (i.e. in order to *acquire* wealth); now Poverty, looking at the same facts from a different angle, claims that they are all practised because of her (i.e. to *avoid* poverty). In each passage eight legitimate occupations (other than agriculture) are mentioned; four of them (the smith, the cobbler, the launderer and the tanner) appear in both passages. Poverty's argument is at first sight self-contradictory, since she assumes that in a world of universal wealth peasants and craftsmen will not work (516) on the way to concluding that in a world of universal wealth Chremylus (who is a peasant) will have to work much harder than he does now (525-6); but she is really only expressing in a dramatic and paradoxical fashion the unhappy (and not yet refuted) truth that if everyone assumes that the needs and comforts of life will be provided for him by others without any effort on his part, then those needs and comforts will not be provided at all. Unhappy truths, however, are of no concern to an Old Comic hero, particularly when he knows that he has for a friend a god who can solve this problem miraculously.

513 **a stitcher:** Greek *rhaptein* "to stitch, to sew" probably suggests primarily the making of leather goods of all kinds (except shoes, which will presently be mentioned separately); cf. *Knights* 783-5 (a cushion), *Clouds* 538 (an artificial phallus), Alexis fr. 103.11 (false buttocks), Xen. *On Horsemanship* 12.9 (the quilted seat of a riding-cloth).

515 **"to break the surface ... the fruits of Deo":** high-flown poetic language (two or three definite articles omitted; *dapedon* "surface, level expanse", used otherwise by Ar. only in lyrics; "the fruits of Deo" = "cereals", Deo being a poetic name for the corn-goddess Demeter found in *h.Hom.Dem.* 47, 211, 492, Soph. *Ant.* 1121, fr. 754, Eur. *Supp.* 290, *Hel.* 1343, *Erechtheus* fr. 65.34, 109 Austin), probably designed (particularly in its circumlocutory style) to be reminiscent of contemporary dithyramb; the dithyrambic style was often parodied in fourth-century comedy, cf. *Eccl.* 1-18, Antiphanes fr. 55, Eubulus fr. 75, Xenarchus fr. 1, Men. *Dysk.* 946-953, and see Nesselrath 242-3, 251, 255-266.

516 **if you're able to live in idleness:** here "you" refers to the new idle rich, whereas earlier in the same sentence, in 512 ("if you have both of these disappear"), it had referred to those who would suffer through these people's idleness; this is not necessarily an oversight (though it may be, cf. on 529), because it is Poverty's case (cf. 509, 525-6) that universal wealth would be disastrous for the very people who desire it and expect to benefit from it.

518 **the slaves will do them for us:** as Praxagora had said when a similar question was asked at *Eccl.* 651; cf. on 461-3.

520 **when he's got money too?:** the presupposition that one who already has as much money as he could possibly need is unlikely to want to acquire more is contrary to common experience and belief (cf. 188-197), and Chremylus is thus able to answer this question (unlike the next) without difficulty.

521 **from Thessaly where all the kidnappers are** (lit. "from Thessaly, from the home of very many kidnappers"): although the typical slave was thought of as being of non-Greek origin (cf. on 461-3), many slaves were in fact Greek; the means by which a free Greek might be reduced to slavery included enslavement for debt (cf. on 147), exposure in infancy (cf. Eur. *Ion* passim, Ter. *HT* 626-7, 640; see W.K. Lacey, *The Family in Classical Greece* [London, 1968] 167, and W.V. Harris, *JRS* 84 [1994] 1-22), capture in war or by pirates, and the method referred to here – the activities of men (called *andrapodistai* "enslavers") who made a profession of abducting persons (most often, no doubt, children) and selling them to slave-dealers. Hermippus fr. 63.18-19 speaks of the Thessalian port of Pagasae alongside Phrygia as the prime sources of slaves for the Athenian market.

524 **to risk his own life:** the kidnapping and selling of free persons was a capital crime at Athens (Arist. *Ath.Pol.* 52.1) and probably everywhere, though the law must have been hard to enforce in regions of large extent and scattered population such as Thessaly. It may well be, too, that if a kidnapper was caught still in possession of his victim, the victim's family might not always allow concern for due process of law to restrain them from immediate revenge.

529   when you bring a bride home: *prima facie* we would expect something like "when you are giving a daughter in marriage", because (i) Chremylus and Blepsidemus (to whom the Greek verb, being dual, ought to be referring) are both old men and both married already (cf. 250, 615) and (ii) the clothing and adornment of a bride was the responsibility of her own family, not of her bridegroom, and they would normally provide a complete wardrobe for her to begin married life with (cf. Isaeus 2.9, 8.8, Dem. 41.27, *SIG*³ 1215 [Myconos]). There is, however, no plausible way of emending the text, and it is best to take *hopotan* "when" as meaning in effect "after", so that the reference is to fabrics and perfumes bought subsequent to the marriage with the husband's money; while incongruity (i) can be accounted for as a confusion resulting from Poverty's incessant, unsystematic and uncoordinated shifts between addressing Chremylus alone, the two old men together, and humanity in general, and between using the singular, dual and plural of the second person.

530   with costly garments in variegated colours: lit. "with costs of dyed garments of variegated appearance", seemingly another touch of "dithyrambic" language (cf. on 515); the adjective *poikilomorphos* "of variegated appearance" occurs otherwise only in a Hellenistic lyric (*Lyr. Alex. Adesp.* 34.1 Powell).

533   as a mistress sits over her slaves: lit. "like a mistress". The picture evoked is that of the lady of a house supervising the work of her female slaves (especially the making of clothes); cf. Xen. *Oec.* 7-10 (esp. 7.6, 7.35 and 10.10)

535-547 Chremylus might simply have pointed out that even if it is true, as Poverty claims, that from her "all ... things that you want are available in ample supply", this is of little benefit to those who cannot afford to buy these things. Instead he leaves this to be inferred from a powerful, emotive tirade in which he graphically portrays the misery of a (very) poor man's life, concentrating on the most basic necessities: warmth (535), food (536, 543-4, 545-6), minimal furniture (545) and, most prominently, the right to a decent night's sleep (537-9, 540-3) of which the poor man is deprived by insect infestation and lack of proper bedding. He imagines a family with no resources and no income, who can buy nothing and have to exist by using what no one else wants.

535   blisters from the bath-house: in the winter, poor people with no adequate heating at home would go to the public bath-houses (cf. 952-4, Alciphron 3.40) and crowd round the water-heating furnaces, more concerned to get themselves thoroughly warmed than to avoid blisters or burns.

536   half-starved little kids and old grannies: a married man would normally have to maintain himself, his wife, his children, his mother if she was a widow (cf. e.g. *Ach.* 817, [Dem.] 59.22), and any slaves he might own.

538-9   around your head, waking you up: "you(r)" in these phrases should be taken as impersonal, equivalent to "one('s)"; Greek in such contexts is able to avoid using any pronoun at all.

539   "You'll starve; up you get!": in place of Poverty's dignified picture of herself as a mistress compelling the worker to his task (532-4) Chremylus assigns the same role to clouds of pestilent insects.

541   a bed of rushes: sc. spread on the floor; in Eur. *Tro.* 507-8 such a bed, with a stone for a head-rest (cf. 542-3), is seen by Hecuba as appropriate to her new status as a slave.

544   mallow shoots: mallow, gathered wild, had been proverbially a food for paupers ever since Hesiod (*Works* 41); cf. also Antiphanes fr. 156, Plut. *Mor.* 158a.

544 **withered radish leaves:** little better than rubbish, since normally the root would be eaten and the leaves discarded. At *Ach.* 469 Dicaeopolis, about to play the role of a beggar, asks Euripides for "some withered leaves for my basket".

545 **a stool:** Greek *thrānos*, a backless seat (corresponding to English "stool" or "bench" according to its shape). The family here imagined is so poor that it does not even *aspire* to possess chairs with back-support.

545 **a ... wine-jar:** Greek *stamnos*, a large jar in which wine was stored and transported; see D.A. Amyx, *Hesperia* 27 (1958) 190-5.

546 **a storage-jar:** Greek *phidaknē* (so always in Athenian inscriptions, see Threatte i 468; *pithaknē* in the ms. tradition of Ar. and other authors), a diminutive of *pithos*, a large, deep earthenware vessel used for long-term storage of grain and other supplies; see Amyx *op.cit.* 168-174, who shows that a vessel that was called a *phidaknē* might have a capacity ranging (at least) from 3 to 12 *amphorês* (roughly from 115 to 460 litres, or from 25 to 100 UK gallons). The jar is imagined to have broken in half longitudinally, and the remains of its lip and its foot will serve as the sides of the trough.

548 **the destitute:** Greek *ptōkhoi* "beggars". Normally beggary/destitution would be thought of as a special and extreme category of poverty (*peniā*); Poverty will choose to treat them as entirely separate concepts (in a manner reminiscent of the quibbling semantic distinctions between close synonyms insisted on by the sophist Prodicus and parodied in Pl. *Prot.* 337a-c; cf. also Andoc. 3.11 on the great difference between a peace and a treaty), redefining *peniā* as the condition in which one can just make ends meet.

549 **that Poverty is the sister of Destitution:** in Alcaeus (fr. 364) she had been the sister of Incapacity (*Amākhaniā*); later in the 380s Plato (*Symp.* 203b-c) made her and Resourcefulness (*Poros*) the parents of Eros. Here "we do say that ..." suggests that the kinship of Poverty and Destitution was proverbial; there is no other evidence of this, but it is as logically appropriate that they should be sisters as it is that Sleep should be the brother of Death (*Iliad* 14.231, 16.672; Hes. *Thg.* 212, 756, 759).

550 **that Dionysius is no different from Thrasybulus:** Dionysius I was absolute ruler of Syracuse from 405 to 367; by 392 he was firmly in control of all of eastern Sicily, and by 389/8 he had conquered the toe of Italy (Iapygia) except for Rhegium. In 394/3, on the initiative of Conon (cf. Lys. 19.19-20), Athens had tried to detach him from his long-standing alliance with Sparta; this initiative met with little success, but one result of it was that the Assembly passed a decree in honour of Dionysius "the ruler of Sicily" and set up a copy of it (*IG* ii^2 18) in the theatre (for Dionysius had some pretensions to be a poet, and indeed won first prize for tragedy at the Lenaea shortly before his death [D.S. 15.74.1-4]). By 388, however, Dionysius' aggressions had made him deeply unpopular throughout much of the Greek world, and at the Olympic Games in the summer, to which Dionysius had sent his brother at the head of a magnificently equipped delegation, an inflammatory speech by Lysias, calling for his overthrow and bracketing him with the King of Persia as an oppressor of the Greeks, led to a riot in which the mob attacked and plundered the Syracusan pavilion (Lys. 33; D.H. *Lys.* 29-30; D.S. 14.109.1-3). Soon afterwards Dionysius at last intervened in the Corinthian War, on the Spartan side, sending twenty ships which formed about a quarter of the fleet with which Antalcidas blockaded the Hellespont and forced Athens to accept peace on Spartan and Persian terms (Xen. *Hell.* 5.1.26, 28).

Thrasybulus, son of Lycus, of the deme Steiria (*PA* 7310; *LGPN* 22), had for many years, until his recent death, been one of the most prominent political and military figures in Athens. He had been a successful naval commander in the later years of the Peloponnesian War, having first come to the fore in 411 when he took a leading role in the suppression of an oligarchic movement in the fleet at Samos and was irregularly elected a general (Thuc. 8.73-76), and soon afterwards promoted the recall of Alcibiades to take command of the fleet (Thuc. 8.81.1). He remained a general until 406 when, probably in consequence of his close association with Alcibiades, he failed to secure re-election; at Arginusae that summer he was a trierarch, and in the dispute which arose afterwards over the fleet's failure to pick up shipwrecked men he was among those who did most to divert public anger from the trierarchs to the generals and thereby bring about their condemnation (cf. D.S. 13.101.2-4, Xen. *Hell.* 1.7.5-6). Under the Thirty he was exiled (Xen. *Hell.* 2.3.42), went to Thebes, and from there, with a handful of followers, seized Phyle on the Attic-Boeotian border (cf. 1146) and began the revolt that led to the overthrow of the Thirty and the restoration of democracy. This naturally made him "one of the most powerful men in the state" (Isoc. 18.23), but as a peacetime politician he seems to have been ineffective: between 403 and 396 we only know of one political action by him, an unsuccessful attempt to give citizenship to all who had fought for the democracy (Arist. *Ath.Pol.* 40.2; a modified version of the same measure was later carried [*IG* ii² 10], whether again on Thrasybulus' initiative we do not know). In 396 Thrasybulus was one of those who persuaded the Assembly to disown an unauthorized attempt to make, through Conon, an alliance with Persia against Sparta (the Demaenetus incident: *Hell.Oxy.* 6.2). In 395, however, he supported the alliance with Thebes, regarding it as dangerous but politically necessary (Xen. *Hell.* 3.5.16), and he was in command of the Athenians who marched to Thebes' aid at Haliartus (Plut. *Lys.* 29.1) and probably again at the battle of Nemea the following year (cf. Lys. 16.15). In 393/2 his popularity seems to have been eclipsed by that of Conon, who was no great friend of his (cf. Arist. *Rhet.* 1400b20); but after Conon's death he apparently returned to favour (a contemporary funeral oration has a strong anti-Conon and pro-Thrasybulus slant [Lys. 2.59-66]), and his opposition to the terms of peace offered by Sparta in 392/1 (*Eccl.* 202-3, 356; cf. R. Seager, *JHS* 87 [1967] 107-8) must have been largely responsible for their rejection. In 390 Thrasybulus was put in command of the main Athenian fleet (Xen. *Hell.* 4.8.25) and gained several military and diplomatic successes (*ibid.* 26-30; D.S. 14.94.2-4; Dem. 20.59-60; *IG* ii² 21, 24), but was killed in a night raid on his camp at Aspendus in Pamphylia. When the expedition returned, Thrasybulus' associate Ergocles was prosecuted for bribery and embezzlement (i.e. for failing to fulfil exaggerated expectations of the revenue the expedition would generate) and sentenced to death (Lys. 28 and 29); and one of his prosecutors insinuated, though he did not openly assert, that Thrasybulus had been plotting to occupy Byzantium as a personal fiefdom, keep his ships there, marry a Thracian princess, and use the area as a base for overthrowing democracy at Athens (Lys. 28.5-8). His reputation for haughtiness and arrogance (Strattis fr. 20; cf. Lys. 16.15) may have helped to make such allegations credible, though even his enemies had to admit that in the past he had done the state some service (Lys. 28.8). On Thrasybulus see R.J. Buck, *Thrasybulus and the Athenian Democracy* (Stuttgart, 1998).

Both the dead Thrasybulus and the living Dionysius, then, were in bad odour with many Athenians in 388: Dionysius was a tyrant, and Thrasybulus was suspected of having aspired to be one; and Lysias, who had himself been intimately involved with the democratic resistance in 404/3 (*POxy* 1606[a].34-38, 157-173; [Plut.] *Lives of the Ten Orators* 835f) and whom Thrasybulus had tried to make a citizen ([Plut.] *op.cit.* 835f-836a), was as ready to write speeches ventilating wild and unsupported allegations against Thrasybulus as he would soon be to incite mob violence against Dionysius. Poverty implicitly condemns any attempt to assimilate the two.

One ancient commentator (in Σ^E), who has been followed in part by P. Funke, *Homonoia und Arché* (Wiesbaden, 1980) 160 n.102, suggested that the reference was not to Thrasybulus of Steiria and Dionysius of Syracuse, but to two men who were generals in 387/6 (Xen. *Hell.* 5.1.26), Thrasybulus of Collytus (*PA* 7305, *LGPN* 14) and a Dionysius (*PA* 4092, *LGPN* 17) who according to this commentator was his brother (there is no other evidence of this, and it is *prima facie* unlikely, since generals were normally, though not invariably, elected one from each tribe). This interpretation can safely be ruled out. Poverty's case is that, while destitution is a bad thing, (moderate) poverty is a good thing; hence, for maximum impact, their human analogues should be two men one of whom could plausibly be regarded as a great villain and the other as a great hero. Nothing that we know either of Thrasybulus of Collytus or of the general Dionysius suggests that either of them could reasonably have been cast in either of those roles; neither, indeed, is known to have done anything of political or military significance between 403/2 and 388, and Aeschines 3.138-9 (who places Thrasybulus of Collytus first on a list of notable pro-Theban statesmen who led embassies to Thebes but failed to secure friendship between Thebes and Athens) strongly suggests that this Thrasybulus had *not* been an ambassador to Thebes during the Corinthian War when Thebes and Athens were in fact allies.

555   **Damater:** it is not clear why here and in 872 Demeter's name is pronounced in the Doric fashion, but it may be significant that both Chremylus here and Carion there are speaking in mocking tones.

555-6   **after toiling and scrimping ... pay for his funeral:** the actual meaning of this clause is virtually identical to that of Poverty's words in 553-4, but its rhetorical impact could hardly be more different. For the tear-jerking theme of the man too poor even to be able to die with dignity cf. *Ach.* 691, *Eccl.* 592.

559-561   Cf. Pl. *Rep.* 8.556d-e where poor men in the army of an oligarchic state contrast themselves, "lean and sun-tanned", with their rich fellow-soldiers, "bred up in the shade, with lots of surplus flesh, full of breathlessness and helplessness", and see how easy it will be to effect a democratic revolution.

561   **wasp-like:** i.e. slim-waisted.

561   **and sting their enemies hard:** lit. "and painful to enemies". The chorus of *Wasps* are old men who now "sting" only in the lawcourts, but in the parabasis (1071-90, cf. 1114-21) they recall their youthful exploits against the Persians, in language that mixes the human ("we charged out 'with spear, with shield'", *Wasps* 1081) and the vespine ("they fled, stung in the jaws and the eyebrows ... there is nothing more manly than an Attic wasp", *ib.* 1088-90).

563   **morality:** Greek *sōphrosunē*, a virtue which can roughly be defined as behaving in accordance with one's place in the scheme of society and of the universe and giving others (both human and divine) the respect due to theirs.

564   **decent behaviour:** Greek *kosmiotēs*, a near-synonym of *sōphrosunē* (compare 89 with 386-7).

564   **wanton insolence:** Greek *hubrizein*, the verb derived from *hubris*, wilful and contemptuous disregard for the rights or dignity of others: see N.R.E. Fisher, *Hybris* (Warminster, 1992), index s.v. "wealth and *hybris*".

565   **to steal or dig through walls:** implicitly accusing Poverty of driving men into crime through need and desperation (cf. Phaleas of Chalcedon *ap.* Arist. *Pol.* 1267a2-5). For "dig through walls" cf. on 204.

[566]   Here the mss. have the following line, evidently to be spoken by Blepsidemus: "Yes, by Zeus, if he has to remain undetected, how is it not decent behaviour?" The line as transmitted is unmetrical, and it has not been convincingly emended: all emendations

yet proposed introduce at least one particle that is worse than redundant. It is true that it could make an effective joke to say that thieves are modest, self-effacing fellows (cf. H.G. Wells, "The Hammerpond Park Burglary", in *The Short Stories of H.G. Wells* [London, 1927] 334: "Being a man of naturally retiring and modest disposition, Mr. Watkins determined to make this visit *incog.*"); but here the joke is so clumsily expressed as to be most unlikely to raise a laugh. Either the line has suffered early and irremediable corruption, or else it is an explanatory note that was mistaken for part of the text and expanded into a rough semblance of an anapaestic tetrameter.

567-570 as long as they're poor ... make war on the people: in very similar terms the contemporary prosecutor of Ergocles says of the defendant and his associates (including by implication Thrasybulus): "As soon as they had had their fill and regaled themselves on your property, they came to regard themselves as not being part of the Athenian community. Once they get rich, they hate you, and make plans to be no longer your servants but your rulers; fearing for their ill-gotten gains, they are ready to occupy strongholds, establish an oligarchy, and do everything to put you in a state of the utmost danger day after day" (Lys. 28.6-7).

569 when they've enriched themselves from the public purse: if that was how they became rich, one would have thought it proved that far from becoming dishonest as a result of being rich, they had become rich as a result of being dishonest; or, otherwise put (cf. 107-9), that while they were poor they *pretended* to be honest servants of the people until they could gain office, influence, and access to public money, and only then did they show themselves in their true colours. Chremylus is not allowed to make this point, though it had been obvious to him even before he met Wealth (cf. 28-38); Ar.'s plan for the *agōn* requires that Poverty shall not lose the argument.

575 flailing the air: lit. "flapping your wings" (i.e. making wild arm gestures?)

577 the children run away from them: sc. when threatened with (corporal) punishment; cf. *Clouds* 1409-10 "Did you beat me when I was a boy?" – "I did, out of benevolence and concern for your good."

578 how hard a thing it is to recognize what's best for you: the mss.' reading would mean "how hard it is to recognize a thing that's in accordance with justice", which is not the sense required by the context. The issue under discussion is not whether being poor is in accordance with justice (whatever that may mean) but whether it is better (for me or you or anyone) to be poor than to be rich (573, 576, 577, 579); that all men flee from poverty (575) shows that they think poverty is bad for them, but nobody could argue that it shows they think poverty is unjust, since people all too often flee from justice! Accordingly *dikaion* "in accordance with justice" must have supplanted some expression meaning "that which is to one's advantage"; Dindorf's suggestion *to kreitton* "that which is preferable" is tempting both because the next line speaks of Zeus not knowing *to kratiston* "that which is most preferable" (the superlative form of the same adjective) and because, to a reader of Ar., the words *kreittōn* "preferable, superior" and *dikaios* "just, righteous" would have an association with each other as alternative designations of one of the two Arguments (*logoi*) who contest the main *agōn* of *Clouds*.

580 *he* has Wealth too: cf. 130-2.

580 and sends *her* off to plague *us*: the mss. treat this as part of Chremylus' speech, but Bentley was probably right to give it to Blepsidemus: (i) Chremylus does not normally use third-person pronouns to refer to Poverty (see on 505) and here he has just been addressing her directly (579); (ii) in her reply Poverty with unusual emphasis says that the two men are *both* mentally purblind (here alone in the entire scene using *amphō /amphoteroi* "both" in reference to them); (iii) there is something to be said for

Holzinger's view (*ad* 566) that Blepsidemus ought to be allowed to "give some sign of life" between 500 and 612.

581   the truly prehistoric purblindness of your intellects, the pair of you: lit. "you who are both truly bleary in your minds with Cronus-like bleariness". Cronus was ruler of the universe before Zeus, and his name was often used to brand people or ideas as antiquated and out of date (*Clouds* 398, 929, 1070; *Wasps* 1480).

583   when he himself holds the Olympic festival: the precinct of Olympia was sacred to (i.e. was the property of) Zeus, and the festival was financed by the sanctuary's funds which likewise belonged to him; therefore he could be spoken of as "holding" the festival and awarding the prizes, in the same sense as (e.g.) Achilles holds the funeral games for Patroclus in *Iliad* 23.

584   every four years: lit. "always at the interval of the fifth year", the usual ancient Greek practice being to reckon time intervals inclusive of both the start and end points. The Olympics were next due to be held in the summer of 388.

586   a crown of *wild olive*: from a sacred tree planted by Heracles, the mythical founder of the festival (Pind. *Olymp.* 3.11-35 with scholia; *AP* 9.357; [Arist.] *Mir.* 834a12-22; Paus. 5.15.3).

592   may Zeus crown *you* with wild olive: sc. since you apparently believe this is a generous favour.

594   Hecate: at the shrines of this goddess, situated at road-junctions (*triodoi*) (Soph. fr. 535; Plut. *Mor.* 193f; Harpocration o25), offerings in the form of cooked food (Plut. *Mor.* 708f-709a) were laid out on the last day of the month (Athenaeus 7.325a); see S.I. Johnston, *ZPE* 88 (1991) 281-222. The food given to Hecate was normally of the poorest kind, e.g. dog meat (Ar. fr. 209, Plut. *Mor.* 290d) and the cheapest kinds of fish (Antiphanes fr. 69.14-15, Charicleides fr. 1).

597   the poor people snatch it away: cf. Lucian, *Kataplous* 7 and *Dialogues of the Dead* 1.1. A client of Demosthenes alleges (Dem. 54.39) that his opponent had, when young, belonged to a club that made a practice of committing wanton impieties, one of which was to collect, and feast on, Hecate's food (cf. also *Frogs* 366). Chremylus' point is that poverty drives people to steal not only from men (cf. 565) but even from the gods.

600   you won't persuade us, not even if you persuade us: in less boldly paradoxical terms, this means that even if Chremylus eventually has to admit that he cannot find any logical flaw in Poverty's arguments, he will still not agree with her conclusions.

601   "City of Argos, hark at what he says!": a quotation from Euripides' *Telephus* (Eur. fr. 713), which Ar. had used many years before in *Knights* (813).

602   Pauson (*LGPN* 4) was a painter who specialized in caricature (Arist. *Poet.* 1448a6, cf. Arist. *Pol.* 1340a36) and in novelty pictures that could be viewed upside down (Plut. *Mor.* 396e; cf. Lucian, *Encomium of Demosthenes* 24) or that gave an illusion of three-dimensionality (Arist. *Met.* 1050a19); he was noted for his jokes and riddles (*Ach.* 854; Heniochus fr. 4) and for his poverty (*Thesm.* 949-952; Eupolis fr. 99.5-8). He is Poverty's "messmate" because they eat the same food (viz. very little) – a useful indication that Poverty has an emaciated appearance. Pauson, who had already been well known in the mid 420s, must now have been an old man.

604   get the hell out of our sight: lit. "go away from us to the ravens" (cf. on 394).

606   to the pillory: cf. on 476.

610   you will one day send for me ... When we do, you can come back: Poverty has thus in effect conceded to men the right to decide whether they want her among them or not; and once men have that right, we may be sure that they will *not* want her, and that "when we do <send for you>" means "never".

611 it's better for me to be rich: reaffirming the position he has taken since the beginning of the *agōn* (498, 506, 572-4, 594-7) despite all Poverty's attempts to refute it (509, 526, 576-8, 593-4).

612 go and boil your head: lit. "howl long for your head", a phrase that had originally implied a threat of a beating (cf. *Lys.* 520) but had long become a generalized malediction that could be directed even at inanimate objects (cf. *Wasps* 584).

615 when I've bathed: bathing in Ar. is typically associated with leisurely and luxurious preparation for festive celebration: cf. *Knights* 50, *Peace* 1139, *Birds* 129-132, *Eccl.* 652, Ar. fr. 111.

616 sleek and gleaming: having oiled my skin after the bath; cf. *Eccl.* 652.

616 from the bath-house: the public baths, hitherto a place to seek warmth and get blisters (535) in the course of a life of misery, will now be a place to get oneself a clean, smooth skin in preparation for parties.

617-8 fart in the face of ... : symbolizing contempt; cf. *Wasps* 618, *Peace* 547, *Frogs* 1074, Epicrates fr. 10.29.

617-8 the craftsmen: see on 162.

624 our bedding: travellers in Ar. usually carry their bedding with them, and *strōmata* "bedding" can sometimes by extension denote the whole of their luggage; cf. *Ach.* 1136, *Birds* 657, *Frogs* 165.

625 in the customary garb: lit. "as is customary", viz. dressed in white (cf. Aristides 48.31 = E&E T486).

626/7 For the choral interlude, see on 321/2; it is particularly appropriate that there should be such an interlude here, since this is the clearest break in the action of the play, covering as it does an interval in which Chremylus and his party go to the Asclepieum in the Piraeus and spend a night there; even longer intervals have to be assumed at *Clouds* 1114/1131 (several days), *Birds* 1469/1494 (about a month? cf. 1515-24), *Lys.* 613/706 (five or six days, cf. 881), 1013/1072 (time enough for a journey to Sparta and back).

627 at the Thesea festival: this festival, held on the 8th of Pyanopsion (approximately corresponding to October), was established in the mid 470s after Cimon brought the bones of Theseus from Scyros to Athens (Plut. *Thes.* 36.4). It was marked by extensive sacrifices (*IG* ii^2 1496 A 134-5), which should imply a distribution of meat to all citizens; but according to the scholia, the food specially associated with the festival, and distributed free, was a humble grain-broth (*athare*), and this is what Carion chooses to mention – not because it was all the poor got at the Thesea (this is most unlikely) but because these old men were so poor that even *athare* was a treat to which they eagerly looked forward.

628 groats: Greek *alphita* (see on 219). The groats were in short supply because, unlike the *athare* (see previous note), they were provided not by the state but by households for themselves, in such quantities as they could afford.

631 of your kind: lit. "of your own friends", i.e. of your fellow-slaves. The preceding vocative *beltiste* "most splendid" is a form of address that would never normally be used by a free person to a slave, and would seem absurdly deferential until undercut by the phrase that follows: Carion is a splendid fellow *for a slave* (cf. 26-27).

632 you seem to have come with some good news: if this reading is correct, Ar. must be parodying the exaggerated caution with which some tragic choruses make inferences which would be obvious to any normal person in real life (e.g. Aesch. *Ag.* 1131-2). But it may not be correct: the endings of the present infinitive and participle (*-ein* and *-ōn*) are often confused in mss. (as at 524), and if we restore a participle here we get the more confident statement "it is clear that you have come with some good news" (sc. but we don't yet know *what* your good news is).

634-6 having been blind till now ... in Asclepius: at least part, and probably all, of this is quoted from one of Sophocles' two plays about the blind seer Phineus (Soph. fr. 710).

635 he has the bright orbs of his eyes restored: lit. "he has been given eyes and his pupils made bright".

637-640 The chorus sing in dochmiacs, a metre typical of tragedy (where it is often associated with moments of high emotion); their lines may be, or may include, a tragic quotation, but if so the source is unknown (probably *not* Sophocles' *Phineus*, since if that were the source, so soon after 634-6, the scholia would surely have been able to say more than merely "this is making fun of tragedy"). Carion's line is a spoken iambic trimeter.

639 that father of fine children: hymns to Asclepius often made mention of his sons Podaleirius and Machaon, surgeons to the Greek army at Troy (*Iliad* 2.731-2), and his daughters, usually named as Iaso, Aceso, Aegle, Panacea and Hygieia; cf. e.g. *PMG* 934 (Erythrae, 380-360 BC) and *IG* ii² 4473 (Athens, 1st c. AD).

641 is there some good news?: the reading of Π83 (*āra prātte[te]*) gives inappropriate sense ("are you doing something good?"; not "have you had some good luck?" which would require an adverb, e.g. *eu* "well", rather than the noun-phrase *khrēston ti* "something good") and is probably an error due to the appearance of the same verb in 629 and 632.

643 waiting for this boy to come implies that it had been agreed, before the party left for the Asclepieum, that when they returned Carion would come on ahead as fast as he could to bring news of how they had fared.

644 bring wine: sc. to celebrate your and our good fortune; cf. *Peace* 1143, Alcaeus fr. 332.

645 you do so love doing that: women in Ar. are insatiable lovers of wine; cf. 737, *Lys.* 194-239, 466, *Thesm.* 347-8, 393, 628-632, 733-757, *Eccl.* 132-157, 227, 1118-24.

647 you'll learn very soon: in fact it will be another 91 lines before she is actually told that Wealth's sight has been restored! There may be parody here of the conventions of the tragic messenger-speech as they had recently been developing. In all undoubtedly Euripidean messenger-speeches, as was noted by M.L. West, *BICS* 28 (1981) 77 n.26, "the speaker ... announces the main point of what has happened before he gives a detailed account"; but in Eur. *IA* 1532ff (from a play that was probably left unfinished by Euripides and completed by his son) a messenger comes to tell Clytaemestra "strange and amazing things" about her daughter, assures her that she will "learn everything clearly ... from the beginning" (1540-1, cf. 649-650 below), and then launches into a detailed narrative which at the point where the fourth-century text ends (1578-1629 being a much later addition) has still not given any clear indication of what the "strange and amazing" news actually is (evidently the miraculous disappearance of Iphigeneia and substitution of a hind at the moment of the sacrifice). Was this pattern typical of tragic messenger-speeches of the early fourth century?

649-652 No English translation of this passage can be both accurate and intelligible. In the Greek, Carion says that he will tell his mistress about the business (*ta prāgmata*) "from the feet to the head" (*eis tēn kephalēn*), i.e. from beginning to end; she misunderstands *ta prāgmata ... eis tēn kephalēn* as referring to troubles (a common meaning of *prāgmata*, cf. 20, 102) falling on her head (cf. 526). Literally rendered, the passage runs:

CARION: ... I will tell you the whole business from the feet to the head.
WIFE: Not, please, to (on) *my* head.
CARION: Not the good things that have now come to pass?
WIFE: Rather, not the business (troubles).

658 **we bathed him:** as a purification rite before entering the sanctuary; bathing is likewise attested as a preliminary to incubation at the sanctuaries of Amphiaraus (Xen. *Mem.* 3.13.3) and of Trophonius (Paus. 9.39.7). Some Asclepiea had sacred springs adjacent to them which were used for this purpose (e.g. at Gytheum, Paus. 3.21.8 = E&E T761; near Pellene, Paus. 7.27.11 = E&E T782); at Zea, where there was none, the sea (across which the god had come to Attica) served instead.

660-1 **and when ... "a sop for Hephaestus' flame":** the language is paratragic (Rau 167), as is shown by the omission of three definite articles and the phrase "Hephaestus' flame" ([Eur.] *IA* 1601, cf. *Iliad* 9.468, 17.88, *Odyssey* 24.71); used again in comic paratragedy at Men. *Sam.* 674).

660 **the preliminary sacrifice of cakelets:** lit. "cakelets (*popana*) and preliminary sacrifices". A *popanon* was a small, flat, round cake, often used in religious offerings (cf. *Thesm.* 285, Men. *Dysk.* 450, schol. Pl. *Rep.* 455c). *IG* ii^2 4962.1-10 (E&E T515) gives the schedule of preliminary offerings at the city Asclepieum: three *popana* each to Maleates (cf. Introduction §3), Apollo, Hermes, Iaso, Aceso, Panacea, the Hounds, and the Hunters.

662 **we made Wealth lie down:** sc. on a couch provided by the sanctuary authorities (whereas the rest of the party had to "cobble together a rough bed" of rushes, straw, grass, etc. [cf. 541] for themselves, and cover themselves with the *strōmata* [cf. on 624] which they had brought with them). A contemporary relief, now in the Peiraeus Museum (405), shows the god healing a sufferer who lies on a couch with legs; see P.T. van Straten in H.S. Versnel ed. *Faith, Hope and Worship* (Leiden, 1981) 98 and pl. 41.

665 **Neocleides** (*PA* 10631, *LGPN* 4) figures in the later comedies of Ar. (cf. *Eccl.* 254-5, 398-407; Ar. fr. 454) as a well-known Assembly speaker; in addition to the allegations made against him in the present scene (embezzlement, procedural obstructionism) he was also accused in comedy, according to the scholia here, of having foreign ancestry and of being a professional prosecutor (*sūkophantēs*). Three years earlier, in *Eccl.*, he had been "that bleary-eyed Neocleides" (*Eccl.* 254, 398); now he is called "blind", but he is evidently not totally sightless (see on 725). There are no known references to him outside Ar.'s plays.

666 **he's got the sighted folk beaten by a distance:** lit. "he has out-javelined the sighted".

669-670 **the god's minister:** possibly the priest, but more likely the sacristan (*neōkoros*); for this official cf. Herodas 4.79-90; Aristides 47.11; 48.35, 46 (E&E T482, 485, 497-8).

677 **cheesecakes:** Greek *phthois*, a round cake made with grated cheese and honey (Ath. 14.647d-e).

678 **the holy table:** almost all Greek sanctuaries had one or more sacred tables which served, among other purposes, to receive "the small, unburnt offerings of private individuals or groups of individuals" (D.H. Gill, *HTR* 67 [1974] 117-137, at p.119; cf. also S. Dow and D.H. Gill, *AJA* 69 [1965] 103-114, and Burkert 68, 96). It was a widespread practice, often specifically recognized in sacred law (e.g. at the Asclepieum of Erythrae: see *IGSK* ii 205.23-25), that when the table was periodically cleared the offerings on it could be consumed by the priest (as, in another cultic tradition, could the "shewbread" of the Jerusalem temple – see Leviticus 24.5-9). Hence Carion's assumption that the priest is *stealing* the offerings would be perceived as either disingenuous or, more likely, comically naïve.

681 **consecrated them:** the Greek verb *(kat)hagizein* properly "designates the burning of victims, annihilation by fire" (Burkert 271); it can be used of any kind of offering that is burnt, from an animal or a human being (Hdt. 1.86.2) to grains (*Birds* 566) or incense (Hdt. 2.130.1). Here and in *Lys.* 238 the verb is humorously used of an officiant who annihilates an offering not by fire but by appropriating it for his/her own consumption.

686 headtire: Greek *stemmata* (cf. also on 39) can denote head adornments of various kinds, usually with religious connotations. Here it probably refers to the thick headband (*corona tortilis*) which Asclepius is often depicted wearing (see e.g. *LIMC* s.v. Asklepios nos. 30, 56, 215, 335).

687 I'd just had a lesson in that from his priest: i.e. since the priest had (as Carion supposed) been stealing food, he assumed that the god would do likewise.

689 she stuck out her hand from under her cover: the rare (indeed, otherwise unattested) Greek verb *hup-heirein* "stick out from underneath" baffled the copyists, who replaced its third-person present form *hupheirei* by the verb form they knew that most nearly resembled it, *hupheirei* "she took away from underneath", which is unintelligible in context. A surviving ancient note, correctly explaining the true reading, itself suffered corruption in all mss. except V, but the Menandrian phrase quoted in it (*exeirantes epikrotēsate* "stretch out your hands and applaud") has turned up on a papyrus published in 1985 (*PHarris* 172 = Men. fr. 908) and confirmed V's reading, enabling Chantry (*Scholia* III 4a 118) to restore the true reading in the text (which appears, no doubt by a lucky error, in at least one fifteenth-century ms.). The simple verb *heirein* (for the aspiration cf. *Et.Mag.* 304.30-31) means basically "thrust" (cf. *exeirein* "stick out", e.g. *Wasps* 423, Men. loc.cit.), whence often "thrust a thread through (beads etc.), string together".

690 a sacred snake: this reddish-brown snake, still called the Aesculapian snake (*Elaphe longissima*), which according to local legend had originally existed only in Asclepius' homeland of Epidaurus (Paus. 2.28.1 = E&E T692), was the most distinctive of the god's attributes (see e.g. *LIMC* s.v. Asklepios nos. 52, 63, 65, 73, 86, 98, 203, 344, 389); together with the staff around which it was often depicted coiling, it has remained an emblem of medicine to this day. Its Greek name *pareiās* was wrongly derived by some ancient scholars from *pareiai* "cheeks", but this snake is not particularly large-cheeked; the alternative form *parouās* (Apollodorus of Alexandria, cited by Aelian *NA* 8.12 = E&E T700) indicates a connection with *parōās* "chestnut" (of horses). The snake is, and was known to be, harmless, but Carion rightly guesses that the half-asleep old woman will forget this and react instinctively to his bite.

693 a ferret: polecats were kept in homes for the purpose of keeping down mice (cf. *Wasps* 1182), despite their propensity to steal meat (cf. *Wasps* 363, *Peace* 1151, *Thesm.* 558-9) and their obnoxious smell (cf. *Ach.* 255-6).

695 I rested: we might *prima facie* be tempted, on the basis of this, to interpret the ensuing narrative as a dream: of the 53 more or less complete cure narratives in *EMI*, 35 mention a dream-vision seen while sleeping in the sanctuary. However, 739-741 shows that Carion was fully awake when he saw the god and his attendants.

696-8 he hadn't yet ... I did do something very amusing: I have adopted Rogers' punctuation of the text; with the punctuation preferred by most editors ("He hadn't yet; but straight afterwards I did actually do something very amusing: as he was approaching ...") a vital event in the narrative, the actual arrival of the god, would be mentioned only indirectly.

701-2 Iaso ... Panacea: two of Asclepius' daughters (cf. on 639 and 660); their names mean "Healer" and "Cure-all", and they were also claimed as daughters by the healing hero Amphiaraus at Oropus on the Attic-Boeotian border (Ar. fr. 21, cf. Paus. 1.34.3).

705 a boorish sort of a god: because he does not find foul smells offensive (cf. *Peace* 131-2 where it is said to be "an incredible tale ... [that] an evil-smelling animal could come among the gods").

706 no, I'm not; I'm calling him a shit-eater: *skatophagos* "shit-eater" was an offensive epithet to apply to anyone, let alone a god (cf. on 305), so Carion is committing, presumably in jest, a worse blasphemy than the one he has just been accused of.

706 oh, you wretched fellow!: this is the only occurrence in Ar. of the interjection *ai*, which becomes more frequent in later comedy (always in the mouths of women) as an expression of sorrow or surprise (e.g. Men. *Epitr.* 468, *Mis.* 177 Sandbach = 577 Arnott; *com. adesp.* 1084.24, 1128.5); see D.M. Bain, *Antichthon* 18 (1984) 35-36.

710 a boy: in patients' visions the god was sometimes accompanied by several servants, e.g. in *EMI* 27, 38 and in Aelian *NA* 9.33 = E&E T422.

713 you blasted liar: lit. "you who will perish miserably" (cf. 456).

716-722 This preparation is very similar to the "prescription" suggested for Neocleides by a hostile fellow-citizen in *Eccl.* 404-6: "Pound together garlic and fig-juice, chuck in some spurge of the Laconian variety, and smear it on to your eyelids before going to bed." Asclepius, however, goes one better (or worse) by applying the medicine to the *inside* of Neocleides' eyelids (721).

718 Tenos garlic: Tenos in the Cyclades (between Andros and Mykonos) was evidently noted for the quality and/or pungency of its garlic.

719 fig-juice: Greek *opos*, the acid latex of the fig-tree, used as rennet in the making of cheese (*Iliad* 5.902-3; Arist. *HA* 522b2-5).

720 mastic: the sap of the mastic or lentisk tree (*Pistacia lentiscus*), described as "mordant" in Galen 11.807.2-3 Kühn. The same Greek word, *skhinos*, can also denote the squill, a very bitter-tasting bulb; but the context here requires a liquid (my note on *Eccl.* 404-6 is to be corrected).

720 Sphettus vinegar: Sphettus was a village about eight miles south-east of Athens, a little to the east of Mount Hymettus; see A.G. Kalogeropoulos, *BCH* 93 (1969) 56-71. Ancient commentators could not agree whether its vinegar really was particularly acrid, or whether Ar. is alluding rather to the reputed character of its inhabitants.

725 disrupting Assembly meetings with sworn objections: lit. "sworn-objectioning the Assemblies". The term *hūpomosiā* (verb *hupomnusthai*) was applied to various procedures by which an objection could be raised on oath which would obstruct or delay an Assembly decision or a court case, but the reference here is to one of these procedures in particular. When the Assembly voted, as it normally did, by show of hands, its presiding officers estimated which side had the majority and announced their decision to the meeting. If any citizen then asserted on oath that the outcome had been wrongly judged, the vote was taken again. This occurred in the notorious Assembly trial of eight generals after the battle of Arginusae in 406, when the vote was first declared to have gone in favour of a proposal to have the generals tried individually, but on a sworn objection being made by one Menecles, and in an atmosphere of intimidation, a second vote resulted in a decision to try them *en bloc* (Xen. *Hell.* 1.7.34). It would appear that Neocleides had been in the habit of challenging vote declarations in this way: Asclepius, by making him totally blind, wishes to make it impossible for him to do so, since no one who had not seen the hands go up could possibly *swear* that the vote had been incorrectly assessed. See M.H. Hansen, *GRBS* 18 (1977) 123-137 (reprinted with addenda in Hansen, *The Athenian Ecclesia* [Copenhagen, 1983] 103-121), esp. 133-4 [113-4].

726 what a very clever, patriotic fellow that god is!: note the implication that Chremylus' wife knows and cares enough about public affairs to be aware that the political disablement of Neocleides is something to be heartily welcomed.

727 Wealth: his name in the Greek is here not *Ploutos* as usual but *Ploutōn*; this is normally the name of the ruler of the underworld (as in *Frogs* 163, 436, etc.), but according to the scholia the god of wealth was so named twice in Sophocles' satyr-play *Inachus* (Soph. fr. 273, 283; cf. [Aesch.] *Prom.* 806, Demetrius of Phalerum ap. Strabo 3.2.9).

733-4 two enormous serpents: not ordinary Aesculapian snakes (see on 690) but their supernatural counterparts. They take an active part in several of the Epidaurus cure narratives (*EMI* 17, 39, 42, 45); cf. also Marinus, *Life of Proclus* 30 = E&E T445.

733-4 out of the temple shows that the pilgrims were not sleeping in the temple itself but in an area adjacent to it. At Epidaurus the *abaton* where the pilgrims slept was a covered portico, open at one side and facing the temple (see R.A. Tomlinson, *Epidauros* [London, 1983] 67), and Carion's account suggests, though it does not prove, that the arrangement at Zea was similar.

736 or so I suppose: Carion says this because the cloth prevented his actually seeing what the serpents were doing.

737 before you could drink off five pints (lit. "ten *kotulai*", cf. on 436): i.e. (given the assumption referred to on 645) in the twinkling of an eye. The quantity of wine mentioned would fill about four modern 70-centilitre bottles.

753 gave him their right hands: thus pledging eternal fidelity to Wealth; cf. *Clouds* 81, *Frogs* 754, 788-9, Soph. *Trach.* 1181, *Phil.* 813, *OC* 1631-2.

758-9 "and old men's shoes with rhythmic tread resounded": the language is poetic, even the everyday word *embas* "shoe" having its register elevated somewhat by being used in the singular: it is not clear whether the sentence is directly adapted from an actual tragedy (cf. Eur. *Med.* 1179-80, *Ba.* 1090-1, both from messenger-speeches) or whether it is pastiche.

763 that there's no groats in the sack: Carion's report ends as it began (627-8) with a reminder of the sheer depth of poverty that some hard-working citizens (are assumed to) have experienced, including the real possibility of sometimes having nothing at all to eat in the house; cf. 253, 504, 536, 539, 543-4, 562, 595.

764 by Hecate: a fairly common oath among women in Ar. (*Thesm.* 858, *Eccl.* 70, 1097), though it could also be used by men (cf. 1070).

764-5 to garland you, in honour of your good tidings: cf. *Knights* 647.

765 with a string of oven-baked loaves: "since he has said that she will no longer be short of bread" (scholia).

768-9 to shower, as it were, on a newly-bought pair of eyes: lit. "as if for newly-bought eyes". The reference is to the practice whereby the mistress of a house threw sweetmeats, nuts, figs, dates, etc. (called *katakhusmata*) over the head of a newly-bought slave when he first arrived at the house: cf. Dem. 45.74, Plut. *Mor.* 753d, *Anecd.Bekk.* 269.9-13, and see M.M. Mactoux, *MEFRA* 102 (1991) 53-81. Bridal couples arriving at the new marital home were also showered with *katakhusmata* (cf. Theopompus com. fr. 15). The ritual was normally (cf. 795) performed at the hearth (to which, and to whose goddess Hestia, a new member of the household was being introduced); but in this case we are led to expect that it will be done outside the house, for reasons that will become apparent at 797ff.

770 *I want to go and meet them:* if, as this *prima facie* suggests, Carion now leaves by the way he came, he must presumably return with his master (not, certainly, with Wealth, who must enter alone – see next note); in which case it may seem surprising that no notice whatever is taken of him in 782-801. Accordingly S.D. Olson, *TAPA* 119 (1989) 196 n.13, has revived an old suggestion that Carion here goes *into the house*, and that *ekeinois* "them" refers not to the party returning from the Asclepieum but to the *katakhusmata* (see previous note) and/or the "oven-baked loaves" of 765. Carion is, however, needed on stage in 782-801. Chremylus and his party set out with him carrying their luggage (624-6): if Chremylus re-enters carrying it himself, he will seem to have been impoverished rather than enriched; if he re-enters without any luggage, there will be an unnecessary inconsistency between the departure and return scenes; therefore Carion must rejoin the party before it arrives.

770/1 For the choral interlude, see on 321/2 and 626/7. Here it is marked (in RV and many later mss.) not as usual by *khorou* but by *kommation khorou* "short section by the chorus", indicating no doubt that we are not dealing with a full "act-dividing" choral song (there will be one soon afterwards at 801/2) but with a short, probably astrophic lyric whose main function is to hail the return of Wealth. That there was indeed a choral song at this point is confirmed by Wealth's opening words: the particle-combination *kai ... ge* "yes, and ...", "more than that, ..." implies (Holzinger's elaborate and unconvincing special pleading notwithstanding) that he is responding to something said to him (unless we suppose, with Rogers and Denniston 158, that he "enters continuing a speech which he has begun off the stage": but it is one thing for a character to enter while muttering to himself or thinking aloud, as Blepsidemus does at 335, and quite another for a character to enter in the middle of a solemn formal address to the gods and Athens). What he is responding to is either a question (e.g. "Do you rejoice in your good fortune?"), or an injunction or exhortation (e.g. "It is proper that you should give thanks to the gods"); the latter gives better closure to the chorus's song. Wealth, the saviour of mankind, enters alone, as do the Sausage-seller in *Knights* 1316ff and Lysistrata in *Lys.* 1108ff; like Lysistrata (and like the Sausage-seller in *Knights* 611ff/624ff, and Peisetaerus in *Birds* 1720ff/1743ff) he is first greeted by the chorus and then speaks in reply to them. He is probably wearing the same white garments in which he was last seen (cf. on 625), since white was the colour appropriate for joyful occasions (cf. *Ach.* 1024, *Thesm.* 841; Aesch. *Eum.* 352; Eur. *Alc.* 923); but the actor will have a new mask, bright-eyed, smiling and probably much younger-looking (cf. Heberlein 132 n.50), with most or all of the "miseries of old age" catalogued by Carion (266) cast off. The scene may to some extent be modelled on that in which Demos (the personification of the Athenian people) appears rejuvenated at the end of *Knights* (1331ff); Wealth's self-condemnation (1374-8) and promise of reform (1379-81) both recall things said by Demos in that scene (respectively, *Knights* 1339-55 and 1357-83), but here they are much less appropriate than in *Knights* because Demos, though more sinned against than sinning, had at least been foolish and gullible in allowing self-interested politicians to deceive him, whereas Wealth had *refused* to cooperate with Zeus' malicious designs towards humanity (87-92) and Zeus had simply forced him to comply by blinding him.

771 **make obeisance:** those who had received a great blessing, experienced a great deliverance, or witnessed a great miracle, "made obeisance to earth and heaven" by kissing the soil and extending their hands to the sky (*Knights* 156; Aesch. *Pers.* 499, *Ag.* 508; Soph. *OC* 1654-5; cf. also *Odyssey* 5.463). Wealth modifies this ritual in several ways appropriate to the situation: (1) he substitutes the Sun (source of the light so long denied him and now restored) for the sky (too closely connected with his persecutor Zeus); (2) instead of saluting the divine Earth, he salutes the land of Attica, with the implication that he will be bestowing special blessings on Athens and its citizens (cf. 1191-3); (3) he addresses the Sun first, so as not to have to turn round twice (for the Sun will be somewhere in the southern half of the sky, whereas the Acropolis is north of the theatre, above the audience seating); (4) the fact that before addressing "the whole land of Cecrops" he addresses the Acropolis (772) – to which he would of course have had to

look *up* – suggests that he does not kiss the ground, which might be thought to demean one who is, after all, a god entering in triumph.

772 **the glorious precinct** (lit. "ground") **of august Pallas**, contrasted as it is with the "whole land" of Attica, must mean the Acropolis; Greek *pedon* "ground" often in poetry denotes a sacred precinct (e.g. Aesch. *Cho.*1036, Eur. *Andr.* 1085) such as "the acropolis of the goddess" was (*Lys.* 241, cf. *Lys.* 480-3). The language of 772-3 is tragic (see Rau 145), but there is no evidence of its being modelled on any specific tragic passage.

773 **Cecrops:** a mythical king of Athens, whose name was often used in poetic designations of Athens, Attica and the Athenians (e.g. *Knights* 1055, *Clouds* 301, Ar. fr. 112, Eur. *Hipp.* 34, *Ion* 1571).

782 Blepsidemus does not reappear with Chremylus and Carion; indeed there has been no mention of him, direct or indirect, since he left with them at 626 – he has served his purpose and is now forgotten (cf. on 321).

782 **damn and blast!:** lit. "throw (yourself) to the ravens" (cf. on 394); this is likewise the first utterance of a newly arriving character at *Clouds* 133, *Wasps* 835. Possibly Chremylus turns and shouts back in the direction of his unwelcome well-wishers (who are not seen by the audience); but Ar. fr. 477 (where it stands between "what's wrong with my stomach?" and "can someone get me a chamber-pot?", all spoken by the same person) shows that the phrase can be a generalized expression of annoyance addressed to no one in particular.

782-3 **"friends" who appear out of nowhere when you're doing well:** and will as swiftly disappear if your fortunes change, as the Honest Man discovered (834-7).

786-7 **who wasn't in that mob of old men who ringed me round ... ?:** lit. "what mob of old men did not ring me round ... ?"

789 **sweetmeats** and "showering" (794) both render Greek *katakhusmata* (see on 768-9).

792 **it is not proper for anything to be taken out of the house:** because that would diminish the family's wealth; cf. 803.

796 **that way we can also avoid vulgarity** (Greek *phortos*): similarly in *Wasps* 56-66 the audience are told that the play they are going to see is "cleverer than vulgar (*phortikē*) comedy" (66) and will not include "a pair of slaves scattering nuts from a little basket among the spectators" (58-59); *phortos* and its derivatives appear in other comments on allegedly crude or inartistic comic techniques at *Clouds* 524, *Peace* 748 and *Lys.* 1218. See *Drama* 1 (1992) 20-21.

797 **it doesn't befit our producer:** implying that Ar. is content and proud to be judged by higher standards than his rivals.

797 **our producer:** when a comic text refers to its author, it may call him indifferently *poiētēs* "poet", *didaskalos* "producer", or both in a single speech (e.g. *Peace* 737, 738 ~ 773), even on occasions when the poet and the producer were actually two different persons (e.g. *Ach.* 628 ~ 634, 644, 649, 654).

799 **make them feel obliged to laugh:** lit. "compel them to laugh", sc. for fear of seeming ungrateful for the favour conferred on them.

800 **Dexinicus** (*LGPN* 1): the scholia make various statements about this man (he was poor; he was a glutton; he was a general) which may well all be no more than guesswork (even the last may be based on nothing more than his name, which means "acquirer of victory"; no general of this name is otherwise known – indeed the name is attested only once again at Athens, *SEG* xix 244). Dexinicus must, however, have been known to the public in some capacity, and it is possible that he was a minor politician who was, or was alleged to be, less well off than politicians usually were (and therefore – it is exaggeratedly assumed – eager to grab any food that was being distributed free). Such

men was vulnerable to the accusation that they presumed to advise the community how to manage its affairs when they could not manage their own competently, and/or that they were especially liable to corruption (cf. on 569), and they were often satirized in comedy (e.g. *Ach.* 614-7, *Wasps* 1267-74), as even the "Old Oligarch" had to admit ([Xen.] *Ath.Pol.* 2.18); it is revealing that Demosthenes (18.171-2) expects a popular jury to take it for granted that the man to advise the people at a moment of crisis must be a loyal citizen *and a rich man*. See J. Ober, *Mass and Elite in Democratic Athens* (Princeton, 1989) 230-240. For satirical comments explicitly directed at named individuals in the audience cf. *Wasps* 74-84, *Peace* 884-6, *Eccl.* 167-8, 364-5.

801 the figs: or, with the Suda, "some of the figs".

801/2 For the choral interlude, see on 321/2: this one, as Wealth finally enters Chremylus' house, marks the moment at which the hero's plan reaches fulfilment, and in the rest of the play we shall see some of the consequences of his success. When the action resumes it is evident that a considerable time has elapsed, since a sumptuous feast is in an advanced stage of preparation (819-821).

802-818 This picture of a state of fantastic wealth and luxury is said by the scholia to be modelled on a scene in Sophocles' *Inachus* (cf. on 727) "when Zeus entered the house and everything became full of good things" (cf. Soph. fr. 276 "pits full of barley" ~ *Wealth* 806); see S.R. West, *CQ* 34 (1984) 298. Inachus, however, did not long exult in his sudden prosperity: the mysterious visitor who was in fact Zeus in disguise turned Inachus' daughter Io into a cow and abruptly departed (Soph. fr. 269a). Well-informed spectators may therefore be led to suspect, wrongly, that some misfortune or danger may yet be in store for Chremylus.

802 gentlemen: possibly addressed to the chorus, but more likely to the audience; cf. *Peace* 13, 244, 276, 1357, *Lys.* 1044, Men. *Dysk.* 666, *Epitr.* 887, *Sam.* 269.

803 without having any outgoings: lit. "taking nothing out of the house" (sc. to pay for it).

804-5 a vast horde of good things ... innocent of any wrongdoing: this sentence can be derived by comic inversion from either of two less paradoxical statements: (a) "a band of *robbers* [or the like] has invaded our house, though we have done no wrong to deserve it", or (b) "we have prospered enormously, though we have done nothing *good* enough to deserve it". It was probably designed to suggest both these ideas simultaneously. The notion of a hostile inroad is strongly evoked by the verb *epeispaiein* "storm into, burst in upon", while (b) reflects the play's basic assumption that in the world as it was before the healing of Wealth, crime was the only way to prosper.

[805a] After 805 all mss. have the line "So delightful a thing it truly is to be rich". The scholia describe this line as "meaningless"; it repeats the content of 802, and breaks the connection between the general statement in 804-5 and the detailed enumeration of blessings in 806-818. Some interpreters (e.g. van Daele, Holzinger, Thiercy) take *houtō* "so, thus" as meaning "under these conditions", viz. without having acquired one's wealth by crime; but that would imply that it was *not* pleasant to possess wealth which *had* been acquired by crime, which would make nonsense of much else in the play (and contradict the opinion strongly expressed by Carion himself in 45-50). The line probably originated from a commentator's paraphrase of 802; indeed a surviving paraphrase of 802 by Tzetzes (in K and P22) runs "*A delightful thing, gentlemen, it is to be* fortunate and *rich*".

806-818 The detailed description of Wealth's blessings consists of two main parts. In 806-811 we hear mainly of a sudden abundance of money (808-9) and of staple foods (corn, wine, oil, figs); thereafter follow a series of instances of materials of high value (bronze, silver, ivory, gold) in which the house so abounds that they are now used for the most common purposes. The last clause (817-8) combines these two themes, with what had been in days of poverty an important food item being treated as worthless waste and put to the meanest use imaginable.

807 with a beautiful bouquet: lit. "flower-scented" (*anthosmiās*), a term applied to wines of exquisite aroma (e.g. *Frogs* 1150, Pherecrates fr. 113.30, Xen. *Hell.* 6.2.6; Hermippus fr. 77.6-11 speaks of a particular variety of wine as smelling of violets, roses and hyacinths).

812-3 every vinegar-cruet ... has turned to bronze: it has not occurred to Carion, and perhaps not to Ar. either, that acidic fluids like vinegar would do damage to metal vessels.

813 cleaning-boards: on which fish were prepared for cooking.

815 an ivory kitchen: i.e. a kitchen decorated with ivory – a fantastic extreme of luxury, since (i) the large-scale use of ivory was almost confined to temples (it had been otherwise, or so men believed, in the heroic age: cf. *Odyssey* 4.73), (ii) any man who *was* rich enough to decorate his house with ivory would certainly give priority to rooms used for entertaining visitors, and (iii) the kitchen, with smoke constantly rising from cooking activities (cf. 821), would be the hardest room in the house to keep clean. Greek *hipnos* ("kitchen" also in *Wasps* 139, 837 and *Birds* 437) can also mean "oven" (Antiphanes fr. 174.3) and "portable lantern" (*Peace* 841); but an ivory oven (unlike a bronze cooking-pot or even a silver cleaning-board) would be totally unusable (I was wrong to defend, and try to explain, this interpretation of *hipnos* in *CQ* 34 [1984] 324 = *Oxford Readings in Aristophanes* ed. E. Segal [Oxford, 1996] 266-7), while one would expect a very wealthy family to have more than one lantern.

816 odd-and-even: "a boyish game, where one holds out his closed hand, and the other guesses whether the articles it contains are of an even or odd number" (Rogers); usually played with, and for, knucklebones (Pl. *Lys.* 206e) or other objects of trivial value (nuts, beans, etc.; see Pollux 9.101). A more difficult variant of the game was *posinda* (Xen. *Hipparch.* 5.10), in which one had to guess the exact number of objects held; at 1055-9 the Young Man mockingly offers to play this game with his aged ex-mistress. Arist. *Rhet.* 1407b2-4 suggests that there was also a third variant in which the guesser could choose whether to say "odd", "even", or an exact number (doubtless standing to win more if he took the last-named option).

816-7 golden staters: except briefly in the last years of the Peloponnesian War, Athens had no gold coinage of its own, but high-value gold (or gold/silver alloy) coins of other states, usually called staters, were widely accepted at Athens as elsewhere; the most common were the Persian gold "daric" (cf. *Eccl.* 602), worth 20 drachmas (cf. Xen. *Anab.* 1.7.18), and the gold/silver stater of Cyzicus (cf. *Peace* 1176), probably worth rather more (cf. Dem. 34.23). Slaves would not normally be in possession of money of their own at all, much less have such a superfluity as to be able to gamble with it.

817 wipe our bottoms with stones: cf. *Peace* 1228-33, Machon 211-7.

818 garlic cloves: garlic was a cheap food (cf. *Ach.* 550, *Knights* 600, *Frogs* 987), and in the new world of affluence it is considered beneath contempt.

819 is making a great sacrifice of: Greek *bouthutei*, lit. "is ox-sacrificing": since an ox was the largest of sacrificial animals, this verb had come to be used of any large sacrifice even if it did not include cattle (cf. the Hellenistic inscription *IG* ii² 1227.5).

820 a boar, a he-goat and a ram: sacrifices of three adult animals of different species, known as *trittoiai*, were offered by the Athenian state on specially important occasions, notably to the Eleusinian goddesses (*IG* i³ 5.5, 78.37). For an individual to make such a sacrifice at home was unheard-of, though a rich man might on rare occasions sacrifice an ox (Poseidippus fr. 28.19, for an upper-class wedding; *com.adesp.* 1138.12; Thphr. *Char.* 21.7, the "man of petty ambition" who afterwards nails up the ox's skull in his courtyard to advertise his wealth). The cooking of the sacrificial food is mentioned at 894 and 1137-8, but it never seems to be consumed, and none of it is ever seen on stage except for some tripe which Carion gives to Hermes at 1169 (the pots of boiled vegetables in the final procession – cf. on 1197 – are something different and much humbler); contrast *Ach.* 1003-1142, *Peace* 1305-15, *Birds* 1579-1693.

821 **I've been forced outside by the smoke:** cf. Men. *Dysk.* 550.

823 **boy:** the Greek has not *pai*, the usual form of address to a male slave (cf. 624), but the diminutive *paidarion*: cf. *Thesm.* 1203; Men. *Aspis* 222, *Mis.* 459 Sandbach = 989 Arnott. Van Leeuwen, followed by Halliwell, takes the boy to be the Honest Man's son, on the ground that he would have been too poor to own a slave; but *paidarion* is never used in addressing one's own children in comedy, or in literary prose down to AD 200 (E. Dickey, *Greek Forms of Address from Herodotus to Lucian* [Oxford, 1996] 71-72). Rather, the Honest Man's (former) poverty is indicated by his not having an *adult* slave.

824 **CARION:** the mss. differ, and the scholia are doubtful, as to whether it is Carion or Chremylus who speaks with the Honest Man and the Informer; all editors since Bergk (1857) have identified this character as Carion, but Thiercy 1318-9 has recently revived the suggestion that he is Chremylus. There are two decisive arguments against this view:

(1) If Ar.'s design had called for Carion to go back into the house at 822 and for Chremylus to come outside shortly thereafter, he would never have had Carion say, a moment before, that Chremylus is busy with a sacrifice and that he himself has been unable to stay inside because of the smoke.

(2) At 874-6 the Informer threatens someone with torture; this must be a slave (since the torture of citizens was illegal, cf. Andoc. 1.43), and if Carion were not present the intended victim could only be the boy servant of the Honest Man. 880, however, makes it clear that up till that point the Informer had not suspected the Honest Man of complicity in the "crime" of healing Wealth (and thereby depriving the Informer and his kind of their riches), and he would therefore have no reason to suppose that the Honest Man's young slave had anything to confess to (876) or any useful information to give; moreover, the threat of torture comes in response to the mocking remarks of 872-3, and these remarks cannot have been made by the Honest Man, since the Informer does not complain of mockery *by him* before 880.

Thiercy is quite correct, however, in noting that "the interaction between the Honest Man and his interlocutor is more like an interaction between two free men than between a free man and a slave"; regarding this, see on 6-7.

831 **believing that that would be to my advantage in life:** for the reason he gives in 834-6. Ancient Greeks did not in general share the widespread modern belief that there is something disreputable about practising generosity if it is done wholly or partly with a view to earning gratitude and the favour of others; they often frankly avowed such motives in court (e.g. Lys. 20.31, 25.13). See C. Gill et al. ed. *Reciprocity in Ancient Greece* (Oxford, 1998), especially ch.10 (G. Herman), ch.11 (P.C. Millett) and ch.14 (C. Gill).

832 Carion is cynical, assuming (rightly) that the Honest Man's friends saw him as a soft touch and milked him dry.

833 **exactly so:** Greek *komidēi men oun*, one of the language's numerous phrases for giving an affirmative answer; it is common in Plato (though not before the *Republic*), but it appears in Ar. only in these three successive utterances by the Honest Man, and it may in 388 have been a novel, voguish, and to some people irritating expression. In Plato the formula is especially associated with Theaetetus, one of the youngest characters in the Platonic corpus (he was in his late teens or early twenties at the time of Socrates' death in 399, Pl. *Theaet.* 142c), who uses it twelve times in the two dialogues in which he speaks (whereas in the *Politicus,* in which he is present but silent, it is used only twice); this tends to confirm that in the early fourth century it was used mainly by younger people, and perhaps also that it tended to be a mannerism of particular individuals.

839   **there was a drought in my stores** (lit. "vessels"): i.e. my resources had run dry (been exhausted) – with a play on the idea of a farmer's being ruined by a literal (meteorological) drought.

840   **but not any more:** most mss., and many editors, have assigned these words to Carion; but if he were the speaker of them, the Honest Man would almost certainly have confirmed this very important statement, at least by using in his reply the assentient particle *ge,* just as he has confirmed the guesses Carion made at 832, 834 and 838.

844   **to dedicate that to the god:** it was a universal custom to dedicate to a god objects symbolic of blessings which the dedicant had received, or perils or sufferings from which (s)he had been saved, through the god's favour; see F.T. van Straten in H.S. Versnel ed. *Faith, Hope and Worship* (Leiden, 1981) 65-151, esp. 92-102. This was done by depositing the object in the god's place of abode, usually a temple but in this case Chremylus' house.

845   **the one you wore for your initiation:** the scholia (citing Melanthius *FGrH* 326 F 4) state that it was "ancestral custom for initiates to dedicate to the goddesses [sc. Demeter and Kore] the clothes in which they were initiated" or to lay them aside to be used as swaddling-clothes for infants, evidently because they had become too holy for ordinary use. As a result it came to be considered legitimate and even semi-obligatory to wear for this occasion clothes that were ready to be discarded in any case and whose dedication would therefore involve no material loss, and the chorus of initiates in *Frogs* (404-8) accordingly wear tattered garments.

845   **the Greater Mysteries** were those celebrated at Eleusis in the month of Boedromion (roughly September), as distinct from the Lesser Mysteries held at Agrae, just to the south-east of Athens (across the Ilissus from the then-unfinished temple of Zeus Olympios), in Anthesterion (roughly February), initiation in which was a prerequisite for admission to the Greater Mysteries (Pl. *Gorg.* 497c, cf. Plut. *Demetr.* 26).

849   **a nice set of presents:** probably said ironically; cf. *Eccl.* 190, 794.

851-2   **thrice wretched, four times ... ten thousand times:** for similar elaborations of the idiomatic use of *tri(s)* "thrice" as an intensifier, cf. *Peace* 242-3 "Oho, Prasiae, thrice wretched, five times wretched, umpteen times wretched", *Knights* 1152-7 "I've been sitting here thrice-long, eager to do you service" – "And I've been sitting here ten-times-long and twelve-times-long and thousand-times-long and aeons-long-long-long" – "And I've been *waiting* for the two of you 30,000-times-long and aeons-long-long-long!"

853   **what a voracious fate has swallowed me:** lit. "with so concentrated (*poluphoros* "capable of bearing a large admixture of water") a fate I have been blended!" In elevated poetry, a person who experiences misfortune or grief may be said to be mixed or blended (*sunkerannusthai*) with it (cf. Soph.*Aj.* 895, *Ant.* 1311, *El.* 1485); Ar. here in effect treats this as a live metaphor from the dilution of wine with water in a mixing-bowl, with the sufferer as the water and his fate as the wine, which in this case is so strong that it absorbs its victim at hardly any cost in potency.

854   **Apollo ... preserve us:** see on 359.

857 I have lost everything that was in my house: just as money and goods magically appeared in fantastic abundance in the house of Chremylus, so they magically vanished from the Informer's house.

859 if my lawsuits don't fail me: it is apparently this expression that reveals to Carion and the Honest Man that the speaker is a *sūkophantēs* (a fact of which they are aware by 873). Blinding was not a legal penalty at Athens (in Aesch. *Eum.* 186-190 it appears in a list of barbaric punishments such as beheading, castration, mutilation and impalement, mostly practised – or thought by Greeks to be practised – in the Persian empire, cf. Xen. *Anab.* 1.9.13); but in the many cases in which the penalty for an offence was not prescribed by law but was decided by the jury (cf. on 480), it was theoretically open to either side to make whatever proposal it chose. If, however, the Informer really envisages proposing the re-blinding of Wealth, it will stamp him as a man of exceptional viciousness and cruelty, just as does his threat to have Carion "racked on the wheel" (875); in addition, since Wealth is a god, it would be an act of gross impiety, for which, unlike the Aristophanic heroes who defy Zeus (Trygaeus, Peisetaerus and Chremylus), the Informer does not have the excuse of acting in the general interest of humanity.

862 a piece of bad coinage: lit. "of the bad minting"; the definite article suggests that there is an allusion to one particular series of coins of very inferior quality, probably the silver-plated bronze coins introduced in 406 as an emergency currency and officially demonetized (or drastically reduced in value) at some time between 403 and 392 (cf. *Frogs* 725-6, *Eccl.* 815-822, Ar. fr. 3, and see J.H. Kroll, *GRBS* 17 [1976] 329-341). For the comparison between bad men and bad coin cf. *Ach.* 517-8, *Frogs* 718-733, Aesch. *Ag.* 390-3.

864-5 who promised that he'd make us all rich: it was in fact Chremylus who held out this prospect (496-7), and even he (as the Informer conveniently forgets) envisaged that at first only the virtuous would become rich, to be joined by the rest of the population as and when they embraced virtue for the sake of the wealth it would bring them. As at 858-9 and 946-950, the Informer puts all the blame on Wealth.

868 this man here: lit. "me, this man here".

869 villains: lit. "burglars" (*toikhōrukhoi*, see on 204), which had come to be used as a generalized term of abuse (cf. 909, 939, 1141, *Clouds* 1327, Ameipsias fr. 23, Dem. 35.9).

870-1 you is plural both times it occurs in these two lines; it refers not to Carion and the Honest Man (for when the Informer begins to speak of them as a pair, he uses the *dual* number [886-894], and in any case it is not until 880 that he even suspects the Honest Man of being a co-conspirator) but to Carion and the household to which he belongs. The Informer, we may presume, has noticed that Carion is remarkably well dressed for a slave, and jumps to the conclusion that he and his master have contrived to enrich themselves at his (the Informer's) expense.

872 Damater: see on 555.

872-3 this informer has certainly blown in like a full gale: cf. *Knights* 430-441 (where a threat by Paphlagon-Cleon to "freshen and sweep down upon [his opponents] like a mighty wind" stimulates his rival the Sausage-seller to shout out a series of nautical orders appropriate to stormy weather), 760.

873 ravenous: *boulimiān* in fourth-century Greek means "to be fainting with hunger" (cf. Xen. *Anab.* 4.5.7-8, [Arist.] *Probl.* 887b38-888a22). Carion affects to suppose that hunger has driven the Informer delirious and that is why he is making these wild allegations.

875 **you'll be racked on the wheel**: a slave, or even a free non-citizen, could be examined under torture by order of the Council or Assembly if it was thought that (s)he might have committed, or be able to give information about, a serious crime, especially one affecting state security (cf. Lyc. *Against Leocrates* 112; Aeschines 3.224; Dem. 18.133; Hypereides in *POxy* 2686). The Informer will later claim that Wealth is plotting to overthrow the democratic constitution (948-950), but as yet the only accusation he has made is one of theft from himself, and on such a matter, and as a private individual, he has no right to order the torture of another person's slave without the master's consent (the procedure involved is fully analysed by G. Thür, *Beweisführung vor den Schwurgerichtshöfen Athens* [Vienna, 1977] and comically exemplified in *Frogs* 616-628). Moreover, "the wheel" was generally regarded as the most extreme form of torture (cf. *Peace* 452, *Lys.* 846, Ant. 5.40, Andoc. 1.43) and resorted to only when other methods had failed; the references, though laconic, suggest that the victim was bound, face upwards, to the broad rim of a fixed wheel, and his extended limbs pulled downwards with cords.

876 **you'll howl if you try**: not only is Carion a slave with the spirit of a free man (cf. on 6-7 and 824), who will not submit to torture without a fight, but he is also sure that his master will do all he can to prevent (or, if the worst comes to the worst, punish) this illegal action.

880 **in on it**: lit. "sharing" (sc. in the Informer's allegedly stolen property).

882 **an old homespun thing**: Greek *tribōnion*, the same word as that translated "old cloak" in 842.

884 **this ring**: evidently a magic one: cf. Eupolis fr. 96; Ameipsias fr. 26; Lucian, *The Ship* 42-43. Those who sold such objects claimed that they protected the wearer "against evil spirits, snakes, and the like" (scholia), or even that they could cure illnesses (Antiphanes fr. 175). See C. Bonner, *Studies in Magical Amulets chiefly Graeco-Egyptian* (Ann Arbor, 1950) 4-5; R. Kotansky in C.A. Faraone & D. Obbink ed. *Magika Hiera* (New York, 1991) 110-1.

884 **Eudamus** is also mentioned in Plato com. fr. 214, a broken papyrus fragment which confirms only that he was a shopkeeper; but he is probably identical with the Eudemus referred to by Theophrastus (*HP* 9.17.2) as one of the most famous of dealers in *pharmaka* (a term of very wide application, covering anything that might be given or applied to a person to alter, for better or worse, his/her physical or mental condition – any medicine, poison, or magical charm). Eudemus and Eudamus are dialectal variants of the same name (in Attic-Ionic and in all other dialects, respectively).

884 **a drachma**: the same price (but a different dealer, Phertatus) is mentioned in Antiphanes fr. 175.

885 **but it doesn't say on it "For informer-bites"**: lit. "but 'of the bite of an informer' is not in/on it". I adopt the explanation of this difficult line proposed by Fritzsche and accepted by Rogers, viz. that magic rings were sometimes inscribed with the name of the evil (e.g. snake-bite) against which they were supposed to give protection, in the genitive case (understood to be governed by *pharmakon* "remedy/prophylactic against ..."), and Carion professes to be alarmed because the Honest Man's ring does not explicitly declare itself to be effective against the "bites" of *sūkophantai*. Cf. the saying of Diogenes the Cynic cited in D.L. 6.51: "Which animal has the deadliest bite? – Of wild creatures, the *sūkophantēs*; of tame ones, the flatterer."

886 **outrageous**: Greek *hubris* (cf. on 564).

887 **here**: viz. just outside a house that has suddenly (and therefore, the Informer presumes, criminally) acquired great wealth.

890 **on my money:** lit. "from <that which is> mine", i.e. on food bought with money that rightfully belongs to me.

892 **from being stuffed full of nothing:** since 891-2 is interpreted by the Informer as a denial of the accusation he has just made, Carion may well here be meaning to imply "because *nothing* of what we'll be dining on is yours".

895 **hnf-hnf, hnf-hnf, hnf-hnf, hnf-hnf, hnf-hnf, hnf-hnf:** in the Greek the sniffs are represented by the letter *upsilon* written twelve times, probably to be interpreted phonetically as six repetitions of [(h)ühü:] – this being the closest approach possible, within the constraints of the Greek phonological system, to a representation of the sound of a hungry man sniffing food. At *Knights* 10 an iambic verse is likewise made up entirely of inarticulate noises (moaning, represented as a sixfold *mumu*).

897 **what with that wretched cloak** (Greek *tribōnion*, cf. on 882) **he's got on:** the Honest Man thinks, or pretends to think, that the Informer is not sniffing but shivering. This line was drastically emended or transposed by several nineteenth-century scholars (and deleted altogether by W.G. Rutherford, *CR* 10 [1896] 99), because at 926-935 the Informer is forced to exchange the cloak he is wearing for a *tribōnion*, which might seem to suggest that up to that point he had been wearing a good-quality garment. This, however, is not an inevitable inference, and it is surely negatived by 861 and 896 – for if the Informer had arrived on the scene well clad, he would not have given the impression of having "fallen on hard times" and would not have been thought to be feeling the cold badly. Rather, his dress is in keeping with the poverty into which he has suddenly fallen – but once it is compared, after 926, with the thirteen-year-old cloak and shoes worn till recently by the Honest Man, we discover that he has not yet fallen as far as he might!

899 **I'm fed up to the teeth:** lit. "Alas (*oimoi*), how I am vexed!"

903-5 **do you work on the land? ... are you a merchant? ... have you learned a trade?:** the farmer supplies the public with food, the craftsman with manufactured goods or with services, the merchant with products imported from abroad; all these three occupational groups are therefore essential to the life of society. The simple society described in Pl. *Rep.* 369c-372c contains these three groups and one other (retailers).

903 **barmy:** lit. "affected by black bile" (cf. on 12).

904 **I claim to be one, when occasion arises:** merchants trading by sea had the right to be tried before a special court (the court of the *nautodikai*) and probably at a time of year convenient to them (cf. Lys. 17.5, where defendants stop a lawsuit by claiming to be merchants and the plaintiff has to bring a new case before the *nautodikai* in the month of Gamelion, during the winter, when sea travel was normally avoided); thus to claim merchant status gave one a chance of delaying an opponent's lawsuit by anything up to six or nine months, and the Informer apparently takes full advantage of this rule when he is sued (but not, of course, when he is suing someone else). One would expect, though we have no explicit evidence on the point, that as a precaution against such abuse of the merchants' privilege, any claim to it would have to be supported by an oath; if so, the Informer is here in effect, with no apparent qualms, confessing himself a perjurer. Cf. *Eccl.* 1027 (where young Epigenes claims to be a merchant in the hope of evading or delaying his legal obligation to sleep with a hideous old woman), and see E.E. Cohen, *Ancient Athenian Maritime Courts* (Princeton, 1973), esp. 42-59, 162-184.

906 **how and where did you get a living ...?:** the past tense is presumably used because he is clearly not getting an adequate living *now*.

907-919 Like Poverty earlier (cf. on 487-618), the Informer is allowed to present an argument which has considerable *prima facie* plausibility and which his antagonists do not refute but merely ignore, as if instinct rather than reason assured them it must be wrong. The argument is that without volunteer prosecutors like himself, law enforcement would be impossible; and in the real world of fourth-century Athens, it was a completely sound argument (since no one envisaged the alternative of creating a state prosecution service). In the new world created by the healing of Wealth, law enforcement will presumably soon become unnecessary, since everyone will become virtuous (497) and lawbreaking will therefore cease; it is noteworthy that Ar. does not allow Carion and the Honest Man to make use of this counter-argument, preferring to have them trust to irrational instinct and deal with the Informer by silencing and abusing him.

908 I am a *wisher*: Greek *boulomai* "I wish, I want", in itself enigmatic, is to be explained in the light of 917-9 (and 929). Many Athenian laws provided that prosecutions for this or that offence could be initiated by "whoever wishes" (*ho boulomenos*); this was regarded as one of the "most democratic" features of the legal reforms introduced by Solon in the early sixth century (Arist. *Ath.Pol.* 9.1; Plut. *Sol.* 18.6). The Informer is saying that his occupation is that of a person who "wishes" in this sense, i.e. a prosecutor. The verb *boulomai* normally always governs an object of some kind (usually an infinitive), though the object may be understood from the context. Its use without any object, as here, in the sense "be a *boulomenos*", "be a prosecutor", is unparalleled, but cannot have been invented by Ar. for this passage, since it would have baffled his audience until explained; it must thus already have been familiar, probably through use in one or more other recent comedies.

910 making enemies for yourself, over things that are none of your business: any man might find he had enemies, and was within his rights if he sought to harm them; but it was considered commendable to forgive wrongs and seek reconciliation, and speakers in the courts frequently claimed credit for such forbearance (see Dover *GPM* 187-194; G. Herman in C. Gill et al. ed. *Reciprocity in Ancient Greece* [Oxford, 1998] 199-225). The *sūkophantēs* is perverse enough to go out of his way to make other men his enemies, by prosecuting them and thereby putting them in danger of death, exile or heavy fines, over wrongs allegedly done by them not to him but to third parties. His response (and that of many prosecutors in court, e.g. Lys. 22.18-22, 28.1, 29.11-14; Aeschines 1.1-2; Lyc. *Against Leocrates* 3-8) is to claim that he is acting on behalf of a wronged *community* (911-9): cf. Dem. 21.45 "The lawgiver thought that anything done by violence was a wrong to the whole community, even those not directly affected by the action ... accordingly he gave the right of indictment for *hubris* to 'whoever wishes' ... because he thought that he who attempts to commit *hubris* wrongs not only his victim but the community".

912-3 isn't it my business ... to work for the good of my own community?: a proposition with which everyone would agree.

912 booby: Greek *kepphos*, a sea-bird (traditionally identified as the stormy petrel, *Hydrobates pelagicus*; cf. the description of its habits by Dionysius, *Ixeuticon* 2.11) that was a byword for imbecility (cf. *Peace* 1067, Archestratus *SH* 154.14, Hesychius κ2242).

914 to go to the aid of the established laws: a typical prosecution speaker's expression, cf. Aeschines 1.2, Lyc. *Against Leocrates* 149. In Lys. 22.3 the same expression is used of a speaker arguing against the illegal summary execution of some alleged offenders.

917 an authority: Greek *arkhē*, properly "a magistracy". Being a juror was not technically an *arkhē* (see M.H. Hansen, *GRBS* 21 [1980] 152-4) but could informally be described as such (cf. *Wasps* 587). The mss.' reading would mean "appoint jurors to hold office (*arkhein*); but the verb *arkhein* "hold office, be a ruler", as distinct from the noun *arkhē*, is not used of jurors even informally (Arist. *Pol.* 1275a23-32, arguing that from the point of view of political theory being a juror ought to be regarded as an *arkhē*, uses only the noun and not the verb; Philocleon's claim in *Wasps* 518-9, 619 that as a juror he rules [*arkhei*] the whole city is meant to be perceived as absurd).

917 who's to bring prosecutions before them?: cf. Lyc. *Leocr.* 4 "The law exists to specify what conduct is forbidden, the accuser to denounce those who have made themselves liable to the penalties of the law, and the juror to punish those whom the first two point out to him as guilty; so that neither the law nor the vote of the jurors has any power without someone to hand offenders over to them".

918 anyone who wishes. – Well, that's me, innit?: see on 908.

921-5 For the attempt to persuade a *sūkophantēs* to pursue a less reprehensible occupation, cf. *Birds* 1430-52. Here, as there, the attempt fails, even though on this occasion the Informer can be offered the option of "liv[ing]" in idleness" (for if he becomes virtuous he will automatically acquire wealth without having to work for it); M.J. Dillon, *Aristophanes' Ploutos: Comedy in Transition* (Diss. Yale 1984) 194-5 argues that his refusal of this option is designed to demonstrate unequivocally, before violent hands are laid on him, that he cannot excuse his behaviour by any plea of necessity – that, in the words of Andocides (1.95), he is not only wicked but *likes* being wicked.

923 if I'm not going to see any activity: implying that for him, it is better to be active in crime (for it was a crime to be a *sūkophantēs*: see Lys. 13.65, Isoc. 15.314, Aeschines 2.145, [Dem.] 58.11, Arist. *Ath.Pol.* 43.5, 59.3) than not to be active at all.

925 all the silphium of Battus: silphium (a wild umbelliferous plant, now long extinct, whose stalk was both eaten as a vegetable and used as a condiment; cf. *Knights* 894-901, *Birds* 534, 1582, *Eccl.* 1171, Eubulus fr. 6.3), was the principal export of the city of Cyrene on the Libyan coast, and was so vital to the Cyrenaean economy that it became an emblem of the city and was used as a device on its coins (see G.K. Jenkins, *Ancient Greek Coins* [London, 1972] 52, 109-110 and pl. 85, 86, 265). Cyrene was founded in the seventh century by one Battus of Thera, who became its first king; thereafter, until the overthrow of the monarchy two centuries later, the kings were named alternately Battus and Arcesilaus (Hdt. 4.150-163). Cyrene was famous for its wealth: Pindar speaks (*Pyth.* 4.260-1) of "Cyrene adorned with gold" (cf. also *Pyth.* 9.8-9, 9.69) and implies (*Pyth.* 5.55-59) that its prosperity has been continuous since the days of its founder; it was later said (Plut. *Mor.* 779d) that Plato had declined to make laws for the Cyrenaeans because so prosperous a people would be too "proud, harsh and ungovernable" to be able to maintain them. Whether "the silphium of Battus" really was, as the scholia claim, a catch-phrase for "immense riches" (like the English phrase "all the tea in China") is uncertain; van Leeuwen not implausibly suggests that Ar. may rather have comically distorted an existing (though unattested) catch-phrase "the *gold* of Battus" – perhaps expecting his audience to think of the tendency of silphium, if consumed in excessive quantities, to cause flatulence of the bowels (cf. *Knights* loc.cit.).

926-934 The distribution of lines between the Informer's two antagonists is uncertain throughout this passage; but since Carion cannot be the speaker of 937, we know that the idea of dressing the Informer in the Honest Man's old cloak is his, and I have therefore hesitantly made him take the lead throughout in despoiling and assaulting the Informer. This has the advantage of maximizing the humiliation the Informer suffers, in being struck and robbed with impunity by a slave. It does require us to accept that at 926 he breaks into the dialogue between the Informer and the Honest Man with a brusque demand in which a threat of violence is barely concealed (and may well have been expressed in gesture); but this is consistent with his character as displayed especially in 56-74.

929   well, that's me, innit?: Carion casts the Informer's own words back at him; cf. *Clouds* 1503 ~ 225, *Wasps* 989 ~ 959, *Birds* 986, 989 ~ 974, 976, 980, and Dionysus' use of Euripidean quotations against Euripides in *Frogs* 1469-78.

931   *you're* the one who sees fit ...: i.e. as one who lives by crime (cf. on 923) you have no right to complain if you become the victim of crime.

932   are you aware (lit. "do you see") **what you're doing?:** reminding Carion that as a clothes-snatcher (*lōpodutēs*) he is committing a crime punishable by death (Arist. *Ath.Pol.* 52.1); the warning has no effect, because the Informer will have no witness to support his accusation.   Most recent editors have accepted a sixteenth-century emendation which has the Informer turn to (where he expects to find) his witness and say "Do you see what he's doing?"; but (i) as Rogers points out, on the five other occasions (see next note) when the cry *marturomai* "witness (this), everyone!" is raised in Ar. by a victim of assault it is never preceded by other words addressed to a known potential witness but always comes as "an ejaculation, wrung from the speaker by the stress of the moment", and (ii) if at this moment the Informer had turned to address his witness, he would have seen that the man was no longer there, and would have felt the shock of being alone among enemies *now* rather than a line and a half later (934).

932   witness this, everyone!: cf. *Ach.* 926, *Clouds* 1297, *Wasps* 1436, *Peace* 1119, *Birds* 1031.   This utterance is a request to anyone in earshot to bear witness to the crime that is being committed; it normally comes as an immediate response to a blow (cf. *Clouds* 494-5).

933   the witness you had: there is little to choose, in terms either of sense or of strength of attestation, between this and the alternative reading "the witness you brought"; but *Wasps* 1408, 1416, 1437 suggest that in this kind of context *ekhein* "have (with one)" rather than *agein* "bring" was the verb that would have come first to Ar.'s mind.

935   "ah, yet another!": the last words (heard from behind the scenes) of Clytaemestra in Soph. *El.* 1415 (which itself echoed Aesch. *Ag.* 1345) as she fell under Orestes' second and fatal sword-thrust.   The scholia are probably right to assume that there is a deliberate reminiscence of the Sophoclean passage (cf. also *Frogs* 1214); and if so, it is reasonable to infer that the Informer likewise falls under his assailants' blows, and remains helpless on the ground, for them to abuse as they will, until 943.   Similar treatment is inflicted on the *sūkophantēs* Nicarchus at *Ach.*926 and on Paphlagon at *Knights* 453-6; at *Knights* 1248-52 the vanquished Paphlagon apparently swoons to the ground spontaneously, as do Philocleon at *Wasps* 995, Dionysus at *Frogs* 479, and probably Euripides at *Frogs* 1478.

935   that old cloak: the one the Honest Man was bringing to dedicate to Wealth (842-6).

937   it's already sacred: if a vow had been made to give a specific object to a god, the object thereupon became the god's property: it had to be dedicated at the first opportunity (once any condition that might have been attached to the vow had been fulfilled), and could not meanwhile be used in any other way.   Thus when, after Peleus had vowed that a lock of his son Achilles' hair would be dedicated to the river Spercheius if he returned safely from Troy, Achilles instead cuts off the lock and puts it in the hands of the dead Patroclus (*Iliad* 23.141-153), Socrates in Pl. *Rep.* 391b complains that Achilles is represented as behaving impiously because the lock is "sacred, the property of Spercheius" and says that on this matter Homer "must not be believed" – even though Achilles knows, and explicitly says (*Iliad* 23.150), that he will never be returning home, and therefore the lock will never be dedicated in any case.

938 where better to have it lie as a dedication ...?: placed on the Informer's shoulders, the cloak will still be "sacred to Wealth", because it will be glorifying him by manifesting the effect of his power in impoverishing the wicked.

939 rogue and villain: lit. "wicked burglar" (cf. on 204 and 869).

940 Wealth ought to be adorned with _stately_ garments: this need not imply that the garments of which the Informer has been despoiled were "stately" (cf. on 897); Carion never says that these are going to be dedicated to Wealth, and there is no need for them to be, since the cloak and shoes originally vowed by the Honest Man remain the property of the god (see on 938). In saying what he says here, Carion has no particular "stately garments" in mind; by "with stately garments" he essentially means "not with shabby garments", which can be better employed in the god's service in other ways.

942-3 I'll nail them to his forehead: since the Informer's "forehead" is, in theatrical actuality, part of the actor's mask, this can in fact be done – and "panoply" (951) shows that it _is_ done, since a single item of accoutrement such as a cloak could not be called, even metaphorically, a panoply. Other than the transfixing of Prometheus in [Aesch.] _Prom._ 64-65, this is the only place in surviving Greek drama where a character is subjected to treatment which in real life would (almost) certainly kill him but which he is allowed to survive by the exploitation of a theatrical convention. It is probably significant that the only person in what is known of Greek comedy who apparently does suffer death during the course of the play is another _sūkophantēs_, in Eupolis' _Demes_ (Eupolis fr. 99.112). Note that in addition to all the other humiliations heaped on him, this treatment forces the Informer to depart _barefoot_, a mark of extreme deprivation (cf. _Lys._ 32.16); no one else in Ar. is left without anything to put on his feet, except for Socrates and his disciples in _Clouds_ (103, 363, 719, 858-9; cf. Ameipsias fr. 9.3), for whom barefootedness is part of the lifestyle of an ascetic philosopher (it was a practice of the real Socrates; cf. Pl. _Symp._ 174a, 220b; Xen. _Mem._ 1.6.2).

943 like a dedication nailed to a wild olive tree (lit. "just as to a wild olive tree"): objects were often dedicated by being hung up on trees, not necessarily in sacred precincts (cf. _AP_ 6.35, 57, 96, 106, 168, 221, 237, 298); wild olive trees are mentioned in this connection by Thphr. _HP_ 5.2.4 and Virg. _Aen._ 12.766-9.

944-5 much stronger than I am: viz. two to one.

945 an ally: to serve as witness. A prosecution could not be begun without the defendant being given a summons to appear before a specified magistrate, and a summons (which was delivered orally) could not be effected without the presence of a witness (_kleter_, cf. _Wasps_ 1408, 1416, 1445, _Clouds_ 1218, _Birds_ 147) who could afterwards, if the defendant failed to appear as required, testify that the summons had indeed been delivered. This was the only outside assistance that was absolutely indispensable to a prosecutor.

946 even a frail one: lit. "even one made of figwood". Figwood is not strong enough to be of any use as timber, and "figwood assistance" (_sūkinē epikouriā_) was an idiomatic expression for "unreliable assistance, 'a broken reed'" (schol. _Lys._ 110; cf. Theocr. 10.45); but the Informer on this occasion does not need a particularly stout-hearted ally, since all he requires is a man to accompany him on a single visit (see previous note). The reference to figwood also embodies a pun on the word _sūkophantēs_, whose literal meaning is "a revealer of figs"; for similar fig-puns cf. _Knights_ 259, 529, _Wasps_ 145, 897, _Birds_ 1699.

946 this mighty god: spoken sarcastically, for the Informer expects to defeat him with the aid of one "frail" assistant; but this only emphasizes yet more his folly, arrogance, and impiety.

948-9 attempting to subvert our democracy: one of the gravest charges that could be
made against anyone: according to a decree passed after the restoration of full
democracy in 410 (Andoc. 1.96-98), a person who attempted to overthrow democracy
became *ipso facto* a public enemy and was not only liable to the death penalty, but
could be killed by anyone without trial and with impunity. The decree (which in
substance, though not necessarily in all its details, doubtless became part of the revised
permanent law-code when this came into force in 403/2) was obviously directed against
attempts to alter the constitution (as was done in 411 and again in 404) by force,
intimidation or fraud, but its language does not require too much stretching to cover the
case of a person who effects a fundamental change in wealth distribution, affecting
virtually everyone in the community, without seeking the community's official approval
(cf. 949-950). Other prosecutors contrived to stretch it much further: in or about 333
one Lycophron was prosecuted for subverting the democracy by ... committing adultery
(Hyp. *Lyc.* 12, cf. Lyc. fr. 10/11.2 Conomis).

948 acting entirely on his own sole authority: lit. "being one alone". One of the most
damaging things that could be said of an opponent was to portray him as an isolated
individual in opposition to the community; cf. *Ach.* 493; Soph. *Ant.* 508; Eur. *Hipp.* 12;
Lys. 7.33; 24.13, 22; Dem. 18.137; 19.113; 21.14, 167, 198; Lyc. *Against Leocrates* 67,
131, 134; Dein. 1.12.

949-950 without obtaining the approval of the ... Council or of the Assembly: the
Informer conveniently ignores the probability that, since at that time most ordinary
Athenians were poor (and virtuous), they would have accepted Wealth's proposal with
the greatest possible enthusiasm.

951 panoply means properly a full set of arms and armour as worn/carried by a hoplite.
There may be an allusion to *Iliad* 16, where Patroclus goes into battle wearing Achilles'
armour and the Trojans initially mistake him for Achilles and panic: by analogy, if the
Informer goes to the bath-house with the Honest Man's "panoply", he may be mistaken
for the Honest Man and allowed to occupy the place hitherto reserved for the latter.

953 run off to the bath-house: cf. 535.

953 in pole position: lit. "as chorus-leader" (Greek *koruphaios*), meaning, evidently,
nearest to the source of heat. In Sophoclean and later tragic choruses, which comprised
fifteen men in three rows of five, the chorus-leader stood in the middle of the front row
(Photius s.v. *tritos aristerou*); but in the pre-Sophoclean tragic chorus of twelve (three
rows of four) and in the comic chorus of twenty-four (probably three rows of eight) no
one could be in the middle of a row, and some evidence (Cratinus fr. 229, cf. Hesychius
α7241, *Anecd. Bekk.* i 445.15) suggests that in these types of chorus the *koruphaios* led
the chorus on and took position at one *end* of the front row. That this was the chorus-
leader's original position is supported by the term *koruphaios* itself, which means "the
man at the extremity", and also by the present passage: if a number of people, more or
less in a line, are crowding to warm themselves near a source of heat, with unequal
success, the warmest is likely to be at one end of the line rather than in the middle of it.
It may well be that Sophocles increased the size of the tragic chorus from twelve to
fifteen (*Life of Sophocles* 4) precisely in order to be able to place its leader in the centre.

955-6 take him by the balls and drag him outside: cf. *Knights* 769-772 "if I do not love
and cherish you ... may I be dragged by the balls with my own meathook to
Cerameicus!"

956 as soon as he sees him, he'll know: because, in Wealth's new world, anyone who
looks impoverished is thereby known to be wicked.

957 one of those "pieces of bad coinage": referring to the Honest Man's words at 862.

958/9 The new information provided by Π83 has made it highly probable that there was a choral interlude here as well as at 321/2, 626/7, 770/1 and 801/2 (see also on 1096/7). The evidence from actor movements points the same way (despite my arguments in *BICS* 31 [1984] 142). If the two scenes are played without a break, the actor playing the Informer, who is not out of sight (down one of the side-passages) until 954, must return either as the Old Woman, by the same side-passage, at 959 (which would give him only four lines to change costume and mask), or as Chremylus at 965 from the stage-house (giving him ten lines to change costume and mask *and* cover the distance between his exit and entrance points); either of these sequences would be quicker than anything comparable in any surviving Greek drama (the quickest change known is at Men. *Dysk.* 873-9, where the actor playing Gorgias, on exiting into the stage-house, has five lines to change and emerge from the same door as Getas).

959 OLD WOMAN: her appearance and manner may make it clear to the audience from the start that she is a courtesan; if any of them are in doubt, it will surely be removed when she addresses a total stranger (and not one for whom she has reason to feel the least affection) as "darling" (967).

962 I assure you, you've come right to his door: a near repetition of *Frogs* 436.

963 you do speak (lit. "ask") in a youthful kind of way: this probably does not refer, as van Leeuwen supposes, to the woman's having addressed the chorus as *gerontes* "old men", for an elderly person may in comedy address another as "old (wo)man" (cf. *Ach.* 1228, *Lys.* 637, Men. *Dysk.* 427, 453, 502, 925, 926); more likely, therefore, it refers to her intonation and voice quality.

964 let me call someone from inside: she would have gone on to call *pai pai* "boy, boy!" or the like (cf. *Ach.* 395, *Clouds* 132, 1145, *Birds* 57, *Frogs* 37), which would have brought out Carion; but Ar. wants to have Chremylus, not Carion, in this scene, and therefore brings him out before the visitor has time to utter the call. That it is indeed Chremylus who appears is shown by 1066 and 1077 (see Dover *AC* 205).

967-9 The second-century papyrus Π83 has an extra line either before or after 968: only faint traces remain of the extra line and of 968, and not a single letter of either can be confidently read. It had never previously been suspected that a line was missing here, and the sense is complete as the text stands: if a line has indeed been lost, nothing can be said with confidence about its exact position, its content or its wording. A metrical scholium on 959 says that there are 84 iambic trimeters (instead of 83) between 959 and 1041 inclusive, but this is mere coincidence, since these scholia were composed by Triclinius and do not appear in any earlier ms. If we were certain that a line of Ar.'s text, of which the medieval tradition knows nothing, had been preserved in this second-century copy, it might have far-reaching consequences for our view of the history of the text; but we cannot rule out the alternative possibility that the extra line was an interpolation (cf. on 566).

969 he's made my life be not worth living: Chremylus at first assumes that she means she has been impoverished, and therefore (970-2) that she is some kind of criminal. The audience probably suspect, from her dress, her make-up, and the attractive foods on the tray her servant is carrying (cf. 995-9), that she is not badly off, and they will be mystified as to what she has to complain of.

970 informeress: Greek *sūkophantria*, coined as a feminine equivalent of *sūkophantēs*. No woman, of course, could bring a prosecution in the Athenian courts; Chremylus (or Ar.) is humorously assuming that the women have a parallel court system of their own, just as in *Thesm.* they are shown as having a parallel Council (*Thesm.* 373) and Assembly.

972 drinking with your letter-class when you hadn't been drawn for a place: for the "letter-classes" into which male jurors were divided, see on 277. Here the participle *(ou) lakhousa* "(not) having been drawn" is singular, and this, together with the phrase "with [lit. in] your letter-class", shows that we are dealing not, as in 277, with a sortition among letter-classes, but with a sortition among individuals within them. It is not difficult to see that such a sortition will at least sometimes have been necessary. Since for any given type of trial the number of jurors required was fixed (a multiple of 100, or a multiple of 100 plus one; whenever the size of an Athenian mass jury is mentioned in any text, it is always specified in one of these two ways), some jurors in one or more letter-classes must often have been surplus to requirements, and at some stage in the allotment procedure a sortition must have been held to decide which of them would actually serve (and thus be paid) that day. Our passage evidently alludes to an abuse (or alleged abuse) whereby some jurors contrived to serve on days when they had been unlucky in this sortition (for another type of fraud likewise aimed at maximizing a juror's opportunities to serve, cf. 1166-7). But Chremylus is speaking of a women's court, and typically assumes that the "jurors" of such a body would not spend their time judging, but drinking (cf. on 645).

973 put right through the mincer: lit. "grated up, grated to shreds".

977 very decent: Greek *khrēstos*, the most common epithet in this play for the virtuous people to whom Wealth gives prosperity (e.g. 92, 93, 239, 490, 826). The following sentence (which in the Greek is introduced by the particle *gar* "for") shows that the Old Woman herself means only that the Young Man was kind to *her*; see also on 1003.

977-8 if ever I wanted anything, he did everything for me: "this is to be understood in an indecent sense" (scholia): in a reversal of normal practice, the *woman* was giving money and goods to the *man* in exchange for sexual services. That this is the Old Woman's meaning was probably made clear by her tone of voice in this sentence; at any rate Chremylus' question at 980 already presupposes it, since in a relationship of the ordinary type there would be no need to ask what it was that the man wanted from the woman. For *ti* "something" as a sexual euphemism, see my remarks in F. De Martino and A.H. Sommerstein ed. *Studi sull'eufemismo* (Bari, 1999) 199, 206.

979 in return I was ready to do any service for him: the mss. read "I did all these services [or: all the same services] for him"; but (i) the (material) services the Old Woman provided for her lover were not at all the same as the (sexual) services he provided for her, (ii) a scholium in M, containing the compound verb *anthupēretoun* "I did services in return", makes it highly probable that this word, rather than the simple *hupēretoun* "I did services", originally stood in the text, emphasizing that the relationship had been one of reciprocity, which the Young Man has violated and which ought to be restored (cf. 1028-30).

982-3 twenty drachmas ... for a cloak, or eight for shoes: since the Old Woman is being presented as having been blindly infatuated, one would expect these prices to be on the high side, but our evidence suggests that they are not absurdly so. In 329/8 the cloaks bought for temple slaves at Eleusis cost 18½ drachmas each, and their shoes 6 drachmas a pair (*IG* ii^2 1672.100-5); over the intervening sixty years the price of wheat under normal conditions had risen from 3 to 5 drachmas per *medimnos* (*Eccl.* 547-8, Dem. 34.39), and if other prices had risen in the same proportion, that would imply that in the early 380s a cheap but respectable cloak might cost about 11 dr. and a pair of shoes about 3½ dr. If the Young Man was taking as much advantage as he dared of his mistress's besotted state, it is not implausible that he might ask for roughly double these sums so as to be able to buy top-quality goods.

984 underdress: Greek *khitōnion*, the inner of the two garments that a woman would normally wear.

984-5 his sisters ... his mother: that he had to maintain them implies (i) that his father was dead and (ii) that his sisters were unmarried and therefore probably not more than about fifteen years old – or at any rate that that is what he wanted his mistress to believe. Note that whereas he asks her for *money* to buy a cloak and shoes for himself, he asks her *to buy* clothes for his mother and sisters, presumably because it would not have been thought proper for a man to buy women's clothing.

986 four bushels: lit. "four *medimnoi*", equivalent to about 200 litres or 6 UK bushels. It was commonly assumed that one *choinix* of wheat (one forty-eighth of a *medimnos*) was a day's ration for an adult male (cf. Hdt. 7.187.2), and the limited evidence we have suggests that a woman was thought to require about half this amount (cf. *GDI* 1884 [Delphi, second century BC]: 4 *hemiekteis* = 16 *choinikes* per month); see L. Foxhall and H.A. Forbes, *Chiron* 12 (1982) 51-62, 86-89. Even if we assume that the Young Man had three sisters as well as his mother to support, 4 *medimnoi* (= 192 *choinikes*) of wheat would therefore still have sufficed the family for two months!

991 my cloak: i.e. the cloak I had paid for.

993 but now he's not thinking that way at all: she does not explicitly say that the Young Man has recently become rich; we (and Chremylus, cf. 1004) are left to infer it from 968 ("since this god began to see again").

995 when I sent him this flat-cake: such a gift, sent by either a woman or a youth to her/his lover, was a recognized signal that (s)he wished for an assignation (cf. Aelian *VH* 11.12, also Ar. fr. 211). The Old Woman is so desperate to ensure that the signal is correctly received that she reinforces it by sending further food gifts and a verbal message too.

997 added: sc. through the mouth of the messenger (presumably the slave who is still carrying the tray).

999 milk-cake: Greek *amēs*, "a kind of milky cake" (scholia; cf. Ath. 14.644f) which was traditionally brought, together with other foods, by a bridegroom to his bride when he came to fetch her from her father's house to his (Alexis fr. 168). If on that occasion it conveyed the message "I want you to come to my house, and I will maintain you", it is here used (together with the return of the other gifts) to say almost exactly the opposite: "I don't need you to maintain me, and I don't want you to come to my house".

1001 he sent back with them the message: lit. "he said, sending them back".

1002 "the Milesians were brave men – once upon a time": with the subtext "and you were beautiful – once upon a time, but not now!" In the early archaic period Miletus had been a warlike and powerful city, waging successful campaigns in the Black Sea region (Ephorus *FGrH* 70 F 183) and intervening in at least one conflict on the west side of the Aegean (Hdt. 5.99.1), and in the early sixth century, under the tyrant Thrasybulus, she emerged undefeated from a long war against the Lydians (Hdt. 1.16-22); but a generation later the Milesians were no more able than the other Asian Greeks to avoid becoming tributary to the Lydian Croesus, and subsequently they made a treaty with Cyrus of Persia and refused to join the other Ionians in resistance to him (Hdt. 1.141.4, 143.1). This comment on their decline, which became proverbial, was ascribed by some to the sixth-century poet Anacreon (*PMG* 426), by some to Timocreon of Rhodes (early fifth century) (*PMG* 733 = Timocreon fr. 7 West), by some to a Delphic oracle given to the Carians (Demon *FGrH* 327 F 16) or to the Cyprians (scholia on 1075) or to Polycrates of Samos (scholia here) in response to an inquiry about the advisability of making an alliance with Miletus.

1003 he obviously wasn't a bad sort, character-wise: to the modern mind an extremely surprising judgement, yet it is not ironical on Chremylus' part. His irony at the Old Woman's expense had previously taken the form of humouring her belief in her own continuing attractiveness and the Young Man's love and respect for her (987-8, 992); now, on the contrary, he speaks of her, honestly and brutally, as "lentil soup" (see next note) and as one whom no man would court except from desperation (1004-5). It follows that the audience – at least the male portion of it, who were the overwhelming majority – are expected to agree that the Young Man is fundamentally one of "the virtuous" and therefore deserves his newly-gained wealth. Since even Chremylus agrees that he has treated the Old Woman unjustly (1071-85) and compels him to resume his relationship with her (cf. 1201), this must imply that justice towards women of inferior social status (and *a fortiori* towards slaves), while it might be *desirable*, was not, in the eyes of the average male Athenian, an *essential* part of what it meant to be a "virtuous" man. It was certainly quite acceptable to treat a *hetairā*, slave or free, in a manner that totally disregarded her dignity, feelings or interests as a person. Thus Eucrates and Timanoridas, having kept Neaera as their joint mistress, apparently for several years, and then wishing to get married, considered they were doing her a kindness when they offered her her freedom at a reduced price on condition that she abandoned either her home town or her profession ([Dem.] 59.29-32); while at Neaera's trial, three arbitrators were ready to testify that they had settled a subsequent dispute between two rivals for her favours on the terms that she should live for half of every month with one of the rivals (Phrynion) who, to use the prosecutor's own words, had been persistently guilty of *hubris* towards her, and there is no mention of any undertaking by him to treat her better in future (*ibid.* 46-47, cf. 33, 35, 37, 40) – and this arrangement is spoken of as confirming that Neaera is "free and her own mistress"! An Athenian might well feel a glow of special virtue if he made provision for his mistress's future welfare when he grew tired of her or wished to marry, just as a nineteenth-century English factory owner might if he did not dismiss half his workforce as soon as trade grew slack; but neither the former nor the latter would expect to incur moral condemnation or social stigma if they acted differently.

1004 lentil soup is likewise linked with poverty in Theocr. 10.54 (where it is being prepared in bulk for a gang of harvest workers) and Antiphanes fr. 185 (where "eating lentil soup" is contrasted with being a king and "sleeping on a soft bed").

1005 he'd lick up anything: Greek *hup-esthiein* is a rare compound meaning either "eat from below" or "eat secretly": cf. schol. *Iliad* 21.271 (commenting on the equally rare synonym *hupereptein*, used of the river Scamander sucking the sand from under Achilles' feet and threatening to sweep him away). The only possible relevance of the prefix here is in the sense "eat (lick up) from below" as an allusion to cunnilingus. Other references to cunnilingus in Ar. suggest that it carried no stigma (cf. *Peace* 716-7, *Eccl.* 846-7) except when practised by one Ariphrades (*Knights* 1280-9, *Wasps* 1275-83, *Peace* 883-5) who may have been a comic poet and therefore a rival of Ar. (cf. Arist. *Poet.* 1458b31); so the point here is probably not that cunnilingus would be *degrading* to the Young Man but that with this particular partner – old, desiccated and no doubt smelly (cf. 1020-1) – it would be even more *physically disagreeable* than intercourse was. Athenaeus (second century AD) read our passage with a different compound, *epesthiein* "eat in addition" (sc. to bread, cf. Kassel & Austin on *com.adesp.* 519), and quotes it as an example of the use of that verb; in itself this would be a perfectly satisfactory reading, but a verb at once so rare and so comically apposite as *hupesthiein* is most unlikely to have entered the text either by corruption or by interpolation.

1006 by the Two Goddesses: at Athens "the Two Goddesses" were Demeter and Persephone (Pherrephatta, Kore), the goddesses worshipped at the women's festival of the Thesmophoria; in comedy, and doubtless in real life, they were invoked in oaths exclusively by women (cf. *Eccl.* 155-8).

1008-37 It has often been suggested that some of Chremylus' remarks in this passage, most of which are (or could be taken as) insulting to the Old Woman, are made "aside" and not meant to be heard by her: thus, of his twelve utterances, van Leeuwen marks eight as asides ("ad spectatores") and Thiercy two (1009, 1035). It is certain, however, that at least some of the time Chremylus *is* addressing himself to the Old Woman, for she responds to him at 1008-9 and throughout 1028-36 – and some of the remarks to which she responds (1008, 1033, 1035) are at least as insulting as any of those to which she does not, yet she never seems to take offence at any of them. I therefore see little reason for distinguishing between moments at which Chremylus is talking to her and moments at which he is talking "only" to the audience; rather, he is throughout talking for the benefit of both. In 1008-24 the Old Woman begins by responding to a direct question, but thereafter Chremylus' comments do not demand a reply, and she ignores them and pursues her account of the Young Man's seemingly lovelorn behaviour in the past. At 1025, having completed this account, she explicitly addresses him with a reiteration of the complaint of Wealth's injustice with which she had begun (967-9), now in her view thoroughly borne out by the evidence she has adduced, and from that point the two engage in a fully interactive dialogue, broken off only when the Young Man is seen approaching.

1008 to join your funeral procession?: the same joke is made at another old woman's expense in *Eccl.* 926, as part of an interminable series of variations on the theme "old = as good as dead" (cf. 277-8 above and 1033, 1035 below); for earlier allusions to the same theme cf. *Clouds* 846, *Wasps* 1365, *Lys.* 372, 599-613.

1009 you mean he wanted to get something out of you: lit. "on the contrary, for the sake of acquiring".

1011 "my little duck" and "my little dove": the Greek words are *nēttarion* and *phattion*, diminutives of *netta* "duck" and *phatta* "ringdove"; cf. Plaut. *Asin.* 693-4 *dic ... med aneticulam, columbam ... , monerulam, passerculum putillum*, Men. fr. 652, Pherecr. fr. 143. Ringdoves, like other birds (cf. *Birds* 705-7; see K.J. Dover, *Greek Homosexuality* [London, 1978] 92), were frequently used as love-gifts (cf. Theocr. 5.96, 133).

1013 at the Great Mysteries: cf. on 845.

1013-4 when I was riding in my carriage: it was fourteen miles from Athens to Eleusis, and women who (or whose husbands) could afford it normally made the journey in a vehicle (cf. Dem. 21.158) until the practice was banned in the 330s, on the proposal of Lycurgus, as being provocatively ostentatious ([Plut.] *Lives of the Ten Orators* 842a).

1015 I'd get a beating that lasted all day: this apparently *increases* her devotion to the Young Man, because it shows the depth of his passion for her. It is unlikely to have told significantly against him with the audience: it was considered as routine for an Athenian to beat his wife for such offences as refusing him sex (*Lys.* 162) or questioning him about things that he thought no concern of hers (*Lys.* 517-521) as it had been in seventh-century Amorgos (Semonides fr. 7.12-18) – and a non-citizen *hetairā*, with no natal family to protect her, could expect to be treated even worse.

1017 being alone at table: lit. "eating alone", i.e. being the sole beneficiary of the Old Woman's bounty.

1021 Thasian wine: the wine of Thasos was a much-praised variety (Athenaeus 1.28e-29c) noted for its dark colour (*Lys.* 205, Ar. fr. 364) and its sweet aroma (*Lys.* 206, *Eccl.* 1118-24; Hermippus fr. 77.3). See F. Salviat, *BCH* Suppl. 13 (1986) 145-196; Davidson 42-43.

1024 randy: strictly "like a sow on heat" (lit. "boar-mad"): a promiscuous woman could be called a "wild sow" (*kapraina*), cf. Hermippus fr. 9, Pherecrates fr. 186, Phryn. com. fr. 34.

1024 life savings: Greek *ephodia*, lit. "journey-money", had the idiomatic sense "savings set aside for one's old age": cf. [Dem.] 49.67, Plut. *Mor.* 8c, and see V. Tammaro, *MCr* 18 (1983) 137-8.

1026 when he claims to always help the victims of wrongdoing: Wealth has not made any such statement explicitly, but he has professed himself the friend of the virtuous and enemy of the wicked, and this commits him to be a friend to anyone who is wronged (unless the victim of wrong is him/herself a criminal – an exception irrelevant to the present case).

1027 say, and it shall be done: for all his merciless teasing of the Old Woman, Chremylus is as good as his word (cf. 1201).

1029 to treat me well in return: cf. on 979.

1030 otherwise, the man has no right ... : Wealth is being asked, through Chremylus, to compel the Young Man to return to his mistress on pain of losing his new-found riches if he refuses. Chremylus in fact tries himself to persuade him to do so, without invoking the authority of Wealth and without explicitly threatening any sanctions; at the end of the scene (1096), when the Young Man goes into the house (where Wealth at present resides), we do not know whether Chremylus' persuasion has succeeded, and when Chremylus in the end does assure the Old Woman (1201) that her lover will indeed come back to her, we are not told by whom or how he was induced to agree to do so.

1034 I've wasted away from grief: cf. Eubulus fr. 102.7, Theocr. 7.76, 11.14, also of the effect of lovesickness.

1037 to be attached to a bread-seller's tray: lit. "to be <the ring> of a *tēliā*" (the mss. other than R read "to be a *tēliā*"; the evidence of the scholia suggests that both variants were current in antiquity). Whichever reading we adopt, the context requires that the reference be to some "ring" that would be big enough to accommodate the Old Woman's bodily circumference (and we may safely assume that she is fat, since otherwise the joke would be feeble; most old men and women in terracottas and vase-paintings illustrating comedy are indeed fat – see Stone 127-143 and figs. 1-5, 8-14). The normal meaning of *tēliā* is "board with a raised rim" (or, equivalently, "lidless box with sides very shallow in proportion to its surface area"); more specifically (see *Et.Mag.* 756.56-757.8 for most of the following usages) it is applied (i) to trays used by itinerant sellers of bread, barley meal, etc. (like the woman who appears in *Wasps* 1388-1414) for displaying their wares (cf. schol. 1037a,d,g Chantry, *Anecd.Bekk.* 275.15-17), (ii) to wooden or wicker trays used as fighting enclosures in the "sports" of quail-tapping (cf. *Birds* 1298-9, Pollux 9.107-9) and cock-fighting (*Anecd.Bekk.* 307.32-33), (iii) to a gambling table (whose raised rim would stop the rolling dice) (cf. Aeschines 1.53, *Anecd. Bekk.* 275.17-18), and (iv) to a board placed over a chimney to cover it against rain when not in use (*Wasps* 147). There was also a word *tēliā*, perhaps of different origin, meaning (v) "hoop of a sieve" (schol. 1037m, Horus ap. *Et.Mag.* 757.1-2; later just "sieve", *Anecd.Bekk.* 382.24-26); but this would not be an appropriate object to mention here, being far too small. It follows that the reading "to be a *tēliā*" must be rejected (since a *tēliā* = board/tray is a solid, not an annular, object, and neither a body nor anything else could be passed through it). Rather, we must seek an object of appropriate size that could reasonably be called the ring (Greek *daktulios*) of a *tēliā*. Greek *daktulios*, like English "ring", can denote objects of widely varying sizes, materials, and uses (see LSJ s.v. *daktulios* II), and I suggest that here it refers to a large leather (less probably metal) ring, attached to a *tēliā* of type (i) above, and used to sling it round the vendor's neck, leaving her hands free, as they would need to be, to hand over or rearrange goods and to receive money. This interpretation has the advantage of increasing the offensiveness of Chremylus' remark: not only is the Old Woman fat, she also reminds him of a market vendor (for whose stereotypical characteristics cf. on 426-7).

1040 going on the revel: i.e. wandering drunkenly around the streets hoping to find a party to gatecrash – as Alcibiades and others do in Plato's *Symposium* (212c-e, 223b) and, metaphorically and destructively, War in *Acharnians* (979-987). The Greek word *kō mos*, used in the text here, denotes a group of such revellers (*kōmastai*) or their activities.

1041 garlands: R's plural (the other mss. have the singular form) is confirmed by 1089.

1041 a torch: this (and indeed the very fact of there being drunken *kōmastai* on the street) indicate that it is now after dark (cf. *Wasps* 1331, *Eccl.* 978). Imaginary darkness, however, is easily forgotten in an open-air theatre, and, to adapt a remark of D.M. MacDowell's (*Aristophanes: Wasps* [Oxford, 1971] 19), it is pointless to ask whether the final procession takes place in the middle of the night.

1042 greeting to you!: Greek *aspazomai se*, cf. on 324. The second-person pronoun is singular, and the addressee is presumably Chremylus: if the Old Woman had been addressed directly (and in what 324 shows to have been a friendly manner), she would certainly have responded directly. As it is, she apparently does not even hear his words clearly (because they are not spoken directly at her and/or because they are drunkenly slurred).

1043 your hair's gone white very quickly: cf. 1051 where he appears shocked at the many wrinkles on her face. We are evidently to suppose *either* that he had actually hitherto been blinded to her physical decay by his desire and need for her money, *or* that, for the same reason, he had pretended not to notice it (see V. Tammaro, *MCr* 18 [1983] 186-7); the former alternative is the more probable, for (i) it does not require the audience to assume, without textual guidance, that the speaker's surprise here and at 1051 is only a pretence, (ii) in any case the unusual invocation in 1050 (where see note) suggests genuine rather than affected surprise and even alarm (at a face as ugly as that of a demon; cf. 422-3, *Eccl.* 1051-73), and (iii) 1059 does not necessarily imply that the Young Man had previously been fully aware that his mistress was nearly toothless (for he might be supposed to have perceived this when she cried out at 1052 as he was peering at her face).

1046 yesterday probably here means "last night": he had spent the night with his mistress as usual, left her as usual in the morning – and soon afterwards found himself rich.

1047 to other people's: so V; other mss. have "to most people's", but several of them have a scholium which quotes part of the line in the same form as V (whereas only late scholia give any positive support to the alternative reading).

1050 Poseidon of the Sea: Greek *Pontoposeidon*, a unique compound (regular would be *pontie Poseidon*, cf. *Thesm.* 322). It was common to invoke Poseidon in moments of amazement, shock or distress (cf. *Knights* 144, 609, *Wasps* 143, *Birds* 294, 1131, *Frogs* 664), and the use of the compound here may be meant to indicate an *exceptional* degree of shock.

1053 catches hold of her: Wakefield's conjecture ("strikes her") may well be right (cf. especially *Wasps* 227).

1054 an old harvest wreath: at the autumn festival of the Pyanopsia, each household made one or more *eiresiōnai* by taking an olive or laurel branch, wreathing it with bnds of red and white wool, and hanging it with all kinds of produce (fruit, bread, oil, wine, honey); the completed wreaths were dedicated to Apollo and then hung on the house door, where they remained (becoming ever drier and harder) until the following Pyanopsia when they were perhaps burnt (see A.H. Groton, *CJ* 86 [1990/1] 21). See Deubner 198-200, Parke 76-77.

1055 it's been quite a time since you did: sc. because the games he is thinking of were normally played by children, and the Old Woman's childhood was a very long time ago indeed. She, thinking that he is talking about love-making (see next note), significantly assumes "quite a time" to mean "nearly a whole day"!

1055 where could we go: the Old Woman, eager to seize on the slightest indication that her ex-lover might still be interested in her, evidently takes *paisai* "play" in a sexual sense (cf. *Birds* 1098, *Frogs* 409-415, *Eccl.* 922), and affects to be shocked that he should make such a suggestion in the street, some distance from either of their homes (cf. *Lys.* 910-1 – but Myrrhine there is being genuinely and deliberately obstructive). She expects, no doubt, the answer "My place or yours?" or the like; the answer she gets makes it evident, even to her, that the Young Man was actually talking about children's games.

1056 some nuts: cf. on 816.

1057 "how many have you got": the game of *posinda* (see on 816) – but instead of "how many nuts in my hand?" it will be "how many teeth in your mouth?". The Old Woman is being invited to guess this herself, on the reasonable assumption that she has never troubled to make a precise check on her dental condition; the Young Man knows the answer (1059; cf. on 1043), and he will pay her if she guesses right (and vice versa).

1061 treating me like dirty washing: lit. "making me a *plunos*"; *plunos* means either "washing-tub or -trough" (if accented on the second syllable) or "item to be washed" (if accented on the first), and the Young Man's response shows that the latter is the sense here. Since clothes were washed by treading them underfoot in a trough filled with water (cf. *Odyssey* 6.92), "treating me like dirty washing" is equivalent to "trampling all over me, humiliating me utterly": *patein* "tread on" is used in a similar sense at *Knights* 166 and Soph. *Aj.* 1146, and at *Ach.* 381 the hero, speaking in the name of Ar. or his producer and referring to a violent invective that had been launched against him by Cleon, says that Cleon had "washed" him (*eplunen*).

1063 she's dolled herself up for sale: lit. "she is in a hucksterly state", i.e. she has disguised her ugliness as a retailer might disguise the shoddiness of his goods when displaying them for sale. Retailing was widely regarded as almost an inherently dishonest activity, and the family of words derived from *kapēlos* "retailer, huckster" often bore a strongly pejorative connotation; cf. 1156, Aesch. fr. 322, Eur. *Hipp.* 953, Pl. *Prot.* 313c-d, Arist. *Pol.* 1258a38-b2. Ancient commentators on our passage appear to have shared this prejudice to the full, informing their readers that retailers "are accustomed to" make old clothes look new and adulterate wine.

1064 white lead: Greek *psimūthion* "lead carbonate" (on its preparation see Thphr. *On Stones* 56), used by younger women to whiten their complexions (cf. Ar. fr. 332-3, Lys. 1.14, Xen. *Oec.* 10.2) and by older women to conceal wrinkles (cf. *Eccl.* 878, 929, 1072, *AP* 11.408).

1065 wreckage: lit. "rags".

1066 at your age: lit. "being an old man". The point may be that she thinks Chremylus is suffering from senile dementia (cf. *Clouds* 844-6, *Wasps* 1364); but since she is as old or older herself, it is more likely to be that his insolence cannot be explained by the irresponsible high spirits of youth (cf. Arist. *Rhet.* 1389a9-11, b2-12) and therefore can only be due to insanity.

1067-79 Throughout this passage, the Young Man is pretending to have perceived that Chremylus has taken a fancy to the Old Woman. At first he makes a show of jealous possessiveness (1067-8, 1072; cf. 1013-6); then he makes a show of respectfulness and magnanimity, and resigns all claim to her (1076-9). We are doubtless meant to conclude, with Chremylus (1080-1), that the whole episode is a ploy on the Young Man's part to provide himself with a "legitimate" excuse for discarding his mistress. The initial accusation, however, need not be supposed to have been plucked completely out of thin air: in 1063-5 Chremylus will certainly have been gesticulating in the vicinity of the Old Woman's face, and when he dropped his hand after doing this, it will have passed near enough to her body for a jealous lover to imagine that he was designedly brushing it against her breasts – or for an excuse-seeking ex-lover to pretend to have so imagined.

1069 by Aphrodite: this oath does not indicate (as e.g. van Leeuwen and Rogers suppose) that the Old Woman is again pretending to be young (cf. on 963), for it is used in *Eccl.* (981, 989, 1008) by a woman who has no need to conceal her age (quite the contrary) because new laws have given special privileges to the old and ugly in matters of sex. What it does indicate, just as in *Eccl.*, is that although the speaker's charms have faded, her sexual desires have not.

1070 by Hecate: see on 764.

1075 "the Milesians were brave men – once upon a time": see on 1002.

1081 and who's going to tell me to?: lit. "and who is the one [masculine] who will *epitrepein*?" Since the verb *epitrepein* was used in 1078 in the sense "allow", it would be a reasonable first hypothesis that it has the same sense here; in which case the speaker would have to be either Chremylus or the Old Woman, and the question would mean "Who will allow you to desert her/me?", i.e. "Nobody will allow you to desert her/me". But neither Chremylus nor the Old Woman can possibly suppose that *everyone*, or even a majority, can be relied on to be against the Young Man abandoning her; on the contrary, most young (or even middle-aged) men would be likely to feel that in his position they would act just as he has done, and the only individuals who *can* be relied on to oppose him are Chremylus and the Old Woman themselves – and possibly Wealth. If, therefore, the text is correct, Holzinger must be right to take *epitrepein* in its later sense "order", which otherwise first appears in Xen. *Anab.* 6.5.11, and to assign the question to the Young Man. The text, however, may not be correct: the use of *epitrepein* in such different senses at such a short interval is not only clumsy but damaging to intelligibility, and it may well be that its future participle *epitrepsōn* has entered the text by error (a scribal eye or mind wandering to 1078) in place of another participle such as *epitaxōn* (van Leeuwen) "(the one) who will order <me to remain with her>".

1082 having anything to do with: Greek *dialegesthai* means literally "converse with", but it can bear the sense "have sexual relations with" (cf. Hypereides fr. 171, Plut. *Sol.* 20.3), and that is probably its meaning here. The Young Man has in effect been urged to "be with" the Old Woman again (1081), i.e. to resume their sexual relationship, and he is refusing to do so: if he were making the stronger statement that he was not prepared (even) to *talk* to her, he would probably have said not *ouk an* ... "I will not ..." but *oud' an* ... "I will not even ..." (cf. *Clouds* 425 where Strepsiades, asked if he agrees to regard no beings as divine except Void, the Clouds and the Tongue, replies "I absolutely wouldn't even speak [*oud' an dialekhtheiēn*] to the others if I met them", sc. much less pay them divine honours).

1082 shagged to pieces by thirteen thousand ... years (lit. "by ten thousand *years* and three thousand"; the particle *ge* places emphasis on the preceding word *etōn* "years"): we expect "by thirteen thousand *men*", and when "years" is substituted for "men" we are forced to reinterpret *diesplekōmene* "shagged to pieces" in the metaphorical sense "ravaged, ruined" (cf. French *foutu*, English "buggered up"; the closest ancient parallel is probably Suet. *Jul.* 51 *aurum ... effutuisti* = both "you squandered money on womanizing" and simply "you squandered money"). Philetaerus (a son of Ar., according to Dicaearchus fr. 83) probably had our passage in mind when, speaking of two elderly *hetairai*, he wrote ""Isn't Cercope already three thousand years old, and ... Telesis ten thousand more than that?" (Philetaerus fr. 9.1-2). The emendations by Rutherford and Willems would give the sense "shagged to pieces by these 13,000 men", referring to the audience; but would that great majority of male spectators who were substantially younger than the Old Woman take kindly the implication that they had been so desperate, or so lacking in discrimination, as to sleep with her even once? Ar. of course often makes disparaging remarks about his audience, but he normally does so in such a way that every *individual* spectator can smugly assume that the insult applies to others but not to himself (cf. *Clouds* 1096-1101, *Thesm.* 814-829, *Frogs* 274-5, 783, *Eccl.*436-440).

1087 a filter-cloth: used to strain solid and semi-solid residues out of wine: cf. Pollux 6.19, 10.75. Possibly as he says this Chremylus holds up his cloak in front of the Old Woman's face, as if to suggest that the Young Man might be able to endure her if he took steps to ensure that he would not have to look at her!

1088 anyway, come inside: all mss. give this half-line to the Young Man; but a visitor cannot invite a householder into the latter's own home, and Chremylus must therefore be the speaker. The verb is singular, so the invitation is addressed to the Young Man only. It is not made clear why Chremylus does invite him in now; we can easily invent a motive for him (e.g. so that the Young Man may meet Wealth, who will be better able than any mortal to persuade him to change his ways), but Ar. does not supply one.

1088-9 right away: lit. "as I am", i.e. without wasting any time in preparing myself (or, in this case, in finding a more appropriate object to dedicate; see next note).

1088-9 and dedicate these garlands to the god: there has been no previous indication that the Young Man knows that Wealth is in Chremylus' house, but we need not ask when or how he learned it; he is merely assumed for convenience to know what the audience know, because the author sees no dramatic or comic advantage that can be gained by assuming otherwise. Nor need we ask why he chooses the garlands as a dedication to Wealth. Finding himself at Wealth's abode, he wishes to make a thanksgiving offering to the god who has (as he believes and hopes) freed him from his thraldom to the Old Woman, and the garlands are the only things he has available at this moment with which to do so.

1090 to him: i.e. to the god. What she wants to say we already know (cf. 967-9).

1092 she won't rape you: some spectators may well be reminded of a scene in *Ecclesiazusae* (938-1111) in which a young man is dragged off screaming by three aged women in succession, each more hideous than the one before, each one claiming a legal right to his sexual services.

1093 working on the underside of that old boat: lit. "pitching her underneath", with reference to the practice of covering the outside of a ship's hull with a coat of pitch (cf. *Ach.* 190, *Frogs* 364; see J.S. Morrison and J.F. Coates, *The Athenian Trireme* [Cambridge, 1986] 188-9); see Henderson[2] 145-6, 164, 178.

1095 determined: the mss.' reading (*eutonōs*) would mean "fit, vigorous, powerful".

1096 was clinging (*proseikheto*, RV) is to be preferred to "is clinging" (*prosiskhetai*, n) as being the less obvious reading: the past tense was "corrected" to a present by a reader who did not realize that the two visitors had at this moment already gone inside (the scholia are silent on the timing of their exit).

1096/7 A choral interlude is necessary here, since otherwise the actor playing the Young Man (who is, by a second or two, the first to exit in the preceding scene) would have less than three lines in which to change and reappear as Carion; and such an interlude is in fact marked in K (see *Scholia* IV.i 267 and W.J.W. Koster, *Autour d'un manuscrit* *d'Aristophane écrit par Démétrius Triclinius* [Groningen, 1957] 120-1, 123), though this evidence has been ignored in all subsequent discussions (including my own in *BICS* 31 [1984] 141-3). See further on 321/2.

1099 it's asking for a thump: lit. "it desires to howl".

1099 HERMES: in each of the three Aristophanic plays in which the hero defies and defeats Zeus (*Peace, Birds* and *Wealth*) an agent of Zeus appears and threatens the hero with terrible punishment. In *Birds* (1199-1261) the agent is Iris (the messenger of Zeus in the *Iliad*) and is sent away with contempt and mockery; in *Peace* (180-726), as here, the agent is Hermes (the messenger of Zeus in the *Odyssey*), his loyalty to Zeus proves merely skin-deep, and he is easily won over to the hero's cause. Hermes will be immediately recognized by the audience thanks to his attributes, especially his broad-brimmed hat (*petasos*) and distinctive wand (caduceus); see Stone 318-320 and fig. 39. Carion too clearly recognizes him at once, never asking who he is and referring to him as the divine Herald at 1110; hence in addressing him at 1100-1 as he would a mortal prankster, he is being knowingly and deliberately insolent to the god, much as Trygaeus is in *Peace* 185-7 and Peisetaerus throughout the whole Iris scene in *Birds*.

1102 no, I didn't: Hermes (notoriously a trickster god, cf. on 1157) may be lying outright, but more probably he is to be understood as equivocating. His words can be taken to mean either "I didn't knock hard" or "I didn't knock"; they are at least arguably true in the former sense, but he expects them to be understood in the latter. This little episode, it will be noted, shows that classical Athens had its counterparts to the mischievous boys of modern times who knock or ring at doors and then run away and hide to enjoy the bafflement of the householder who comes to answer the door; unlike them, however, Hermes, being both ingenious and divine, is able to play this trick even when he really does want to pay a call at the house!

1106 the pig: many Athenians kept pigs in pens in the courtyards of their houses (cf. *Wasps* 844) as an efficient recycling device for disposing of much household rubbish and ultimately converting it into food for the family.

1108 hash you ... up: lit. "stir you together"; cf. *Peace* 228-288 where the ogre War throws (foods representing) the states of Greece into a giant mortar to be pounded into a mash.

1108 a bowl (Greek *trublion*) is ludicrously anticlimactic. A *trublion* was a smallish, shallow vessel which could be used as an individual soup-bowl (*Ach.* 278, *Knights* 905) or for carrying small amounts of food (*Knights* 650, *Birds* 77, *Eccl.* 1176); it is never mentioned as being used for any kind of food *processing*, let alone the preparation of a dish made from at least seven whole humans and two animals!

1109 into the Barathron: cf. on 431; but here the threat is of limited punitive value, since the offenders will apparently have been made into a mash or stew already.

1110 this herald needs a tongue cutting out: lit. "the tongue is cut for this herald". When an animal was sacrificed, the tongue was cut out and set aside until the end of the meal, when it was either cut up and burnt on the altar (*Odyssey* 3.332-341; Athenaeus 1.16b-c; cf. *IG* ĭ² 255.B8-9), or given to the officiating priest or herald (scholia, citing the Alexandrian scholar Callistratus; *Peace* 1109; *Inschr. Priene* 174.9, 364.4); sometimes the tongue was offered, or a libation poured over it, to Hermes (scholia, Athenaeus *loc.cit.*) Hence "the tongue is [i.e. must be] cut out by itself" (*Peace* 1060, *Birds* 1705) and "the tongue for the herald" (either a human herald, or Hermes the divine Herald, cf. Aesch. *Ag.* 515, *Cho.* 165 [123a]) became catch-phrases. Here Carion is adapting these phrases to tell Hermes that, for bringing so unfriendly a message, *his* tongue is [i.e. ought to be] cut out.

1114-6 no one sacrifices ... no nothing: cf. 137-9. The result, as in *Birds* 1514-1693, is that the gods are starving.

1114 laurel: near the pillar and altar of Apollo Agyieus which regularly stood in front of Athenian houses (cf. *Wasps* 869-878) there was often planted a laurel-bush (cf. *Thesm.* 489), and our passage suggests that branches from this bush were periodically burned (as was incense, cf. *Wasps* 861) on the altar of the god to whom this plant was sacred. The stage-house of the Theatre of Dionysus likewise had a pillar and altar of Apollo Agyieus in front of it (cf. *Thesm.* 748; Pherecrates fr. 92; Men. *Dysk.* 659, *Mis.* 314 Sandbach = 715 Arnott, *Sam.* 309, 444, fr. 884; Aesch. *Ag.* 1081; Eur.*Phoen.* 631), and Hermes probably gestures towards it as he speaks.

1119 very thoughtful of you: lit. "you are sensible". This is taken by Rogers as expressing approval of Hermes' self-centredness; but that would be out of keeping with Carion's attitude everywhere else in the scene, where he frequently insults Hermes, never displays any sympathy with him, does all he can to avoid giving him any help, and – when Hermes eventually does secure admission to the household – immediately offloads a messy job on to him (1168-9). Rather, Carion is ironically commending Hermes for having had the "good sense" to suffer ruin when he had so richly deserved it; cf. 863, *Peace* 271-2.

1120 the women tavern-keepers would make offerings to Hermes as the god of trade (cf. on 1155).

1123 I just rest with my feet up: sc. rather than going the rounds of the taverns to collect the offerings. G. Mastromarco, *Vichiana* 12 (1983) 249-252, argues that Greek *anabadēn* here means "upstairs", i.e. "in heaven" (cf. Plaut. *Amph.* 863); the meaning of this word is likewise uncertain at *Ach.* 399, 410, but *anapauomai* "I rest" suggests that here the sentence as a whole is making an implicit contrast, not between being on earth and being in heaven, but between activity and inactivity.

1124-5 and then sometimes do them damage: possibly by giving assistance to thieves (cf. on 1139-40); possibly the point is merely the general one that sacrifice and prayer (to whichever god directed) often fail to avert misfortune.

1126 the fourth of the month was Hermes' birthday (*h.Hom.Herm.* 19) and a day for public as well as private offerings to him; see e.g. *SEG* xxi 541 v 47-58 (Erchia, Attica), *SIG*[3] 714.28-31 (Rhegium), *IGSK* ii 207.1-3 (Erythrae), and cf. Thphr. *Char.* 16.10 (on the 4th and 7th of the month, the superstitious man "buys myrtle, frankincense, cakelets, and then ... spends the whole day garlanding the Hermaphrodites").

1127 "you yearn ... and call in vain": almost certainly a quotation from tragedy (*trag.adesp.* 63). Tzetzes (twelfth century) and later medieval commentators associate the line with the story of how, during the voyage of the Argonauts, the beautiful youth Hylas was snatched by water-nymphs, and how his lover Heracles searched long and vainly for him; no specific reference to a tragedy about Hylas survives, but Ovid, *Tristia* 2.406, confirms that the story was used by tragic dramatists.

1128 legs: strictly "thigh, ham" (Greek *kōlē*). The thigh-bones, wrapped in fat, were the most important of those portions of a sacrificial animal that were not consumed by the worshippers but were burnt on the altar for the god (cf. *Peace* 1021, 1039, 1088; *Odyssey* 3.456-461; Hes. *Thg.* 535-557); and the flesh of one thigh (*kōlē*), was often also assigned to the god and placed on the holy table (cf. Ameipsias fr. 7, *IG* ii[2] 1356.3-4 and passim).

1129 up on *one* leg with you ... and hop it!: the Greek says simply *askōliaze* "hop!" (cf. Pl. *Symp.* 190d, Arist. *Inc.An.* 705b34), with an extremely feeble pun on *kōlē* (see previous note). The phrase "in the open air" shows that there must be an allusion to some specific, culturally recognized activity that occurred outdoors and involved hopping on one leg (for hopping in itself is not something that can only be done outdoors); and the scholia take the reference to be to a competition held "in honour of Dionysus" which consisted of jumping up and down, one-legged, for as long as possible on an empty, inflated, greased wineskin (cf. Pollux 9.121). Ancient references to the association of this game with one or more specific festivals are under strong suspicion of being based on Hellenistic scholarly constructions (see K. Latte, *Hermes* 85 [1957] 385-391), but the game itself certainly existed in classical Athens (Eubulus fr. 7), and there is no reason to doubt that Carion is indeed alluding to it. Perceiving apparently from Hermes' repeated references to food that the god is anxious to go into the house and share in the sacrificial meal, he pretends to have misheard 1128 as a lament, not for the hams of yore, but for the hopping games of yore, and reminds Hermes that such games were always played "in the open air" so that he cannot use them as an excuse to go inside.

1130-1 innards: Greek *splankhna*, in sacral language, denoted the liver, kidneys, heart, etc., of the victim (but not the stomach or intestines); these organs were roasted over the altar fire and partaken of by all present (see e.g. *Odyssey* 3.9, 3.40), the god also being given a share (cf. Athenion fr. 1.18). When Carion repeats the word, he is speaking non-sacral language.

1132 of fifty-fifty blend: lit. "mixed equal with equal", i.e. containing wine and water mixed in equal proportions. This was a fairly strong mixture (cf. Alexis fr. 59, 246.4; Sophilus fr. 4; Timocles fr. 22; Xenarchus fr. 9); according to *com.adesp.* 101.12, regular drinking at this strength would lead to insanity. Athenaeus (10.426b-427a, 430d-431b) collects much classical (mainly comic) evidence on wine mixture strengths, from which it emerges that the most common proportions of water to wine were 3:1 (cf. Hes. *Works* 596) and 5:2.

1133 drink *this* with your meal: Greek *epipīnein* means "drink with or after something" (cf. *Knights* 354, 357, *Peace* 712, Pl. *Rep.* 372b); hence by using this word Carion is deliberately ignoring the fact that Hermes has no food. Carion's general attitude to Hermes (cf. on 1119) suggests that the drink he offers him should be something unpleasant; my conjecture that it is urine is influenced by the parallel of *Birds* 1495-1552 where Peisetaerus comes out of the stage-house carrying a *diphros* (night-stool), presumably in order to empty it on a dung-heap, and at the end of the scene gives it to the god Prometheus.

1134 your dear old friend: Hermes does not explain why he should be regarded as such, and his appeal makes little impression on Carion (see next note).

1135 yes, if you need something that I'm *able* to help you with: this sounds friendlier than it is; Carion will be very good at finding reasons for being *un*able to help Hermes!

1138 "not to be taken out": Greek *ouk ekphorā*, a regular expression in sacrificial regulations indicating that meat from the sacrifice was not to be taken out of the sacred precincts (cf. *SIG*³ 1004.32, 1026.10); in *SEG* xxi 541 (Erchia, Attica) the phrase appears in the variant form *ou phorā* (i 5, 10-11, 21, etc.)

1139-40 when you nicked some little thing of your master's: cf. 26-27. Hermes was the god of thievery: cf. *Peace* 401-2, *Iliad* 24.24, *Odyssey* 19.395-7, *h.Hom.Herm.* 175, 292, Hipponax fr. 3a.

1141 crook: lit. "burglar"; cf. on 869.

1142 a well-baked stuffed loaf (Greek *nastos*, a large conical white loaf stuffed, before baking, with crushed almonds and raisins: Pollux 6.78, cf. Nicostratus fr. 13, *Et.Mag.* 597.56-598.5): a thanksgiving offering, either itself purloined from the kitchen or bought from a pastrycook with the proceeds of sale of the article originally stolen. For *nastoi* as official sacrifices cf. *IG* ii² 1366.23-24, 1367.14.

1143 you'd eat that up yourself: had an offering like this been made at a temple, it would have been placed on the holy table (see on 678) and ultimately eaten by the priest or his staff. Carion evidently made his "offerings" at home – and then assumed the role of priest himself.

1144-5 Carion's point is that when he stole, he was the one to suffer if he failed and therefore he should be the one to profit if he succeeded.

1144 hit: or "whipped"; the Greek means literally "you did not share an equal number of blows/strokes to me" and does not specify how they were inflicted.

1146 now you've seized Phyle, it's time to forget old grudges: alluding, in a telescoped fashion, to events of the year 403. The process that led to the overthrow of the Thirty, and the restoration of democracy at Athens, began with the occupation of Phyle by Thrasybulus (see on 548); it ended, probably about eight months later, with a settlement (Arist. *Ath.Pol.* 39-40; cf. Andoc. 1.81-91) under which, *inter alia*, all citizens swore "not to remember any grudges about the past", i.e. not to attempt to exact punishment for any offence committed before the restoration (except against the Thirty themselves, members of a few boards of officials closely associated with them, and anyone who had committed homicide or wounding with his own hand). See T.C. Loening, *The Reconciliation Agreement of 403/402 BC in Athens* (Stuttgart, 1987); R.J. Buck, *Thrasybulus and the Athenian Democracy* (Stuttgart, 1998) 71-83. Carion (who here, as in 823-958, in effect represents his master) has risen in revolt against the gods, as Thrasybulus did against the Thirty, and defeated them; now he should emulate the magnanimous forgiveness shown by the democrats in 403.

1151 "my homeland's any land where I can prosper": the sentiment was proverbial (cf. Eur. *Phaethon* 163 Diggle = fr. 777 Nauck, Ar. fr. dub. 925, Lys. 31.6, Cic. *TD* 5.108); this particular formulation of it may well be a tragic quotation (not in *TrGF*).

1153-63 Hermes offers his services to Chremylus' household under five of his numerous cult-titles. Carion rejects the first four on a variety of grounds, but can find no objection to make to the fifth offer. In my translation I have incorporated glosses of the five titles (and also of a sixth which Carion invents at 1170: see note there).

1153 Hermes Strophaios stood by the house door to protect it against thieves (scholia); the ithyphallic pillar-images of Hermes which stood "before many private doors" in Athens (Thuc. 6.27.1, cf. *Clouds* 1478) may or may not have been thought of as representing Hermes Strophaios.

1154 turners and twisters: Greek *strophai* "twists, evasions, duplicities" (cf. *Eccl.* 1026), possibly in origin a metaphor from wrestling (cf. *Ach.* 385, *Frogs* 775, 957).

1155 Hermes Empolaios: cf. *Ach.* 816 (a Megarian trader who has just made what he thinks is a good sale), *SEG* xxx 908.

1156 huckster: Greek *palinkapēlos* (cf. [Dem.] 25.46, 56.7), an even more pejorative term than *kapēlos* (cf. on 1063); the prefix means "again, a second time" and implies that the trader so designated bought his wares not from the producer but from another middleman, so that at least two rounds of profit had been added to their price before they reached the consumer. Carion's point is that no one would live on the proceeds of so despised an occupation unless he was so poor as to have no alternative.

1157 Hermes Dolios: cf. *Thesm.* 1202, Soph. *Phil.* 133, [Eur.] *Rhes.* 217, Aen.Tact. 24.15, Paus. 7.27.1, *SEG* xxxvii 1673.

1158 honest behaviour: lit. "simple ways".

1159 Hermes Hegemonios: cf. *IG* ii² 1496 A 84-85, 115-6, *SEG* xxiii 547.53. Hermes acts as guide to Priam in *Iliad* 24.333-694, and to the souls of Penelope's suitors in *Odyssey* 24.1-10; he "is more angered than any other god if one refuses to help a traveller who needs to know the way" (Theocr. 25.4-6).

1159 Wealth: lit. "the god".

1161 Hermes Enagonios: many gods were patrons of contests of various kinds, but Hermes in this capacity took an interest in them all and could bestow victory in any of them. Cf. Aesch. *Cho.* 727-9, fr. 384; Simonides *PMG* 555.1; Pind. *Olymp.* 6.79, *Pyth.* 2.10, *Isthm.* 1.60; Paus. 5.14.9; *IG* i³ 5.3.

1162 nothing more appropriate for Wealth than ... holding competitions: in classical Greece, individuals might (e.g. as *khorēgoi*) sponsor particular entries for a competition, but an individual, unless he was a monarch or a tyrant, would no longer "hold" (*poiein*) an entire competition himself (i.e. decide the programme and provide the prizes), as Achilles does in *Iliad* 23 or as the sons of Amphidamas did on an occasion recalled by Hesiod (*Works* 650-9); competitions were said to be "held" either by a state, or by a cult-association, or by their patron god (cf. 583). In principle, therefore, Hermes could be envisaging either (i) that Wealth/wealth will enable the Athenian state to hold new festival competitions (or expand existing ones) in honour of whatever gods they see fit, or (ii) that new festivals with new competitions will be established in honour of Wealth himself. Since Hermes is using his title of Enagonios to secure a job in Chremylus' household (where Wealth at present resides), not one with the Athenian state, his meaning here must be (ii).

1164-70 Note the grudging, discourteous way in which Carion at length accepts Hermes into the household. He does not tell Hermes directly that he has been accepted, but turns away to address the audience, telling *them* that Hermes has "f[ou]nd himself a nice little living"; and when Hermes asks whether this means he may now come in, Carion replies by giving him his first orders before he has even got through the door.

1166 all: an exaggeration of a kind typical when allegations are made, in ancient or modern times, that public money is being fraudulently diverted into hands that have no right to it.

1167 to get themselves registered under several letters: see on 277 and 972. The most obvious way to achieve this (thereby increasing one's chances of being selected to serve, and earn pay, on any given day) was to register repeatedly in different names; there was no central master register of citizens (only 139 separate registers in the various demes), so it was difficult for the authorities to check this type of fraud (which in any case involved no financial loss to the state, only to the honest majority of jurors).

1168 yes: this is more explicit than the Greek, which has only the emphasizing particle *ge* and means literally "*and*, going yourself to the well, wash the offals".

1169 offals: Greek *koiliai*, strictly stomachs and/or intestines (often used as sausage-skins, cf. *Knights* 160, 302, 488).

1170 Hermes Diakonikos is not a cult-title, but Hermes traditionally has in comedy the role of a servant in the Olympian household (cf. *Peace* 180-202, and Mercury in Plautus' *Amphitruo*) and can be referred to as such in satyr-drama and even tragedy (cf. [Aesch.] *Prom.* 941-2, 954, 966, 983; Soph. fr. 269c.21, 35; 269d.21; Eur. *Ion* 4). Carion gives Hermes a thoroughly menial task the instant he joins Chremylus' household: the god who began the scene by threatening the whole family with destruction is now the lowliest of the slaves within it, ordered about by that Carion whom earlier (1106) he had ranked just above the pig.

1170/1 Some editors, following a proposal by Bergk, have posited a choral interlude here (cf. on 321/2, 626/7, 770/1, 801/2, 958/9, 1096/7); but no ms. indicates one, and neither do the Triclinian metrical scholia (on 1097) relating to the scene just ended. Nor is an interlude necessary here from the performance point of view, provided that four actors are available: neither of the two who went into the house at 1170 will be required again until 1197. In New Comedy there are frequently brief intervals when the stage is empty of actors without there being any choral performance (this occurs no less than eight times in Menander's *Dyskolos*); cf. also *Clouds* 1212/3, *Wasps* 1325/6 (though one of these directly follows, and the other directly precedes, a solo lyric sung by an actor) and possibly *Eccl.* 1111/2.

1172 That it is Chremylus, not Carion, who converses with the Priest is evident from the orders he gives in 1194ff and from the Old Woman's appeal to him in 1200-3 which takes up the thread of the scene 959-1096. As at 965, he makes a convenient (and unmotivated) appearance just when someone has come to see him, but in this scene the preparation for his entry is even scantier\than it was then.

1173 **this god**: the mss. have "this Wealth" (*ho Ploutos houtos*), but it is very unlikely that Ar. perpetrated such a cacophonous monstrosity when he had no need to; more probably *Ploutos* is a gloss by a reader who wished to remind himself or others that the reference was not to Hermes. No spectator could be in the slightest danger of such misunderstanding, any more than at 1159 (where see note) when Hermes is actually present. Rogers and Holzinger argue that the cacophony is intentional and designed to give the Priest's words a disparaging tone; but the Priest would not speak disparagingly of Wealth (any more than Hermes does) when he wishes to become a follower of Wealth himself (1186-7). As emended by Elmsley the line is identical with 968 (cf. also 1113-4).

1175 **Zeus the Saviour**: there was an important sanctuary of Zeus the Saviour (*Sōtēr*) and Athena the Saviouress (*Sōteira*, cf. *Frogs* 378) in the Peiraeus (Paus. 1.1.3, cf. *IG* ii² 783.7), and a statue of Zeus in the Agora that was sometimes called Zeus the Saviour and sometimes Zeus the Liberator (*Eleutherios*) (cf. Isoc. 9.57, Men. fr. 482, Harpocr. ε35); his festival, the Diisoteria (on an unknown date in the last month of the year, Scirophorion), had become the most popular of all Athenian festivals by the 330s, to judge by the proceeds of the sale of sacrificial victims' skins (*IG* ii² 1496 A 88-89, 118-9). It is not clear when the cult was founded, though Zeus the Saviour had for generations received the third libation after a meal (Aesch. *Ag.* 1386-7, *Cho.* 244-5, 1073, *Eum.* 759-760, *Supp.* 26, fr. 55.4; Soph. fr. 425); it is striking, however, that the nine references to Zeus the Saviour in Ar. (counting the present scene as a single reference) are all from 411 or later (the earliest is *Thesm.* 1009). See R. Parker, *Athenian Religion: A History* (Oxford, 1996) 238-241. Our priest has presumably come from the Peiraeus sanctuary, so I have brought him on from the left (west) side (see Introduction §7).

1179-82 All the worshippers mentioned had either recently been, or expected soon to be, in peril of their life or property, so that Zeus the Saviour was a particularly appropriate recipient of their prayers or thanks.

1181 **seeking favourable omens for a journey** (or other hazardous undertaking; the Greek does not specify its nature): i.e. making a sacrifice in the hope that the omens derived from inspection of the internal organs, the manner in which parts of the offering burned on the altar, etc., would be auspicious: cf. Hdt. 7.113.2, Xen. *Hipparch.* 3.1, *Poroi* 6.3.

1182 **and would also invite me**: the man is making the sacrifice at his home, but since on this occasion it is particularly important that the omens be correctly interpreted, he invites the Priest along as an expert in this field.

1184 **thousands on thousands**: lit. "more than ten thousand".

1185 **you get your customary portions of *their* offerings**: implicitly calling the Priest a *skatophagos* (cf. on 305 and 706).

1189-90 **Zeus the Saviour ... is with us here**: it has traditionally been assumed (following a brief and ambiguous scholium) that by "Zeus the Saviour" Chremylus here means Wealth, since he is the *real* Saviour of humanity, and this interpretation has recently been defended by S.D. Olson, *HSCP* 93 (1990) 237-8 n.50, who points out that whereas Wealth is certainly in Chremylus' house, Zeus has not been seen to enter it and "Aristophanic gods do not [just] magically appear somewhere". It is hardly likely, however, that an audience would instantly, and without any textual guidance, understand that the name Zeus, which has throughout the play been that of Wealth's antagonist, now denotes Wealth himself: even at the end of *Birds*, where Peisetaerus has acquired the thunderbolt and the power of Zeus and is repeatedly compared to Zeus, he is never himself *called* Zeus. In Chremylus' next speech, moreover (1192), as Rogers points out, he says not "we're going to install him" (viz. the new Zeus I mentioned a moment ago) but "we're going to install Wealth" as if he had not spoken of Wealth previously. Nor does Olson explain how the Priest, who (as Chremylus' "Don't worry" indicates) had shown signs of apprehension about the possible consequences of deserting *Zeus*, could feel reassured (1190) by being told that *Wealth* was in Chremylus' house (a fact, after all, which he must have already known, otherwise he would not have come there in the first place). I accordingly regard it as certain that when Chremylus says that Zeus the Saviour is "with us here", he means precisely that. No one is sacrificing to the gods (1113-6, 1173-83), so all of them, including Zeus, are starving. In *Birds*, faced with a similar predicament, Zeus had surrendered his power to Peisetaerus and the birds; here he has followed the example of his son Hermes and his priest, and himself gone over to the winning side. That he has not been seen to enter Chremylus' house is not decisive evidence; the departure of Zeus from the house of Inachus in Sophocles' satyr-play of that name (cf. on 802-818) provides a likely parallel (Soph. fr. 269a; cf. S.R. West, *CQ* 34 [1984] 297 "the visitor's departure ... was surely left to the audience's imagination") – and if food, metals and money can "magically appear" in Chremylus' house, as they did earlier in the play, we can hardly deny a god the power to do so!

1191 **wait a moment!:** the Priest evidently assumes that Chremylus intends to install Wealth in his, Chremylus', own house (i.e. to establish within his house a sanctuary of Wealth), as Trygaeus installs Peace in *his* house in *Peace* 922ff., and accordingly he is eager to get inside, proceed with the installation-sacrifice, and (above all) partake of the meal that will follow. Chremylus, however, has other intentions.

1192 **before:** in the days of the Athenian empire, when the tribute of the "allied" states, together with other sources of income, annually brought 1000 talents or more into the Athenian state treasuries (Xen. *Anab.* 7.1.27, referring to 431; *Wasps* 660 gives a figure of "nearly 2000 talents" for 423/2, by which time the tribute assessments had been greatly increased; in 392/1 Andocides [3.8-9] told the Athenians that after the Peace of Nicias in 421 they had been receiving more than 1200 talents annually in tribute alone). On the current state of Athenian public funds, cf. on 408 and see Introduction §1.

1193 **the inner chamber** (Greek *opisthodomos* "rear chamber") **of the Goddess:** the *opisthodomos* mentioned, without further specification, in various fifth- and fourth-century texts as a state treasury on the Acropolis is usually taken to have been the western chamber of the "old temple" of Athena Polias, whose surviving foundations lie between the Parthenon and the Erechtheum (cf. scholia here: "at the back of the temple of the Athena who was called Polias, there was a double wall with a door, where there was a treasury"). This temple, built probably in the 520s, was burnt in the Persian sack of 480/79, but the *opisthodomos* was apparently rebuilt as a treasury, and from 434/3 (*IG* i³ 52 A15-18, B23-25) it contained all the funds administered by the state treasurers, both those of Athena and those of "the Other Gods". The old temple was badly damaged by fire in 406 (Xen. *Hell.* 1.6.1), but the *opisthodomos* continued to be used as a treasury until it suffered a second fire, possibly in the 370s (Dem. 24.136 with scholia;

this cannot refer to the fire of 406, since it is said to have happened "after the archonship of Eucleides" who was archon in 403/2, *ibid.* 134). See Travlos 143-7; R.J. Hopper, *The Acropolis*[2] (London, 1974) 110-5. Another view (J.M. Hurwit, *The Athenian Acropolis* [Cambridge, 1999] 143-4, 162-3) is that the *opisthodomos* (which is not mentioned in any text earlier than 434/3) was the western chamber of the (then recently completed) Parthenon; we hear of "the *opisthodomos* of the Parthenon" in connection with the visit of Demetrius Poliorcetes to Athens in 307 (Plut. *Demetr.* 23.5).

1194-1209 Who takes part in the final procession? Wealth, Chremylus, the Priest, the Old Woman, and (following behind) the chorus are known participants. One might be tempted to suppose that all the other characters whom we know to be in Chremylus' house – his wife, children and servants; the Honest Man; the Old Woman's reluctant young lover; Hermes; and perhaps even Zeus the Saviour – should also join in honouring a god to whom they have all given their allegiance. It is, however, virtually certain that the Young Man at least does *not* join in the procession, since if he were in it, the Old Woman, who was earlier described (1095-6) as sticking to him "like a limpet", would certainly have joined in without question; and there is no indication in the text that any large number of persons have come out of the house, or that the procession needs careful marshalling by Chremylus – rather, once Wealth has come out and the Old Woman has been persuaded to carry the pots, the procession is ready to move. I therefore prefer to suppose that the procession comprises only the "known participants" listed above, with the addition of Carion. At least one slave must be present on stage from 1194/5 onwards, and Carion (whom both Wealth and the audience have known for so long) is the appropriate person to be asked to "call out Wealth" (1196); the fact, too, that he is to *call* (not *send*) him out implies that he thereafter remains outside himself. Since Carion and Wealth do not speak, they may, as in 624-6, be represented by supernumeraries. The pots (1197) must be brought by other slaves (never actually referred to in the text), who may also join the procession or may go back inside.

1194 lighted torches: since only one person is told to bring the torches, there can hardly be more than four of them, so they cannot be distributed to the whole chorus as they are at the end of *Frogs* (cf. *Frogs* 1524-5). One of them, we know, goes to the Priest; and since Carion apparently has no torches in his hands by 1196, it is most likely that he brought only two torches altogether and that Chremylus, the only other character on stage at this point, has been given the other. Torches also appear at the end of *Clouds* (1490ff), *Peace* (1317ff), *Frogs*, and *Ecclesiazusae* (1150), and of all the Menandrian plays whose closing lines survive (*Dysk.* 964, *Mis.* 459 Sandbach = 989 Arnott, *Samia* 731, *Sik.* 418).

1197 and what am I supposed to do?: Chremylus takes her to mean "what should be my role in the procession?", but it is clear from 1200, 1202-3 that she is far from eager to join the procession at all and that her overriding concern is to be reunited with the Young Man; from which it follows that her question actually meant in effect "are you going to leave me behind without solving my problem?"

1197 the pots: at the installation of a cult-image in a temple or shrine, or at the dedication of an altar, it was customary, if there was no animal sacrifice, to offer pots of boiled vegetables to the god: cf. *Peace* 923-4, Ar. fr. 256. This might well seem an unduly cheap offering when the honorand is Wealth (cf. 940) and the location is to be the oldest sanctuary of the city's patron goddess; does it serve as a gentle reminder, as the play nears its end, that the universal enrichment we have witnessed is after all a comic fantasy? This may possibly also be the explanation of *Eccl.* 1178 where, after singing of the splendid feast that may be waiting for them in the Agora, the chorus urge Blepyrus to go there quickly "but take some porridge to dine on".

1198 carry them on your head: as women carry water-jugs and other vessels in countless vase-paintings (and cf. *Eccl.* 222); Herodotus (2.35.3) asserted that in Egypt, where "most of the customs and usages [are] entirely opposite to those of other people", men carried loads on their heads and women on their shoulders. The Old Woman is a grotesque comic counterpart of the *kanēphoros*, the young virgin who carried the ritual basket (*kanoun*) in many a sacrificial and festival procession (cf. *Ach.* 253-260, *Lys.* 646-7, 1188-94, *Eccl.* 730-3).

1201 the young man will come to you: see on 1030.

1201 tonight: Greek *eis hesperān* means literally "towards evening", but this does not necessarily imply anything about what the time of day is now supposed to be (cf. on 1041). In *Eccl.* 1047-8 a young man who has come from dinner carrying a torch (indicating that it is well into the evening) promises his girlfriend that "towards evening ... I'll be giving you a long thick reward"; in amatory contexts, in other words, *eis hesperān* meant something like "at bedtime".

1206 wrinkly skin: Greek *graus*, which means both "old woman" and "the skin that forms on the surface of boiled liquids in pots, especially milk" (cf. Ath. 13.585c, Nic. *Alex.* 91). I owe this rendering to Holzinger.

1208-9 Metre: anapaestic tetrameters.

1209 singing: the words of their song, like the words of most earlier choral songs in this play, were not included in the book-text that went into circulation. The practice, however, of having choruses make their final exit singing a traditional song whose words were not treated as part of the play-script went back at least to the beginning of Ar.'s career: in *Acharnians* (1233-4) and in *Lysistrata* (1320-1) the last transmitted lines of the play are an instruction to the chorus to sing, evidently designed to introduce an exit-song which does not appear in the text, and a choral exit-song may also have been omitted from the script of *Knights* (which, as transmitted, ends with spoken dialogue).

Addenda to Previous Volumes[1]

General Introduction (Acharnians, pp. 2-20)[2]

page 2 *His first play* ... : G. Mastromarco, *QSt* 10 (1979) 153-196, and S. Halliwell, *CQ* 30 (1980) 33-45, have argued that *Wasps* 1018-22 is best interpreted to mean that even before 427 Ar. had been actively collaborating in the writing of comedies that were mainly composed by, and presented in the name of, others: see commentary on *Wasps* 1018-29.

2   *produced ... by Callistratus:* so *Proleg.* III 38 Koster, which gives the date and is doubtless ultimately derived from the official production records (*didaskaliai*). One scholium to *Clouds* 531 names Philonides as the producer of *Banqueters* (cf. D. Welsh, *CQ* 33 [1983] 52-53, and H. Lind, *Der Gerber Kleon in den Rittern des Aristophanes* [Frankfurt, 1990] 141-8, esp. 147); but this statement (which appears in only one ms.) may well be no more than a late commentator's attempt to make sense of another scholium on the passage which (absurdly) glosses "another girl" as "Philonides and Callistratus" (as if one play could have two official producers).

2 n.4 I should not have stated as a fact that *IG* ii² 2325 names Ar. as a Dionysian victor in the mid 420s, since only the first three letters of the name survive and Aristomenes remains a theoretical possibility (D. Gilula, *CQ* 39 [1989] 332-8). However, the next twelve names on this victor-list do not include Ar.'s, and the twelfth of them, the very minor dramatist Cephisodorus, won what was probably his only victory in 402 (*Lys.* 21.4); hence if Ar. did not win his first Dionysian victory in 426 or 425 he cannot have done so before 401, which may be thought extremely unlikely.

3   *we have little information:* we know, however (thanks to a discussion by Galen preserved only in a ninth-century Arabic translation of a Syriac translation), that Ar. had, or claimed to have had, a serious illness in the months leading up to the production of *Thesmophoriazusae II* (Ar. fr. 346).

3   *his prolific and successful dramatic career:* it is striking that Ar.'s productivity varied considerably over the years: eleven plays belong certainly or probably to the seven years 427-421, ten to the seven years 411-405, but only five, plus the revised *Clouds*, to the nine years between.

---

1   These Addenda are based on the original printings of the several volumes; in subsequent printings some corrections had already been inserted, where this was possible without affecting pagination. No attempt has been made to update references in the original where new editions of fragments, inscriptions, etc., have been published meanwhile, but references in the Addenda follow the conventions of the present volume.

2   Endnotes to the General Introduction (pp.24-29) are referenced not by the page on which they appear, but by the page in the Introduction itself on which they are referred to.

3 n.10 I do not now believe that the restaging of *Frogs* can have taken place so late as 403; there are strong reasons for assigning it to Lenaea 404. See Introduction to *Frogs*, pp.21-23 (more fully, my discussion in A.H. Sommerstein et al. ed. *Tragedy, Comedy and the Polis* [Bari, 1993] 461-476).

3 n.12 The reference should be to *IG* ii² 1740.24 = *Agora* xv 12.26.

4-5 There is a play-by-play discussion of Ar.'s lost works by L. Gil, "El Aristófanes perdido", *CFC* 22 (1989) 39-106.

4 *Aeolosicon:* the "first" and "second" play of this name may have been merely two forms of the script of one and the same play, respectively with and without the choral songs; see Introduction to *Wealth*, p.24 n. 98 and p. 28 n. 113. If so, this play was produced in 386 or later.

4 *Anagyrūs* should be *Anagyrus*: the play was named after the eponymous hero of the village of Anagyrus, not after the village itself. This hero was said (Suda α1842) to have avenged an act of sacrilege against himself by making the offender's mistress fall in love with her stepson; there followed a sequence of events reminiscent of those in the story of Phaedra and Hippolytus, ending with the suicide of the offender and his mistress; the play, significantly, contained a parody of Euripides' *Hippolytus* (Ar. fr. 53). The attack on Eupolis for a threefold act of plagiarism (fr. 58) dates the play after the revised *Clouds* (for *Clouds* 553-4 refers to only one such offence by Eupolis) and hence probably no earlier than 417 (see below on *Clouds*).

4 *Cocalus:* cf. Clement of Alexandria, *Stromateis* 6.26.6, who says that the plot of this play was taken over, with slight changes, by Menander's contemporary Philemon in his *Hypobolimaios (Changeling).*

4 *Danaids* had a parabasis (Ar. fr. 264-5) and is therefore likely to date from before 400.

4 *Dramas or Centaur:* a scholium to *Wasps* 61, speaking of references to the gluttony of Heracles "in the dramas produced before this" (or "in the *Dramas*, produced before this"), makes it highly likely that *Dramas or Centaur*, which did feature a gluttonous Heracles (cf. Ar. fr. 282, 284; the centaur was Pholus, cf. [Apoll.] *Bibl.* 2.5.4), was produced before 422, probably in 426 (Len.) or 425 (Dion.)

4 *Peace II:* on this play, which I would now date with fair confidence to 410-405, see Introduction to *Peace*, pp. xix-xx.

5 *Seasons:* Gil *op.cit.* 106 favours a date nearer 411 than 421 because the iambic tetrameters in fr. 581 use anapaestic feet more freely than is normal in Ar.'s earlier plays.

6 n.30 For "a chaser of conceits" (*gnōmidiōktēs*, a word of very dubious formation) read (with the best ms. of the commentary on Plato in which the passage is preserved) "a man of mini-maxims" (*gnōmidiōtēs*); see W. Luppe in F.D. Harvey and J. Wilkins ed. *The Rivals of Aristophanes* (London/Swansea, 2000) 19.

7 n.36 The "fourth of the month" joke is probably designed to turn against Ar. his comparison of himself to Heracles in *Wasps* 1029-43 and *Peace* 751-760; see G. Mastromarco, *RFIC* 117 (1989) 410-423, and H. Lind, *Der Gerber Kleon in den Rittern des Aristophanes* (Frankfurt, 1990) 220-230.

7 In the *Symposium:* on the date of the *Symposium* (between 385/4 and 378) see K.J. Dover, *Phronesis* 10 (1965) 2-20 = *The Greeks and their Legacy* (Oxford, 1989) 86-101; on the portrayal of Ar. therein, see K.J. Reckford, *Aristophanes' Old-and-New Comedy* (Chapel Hill, 1987) 70-75; C.J. Rowe, *Plato: Symposium* (Warminster, 1998)

9, 136, 146, 153-160, who finds Plato's treatment of him more disparaging than is assumed here; and S. Avlonitis, *RhM* 142 (1999) 15-23.

8   *Old Comedy:* a brilliant insight into the origins and development of Old Comedy in its relations with Athenian democracy is provided by A.T. Edwards in R.S. Scodel ed. *Theater and Society in the Classical World* (Ann Arbor, 1993) 89-117. Edwards suggests that comedy, originally a form of unofficial popular entertainment, was introduced to the City Dionysia in the 480s "in part ... as a check upon the authority and prestige of ... the aristocrats" who at that time supplied most of the political leaders. I would add that the year 488/7, in which the decree authorizing these first official comic performances must have been passed, was also the year in which began a series of almost annual ostracisms of these same aristocratic leaders, and the year in which another decree provided for the choice of the nine archons by lot instead of election (put into effect for the new year 487/6). This whole complex of measures seems likely to represent a shift to a more populist brand of politics probably to be associated with the first Athenian demagogue, Themistocles. Thirty or forty years later, however, in a time of intenser class-feeling caused by the Ephialtic revolution and its aftermath, a new generation of poets, of whom Cratinus was the most prominent, "appropriated" — or hijacked — this demotic entertainment and used it against "the leaders whom the demos ha[d] chosen for itself". There was thus a permanent tension in Old Comedy between its "popular-grotesque" origins and its "political-aesthetic agenda", which may explain many of the seeming contradictions or deconstructions that recent critics have found in plays of the genre. At the same time other dramatists such as Crates were tending to abandon the popular-grotesque tradition in another way, by moving towards a comedy based on myth or on private life with little or no link to the civic world. Both these trends, in Edwards' view, by cutting Old Comedy away from its social roots, condemned it to decline. I would maintain that these trends were unintentionally encouraged by decisions taken probably also in the 450s or 440s, as a result of pressure on seating space, which created a theatre audience that was no longer socioeconomically representative of the citizen body. I have discussed these issues in *Aeschylean Tragedy* (Bari, 1996) 18 and in J.A. López Férez ed. *La comedia griega y su influencia en la literatura española* (Madrid, 1998) 46-57.

8   *Magnes ... did not attain a high level of artistic sophistication:* at this period, however, a form of comic drama with significant literary ambitions was flourishing in Sicily, its principal exponent being Epicharmus, and it is increasingly being recognized that the Sicilian school of comedy was an important influence on the development of the Attic; see especially A. Melero Bellido, "Epicarmo y la comedia ática", in *Primeras jornadas internacionales de teatro griego* (Valencia, n.d.) 25-42; "La comedia prearistofánica", in *Actas del IX Congreso Español de Estudios Clásicos* (Madrid, 1998) 3-25; and "La formación de la poética cómica", in *Cuadernos de literatura griega y latina* 2 (1998) 183-207. Another influence much stressed in recent scholarship, particularly in regard to the development of comic satire, is that of the tradition of iambic "blame-poetry" going back to Archilochus in the seventh century; see R.M. Rosen, *Old Comedy and the Iambographic Tradition* (Atlanta, 1988); E. Tz-Y. Lee, *The Iambike Idea from Iambic Poetry to Attic Old Comedy* (Diss. Yale 1993); E. Degani in E. Corsini ed. *La polis e il suo teatro* ii (Padua, 1988) 157-179, and in *Entretiens Hardt* 38 (1993) 1-49. These two sources can be seen as respectively fuelling the "two divergent trends" of the 440s and

430s, and both have contributed to the complex mosaic that is Aristophanic comedy; see G. Mastromarco in J.A. López Férez ed. *La comedia griega y su influencia en la literatura española* (Madrid, 1998) 23-42.

9   *Parodos:* on the Aristophanic *parodos* see B. Zimmermann, *Untersuchungen zur Form und dramatischen Technik der aristophanischen Komödien* i (Königstein im Taunus, 1984) 6-149, and his article "The parodoi of the Aristophanic comedies", *SIFC* (3rd ser.) 2 (1984) 13-24 (reprinted with revisions in E. Segal ed. *Oxford Readings in Aristophanes* [Oxford, 1996] 182-193).

10 n.49   In addition, in *Acharnians* Ar. seems to play with his audience's expectation of an *agōn*; the choral strophes both at 358ff and at 490ff each give the impression of being introductory to an *agōn*, and each time the expected sequel fails to materialize. See M.E. Aria, *The Dynamics of Form and Genre in Aristophanic Comedy* (Diss. Columbia 1997) 130ff.

10   *After the agōn* ... : on the organization of this section of an Aristophanic comedy, see T. Gelzer in *EH* 38 (1993) 65-86.

10   *The second parabasis:* see now P. Totaro, *Le seconde parabasi di Aristofane* (Stuttgart, 1999).

11   *the functional structure:* see now G.M. Sifakis, *JHS* 112 (1992) 123-142.

13   *what Aristophanes liked to present:* N.J. Lowe, in J. Redmond ed. *Themes in Drama 10: Farce* (Cambridge, 1988) 33-52, at p.49, defines what he sees as the five basic aims of Aristophanic comedy: to provoke laughter; to engage with issues of concern; to enact a good story ("the fulfilment of narrative"); to present attractive innovations in technique and showmanship; and to gratify fantasy, especially fantasies of power and subversion.

14   *only five of their voting-tablets ... were read and counted:* for another interpretation of the ancient evidence on this subject see M. Pope, *CQ* 36 (1986) 322-6; the evidence is reviewed afresh by Csapo & Slater 157-160. The following procedure would in my view both account for the ancient evidence and produce a clear and fair result without undue delay: (i) each of the ten judges writes down a complete ranking of the contestants and "signs" his tablet with the name of the tribe to which he belongs; (ii) the presiding magistrate successively chooses five of the ten tablets at random; (iii) the rankings awarded by these five judges are announced, and a tally kept of all rankings awarded to each contestant; (iv) the contest result is then decided by giving precedence to the contestant(s) with the greatest number of first-place votes, then (if first-place votes are equal) to the contestant(s) with most second-place votes, and so on down; (v) if two contestants have exactly the same vote profile, a sixth tablet is drawn and read (this will *always* break the tie). The rule that only five votes were normally counted is rightly seen by Csapo & Slater as a precaution against corruption: anyone who tried to bribe a judge was as likely as not to have wasted his money.

14   *a circular dance-floor:* there is now widespread support for the view that the *orchēstrā* in the Theatre of Dionysus was rectangular or trapezoidal in shape and much wider than it was deep; see E. Pöhlmann et al., *Studien zur Bühnendichtung und zum Theaterbau der Antike* (Frankfurt, 1995), especially Pöhlmann's own fundamental article (pp.49-62; originally published in *MH* 38 [1981] 129-146) and the review of the archaeological evidence by H.R. Goette (pp.9-48). The proponents of this view have never, however, explained how an *orchēstrā* of such a shape could accommodate the performance of

dithyrambs, with their choruses of fifty dancers in circular formation; and S. Scullion, *Three Studies in Athenian Dramaturgy* (Stuttgart, 1994) 3-42 has argued powerfully that the hypothesis of a rectilinear *orchēstrā* in the Theatre of Dionysus is inconsistent with "the clear evidence of the remains".

14   *its chorēgos:* on all aspects of the *chorēgiā* system see now P.J. Wilson, *The Athenian Institution of the Khoregia* (Cambridge, 2000). At the City Dionysia the *chorēgos* was always a citizen; at the Lenaea he could be a metic – and as Wilson (29-31) points out, *most* of the Lenaean *chorēgoi* known to us in fact were metics.

15   *by Callistratus:* see Addenda to p.2 (above).

15   *choruses were composed of ordinary citizens:* more specifically, of *young* male citizens. The characters of Plato's *Laws* (665b) take it as self-evident that the idea of a Dionysiac chorus of old men, or even of men over thirty, is *prima facie* absurd, and chorus members on vase paintings are nearly always beardless; cf. also *Wasps* 1060-2 which implies that a man is in his choral, his military and his sexual prime more or less simultaneously.

15   *a fourth actor:* D.M. MacDowell, *CQ* 44 (1994) 325-335, argues convincingly that the official limit for comedy in Ar.'s time was four actors, not three, and that it was strictly enforced. C.W. Marshall's attempt to refute MacDowell in *CQ* 47 (1997) 77-84 has to resort to desperate measures (impossibly quick costume changes, ventriloquial performance of certain parts by actors taking other parts) and fails to explain why the phenomena on which MacDowell had relied to show the necessity for four actors in Old Comedy do not exist in New Comedy.

15 n.84   Delete second sentence of note; for the comic phallus in *Eccl.* and *Wealth* see commentary on *Eccl.* 470, 622, 969, 978, and *Wealth* 295.

15-16   *The solution adopted ... :* Ruschenbusch (see note 88) was right to argue that there is no contemporary evidence for theoric distributions, or anything equivalent to them, before the mid fourth century. If any step was taken in the 440s to ease pressure on seating space, it is more likely to have been an increase in the admission charge; see my discussion in C.B.R. Pelling ed. *Greek Tragedy and the Historian* (Oxford, 1997) 65-71.

16   *our evidence ... that citizen women did not attend:* this statement is not refuted by any of the evidence cited by J.J. Henderson, *TAPA* 121 (1991) 133-147. Indeed, the fact that in Alexis fr. 42 women are apparently envisaged as attending the theatre *in a comic gynaecocracy* should actually be regarded as *prima facie* evidence that they did *not* normally attend it in reality. In *Thesm.* 386 ("seeing how you were being vilified by Euripides") "seeing" need not, and probably should not, be taken literally; see commentary *ad loc.*

16   *TRANSMISSION:* there is an excellent account of the transmission of, and the ancient and medieval commentators on, Aristophanes' text in N.V. Dunbar's edition of *Birds* (Oxford, 1995) 31-51.

17   *it is primarily to the schools ... that they owe their survival:* in the fourth century AD the rhetorician Libanius (*Or.* 1.9) recalls reading *Acharnians* as a school text.

17 n.100   Add N.G. Wilson, *Scholars of Byzantium* (London, 1983) 33-36; K. McNamee, *GRBS* 36 (1995) 399-414 and *CQ* 48 (1998) 269-288.

17 n.102   Π13 must now be credited with *four* good readings in *Thesm.*: a re-examination of the papyrus by S.M. Medaglia (see *Bollettino dei Classici* 3 [1982] 154-9) yielded a

new reading in *Thesm.* 242 with whose help Medaglia brilliantly solved this long-standing textual crux.

17   *in the Byzantine Empire:* my statements about the "period of religious extremism" and the ensuing Byzantine renaissance are somewhat oversimplified; for an authoritative account of classical scholarship and education in this period, see Wilson *op.cit.* 61-135.

18   *Maximus Planudes ... Manuel Moschopoulos:* neither of these scholars can be conclusively proved to have made any emendations in Ar.'s text, though both produced some annotations on *Wealth* (and Moschopoulos at least wrote some on *Clouds* too); see Wilson *op.cit.* 238, 244-7. On the textual tradition of the Byzantine triad see further K.J. Dover, *The Greeks and their Legacy* (Oxford, 1989) 223-265.

19   *The text of the Aldine:* Musurus' main copy-text is now known to have been the fifteenth-century Selestadiensis 347 (now at Sélestat [Bas-Rhin]), a copy of (or at least closely related to) the Triclinian ms. L; he also used E (which supplied corrections and scholia) and a ms. related to Γ (but having the endings of *Peace* and *Eccl.* intact) which enabled him to print *Peace* and *Eccl.* and supplied further corrections in other plays. See M. Sicherl in B. Haller ed. *Erlesenes aus der Welt des Buches* (Wiesbaden, 1979) 189-231 (revised in Sicherl, *Griechische Erstausgaben des Aldus Manutius* [Paderborn, 1997] 114-154), and S.D. Olson, *CQ* 48 (1998) 72-74.

ACHARNIANS

Introductory Note

page 32 *the restoration ... of the old country life:* G.L. Compton-Engle, *Sudden Glory: Acharnians and the First Comic Hero* (Diss. Cornell 1997) 53ff notes that in the second half of the play, we actually see Dicaeopolis function as a successful *urban* citizen, trading in (his own version of) the Agora and cooking eel and squid (unobtainable in inland country districts). This does not necessarily mean, however, that he has severed himself from his rural roots; it can be taken as showing the former underdog beating the arrogant city folk at their own game. L. Bertelli, *SRCG* 2 (1999) 39-62, points out that the play shows a strong tendency to hark back to events of the period 446-431; I would interpret this as showing that Ar.'s design is to elide the intervening years so as to make the spectator feel that the question at issue is not "should we now try to end the war?" as "should we have gone to war in the first place?"

33 n.1 Add M.H. Hansen, *The Athenian Democracy in the Age of Demosthenes* (Oxford, 1991) 212-8, 221-2.

33 *Editions:* an edition in the Clarendon series is being prepared by S.D. Olson.

Bibliography

W.G. Forrest, "Aristophanes' *Acharnians*", *Phoenix* 17 (1963) 1-12.

L. Edmunds, "Aristophanes' *Acharnians*", *YCS* 26 (1980) 1-41.

D.M. MacDowell, "The nature of Aristophanes' *Akharnians*", *G&R* 30 (1983) 143-162.

W. Kraus, *Aristophanes' politische Komödien* (Vienna, 1985) 31-111.

H.P. Foley, "Tragedy and politics in Aristophanes' *Acharnians*", *JHS* 108 (1988) 33-47.

S.D. Goldhill, *The Poet's Voice: Essays on Poetics and Greek Literature* (Cambridge, 1991) 167-222.

S.D. Olson, "Dicaeopolis' motivations in Aristophanes' *Acharnians*", *JHS* 111 (1991) 200-3.

A. Grilli, *Inganni d'autore: due studi sulla funzione del protagonista nel teatro di Aristofane* (Pisa, 1992).

C. Carey, "The purpose of Aristophanes' *Acharnians*", *RhM* 136 (1993) 245-263.

N.R.E. Fisher, "Multiple personalities and Dionysiac festivals: Dicaeopolis in Aristophanes' *Acharnians*", *G&R* 40 (1993) 31-47.

N.W. Slater, "Space, character, and ἀπάτη: transformation and transvaluation in the *Acharnians*", in A.H. Sommerstein et al. ed. *Tragedy, Comedy and the Polis* (Bari, 1993) 397-415.

G.A.H. van Steen, "Aspects of 'public performance' in Aristophanes' *Acharnians*", *AC* 63 (1994) 211-224.

M.W. Habash, "Two complementary Dionysiac festivals in Aristophanes' *Acharnians*", *AJP* 116 (1995) 559-577.

K. Vanhaegendoren, *Die Darstellung des Friedens in den Acharnern und im Frieden des Aristophanes* (Hamburg, 1996).

P. Demont, "Aristophane, le citoyen tranquille et les singeries", in P. Thiercy and M. Menu ed. *Aristophane: la langue, la scène, la cité* (Bari, 1997) 457-479.

L. Bertelli, "Gli *Acarnesi* di Aristofane: commedia di memoria?", *SRCG* 2 (1999) 39-62.
C.B.R. Pelling, *Literary Texts and the Greek Historian* (London, 2000) 141-163.

Note on the Text

page 34 to papyri add Π71 (Berlin Papyrus 21200; sixth century; contains 76-78) and Π73 (Oxyrhynchus Papyrus 4510; second century; contains fragments of 55-825 totalling 111 lines). In addition, considerable further fragments of Π19 have been published by H.G.T. Maehler, *APF* 30 (1984) 17ff. Significant readings of these papyri are given below in their places.

Text and Translation

Dramatis Personae: S.D. Olson, *CQ* 42 (1992) 310 with n.23, points out that the text gives us no reason to suppose that the man whom I have designated "Groomsman" is anything but a slave; he should therefore be labelled "Bridegroom's Slave". The speaker of 1174-89 (my "Third Messenger") is probably Lamachus' slave, who went to war with him at 1141.

Initial stage-arrangements. [The performing area at first represents the Pnyx, where the Assembly meets. The stage-platform represents the speaker's platform; close to it are benches for the Prytaneis. The stage-house is at present ignored; later its doors will at various moments represent the houses of Dicaeopolis, Euripides and Lamachus. Dicaeopolis arrives by a side-passage and sits on the ground, well away from the platform. He waits patiently for a minute or two; then, finding himself still alone, begins fidgeting, yawning and showing other signs of boredom; then turns to address the audience.]

line

40 There is probably no stage-crowd, since the citizen body can be represented by the theatre audience; see N.W. Slater in A.H. Sommerstein et al. ed. *Tragedy, Comedy and the Polis* (Bari, 1993) 399.

55 It is possible that Godschild is removed before he can complete his sentence (see W. Kraus, *Aristophanes' politische Komödien* [Vienna, 1985] 35); if so, the question-mark at the end of the line should be preceded by a dash, and the translation should read "Triptolemus and Celeus, will you stand idle while I'm—".

78 The position of the surviving letters]φαγειν[in Π71 makes it likely that this papyrus had originally the same reading as the medieval mss.

91-97 In view of new evidence as to the meaning of "eye" in connection with ships (see Addenda to Commentary) I would now suppose that Pseudartabas' mask had no nose or mouth, only an enormous eye set roughly where the mouth should be and partly swathed. Dicaeopolis' last sentence (97) should be rendered "I suppose that's an oarport sleeve you've got down there round your eye!"

125 For "Doesn't this make you want to hang yourself?" read "Doesn't that just choke you?"

189, 192 Note that Dicaeopolis does not taste the first two samples (as he is invited to do), but rejects them on their aroma alone: cf. P. Thiercy in Sommerstein et al. *Tragedy, Comedy and the Polis* 513-4.

193 For "as if the allies were being ground down" read "as if the allies were playing for time": as a ten-year treaty neared its end, it would become more and more tempting for allied states to withhold or delay tribute payments in the hope, either that Athens would be reluctant to send out punitive expeditions when a major war might erupt at any time, or that in the event of such a war the recalcitrant allies might secure help from Sparta.

203 Henderson (LCL) adopts Elmsley's transposition of this line to precede 201; this expeditiously disposes of the no longer relevant Godschild and gives stronger contrastive force to the first-person pronoun in 201 (where for "Myself ..." read "And as for me ...").

231 Insert <καὶ σκόλοψ> (Hermann, cf. Suda) "or like a stake" after ἀντεμπαγῶ (in trans. after "like a reed"); see Addenda to Commentary.

255 For "marries" read "inseminates"; cf. Ar. fr. 233, Arist. *EN* 1148b32, Hesychius β466 (citing Solon), and see M.G. Bonanno, *Sileno* 10 (1984) 93-96.

291-2Π73 has ἐπειτα.

293 Π73 has ουκ ιστε[. W.G. Clark's conjecture οὐκ ἰστέ'; "but oughtn't you to learn ...?" deserves consideration.

298 Hermann's conjecture is now confirmed by Π73 which has]ι συ.

301, 302 Π73 reads κατατεμω and πρτ' ες καττυ[with the medieval mss.

323 Π73 reads τ αρα, supporting Elmsley's conjecture τἄρα (γ' ἄρα most mss.: χ' ἄρα A).

325 The true reading, hitherto known only from the late ms. Vb1, is now confirmed by Π73 (δηξομ' αρ ὑμας).

343 Restore smooth breathing on ἐκσέσεισται.

347-8 The difficulties of this passage have been largely solved by W. Lapini, *SIFC* 92 (1999) 3-11. He reads ἆρα πάντες ἀνασείσειν (Dindorf) βοήν (R²) (better in my view βοάς [Clark] which keeps the number of the expected λίθους and accounts more easily for the ms. tradition), the latter a surprise substitute for λίθους "stones" and referring to the cries of distress that the Acharnians would have raised at the "death" of their "beloved" coal-basket; this interpretation enables us to keep the transmitted τ' in 348 instead of emending it to δ'. Render "So you were all on the point of brandishing ... cries, and some coals from Mount Parnes very nearly died".

348 Read Παρνήσσιοι (Wordsworth), cf. *SEG* xxxiv 39.

412 For "are you wearing" read "have you got"; there is no other evidence that Euripides is *wearing* one of his own costumes (as Agathon, for artistic reasons which he explains, does in *Thesmophoriazusae*). N.W. Slater in Sommerstein et al. *Tragedy, Comedy and the Polis* 405-6 suggests that the point is that Euripides would not (still) have these costumes in his possession unless they "were so worthless that no one else wanted them" – since otherwise the *chorēgos*, who had had them made, would either have kept or sold them.

485   For "you silly heart" read "my daring heart"; see L. McClure in F. De Martino and A.H. Sommerstein ed. *Lo spettacolo delle voci* (Bari, 1995) ii 46 who compares Eur. *Med.* 1244, *IT* 466.

541   Triclinius' conjecture is confirmed by Π73: only]ι survives at the relevant point, but the space available is only enough for [ε]ι, not for [ει κα]ι.

551   For "anchovies" read "pilchards": cf. A. Dalby, *Siren Feasts: A History of Food and Gastronomy in Greece* (London, 1996) 72.

611   Restore smooth breathing on ἐστί.

615   Π19 has υπερ with the medieval mss.

615   For "contributions" read "whip-rounds".

623   B's conjecture is confirmed by Π19 (γε πελ[).

636   Bentley's conjecture is confirmed by the position of οι πρεσβεις in Π19.

642   For "meant" read "means".

674   Restore smooth breathing on ἀγροικότερον.

731   Since in Megarian /VCw/ became /VC/ as in Attic, not /V:C/ as in e.g. Argolic, and since elsewhere Ar. reproduces this feature of the dialect correctly, Robertson's conjecture cannot be right (see B.M. Palumbo Stracca, *Helikon* 29/30 [1989/90] 385-6). I would now prefer κορίχι', which is also closer to R's reading.

732   For μᾶδδαν read μάδδαν (codd.): see S. Colvin, *Dialect in Aristophanes* (Oxford, 1999) 133-4.

741   εἶμεν is a conjecture by Dindorf (εἰμὲν Vp3): R*aj* have ἦμεν vel sim.

750   Π19 has]ρασου[with most of the medieval mss.

767   Π19 has ναι μα with *aj*.

771   εἶμεν is a conjecture by Dindorf: R*aj* have ἦμεν, Π19]μεν.

779   For τ' read τυ (Blaydes: τ' R: τύ γ' rell.); see Colvin *op.cit.* 193.

795   Π19 has]ανδε [with R*aj*.

797   τοῦ is a conjecture by Elliott: R*aj* have τῶ vel sim.

803   Only the end of the line survives in Π19, but the position of these letters suggests that it had the same readings earlier in the line as the medieval mss.

835   For μᾶδδαν read μάδδαν: cf. on 732 above.

841   For "he'll smart when he sits down" read "he'll be set howling": see LSJ s.v. *kathizō* I 5 (but the mediopassive usage occurs only here).

860   The text strongly suggests that there is only one sack of goods, and that the trader (being Boeotian and therefore stupid, cf. on 902) is carrying it himself, while his slave carries only a few sprigs of pennyroyal.

864   After "Away from the doors, you wasps!" insert stage-direction: [*He waves his arms as if shooing away the pipers, and they run off.*]

871   For the second τῶν read τᾶν; see Colvin *op.cit.* 150.

873   For "Absolutely all" read "Quite simply, all".

888   I was wrong to bring out Dicaeopolis' children here; the "children" he addresses are in fact the brazier and fan (hence the promise of a gift of coals; cf. 326ff) – it is *they*, his cooking utensils, that are asked to greet the eel as a long-lost friend.

905   For σιώ read θιώ (Blaydes), which was corrupted owing to the familiarity of the similar Laconian oath; see Colvin *op.cit.* 169 n.43.

910 It is possible, though by no means certain, that Ar. wrote Θείβαθε (as in 868), intending the next word to be pronounced ϝίττω: see Colvin *op.cit.* 177-8.

948-9 For "reap it and gather it in" read "cut down your crop"; there is a pun based on the fact that when applied to objects other than actual crops, θ(ε)ρίζω and its compounds tend to mean "destroy". See C. Romano, *Responsioni libere nei canti di Aristofane* (Rome, 1992) 95.

958/9 It is more likely that Lamachus' slave comes out of one of the side doors, thus helping to prepare for the scene 1071ff when this door will explicitly represent Lamachus' house.

960 Dobree's conjecture is confirmed by Π19 (ἰσι δραχμης).

1048 For ΠΑΡΑΝΥΜΦΟΣ (GROOMSMAN) read ΟΙΚΕΤΗΣ ΝΥΜΦΙΟΥ (BRIDEGROOM'S SLAVE); see above on *Dramatis Personae*.

1055 For χιλίων read χιλιῶν: cf. scholia and Herodian 1.426.11-12.

1079 For ἑορτάσαι read ἑορτάσαι: see Threatte i 500.

1096 For "close up" read "lock up the stuff" (i.e. the cooking equipment etc.); see Thiercy ad loc.

1104 Restore smooth breathing on ἐμοί.

1108-18 I have argued in *MCr* 25-28 (1990-3) 139-144 that 1109-12 ("Bring out the crest-case ... before dinner?") should be transposed to stand after 1117 ("He greatly prefers the locusts"); this transposition has since been adopted by Henderson (LCL).

1112 For "jugged hare" read "hare stew" (strictly, a stew made from hare offal and blood); see Dalby, *Siren Feasts* 62.

1121 *hold on to this:* an alternative possibility is that "this" is Dicaeopolis' phallus; see A. López Eire, *La lengua coloquial de la comedia aristofánica* (Murcia, 1996) 118.

1126 Add stage-direction: [*resting his shield on its stand*].

1174-89   For ΑΓΓΕΛΟΣ Γ (THIRD MESSENGER) read ΟΙΚΕΤΗΣ ΛΑΜΑΧΟΥ (LAMACHUS' SERVANT); see on *Dramatis Personae* above.

1196 This line (Δικαιόπολις εἴ μ' ἴδοι τετρωμένον) was accidentally omitted (from the Greek text only) in earlier printings; it should follow αἰακτὸν ἂν γένοιτο.

1216 For "midway" read "right round".

Commentary³

1   The hero's name is in effect etymologized at 499-501 ("I speak before *the Athenians* about *public affairs* [lit. the city] ... with *justice*") and at 595 ("What am I? A *decent citizen*"). See L. Lenz, *Gräzer Beiträge* 14 (1987) 95, and M. Menu in Menu ed. *Théâtre et cité* (Toulouse, 1994) 25.

6   This passage has been discussed by E.M. Carawan, *CQ* 40 (1990) 137-147, who derives the following scenario from Theopompus *FGrH* 115 F 93-94: Cleon accused the cavalry (either all of them, in a political speech, or some of them, in a prosecution) of desertion or dereliction of duty; they, or some of them, retaliated by charging him with taking bribes, and he avoided trial by relinquishing the money he had received. That the reference in Ar. is to "a recent theatrical event" is most unlikely, because (i) "among the extant fragments of Theopompus ... we have no reliable evidence of an historical account wholly fabricated from comedy" (Carawan *op.cit.* 140) and (ii) as Henderson

---

3   An asterisk denotes an entirely new note.

(LCL) points out, *Knights* 507ff implies that the Knights had not figured in comedy before 424.

10-11 If this passage refers to an actual incident (and it probably does), what was the incident? Half a dozen hypotheses are reviewed by G. Mastromarco in P. Thiercy and M. Menu ed. *Aristophane: la langue, la scène, la cité* (Bari, 1997) 541-8. He favours a suggestion previously made, in a somewhat different form, by R. Böhme, *Bühnenbearbeitung äschyleischer Tragödien* ii (Basle, 1959) 122: Theognis had been granted a chorus to produce plays by Aeschylus, and Dicaeopolis was appalled to learn that this honour had been given to so unworthy a person (alternatively, and perhaps better, we may be meant to suppose that he momentarily imagines he is about to have to sit through four plays *by* Theognis!).

16 For "equally badly it would see[m]" read "equally badly it was alleged".

19 See M.H. Hansen and F. Mitchel, *Symbolae Osloenses* 59 (1984) 16; M.H. Hansen, *The Athenian Democracy in the Age of Demosthenes* (Oxford, 1991) 133-4.

45 On Amphitheus see also D. Welsh, *CQ* 33 (1983) 51.

47-5 For "the son, not the father" read "the son, not the grandfather".

63 On Pyrilampes' peacocks see P.A. Cartledge in Cartledge et al. ed. *Nomos: Essays in Athenian Law, Politics and Society* (Cambridge, 1990) 41-61.

*66 **two drachmas a day:** L. Bertelli, *SRCG* 2 (1999) 43 n.22, points out that this would be an abnormally high rate: cf. *IG* i^3 37.25 (447/6: 1 dr.). As late as 346, after a century's inflation, the standard rate was still 1 dr.: the ten-man embassy to ratify the peace with Philip II was away for 84 days (Dem. 19.57-58) at a total cost quoted as 1000 dr. (Dem. 19.158, rounding up the time to "three whole months" and doubtless rounding up the cost as well). After eleven years, the present ambassadors would have "earned" about 8000 dr. each.

79 After "male prostitutes" insert "(lit. 'cock-suckers')".

88 Cleonymus also appears as the mover of decrees or amendments in *IG* i^3 70.5 (not otherwise datable) and 1454 bis (426/5?). To the comic references to him, add *com.adesp.* 1151.5. His treatment by the comic poets is discussed by I.C. Storey, *RhM* 132 1989) 247-261, who is, however, wrong to dismiss as a comic invention the allegation that he had thrown away his shield: if it is an invention, why is no similar accusation ever made in comedy against anyone *else*?

92 The title "King's Eye" appears as early as Aesch. *Pers.* 979. There is no evidence for it in Persian sources; cf. D.M. Lewis, *Sparta and Persia* (Leiden, 1977) 19-20.

95-97 The claim that "the oarports of a warship were called 'eyes'" was one based on inference rather than direct evidence, and the inference was never very safe, particularly as Greek warships regularly had large eyes on their port and starboard bows (sometimes painted on the timbers, sometimes, it is now known, on marble blocks fitted to the hull; see J.S. Morrison and J.F. Coates, *The Athenian Trireme* [Cambridge, 1986] 150 n.21). Dicaeopolis, speaking of Pseudartabas as if he were a ship, observes that he has an *askōma* not, like ordinary ships, around his lower oarports, but around his eye (which on a real ship needed no such protection, not being an orifice).

100 L. Bertelli, *SRCG* 2 (1999) 45, reasonably suggests that another name that might be perceived amid the gibberish is that of Pissuthnes, the satrap of Sardis, who had supported the Samian rebellion in 440 (Thuc. 1.115.4-5) and an anti-Athenian faction at Colophon between 430 and 427 (Thuc. 3.34.2).

118 Henderson (LCL) points out that the Greek (lit. "Cleisthenes of Sibyrtius") could also be taken to imply that Sibyrtius was, or had been, Cleisthenes' lover.

120-1 My interpretation is not wholly satisfactory, because in the original Archilochean context "a rump like thine" must have meant "no rump" (cf. Semonides fr. 7.76), so that 120 would inevitably be taken not as a sarcastic, but as a direct, reference to Cleisthenes' beardlessness; see P. Demont in Thiercy & Menu *Aristophane* 467-8, and Kugelmeier 172-4. The point of 121, and of Dicaeopolis' indignation, is presumably therefore that Cleisthenes, like the "monkey" (trickster) that he is, has taken advantage of his unmanly appearance to masquerade as a Persian eunuch for the purpose of deceiving the Athenian people.

125 The Prytaneum is more likely to have been somewhere below the east end of the Acropolis; see G.S. Dontas, *Hesperia* 52 (1983) 48-63. On the categories of persons who might be entertained there, see M.J. Osborne, *ZPE* 41 (1981) 153-170.

*133 you lot: taken by M.A. Levi, *RIL* 112 (1978) 92, to refer to the Prytaneis; by A. Grilli, *Inganni d'autore: due studi sulla funzione del protagonista nel teatro di Aristofane* (Pisa, 1992) 53 to refer to the gullible public. The former is more likely, because, as Grilli himself stresses elsewhere (61ff), it is Ar.'s concern in the prologue to *identify* Dicaeopolis' opinions and interests with those of the average spectator, thus ensuring in advance that the audience will side with him when he pleads a possibly unpopular cause.

146 For "phraties" read "phratries".

162 It is not true that thranite oars were longer than others (see Morrison & Coates *op.cit.* 138-9); when bonuses were paid to thranite rowers, it was probably because they were more exposed to danger from "collision and missiles" than the lower tiers (see Dover on Thuc. 6.31.3).

164 G. Mastromarco, *Commedie di Aristofane* i (Turin, 1983) 93, points out that one could not always know if an Assembly meeting was going to last a long time: one might bring food along in case it did, and if the meeting ended early one could always take the food home and use it in other ways.

*196 ambrosia and nectar: the food and drink of the gods; to make peace, it is implied, is a way to attain almost divine bliss (cf. K. Vanhaegendoren, *Die Darstellung des Friedens in den Acharnern und im Frieden des Aristophanes* [Hamburg, 1996] 86-87).

202 On the Country Dionysia and the Anthesteria in *Acharnians* see M.W. Habash, *AJP* 116 (1995) 559-577.

*216 treaty-bearer: Greek *spondophoros*, normally used of those who travelled to the various cities to announce the "sacred truce" for the Olympic games (note the mention, just before, of a famous athlete) or similar festivals (including, significantly in view of Godschild's genealogy, the Eleusinian Mysteries): cf. Pind. *Isthm.* 2.23, Aeschines 2.133. To offer violence to such a person would be sacrilege, yet the chorus are willing to do so. See A.M. Bowie, *Aristophanes: Myth, Ritual and Comedy* (Cambridge, 1993) 21, and Vanhaegendoren *op.cit.* 82.

231 While I would still maintain that there are some "discrepancies of one metrical unit between strophe and antistrophe" in Ar. that are not readily removable by emendation, this one *has* to be removed, since otherwise we would have to posit at 215 a major metrical break between article and noun; moreover an entry in the Suda lexicon for *skolops* "stake" seems to indicate that the compiler, or his source, knew a version of the text that included that word. See L.P.E. Parker, *The Songs of Aristophanes* (Oxford, 1997) 115-9, 124-5.

255 It should have been mentioned that by "ferrets" Dicaeopolis here actually means "girls"; cf. Strattis fr. 75, Babrius 32.

263-279 There survive fragments of two actual phallic hymns (*PMG* 851a,b), one of them addressed to Dionysus.

*266-7 returning ... to my deme: the idea that Dicaeopolis' private peace has magically enabled him to return to his country home appears only here; in typical Aristophanic fashion, it is forgotten as soon as it becomes dramatically inconvenient.

284-302 P. Mazon, *Essai sur la composition des comédies d'Aristophane* (Paris, 1904) 20 suggested that on 285 the chorus took five menacing steps towards Dicaeopolis; cf. now R. Pretagostini in B. Gentili & F. Perusino ed. *Mousike: metrica, ritmica e musica greca in memoria di Giovanni Comotti* (Pisa, 1995) 265-276. It is not clear whether at 336 this movement is repeated or whether (as I would prefer to suppose) it is reversed.

326 On Euripides' *Telephus* see now M. Heath, *CQ* 37 (1987) 272-280, and M.J. Cropp in C. Collard et al. *Euripides: Selected Fragmentary Plays* i (Warminster, 1995) 17-52. E.G. Csapo, *EMC* 28 (1994) 53 and pl.1, has suggested that this scene of *Acharnians* may be portrayed on a series of Apulian relief *gutti* from the 320s; if so, they would indicate that the "sword" of 342 is a real sword, rather than a kitchen knife as I have assumed.

346 Alternatively "this" might be the comic phallus (cf. *Wasps* 1062); see L. Gil, *MCr* 18 (1983) 78-80.

377 For a comic character to speak in the name of the author is not quite unique: in the last line of Menander's *Samia* the conventional prayer for victory (here put in the mouth of the old man Demeas) asks that victory should "always follow my choruses".

388 *PA* 7556 is not the Hieronymus mentioned here but his grandson.

406 The assignment of Cholleidae to "the inland division [*trittys*]" of the tribe Leontis depends mainly on the evidence of this very passage; two inscriptions, contrariwise, seem to assign it to the (very scattered) city division (see J.S. Traill, *Hesperia* 47 [1978] 99-100). However, the northern Attic local colour in this play (Acharnae, Parnes [348, cf. 1075], Phyle [1023]) does strongly suggest that the deme was located in that region.

424 The Euripidean Philoctetes was dressed in animal skins (Dio Chrys. 59.5).

430 On Ar.'s paratragic exploitation of *Telephus* see W.G. Arnott in J.H. Betts et al. ed. *Studies in Honour of T.B.L. Webster* i (Bristol, 1986) 6-8; H.P. Foley, *JHS* 108 (1988) 33-47; and F. Jouan in P. Ghiron-Bistagne ed. *Thalie: Mélanges interdisciplinaires sur la comédie* (= *CGITA* 5 [1989]) 17-30

483-8 Dicaeopolis' apostrophe to his "soul" or "heart" appears (appropriately) to be modelled on Eur. *Med.* 1242-50; see A.N. Michelini, *TAPA* 119 (1989) 120. The metaphor of a race is implicit not only in *grammē* "finishing line" but also in *probaine* (483) "run on", *hestēkas?* (484) "you stand still?" (i.e. "haven't you started yet?") and *apelthe* (486) "start!"; see F. García Romero, *CFC* 6 (1996) 78-81.

*504 for we are by ourselves: the same phrase appears, with a change of gender, in *Thesm.* 472, and it may well come from *Telephus* (cf. M. Heath, *CQ* 37 [1987] 278). C.B.R. Pelling, *Literary Texts and the Greek Historian* (London, 2000) 149, points out that this probable link to *Telephus*, combined with the fact that Dicaeopolis has to take some trouble *explaining* that, and why, "there are no foreigners here yet", shows that, contrary to the view of many scholars, it was *not* already a familiar assumption that Lenaean comedies could be expected to have a more "Athenian" and less "international" flavour than Dionysian ones.

507-8 For "gound" read "ground".

510-1 There may also be an allusion to a more recent event. A series of major earthquakes in the spring of 426 had caused the cancellation of that year's Peloponnesian invasion of Attica (Thuc. 3.87.4, 3.89); they appear, however, to have had serious effects only north of the Isthmus.

519 On the *sūkophantēs* see commentary on *Wealth* 31.

522 Read straightforwardly, the passage implies that any goods imported from Megara were *ipso facto* liable to be confiscated, i.e. that Athens had placed an embargo on all or most imports from Megara well before the famous decree of Pericles (which intensified the embargo by extending it to the whole empire and by effectively preventing Megarians from buying, as well as from selling, in the Athenian market). Ar. is careful to say that he does not hold "the city" responsible for the denunciations (515-6), but this is not necessarily incompatible with the existence of such an embargo (which could only be *enforced* by the actions of individual accusers). See Pelling *op.cit.* 156-7.

524-5 For "thowing" read "throwing". It is appropriate to this play that the war is seen as originating from a symposium that went wrong; symposia, successful and flawed, feature strongly in the play's wine/war opposition, cf. 72-78, 263-279, 551, 751-2, 979-989, 1000-end — and note that *spondai* (in different senses of the word, cf. on 179) mark both the end of a war and the beginning of a symposium. See R. Scaife, "From *kottabos* to war in Aristophanes' *Acharnians*", *GRBS* 33 (1992) 25-35, esp. 34-35. Pelling *op.cit.* 153-4 argues that the entire Simaetha story could have been invented by Ar. on the model of what the Euripidean Telephus (must have) said about the abduction of Helen; but he ignores the fact that Simaetha is named and the audience are apparently expected to know something about her (cf. T.D. Braun in F.D. Harvey and J. Wilkins ed. *The Rivals of Aristophanes* [London/Swansea, 2000] 213-4). I have little doubt that a *hetairā* named Simaetha did come from Megara to Athens, some time before the war, in the company of some young Athenians (just as Neaera came from Megara to Athens in the company of Phrynion in 371/0, cf. [Dem.] 59.35-39); what Ar. will have invented is the association between this episode and the outbreak of war, as in *Peace* he invented the association between a scandal involving Pheidias and the outbreak of war.

528 The absurdity of these accounts of the origins of the war in no way proves that Ar. did not intend or expect them to be taken seriously as arguments against the justice and expediency of beginning or continuing it. Half the conflicts in modern history have been alleged, by politicians and political commentators as much as by comedians and satirists, to have been stirred up by political leaders (or by sinister forces behind them) to distract public attention from some crime or scandal — and such allegations have often been widely believed.

*548-554 rations being measured out ... warbling and piping: of 25 Greek words (other than monosyllables) in these six and a half lines, no less than 22 end in -*ōn*.

566 On Ar.'s portrayal of Lamachus see G. Cortassa in E. Corsini et al. ed. *La polis e il suo teatro* (Padua, 1986-8) ii 233-263.

567 Similarly "who glancest lightning" suggests that "Olympian Pericles has ... passed his thunderbolts into the hands of Lamachus, his destined successor" (B.H. Kraut, *I Aristophanes: Poetic Self-Assertion in Old Comedy* [Diss. Princeton 1985] 82). But as the scene proceeds Lamachus is steadily downgraded, from quasi-god to hero (575, 578) to general (593) to placeman (597) to upstart "youngster" (601) to bankrupt (614-7) to outcast (625).

*577 been openly defaming our whole city: quoted or adapted from Euripides' *Telephus* (Eur. fr. 712).

593 A third possible explanation is that Lamachus calls himself a general because, though not actually holding the office at present, he has often held it in the past (so Kraus, *Aristophanes' politische Komödien* 57; L. Bertelli, *SRCG* 2 [1999] 56).

603 The Teisamenus who was "prominent in the last years of the fifth century" was the subject of an entire comedy by Theopompus, which makes it even more likely that the comic references noted by the scholia are to him.

604 The implication of my note (mislabelled 603) that Chares is the name of an Athenian is wrong. The use of the Greek phrase *para Charēti* (rather than *meta Charētos*) shows that he must be a ruler to whom the Athenians had sent an embassy, and probably (like the Thracians, Chaonians and Sicilians) one outside Greece proper (we cannot tell where).

614 Coesyra appears, from the evidence of ballots cast against the elder Megacles on one of the two occasions when he was ostracized (Lys. 14.39), to have been his mother, not (as I implied) his wife; she may have been the daughter of the tyrant Peisistratus by an Eretrian wife (Peisistratus was in exile at Eretria for ten years: Hdt. 1.61.2-62.1). See B.M. Lavelle, *GRBS* 30 (1989) 503-513; F. Willemsen, *MDAI(A)* 106 (1991) 144-5; D.M. Lewis, *ZPE* 96 (1993) 51-52; G.R. Stanton, *ZPE* 111 (1996) 69-73.

615 My definition of *eranos* was wrong; it should read "a friendly loan made by an *ad hoc* group of individuals ... without interest, and with an arrangement for repayment over a period of years in regular installments" (M.I. Finley, *Studies in Land and Credit in Ancient Athens 500-200 BC* [New Brunswick NJ, 1951] 100; see also P.C. Millett, *Lending and Borrowing in Ancient Athens* [Cambridge, 1991] 153-9). The coupling, in our passage, of *eranoi* with ordinary "debts" strongly suggests that Megacles and Lamachus are being accused of having failed to keep up their repayments (until their financial plight was eased by appointments to lucrative ambassadorships).

626-718 For discussions of the parabasis of *Acharnians* and its relation to the rest of the play, see A.M. Bowie, *CQ* 32 (1982) 27-40; F. Perusino, *Dalla commedia antica alla commedia di mezzo* (Urbino, [1987]) 17-33; K.J. Reckford, *Aristophanes' Old-and-New Comedy* (Chapel Hill, 1987) 187-191; T.K. Hubbard, *The Mask of Comedy* (Ithaca NY, 1991) 41-59.

628 Note that *didaskalos* can also mean "teacher, educator", and the related verb *didaskein* is used in the sense "give instruction" in 656 and 658; see commentary on *Frogs* 1053-6.

*633-645 It is *prima facie* inconsistent that Ar. is said to have deserved praise both from the Athenians, for opening their eyes to the deceptions practiced by "ambassadors from the allied states", and from these states themselves, for telling the Athenians the unpalatable truth about "what democracy means" for them. But there is no real inconsistency: Ar.'s point is that the allies, who previously tried to evade payment of tribute by diplomatic chicanery, are now happy to pay in full and honestly because they so much admire Ar.'s willingness to speak up on their behalf.

653 That the Athenians are here advised not to make peace if it means surrendering Aegina is not inconsistent with what I take to be the general message of the play. Dicaeopolis had implied (cf. on 538) that the Spartans had been sincere in 432/1 when they claimed that there would be no war if the Megarian decree was repealed, i.e. that the demand they had made at that time for Aegina to be independent had been merely a bargaining ploy; supporters of peace in 426/5 may well have been arguing (perhaps naively — but that is another matter) that things were still the same.

654   Conceivably, as R.G. Tanner has pointed out to me, it may be significant that the name Aristophanes is found in a distinguished Aeginetan family (Pind. *Nem.* 3.20); might the poet's grandmother have been a member of that family?

*659-662 let Cleon contrive ... shall I be convicted: adapted from a play of Euripides (Eur. fr. 918), very possibly *Telephus*.

704   On the accusation of barbarian ancestry see D.M. MacDowell in A.H. Sommerstein et al. ed. *Tragedy, Comedy and the Polis* (Bari, 1993) 362-4, who argues, in view especially of 712 ("the kinsmen of the advocate's *father*") that it was Euathlus' paternal grandmother who was a Scythian. Similarly, in the following century, Demosthenes, whose maternal grandmother had been of Scythian origin (Aeschines 3.171-2), is described as "this Scythian speech-writer" (Aeschines 2.180), "a barbarian *sūkophantēs*" (*ib.* 183), "this abominable Scythian" (Dein. 1.15).

726   Delete "Soviet".

729   Ar.'s representation of Megarian dialect is analysed in detail by S. Colvin, *Dialect in Aristophanes* (Oxford, 1999), who concludes (p.297) that its features are reproduced fairly accurately except in some details of verb morphology. Colvin argues (pp.302-6) that non-Attic dialect in Ar. is not normally treated as in itself laughable; its main function is rather to serve as a regional/political label alongside other stereotypes.

774   In Eupolis fr. 192.170 (a passage cited as a heading to a commentary note, not part of a continuous text) a character swears "by Diocles" in an unknown context.

819   On *phasis* see now D.M. MacDowell in M. Gagarin ed. *Symposium 1990: Papers on Greek and Hellenistic Legal History* (Vienna, 1991) 187-198.

*822 let go that sack: the sack is now empty, but the Informer, after the manner of his kind, takes it for granted that it must contain more contraband goods.

843   For "421/0" read "422/1". Prepis may have belonged to the deme of Xypete (*IG* i³ 894).

846   Ar. likes to mention the removal of Hyperbolus, as here, as the last of a series of blessings: cf. *Knights* 1363, *Wasps* 1007, *Peace* 921, 1319. According to one source (Theophrastus, cited by Plutarch) it was Phaeax, not Nicias, who plotted with Alcibiades to secure Hyperbolus' ostracism; I have suggested in *CQ* 46 (1996) 332-3 that Hyperbolus' comic reputation may have made him an attractive target for such a plot.

849   C. Carey, *LCM* 18 (1993) 54, has provided a palmary interpretation of "the adulterer's cut": he suggests that one of the punishments that might be unofficially inflicted on an adulterer was *to have his head shaved*. In support of this one may note (i) that this would be particularly disgraceful because the shaven head was associated with slaves (cf. *Birds* 911) and (ii) that this humiliation is elsewhere associated with *women* who are (or are believed to have been) sexually unfaithful to their male possessors (cf. Eur. *Tro.* 1026 and above all Menander's *Perikeiromene*). Cratinus, in other words, is totally bald.

855   The Lysistratus of *Lys.* 1105 was probably of the deme Amphitrope, not Cholargus, and if so was certainly not the man mentioned here; see commentary *ad loc.*

860 Colvin, *Dialect in Aristophanes* 297-8, comes to much the same conclusions as I had done about Ar.'s representation of Boeotian dialect.

*878-880 geese, hares ... Copaic eels: with the exception of the first, second and last items, this list consists entirely of animals that were considered neither edible nor useful nor decorative (see P. Thiercy in Thiercy & Menu *Aristophane* 162-3). We are probably meant to infer already that this Boeotian, with the dull intellect of his race, cannot distinguish between valuable and worthless goods — is in fact just the sort of person to be willing to exchange the whole lot of them for a Nicarchus.

887 Morychus had an imposing town house near the unfinished temple of Olympian Zeus (Pl. *Phdr.* 227b) to which his name remained attached even after his death. It is tempting to identify him with the trierarch of *IG* i³ 1032.409 (navy-list, probably of 406), and to suppose that he was the Morychus whose tomb was imposing enough to have its bounds marked by boundary-stones (*horoi*) (cf. *IG* i³ 1135).

893-4 Similarly in *Peace* 1013-4 a Copaic eel is spoken of in terms appropriate to a lost wife or bride; Davidson 10 cites evidence that "the practice of comparing women to mouth-watering fish and fish to women [or boys] seems to have been rather more general in Athenian society", e.g. Eubulus fr. 34 and 36 (eels again), Antiphanes fr. 27.

907 On the qualities associated with the monkey in Ar. see P. Demont in Thiercy & Menu *Aristophane* 457-479.

920 It was suggested many years ago by P.N. Ure, *AE* 100 (1937) 258-262, that *tiphē* here meant a type of lamp with a large, round, shallow bowl, known to have been used in Boeotia, which could easily (in theory) have been floated down a drain as a miniature fireship.

961 On the Anthesteria, see also W. Burkert, *Homo Necans* tr. P. Bing (Berkeley, 1983) 213-247; on its role in the structure of this play, see M.W. Habash, *AJP* 116 (1995) 559-577.

982 R.M. Harriott, *Aristophanes, Poet and Dramatist* (London, 1985) 96, notes that the destruction of vines, formerly blamed on Sparta (183, 233, 512), is now seen as due to the Athenians' own error in treating War as a friend.

1017 D. Auger in Thiercy & Menu *Aristophane* 370-3 notes that in Ar. sympathetic characters (e.g. Dicaeopolis, Trygaeus, Peisetaerus) generally cook meals themselves, while the bad citizen (e.g. Demos, Paphlagon and the Sausage-seller in *Knights*) appropriates food made by others. Cooking can thus be seen as a metaphor for civic activity: the good citizen is an active contributor, the bad citizen a passive consumer.

1028 L.P.E. Parker, *CR* 33 (1983) 11, and D.M. MacDowell, *G&R* 30 (1983) 159-160, suggest, no doubt rightly, that the Dercetes of the play and the Dercetes of the inscriptions are one and the same, and that there is some reason, well known to the audience, why it is appropriate that he should be satirized and refused a share of the peace.

*1029 anoint my eyes with peace: in this part of the play the peace-liquid seems to have metamorphosed from wine to oil (cf. 1053, 1063-6), which is equally appropriate since olive trees suffered as much as vines from the Spartan invasions (cf. 995-9); see D.M. MacDowell, *Aristophanes and Athens* (Oxford, 1995) 76.

*1066 anoint her husband's cock: for this form of (normally aphrodisiac) magic see J.J. Winkler, *The Constraints of Desire* (New York, 1990) 79 who cites *PGM* vii 191-2, xxxvi 283-294.

1093 The three lines "Since the famous Harmodius ... of dancing-girls" should be deleted. There was in fact said to have been a courtesan, Leaena, sometimes described as Harmodius' mistress (Athenaeus 13.596f) and sometimes as Aristogeiton's (Paus. 1.23.2-3, Polyaenus 8.45), who after the assassination of Hipparchus died under torture without revealing anything about their plot; afterwards she was commemorated by a bronze lioness (symbolically tongueless, it was said) in the Propylaea (Pliny *NH* 34.72; Plut. *Mor.* 505d-f; Paus. loc.cit.; Polyaenus loc.cit.). See W.G. Forrest, *CQ* 45 (1995) 240-1 (who however does not refer to *Ach.* 1093).

*1128-9 reflected in the bronze I see ... : Lamachus, and after him Dicaeopolis, are here practising the form of divination known as catoptromancy (mirror-gazing); cf. comm. on *Wealth* 382.

1154-5 Since for Ar. it is axiomatic that his own comedies are the only ones worth seeing, it is not unlikely that the reference would be understood as being to *his* only previous Lenaean play, a year earlier (426) — probably *Dramas or Centaur* (see Addenda to General Introduction p.4); and since a *chorēgos* would hardly wish to offend his entire chorus by refusing to give them the customary dinner, it is possible that his offence was actually that of not inviting *Ar.* (on the ground, presumably, that he had had no *official* responsibility for the performance) and that here, as at 659-664, the chorus are speaking in the name of the author.

KNIGHTS

Introductory Note
page

2   *the Athenian people ... is shown as being so stupid and gullible:* this aspect of *Knights*,
the satire on Demos (and therefore on the audience), is strongly stressed by P. Reinders,
Drama 3 (1995) 1-20, and by B. Effe in G. Binder and B. Effe ed. *Das antike Theater:
Aspekte seiner Geschichte, Rezeption und Aktualität* (Trier, 1998) 49-68.

3 n.1   On the portrayal of Cleon see also, with particular reference to his business activities
and to possible personal and local feuds between him and Ar., H. Lind, *Der Gerber
Kleon in den Rittern des Aristophanes* (Frankfurt, 1990).

3   *the Athenian cavalry:* see now G.R. Bugh, *The Horsemen of Athens* (Princeton, 1988)
and I.G. Spence, *The Cavalry of Classical Greece* (Oxford, 1993).

4   *if Eupolis had any share in the composition of Knights:* see Addenda to Commentary
on 1225.

4   *There is an edition ...:* an edition in the Clarendon series is being prepared by J.J.
Henderson.

Bibliography

H.J. Newiger, *Metapher und Allegorie: Studien zu Aristophanes* (Munich, 1957) 11-49.

M. Landfester, *Die Ritter des Aristophanes* (Amsterdam, 1967).

E.R. Schwinge, "Zur Ästhetik der aristophanischen Komödie am Beispiel der Ritter", *Maia* 27
(1975) 177-199.

W. Kraus, *Aristophanes' politische Komödien* (Vienna, 1985) 113-192.

R.W. Brock, "The double plot in Aristophanes' *Knights*", *GRBS* 27 (1986) 15-27.

L. Edmunds, "The Aristophanic Cleon's 'disturbance' of Athens", *AJP* 108 (1987) 233-263.

L. Edmunds, *Cleon, Knights, and Aristophanes' Politics* (Lanham MD, 1987).

R.M. Rosen, *Old Comedy and the Iambographic Tradition* (Atlanta, 1988) 59-82.

H. Lind, *Der Gerber Kleon in den Rittern des Aristophanes* (Frankfurt, 1990).

S.D. Olson, "The new Demos of Aristophanes' *Knights*", *Eranos* 88 (1990) 60-63.

J. Wilkins, "The regulation of meat in Aristophanes' *Knights*", in H.D. Jocelyn ed. *Tria
Lustra: Essays and Notes Presented to John Pinsent* (Liverpool, 1993) 119-126.

P. Reinders, "Der Demos in den *Rittern* des Aristophanes am Beispiel des Amoibaions in den
Vv. 1111-1150", *Drama* 3 (1995) 1-20.

R.E. Harder, "Der Schluss von Aristophanes' Rittern", *Prometheus* 23 (1997) 108-118.

B. Effe, "Das Theater als politische Anstalt: Aristophanes' 'Ritter' und Euripides'
'Schutzflehende'", in G. Binder and B. Effe ed. *Das antike Theater: Aspekte seiner
Geschichte, Rezeption und Aktualität* (Trier, 1998) 49-68.

F. Muecke, "Oracles in Aristophanes", *SRCG* 1 (1998) 257-274.

A.H. Sommerstein, "Monsters, ogres and demons in Old Comedy", in C. Atherton ed.
Monsters and Monstrosity in Greek and Roman Culture = NCLS 6 (2000) 19-40, esp.
28-31.

Note on the Text

page 5 *seven papyri:* two more have been published since: Π64 (Bingen Papyrus 18, containing 1040-58) and Π74 (Oxyrhynchus Papyrus 4511 [3rd c.], containing 736-746)

Text and Translation
line
1-9 W. Kraus, *Aristophanes' politische Komödien* (Vienna, 1985) 119, following van Leeuwen, plausibly argues that the speaker-assignments in this passage should be reversed, since the same person ought not to speak 8b-9 (recommending wailing) and 11-12 (rejecting wailing).

16 The transposition is due not to Richards but to C.F. Hermann.

77 For "with his feet *this* far apart; so that ..." read "and when he takes a stride *this* long ...": Greek *diabainein* can refer to back-to-front as well as to sideways separation of the feet. See B.D. MacQueen, *AJP* 105 (1984) 456.

107/8 After *He drinks the whole cup,* insert *and leaps excitedly to his feet.*

146 After "Let's look for him", Thiercy *ad loc.* plausibly makes the two slaves scan the audience in search of a sausage-seller (Ar. of course is confident that no practitioner of so despised a trade, even if present, would wish to declare himself).

235 After *coming out of the house,* insert *a garland on his head:* cf. 1227, and see M.C. English, *The Stage Properties of Aristophanic Comedy* (Diss. Boston Univ. 1999) 445.

271 A possible solution of the textual crux is γ' ἐνιῇ "charges", a cavalry term (cf. Xen. *Cyr.* 7.1.29, *Hell.* 2.4.32); this line of emendation was suggested to me by P.T. Eden (whose own proposal, ἐνῆται, gives equally good sense but is further from the transmitted text).

272 For "duck out *this* way", read "wheel away in *this* direction" (cf. Thuc. 5.73.3), the chorus once again thinking in terms of cavalry manoeuvres.

274 The last word of the line should probably be καταστρέφεις (V*aj*: καταστρέφει R); in translation, for "try to make yourself master of the city" read "turn the city upside down" (cf. 309-312).

340 The emendation here should be credited to Bentley, not Tyrwhitt; see J.J. Henderson in H.D. Jocelyn ed. *Tria Lustra: Essays and Notes Presented to John Pinsent* (Liverpool, 1993) 116.

358 For "ruffle Nicias" read perhaps "make Nicias shit himself" (cf. LSJ ταράσσω I 4, τάραξις II 1, and, for the idea, 69-70, *Wasps* 941, *Lys.* 440, *Thesm.* 570, *Eccl.* 640).

370-3 Henderson (LCL) transposes these lines into the order 373-0-2-1, since 370 is more appropriate to a leather-worker than a butcher; but the same is true of 373 (bristles are plucked out of hides, not out of meat). It may therefore be preferable to retain the transmitted order but suppose that a line has been lost after 369 and another after 370.

382-6 Rather than insert οὐδ' ἐλαφρόν after 386, it may be preferable, with Hermann, to read in 383 καὶ <λόγοι τῶν> λόγων: this improves the syntax of the sentence, makes it easier to understand how the analysis found in the metrical scholia was arrived at, and posits an all too easy corruption.

474 For "revealing this" read "revealing *this*": D.M. Lewis, *CR* 33 (1983) 176, points out that there is an implicit contrast with the Sausage-seller's willingness to accept a bribe to keep quiet in 440.

525 For "he was found wanting in satirical power" read "his jokes had lost their bite". A. Melero (Bellido) in J.A. López Férez ed. *La comedia griega y su influencia en la literatura española* (Madrid, 1998) 66 points out that σκώπτειν in Ar. regularly refers not to political or social satire but to low-comic jokes and routines of the kind that Ar. affects to regard as beneath him.

532 For "pegs" read "studs", pieces of amber mounted as ornaments on the arms of a lyre; pegs for tuning were a later invention. See F. Perusino, *Corolla Londiniensis* 2 (1982) 153-6.

545 F. Ademollo, *Atene e Roma* 39 (1994) 177-180, argues convincingly that the sense given by my translation (which he agrees is that required by the context) cannot be got out of the transmitted text, and proposes the simple and effective emendation (once considered and rejected by van Leeuwen) οὐκ for κοὐκ, making the line mean literally "because, in a self-controlled way, he did not [i.e. he refused to] leap in foolishly and talk nonsense".

546 The emendation I adopted is due not to Meineke but to Bentley.

605 στρώματα (*vaj*M) is probably the better reading; the "youngest" – who often in military units get the jobs no one else wants – could be engaged, in preparation for a night in open bivouacs, in the tedious but necessary task of collecting leaves under which to sleep (cf. *Odyssey* 5.482-7, 16.46-48, Eur. *Cycl.* 386-7). R's reading is tempting because it seems to look forward to 606-7; but the horses are there described, not as foraging for food for their mess, but as eating it themselves, and the understood subject is therefore not "the youngest" but the horses generally.

610 Bentley's emendation was proposed independently by Daubuz at about the same time; see Henderson (cited on 340) 116.

662 For "anchovies" read "pilchards" (see Addenda to *Ach.* 551).

697 For [*skipping about*] read [*dancing mockingly round Paphlagon*], and for "I scout you and flout you!" read "Cock-a-doodle-doo!" (cf. Dem. 54.9, and Thiercy's translation).

755 For "chewing" read "stringing" (lit. "tying by the foot"), a boring job requiring no skill; figs were strung together to make necklaces used in certain rituals (see comm. on *Lys.* 646-7).

814-6 This difficult metaphor has been discussed by J.L. Marr, *CQ* 46 (1996) 562-3. He is probably right to assume that the liquid (not named in the Greek text) with which Themistocles "filled [Athens] to the brim" was not water but wine (which, with barley-cake and fish, would make a complete meal). He also suggests that 814 and 816 refer to Themistocles' rebuilding of the city walls to enclose a greater area than before (cf. Thuc. 1.93.2) in contrast with Cleon's alleged attempt to make the city smaller (817).

1026 The transmitted reading θύρας should be retained: trans. "this dog is nibbling away at your oracle as if it were a door". Dogs do worry at doors (as they do at bones), and the verb does not imply that the door has actually been eaten away. See Nemesianus, *Cynegetica* 168.

1046, 1049 Π64 reads]οιδηροῦν τειχ[and εκελευε πεντ[, in both cases agreeing with the medieval mss.

1075 The apparatus entry for 1075 should be relabelled 1074.

1091 The last word should be accented πλουθυγιείαν: see comm. on *Birds* 731.

1215 Read παππίδιον (so almost all mss.; cf. *Wasps* 609, *Peace* 120, *Odyssey* 6.57, etc.). N.W. Slater, *AJP* 120 (1999) 366, very plausibly suggests that the Sausage-seller turns his hamper over and shakes it out to show that it is empty (I doubt if he is right to suppose that the same is done with Paphlagon's hamper at 1218 – this would leave its contents littering the ground; at most the Sausage-seller might ostentatiously strive in vain to lift it with one hand, thus demonstrating what a weight of food it still held).

1286 For "beard" read perhaps "moustache" (cf. Eubulus fr. 98.2-3).

1294 Another emendation worth recording is φασὶ <μὲν> γὰρ αὐτὸν (Bentley).

1389 There is something to be said for having *three* girls appear here, partly because superhuman feminine beings often come in threes (e.g. the Fates, the Graces; cf. *Peace*, Fullfruit and Showtime in *Peace*) and partly because of the considerations mentioned in comm. on 1391.

Commentary
line

61 On Sibylla see H.W. Parke, *GRBS* 25 (1984) 224-232, and his *Sibyls and Sibylline Prophecy in Classical Antiquity* (London, 1988).

83-84 On Themistocles' death, and on why bull's blood was thought deadly (because of the rapidity with which it coagulates), see now J.L. Marr, *G&R* 42 (1995) 159-167; he suggests that the suicide story originated as an attempt by Themistocles' sons, after their recall to Athens, to give their father (who had been condemned *in absentia* for treason) a heroic end.

*100 **with little plans and thoughts and ideas:** possibly a surprise substitute for "with piss"; cf. 400, and see Kraus, *Aristophanes' politische Komödien* 107.

*122 **that's in the oracles, "pour me another":** part of the joke is that Demosthenes is reading the oracle-text silently but Nicias thinks he is reading it aloud: on silent reading see B.M.W. Knox, *GRBS* 9 (1968) 421-435; A.K. Gavrilov, *CQ* 47 (1997) 56-73; and M.F. Burnyeat, *ibid.* 74-76. J. Svenbro in J.J. Winkler and F.I. Zeitlin ed. *Nothing to do with Dionysos?* (Princeton, 1990) 367 argues that our passage shows that in the 420s silent reading was still "not familiar to everybody", but such an inference is unjustified: reading aloud, even to oneself, continued to be a common practice throughout antiquity, and it was therefore always possible, when someone was overheard speaking while perusing a text, for the overhearer to make the mistake that Nicias makes here.

129 For Eucrates the bran-seller, hemp-seller, and "hog from Melite", cf. also Ar. fr. 149, Cratinus fr. 339, Hesychius μ728.

143 On the Sausage-seller's occupation, and the whole theme of food (especially meat and offal) preparation in this play, see J. Wilkins in Jocelyn ed. *Tria Lustra* 119-126.

*147 **by the grace of god:** spoken more truly than he knows; cf. 903, 1338.

179 For "a man" = "a man of worth" cf. also Dem. 19.265.

191 An occurrence of [*dēm*]*agōgos* in *P.Heid.* 182.a.4, seemingly a fifth-century political tract, may possibly be earlier than this. It is doubtful whether the word was ever "not ... in itself pejorative"; outside comedy, no one ever uses it in reference to himself or to a political ally.

197, 204 Most mss. read not *ankulokhēlēs* "crook-taloned" but *ankukokheilēs* "hook-beaked"
(lit. "with crooked lips") as in *Odyssey* 19.538; "crook-taloned", however, is required
here in view of 205.

214-5 For valuable discussions, from various points of view, of the use of the concept of
tarattein/kukān in *Knights*, see L. Edmunds, *AJP* 108 (1987) 233-263; B. Marzullo,
MCr 23-24 (1988/9) 209-221; and M. Heath in G.W. Dobrov ed. *The City as Comedy*
(Chapel Hill NC, 1997) 234-6.

225 In the fourth century the nominal establishment of the Athenian cavalry is known to
have been 1000 (Xen. *Cavalry Commander* 9.3).

231-3 The Cratinus reference is now fr. 228 K-A. S.D. Olson, *CQ* 49 (1999) 320-1, noting
that this "fragment" is not an actual quotation and that Ar. himself never refers to
Cleon's eyebrows, persuasively argues that Cratinus was probably speaking not of
Cleon's *appearance* as such but of a terrifying facial *expression* (frown, scowl or sneer)
supposed to be typical of him. Olson is, however, wrong to infer that our passage
"cannot be taken as evidence for the use of portrait-masks": the very fact that Ar. draws
attention to, and explains, the *absence* of a portrait-mask of Cleon is evidence that, for
characters representing well-known contemporaries, portrait-masks were the regular
thing.

242-3 Part of Simon's treatise on horsemanship survives; for a text and French translation, see
E. Delebecque, *Xénophon: de l'art équestre* (Paris, 1950) 155-168. As to Panaetius,
there were *two* men of this name denounced for impiety in 415 (see MacDowell on
Andoc. 1.13), one of them (we do not know which) the son of Polychares of Aphidna
(*IG* i³ 422.204-5); our man could be either (or neither).

248 The general unpopularity of tax-farmers is evidenced by the law empowering the
Council to confine them in the stocks if they failed to hand over to the state, at the
specified time, the sum for which they had contracted (Andoc. 1.92-93); shortly before
400 this penalty was replaced by simple imprisonment (cf. Arist. *Ath.Pol.* 48.1), but
even this put defaulting tax-farmers in the same category as those guilty of treason or of
conspiring against the democracy (Dem. 24.144, 147).

281 On the categories of persons who might be entertained in the Prytaneum, see M.J.
Osborne, *ZPE* 41 (1981) 153-170; Cleon's is the only known case of this honour being
awarded for a military success until it was conferred on Iphicrates in 371/0 (Dem.
23.130, 136, D.H. *Lys.* 12).

300, 301-2 On *phasis* see now D.M. MacDowell in M. Gagarin ed., *Symposium 1990: Papers
on Greek and Hellenistic Legal History* (Vienna, 1991) 187-198. The procedure was
initiated by "pointing out some object or property with which an offence had been
committed". It seems likely that down to the 390s at least all *phasis* cases were tried by
the Council (cf. Isoc. 17.42, 18.6), which accounts for the mention of the Prytaneis in
Knights 300; later the procedure seems to have been assimilated to that for other types
of prosecution, but the successful prosecutor continued to receive half the proceeds of
confiscation. In our passage, MacDowell (p.191) thinks the tripe is supposed to come
from sacrificed animals; "it is known that payments were made to a sacred treasury for
the hides from sacrificed animals", and here a comic *sūkophantēs* assumes that the same
is true of their intestines.

*303-460 constitutes a formal epirrhematic *agōn*, the first of two in the play, but a peculiarly
chaotic one. The *ōdē* (303-332) and *antōdē* (382-406) are both interrupted by

altercations (in trochaic tetrameters) between the contestants; the couplet 407-8 has the form but not the content of an *antikatakeleusmos*; when the *epirrhēmata* begin (335 and 409 respectively) the antagonist each time breaks in after a line or two; and uniquely, the contestant who begins the first *epirrhēma* (the Sausage-seller, at 335 — though Paphlagon, jumping the gun, had actually been the first contestant to speak, at 314) wins the contest, though only by physical force (451-6). This analysis is based on, but in some respects goes beyond, that of M.E. Aria, *The Dynamics of Form and Genre in Aristophanic Comedy* (Diss. Columbia 1997) 196ff.

327 On Hippodamus and Archeptolemus see now P. Benvenuti Falcini, *Ippodamo di Mileto architetto e filosofo* (Florence, 1982).

336 F. Ademollo, *Atene e Roma* 39 (1994) 173-5, sees Paphlagon's *au* as referring back to 315, where the Sausage-seller had interrupted him almost as soon as he had begun to speak; Paphlagon has not spoken since, and now in effect complains that he has been "interrupted" again *before* he has had a chance to start speaking.

362 On the Laurium mines see R.J. Hopper, *ABSA* 48 (1953) 200-254; *G&R* 8 (1961) 138-151 (a good introduction); *ABSA* 63 (1968) 293-326; and R.G. Osborne, *Demos: The Discovery of Classical Attika* (Cambridge, 1985) 111-126. It was only the underground resources themselves that were treated as state property; the land above them was owned by individuals, to whom the mine-lessees may have had to pay a rent in addition to the price they paid to the state for the lease (see Osborne *op.cit.* 118). The highest known price for a lease is now 17,550 dr. (*SEG* xvi 126.15).

394 In view of the law cited in Lys. 10.16 and Dem. 24.105 (cf. also the story of Hegesistratus in Hdt. 9.37), it is likely that "the wood" was a generic term which covered *both* the five-holed frame (designed for punishment and degradation) *and* a one-holed ankle clamp (designed primarily as an anti-escape device; sometimes used to restrain slaves if it was feared they might run away while unsupervised, cf. Dem. 18.129). See V.J. Hunter, *Phoenix* 51 (1997) 310-1 (who discusses the ankle clamp only).

407 The reference to Arist. *Ath.Pol.* 51.3 (written at a time when some of the duties of the corn-controllers had been transferred to other officials) should be supplemented by references to Lys. 22 *passim* and to a currency law of 375/4 published in *Hesperia* 43 (1974) 157-188 (at lines 18-23).

410 My note did not explain the relevance of sacrificial meats (Greek *splankhna*, properly the liver, kidneys, heart, etc., of a sacrificial animal, which were roasted over the altar fire and partaken of by all present at the sacrifice with the god also being given a share). The best explanation of the phrase is to suppose that a sacrifice was offered to Zeus Agoraios before meetings of the Assembly, so that "to share the sacrificial meats of Zeus Agoraios" means in effect "to take part in the proceedings of the Assembly"; see H.A. Thompson, *Hesperia* 21 (1952) 93.

416 See Addenda to comm. on *Ach.* 907.

448 The charge of being the grandson of a tyrant's "spear-bearer" seems to have been made against the speechwriter and oligarch Antiphon at his trial for treason in 411 (cf. Ant. fr. 1).

449 Myrrhine probably owed her place in Athenian folk-memory chiefly to the fact that at some time subsequent to her husband's expulsion she was assassinated: her killers were rewarded with Athenian citizenship and (probably) a gift of land on Salamis (see the

Patmos scholia to Dem. 23.71 [*BCH* 1 (1877) 138] and R. Parker, *Miasma* [Oxford, 1983] 368-9).

517 This is the earliest known, and quite possibly the very first, occurrence of the trope whereby the relationship between an artist and his art was spoken of in sexual terms; I discuss this in my contribution to E.J. Stafford and J. Herrin ed. *Personification in the Greek World* (forthcoming).

522 An alternative (and possibly better) interpretation is that the actions of the persons in Magnes' plays (characters or chorus or both) are being ascribed to the author; cf. *Frogs* 13-15 where Phrynichus, Lycis and Ameipsias are said to "carry luggage" in their plays, meaning that they often have scenes featuring luggage-carrying slaves.

526-8 Cratinus in his *Wine-flask*, produced just over a year later, in which he made himself a character, adapted this description of his poetry in a passage (fr. 198) where someone compares his eloquence to a multiple fountain or to a river which, unless dammed, "will flood the whole place with poetry". He also accused Ar. of plagiarism (fr. 213)!

532-3 The words can also be taken literally as referring to Cratinus' physical state: "his pegs/studs (teeth) are falling out, his strength is gone, and his frame is sagging". Cf. Epicrates fr. 3.15 (of the ageing courtesan Lais) "she is loose in the joints [*harmoniai*, the same word as here] of her body".

534 On Connus see R.P. Winnington-Ingram in B. Gentili and R. Pretagostini ed. *La musica in Grecia* (Rome/Bari, 1988) 246-263. There were no musical contests at the Olympic Games, so either "Olympic" is an error by the scholiast for e.g. "Pythian", or else Connus' withered garland is to be explained in some other way (e.g. as the one he had worn on the last occasion, a long time ago, when he had had the opportunity of performing at a public festival).

547 After "with ... eleven oars", *Lēnaïtēn* "Lenaean" probably puns on *naïtēn* "nautical"; nautical themes constantly recur in this parabasis (cf. 542-4, 554-5, 559-564, 567, 598-610) and elsewhere in the play. See K.J. Reckford, *Aristophanes' Old-and-New Comedy* (Chapel Hill NC, 1987) 128-9.

562 Phormio's deme was probably Paeania (cf. Paus. 1.23.10); his death can be more precisely placed in the spring of 428 (cf. Thuc. 2.103).

566 For "the annual festival of the Panathenaea" read "the quadrennial festival of the Great Panathenaea"; see T.L. Shear, *Hesperia* Suppl. 17 (1978) 36 n.89.

567 The phrase is not necessarily "of a poetic cast"; cf. *IG* i³ 365.30.

580 In support of the suggestion that *stlengis* here means some kind of head-dress, D.M. MacDowell, *Aristophanes and Athens* (Oxford, 1995) 94 n.29 compares the circlets worn by the horsemen in the procession on the Parthenon frieze.

*586-9 bringing ... Victory: "when Athena is asked to bring Nike with her, every contemporary spectator must have thought of the cult-image of Athena Parthenos (cf. also 1169f), who was represented with Nike in her hand" (Zimmermann ii 208).

608 S. Halliwell, *LCM* 7 (1982) 153, rightly points out the relevance of *PMG* 892, the only other passage in archaic or classical Greek literature which purports to quote the words of a crab: "This is what the crab said when he seized the snake with his claw: 'A friend should be straight and not think crooked thoughts'." Thus in the words ascribed to Theorus two well-known drinking-songs are blended — with the implication that Theorus is a crook and/or a treacherous friend (cf. *Wasps* 1241-2).

*624-682 In a play which consists almost entirely of altercation, this and Demosthenes' exposition-speech at the start (40-72) are the only two set speeches (other than those by the chorus-leader in the two parabases) of any significant length (the next longest, also by the Sausage-seller, is of only 11 lines [847-857]). The opportunity to make it only arises because, here and here alone between 235 and 1252, one of the two main characters is absent; and even so, it proves to be largely a report of yet another slanging match between the Sausage-seller and Paphlagon, containing within itself verbatim quotations from five different speeches and reports of, or explicit references to, four more. See Aria *op.cit.* 232-3.

639 The idea of the auspicious fart comes from *h.Hom.Herm.* 294-7 where a deliberate fart by the baby Hermes is called an omen (*oiōnos*): see J.T. Katz, *CQ* 49 (1999) 315-9.

*648 in strict secrecy: compare the account in *Hell.Oxy.* 6.1 of how, in 396, Demaenetus, "having communicated his plan secretly to the Council", attempted to establish contact with Conon and the Persians with a view to forming an alliance with them against Sparta, "without the sanction of the people": when his action became public knowledge, the Council claimed to have had nothing to do with it.

697 On the *mothōn* see further L.B. Lawler, *TAPA* 75 (1944) 31-33.

732 By calling himself Demos' "lover", Paphlagon casts himself as sexually aggressive and dominant (cf. 352, 355) and allots the passive role in the relationship to Demos; at the end of the play this will be reversed as Demos is presented with one boy and two or three girls for his use and pleasure (1384-94) while Paphlagon is consigned to the haunts of prostitutes (1400-3). On the paradoxical portrayal in this play of the politician as simultaneously slave, friend, flatterer and lover of the people, and its implications, see further A. Scholtz, *Erastes tou demou: Erotic Imagery in Political Contexts in Thucydides and Aristophanes* (Diss. Yale 1997) ch.5. The idea that the good citizen is "in love" with his community was probably a favourite with Pericles (cf. Thuc. 2.43.1) and goes back at least as far as 458 (cf. Aesch. *Eum.* 852).

759 The language used here about Paphlagon recalls descriptions of Prometheus in [Aesch.] *Prom.*; he is called "artful" (*poikilos*) in *Prom.* 308 and "clever at finding resources (*poros*) in impossible situations (*amēkhana*)" *ibid.* 59. Cf. comm. on 836.

774 Alternatively or additionally, Paphlagon-Cleon may mean that as a councillor he had been active in promoting prosecutions by way of *eisangelia* (see Introductory Note to *Acharnians*); cf. Lys. 30.22 "When the Council is in financial difficulties, it is compelled to accept *eisangeliai*, confiscate citizens' property, and follow the advice of those orators who make the basest proposals".

786 Davies' identification of Cleon's wife has been challenged by F. Bourriot, *Historia* 31 (1982) 404-435. There was, however, another connection between Cleon and Harmodius: the nearest living kinsman of Harmodius (and likewise of Aristogeiton) was entitled to maintenance in the Prytaneum (*IG* i³ 131.5-7), the same honour that had recently and controversially been awarded to Cleon.

830 In lemma, for "hand" read "oar".

835 Another possibility is that the sum of forty minas is mentioned because this is the precise amount that Cleon had accused Diodotus of having received from the Mytileneans in 427. I owe this suggestion to a student, Alex Firth.

*852-7 H. Lind, *Der Gerber Kleon in den Rittern des Aristophanes* (Frankfurt, 1990) 94-131, gives a brilliant topographical interpretation of this passage. There are known to have been tanneries in Cleon's deme of Cydathenaeum (*IG* ii^2 1556.34-5, 1576.5-6), almost certainly beside the Eridanus stream (since leather-making requires a good supply of water, and at all times and places has normally been carried on near streams or rivers). This stream flowed past the north end of the Agora directly adjacent to the Stoa Poikile (cf. T.L. Shear, *Hesperia* 53 [1984] 1-19); in this area, then (probably to the east of the Stoa), the leather, honey and cheese sellers were concentrated. There is evidence too that at ostracisms (855) the votes were collected and counted in an area called the Perischoinisma which also lay at the north end of the Agora (cf. Pollux 8.20; Alciphron *Ep.* 2.3.11; Paus. 1.8.4; [Plut.] *Lives of the Ten Orators* 847a). And the main corn-market was in the Stoa Alphitopolis which may (cf. *Eccl.* 684-6 — though see comm. on that passage) have lain near the Stoa Basileios at the north-west of the Agora. Hence all the key points referred to were within a stone's throw of the tanning district, if this lay along the Eridanus a little to the east of the Stoa Poikile (i.e. roughly along the line of the present Adrianou Street eastward of Aghiou Philippou). A deme decree found in 1938 close to Aghiou Philippou, and published in 1997 as *Agora* xvi 68, makes it likely that the deme of Cydathenaeum extended this far to the west.

852-3 For other explicit or implicit references to factions sitting together in blocks in Assembly, Council and courts, see P.J. Rhodes, *JHS* 106 (1986) 139.

855 On "the potsherd game" cf. also Pl. *Phdr.* 241b. Ar. was probably not the first to speak jocularly of ostracism in terms of this game. In the game, a player who was caught had to sit down and was called *onos* "donkey" (Pollux 9.112), and a surviving ostracism ballot is inscribed "Agasias son of Phanomachus is a donkey"; see P.J. Bicknell, *ZPE* 62 (1986) 183-4.

862 Cf. [Dem.] 25.64 "He shouts at every meeting of the Assembly 'I alone am loyal to you; all these others are in a conspiracy; you have been betrayed; my loyalty is your only hope". The portrait of the politician Aristogeiton painted in that speech has several other features in common with the Aristophanic Cleon (e.g. [Dem.] 25.40 "some folk say he's the People's watchdog", cf. 1014-35).

892 This is, surprisingly, the last reference in the play to Paphlagon's trade as a tanner (Lind, *Der Gerber Kleon* 73).

901 Pyrrhander may have been the grandfather of Pyrrhander of Anaphlystus (born before c.410, died after 330), who was active in the formation of the Second Athenian League and the alliance with Thebes in 378/7 (Tod 121, 123, 124) and was a respected elder statesman in 346 (Aeschines 1.84).

908 "The first hint of rejuvenation", to be sure, but also a classic piece of toadyism (*kolakeia*); cf. Ar. fr. 416, 689, and especially the behaviour of Theophrastus' Flatterer (*Char.* 2.3) who "picks a flock of wool off his patron's cloak, and if a bit of chaff is blown on to the top of the man's head, plucks it off, laughs and says 'You see? You've got a beard full of grey hairs just because I haven't met you for two days'" (*pretending*, that is, that the chaff is a grey hair from his beard).

925-6 The theory that fourth-century *eisphorai* were "levied on a progressive basis" was long ago disproved by G.E.M. de Ste Croix, *C&M* 14 (1953) 30-70. In our passage "the rich" are not those who pay *eisphorai* at a specially high rate, but simply those who are rich enough to be assessed for it at all, in contrast with the majority who are not (cf. Lys. 27.10, [Dem.] 10.37).

941-2 For the threefold oath "by Zeus, Apollo and Demeter", cf. [Dem.] 52.9.

958 See Addenda to comm. on *Ach.* 88.

964 The reference is probably not to circumcision but to adhesion of the foreskin; see comm. on *Wealth* 267.

969 The councillor Smicythus cannot be proved to have served in 427/6, and the secretary of 424/3 could equally well have been called Smicythion (D.M. Lewis, *CR* 33 [1983] 176); it is better to admit that, if the scholia are right in their interpretation of the passage, we cannot identify the man concerned.

979 "The place where notices of impending lawsuits were displayed" was probably the monument of the *eponūmoi* (the heroes who gave their names to the ten tribes) in the Agora; cf. Dem. 21.103 and see T.L. Shear, *Hesperia* 39 (1970) 145, 203-4. In Eubulus fr. 74 a list of goods for sale "all in the same place" at Athens (i.e. the Agora) is composed partly of foodstuffs, flowers, etc., and partly of items like lawsuits, witnesses and indictments.

989-990 See now M.L. West, *Ancient Greek Music* (Oxford, 1992) 172-184, esp. 174-5 and 179-180.

*997-1099 On this "*agōn* of oracles" see E. Suárez de la Torre in López Férez ed. *La comedia griega ...* 191-4.

1038 The line alludes to an Aesopic fable (255 Perry) in which a gnat challenged a lion to single combat, and the lion, vainly trying to lay hold on the gnat, succeeded only in injuring himself and eventually had to admit defeat. Paphlagon clearly does not remember the story very well!

1053 For another play on the ambiguity of *korakīnos* cf. Ar. fr. 550.

1056 The last sentence of my note is far-fetched and should be deleted; for a better interpretation of the *Little Iliad* line see A.D.Fitton Brown, *LCM* 9 (1984) 72.

1085 Diopeithes may be the man described in Eupolis fr. 264 (from *Prospaltioi*, produced in 429) as "lame in one hand".

*1095 ambrosia: the food of the gods, which can confer immortality: cf. *h.Hom.Dem.* 235-242, Pind. *Pyth.* 9.63, Theocr. 15.106-8, Ap.Rh. 4.871. See C.A. Anderson, *TAPA* 121 (1991) 152-3.

1099 The same Sophoclean line is parodied, but with Cleon as the subject, in *com.adesp.* 740 ("being the guide and counsellor of their old age, and giving them fresh opportunities to earn pay").

1119-20 The expression "present and yet absent" was proverbial, cf. Heraclitus fr. 34 D-K.

1185 F. Salviat, *Archaeonautica* 2 (1978) 259-260, plausibly linked *enteroneia* with *entorneia* "rail, gunwale" (better perhaps "frame-timbers" of a ship; see S. Amigues, *RA* [1990] 92-96), which is found in a papyrus letter of early Ptolemaic date (*Chronique d'Égypte* 24 [1949] 289-290) and may be restored by conjecture in Thphr. *HP* 5.7.3. Ar.'s *enteroneia* will be a pun on this technical term.

1225 S. Halliwell, *GRBS* 30 (1989) 523-4, thinks that the evidence of the Cratinus and Eupolis fragments, taken together with other scattered evidence on collaboration between comic dramatists in the 420s, is sufficient to justify the hypothesis that Eupolis made a substantial contribution to *Knights*. The only such evidence that I find cogent is a detail on which Halliwell (524 n.17) curiously puts no weight at all: that in the course of his attack on Eupolis (*Clouds* 554) Ar. refers to *Knights* as "our" play — a very careless thing to do, unless it was designed as a tacit admission that there *had* been collaboration.

1246 Lind, *Der Gerber Kleon* 175-184 shows that the reference is probably to one specific gate, the Sacred Gate, which stood just west of the Dipylon Gate and about 150 metres east of where the Cerameicus Museum now stands. This gate was the most convenient for travellers to and from the Peiraeus (the "foreigners" of 1408), and the outer Cerameicus, into which it led, was a notorious haunt of prostitutes (cf. Alexis fr. 206; Luc. *Dialogues of Courtesans* 4.2; Alciphron *Ep.* 3.12.3). Parts of a building adjacent to this gate have been identified as brothels (U. Knigge, *AA* 1980:265, 1981:387-8, 1983:212; Davidson 84-86), and there was a circular bathing-place (cf. 1401) outside the walls between it and the Dipylon (cf. Isaeus fr. 21 Thalheim).

*1248 Ah me, fulfilled is the god's oracle: a quotation from Sophocles (fr. 885a).

1249 possibly comes from *Stheneboea* (parodying Eur. fr. 671.1) rather than *Bellerophon*: see A.C. Clark, *Euripides in a Comic Mirror: The Tragodoumenai* (Diss. U. of N. Carolina 1998) 74 n.59.

1250-2 There may also be a reminiscence of Sappho fr. 94.5-7 ("'Sappho, truly I leave you against my will' ... 'Depart in peace, and remember me'"); see Kugelmeier 159.

1277 P. Totaro, *Eikasmos* 2 (1991) 153-7 (see now also Totaro, *Le seconde parabasi di Aristofane* [Stuttgart, 1999] 40-43, 94-97), points out some features in this passage and *Wasps* 1277-8 suggesting that the compliments to Arignotus are to be taken ironically and that he is really being accused of passive homosexuality: (1) the *Wasps* phrases "dear to everyone" and "on whom delight attends" can be interpreted in that way (cf. Henderson[2] 160 and the hetaira-name Pasiphile in [Archil.] fr. 331); (2) *Eq* 1279 suggests that Arignotus is white-skinned like a woman (cf. *Thesm.* 191; see Henderson *op.cit.* 211), and *leukon* is followed by the suggestive *orth-ion* (cf. Henderson *op.cit.* 112).

1286 The second sentence of my note should be deleted.

1287 The explanation for the sudden mention of Polymnestus and Oeonichus may be that Ar. has abruptly changed the subject and is now criticizing, not Ariphrades' morals, but his music, which is (he suggests) equally bad (or perhaps old-fashioned).

1300 Just as *Acharnians* (7-8, 299-302) contains foreshadowings of *Knights*, so the personification of the triremes here may be seen as a kind of preliminary sketch for Ar.'s *Merchant Ships*, produced twelve months later.

1302 According to the scholia this line comes from Euripides' *Alcmeon* (fr. 66); it will have been an adaptation rather than a quotation.

1304, 1363 See Addenda to comm. on *Ach.* 846.

1310 For pine as ship-timber, cf. Eur. *Med.* 4, *Andr.* 863-4, *Hel.* 241, and see J.S. Morrison and J.F. Coates, *The Athenian Trireme* (Cambridge, 1986) 180-191.

1312 The Theseum, like the Prytaneum (see Addenda to comm. on *Ach.* 125), is now considered by many to have lain below the east end of the Acropolis; see G.S. Dontas, *Hesperia* 52 (1983) 62 n.42. On its role as a "slave refuge" see K.A. Christensen, *AJAH* 9 (1984 [1988]) 23-32.

1321 On the rejuvenation (for such it is) of Demos see S.D. Olson, *Eranos* 88 (1990) 60-63 and R.E. Harder, *Prometheus* 23 (1997) 108-118, who also emphasizes (i) the appropriateness of the method in a play where cookery has been so prominent a theme, (ii) the transformation of Demos from an (inappropriately) old *eromenos* (732-748) into a vigorous *erastes*, and (iii) his new-found ability to think for himself (1357-83) rather than merely assenting to whatever the favourite of the moment may propose.

1327-8 I should have noted that my proposals about the use of the *ekkyklēma* here and at 1249 were anticipated, with a few differences, by S. Srebrny, *Studia Scaenica* (Wrocław, 1960) 87-89.

1331 On the cicada brooch see especially A. Rumpf in *Symbola Coloniensia Iosepho Kroll ... oblata* (Cologne, 1949) 85-99.

1359 The speaker of Lys. 27 does not actually use the "crude argument"; rather, he asserts that the defendants have often used it in cases where *they* were prosecuting.

1370 It seems that in the fifth and early fourth centuries conscription lists for military expeditions were not drawn up on the basis of age; rather, *ad hoc* lists were made by the generals, with those who had not recently served being taken first; cf. Thuc. 6.26.2, 6.31.3, Lys. 9.4, 9.15, Aeschines 2.168, and see A. Andrewes in G.S. Shrimpton and D.J. McCargar ed. *Classical Contributions: Studies in Honor of Malcolm Francis McGregor* (Locust Valley NY, 1981) 1-3. Hence "another list" here will mean either (as my note suggested) the roll of the cavalry, or the roll for the less dangerous of two expeditions being sent out at the same time.

1382 To references add Xen. *Cyr.* 8.1.34-38. The combination in 1382-7 of hunting, luxurious living and pederasty suggests that Demos is henceforth going to adopt a lifestyle previously associated with the class to which the Knights belong.

1399 It can hardly be a coincidence, given that Paphlagon is being sent to a haunt of prostitutes, that both *kūon* "dog" and *prāgma* "thing" could denote either the male or the female genitals (donkeys, be it noted, are notoriously well endowed as far as the former are concerned) — see Henderson, *The Maculate Muse* 116, 127 (male) and 133, 134 (female) — and that *meignunai* "mix" could mean "cause to unite sexually" (cf. comm. on *Frogs* 944).

1405 Add references to W. Burkert, *Structure and History in Greek Mythology and Ritual* (Berkeley, 1979) ch.3 and *Greek Religion* (Eng.tr. Oxford, 1985) 82-84), and J.N. Bremmer, *HSCP* 87 (1983) 299-320.

1406 The scholia, and the inscription cited, suggest that this robe (the *batrachis*) was often richly decorated, perhaps with floral patterns, and L.J. Bennett and W.B. Tyrrell, *Arethusa* 23 (1990) 251, perceive the Sausage-seller as thus "transformed ... into an embodiment of fertility and reawakening of life symbolized by the flowers of the green meadow", and contrast this image of springtime with the withered autumnal *eiresiōnē* that fell to the ground at 729.

CLOUDS

Introductory Note
page
2   *it was placed third and last:* the failure of *Clouds* is convincingly explained by M.
Hose, *Drama* 3 (1995) 27-50, as being due to its sharp deviation from the normal
patterns of contemporary comedy, which Hose describes, on the basis of Ar.'s other
plays of the 420s, as embodying the triumph of a representative of the Athenian ideal
over a flawed reality. In *Clouds* no one represents the Athenian ideal, and the
dénouement is typically *tragic.*

2 n.1 Against the attempt by E.C. Kopff, *AJP* 111 (1990) 318-329, to downdate the revision
to c.414, see J.J. Henderson in R.M. Rosen and J.J. Farrell ed. *Nomodeiktes: Greek
Studies in Honor of Martin Ostwald* (Ann Arbor, 1993) 591-601. I have argued in P.
Thiercy and M. Menu ed. *Aristophane: la langue, la scène, la cité*(Bari, 1997) 276 n.22
that the new parabasis, which assumes (534-6) that mention of Electra will call
Aeschylus to mind rather than Sophocles or Euripides, must have been written between
Dionysia 419 and Dionysia 417 and most likely in the first twelve of those twenty-four
months.

2 n.3 Eupolis' *Baptai* does not directly give a *terminus ante quem* for the revision of *Clouds*,
since it is probably responding not to *Clouds* but to *Anagyrus* (Ar. fr. 58).

2   *"making the worse argument into the better":* O. Imperio in A.M. Belardinelli et al.
Tessere. Frammenti della commedia greca: studi e commenti (Bari, 1998) 43-130, at
101-2, points out that the basic idea of *Clouds* was already present in a comedy of
Epicharmus (Epich. fr. 170; cf. Plut. *Mor.* 559b) which included (i) a man seeking to
evade his debts with the help of a philosophical argument (that according to Heraclitus
everything is in flux, therefore he is not the same man who borrowed the money), (ii)
this man then being beaten up (by his creditor) and the assailant then avoiding
punishment by exploiting (the same) philosophical argument, and (iii) a debate between
a Heraclitean and an anti-Heraclitean.

2 n.4 On the portrayal of intellectuals in comedy, see B. Zimmermann (and discussants) in
EH 38 (1993) 255-286, Imperio *op.cit.*, and C. Carey in F.D. Harvey and J. Wilkins ed.
The Rivals of Aristophanes (London/Swansea, 2000) 419-436. Carey notes (pp.427-
431) that there is little sign that Old Comic dramatists other than Aristophanes took
much interest in the major rationalist thinkers of their day, other than Socrates and to
some extent Protagoras, and that they, and presumably their audiences, seem to have
been more interested in the allegedly parasitic role of intellectuals in society (cf. *Clouds*
331-4) than in their innovative ideas. This "avoidance of sustained engagement with the
intellectual content of contemporary thought by [other] comic poets suggests that
Aristophanes was taking a calculated risk in offering his audience [in *Clouds*] a play
with so much intellectual meat. ... *Clouds* may have failed in part because it was too
much concerned with ideas in which the audience had little interest" (Carey *op.cit.* 431).

3   *their dupe Strepsiades:* A. Grilli, *Inganni d'autore: due studi sulla funzione del
protagonista nel teatro di Aristofane* (Pisa, 1992) contains a valuable discussion of the
presentation of Strepsiades in *Clouds*. He regards Strepsiades, not Socrates, as the

centre of interest in the play, holding that the immorality of the sophists, being axiomatic in Old Comedy, is not so much asserted as assumed. Strepsiades differs from all normal Aristophanic heroes (1) in his weakness, passivity, and ineffectiveness, and (2) in explicitly accepting the immorality of his own project; once this begins to become apparent (from somewhere between 73 and 98-99), there are only two subsequent scenes in which he regains some heroic traits, viz. the creditor-scene and the (new) ending.

3   *the unfair image of Socrates created by comedy:* Guidorizzi on 223ff, analysing Ar.'s image of Socrates, sees it as having been compounded from five elements: the priest of an exotic mystery religion (see comm. on 140); a Pythagorean ascetic; an atheistic scientist; a sophist teaching grammar; and, to an uncertain extent, the real Socrates. To these one should surely add, as a sixth element, a teacher of rhetoric (such as Antiphon).

3   *this prejudice is more dangerous to him:* the "indictment" brought against Socrates by this "first set of accusers", which he states twice *in extenso* (*Apol.* 18b, 19b-c) each time with a reference to comedy (18d, 19c), contains precisely the main elements of the portrayal of Socrates in *Clouds* ("studying things below the earth and in the sky, and making the weaker argument into the stronger, and instructing other people in these same things", 19b-c tr. M.C. Stokes) with the exception of his rejection of the traditional gods in favour of the Clouds and other novel deities, which for obvious reasons it does not suit the Platonic Socrates to highlight at this stage of his defence.

4   *revised in details:* better "partly revised"; see R.K. Fisher, *Aristophanes' Clouds: Purpose and Technique* (Amsterdam, 1984) 23 n.16.

4 n.10 I.C. Storey, *AJP* 114 (1993) 71-84, seeks to identify other elements in the surviving text which belong to 423 rather than later. His conclusion is that except as noted by the ancient commentators, revision had not progressed far and the play was a long way from being ready for restaging. In Thiercy & Menu ed. *Aristophane* 269-282, I argue that in the original play Strepsiades was not present during the *agōn*; that 1105-14 were inserted as part of the revision; and (in agreement with Storey) that outside the sections now represented by 518-562, 886-948, 1105-1115 and 1437-end there were few if any substantial changes (only one fragment of the first *Clouds*, viz. Ar. fr. 392, seems to come from outside these sections, and that may be wrongly attributed). For other recent views on the extent and nature of the revision, see H. Tarrant, *Arctos* 25 (1991) 157-181; MacDowell 134-149 (whose reconstruction of the original ending ignores the attested presence in the first *Clouds* of part of what is now line 1417); and A. Casanova, *Prometheus* 26 (2000) 19-34.

Bibliography

Editions: W.J.M. Starkie (London, 1911); K.J. Dover (Oxford, 1968); G. Guidorizzi and D. Del Corno (Milan, 1996).

Books and articles

C.P. Segal, "Aristophanes' cloud-chorus", *Arethusa* 2 (1969) 143-161. Reprinted in H.J. Newiger ed. *Aristophanes und die alte Komödie* (Darmstadt, 1975) 174-197, and in E. Segal ed. *Oxford Readings in Aristophanes* (Oxford, 1996) 162-181.

A.W.H. Adkins, "Clouds, mysteries, Socrates and Plato", *Antichthon* 4 (1970) 13-24.

E.A. Havelock, "The Socratic self as it is parodied in Aristophanes' *Clouds*", *YCS* 22 (1972) 1-18.

K.J. Reckford, "Father-beating in Aristophanes' *Clouds*", in S. Bertman ed. *The Conflict of Generations in Ancient Greece and Rome* (Amsterdam, 1976) 89-118.

P. Green, "Strepsiades, Socrates and the abuses of intellectualism", *GRBS* 20 (1979) 15-25.

M.C. Nussbaum, "Aristophanes and Socrates on learning practical wisdom", *YCS* 26 (1980) 43-97.

J. Hanus, "The gods in the *Clouds*", *Graecolatina Pragensia* 8 (1980) 11-23.

L. Woodbury, "Strepsiades' understanding: five notes on the *Clouds*", *Phoenix* 34 (1980) 108-127.

D. Ambrosino, "Nuages et sens: autour des *Nuées* d'Aristophane", *QSt* 18 (1983) 3-60.

R.K. Fisher, *Aristophanes' Clouds: Purpose and Technique* (Amsterdam, 1984).

R.K. Fisher, "The relevance of Aristophanes: a new look at *Clouds*", *G&R* 35 (1988) 23-28.

T.K. Hubbard, *The Mask of Comedy* (Ithaca NY, 1991) ch.5.

A. Grilli, *Inganni d'autore: due studi sulla funzione del protagonista nel teatro di Aristofane* (Pisa, 1992)

M.C. Marianetti, *Religion and Politics in Aristophanes' Clouds* (Hildesheim, 1992).

D.E. O'Regan, *Rhetoric, Comedy and the Violence of Language in Aristophanes' Clouds* (New York, 1992).

E.G. Csapo, "Deep ambivalence: notes on a Greek cockfight", *Phoenix* 47 (1993) 1-28, 115-124.

I.C. Storey, "The date of Aristophanes' *Clouds II* and Eupolis' *Baptai*: a reply to E.C. Kopff", *AJP* 114 (1993) 71-84.

J.J. Henderson, "Problems in Greek literary history: the case of Aristophanes' *Clouds*", in R.M. Rosen and J. Farrell ed. *Nomodeiktes: Greek Studies in Honor of Martin Ostwald* (Ann Arbor, 1993) 591-601.

S.D. Olson, "*Clouds* 537-44 and the original version of the play", *Philologus* 138 (1994) 32-37.

P. Vander Waerdt, "Socrates in the *Clouds*", in Vander Waerdt ed. *The Socratic Movement* (Ithaca NY, 1994) 48-86.

M. Hose, "Der aristophanische Held", *Drama* 3 (1995) 27-50.

R. Janko, "The physicist as hierophant: Aristophanes, Socrates and the authorship of the Derveni-papyrus", *ZPE* 118 (1997) 61-94.

R.M. Rosen, "Performance and textuality in Aristophanes' *Clouds*", *Yale Journal of Criticism* 10 (1997) 397-421.

A.H. Sommerstein, "The silence of Strepsiades and the *agon* of the first *Clouds*", in P. Thiercy and M. Menu ed. *Aristophane: la langue, la scène, la cité* (Bari, 1997) 269-282.

O. Imperio, "La figura dell'intellettuale nella commedia greca", in A.M. Belardinelli et al. *Tessere. Frammenti della commedia greca: studi e commenti* (Bari, 1998) 43-130, esp. 99-120.

A. Casanova, "La revisione delle *Nuvole* di Aristofane", *Prometheus* 26 (2000) 19-34.

C. Carey, "Old Comedy and the sophists", in F.D. Harvey and J. Wilkins ed. *The Rivals of Aristophanes* (London/Swansea, 2000) 419-436.

Note on the Text
page

5 n.1 Another papyrus not cited in the apparatus is Π65 (Rainer Papyrus III 20), a fragment of a commentary on *Clouds* 186-211, incorporating a few words of the text.

Table of Sigla
page

6 U should be dated "late 13th": L. Battezzato, *Prometheus* 22 (1996) 29-34, has shown that it was produced in the same environment, and probably close to the same time, as Φ (Laurentianus *conv. soppr.* 66), whose date is now known (see K. Matthiessen, *Scriptorium* 36 [1982] 255-8) to be 1291.

Text and Translation
line

1-18 Since at 18 *pai* "boy" is second, not first, word in the sentence, it is *not* being used to call the slave's attention, and therefore, as Thiercy has seen, he must be on stage from the start. Presumably he is asleep (cf. 5); Strepsiades must therefore wake him up with a nudge or kick before speaking to him. His first words to the slave should be rendered "Light a lamp, boy, ...".

35 K.J. Dover, *The Greeks and their Legacy: Collected Papers, Vol. II* (Oxford, 1989) 265, points out that V3 has the true reading in its text (doubtless an emendation made with the help of the scholia).

53-55 Lucian, *On Mourning* 17, shows that Greek *spathān* "weave closely, be extravagant" could also mean, in the middle voice (*spathāsthai*), "spend oneself sexually", and J.J. Henderson, *The Maculate Muse*[2] (New York, 1991) 171-2 sees here a play on this sense: Strepsiades' wife is being extravagant *both* with his money *and* with his sexual energies. This provides a much-needed punch-line (trans. e.g. "You're squandering my resources"); but in order to make it work, the business of displaying the cloak must be so managed as to draw attention not only, or even mainly, to the garment (under which Strepsiades has no doubt been sleeping, or trying to sleep), but to the flaccid phallus that is revealed when the garment is lifted up.

142 In the first hardcover printing this line (ἥκω μαθητὴς εἰς τὸ φροντιστήριον) was accidentally omitted from the text.

172-3 For "gazing open-mouthed at the sky" read "gazing up open-mouthed", and for "eaves" read "ceiling", for the following reasons: (1) "ceiling" (or "roof as viewed from within") is the normal (though not the invariable) meaning of Greek *orophē*; (2) geckos do walk upside down on ceilings (see e.g. H.S. Ngor and R. Warner, *Surviving the Killing Fields: The Cambodian Odyssey of Haing S. Ngor* [London, 1988] 421); (3) a person who went outside to look up at the moon would not stand directly under the eaves of a house; (4) this is how Plato seems to have interpreted the passage, to judge by *Rep.* 7.529a-b where the phrases "decorations on a ceiling" and "gazing up open-mouthed" (*anō kekhēnōs*, the same words used here) appear within a few lines of each other in a discussion of the study of astronomy. Until the end of 172 the story sounds like a little-altered version of that of Thales and the well (see comm.); then, as in 179, the scene suddenly changes, as it turns out that Socrates is conducting his astronomical investigations *indoors* (the preferred space of these pale-faced thinkers). Possibly we are to understand that he is so intent on his thoughts that he has forgotten it is the ceiling, not the sky, above him. The point of "in the dark" is that in a dimly-lit ancient room at night, with any lamp placed relatively low, a small animal high up would be very hard to see (especially if one's mind was elsewhere!).

178-9 The best solution for this crux (see comm.) may well lie in Guidorizzi's suggestion (in his commentary) of a lacuna (presumably after 178).

226 For "wicker cage" read "cheese-rack"; D. Ambrosino, *MCr* 19/20 (1984/5) 51-69, has argued convincingly (i) that this is what Greek *tarros* means here and (ii) that in view of 232-4 it is significant that fresh cheeses were put on racks *to dry out*. Socrates, it may thus be supposed, is standing on a four-cornered rack of stiff wickerwork which hangs by four cords from the hook of the stage crane. (Ambrosino places him on a rack *which stands on the stage-house roof*; but he would then need to go briefly offstage in order to get down to ground level, and 237-9 gives him no time to do so — contrast *Wasps* 155-168, *Lys.* 884-9.)

275-328 On the entrance of the chorus see now P. von Möllendorff in E. Pöhlmann et al. *Studien zur Bühnendichtung und zum Theaterbau der Antike* (Frankfurt, 1995) 147-151; his crucial contribution is to propose (adapting to *Clouds* a suggestion made in relation to *Peace* by P. Thiercy, *Aristophane: fiction et dramaturgie* [Paris, 1986] 127-8) that the actual entrance of the chorus is made, not via a wing-entrance (*eisodos*), but *coming down through the audience area*[4]. This accounts for the mention of Parnes at 323 (for the audience were on the *north* side of the theatre), for the phrase "coming gently down" (323-4), and for the phrase *para tēn eisodon* "by [not 'at' or 'in'] the wing-entrance" at 326. The Clouds may have sung their offstage entry-song behind the stage-house façade (Möllendorff 150), which gives them from 313 to 323 to get round and up to their entry position (in the fourth-century theatre there were steps linking the western *eisodos* and the western spectator entrance, Möllendorff 154 n.40); it may, however, be better to assume that they start this movement earlier and that the antistrophe (whose words must be heard clearly; see comm. on 302-310) is sung near the western *eisodos*.

327 For "unless you've got styes the size of pumpkins" read "unless your eyes are running bottlefuls of rheum"; the *kolokuntē* is the white-flowered bottle-gourd, *Lagenaria vulgaris*, the husk of whose fruit made a handy container for various liquids. Cf. J.L. Heller, *ICS* 10 (1985) 111.

---

4 Möllendorff (150) actually proposes that only *half* the chorus come on by this route, but nothing whatever in the text indicates that the chorus divides in two; *hautai ... hautai* in 324-5 denotes not two different groups (that would be *hautai men ... hautai de*) but one single group.

337 If we read διερᾶς (Reisig) and assume that it is here used as a noun meaning "water, sea" (as its synonym ὑγρά often is: cf. *Wasps* 678, *Iliad* 24.341) we can omit the comma after this word and create a single phrase which may be rendered "the crook-taloned air-floating birds of the airy sea" (so Thiercy): not a very elegant phrase, but it's not meant to be!

340 Read λέξον νύν μοι (K°: probably a variant rather than a supplement), since δή is more likely to be a gloss on νυν than vice versa (this gloss is often added to remind readers that this is the particle νυν and not the temporal adverb νῦν).

385 For "who do you expect to believe that?" read "what reason is there for believing that?"; see D.M. MacDowell, *CR* 33 (1983) 175.

398 For "the age of Cronus" read "the Cronia" (see Addenda to comm. *ad loc.*)

411-427 F.W. Fritzsche, *De fabulis ab Aristophane retractatis III* (Rostock, 1851) 6-7 suggested transposing 423-6 to stand between 411 and 412, which gives a much smoother sequence of thought: having completed his demonstration that the Clouds are the cause of natural phenomena traditionally attributed to Zeus, Socrates asks Strepsiades whether he will henceforth regard them (with Chaos and the Tongue) as the only gods (423-4), and on Strepsiades' assenting to this (425-6) the Clouds invite him to become their pupil if he can accept their discipline (412-9), he assures them he can (420-2), and they then ask him what he wants them to do for him (427-8). The displacement of 423-6 will have been due to the near-homoeoteleuton between 411 and 426 causing the four lines to be omitted, later to be restored to the text in the wrong place.

439 Cobet's deletion of χρήσθων leaves ἀτεχνῶς ὅ τι βούλονται almost without a syntactic construction; better, with Hermann and Guidorizzi, posit a lacuna after νῦν οὖν. Reisig's <οὗτοι> (= the members of the school) is plausible, but <μοὗτοι> would be even better.

509 For "hanging" read "peering".

554 For ἡμετέρας read ἡμετέρους.

561 For εὐφραίνεσθ᾽ read εὐφραίνησθ᾽.

638 E. Degani, *GFF* 11 (1988) 55-56, strongly commends Hermann's conjecture ἢ ῥυθμῶν ἢ περὶ ἐπῶν, which is in keeping with the structure of the passage and the logical relations of the topics, "measures" and "rhythms" (which together form what we would call metrics) being discussed first and in that order (639-645, 647-654) and followed by "words", i.e. grammar (658-693).

The apparatus should read:

> ῥυθμῶν ἢ περὶ ἐπῶν Hermann: περὶ ῥυθμῶν ἢ ἐπῶν ΝΘ: περὶ ἐπῶν ἢ ῥυθμῶν REK: περὶ ἐπῶν ἢ περὶ ῥυθμῶν Longinus *Prolegomena to Hephaestion* 83.19, Choeroboscus *in Heph.* 179.6: ἐπῶν ἢ περὶ ῥυθμῶν V ᵛˡChoeroboscus *loc.cit.*: ῥυθμῶν Choeroboscus *in Heph.* 203.2.

The translation should read: "About measures or rhythms, or about words?"

723-6 The rapid exit and re-entry I posit for Socrates is implausible; more likely he first appears at a window, coming out of the door only at 731 (so Guidorizzi).

740-1 For "slice your thought into minute parts" read "open out your thinking and refine it"; see D.M. MacDowell, *CR* 33 (1983) 175.

819 For τὸν (codd.) read τὸ (Valckenaer): Symmachus (in Σᴱ) seems not to have had an article at all in his text, for he says the second syllable of Δία should be scanned long!

849 The true reading ταὐτό is also in Θ (Dover, *The Greeks and their Legacy* 265).

894 For "I'll defeat you", since the Greek verb is present, read "I can beat you".

953 For the obelized words read ἀμείνων λέγων (Dover); cf. on 1028-9 below.

975 The second and third apparatus citations should read:]νους Π8:]νοις Π8ˢ.

983 For "dainties" read "fancy fish".

995 Henderson (LCL) conjectures οὗ for ὅ τι, retaining μέλλεις and ἀναπλήσειν: the language is strained and probably refers euphemistically to sexual transgressions which this speaker finds too gross to mention.

1005-8 This passage has been discussed by J. Taillardat, *REG* 95.2 (1982) xvi-xviii; E.K. Borthwick, *Nikephoros* 2 (1989) 125-134; and (most convincingly) J. Jouanna, *BCH* 118 (1994) 35-49, who argues that (1) ἀποθρέξει means "you will go for a training run" (cf. Ar. fr. 645); (2) *pace* Taillardat and Borthwick, athletes are occasionally shown in vase-paintings wearing garlands or headbands; (3) for λευκῷ read λεπτῷ (van Leeuwen), not γλαυκῷ nor λιτῷ (Borthwick); (4) φυλλοβολούσης is correct and bears its ordinary meaning, since 1007 refers to autumn as is proved by the reference to green-brier (μῖλαξ) which flowers in October/November. The only weakness in this analysis is that the text offers no particle or particles to mark the alleged contrast between autumn (1007) and spring (1008); this can be remedied by reading in 1008 e.g. ἦρός θ' ὥρᾳ χαίρων. The translation should read: "no, you will go down to the Academy and take a training run under the sacred olive-trees, wearing a light reed chaplet, together with a good decent companion of your own age, fragrant with green-brier and leaf-shedding poplar and freedom from cares, or delighting in the season of spring, when the plane tree whispers to the elm."

1028-9 Zimmermann ii 126-7 proposes the excellent emendation εὐδαίμονες ἄρ' ἦσαν (Ω = Laurentianus XXXI 35 [15th century]) οἱ ζῶντες ἐπὶ Κρόνου τότε "Happy, I see, were they who lived then, in the days of Cronus". Elsewhere in the play the name of Cronus labels people and practices as archaic or obsolete (398, 929, 1070); but it was also associated with the felicity of the Golden Age when Cronus had ruled the universe, before the harsh reign of Zeus (cf. Telecleides fr. 1; Cratinus fr. 176; Hes. *Works* 109-119; *Alcmeonis* fr. 7 Davies; Pl. *Polit.* 271c-272b; [Pl.] *Hipparchus* 229b; Arist. *Ath.Pol.* 16.7).

1119 Coraes' emendation is far from satisfactory, but the transmitted text (accepted by Guidorizzi) lacks an essential definite article (as witness Del Corno's translation, "*le* vite gravide di grappoli"). Might one read τὰς καρπὸν τεκούσας ἀμπέλους ("your vines when they have borne their fruit")?

1137 The transmitted text is defensible; the lack of connection with the previous sentence (asyndeton) can be explained on the ground that 1137-41 is essentially a fuller statement of what is said in 1135-6. In translation, for "crush and destroy me; and when I make ..." read "crush and destroy me: when I make ...".

1155-6 For "moneylenders" read "loan-sharks"; an *obolostatēs* was one who made a living by lending small sums for short periods at very high rates of interest. See P.C. Millett, *Lending and Borrowing in Ancient Athens* (Cambridge, 1991) 179-188, 303 n.10. It does not follow from Strepsiades' use of this term that the creditors whom we see later are actually to be regarded as professional moneylenders; see comm. on 1216.

1308 Add to apparatus: λήψεταί τι Bergk: λήψεται RVEᵃᶜK: τι λήψεται EᵖᶜNΘ.

1494 For "*He sets fire to the rafters*" read "*He throws the torch down into the house*" (so Thiercy): a fire that starts at or near floor level, if it takes hold quickly, is more dangerous to life than one that starts at roof level, because the rising flame and smoke are more likely to trap and/or suffocate those in the building. Care would have been taken (if the revised script had ever been produced) to have some combustible material strategically placed so that the torch, falling on it, could kindle a realistic blaze (and also, one hopes, to place plenty of water within easy reach); cf. Addenda to comm. on 1484-5.

Commentary
lines

21 Twelve minas appears to have been a not untypical price for a top-class horse (cf. Lys. 8.10, Xen. *Anab.* 7.8.6 [50 darics = 10 minas]) and also, at least in the later fourth century, the maximum allowable compensation for a cavalry horse disabled or killed in service (see G.R. Bugh, *The Horsemen of Athens* [Princeton, 1988] 158, 169).

23 See also J.H. Kroll, *Hesperia* 46 (1977) 86-88.

37 Replace the reference to Harrison by one to D. Whitehead, *The Demes of Attica* (Princeton, 1986) 125-7, 131-2.

48 See Addenda to comm. on *Ach.* 614.

67 The name Pheidippides is "internally contradictory" only from the peasant's point of view; to an aristocrat *pheidesthai tōn hippōn*, lit. "sparing one's horses", would merely suggest managing them well, feeding them properly and not over-straining them (cf. *Iliad* 5.201-3). See O. Panagl in P. Händel and W. Meid ed. *Festschrift für Robert Muth* (Innsbruck, 1983) 297-306.

*83 **by Poseidon here:** it may seem surprising that Strepsiades should have an image of Poseidon in his home, but this is doubtless to be viewed as further evidence of the extent to which his wife dominates the household.

91 Further evidence for the use of the *ekkyklēma* in this scene comes from other passages where there is ambivalence as to whether the characters are supposed to be inside or outside the house, notably 19 ("bring *out* my accounts"); see P. von Möllendorff, *Grundlagen einer Ästhetik der Alten Komödie* (Tübingen, 1995) 119-121.

103 Delete reference to Ar. fr. 377 Kock (= 393 K-A).

103 Not only Socrates' habit of going barefoot, but virtually all his outward and visible characteristics as described in *Clouds*, are referred to also by Plato: see comm. on 362, 415-6, 838. No doubt too his mask showed the ugly features remarked on by Alcibiades in Pl. *Symp.* 215a-b, Critobulus in Xen. *Symp.* 4.19, and Theodorus in *Theaet.* 143e (snub nose, protruding eyes). Nowhere outside *Clouds*, however, is it said or implied that Socrates was pale, and it is probably significant that he himself (as distinct from Chaerephon and the students) is never specifically described as pale in *Clouds* itself either. See D.F. Leão, *Humanitas* (Coimbra) 47 (1995) 327-339.

*126-132 It is acutely noted by Guidorizzi (on 1476-1511) that every major new turn taken by the plot of *Clouds* is preceded by a soliloquy from Strepsiades (cf. 791-2, 1131-44, 1201-5, 1476-85).

*137 rendered abortive an idea that had been discovered: many scholars have succumbed to the temptation to see here a parody of Socrates' well-known comparison of himself to a midwife in Pl. *Theaet.* 148e-151d, and hence evidence that the analogy was actually used by Socrates; but see M.F. Burnyeat, *BICS* 24 (1977) 7, who shows that Plato in the passage referred to does all he can to "make it abundantly clear that the comparison is *not*, in any sense, to be attributed to the historical Socrates".

229 On Diogenes of Apollonia, see now A. Laks, *Diogène d'Apollonie* (Lille, 1986). On the relationship between him and the Aristophanic Socrates, see P. Vander Waerdt, "Socrates in the *Clouds*", in Vander Waerdt ed. *The Socratic Movement* (Ithaca NY, 1994) 48-86 (esp. 61-64, 71-75), who however goes much too far in claiming that *all* the physical doctrines ascribed to Socrates in the play come from Diogenes. We may have recovered part of a work of Diogenes in the shape of the Derveni papyrus; see R. Janko, *ZPE* 118 (1997) 61-94, esp. 80ff (though he prefers, less plausibly in my view, to attribute the text to Diagoras of Melos).

*245 the one that never pays its debts: it is ironic that Strepsiades should immediately offer to swear that he will pay Socrates' fee for learning this Argument!

252 There is more to the Clouds than this; see especially D. Ambrosino, *QSt* 18 (1983) 3-60, who sees them above all as embodiments of the power of speech, which she finds to be the dominant idea of the play.

270-3 W.S. Teuffel in his edition (Leipzig, 1863) suggested, no doubt rightly, that while reciting these lines Socrates turns to face successively the four cardinal points.

302-310 For this view of the role of the Clouds in the play, see also J. Hanus, *Graecolatina Pragensia* 8 (1980) 19-22. M.C. Marianetti, *Religion and Politics in Aristophanes' Clouds* (Hildesheim, 1992) 79-81, 96-97 notes that already in the strophe (275-290) the Clouds' association of themselves with nature, brightness, agriculture, etc., tends to distance them from the urbanized, light-shunning Socratics, and that similarly in 1115-30 their blessings and curses are mostly of an agrarian nature.

303-4 A preferable interpretation, taking fuller account of the fact that the word translated "is opened" (*anadeiknutai*) means more precisely "is displayed by opening", is offered by C. Sourvinou-Inwood in M.Golden & P. Toohey ed. *Inventing Ancient Culture: Historicism, Periodization, and the Ancient World* (London, 1996) 140: the passage "indicates that the rite of the Eleusinian Mysteries included a ceremonial opening of the gates of the Telesterion to display its interior to the *mystai* who will be received in it, and probably also that this was a significant moment in the initiation ceremony".

323 Why did Ar. make Socrates point to Parnes when he knew Parnes could not be seen from the theatre? Because of all Attic mountains it is over Parnes that clouds most often gather; see G.V. Lalonde, *Hesperia* Suppl. 20 (1982) 80-81, citing Thphr. *On Weather Signs* 47.

332 (on medicine): Also relevant is the tendency for leading fifth-century medical men to be at least as concerned about the rhetorical success with which they promoted themselves and justified their theories as about the actual therapeutic success of their practice; relevant texts include Xen. *Mem.* 4.2.5, Pl. *Gorg.* 456b-c, 514d, and Hippocr. *On the Nature of Man* 1. On doctors and medicine in comedy see Imperio in Belardinelli et al. *Tessere* 63-75.

333 See now B. Zimmermann, *Dithyrambos* (Göttingen, 1992) 117-136.

349 See Addenda to comm. on *Ach.* 388.

353-4 See Addenda to comm. on *Ach.* 88.

361 Prodicus' *Choice of Heracles* seems in several respects to have provided a model for the debate between the Better and Worse Arguments in *Clouds* itself: see A.M. Bowie, *Aristophanes: Myth, Ritual and Comedy* (Cambridge, 1993) 109-110.

380 The references to Democritus should be supplemented by Leucippus A1 D-K = D.L. 9.31-32; Epicurus ap. D.L. 10.90, ascribing a cosmogonic *dinos* to "one of the so-called physicists", may be referring to either of the two. Hence our passage cannot be regarded as evidence that Democritus had published anything before 423; Leucippus on the other hand had written early enough to influence Diogenes of Apollonia (Diogenes A5 D-K).

398 Delete note and substitute: **the Cronia:** a festival in honour of Cronus, held on 12 Hecatombaeon (approximately July), and by the classical period considered of so little importance that legislative sessions could be held on that day (Dem. 24.26-31); see Parke 29-30. Similarly at 984 old-fashioned ways of thought are linked with another archaic ritual occasion, the Dipolieia.

*463-5 with me ... you will lead the most envied life in the world: cf. Pl. *Phd.* 81a "Such a soul ... , in the words used of those initiated in the mysteries, will truly dwell with the gods for the rest of time", also 69c. In Plato, however, and almost certainly in its original religious context too, this promise referred to the afterlife; the Clouds' promise refers to this world.

518-562 On eupolideans see also L.P.E. Parker, *PCPS* 34 (1988) 115-122. E.M. Hall in F.D. Harvey and J. Wilkins ed. *The Rivals of Aristophanes* (London/Swansea, 2000) 407-8 notes the extraordinary confusion of genders and identities in this parabasis: the speakers are directly or indirectly identified as (male) theatre performers, as (feminine) clouds, as Aristophanes, as an unmarried mother, as a (feminine) comedy (the shape of whose phallus, however, is a matter of concern), as Electra ... .

521-3 Old Comedy was almost certainly performed in southern Italy in the fourth century, and may have been introduced there as early as the foundation of Thurii in 444/3; see O.P. Taplin, *Comic Angels* (Oxford, 1993), esp. 14-17, 89-99. It is, nevertheless, unlikely that at this time any Athenian comic dramatist would choose to have his play performed for the *first* time anywhere but Athens — though at the very end of the fifth century at least two comedies may indeed have received their first performance in Italy, Metagenes' significantly named *Thurio-Persians* and Nicophon's *Sirens* (both of which, according to Athenaeus 6.269f-270a, were "unproduced", sc. at Athens).

*533 since that time ... of your good opinion: as is noted by D. Welsh, *Hermes* 118 (1990) 424, this line proves that "at least some of the spectators at the 'Banqueters' already knew that Aristophanes had written the play".

537 On Ar.'s practice of both disowning and employing "cheap and vulgar laughter-raising devices", see G.W. Dobrov in J. Redmond ed. *Themes in Drama 10: Farce* (Cambridge, 1988) 15-31.

551 See Addenda to comm. on *Ach.* 846.

553 *Demes* was more probably produced in 417 or 416, when the battle of Mantinea (Eupolis fr. 99.30-32) was still topical; see I.C. Storey in Harvey & Wilkins ed. *The Rivals of Aristophanes* 173-190.

554 I certainly underestimated the extent to which *Maricas* can be shown to have imitated *Knights:* see I.C. Storey in Sommerstein et al. ed. *Tragedy, Comedy and the Polis* (Bari,

1993) 381-4, and my contribution to Harvey & Wilkins ed. *The Rivals of Aristophanes*, at pp.440-2.

555 Eupolis seems to have portrayed Hyperbolus' mother as an itinerant bread-seller (cf. Eupolis fr. 209), as probably did Hermippus (see comm. on 557).

556 On Phrynichus see now F.D. Harvey in Harvey & Wilkins ed. *The Rivals of Aristophanes* 91-134.

562 This is the only place where Ar. alludes to the judgement of posterity *on his own work*, and is thus precious evidence that he expected his plays to survive, presumably *in the form of texts* which future generations would read (just as he himself read Homer or Aeschylus); see R.M. Rosen, *Yale Journal of Criticism* 10 (1997) 397-421, esp. 410-1.

570 The reference to *trag. adesp.* 112 should be to Eur. fr. 908b Nauck-Snell.

621 After the death of Patroclus, Achilles insists on eating nothing until sunset the next day, even though he is going into battle (*Iliad* 19.209-214, 305-8); similarly Alexander ate nothing for two days after the death of Hephaestion (Arr. *Anab.* 7.14.8).

686 I.C. Storey, *JHS* 115 (1995) 182-4, adduces strong arguments to distinguish the Philoxenus of these passages both from the glutton referred to by later authors and from the father of the Eryxis of *Frogs* 934. Noting that almost all the other persons satirized in the opening scene of *Wasps* are politicians, he is inclined to identify our man with the mover of a decree on the cult of Apollo c.422-416 (*IG* i³ 137).

730 Note that Greek *epiballein* (which I have here rendered "throw over [me]") has as one of its meanings "bring (a woman) into sexual union with (a man)", cf. Diogenianus 2.72, and that the preposition *ex* "instead of" (lit. "out of") half suggests the idea that the blankets are to be *transformed* into a girl. See E. Degani, *Eikasmos* 1 (1990) 135.

749 On "drawing down the moon" cf. also Hippocr. *On the Sacred Disease* 4.

889 The "fighting-cock scholium" may be more simply explained as due to confusion with 847ff; see my discussion in Thiercy & Menu *Aristophane* 281-2. In the 1980s and 1990s there was a tendency to take this scholium seriously and to see the "Getty Birds vase" as illustrating this *agōn* (see especially E.G. Csapo, *Phoenix* 47 [1993] 1-28, 115-124); but there are serious difficulties with this view, to which attention has been drawn by Taplin, *Comic Angels* 103-4.

968 See Addenda to comm. on *Knights* 989-990.

969-971 Phrynis cannot have won a Panathenaic victory in 456, since that was not a Great Panathenaic year, and M. Hose, *Philologus* 137 (1993) 3-11, argues that the "archonship of Callias" referred to by the scholia here was that of 406/5; *pace* Hose, however, a victory in that year (seventeen years after *Clouds*) could hardly have been Phrynis' *first*, particularly as Arist. *Met.* 993b15 implies that Phrynis was famous well before Timotheus. Another possibility, first canvassed by M.H.E. Meier, is that "Callias" is an error for "Callimachus" (446/5), in which case the rather curious statement of the scholia that he was "the first to play the lyre at Athens" may be a garbled abbreviation of a statement that he was the first to win the competition in singing to the lyre at the Panathenaea after its reorganization, inspired by Pericles, at about this time; see J.A. Davison, *JHS* 78 (1958) 40-41.

972 Add: i.e. "obscuring the poetry and its intimate connection with the traditional music" by introducing melodic complexities (A. Andrisano, *MCr* 23/23 [1988/9] 194-7).

983 Greek *opsa* denoted especially fish (modern Greek *psari* "fish" is descended from its diminutive, *opsarion*). On the association, in Athenian democratic thinking, between fish-eating, luxury, arrogance, subservience to bodily desires, and other deplorable qualities, see J.N. Davidson, *CQ* 43 (1993) 53-66, and his book *Courtesans and Fishcakes* (London, 1997).

984 See Addenda to comm. on *Knights* 1331.

985 On the Dipolieia see also W. Burkert, *Homo Necans* (Eng. tr. Berkeley, 1983) 136-143.

989 In fact *kōlē* "penis" does appear to be attested on two magical amulets (C. Bonner, *Studies in Magical Amulets chiefly Greco-Egyptian* [Ann Arbor, 1950] 215; id., *Hesperia* 20 [1951] 335-6 #51); see D.M. Bain, *Eikasmos* 3 (1992) 149-152.

997 On the erotic symbolism of apples cf. also Sappho fr. 105a, Stesichorus *PMG* 187, and Berlin Papyrus 21243 (published by W. Brashear, *ZPE* 33 [1979] 261-278), and see A.P. Burnett, *Three Archaic Poets* (London, 1983) 267-8. The symbolism survives in Greece to the present day, but the apple is virtually always thrown at the woman (as in the myth of Melanion and Atalanta), not by her.

1001 The "tasteless vegetable" is now officially named *Amaranthus lividus*. On the use of its name as a term of abuse in Greek, Latin and Italian, see M.G. Carilli, *Studi e Ricerche dell'Istituto di Latino* (Genoa) 4 (1981) 23-30.

1075 On *phusis* = "genitals" cf. also Hippocr. *Mul.* 2.143, *PGM* xxxvi 284, and see K.McLeish, *CQ* 27 (1977) 76-79, and J.J. Winkler, *The Constraints of Desire* (New York, 1990) 217-220.

1083 On how the use of wood-ash would facilitate depilation (and render it extremely painful), see comm. on *Thesm.* 537. These punishments for adulterers (or, more accurately, forms of private revenge licensed by custom) are, not surprisingly, never mentioned outside comedy, but Xen. *Mem.* 2.1.5 alludes to them as plainly as is consistent with the dignity of serious literature. They constituted in theory the serious crime of *hybris* (cf. Xen. *loc.cit.*), but a prosecution would have no chance of success unless the victim/accuser could convince the jury that he was not in fact guilty of adultery. See C. Carey, *LCM* 18 (1993) 53-55.

1102 I have discussed this passage in *MCr* 25-28 (1990-3) 175-9. My original interpretation was not fully satisfactory, as had been pointed out by R.K. Fisher, *Aristophanes' Clouds: Purpose and Technique* (Amsterdam, 1984) 205 n.8, since after 1096-1100 one would have expected "you buggers" to be an address to (the majority of) the audience. I therefore suggested that the Better Argument flung his cloak towards the audience (or perhaps rather towards one of the individuals in it who had been singled out in 1099-1101) and thereby revealed that he was wearing beneath it an inner garment (*khitōn*) of an effeminate style and colour, probably a saffron-dyed *krokōtos* (cf. *Thesm.* 138, 253, 941, 945, 1044, 1220; see Stone 174-5). I would now be inclined, additionally, to adopt, or adapt, a proposal made by Möllendorff in Pöhlmann et al. *Studien zur Bühnendichtung* ... 147 and suggest that after throwing the cloak (as a right-handed man naturally would) towards the spectators on his *right* side, the actor ran up one of the gangways in the *left* (western) part of the auditorium (perhaps pausing to dally flirtatiously with a spectator or two?), eventually disappearing from view to return to the performing area round the outside of the theatre complex (cf. Addenda to text/translation of 275-328).

1115-30 P. Totaro, *Le seconde parabasi di Aristofane* (Stuttgart, 1999) 66-67 n.8 points out that in this second parabasis, just as in the first, the chorus speak in the name of justice and religion. One may also note that the threats in the latter part of the speech foreshadow the end of the play (stoning, 1508; breaking down roofs, 1488ff); this *may* indicate that the speech is a new one written for the revised version of the play.

1154-70 It is striking that in all the known tragic songs which provide partial parallels to this one, the character who sings is a *woman*. J. Angel y Espinós, in A. López Eire ed. *Sociedad, política y literatura: comedia griega antigua* (Salamanca, 1997) 243-8, argues that the play parodied in 1154-5 is likely to be Euripides' *Peleus* rather than Sophocles', since the continuation of the tragic passage as cited in the scholia ("Oho, who is at the door or in the house?") shows typically Euripidean features (cf. *Phoen.* 1067, *Ba.* 170, and numerous passages in which *pule* "door, gate" and *domos* "house" appear in close proximity); if he is right, it is reasonable to suppose that much in 1156-64 is modelled on Euripides too.

*1162 who will dispel the grief: Greek *lūsaniās*, which is also a fairly common personal name, and which I.C. Storey, *CQ* 39 (1989) 549-550 suggests may allude to one of two actual contemporaries of that name. The more promising of the two, in my view, is Lysanias of Thoricus (*PA* 9312, *LGPN* 54), father of the cavalryman Dexileos (*IG* ii² 6217) born in 414/3, killed at Corinth in 394/3, and commemorated by a famous surviving monument; this Lysanias would probably be in his early or middle twenties in 423 and thus of similar age, status and original tastes to Pheidippides. "The reader for *CQ*" (viz. myself) speculated that Lysanias might recently have won renown by saving his father's life in battle (at Delium?) and that this was why it was appropriate for Strepsiades to compare *his* son and potential saviour to Lysanias. Storey's own preference was for Lysanias of Sphettus (*PA* 9324, *LGPN* 53), whose son Aeschines became a well-known associate of Socrates and later a writer of Socratic dialogues, and who was himself present to support Socrates at his trial in 399 (Pl. *Apol.* 33e).

*1214 so ought a man ... his own money away?: the witness has apparently been trying to persuade the creditor not to press for payment.

*1234 Zeus, Hermes and Poseidon: Zeus as the supreme god, Hermes as the god of trading (*Empolaios*, cf. *Ach.* 816, *Wealth* 1155), Poseidon because the loan was for buying a horse (so Hermann).

*1269 particularly when I'm in distress: we may be meant to assume that the man urgently needs his money back to pay for medical treatment.

1299 For "his forthcoming book *Hybris*" read "his book *Hybris* (Warminster, 1992)".

1300 Alternatively the point of *seiraphoros* may be that the offside trace-horse, because of its role in the race, was the one most likely to need goading; see F. García Romero, *CFC* 6 (1996) 94-95.

1356 On the Crius-ode see now further J.H. Molyneux, *Simonides: A Historical Study* (Wauconda IL, 1992) 47-54.

1358 In his objection to singing at table, Pheidippides significantly has the support both of his admired Euripides (cf. *Medea* 190-203) and of the Platonic Socrates (cf. *Prot.* 347c-348a, *Symp.* 176e). See G. Crane, *Mnemosyne* 43 (1990) 435-8.

1380 D.E. O'Regan, *Rhetoric, Comedy and the Violence of Language in Aristophanes' Clouds* (New York, 1992) 120 notes the irony of Strepsiades' appeal to the "debt of nurture" due to him as parent (cf. also 861-4, 999) when he has been trying to evade paying *his* debts to others. Presently Pheidippides will claim the right (duty?) to repay a somewhat different kind of "debt" to his father by giving him beatings in return for the beatings he received as a child.

1382, 1383, 1384 All these nursery words are still in use in Greece in almost the same form; see Th. Stephanopoulos, *Glotta* 61 (1983) 12-15 (who notes that in modern usage *mamma* often refers specifically to bread). For a comprehensive overview of what is known about "baby talk and child language" in ancient Greece, see M. Golden in F. De Martino and A.H. Sommerstein ed. *Lo spettacolo delle voci* (Bari, 1995) ii 11-34.

1484-5 The burning of Troy had been the final catastrophe of at least one earlier tragedy, the *Sack of Troy* by Iophon (son of Sophocles); cf. Ar. fr. 234 "Hecuba wailing and the heap of straw burning" (sc. backstage to simulate the conflagration).

WASPS

Introductory Note
page

xv   *this is probably an error:* which play, then, did Philonides produce? Most critics have supposed it was *The Preview*, and some have deleted from the text of the Hypothesis the words *dia Philōnidou* "through Philonides" referring to *Wasps*. But how could these words have come to be inserted? It is better, with Hermann, to delete Philonides' name from the following statement about *The Preview*, which will then read "And he [i.e. Ar.] won first prize with *The Preview*". The first-prize winner's name was omitted because he was also the author of the play to which the Hypothesis itself refers; a later scribe, thinking the omission accidental, misguidedly "corrected" it.

xv n.1   Mastromarco's hypothesis has been refuted by R.M. Rosen, *ZPE* 76 (1989) 223-8. It remains true, however, that the responsible magistrate might very well think it a reasonably safe exercise of his discretion to refuse a chorus to a dramatist whose last production at the festival in question had been a failure.

xviii   *political pessimism:* Cf. S.D. Olson, *TAPA* 126 (1996) 145, after an insightful analysis drawing parallels between the treatment of Laches/Labes, of Bdelycleon and of the poet (in the two parabases) by the Athenian people (as represented, in the first two cases, by Philocleon): "The picture of the Athenian people which emerges here is ... not a particularly happy or encouraging one. At best, they can be protected from their enemies [viz. Cleon and his like] by those who see the nature of things more clearly than they do; at worst, they alternate between being exploited by those whom they foolishly regard as their leaders and lashing out against those who make a conscientious effort to help them." Olson rightly sees the play (and Ar.'s earlier work in general) as favouring government by an élite, and as encouraging the masses to believe that such a régime would be more in their interests than the existing one; Olson sees this as the position of a sincere "conservative democrat", but it could just as easily be the position of a dissembling anti-democrat (essentially the view of Konstan whom Olson is opposing). For another, more optimistic view of Philocleon as typical Athenian see A.C. Purves, *Drama* 5 (1997) 5-22.

xviii   *Philocleon ... has defeated ... his son:* on Philocleon's final triumph see K.J. Reckford, *Aristophanes' Old-and-New Comedy* (Chapel Hill NC, 1987) 277-281. The strong heroic, and Dionysiac, element in Philocleon, set against the humourless killjoy (and father-beater) Bdelycleon, make me somewhat doubtful of the thesis persuasively advanced by Z.P. Biles, *Aristophanes' Wasps: A Study in Competitive Poetry* (Diss. U. of Colorado 1999) that Bdelycleon is to be understood as representing Ar. himself, the one struggling to educate his father, the other to educate the Athenian people (both with limited success, as is shown, respectively, by the ending of the play and by the failure of *Clouds*).

Bibliography

J. Vaio, "Aristophanes' *Wasps*: the relevance of the final scenes", *GRBS* 12 (1971) 335-351.

G. Mastromarco, *Storia di una commedia di Atene* (Florence, 1974).

G. Paduano, *Il giudice giudicato* (Bologna, 1974).

W.T. MacCary, "Philokleon *ithyphallos*: dance, costume, and character in the *Wasps*", *TAPA* 109 (1979) 137-147.

L. Lenz, "Komik und Kritik in Aristophanes' 'Wespen'", *Hermes* 108 (1980) 15-44.

D. Konstan, "The politics of Aristophanes' *Wasps*", *TAPA* 115 (1985) 27-46; revised version in Konstan, *Greek Comedy and Ideology* (New York, 1995) 15-28.

A.M. Bowie, "Ritual stereotype and comic reversal: Aristophanes' *Wasps*", *BICS* 34 (1987) 112-125.

G. Mastromarco, "L'eroe e il mostro (Aristofane, *Vespe* 1029-1044)", *RFIC* 117 (1989) 410-423.

K.C. Sidwell, "Was Philokleon cured?: the *nosos* theme in Aristophanes' *Wasps*", *C&M* 41 (1990) 9-31.

M. Menu, "Philocléon: une initiation de la vieillesse dans les comédies d'Aristophane?", in A. Moreau ed. *L'initiation* (Montpellier, 1992) 165-184

A. Crichton, "'The old are in a second childhood': age reversal and jury service in Aristophanes' *Wasps*", *BICS* 38 (1993) 59-80.

K.S. Rothwell, "Aristophanes' *Wasps* and the sociopolitics of Aesop's fables", *CJ* 90 (1994/5) 233-254.

S.D. Olson, "Politics and poetry in Aristophanes' *Wasps*", *TAPA* 126 (1996) 129-150.

N.W. Slater, "Bringing up father: *paideia* and *ephebeia* in the *Wasps*", in A.H. Sommerstein and C. Atherton ed. *Education in Greek Fiction* (Bari, 1997) 27-52, with response by A.H. Sommerstein (53-64).

A.C. Purves, "Empowerment for the Athenian citizen: Philocleon as actor and spectator in Aristophanes' *Wasps*", *Drama* 5 (1997) 5-22.

J. Vaio, "Assembling wasps", *Drama* 5 (1997) 23-33.

G. Colesanti, "Il δέχεσθαι τὰ σκόλια in Aristoph. *Vesp.* 1208-1250", *SRCG* 2 (1999) 243-262.

Note on the Text

page

xx *its (indirect?) copy C:* Koster in his edition of the scholia (xl-xli) gives evidence showing that C is probably *not* a descendant of Vp3, but rather that both derive from a common source.

Table of Sigla

Three new papyri were published by N. Gonis in *The Oxyrhynchus Papyri* LXVI (1999): Oxyrhynchus Papyri 4509 (Π72; second century; contains scholia on 36-41, but no text), 4512 (Π75; third century; contains 96-116), and 4513 (Π76; fifth century; contains 1066-

1108). The last-mentioned is the most important, confirming at 1085 a reading previously known only from a grammarian's quotation and supplying a new and excellent reading at 1102.

Text and Translation
line

7-8   For [*He yawns and stretches*] read [*He begins to nod off, but abruptly jerks himself awake again*]. It is the sudden, almost convulsive head movement that makes Xanthias wonder if his companion is "having a mad fit, or ... in a Corybantic frenzy"; see E.K. Borthwick, *CQ* 42 (1992) 275-6, who cites *inter alia* Men. *Thph.* fr. dub. (p.146 Sandbach) 7-8 (= *Thph.* 37-38 Arnott), where, in a hymn to the "Phrygian Queen" or "Mountain Mother", there is mention of "head-shakers" and of "sweet-faced Corybantes" in successive lines.

113   Π75 has only]ησαντες, which is, however, more likely to represent the reading of RV than that of *j*.

179   Thiercy notes that the donkey's panniers must be covered with a cloth hanging down on both sides, the better to conceal Philocleon; Xanthias lifts the cloth at 181, as soon as he is reminded of the Odysseus-Cyclops episode.

204   For "made it drop" read "dropped it" (sc. as excrement); cf. *Clouds* 173, *Birds* 1114-7.

282   L.P.E. Parker, *The Songs of Aristophanes* (Oxford, 1997) 218-9, gives strong metrical reasons for regarding διεδύετ' as corrupt. The best emendation is διέδυ <πως> (Dindorf) "somehow gave us the slip", which also gives better sense. If Philocleon were driven sick with indignation every time a defendant *tried* to lie his way out of trouble, he would be in a fever almost every day; rather, what his friends think may have affected him so deeply is the fact that one of them has *succeeded* in deceiving a majority of the jurors (Philocleon himself will have voted guilty as he always does, cf. 278-280).

297   Read παππία (Bentley); see Addenda to *Knights* 1215.

308   The imperfect response with 296 can be obviated, and syntax and sense slightly improved, by Blaydes's emendation πόρον Ἑλλας ἱερὸν <εὑρεῖν> "can you find any fair hope for us, any chance ... ?" And if we are thus going to assume that something has been lost from the text here, we might as well improve the strophic correspondence further by positing that Ar. wrote ἀπαπαῖ φεῦ twice (Hermann).

394   For "fart" read "shit"; see comm. on *Frogs* 10, and Dunbar on *Birds* 791 ("had a good fart ... presumably with solid results").

407   Both my emendation and Bergk's require final -*ai* to be scanned short before a vowel ("epic correption"), a device which, while quite common in Aristophanic lyric, would be unparalleled in this particular type of metrical context (see Parker *Songs* 234-5); better therefore replace ἐντέτατ(αι) "is braced" by ἐντατέον (D.M. Jones) "must be braced".

455/6   Delete the last sentence of my stage-direction: if the chorus have remained passive against three unarmed slaves, it is unlikely that they would attack opponents who are now more numerous and better equipped. Rather, they remain all noise and no action (cf. 436); their "sting" is effective only when they are in court.

493   For "perch" (Greek *orphōs*) read "grouper" (*Epinephelus* spp.; today *rofós* in Greek and *orfoz* in Turkish).

537 Parker *Songs* 239 shows that the Platonic parallels (*Rep.* 370b, 375a), on which I relied in my 1977 article (cited in the commentary) to show that ἐθέλειν + infinitive could function in Attic as a periphrastic future tense, are invalid, and hence ἐθέλει must be corrupt. Suitable sense is given e.g. by γένοιθ', οὗτός (Bentley) σε λέγων κρατήσει (Blaydes), "for if, which heaven forbid, he beats you in the debate– ".

542-5 Wilamowitz's emendation, which *increases* the irregularity of responsion with 646-7, is hardly justifiable, and it is best, with Porson, to delete ἂν and ἁπάσαις and read σκωπτόμενοι δ' ἐν ταῖς ὁδοῖς θαλλοφόροι καλούμεθ' "and we'll be mocked in the streets and called ...".

636 Parker *Songs* 238 strongly supports Porson's emendation ὡς δ' ἐπὶ πάντ' ἐλήλυθεν, which restores both metrical coherence within the stanza and strophic responsion with 531.

646-7 Porson's supplement χαλεπὸν <νεανίᾳ> improves syntax as well as strophic responsion; in translation, for "one who" read "a young man who".

655 Read παππίδιον (Suda); see Addenda to *Knights* 1215.

677 Read πλουθυγιείαν; see Addenda to *Knights* 1091.

807, 933 Read ἁμίς, ἁμίδα; this word was aspirated in Attic (Aelius Dionysius α98, Photius α1197).

810 For "a full bladder" read "slow leakage"; Greek *strangouriā* means "difficulty in passing urine" (often due, no doubt, to such conditions as prostate enlargement).

828 Before "Thratta" insert [*Aloud*]: Philocleon's deliberate interruption ("Stop, you!") shows that at that point Bdelycleon was no longer musing to himself but was speaking for his father to hear.

862 Read πρῶτα (codd.): πρῶτον is my error.

863-7 It is probably preferable to assign these anapaests to the chorus-*leader* (so M. Kaimio, *The Chorus of Greek Drama within the Light of the Person and Number Used* [Helsinki, 1970] 175 n.4).

873 For "and may our wanderings have an end" perhaps read "now that we have ceased to go astray": cf. Pl. *Phd.* 79d, 81a.

928 Henderson (LCL) has provided the definitive English rendering of this line: "one copse can't support two robbers".

995 Reckford, *Aristophanes' Old-and-New Comedy* 259, suggests that the "water" may in fact be the liquid most readily at hand, viz. the contents of the "water-clock"; an idea both funny and economical.

1011 μὲν should be deleted (Burges) to avoid a transition from iambic to trochaic rhythm without a proper word-break at 1012/3; in translation, for "for the time being take care" read "take care now".

1056 For "citrons" read "quinces". The citron (*Citrus medica*) had not yet reached the Mediterranean region (it was still unfamiliar to Greeks at the end of the fourth century, cf. Thphr. *HP* 4.4.2). Quinces are known to have been used to make perfumes (cf. Hicesius ap. Athen. 15.689c, Thphr. *On Odours* 26, 31).

1085 Π76 has]ϵωσᾳ[με(σ)θα, and the space available would not be sufficient for ἀπ-to have preceded; the papyrus thus confirms the reading of *Anecd.Oxon.*

1102 Π76 has πολλαχη (i.e. πολλαχῇ), which gives exactly the sense required here ("in many ways", "from many points of view"); πολλαχοῦ, the reading of the medieval mss., ought properly to mean "in many places".

1116 E.K. Borthwick, *BICS* 37 (1990) 57-60, gives strong reasons for adopting Dobree's conjecture τὸν πόνον, which is supported by Homeric and Hesiodic passages suggesting that the idea "drones eat <the produce of> the working bees' labour" was a commonplace (*Odyssey* 14.417; Hes. *Thg.* 594ff, *Works* 302-4) and by many passages, two of them fifth-century (Pind. *Pyth.* 6.55, Eur. *IT* 165), in which honey is spoken of as the "labour" of bees. Trans. "eat up the tribute, the fruits of our labour" (lit. our labour consisting in the tribute).

1153 For "oven" read "baking-crock".

1226-7 G. Colesanti, *SRCG* 2 (1999) 251-6, revives a suggestion by Dobree that both these lines should be given to Philocleon, noting that Bdelycleon uses the present (not the future) tense in 1225 to refer to his own singing of *Harmodius*, as if that song, in its various forms, were so well known that it could be "taken as read"; Philocleon does not interrupt and continue Bdelycleon/Cleon's song, but (as in 1232-5 and 1241-2) sings another as a rejoinder to it.

1251 The slave's name should be accented Χρῦσε: see T. Gelzer in *EH* 38 (1993) 80 n.18.

1263ff Thiercy provides further arguments in support of Stephanis' suggestion (see comm.) that the slave who accompanies Philocleon and Bdelycleon to the party, and who reports on it in 1292-1325, is not Xanthias but the Chrysus of 1251; he notes in particular that 1297-8 *prima facie* implies that this slave is elderly, whereas Xanthias is clearly young and strong (cf. e.g. 152-5, 199-202).

1388 For [*carrying an empty tray*] read [*with an empty tray slung from her shoulders*]; see comm. on *Wealth* 1037.

1412 Thiercy here follows, as I should have done, the excellent suggestion of MacDowell that Myrtia, in turning to go, accidentally hits Chaerephon (with her display tray?) who falls at her feet (or perhaps at Philocleon's?)

1473 Parker *Songs* 257 finds κατακοσμῆσαι metrically unacceptable (it implies an aeolic base of the form ∪∪–) and suggests it may be a gloss – in which case the word it displaced may have had some such sense as "train for" rather than "equip with".

Commentary
lines

9   On Sabazius see now S.E. Johnson in *Aufstieg und Niedergang der römischen Welt* II xvii (Berlin, 1981-4) 1583-1613.

19   See Addenda to comm. on *Ach.* 88.

35-36 The insult to Cleon is intensified by this implicit comparison of him to a woman; similarly in 1032-5, all the beings and objects to which the Cleon-monster is compared are either biologically or grammatically feminine.

63   In fact the play *will* attack Cleon (and at 1291 Ar. will even boast of having done so); the promise is as false as the statements made in *Clouds* 541-3 about the low-comic features allegedly absent from that play. See L. Edmunds, *Cleon, Knights and Aristophanes' Politics* (Lanham MD, 1987) 51-57.

74   Amynias was also satirized as an uncultured boor (Eupolis fr. 222).

80   As is pointed out by B.H. Kraut, *I Aristophanes: Poetic Self-Assertion in Old Comedy* (Diss. Princeton 1985) 167, Philocleon himself will become a philoeniac in the end — and therefore, comically speaking, one of "the best people".

82   See Addenda to comm. on *Clouds* 686.

118   Add reference to R.C.T. Parker, *Miasma* (Oxford, 1983), esp. 207-234.

123   See further Introduction to *Wealth* (§3) and references cited there.

*139   gone into the kitchen: from his position on the roof Bdelycleon "has a bird's-eye view of the whole establishment, including the yard and the kitchen ... at the back of the house" (D.M. MacDowell in J. Redmond ed. *Themes in Drama 10: Farce* [Cambridge, 1988] 1). Hence Philocleon cannot move from one part of the house to another without being seen by his son while crossing the yard.

188   E.L. Bowie in E.M. Craik ed. *"Owls to Athens": Essays on Classical Subjects for Sir Kenneth Dover* (Oxford, 1990) 33 points out that "all painted and plastic representations of the famous scene from the *Odyssey* have Odysseus clinging to the underside of the ram, *his head forwards* [italics mine]". It does not necessarily follow, however, as Bowie supposes, that Philocleon must be in the same position; it would be at least as funny for him to be hanging on the wrong way round, with his head at the dirtier end of the donkey.

233   Delete the reference to the two "broken names".

240   *vague threats of prosecution made by ... Cleon:* see I. Moneti, *Civiltà Classica e Cristiana* 14 (1997) 245-254.

273-289   Zimmermann i 97-99 places the "shift into dactylo-epitrite metre" as early as the third colon; Parker *Songs* 216-9 agrees.

314-5 How is the boy carrying the bag? Not in his hand, for, as is pointed out by G. Mastromarco, *Commedie di Aristofane* i (Turin, 1983) 93, we know from 249-250 that one hand is holding the lamp and the other is free. If the bag had draw-strings or the like, he could have carried it on his wrist while it was empty; this solution is preferable to Mastromarco's transfer of 314-5 to the father, since in this lyric dialogue it is regularly the son who uses high-poetic tropes such as this apostrophe to an inanimate object.

389   J.S. Rusten, *HSCP* 87 (1983) 289-297, citing Pind. *Nem.* 7.86-101, *Pyth.* 8.56=60, Hdt. 6.69.3, Eur. *Hel.* 1165-8, Thphr. *Char.* 16.4, argues that "a hero whose shrine was near an individual house might be 'domesticated' and receive regular greetings and offerings from his mortal neighbors; in return, the hero was expected to influence the fortunes of 'his' family". The present prayer parodies this practice.

*395   Here, you, wake up!: B. Zimmermann, *SRCG* 1 (1998) 280, notes that 334-394 is formally a perfect epirrhematic syzygy *except* that the *pnigos* in 358-364 lacks a responding *antipnigos*, and plausibly suggests that the audience are meant to perceive that the syzygy, like the escape of Philocleon which it enacts, is cut short by the awakening of Bdelycleon.

421   *the pair are said to haunt the law-courts:* Philippus may have been haunting the law-courts in 414, but hardly Gorgias, who (even had he been in Athens) could not, as a foreigner, bring prosecutions in the Athenian courts except for wrongs committed against himself; see comm. on *Birds* 1701.

433   To references for the name Midas, add *com. adesp.* 1132.32, Hyp. *Ath.* passim, and Terence, *Phormio* 862. Note that Bdelycleon has seven identifiable slaves (Sosias,

Xanthias, Midas, Phryx, Masyntias, Thratta [828] and Chrysus [1251]; the steward mentioned at 613 may be yet another), almost twice as many as any other major character in Aristophanes; see E. Lévy in *Actes du colloque 1972 sur l'esclavage = Annales littéraires de l'Université de Besançon* 163 (1974) 33-34.

*500 at midday: i.e. during the siesta period (Nicophon fr. 20.1-2; Aesch. *Ag.* 565-6; Pl. *Phdr.* 259a); a domestic slave probably could not have gone out alone in the evening. C. Catenacci, *QUCC* 58 (1998) 28-29, suggests that there is also an allusion to the alleged (perverse) preference of barbarians for daytime sex (cf. *Peace* 289-290, and add Hdt. 4.113 to the references there cited); but the taste was not confined to barbarians (cf. *Birds* 793-6, *Lys.* 414-9).

506 See Addenda to comm. on *Ach.* 887.

523 See also Aesch. *Eum.* 746 where Orestes seems to be threatening to hang himself if found guilty.

538 For "cf. 599" read "cf. 559".

574 The gloss "slacken the peg" is misleading: early Greek lyres were not tuned by pegs. Rather, the end of each string was laid on a strip of cloth or leather (*kollops*) which was then wound round the yoke of the lyre and could be tightened or loosened. In the later fifth century these strips were replaced by wood or metal rings (still called *kollopes*) around which the string was looped. See A. Bélis, *BCH* 109 (1985) 201-220, and M.L. West, *Ancient Greek Music* (Oxford, 1992) 61.

616 Alternatively the "donkey" may be a horn-type drinking-vessel (or *rhyton*) in the shape of a donkey's head, like the "elephant" and "Pegasus" of Epinicus fr. 2, the "griffin" of Astydamas II fr. 3.3-4, etc. (see P. Nencini, *SIFC* 2 [1894] 381 n.1 and U. Lesi, *GFF* 13 [1990] 123-4); for actual examples see *ARV²* 382 #189-195, 445 #259.

625 Thiercy notes that Greeks still say *popo* to exorcize bad luck.

*656 not with counters but just on your hands: or perhaps (with a metaphor from the two principal methods of voting at Athens) "by show of hands, not by ballot", i.e. "just to a good approximation"; see M.H. Hansen, *The Athenian Democracy in the Age of Demosthenes* (Oxford, 1991) 147-8.

659 See Addenda to comm. on *Knights* 362.

675 See Addenda to comm. on *Knights* 534, and, on the phrase "a half-brain of Connus", *CQ* 33 (1983) 488-9.

769 For the imposition of one-drachma fines for minor offences cf. [Dem.] 25.71.

*863-890 This passage is discussed by K.C. Sidwell in *Hermes* 117 (1989) 271-7 and *C&M* 41 (1990) 9-31, with emphasis on what Sidwell sees as the (psycho)therapeutic aspects of the ritual, of the ensuing trial scene, and of the play as a whole.

1007 See Addenda to comm. on *Ach.* 846.

*1023 honoured as nobody has ever been among you: this may well be not a vague assertion of the poet's prestige, but a precise claim (modelled on those often made by athletes; cf. H.A. Harris, *JHS* 82 [1962] 24) that he had achieved a well-defined feat which no one had achieved before him. C. Neri, *Annali della Facoltà di Lettere, Univ. di Bari* 37-38 (1994/5) 284, tacitly rejecting the Mastromarco-Halliwell thesis, suggests that Ar. is here referring to his having won both the Lenaean and Dionysian contests in the same year (424 – though a Dionysian victory in that year is not otherwise attested). The claim is also, however, capable of an interpretation consistent with the Mastromarco-Halliwell thesis: it might refer to Ar.'s having won both the Dionysian contest of 426 and, ten months later, the Lenaean contest of 425. The Lenaean contests had begun c.440, so it is quite possible that no one before 425 had been victorious at one of the two festivals while still the "reigning" victor of the other.

1031 For "may be" read "is probably"; see G. Mastromarco, *Dioniso* 57 (1987) 91, who cites Bacch. 5.60 where Cerberus is called "jag-toothed" in a context concerned with Heracles.

1038 G. Mastromarco, *RFIC* 117 (1989) 421-2 notes that the demon Epialus (Epiales, Epioles) was said to have *strangled his father* and was killed *by Heracles* (cf. Sophron fr. 68, 70; [Apoll.] 1.6.2).

1042 R.G. Osborne in P.A. Cartledge et al. *Nomos* (Cambridge, 1990) 94-95 n.37, and F.D. Harvey, *ibid.* 106 n.13, agree that the law referred to in *Ath.Pol.* 43.5 probably in fact related, not to charges brought against metic *sūkophantai*, but to charges brought by metics against citizen *sūkophantai*.

1056-7 Delete second sentence of note.

1087 There is a pun on Greek *thūlakos* "bag" which can denote both trousers (Eur. *Cycl.* 182) and the egg-sac of the tunny (Arist. *HA* 571a14); see T. Long, *Barbarians in Greek Comedy* (Carbondale IL, 1986) 89.

1182 Polecats and mice seem to have been a favourite subject for animal fables, and we now have fragments of a mock epic describing a war between them, a parallel to the long-known *Battle of the Frogs and Mice* ascribed to Homer; see H.S. Schibli, *ZPE* 53 (1983) 1-25.

1208 Cf. Eur. *Cycl.* 543 where the Cyclops, likewise being taught on stage (i.e. out of doors) how to behave at a symposium, is explicitly told "Now recline, please, laying your side on the ground".

*1253-5 From wine come ... while the hangover's on you: cf. Epicharmus fr. 148, Eubulus fr. 93, Alexis fr. 160.

1259 We also hear of other classes of what might be called "ethnic anecdotes" of this kind, such as Libyan tales (e.g. Aesch. fr. 139) or Cyprian, Sicilian and Carian tales (Timocreon *PMG* 730, 732, 734); see M.L. West, *Entretiens Hardt* 30 (1984) 114-6.

1270 I.C. Storey, *Phoenix* 39 (1985) 319-322, suggests that the man meant may rather be Antiphon son of Lys(id)onides (*PA* 1283, *LGPN* 5), a wealthy man, later put to death by the Thirty (Xen. *Hell.* 2.3.40; cf. [Plut.] *Lives of the Ten Orators* 833a), who had been satirized by Cratinus (fr. 212) in 423.

1278 See Addenda to comm. on *Knights* 1277.°

1290 It is ingeniously suggested by P. Demont in P. Thiercy and M. Menu ed. *Aristophane: la langue, la scène, la cité* (Bari, 1997) 477 that what Ar. did to make people think he had come to terms with Cleon was to let it be known, in advance of the production of *Wasps*, that his lead actor was playing a character called Philocleon. If this is not right, it ought to be! On this *antepirrhēma* as a whole, see P. Totaro, *Le seconde parabasi di Aristofane* (Stuttgart, 1999) 179-195 (though his interpretation of it, according to which the "vine" of 1291 is not Cleon but supposed friends of Ar. who had failed to support him when he needed support, is not acceptable, since at no time, according to the scenario he reconstructs, had these men *relied on* Ar. as a vine relies on its stake).

1301-2 Storey *op.cit.* 332 sees in those named here a group of "men of superior station, mocked for their style of living and arrogant behaviour" (though men like Thuphrastus and Lysistratus could surely at most only be hangers-on of such a group). He observes that Eupolis' plays *Flatterers* (421) and *Autolycus* (420) show that the social life of this circle was a regular target for comic satire in the late 420s. Phrynichus the demagogue (as he then was) would not fit in well with such a coterie, and Storey (328-330) suggests that the Phrynichus here referred to is the man mentioned in Andoc. 1.47 (see further my note in *Phoenix* 41 [1987] 189-190). If this is right, then the group mentioned here contains no political figures, in contrast with the mainly Cleonist group of 1220ff. Jeffrey Henderson has suggested to me that these men's alleged "arrogant behaviour" may have consisted in "carousing in the streets" as Philocleon does later.

1301 Lycon's "wife Rhodia" may rather have been a mistress from Rhodes; see comm. on *Lys.* 270. The reference to Eupolis fr. 63 should be to fr. 53 Kock = 61 K-A.

1372 The seemingly vague phrase "in honour of the gods" may well mean "in honour of the Twelve Gods", an altar to whom stood in the Agora; see comm. on *Birds* 95.

1410 On Lasus see G.A. Privitera, *Laso di Ermione nella cultura ateniese e nella tradizione storiografica* (Rome, 1965).

1411 Before "*lāsisma*" insert "comically banal".

1418 See Addenda to comm. on *Clouds* 1299.

***1465 filial love:** Greek *philopatriā*, which can also mean "patriotism", and which according to Biles, *Aristophanes' Wasps* 111 should be understood in both senses simultaneously. The chorus had previously praised Bdelycleon as one who "love[s] the people as no other man does" (887-890) — though earlier they had repeatedly condemned him as pro-Spartan and anti-democratic!

1493 As P.T. Eden has pointed out to me, the meaning is much more likely to be "Mind you don't get buggered", making a comic climax to Xanthias' interventions; for parallels see J.J. Henderson, *The Maculate Muse*[2] (New York, 1991) 211, esp. *Ach.* 104, *Knights* 78.

1518-37 The archilochean was apparently used by the tragedian Phrynichus (fr. 13); cf. 1490, 1524.

PEACE

Introductory Note

page

xvii *the comic exploitation of ... other genres of poetry:* and also of familiar mythical patterns, especially that of the *anodos* – the bringing up of a goddess (e.g. Persephone, Pandora) from the underworld, normally with the assistance of Hermes; see S.D. Olson, *Aristophanes: Peace* (Oxford, 1998) [hereafter "Olson"] xxxv-xxxviii.

xvii *his decision to represent the goddess Peace ... by a statue:* why did Ar. so decide? One possible explanation is that in Old Comedy a beautiful *living* female (even though impersonated by a male performer) almost always ends up (as Fullfruit and Showtime do) as a sex-object, i.e. as a subordinated being, and that Ar. did not wish to represent Peace as being in any way subordinate to anyone or anything.

xix *some change in the stage-picture:* A.C. Cassio, *Commedia e partecipazione* (Naples, 1985) 76, and independently P. Thiercy, *Aristophane: fiction et dramaturgie* (Paris, 1986) 213, suggest that a few members of the chorus (perhaps six) withdraw from the ropes at 508, to be quietly reabsorbed into the chorus after the end of the hauling-scene.

Bibliography

Editions of the play: add S.D. Olson (Oxford, 1998), which supersedes Platnauer.

Other publications since 1985[5]

H.J. Newiger, "War and peace in the comedy of Aristophanes", has been reprinted with minor revisions in E. Segal ed. *Oxford Readings in Aristophanes* (Oxford, 1996) 143-161.

A.C. Cassio, *Commedia e partecipazione: la Pace di Aristofane* (Naples, 1985).

K. Vanhaegendoren, *Die Darstellung des Friedens in den Acharnern und im Frieden des Aristophanes* (Hamburg, 1996).

Note on the Text and Table of Sigla

xxii *three papyri:* the following additional papyri have appeared subsequently; they offer between them only one or two new readings of any interest.

Π66	Rainer Papyrus I 34 (5th century; contains commentary on 410-5, 457-466)
Π67	Berlin Papyrus 21223 (6th century; contains 141-152, 175, 178-187, 194-200)
Π70	Duke Papyrus, inv. 643 (3rd century; contains 474, 476, 507-523, with scholia)

---

5   I cannot refrain from drawing attention to the extraordinary dearth of significant recent interpretative articles dedicated to this play, a neglect unparalleled for any of Ar.'s other surviving comedies.

Π77   Oxyrhynchus Papyrus 4514 (4th century; contains 1195-1211, 1233-47)

xxii   *the remaining mss. ....:* this branch of the textual tradition is superbly analysed by S.D. Olson, *CQ* 48 (1998) 62-74 (see also his edition, pp. liii-lxv), who shows that *y* (called by Olson β) became the ancestor of several subfamilies *successively* as it progressively lost more and more of the folios containing *Peace*:

(i)   after the loss of 948-1011, the ancestor of *p* and of a ms. used by the Aldine editor, Musurus, to supplement his main copy-text (see Addenda to General Introduction, p.19);

(ii)   after the loss of 1301-end, the ms. used by Triclinius (my *t*); the loss of 1228-1300 in L is due to damage to that ms. after it was copied;

(iii)   after the loss of a further ten folios (by which time only twelve of the original twenty-four remained), either Γ or a lost ms. from which Γ was afterwards copied.

Dramatis Personae

For SICKLE-MAKER read PRUNINGHOOK-MAKER; see Addenda to 1197ff.

Text and Translation
line

6   Olson punctuates οὐ κατέφαγεν; "didn't he eat it?", i.e. "did he reject it? is that why he wants another so soon?" For the beetle's fastidiousness cf. 12, 25-28.

16   Olson reads ἑτέρας γε, which is in H as well as *t* and was probably therefore the reading of *y*: I would prefer καὶ τρῖβέ γ' ἑτέρας.

67   ἐνθαδί may be retained; Olson points out that Lenting's conjecture puts ἄν in an abnormal position. Trans. "He used to say to himself, standing here where I am now", and add stage-direction: [*gazing and gesticulating towards the sky*].

83   Read σοβαρὸς (so the lemma to *Rhetorikai Lexeis* 161 Naoumides); Ar. always uses the adjectival, not the adverbial, form of this lexeme with verbs of motion (*Clouds* 406, *Wealth* 872), and indeed there seem to be no pre-Hellenistic attestations of the adverb. See B. Marzullo, *I sofismi di Prometeo* (Florence, 1993) 397.

186-7 Olson, following a suggestion by B. Millis, reverses the order of these lines (V has 186 in the margin; R and the Suda omit 187), thus restoring the standard sequence name-patronymic-ethnic.

195   Π67 reads ἰην ἰην ἰη[υ, and this should be preferred as *lectio difficilior*; see M.L. West, *ZPE* 60 (1985) 10.

223/4 After 223 Σ^V 173 report the presence of a short line τί φησὶ (τί φής; Zacher: "what are you saying?"), and Olson prints this; but εἰς ποῖον; ought surely to follow directly on εἰς ἄντρον βαθύ, and I suspect that τί φησι; started life as an attempt to fill a lacuna caused when εἰς ποῖον; dropped out of some copies.

239   Olson rightly inserts punctuation after ὅσον κακόν: trans. "what a menace! and that expression on War's face!"

246 In *CQ* 36 (1986) 353-8 I proposed to read ἰὼ Μέγαρ', ὡς <ξυν>επιτετρίψεσθ' αὐτίκα, in order that the line could begin in the same way as 236, 242 and 250. Olson reports ἐπιτετρίψεσθ' as the reading of ᴸΣᴿ.

253 The crasis χρῆσθάτέρῳ (Brunck) accounts better for the transmitted text.

261/2 After 261 Σᵛ 173 report the presence of a short line ἰή ἰή (cf. 223/4), which can be accounted for if War (most unreasonably, but then that's his nature) strikes his servant again as an accompaniment to his order to fetch a pestle from Athens; trans. "Aagh!"

262 Here, as Olson notes, Hurlyburly exits into the *near* wing; at 275 he exits into the *far* wing, which is why War has time there to call after him.

300 Peter Jones (personal communication) suggested that the transmitted text conceals the verb ἀνασπάσαι (both "to draw up" and "to drink up"); perhaps therefore we should read e.g. νῦν γὰρ <οὖν> ἀνασπάσαι.

301 P. von Möllendorff in E. Pöhlmann et al. *Studien zur Bühnendichtung und zum Theaterbau der Antike* (Frankfurt, 1995) 147-151 suggests — modifying a proposal made by Thiercy, *Aristophane* 127-8 — that the chorus enter by descending through the audience area (cf. Addenda to *Clouds* 275-328); this would help to explain their identification with the audience in 296-8. If it were important to remember that the action is set in heaven, it would be inappropriate for the chorus to move *downwards* to join in it; but in fact the heavenly setting has been entirely forgotten (already in 279 Trygaeus has assumed that Hurlyburly will travel to Sparta on foot) and is not recalled until Trygaeus is about to go home (720).

303 For "scarlet" read "crimson".

316, 326, 337 It is most unlikely that καί should have found its way into the text by mistake three times in similar phrases within 21 lines, and although the emphatic use of καί *after a negative* cannot be exactly paralleled, Olson is doubtless right to retain the transmitted text in all three passages. Trans. (316) "This time there is no one who will take her away from us"; (326) "Well, put a stop to it, *now!*"; (337) "Don't go over the top right away".

337-345 The chorus probably still continue their frenzied dance until 345 when, with the commencement of their first lyric strophe, they fall into a more measured step (so Thiercy).

348 For "palliasses" read "beds of leaves"; see Addenda to *Knights* 605.

365 may be retained (as by Olson) provided we read κλῆρον "a lottery" (van Herwerden, cf. LSJ κλῆρος I 2); trans. "because, being Hermes, you'll hold a lottery, I know". Trygaeus is making a desperate attempt (which Hermes ignores) to escape death by persuading Hermes to follow his usual custom and draw lots even though there is only one "candidate" for execution: instead of (say) ten lots with ten different names on them, there would this time be one lot marked for Trygaeus' destruction and (say) nine blanks.

402 On stemmatic grounds Olson prints νῦν εἰσι μᾶλλον preceded by a one-syllable lacuna; he does not suggest what could have stood there, and the only possibility I can see is <οὖν> (which certainly could have fallen out easily enough before νῦν).

440/1 *p* here report a lacuna of 7-9 lines; if such a passage has indeed been lost here, it must have contained further blessings on those who work for peace (making a total of 11-13 lines of blessings to match the 12 lines of curses that follow).

469 Alternative emendations are ἄγε νυν (Austin) and ἄγε δὴ (Zimmermann).

493 Meineke's emendation, whose sole justification is consistency with 466, certainly does not deserve to be in the text.

518, 519 Π70 marks change of speaker before both these lines; comparison with 459-463, 467-8, 484-490, 494-6 suggests that 518 should be assigned to the chorus-leader (and dashes therefore inserted at 518 and 519 in my text).

542 For "cupping-vessels" read "ladles": the Greek for cupping-vessel is not *kuathos* but *sikuē*, and the reference is to the use of the (cold) convex side of a ladle to ease the inflammation "as we would ... apply ice or a cold compress" (L.J. Bliquez and P. Rodgers, *CP* 93 [1998] 236-241, at p.240).

550-5 Olson makes a good case for giving 550 to Trygaeus and 551-5 to Hermes; 551-5 is a herald's proclamation, and Hermes (as always) carries a herald's wand. The "agricultural tools" of 552 are not produced *ad hoc*, but are the same tools which the chorus had when they first entered; they had laid these aside in order to haul on the ropes, and now they take them up again and keep them until 732. My stage direction at 563/4 should be corrected accordingly.

605 Olson finds no emendation satisfactory, but thinks the context requires "a v[er]b implying some sort of abuse". This desideratum is met by ἥψατ' αὐτῆς (Herington), which is adopted by Henderson (LCL); trans. "it was Pheidias who first violated her purity [lit. touched her] when he got into trouble".

628 For "raven-fig" read "crow-fig".

660 Better "Well, let her speak in a whisper just to you".

726 Trygaeus' exit is more likely to be into the far wing (i.e. passing in front of Peace, not round the side of her): "his address to [Fullfruit and Showtime] in 726-8 is most easily taken as intended to cover [this] movement" (Olson xlvii).

749 ὑμῖν was not proposed by Blaydes, and Olson credits it to me (though he does not himself accept it).

832 We should surely read κατὰ τὸν αἰθέρα – not because my translation "in the sky" would otherwise be incorrect, but because in Euripides it is always in the *aithēr* (the bright substance that fills the upper part of the space between the earth and the firmament) and not in the *āēr* (the cool, damp, often misty vapour that we mortals breathe) that both stars and (when they are thought of as going above rather than below) departed souls have their being: ἀέρα slipped in here from 827. (This proposal of mine made its first public appearance in Olson's apparatus and commentary.)

866 Triclinius' emendation, or something like it, should be accepted; cf. below on 920.

886 Meineke's conjecture must be wrong, since 875-880 makes it overwhelmingly probable that Showtime has no clothes to remove; read τὰ σκεύη, and trans. "that stuff". The scholia are probably on the right track in supposing "that stuff" to be "some symbols of peace and agriculture"; they must, when held motionless in front of her, be large enough to conceal what is displayed at 891, but 879-880 suggests that a fair amount of thigh is already exposed. A skin or two of wine would be appropriate; of the fragrances of Showtime, as listed in 530-7, at least six had some connection with wine (cf. also 874).

893 For "used to keep their trivet there" read "used to put their pot-props there"; *lasana* have been identified by S.P. Morris, *Hesperia* 54 (1985) 393-409, with a class of coarse earthenware objects, shaped like bent cylinders with handles, which seem well fitted to be used, in pairs or in threes, to support a cooking-pot over a fire. Morris, and likewise Olson, think the reference is to Showtime's legs; but the (roughly cylindrical) *lasana* are said to belong, not to her, but to the Council, and in this context they are therefore likely to be phallic.

913 For "qualitites" read "qualities".

916 Olson prefers to retain τιv δῆ" ("Well, what will you say when ... ?") rather than φήσεις, because the latter is easier to explain as a gloss; note that 917 need not be an answer to 916 − it may merely continue 915 ("And we'll always ..."), ignoring the interruption.

920 Deletion of ὅμιλον is unjustifiable, because it was not a word in ordinary use in Hellenistic and later times and would not have been written in as a gloss.

924-936 In view of the second person plural in 925, Trygaeus' interlocutor in this passage should probably be the chorus-leader (so Olson).

953 Olson makes the excellent emendation τοῦδ': in translation, for "give him something" read "give him some of this beast".

956-962 In accordance with the chorus's advice (950), the sacrificial preparations are made at breakneck speed (to great comic effect), until the action is slowed for the sake of other jokes in 963-972 (so Thiercy).

978-986 Olson prefers to give this to the chorus-leader, because (i) a description of the behaviour of "adulterous wives" is more appropriate to him than to a slave and (ii) "it is not the business of a slave to pray for the welfare of the *polis*[6]" (van Leeuwen); but (i) the behaviour being described would be visible to anyone, slave or not, passing along the street, and (ii) the prayer is not for the Athenian *polis* (which is not mentioned once) but for the Greek people as a whole (996), and slaves are among those envisaged as benefiting from Peace's return (1002).

995 For "to one another" read "about one another".

1013-4 See Addenda to comm. on *Ach.* 893-4.

1025 Better "and all the other requisites for this job" (so in effect Olson); my previous rendering would require not τούτοις but ταύταις. The "requisites" will then include the utensils that are brought out presently on the table.

1031 For "Stillbides" read "Stilbides".

1066 Olson gives the question "Why are you laughing?" to the slave, "since Hierocles nowhere else acknowledges [Trygaeus'] comments".

1081 For "cast lots" (Greek *diakauniasai*) read "throw dice": a *kaunos*, as Olson points out, was not an object but a numerical score (Ar. fr. 673, Cratinus fr. 207), so the reference is probably to a form of lottery by dice, in which two or more players each threw two or three dice with the highest (or, less likely, the lowest) total winning.

1102 Before "*a portion of each part of the offals*" add "*a platter on which is*" (so rightly Olson).

1103 For "if it's all right with you" read "if that's your attitude"; see D.M. Bain, *CR* 36 (1986) 200.

1135 For "grubbed up" read "lopped"; Olson compares Dem. 43. 69-70 where *ekpremnizein* (the verb used here) is something distinct from *exoruttein* "uprooting".

1144 For "parch" perhaps read "scoop out"; cf. E.K. Borthwick, *CQ* 19 (1969) 311.

1173 For "scarlet" read "crimson" (cf. 303 above).

1191-6 Olson has attendants bring out tables, food, cooking gear, etc., before or during this speech, and in view of 1312-4 (cf. 1196) this is likely. The chorus will eventually take

---

6   van Leeuwen actually used the Latin word *civitas*.

away the food with them, but the other properties will remain (to be cleared away when the play is over).

1193-4 A headband would probably not be large, conspicuous or distinctive enough to be effective as a prop here. Olson suggests that Trygaeus (whom he assumes to be already dressed as a bridegroom) gives the slave his old inner garment (*exōmis*); but he is still a farmer, and will need working clothes.

1197ff For "sickle" read "pruning-hook" throughout: the Greek word is *drepanon*, and Pl. *Rep.* 333d (cf. Hes. *Shield* 292) shows that when one thought of *drepana* one thought primarily of the cultivation of vines, not of cereals, and this is appropriate both to the Dionysiac ethos of comedy and to Trygaeus' name and occupation.

1222 For "take the away" read "take them away".

1248 For "you'll have the very thing to ..." read "it'll do, all on its own, to ..." (so in effect Olson).

1250 The objects displayed here are probably not helmets, since helmets are too big to be used for measuring drugs and since 1255-7 strongly suggests that no alternative use for helmets has been mentioned up to that point; Olson suggests scabbards (*kolea*).

1268-94 Olson suggests that Boy 2 is urinating (or pretending to) while Trygaeus is engaged with Boy 1 (cf. *Wasps* 936-941).

1305-end Note that the line-numbering in this passage, which has never been completely standardized, is altered by Olson so as to correspond strictly to the versification and to allow space for attested lacunae (see below); the following table shows the correspondences, for all verses other than hymeneal refrains:

Sommerstein	Olson	
1305-10	1305-12	
1311-28	1313-30	
1329-31	1331-3	
1333-4		1336-7
1337-43	1340-6	
1346-8		1354-6
1351-4		1359-62
1357-9		1365-7

1307 The emendation which I ascribed to Portus was taken by him from the marginalia of Biset; see C. Austin, *Dodone* 16 (1987) 63 n.2.

after 1345 *p* mark a lacuna of 5-7 lines, and a confused note in Σ^V may or may not indicate that its author also knew of such a lacuna; so it is possible that a stanza plus refrain, probably in praise of Trygaeus, has dropped out here. In that case 1346-8 may be addressed by Trygaeus to the chorus ("You, at any rate, will live happily ..."; the Greek verbal forms in this sentence are all plural, not dual).

1359 A scholium at the very end of the text reports that Heliodorus read ὑμὴν ὑμέναι' ὦ, and this (presumably doubled) should therefore be restored to the text (Schrader — though Olson does not actually insert the words).

Commentary
lines
6-7, 33-37 Ar.'s description of the dung-beetle's method of eating may derive from a misinterpreted observation of its method of making a ball of dung: see N. Davies and J. Kathirithamby, *Greek Insects* (London, 1986) 88-89. He could not have observed the creature actually eating, since it feeds underground.

45-46 The Ionians, one of whom is made to liken the dung-beetle to Cleon, are seen by Cassio *Commedia ...* 106 as representing "those allies who suffered so much at the hands of the demagogues" (cf. comm. on 639 and 760); Cassio also discusses (105-118) the many other references to, and jokes about, Ionia and Ionians in the play.

*****69-71 then he'd have light little ladders made ... :** Olson compares Polyaenus 7.22; also relevant is Σ Eur. *Phoen.* 1173 (on Capaneus).

83-86 Olson draws attention to several echoes in this passage of expressions commonly used in relation to horses; cf. Xen. *On Horsemanship* 7.10, 8.5, 9.6, 10.17.

126 *Stheneboea* is much the more probable source, since only in that play (where Bellerophon invited Stheneboea to fly with him to Caria/Lycia, and then threw her into the sea) could the option of a sea-voyage have been considered, and moreover the scholia here cite a passage about Lycia as having preceded our line in the Euripidean text; both Nauck (Eur. fr. 669.4) and C. Collard (in Collard et al. *Euripides: Selected Fragmentary Plays* i [Warminster, 1995] 96, 119) ascribe the line to *Stheneboea*.

*****128 harness ... and ride:** lit. "yoke ... and drive", which would suit a chariot better than a steed; the phrase is therefore probably paratragic (so Olson).

*****140 what if it falls into the watery depths of the sea?:** the phraseology is paratragic, and the line could well come from *Stheneboea* (so A.C. Clark, *Euripides in a Comic Mirror: The Tragodoumenai* [Diss. U. of North Carolina 1998] 65 n.38); Stheneboea herself would be the speaker, expressing apprehension about Bellerophon's invitation to her to elope with him on Pegasus.

151 For another religious regulation requiring three days' chastity cf. *SEG* xiv 529.15-17 (Cos, second century BC).

277-8 On the "Samothracian gods" see also S.G. Cole, *Theoi Megaloi: The Cult of the Great Gods of Samothrace* (Leiden, 1984).

279 The pun expounded in my note explains why Ar. used the verb *apostrephein* instead of *diastrephein*, the normal verb for twisting or spraining a limb.

291 Timotheus' *Persians* was not a dithyramb but a nome.

296-8 On satyric features in this scene, and in *Peace* generally, see F. Jouan in P. Thiercy and M. Menu ed. *Aristophane: la langue, la scène, la cité* (Bari, 1997) 222-4.

301 The omitted reference should be to pp. xviii-xix. The note on **liberation** should be keyed to 301, not 302.

304 See Addenda to comm. on *Ach.* 566.

319 The line probably does refer to Cleon: see B. Marzullo, *MCr* 23-24 (1988/9) 209-221 (cf. Addenda to comm. on *Knights* 214-5). Cleon can perfectly well be envisaged as "rushing out" or "making a sortie" from his abode in the underworld, and in the absence of an expressed subject the hearer will inevitably take the subject to be the same as in 313-5. War's occupation of the stage-house is now forgotten; henceforth it represents the entrance to the cave in which Peace is confined.

348 See Addenda to comm. on *Knights* 562.

374-5 The price of three drachmas is realistic; Olson compares e.g. *IG* ii² 1358 a.55, b.4, and *Hesperia* 7 (1938) 5 no.1.86-91.

395 Eupolis fr. 35, as plausibly emended by Hanow, locates the "single incident" at the battle of Spartolus in 429 (Thuc. 2.79), when the Athenians were routed, losing 430 dead including all three commanders; Peisander, according to the speaker of this fragment, was on that occasion "the most cowardly man in the army".

420 See Addenda to comm. on *Clouds* 985.

433-457 There would be nothing unheard-of in the idea of a god making libation: see Cassio *Commedia ...* 64, and Olson *ad loc.*

446 See Addenda to comm. on *Ach.* 88.

479 See Addenda to comm. on *Knights* 394.

520 K. Vanhaegendoren, *Die Darstellung des Friedens in den Acharnern und im Frieden des Aristophanes* (Hamburg, 1996) 121, notes that in this seven-line speech there are at least eight expressions linking Peace/peace with wine; cf. also Addenda to 886 (text).

523 Opora and Theoria both seem to have been names used by courtesans. One named Opora was the title-character of comedies by Alexis and Amphis; for Theoria cf. *Defix.* 15 (Sophocles had a mistress named Theoris, cf. Athenaeus 13.592a, *Life of Sophocles* 13). On the concept of *theoriā*, especially in my sense (ii), and its relevance to this play, see I.C. Rutherford, *PLLS* 10 (1998) 141-5, and S. Scullion in E.J. Stafford and J. Herrin ed. *Personification in the Greek World* (London, forthcoming), who brilliantly renders Theoria's name as "Junket".

*551-2 the peasants may go off home to the country: they do not in fact do so until the end of the play, after a second proclamation and a fresh distribution of agricultural equipment (1316-8); on the "abortive finale" here, see Cassio *Commedia ...* 74-75.

616-8 This passage is evidence that Pheidias was remembered as being strikingly handsome.

*629 which I'd planted (Greek *ephuteusa*) **and nurtured:** adapted from Euripides' *Medea* (1349) where Jason laments the death of the children "whom I begot (*ephūsa*) and nurtured".

681 See Addenda to comm. on *Ach.* 846.

682 Halliwell's proposal and mine were both anticipated by Sharpley.

699 This passage was explained many years ago by Henri Grégoire (in L. Parmentier & H. Grégoire, *Euripide* [Paris, 1923] 162-3 n.5) as alluding to a speech in Sophocles' *Creusa* (Soph. fr. 354) in which someone says:

> And do not be surprised, my lord, if I hold on to my profit as I do! For even mortals who have great wealth grasp at profit, and for human beings all other things rank after money. There are those who exalt the man who is free from sickness, but I think that no poor man is free from sickness; the poor man is always sick (tr. Lloyd-Jones).

In typical comic fashion, the opinions of a character are here ascribed to the author. The same ideas are distantly echoed in *Birds* 605 and *Wealth* 146, 188-197. In the last sentence of my note, as Peter Jones (personal communication) has pointed out, "and unsuccessful" should be deleted, in view of 696 ("he's prospering").

714 I should have made it clearer that the *theōroi* referred to in Dem. 19.128 were *members* of the Council, who thus had a fair chance of getting a free trip abroad during their term of office: comedy shows no hostility to this "perk", such as it does e.g. to the salaries and entertainments of (elected) ambassadors, no doubt because the lottery for membership of the Council was open to all citizens who chose to apply. See MacDowell 194.

741 I failed to notice that *Proleg.* XIc (p.45.50 Koster) and XIIa (p.35.65) actually state that in *Syleus* Heracles' tasks included the making of loaves; see E. Degani, *Eikasmos* 6 (1995) 67-69.

749 Similar language is also used of Aeschylus in Pherecrates fr. 100, and that passage is more likely to have been the model for ours than vice versa; see N. O'Sullivan, *Alcidamas, Aristophanes and the Beginnings of Greek Stylistic Theory* (Stuttgart, 1992) 15.

775-818 Ts. Uchida, *RhM* 135 (1992) 225-234, argues convincingly that the "I" of these songs is not the chorus (as in similar parabatic songs in Ar.'s other early plays) but the poet, who thus, having asserted in the "anapaests" his superiority to all other comic dramatists, now claims superiority over almost all tragic poets as well.

775-780 The scholia do *not* in fact say this passage comes from the *Oresteia* (only that it comes from Stesichorus), and as Platnauer pointed out (cf. Kugelmeier 84-86) its content and tone seem hardly appropriate to so dark a theme.

*789 dwarfish: "not merely small but disfigured as well" (Olson): cf. Arist. *PA* 686b4-11 (large head, small legs).

804-6 The vocabulary is tragic: Olson thinks this passage may be, or may include, a quotation of or allusion to a play by Melanthius, but it could also be a mere pastiche in tragic style appropriate to the description of a tragic poet.

829 See Addenda to comm. on *Clouds* 333.

*830 preludes: see comm. on *Birds* 1385.

832-3 To the list of early-attested "catasterisms" add Ursa Major (= Callisto) and probably also Bootes (cf. Hes. fr. 163). In 412 Euripides made Athena as *dea ex machina* inform almost the entire cast of his *Andromeda* (Cepheus, Cassiepeia, Andromeda, Perseus — possibly even the sea-monster that had been about to devour Andromeda, now the constellation Cetus) that they would eventually be translated to the skies (Eratosthenes, *Catast.* 15, 17). For the Hyades add Eur. *Erechtheus* fr. 65.107-8 Austin with schol. Aratus 172. My belief (2) appears first in Epicharmus fr. 245, 265, and is combined with (1) in Pl. *Tim.* 42b as part of a quasi-Pythagorean theory of metempsychosis.

835 On Ion see also M.L. West, *BICS* 32 (1985) 71-78, who puts his birth "c.484-1"; K.J. Dover, *The Greeks and their Legacy* (Oxford, 1989) 1-12; and A. Leurini, *Ionis Chii testimonia et fragmenta* (Amsterdam, 1992).

*868 her bottom part (Greek *ta tēs pūgēs*) is, as Olson has perceived, a surprise substitute for "the things in Fortune's power" (*ta tēs tukhēs*); cf. Eur. *Phoen.* 1202, *IA* 1403.

890 Olson shows that my interpretation of *anarrhusis* is wrong; I would now take the word as bearing its usual cultic meaning of "drawing back", but with the *thighs* (rather than the head/neck) as its implied object, so that it becomes equivalent to *diamērizein* "get between the thighs [of a woman or boy]"; cf. especially *Birds* 1254 "raise up her legs and screw her (*diamēriō*)".

924 For "sood" read "stood".

933 Trygaeus hopes that, by a kind of name-magic, the use of an *ois* for the sacrifice to Peace will bring it about that people utter the cry *oī* when the cause of Peace will be served by their doing so.

962 The throwing of the barley seeds to the spectators also serves to make them part of the action; similarly at 1115-6 they are invited to share in the ritual eating of the offals. See Cassio *Commedia ... 126*.

969 For "drenching" read "wetting": as Olson points out, there would not be nearly enough water in the bowl to soak twenty-four *choreutai* — but at least its whole contents can be thrown at them!

1008 See Addenda to comm. on *Ach.* 887.

1014 Evidently in Melanthius' play Jason's new wife, Glauce, died in childbirth (poisoned, suggests Olson attractively, with drugs supplied by Medea ostensibly to ease her delivery).

1031 N.D. Smith, *CA* 8 (1989) 143, notes that Stilbides will lose not only prestige but also perquisites (such as those claimed by Hierocles in the ensuing scene) if sacrificers find they can dispense with his services.

1054-5 Cf. M.H. Jameson in M. Cropp et al. ed. *Greek Tragedy and its Legacy: Essays Presented to D.J. Conacher* [Calgary, 1986] 60-61, citing many relevant vase paintings: "Omens are taken from the behaviour of the ... tail in the fire. With the heat of the flames the tip of the tail turns up and the whole tail forms a curve ... no doubt significance was read into the particular curve that appeared."

*1077-9 "So long as ... peace to have been made": the points Hierocles is seeking to make are (1) that "sometimes a danger is at its worst when it seems to be receding" and (2) that "unwarranted haste ... can have disastrous consequences" (Olson).

1084 The right of certain religious experts to maintenance in the Prytaneum may be mentioned in a damaged, and very variously restored, passage of *IG* i³ 131 (lines 9-10). According to schol. *Birds* 521 the same privilege had been granted to Lampon.

1085 The proposal which I ascribe to Carey had in fact been made before, e.g. by Verrall (*ap.* Sharpley), van Daele and Cantarella: Carey's contribution was to point out that it already appeared in a scholium (now wrongly attached to 1101).

1095 See Addenda to comm. on *Knights* 61.

1127-90 P. Totaro, *Le seconde parabasi di Aristofane* (Stuttgart, 1999) analyses in detail the relationship between this parabasis and Hesiod's *Works and Days*, especially two passages (504-560, 582-596) describing two seasons of the farmer's year (deep winter, cf. 1131-58; high summer, cf. 1159-71) when there is little work to be done.

1146 The name Syra has now turned up in a new papyrus of Menander's *Misoumenos* (*Mis.* 555 Arnott). For Manes, add [Dem.] 53.20 and *SEG* xxxiv 122.37 (a freedman?)

1192 It is far better, with Thiercy, to identify the "crowd" with the theatre audience.

*1263 a drachma for a hundred: a good price for stakes (though not, of course, for spear-shafts); in *IG* i³ 422.305, fifty-nine drachmas buy 10,200 stakes (at which rate one drachma would have bought 173).

*1301 and put your parents to shame: cf. Alcaeus fr. 6.13-14 "And let us not put to shame ... our noble parents who lie under the earth"; both passages use the same dialectal form (*tokēas*) of the accusative plural of *tokeus* "parent". There and elsewhere (e.g. *Iliad* 6.206-210), however, it is the coward who puts his parents to shame (by showing the world that they have begotten and reared an unmanly son); here it is the coward's *son* who puts (one of) his parents to shame (by publicizing his cowardice).

1306 The allusion is rather (so Olson, following a scholium) to oarsmen who only pretend to row, pulling at their oars without dipping them into the water (lit. "pulling <the oars> empty [i.e. with no water in their hollows] past <the sea surface, instead of under it>").

BIRDS

Introductory Note
page

2 n.4 Add to references T.K. Hubbard in G.W. Dobrov ed. *The City as Comedy* (Chapel Hill NC, 1997) 23-50, who argues that *Birds*, while seeming at first to promise an Age-of-Cronus fantasy like those in the plays mentioned, presents in the end "a hypercivilized, overstructured totalitarian state, a dystopian nightmare vision of grandiose proportions". There is much truth in this from a bird's point of view – but Ar.'s audience consisted of humans, and after 1469 Peisetaerus is the only human in the play and hence the only character with whom they can identify.

3 *Animal Farm:* cf. A. Ničev, "L'énigme des Oiseaux d'Aristophane", *Euphrosyne* 17 (1989) 9-30, who (thinking, I am sure, as much of his own land in his own day as of Aristophanic Athens) sees the play as embodying the belief that "the dreams, the efforts and the sacrifices made in the name of a splendid cause are [always] exploited by pragmatists inspired solely by the thought of personal gain".

3 *the established hierarchy of the universe:* P. Thiercy in J.A. López Férez ed. *La comedia griega y su influencia en la literatura española* (Madrid, 1998) 95-96, notes that the play itself has a structure that reflects this hierarchy: Peisetaerus interacts first with birds (59-894), then with men (903-1469), and finally with gods (1494-end).

6 *a ... vase ... in the J. Paul Getty Museum:* few would now maintain that the "Getty Birds" vase was related to this play: the birds on the vase have erect phalli, which comic performers do not wear except for specific reasons (sexual frustration or sexual anticipation) and for which the text of *Birds* offers no support, and they are domestic fowls, whereas all the chorus of our play (listed in 297-304) are wild birds. The most popular view (first put forward by O.P. Taplin, *PCPS* 33 [1987] 95-96; most fully developed by E.G. Csapo, *Phoenix* 47 [1993] 1-28, 115-124) has been that the Getty Birds represent the Better and Worse Arguments in the first version of *Clouds*, but Taplin in a later treatment (*Comic Angels* [Oxford, 1993] 103-4) gave good reasons for rejecting this view, and offered (with unnecessary hesitation) what remains the most persuasive explanation of the painting – that it represents a chorus of *satyrs* costumed as birds, or transformed into birds, from an unidentifiable comedy.

Bibliography

Editions of the play: add G. Zanetto and D. Del Corno (Milan, 1987); N.V. Dunbar (Oxford, 1995).

Editions of the scholia: the scholia to *Birds* have now appeared as Pars II Fasciculus III of Koster's *Scholia in Aristophanem* (ed. D. Holwerda [Groningen, 1991]). I have included below corrections to the apparatus where, but only where, improved information about the scholia has significantly affected the balance of evidence bearing on the constitution of the text.

Other publications since 1986

T. Gelzer, "Some aspects of Aristophanes' dramatic art in the *Birds*", is reprinted with minor revisions in E. Segal ed. *Oxford Readings in Aristophanes* (Oxford, 1996) 194-215.

D.C. Pozzi, "The pastoral ideal in the *Birds* of Aristophanes", *CJ* 81 (1986) 119-129.

E. Corsini, "Gli 'Uccelli' di Aristofane: utopia o satira politica?", in R. Uglione ed. *Atti del convegno nazionale di studi su la città ideale nella tradizione classica e biblico-cristiana* (Turin, 1987) 57-136.

B. Zannini Quirini, *Nephelokokkygia: la prospettiva mitica degli Uccelli di Aristofane* (Rome, 1987).

A. Ničev, "L'énigme des Oiseaux d'Aristophane", *Euphrosyne* 17 (1989) 9-30.

D. Konstan, "A city in the air: Aristophanes' *Birds*", *Arethusa* 23 (1990) 183-207; revised version in Konstan, *Greek Comedy and Ideology* (New York, 1995) 29-43.

C. Perkell, "On the two voices of the birds in *Birds*", *Ramus* 22 (1993) 1-18.

G.W. Dobrov, "The tragic and the comic Tereus", *AJP* 114 (1993) 189-234.

N.V. Dunbar, "*Sophia* in Aristophanes' *Birds*", *Scripta Classica Israelica* 15 (1996) 61-71.

N.V. Dunbar, "Aristophane, ornithophile et ornithophage", in P. Thiercy and M. Menu ed. *Aristophane: la langue, la scène, la cité* (Bari, 1997) 113-129.

G.W. Dobrov ed. *The City as Comedy: Society and Representation in Athenian Drama* (Chapel Hill NC, 1997) 1-148 (articles on *Birds* by D. Konstan, T.K. Hubbard, F.E. Romer, N.W. Slater, G.W. Dobrov and J.J. Henderson).

A. Tsakmakis and M. Christopoulos ed. *Ornithes: opseis kai anagnoseis mias Aristophanikes komodias* (Nicosia/Athens, 1997).

P. Ceccarelli, "Life among the savages and escape from the city", in F.D. Harvey and J. Wilkins ed. *The Rivals of Aristophanes* (London/Swansea, 2000) 453-471.

I.A. Ruffell, "The world turned upside down: utopia and utopianism in the fragments of Old Comedy", *ibid.* 473-506.

Note on the Text and Table of Sigla

page

8 *three papyrus fragments:* two further papyri were published by N. Gonis in *The Oxyrhynchus Papyri* LXVI (1999): Π69 (Oxyrhynchus Papyrus 4516; 2nd century; contains 1661-76), one or two of whose readings had already appeared in Dunbar's edition, and Π78 (Oxyrhynchus Papyrus 4515; 5th/6th century; contains 1324-8 and 1357-61).

8 *a palimpsest in Florence:* Dunbar (pp.20-21) shows that in the text, as more clearly in the scholia, F's affiliations are with the *a* group.

8 *V and E:* now that a good reading previously known only from E (at 1670) has turned up in Π69, there is increased reason to suspect that some other readings of E (e.g. at 992, 1090, 1691, 1710; also M9's reading at 593) may derive from an ancient source of which no other trace survives; see Dunbar, p.27.

9 *Triclinius' recension:* Dunbar (pp.46-47) shows that Triclinius' main exemplar had a text close to that of ΓU.

10 U should be dated "late 13th": see Addenda to *Clouds* Table of Sigla.

11 *see White's edition of the scholia:* the reference should now be to Holwerda's edition, pp. xxiv-xxvii.

Text and Translation
line

1-9   Dunbar reverts to the traditional assignments here (noting that 3-4 should be spoken by the subordinate partner, and holding that τηνδεδί "this other one" in 18 indicates that Peisetaerus has the crow), then continues 10 to Peisetaerus. This, however, requires her to suppose that Peisetaerus' "what's making you gape like that?" in 20 is addressed to his companion's bird rather than his own (since the bird in question must be the jackdaw); it is therefore preferable to leave the jackdaw with Peisetaerus and assign the opening lines as follows: 1 E, 2 P, 3-6 E, 7-8 P, 9-10 E, 11 P, 12a E, 12b-22a P.

9   The conjecture I ascribed to myself was actually first made by Bothe.

61   Dunbar suggests that the two slaves, of whom nothing is heard for a long time and who are not called on to assist their masters during the battle-scene 327ff, here drop the luggage and run away — though there is no obvious moment at which they can return.

65, 68   No doubt Peisetaerus and, following his lead, Euelpides here mimic the posture and movements of birds. I owe this point (obvious once perceived) to Dictynna Hood's production of the play at Cambridge in February 1995.

129   The reading πρῴ is implied by Σ^R as well as by $\Sigma^{VEΓ^2M}$.

134   The scholia should not be cited in support of the reading τότ'.

156   For "Not a disagreeable life to lead" read "It's got quite good wearing qualities"; as the scholia see, Tereus is speaking in the terms a tailor might use in commending a garment to a customer (cf. 121-2). See G.W. Dobrov, *Winged Words/Graphic Birds* (Diss. Cornell 1988) 96.

160   For "bergamot" (a variety that did not exist in antiquity) read "water-mint"; see A. Dalby, *Siren Feasts* (London, 1996) 83.

194   For "snares" read "traps"; Dunbar points out that Greek *pagis* must denote "a solid structure", as is shown by its etymology (lit. "something fixed together") and by e.g. [Homer], *Battle of the Frogs and Mice* 116-7 (a wooden mousetrap).

202, 266   Dunbar defends the transmitted reading ἔμβα;" in both passages, taking it to mean "go up on to" and supposing that Tereus sings from the stage-house roof; εἴσβαινε "go in" at 208 (on which she does not comment) need not contradict this, since the actor would have to go into the stage-house before climbing to the roof. Apart from avoiding two emendations, and avoiding having a major song sung offstage, we may note that this puts Tereus in the best possible position to summon the other birds, as he does, *from far and wide*; 209-222, on the other hand, ought surely to be sung from within the stage-house, since (i) that is where we would expect Tereus' wife to be and (ii) there is no time between 208 and 209 (as there is between 222 and 225) for the actor to get up to roof level.

204   καλοῦμεν is also read by Photius.

226   For "to sing again" read "to sing an aria this time".

241   The metrical objections to Dale's emendation (see comm.) are not fatal, and are perhaps outweighed by Dale's (and Dunbar's) point that any bird that eats oleaster berries will eat arbutus berries as well and vice versa.

270   Tereus may now be wearing armour (being about to act in his official capacity as ruler of the birds) and have two attendants; cf. on 434 below.

299 The scholia provide the following evidence about the text: (1) In the lemma, VΓ have -η-, Γ² -ει-, and each reports Didymus as supporting its own reading. (2) Euphronius held -ει- to be the Attic form, as (E) makes explicit. (3) When the word appears elsewhere in the note, V always has -η-, as does (E) which has the word only once; Γ² varies.

303 For "stockdove" read "redshank". The stockdove has *bluish-purple* feet. Aristotle's bird is fairly certainly identifiable as the palm dove (*Streptopelia senegalensis*), but this is (now at any rate) confined, in Europe, to eastern Thrace. There are some half-dozen red-footed species which are or were common in central Greece and for which no other ancient name is known (redshank, chough, red-footed falcon, lapwing, oystercatcher, black-winged stilt); Ar.'s *eruthropous* is likely to have been one of these. See W.G. Arnott in H.D. Jocelyn ed. *Tria Lustra: Essays and Notes Presented to John Pinsent* (Liverpool, 1993) 131.

303 For "firecrest" read "woodchat" (*Lanius senator*); see Dunbar *ad loc.* and in Thiercy & Menu *Aristophane* 126-7[7].

310-6 Dunbar prefers to analyse 310-2 and 314-6 as dochmiac; in 310-2 this requires the syllable πο to be iterated eight times (as in A) and ἄρ' to be deleted (Haupt).

322 In apparatus, for Σ^M read Σ^(E).

363 Dunbar (on 352-385) argues that since there is only one pot and one spit (cf. 387-391), it is probably only Euelpides who puts on "armour", while Peisetaerus, like a true general (cf. 362), uses his subordinate's body as his shield. Dunbar offers several possible equations of the utensils with items of military equipment; most plausible perhaps is that at first pot = helmet, spit = palisade, plates = shields-cum-eyeguards, while after 386 the spit becomes a spear and the other items are grounded to become boundary-markers of the "camp".

364 In apparatus, to witnesses for ἐλελελεῦ add ^ΛΣ^Γ; to those for ἐλελεῦ add Σ^V(EΓM.

386-7 Dunbar accepts Blaydes' νὴ Δι" with change of speaker, and rejects van Leeuwen's deletions, which are certainly somewhat arbitrary. We can assume that at 361-2 Euelpides, instead of taking one plate "for his eyes" (which might not be big enough), very sensibly took two. Trans. "(Eu.) They're behaving more peaceably. (Pe.) Yes, they are; so lower the pot and the two plates. Now we must mount a patrol ..."

403-5 Dunbar proposes τούσδε τίνες πόθεν (ποτὲ καὶ del. Bothe) ἐπὶ τίνι τ' ἐμόλετον ἐπινοίᾳ: but the ending -τον in the 3rd person dual of past indicative tenses is otherwise confined to a few Homeric passages (the normal ending is -την), and it is very unlikely that Ar. would have used it in a word-form which does not, and with its three successive short syllables could not, appear in Homer.

423 In apparatus, for Σ^ΓΓ³M read Σ^Γ³.

---

7 On this and other passages, it should be pointed out that many bird-names in my translation are deliberately vague; e.g. I say "francolin" (248, 297) rather than "black francolin" and "lark" rather than "crested lark". This is to avoid creating the impression that the attitude of Ar.'s audience to a passage like 297-304 would have resembled the attitude of a bird-lover of today. In many cases classical Athenians may indeed have supposed what are now considered two or more separate species to be one and the same.

434 Dunbar rightly argues that Tereus is more likely to be addressing his own slaves than his visitors' (who may not even be present; see Addenda to 61 above); if so, the "panoply" is probably also his (see Addenda to 270 above; cf. *Lys.* 563, Soph. fr. 581.3), and in that case it is hung in the kitchen not because it consists of kitchen utensils but because "a room with a regular fire seems to have been the normal place ... to hang for storage ... articles not in constant use", since it gave the best protection against damp (Dunbar, comparing Hes. *Works* 45).

460 The emendation which I ascribe to Brunck had been made before him by Bentley.

484 Σ(ii)^{Γ2} reads Μεγαβάζ-, not Μεγαβύζ-.

489 In apparatus, to witnesses for ὄρθριον add Σ^R.

527 For "springes" read "traps"; see on 194 above.

531 For κοὐδ ' οὖν Dunbar proposes κοὐ μόνον, which deserves serious consideration; trans. "And even granted they're determined to do so, they don't just have you roasted ..."

535-8 Dunbar makes drastic changes in the text at the end of this *pnīgos*, partly on metrical and partly on syntactic grounds. I discussed these briefly in *CQ* 48 (1998) 9, but the text that I there implicitly advocated is unacceptable metrically. Read rather:

$$... \text{καὶ τρίψαντες}$$
κατάχυσμ' ἕτερον γλυκὺ καὶ λιπαρόν,
κᾆπειτα κατεσκέδασεν θερμὸν
θερμῶν, ὥσπερ κενεβρείων.

γλυκὺ καὶ del. Dunbar   θερμῶν Sommerstein: τοῦτο καθ' ὑμῶν αὐτῶν codd.: τοῦτο καθ' ὑμῶν ἀτεχνῶς Blaydes: θερμῶν ἀτεχνῶς Dunbar: θερμῶν ὑμῶν αὐτῶν Henderson (LCL)

576 Tyrwhitt's conjecture was anticipated by "Anon. Par.", the unidentified writer of some marginalia in a copy of the Rapheleng edition of Ar. (Leiden, 1600) in the Bibliothèque Nationale, Paris; see Dunbar, p.51, and C. Austin, *Dodone* 16 (1987) 71.

584 Brunck's conjecture was anticipated by Faber.

586 Dunbar deletes σὲ βίον "you as their life" as a gloss[8], alien to classical Greek usage, and continues σὲ Κρόνον, σὲ Ζῆνα, σὲ Γῆν, σὲ Ποσειδῶ: this is, however, a bizarre order, and in *CR* 48 (1998) 9-10 I proposed σὲ Ζῆνα, σὲ Γῆν, σὲ Κρόνον, σὲ Ποσειδῶ (i.e. supreme god, then three others in generational sequence; the absence of medial caesura is unobjectionable, cf. 600). Note that (E)^{ac}ΓU omit δὲ before Γῆν, while V(E)M insert another, unmetrically, before Κρόνον. Trans. "*you* as god, *you* as Zeus, *you* as Mother Earth, *you* as Cronus, *you* as Poseidon".

659 Dawes's conjecture was anticipated by Anon.Par.

676 Nothing in the text indicates when Procne exits, but probably she goes back inside at the end of the parabasis (so Thiercy 1185).

704 Brunck's conjecture was anticipated by Daubuz.

731 εὐδαιμονίαν "happiness" should be deleted (Hamaker); it is clear from Σ^{RVEΓM} that the ancient commentators did not have this word in their text.

---

8   On σὲ (δὲ) Γῆν, Dunbar assumes; but it could also be a gloss on σὲ Ζῆνα, with reference to the supposed etymological link (Pl. *Crat.* 396a-b) between Ζῆνα and ζῆν "to live".

763, 873 For "frigate-bird" read "pigeon", which is no truer a translation but (as noted by W.G. Arnott, *CR* 38 [1988] 212) gives a much neater English pun.

766 Dindorf's conjecture was anticipated by Daubuz.

792 For "let off a fart" perhaps read "blown it all out"; see Addenda to *Wasps* 394.

887 For "Marsh Tit" read "Coal Tit", in view of Aristotle's statement (*HA* 616b4ff) that the *melankoruphos* lays more eggs than any other bird except the ostrich, with a maximum of over 20; the coal tit (*Parus ater*) is the only black-headed or black-capped bird regularly breeding in Greece in whose nest over 20 eggs have been found. See Arnott in Jocelyn ed. *Tria Lustra* 133-4.

996 Read with Dawes κατὰ γύας "into field-blocks" (R^ac^ has κατ' ἀγυάς): as Dunbar points out, ἀγυιά is not an Attic word except in a few religious contexts, and a *polis* includes landholdings (cf. γεωμετρῆσαι in the same sentence!) as well as houses and streets.

1001-9 Dunbar solves the apparent inconsistency between 1001 ("baking-cover", i.e. hemisphere) and 1005 (circle) by supposing that the city as a whole is hemispherical (or, in two-dimensional representation, semicircular) and identifying the "circle" of 1005 with the agora (as is grammatically possible: trans. "apply a straight ruler and draw lines across, so that your circle may become quadrangular and be a central Agora with straight streets leading to it ..."); the agora is "quadrangular" simply because of the angles formed by the four principal avenues that meet there. Dunbar supposes that Meton "draws" his diagram in the air; but if this were so there would be no need for the description to be geometrically coherent as she has convincingly shown it to be.

1033 To witnesses for ἤδη add Σ^E^.

1040 The sequence τοῖς αὐτοῖς ... καθάπερ is perfectly idiomatic (cf. *IG* ii² 244.32), and τοῖς αὐτοῖς should be read: see S. Grimaudo, *Sileno* 20 (1994) 359-368 (published several years after its nominal date, and not available to Dunbar). Trans. "shall use the same measures, weights and decrees as the Olophyxians".

1064 Dunbar's conjecture had previously been entertained, but rejected, by Dindorf.

1149 The list of scholiastic witnesses for ὑπαγωγέα should read Σ^VEΓM^ ^λ^Σ^RVEΓ^: for ἐπαγωγέα, ^λ^Σ^M^.

1149-51 Dunbar in her edition, as earlier in E.M. Craik ed. *"Owls to Athens": Essays ... presented to Sir Kenneth Dover* (Oxford, 1990) 61-68, argues very persuasively that the swallows' role in the building work is that of *plasterers* – appropriate to them because of their habit of using mud as plaster in building their nests, and appropriate also to their being mentioned last: the ὑπαγωγεύς must then be (the bird's tail used as) the plasterer's trowel; my objections relating to the shape of the swallow's tail, and to the textual emendation required, are shown not be insuperable. It is hard on this view to account for ὥσπερ παιδία, but I suggested in *CR* 48 (1998) 10 that there might be an allusion to an (otherwise unattested) children's game in which one player held an object behind his/her back and the others tried to guess what it was or which hand held it (the speaker's own hands could be used to make such an allusion obvious). If this, or something like it, is correct, we can render: "And the swallows flew up holding their trowels behind them, like children playing a game, and carrying mud in their beaks."

1208 Elmsley's conjecture was anticipated by Daubuz.

1212 Bachmann's textual proposals are accepted by Dunbar, probably rightly, on the ground that they account best for the state of the transmitted text; trans. "Did you make an approach to the Chief Jackdaws? (Iris) What are you talking about?"

1240/2 Dunbar reads the future indicatives ἀναστρέψει (Porson) and καταιθαλώσει (R Suda); this is Ar.'s usual practice in final clauses introduced by ὅπως without ἄν.

1242 In apparatus, to witnesses for Λικυμνίαις add $^Λ Σ^P$. There is no mention of Callimachus in $Σ^M$.

1288-9 Dunbar points out that the iterative aorist ἄν ... κατῆραν can coexist quite happily with the surrounding imperfects (cf. *Lys.* 510-9), so that Kappeyne van de Coppello's emendation is unnecessary. There is a case for retaining the mss.' ἀπενέμοντ', since this verb can mean "read" (cf. Soph. fr. 144 codd.); see C. Catenacci, *QUCC* 62 (1999) 49-61.

1325 Π78 reads πτερων.

1328 Bentley's conjecture is confirmed by Π78 (βραδυς ϵ[στι τις).

1358 Π78 reads γα[ρ αν νη] Δι.

1360-9 Many scholars, following Didymus (in the scholia), have taken the "wing", "spur" and "comb" of 1364-6 for a shield, spear and helmet. This is attractive, and there is no reason why these items could not have been lying among the wings in the baskets ready for Peisetairos to fish out. If so, as Dunbar notes, *none* of the visitors who come in quest of wings actually get them.

1492 There should be no comma after "naked", since "all down his right side" has to be taken *both* with "stricken" (as in my note) *and* with "naked": the mugger's victim is stripped of his *himation* and left wearing an *exōmis* fastened at the left shoulder and leaving the right side of the upper body bare — the form of *chitōn* worn by most humbler Athenians, even in winter (cf. *Knights* 882-3 and Stone 175-6). See Thiercy 1198.

1549 Τίμων καθαρός "a downright Timon" should be continued to Peisetaerus (Kock, Dunbar): had Prometheus been the speaker, Ar. would certainly have inserted the particle γε.

1652 Dunbar reads with Cobet γ' ἐκ ξένης, this being the usual expression denoting maternal descent in the context of citizenship and inheritance laws.

1656 In apparatus, to witnesses for νόθῳ 'ξαπο- add $^Λ Σ^{Εγ}$.

1665 Π69 has εγγυτατα, but this is probably a banalization (see Dunbar *ad loc.*).

1670 Π69 has κ]αι τουτ, giving strong support to E's reading; in translation, delete "actually".

1671 For αἴκειαν read ἄκειαν: see M.L. West, *Aeschylus: Tragoediae* (Stuttgart, 1990) xlv.

1672 Hirschig's conjecture is confirmed by Π69 (καταστησας).

1674 Π69 has παλαι.

1712 The grammar is simplified, and the stylistic level raised, by οἷος (Blaydes: οἷον VEAMΓ: οἷον δ' U: ἔνδον R).

1720 A.M. Bowie, *Aristophanes: Myth, Ritual and Comedy* (Cambridge, 1993) 165, and also Dunbar, suggest that Peisetaerus and Princess arrive, as a bridal couple of rank and wealth normally would, and as Zeus and Hera once did (see on 1738-40), in a carriage or chariot. This is a very tempting proposal, and would make a maximal contrast with Peisetaerus' first entry in the play, as well as providing a link (as Bowie notes) with the return of the similarly-named tyrant Peisistratus to Athens accompanied by Phye/Athena (Hdt. 1.60). Possibly at 1759-62 the couple stood up in the vehicle (if not already standing), their "dancing" being largely symbolic; Dunbar has them "leaping down ... to exit dancing with the Chorus", but this would leave the vehicle stranded on stage at the end of the play.

1755-8 should be sung by Peisetaerus, not the chorus-leader: (i) as Dunbar points out, it is parallel to the invitations by hero to chorus at *Ach.* 1231 and *Peace* 1357-9; (ii) it is for Peisetaerus, now "most exalted of gods" (1765), to invite the birds to his home, not for them to invite themselves.

Commentary
lines

1-161 Marzullo's reassignments are well defended by D. Del Corno in Thiercy & Menu *Aristophane* 249-250, who argues that they give Euelpides precisely the same kind of part that he has in later scenes, contrasting in a consistent manner with that of Peisetaerus; *contra*, H.G. Nesselrath, *MH* 53 (1996) 91-99.

15-16 For a fuller discussion of Sophocles' *Tereus* in its relation to *Birds*, see G.W. Dobrov, *AJP* 114 (1993) 189-234. The plot and structure of Sophocles' play are discussed by D.G. Fitzpatrick, *CQ* 51 (2001) 90-101.

43 The early scenes are ambiguous as to whether the travellers' aim is to settle in an existing city (cf. 120-154) or to found a new one; but (*pace* Bowie *Aristophanes* 152) the idea of a sacrifice is appropriate only to the latter, and in 44-45 they speak of hoping to find a "*place* where we can settle" as if their plan was to found a city of which they would be the sole inhabitants. The whole plot of the play is shown by Bowie *Aristophanes* 153-166 to be closely modelled in many ways on the genre of city foundation-myths.

*86-87 the fright made my jackdaw flit: M.C. English, *The Stage Properties of Aristophanic Comedy: A Descriptive Lexicon* (Diss. Boston U. 1999) 235, noting that the disappearance of the birds is not mentioned until 26 lines after it is supposed to have happened, suggests that the delay is designed to allow for any possible reluctance they might show to fly away on cue.

102-3 On Demos' peacocks see P.A. Cartledge in Cartledge et al. ed. *Nomos: Essays in Athenian Law, Politics and Society* (Cambridge, 1990) 41-61.

105-6"The joke makes a virtue of necessity and/or choregic parsimony" (N.W. Slater in Dobrov *The City as Comedy* 77); cf. *Peace* 1018-22, *Frogs* 404-9.

149 On relations between Elis and Lepreum, see now J. Roy in M.H. Hansen ed. *The Polis as an Urban Centre and as a Political Community* (Copenhagen, 1997) 282-320, and T.H. Nielsen, "A polis as part of a larger identity group: glimpses from the history of Lepreon", in J. Roy ed. *Belonging: Ethnicity, Citizenship and Group Identity* (London, forthcoming).

153-4 Opuntius (*LGPN* 1 = 2) belonged to the deme Oa, as ostracism ballots cast against him in 417 or 416 have revealed; see F. Willemsen, *AD* 23 (1968) B 29.

172 Simon Hornblower has pointed out to me that the phraseology used here suggests the idea of a "synoecism", the union of a number of communities into a single *polis* with a fortified urban centre; cf. Thuc. 1.58.2 "Perdiccas persuaded the Chalcidians to abandon and demolish their coastal cities, resettle at Olynthus, and make this *single city* a strong one", 2.15.2 "Theseus ... abolished the councils and magistracies of the other towns ... and compelled the people to have a *single city*", Hdt. 1.170.2 "Bias ... advised the Ionians to emigrate in a body, sail to Sardinia and then found a *single city* comprising all Ionians".

209-222 Add to references D.C. Pozzi, *CJ* 81 (1986) 123-4, and G. Mathews, *Maia* 49 (1997) 6-15. The wording of 226 does not necessarily imply that 209-222 were sung: Greek *au* means not "again" but "on this second occasion", so that 226 indicates that there is going to be a song, and that this will be Tereus' second performance, but not necessarily that the first performance was also a song in the full sense.

227-262 Add to references R. Pretagostini in B. Gentili and R. Pretagostini ed. *La musica in Grecia* (Rome/Bari, 1988) 189-198, and L.P.E. Parker, *The Songs of Aristophanes* (Oxford, 1997) 298-305. At a seminar in or about November 1999, my student Themelis Glynatsis pertinently asked what Peisetaerus and Euelpides were doing during the song, and I speculatively suggested that they were scanning the sky for the approach of birds in four different directions successively: in 230-7 to the north-west (towards the corn-lands of the Attic plain); in 238-242 to the south-east (towards the nearest mountain range, Hymettus); in 243-9 to the north-east (towards Marathon and the marshes of the east coast); and in 250-3 to the south-west (towards Peiraeus and the sea).

249 For "the last few centuries" read "the last century or so".

268-292 P. Thiercy, *Aristophane: fiction et dramaturgie* (Paris, 1986) 75 notes that one reason for the insertion of this dramatically unnecessary scene will have been to give the piper, who has been accompanying Tereus' song from the "thicket" in the "role" of Procne, time to get down to the wing-entrance in order to lead the chorus on as was customary. Dunbar and S. Halliwell, *Aristophanes: Birds, Lysistrata, Assembly-Women, Wealth* (Oxford, 1997) xxxiii, have both adopted Dover's staging, which has the advantage that it bluffs the audience into half expecting that the whole chorus may enter at roof level; Dunbar meets my objection by arguing that "'hill-crest' could appropriately describe the top of a building whose front represents rock ... and wood", but 293 implies that the birds have occupied *more than one* hill-crest. Perhaps it is only the Mede and the Second Hoopoe who appear on the roof, while the other two birds (who are *not* said to have occupied hill-crests, nor to have arrived flying) enter at ground level; note that these two (the Flamingo and the Gobbler/Cleonymus bird) are both large and heavy, which the Mede and the Second Hoopoe need not be. *Two* birds on the roof might be occupying corner-turrets of the stage-house which could reasonably be called "crests".

285 On *sūkophantai* see comm. on *Wealth* 31.

289 See Addenda to comm. on *Ach.* 88.

*297-304 The twenty-four birds named in this passage are discussed in detail by N.V. Dunbar in Thiercy & Menu *Aristophane* 113-129. For the *hupothumis* she suggests, as alternative possible identifications, a bunting (*Emberiza* spp.) or a pipit (*Anthus* spp.).

299-300 Dunbar believes that the mythical association of the *kērulos* with the halcyon (which first appears in Antigonus of Carystus *Wonders* 23 Giannini) is based on Hellenistic misinterpretation of Alcman, and that, as implied by Archilochus (fr. 41) and Aristotle

(*HA* 593a12) the bird was a real one, though probably one unfamiliar in Attica; one possibility (put forward by Dunbar on the tentative suggestion of W.G. Arnott) is the pied kingfisher (*Ceryle rudis*), a resident today of Anatolian but not of European shores, whose modern Greek name is *lophokirylos*.

306 Or does the use here of *kopsikhoi* indicate that the chorus, or most of them, were wearing identical costumes that made them more or less resemble blackbirds? My student Thomas Talboy acutely pointed out in a seminar that nowhere in the play is anything whatever said about the actual appearance of individual members of the chorus.

357-361 J. Wilkins in F.D. Harvey and J. Wilkins ed. *The Rivals of Aristophanes* (London/Swansea, 2000) 344, points out the appropriateness of men using cooking and eating utensils as armour/weapons against this eminently edible enemy.

*441-3 that they're not to bite me ...: there is probably an allusion to the rules of the *pankration*, which forbade biting (Luc. *Demonax* 49) and eye-gouging (Philostratus, *Imag.* 2.6.3); see R. Campagner, *Nikephoros* 3 (1990) 141-4.

*444 I agree to the pact: this is the first time the chorus have ever addressed (or been addressed by) the two men directly; hitherto all communication between them has passed through Tereus.

451-9 = 539-547 Parker *Songs* 312-5 prefers to describe the metre as a variety of dactylo-epitrite in which most verses are acephalous (i.e. docked of what would normally be their initial syllable).

*464 are we going to have a dinner, or what?: N.W. Slater in Dobrov *The City as Comedy* 80 notes that Peisetaerus at least *is* going to be dining before the play ends — dining on some of the birds!

471 B. Zannini Quirini, *Nephelokokkygia* (Rome, 1987) 94-95, notes that the same fable is attested in various parts of Africa, attached to a different bird in each region, and that in these versions the idea "there was no earth" appears just as it does in Ar. He may thus have had the story available to him in precisely the form he needed.

507 In *Frogs* 1380-4 *kokkū* may represent the call of the cock (cf. *Eccl.* 31) rather than of the cuckoo, so that the joke here will include a play on the fact that the different calls of these different birds were conventionally represented by the same Greek syllables. Dunbar suggests the expression *kokkū, psōloi pedionde* may have originated "among Athenian soldiers as a jocular reveille call" meaning "get out of bed and prepare for the battlefield"; but it would be odd for a semi-obscene jocularity to use the word *pedion* without reference to its sexual sense, and the expression is at least as likely to derive from the world of the symposium as an invitation to the participants to transfer their attention from the gifts of Dionysus to those of Aphrodite.

516 On Apollo's connection with hawks cf. also *Iliad* 15.237 where he takes the form of one.

525 Dunbar plausibly suggests that while birds in sanctuaries were generally protected, *the sanctuary staff* were permitted to shoot or stone birds *"not established in the [sanctuary] as resident nesters"* (for the exception cf. Eur. *Ion* 1196-8); they would not themselves set traps (not being experts at this), but might hire professionals (the "fowler[s]" of 526) to do so if bird nuisance (from droppings) became particularly serious.

540-3 Cf. R. Tosi, *MCr* 13/14 (1978/9) 239-240. Other parallels include Thuc. 1.71.7, 1.144.4, 2.62.3; Isoc. 8.94; Dem. 3.36. The *topos* is no doubt related to the Athenian citizen's oath of allegiance, which included the clause "I will bequeath the fatherland (sc. to the next generation) not smaller, but greater and better, to the best of my own ability and with the help of all": see P. Siewert, *JHS* 97 (1977) 102-4.

586   Poseidon may owe his place in this passage to a reminiscence of Empedocles fr. 128.2 D-K (which comes, significantly, in a description of that philosopher's own version of the Golden Age): "nor was Zeus king, nor Cronus *nor Poseidon*, but Cypris was queen."

590   Ar. can hardly have been ignorant of the practice of caprification (planting wild and cultivated fig-trees close together, or else hanging wild fruits on the branches of cultivated trees, so that in either case gall-wasps could easily pass from the former to the latter), since Herodotus (1.193.4-5) treats it as common knowledge (and asserts, wrongly, that an analogous practice was followed in the cultivation of date-palms in Babylonia). It may, however, have been thought that if too many gall-wasps got on to a fig-tree they might damage its wood or bark as the *knīpes* did.

619   Although there is no explicit evidence that Greek *states* (except of course Cyrene) consulted Ammon in the fifth century, it is likely that Sparta at least did so sometimes (cf. Paus. 3.18.3). See C.J. Classen, *Historia* 8 (1959) 349-355; I. Malkin, *CQ* 40 (1990) 541-5.

672   A.D. Barker, in a conference paper at Warwick (April 1999), going beyond Romer, made a strong case for the view that Procne is impersonated by the regular theatrical piper, who instead of coming on with the chorus had stayed offstage after accompanying the Hoopoe's song and now appears in the guise of a woman, possibly also with a bird's head under his *phorbeiā* – and remains, still in this guise, to the end of the play. Cf. E.G. Csapo ap. Taplin, *Comic Angels* 107 n.6. To any such suggestion Dunbar objects that the official piper's "long, fancy tunic ... strongly suggests a professional dignity incompatible with his playing costumed as a bird", but pipers in dithyramb, at least, sometimes went to much greater extremes (cf. Arist. *Poet.* 1461b30-32). A stronger objection may be that 268-292 seems designed to give the piper time to take his place at the head of the chorus after the end of the Hoopoe's song (see above on that passage).

673-4 If the "shell" is the mask there is an extra dimension to the joke, since if Euelpides puts his suggestion into practice he will, on unmasking the performer, find himself kissing a *man*! Cf. L.K. Taaffe, *Aristophanes and Women* (London, 1993) 41.

685-702 The Orphic connections of this ornithogony are further examined by A. Pardini in A. Masaracchia ed. *Orfeo e l'orfismo* (Rome 1993) 53-65, and by A. Bernabé in J.A. López Férez ed. *De Homero a Libanio* (Madrid, 1995) 195-211, who concludes that the passage is proof of "a fairly extensive knowledge of [Orphic] literature on the part of Aristophanes and his public". On Orphism and its relation to other religious and intellectual currents of archaic and classical times, see further R. Parker, "Early Orphism", in A. Powell ed. *The Greek World* (London, 1995) 483-510.

695   Night is spoken of as winged in Eur. *Or.* 176 (produced six years later than *Birds*), and is sometimes so represented in art (see E. Bernet, *RE* xvii 1672; *LIMC* s.v. Astra 5, 7, 8, 10).

737-752 = 769-784 There is an interesting discussion of these lyrics by J.M. Bremer in *EH* 38 (1993) 156-9.

771-2 Ar. is here following an established poetic tradition (cf. *h.Hom.* 21.1-3) which conflated the behaviour of two species of swan both of which still winter on the Hebrus delta; the vocal song comes from the whooper swan (*Cygnus cygnus*), the wing-beat noise from the mute swan (*C. olor*). The two species were never distinguished in antiquity. See W.G. Arnott, *G&R* 24 (1977) 149-153.

789 Dunbar (on 786-9) argued that no inference could be drawn from this passage regarding the Dionysia programme, because "us" might refer generally to the performers (or the performers and audience) in the theatre without distinguishing between tragedy and comedy; but G. Mastromarco, *Eikasmos* 9 (1998) 61-68, has shown that in parabatic epirrhemata and antepirrhemata spoken (as this one is) in character, the first person plural, which appears at least 50 times, *always denotes specifically the chorus of the play in question*. W. Luppe (*Eikasmos* 10 [1999] 57-59) argues that a spectator wishing to take a lunch break, and return in a couple of hours, would not need wings to do so; but in this passage the power that wings give is not that of *rapid* movement but that of movement *in the vertical dimension* (five of the eight lines 789-796 end with *aneptato* "he'd fly up" or *kateptato* "he'd fly down"), which alone could make it possible for the spectator to leave the theatre in the middle of a performance without annoying others.

858 My assumption that the "raven in a piper's muzzle" (861) is in fact the regular theatrical piper would of course be ruled out if Barker's suggestion about Procne (see on 672 above) were correct; in any case 859-861 imply that the raven-piper is permanently silenced, which the theatrical piper cannot be. More likely, therefore, with Dunbar, we should assume that the raven-piper is a supernumerary performer who brought up the rear of the sacrificial procession (the piper's regular place in such processions), wearing a raven costume and mask with *phorbeiā* and pipes, and *miming* the action of piping. The implication of calling a raven Chaeris would be precisely the same as the implication of calling Chaeris a raven (see comm. on 861).

893 The *stemmata* may rather (so Dunbar) be a ribboned garland on the priest's head (cf. Eur. *Ion* 522).

904-953 Dunbar notes that in one respect — his need of warm clothes — the Poet is also reminiscent of Hipponax (frr. 32, 34).

967-8 As W.G. Arnott, *CR* 38 (1988) 212 points out, the common Greek crow, namely the hooded crow (*Corvus corone sardonius*), *is* steel-grey, so this oracle contains only two impossibilities, not three.

*974 here, have the book: this refrain implies the existence in some circles of an unreflecting belief that anything that is in a book must be true; see N.J. Lowe, *Annals of Scholarship* 10 (1993) 63-83.

1007 The Place de l'Étoile is now the Place Charles de Gaulle.

1046-7 Add reference to N.R.E. Fisher, *Hybris* (Warminster, 1992).

1072 Dunbar points out that "on this day" implies that *Birds* was produced on the *first* day of the dramatic competition; if my and Mastromarco's interpretation of 786-9 is correct (see above on 789) it must follow that the present speech, like *Eccl.* 1154-62, was written after the draw for order of performance (so N.W. Slater in Dobrov ed. *The City as Comedy* 91 n.33).

1073 "All this must have happened no later than about 417 ...": Dunbar argues that my inference is a *non sequitur*, since the proclamation may have been made several times in a year. This will still, however, not allow us to accept the statements of D.S. 13.6.7 and Al-Mubashir, *Life of Zeno* ed. G. Rosenthal (*Orientalia* 6 [1937] 21-67, at p.33), that the decree of outlawry was passed during the Athenian year 415/4; for the speaker here does not say merely that the proclamation against Diagoras *has often been* repeated, or that it *was* repeated earlier on this (sc. particular) day, but that it *is* repeated especially on this (sc. annually recurring) day — which could not be said if this was the first time the proclamation had been heard at the City Dionysia. Hence the latest possible date for the decree would be the early spring of 415. Either Diodorus, and Al-Mubashir's source, wrongly deduced the date of the decree from the date of *Birds* or of the Mysteries scandals of summer 415, or else there were two decrees, one passed in 416/5 or earlier against Diagoras alone and a later one, passed in 415/4, condemning the people of Pellene also.

*1088-1101 G. Mathews, *Maia* 49 (1997) 7-9, notes some resemblances between this passage and Soph. *OC* 668-678 (written about eight years later) and suggests that they may have a common source.

1114-5 See now however B.S. Ridgway, *AJA* 94 (1990) 583-612, who shows that the material evidence for such "head-protectors" for statues is scanty. Our passage shows only that some statues had crescent-shaped metal objects over their heads, not that these had a protective (or any other functional) purpose; Ridgway suggests that the reference may be e.g. to the helmet-crests worn by some Athenas.

*1122-63 FIRST MESSENGER: P. Thiercy, *Pallas* 38 (1992) 294-8, argues that this character should be identified with Euelpides, who was sent to help with the building of the wall (837-842) and now reports that this job is complete; note especially his last words, "you do the rest now yourself", which suggest that he had previously been a partner or assistant to Peisetaerus. Would Euelpides, however, refer to his companion as "Governor Peisetaerus"?

*1128 the wooden horse of Troy: the reference may, as the scholia suggest, be not so much to the original Wooden Horse as to the bronze statue of it on the Acropolis, made by Strongylion and dedicated by Chaeredemus at an unknown date but earlier than 403 (*IG* i[3] 895, Paus. 1.23.8).

1148 As pointed out by W.G. Arnott, *CQ* 38 (1988) 212, the mallard's "apron" consists not only of a neckband but also of a "purple-brown chest patch". Arnott now, however, prefers to render Greek *periezōmenai* (lit. "girded round") as "with their tunics belted", i.e. with their clothing suitably adjusted for manual work (see Arnott on Alexis fr. 179.11); depending on the precise type of clothing style envisaged, several different duck species might be seen as having appropriate markings (see Dunbar on this passage).

1203 Cf. Shakespeare, *Romeo and Juliet* II iv 108, where the sight of Juliet's ample Nurse rapidly approaching prompts the waggish Mercutio to cry "A sail, a sail!"

*1212-6 Cf. Aen.Tact. 10.8-11, on how to control entry to and exit from a city in time of siege: no inhabitant is to leave by ship without a pass (*sumbolon*, cf. 1214); foreigners who arrive are to be disarmed and a strict watch kept on their lodgings and their dealings with the population.

*1216 my man: this and "mister" (1257) render Greek *ō mele*, which, as is noted by J.D. Hague, *Presenting the Divine: Stagecraft and Politics in Aristophanes' Birds* (Diss. Boston U. 1997) 38-40, is hardly an appropriate form of address for a deity who is supposed to be reproving and threatening a rebellious mortal; it is almost entirely confined to Old Comedy (23 times in Ar.; never in Menander; once among 11,878 address-tokens in the prose corpus studied by E. Dickey, *Greek Forms of Address* [Oxford, 1996]) and serves essentially as a sentence-adverb indicating that the speaker is enlightening the addressee about an important matter of which (s)he is, and ought not to be, ignorant, comparable to English expressions like *I'd have you know* or *the thing is*.

*1253-4 I'll take on the servant first: this third-person reference to Iris is surprising; is there an allusion to some story of a man who found his bride less attractive than her maidservant, and acted accordingly? Peisetaerus' threat to rape Iris recalls her treatment in (probably) two or more satyr-plays, of which only Achaeus' *Iris* is now identifiable: see A. Kossatz-Deissmann, *LIMC* v.1.751-2; E.W. Scharffenberger, *JHS* 115 (1995) 172-3. The story may actually be older than satyric drama itself, since it seems to appear in art as early as 540.

*1257 mister: see above on 1213.

1296 (on Lycurgus): it is probably this Lycurgus who was called a *kerameus* by an unknown comic dramatist (*com. adesp.* 362). See H. Heftner, *ZPE* 119 (1997) 13-19, who considers various possible primary and secondary meanings that *kerameus* may have had; the least unlikely is probably "inhabitant of Cerameicus" (cf. *Frogs* 1093) with the implication "(former) male prostitute" (cf. Hesychius κ2267, also Addenda to comm. on *Knights* 1246) — for (this is not noted by Heftner) Lycurgus seems to be portrayed as effeminate in Cratinus fr. 32 where he is cast for a maiden's role (that of *diphrophoros*, see *Birds* 1552) in a mock Panathenaic procession.

1296 (on bats): compare the riddle alluded to by Pl. *Rep.* 479b-c and quoted, in two versions, by the scholia there: "A man who was not a man killed a bird that was not a bird, perched on wood that was not wood, with a stone that was not a stone" (answer: eunuch, bat, fennel, pumice). The phraseology seems to imply that a bat was thought of as a special kind of bird rather than of beast, just as a eunuch is a special kind of man rather than of woman.

1297 (on the decree of Syracosius): see now S. Halliwell, *JHS* 111 (1991) 59-63; J.E. Atkinson, *CQ* 42 (1992) 61-64; MacDowell 25; A.H. Sommerstein, *CQ* 46 (1996) 332 n.28; J.C. Trevett, *CQ* 50 (2000) 598-600. It is certain, *pace* Halliwell, that Syracosius took some kind of action which deprived comic dramatists of possible satirical targets. In principle, to be sure, the words quoted in my note, to the effect that Syracosius had (literally) "taken away those whom I [*or* they] wanted to satirize", might be not the words of Phrynichus but those of the commentator who cites him; but why should a commentator have conjectured that Syracosius had *carried an anti-comedy decree* on the basis merely of the fact that he (like countless others) had been the subject of insulting remarks in a comedy? Rather, we should accept that Phrynichus did indeed complain of having been deprived of satirical targets. Whether this was done through an anti-comedy decree or by other means, the Phrynichus fragment does not reveal and the scholiast clearly did not know. My 1986 proposal about the content of the decree is unsatisfactory (MacDowell reasonably points out that "immunity from satire would have been a privilege, not a penalty"), and I would now prefer to revert to a suggestion I then rejected (pp.106-7), that Syracosius had deprived Phrynichus and others (not of the *right* but) of the *opportunity* to satirize certain persons (who may or may not have been those implicated in the religious scandals, or some of them) by bringing about their execution or exile. Trevett suggests that Phrynichus was really making a punning reference to the war against the Syracusans, which had resulted in many potential satirical targets being away from Athens on campaign; this is unlikely, since (for one thing) such absence was no bar to comic satire of them (one of the two remaining commanders of the expedition is mentioned twice in *Birds* itself).

1313-1322 = 1325-34 Parker *Songs* 336-341, noting that the "anapaestic" elements are not of types characteristic of true anapaestic verse, explains the metre as based on a dicolon used by Archilochus and found in Cratinus fr. 256 and 257,

$$\cup\cup-\cup\cup-\cup\cup-\cup\cup-x-\cup-\cup--$$

This dicolon appears to have no name, and I suggest calling it, after the Cratinus play in which it appears, the *chironean*.

*1313-4 populous: lit. "with many men". As is noted by N.W. Slater in Dobrov ed. *The City as Comedy* 85, this ought not to be something that the birds should welcome, for it will mean their being outnumbered in their own city; but as always they allow Peisetaerus to lead them by the beak.

1321-2 The praise of Tranquillity has a Pindaric ring; cf. *Olymp.* 4.20, *Pyth.* 8.1 and especially Pind. fr. 109.3 "the shining light of high-souled Tranquillity".

*1346 laws: Greek *nómoi* can also mean "songs", and it is possible that Peisetaerus misunderstands, or professes to misunderstand, what the Young Man is saying.

1372-1409 On the "new" dithyramb, see Addenda to comm. on *Clouds* 333. On Cinesias, see now C. Kugelmeier, *Reflexe früher und zeitgenössischer Lyrik in der alten attischen Komödie* (Stuttgart, 1996) 208-248. On his illness, add Strattis fr. 17.

1403 Antiphon 6.11 is consistent with the supposition (preferred by A.W. Pickard-Cambridge, *The Dramatic Festivals of Athens*[3] [Oxford, 1988] 75-76) that the tribes *chose* from among the ten appointed trainers in an *order* determined by lot, so that the lucky tribes had a wider choice than the unlucky; in the mid fourth century pipers were assigned to tribes for this contest in this way (Dem. 21.13). If this interpretation is correct, Cinesias would in effect be claiming that he was (nearly) always chosen as trainer by the tribe that won the right of making the first choice.

1470-81 This is the first of three choral interludes which serve to separate the final scenes of the play (the others are 1553-64 and 1694-1705). As Bowie *Aristophanes* 175 n.107 notes, each has a thematic link to the scene that precedes it: here the link is sykophancy (1479); in 1553-64 the "Shadefeet" and the cowardly Peisander mirror Prometheus skulking under his parasol; in 1694-1705 the "Tongue-to-Belly Men" are linked by their "barbarian stock" with the Triballian god, by their devotion to the belly with Heracles, and by their "philippic" (lit. horse-loving) nature with Poseidon who *inter alia* was god of horsemanship.

1494-1552 Hague, *Presenting the Divine* 44-51, points out that Prometheus' veiled face, and his parasol, are both *feminine* attributes; but he is unable to suggest convincingly why Ar. should want to portray Prometheus in this way. Perhaps the object is simply to mislead the audience into believing at first that the new arrival is in fact a woman (just as before the entry of Iris we were led to expect a *male* divine intruder, see comm. on

1176); no word spoken either by Peisetaerus, or by Prometheus before he unveils, is specific as to the visitor's gender.

*1595 with full powers: it is only at these words — which tell him that Zeus has committed himself in advance to accept any terms the ambassadors can obtain — that Peisetaerus condescends to take any notice at all of their official démarche.

1615 A. Loma, *Živa Antika* 47 (1997) 87-110, ingeniously, if improbably, explains *nabaisatreu* as Iranian **nabahi xšaθra vahu* "the realm in the clouds is good". One may certainly note that in very many ancient Indo-European languages the word for "cloud" would be something that a Greek might pronounce as *naba-*.

1619 Strictly speaking, as Dunbar points out, the proverb (*menetoi theoi, ouk apateloi*) meant "The gods take their time, but they do not deceive", i.e. the fulfilment of their promises may be delayed but is none the less sure. This interpretation, however, would be of no use to a man who is concerned, not with whether the gods will default on their promises to *him*, but whether *he* can safely procrastinate regarding his promises to *them*: he must be taking *menetoi theoi* to mean, not "the gods are apt to make people wait", but "the gods may be made to wait", and correspondingly the words he ignores — if we are meant to recall them at all — must here be understood as meaning "one cannot deceive the gods", even though *apatelos* is nowhere else found in a passive sense.

1628-9 Alternatively, *naka* may represent a negative in the Triballian's native language, which would certainly be Indo-European; see C. Brixhe in R. Lonis ed. *L'étranger dans le monde grec* (Nancy, 1988) 116-7.

1701-3 Not only *Philippoi* but also *Gorgiai* may conceal a pun, since the latter could suggest *gorgos* "fierce", thus picturing the Tongue-to-Belly Men as a ferocious tribe of barbarian horsemen. For the association between the word *gorgos*, horses, and horsemen cf. Xen. *Cyr.* 4.4.3, *Eq.* 1.10, 1.14, 10.4, 10.5, 10.17, 11.12, *Hipparch.* 3.11.

1731-6 = 1737-42 On this song see G. Mathews, *Maia* 49 (1997) 16-20.

1738-40 Dunbar notes, however, that in art the bridal car is driven not by a friend of the groom, but either by the groom himself or by a professional driver.

LYSISTRATA

Introductory Note
page

2 n.9 The alleged affair was no mere "later legend"; in a comedy produced during Alcibiades' lifetime (most likely during his years of naval command between late 411 and 407) someone spoke of "the delicate Alcibiades ... whom Sparta is eager to seize as an adulterer" (*com. adesp.* 123).

2 *Peisander ... had not yet come forward in public:* H.C. Avery, *CP* 94 (1999) 127-146, thinks that *Lys.* ignores the possibility of radical constitutional change not because Peisander was keeping his plans secret, but because Peisander was not yet in Athens at all. He doubts whether the plans could have remained secret for long once Peisander had arrived (since they had been publicly aired in Samos, cf. Thuc. 8.48.2-3, and were therefore known to the crew of his ship), and suggests that his mission to Athens was delayed (note the imperfect tense in Thuc. 8.49) by perceived naval threats to Samos (cf. Thuc. 8.50.5-51.2 and 41.3-43.1) and that he only sailed for Athens when it was clear that the Peloponnesian fleet at Rhodes did not intend to put to sea for some time (cf. Thuc. 8.44.4) – which, Avery calculates, would be just about the time of the Lenaea.

4 n.22 I would now add the concluding scene of *Peace* and at least one, probably two, scenes in *Ecclesiazusae*; see comm. on *Eccl.* 969 and Introduction to *Eccl.*, p.32.

5 n.31 The Myrrhine epitaph is now *IG* i^3 1330.

Bibliography

Editions of the scholia: the scholia to *Lys.* have now appeared as Pars II Fasciculus IV of Koster's *Scholia in Aristophanem* (ed. J. Hangard [Groningen, 1996]). I have included below corrections to the apparatus where, but only where, improved information about the scholia has significantly affected the balance of evidence bearing on the constitution of the text.

Other publications since 1990

L.K. Taaffe, *Aristophanes and Women* (London, 1993) 48-73.

D. Konstan, "Aristophanes' *Lysistrata*: women and the body politic", in A.H. Sommerstein et al. ed. *Tragedy, Comedy and the Polis* (Bari, 1993) 431-444; revised version in Konstan, *Greek Comedy and Ideology* (New York, 1995) 45-60.

F.D. Harvey, "Lacomica: Aristophanes and the Spartans", in A. Powell and S.J. Hodkinson ed. *The Shadow of Sparta* (London, 1994) 35-58.

R.L. Fowler, "How the *Lysistrata* works", *EMC* 15 (1996) 245-9.

C.A. Faraone, "Salvation and female heroics in the parodos of Aristophanes' *Lysistrata*", *JHS* 117 (1997) 38-59.

G. Mastromarco, "La *Lisistrata* di Aristofane: emancipazione femminile, società fallocratica e utopia comica", in A. López Eire ed. *Sociedad, política y literatura: comedia griega antigua* (Salamanca, 1997) 103-116.

A.H. Sommerstein, "Nudity, obscenity and power: modes of female assertiveness in Aristophanes", in S. Carlson and J. McGlew ed. *Performing the Politics of European Comic Drama* (Cedar Falls IA, 2000) 9-24.

Text and Translation
line

64 The evidence from Σ^R is more complex than my apparatus implies. There are two annotations, in both of which the word ἀκάτιον appears; but while one of them is clearly explaining the reading τἀκάτ(ε)ιον, the other is equally clearly explaining a text which referred to a shrine of Hecate.

69-253 G. Mastromarco, *Eikasmos* 6 (1995) 71-89, proposes an alternative division of roles between Calonice and Myrrhine in this scene, which has the advantage of being based on observable data within the scene itself. The speaker of 95b-96 ("Yes, indeed, dear lady ...") should be Myrrhine, since Calonice has already asked the question (21-23) and been given an answer. Hence Myrrhine is, as 69 and 73 already suggested, the leader and spokeswoman of the Athenian wives who arrive at and after 65; and accordingly Mastromarco gives her all the neutral, "straight" interventions, leaving for Calonice mostly those which are distinctively boozy or bawdy, viz. 83, 88b-89, 91b-92, 104, 112b-114, 130 [*sic*; I would prefer 129], 136b, 201, 207, 238b-239. This, as he notes, prepares well for the role that Myrrhine (but not Calonice) will have later in the play.

106 Hangard reports $^\lambda\Sigma^o$ as reading πορπακισ⁻.

107-110 MacDowell 230 n.4 plausibly assigns these lines to Calonice on account of their "vulgar tone" (cf. above on 69-253); indeed one might well claim that they are positively wrong for Lysistrata who elsewhere, while expertly exploiting the sexual desires of others, never gives any indication of being subject to them herself. One may further note that the speaker's "us" (110), referring to the frustrated wives, contrasts with Lysistrata's "you" (99-101); that the particle *oun* "then, in that case" in 111 appears to mean "in view of these complaints of yours"; and that to take these lines away from Lysistrata adds to the shock-value of her obscenity in 124, which will then be the first she has intentionally uttered in the play.

116 Hangard reports παρα⁻, not παρ⁻, as the reading of Σ^o and its lemma.

126 Hangard reports that $^\lambda\Sigma^o$ reads μοιμυᾶτε, though the scholium itself implies that μυᾶτε stood in the commentator's text.

133-6 There is no need to posit a fifth actor here (or at 447-8, see below); the speaker of 136b is not merely "repeat[ing] her refusal" (Henderson xlii) but intensifying it and thereby showing that the speaker of 133-5 is not isolated in her extreme reaction. See D.M. MacDowell, *CQ* 44 (1994) 331.

152 In first apparatus entry, before "codd. Suda" insert "vel sim."

173 The *lemmata scholiorum* are ἃς σπουδᾶς in Γ, ἃς σποδᾶς in one scholium in O, ἃς σπονδᾶς in another; but in both mss., and also in R, the scholium itself gives the gloss σπουδῆς.

200 Hangard reports $^\lambda\Sigma^o$ as having a circumflex, not a grave, accent.

206 S. Colvin, *Dialect in Aristophanes* (Oxford, 1999) 175-6, revives a suggestion by Bergk that Ar. wrote ποτόδδει Ϝαδύ: digamma (Ϝ) and gamma (Γ) are frequently confused by scribes unfamiliar with the former.

259 The list of *dramatis personae* prefixed to the play in Γ includes the name Στρυμοδώρα: no woman named Strymodora is mentioned anywhere in the text, so it is likely that the reference is to this passage and that Γ or its source, before mutilation, had the true reading in its text here.

444 For "cupping-vessel" read "ladle"; see Addenda to *Peace* 542.

447-8 There is again (cf. on 133-6 above) no need for a fifth actor; the speaker of 447-8 may be the women's chorus-leader (so Rogers, Dover *AC* 156, Thiercy), intervening from an unexpected direction.

514 The reading of ᴬΣᶠ is ἦδ': the scholium in R has no lemma.

539 There is no relevant scholium in R: that in Γ has αἵρεσθ' as its lemma.

564 ἐδεδίσκετο is also read by Photius.

601 To witnesses for δημάζω add Σ(ii)ᶠ.

664 It is not certain that the transmitted reading λυκόποδες "Wolf-feet" would be unmetrical: F. Perusino, *QUCC* 58 (1998) 57-67 (cf. I. Rodríguez Alfageme, *CFC:egi* 9 [1999] 129-138), arguing that λευκόποδες "Whitefeet" would carry connotations of effeminacy hardly appropriate for this semichorus, notes that elsewhere in Ar. a dochmiac may respond to two cretics (cf. Parker *Songs* 47; I have accepted such responsions in my text at *Wasps* 339 ~ 370 and *Birds* 333-5 ~ 349-351). However, Hesychius clearly read "Whitefeet", and, in broad agreement with R.J. Hopper, *CQ* 10 (1960) 246, I would now interpret this as *synonymous* (not, as formerly, antonymous) to "Dustyfeet" (*konīpodes*) and as referring to peasant soldiers (the underlying assumption, historically mistaken but implicit e.g. in *PMG* 893 and 896, being that all foes of the tyrants were democrats).

715 R's reading should be given as ἦ.

761 For "hooting" read "honking".

809 Parker *Songs* 379 argues that Bentley's emendation is unnecessary, since the irregular responsion which it is designed to avoid has a precise parallel at 1062 (~ 1048, 1193, 1207); read ἦν τις ἀίδρυτος with the mss. other than R.

917 For "let you lie" read "lay you"; see Addenda to comm. on this passage.

998 Σᴿᴳ gloss the verb in the aorist, not the imperfect tense, implying a reading ἆρξε μέν or simply ἆρξεν (conj. Blaydes).

1063-4 Add to apparatus: γεύεσθ' Holwerda.

1153 Hangard reports ᴬΣᴿ as reading ἱππίους.

1220 The reading σομεν should be ascribed not to Florent Chrestien but to ᴵΣᴿ.

1273 It is possible that in this scene Lysistrata wears the *aegis* of Athena. The priestess of Athena Polias sometimes wore this garment, in particular when she visited brides shortly after their marriage (Suda αι60) – and Lysistrata is presiding over what is in effect a mass renewal of marriage. If Lysistrata is thus, as it were, the embodiment of Athena (cf. E.J.S. Sibley, *The Role of Athena in Fifth Century Athenian Drama* [Diss. Nottingham 1995] 61-62), it accounts for the otherwise curious fact that the many deities invited to join the dance in 1279-90 do not include Athena (for Athena is already present and, if my assignment of the song in 1279-90 is correct, she is actually issuing the invitation); and the final hymn (see comm. on 1320-1) will be virtually a hymn to her, the maker of peace, as Athena incarnate. It is probably also significant that the heroine's name is reminiscent of Athena's epithet or cult-title *Phobesistratē* "she who puts armies to flight" (*Knights* 1177), which is itself associated with the aegis (Hes. fr. 343.18).

1279 My metrical characterization of this song (see comm. on 1279-90) requires the adoption here of Enger's conjecture ἔπαγε <δὲ> Χάριτας.

1307 Add to apparatus· ἦτε and εἶτε Σ^R.

1315 N.C. Conomis, *Hellenika* 38 (1987) 139-140, makes the very tempting conjecture ἐκπρεπής, comparing Alcman *PMG* 1.46 (which refers to the leader of a chorus of Spartan maidens!); a similar corruption has occurred in almost all mss. at Eur. *Hec.* 269, and in most at Aesch. *Pers.* 184, Eur. *Alc.* 333. Trans. "and pre-eminent at their head is the daughter of Leda, the unsullied chief of their chorus".

1320 The lemma in Np is simply καὶ τὰν σιὰν: in O it is καὶ τὰν δίαν [*sic*] δ' αὐτὰν.

Commentary

line

81ff See now Colvin, *Dialect* for a detailed analysis of Ar.'s representation of Laconian, which Colvin (p.297) finds to be carefully and, on the whole, consistently depicted.

*254-387 Important new light is shed on this *parodos* by C.A. Faraone, *JHS* 117 (1997) 38-59, who shows that the male chorus's attempt to burn the Acropolis with the women inside it, and the female chorus's dousing of the flames, is reminiscent (i) of several episodes of myth (Zeus and the Hyades saving Alcmene from the rage of Amphitryon; the dousing of Heracles' pyre by nymphs before Athena [n.b.] conveys him to heaven; the dousing of Croesus' pyre), (ii) of the role of water-carrying nymphs in various mystery-cults (cf. *h.Hom.Dem.* 105-110, 288-290; Paus. 8.31.3-4; *Clouds* 270-1; and vast numbers of votive hydriai and hydriaphoroi in Demeter sanctuaries), and (iii) of the Persian sack of the Acropolis itself (even though the men pose as its defenders, recall the two-day siege that ousted Cleomenes in 508, and invoke the glory of Marathon).

435-6 On the status of public slaves cf. also *IG* ii² 1570.78-79 which appears to show that public slaves could themselves be the owners of slaves. It is, however, by no means certain that these privileges were enjoyed by the Scythian archer-policemen, and the point here is probably rather that as a public slave *acting under a magistrate's orders* the archer is an agent of the state's authority and violence against him by a private person is therefore tantamount to violence against the *polis*.

804 On the date of Phormio's death, see Addenda to comm. on *Knights* 562.

917 The fact that Myrrhine uses what is "normally a men's oath" is one of numerous touches, in this scene and elsewhere, indicating that the usual power relations between men and women have been reversed; see G. Mastromarco in A. López Eire ed. *Sociedad, política y literatura: comedia griega antigua* (Salamanca, 1997) 109-116, esp. 115, where he shows that this sentence is based on one that might be spoken by a *man* to a *prostitute* (note that a common term for a cheap prostitute was "ground-banger" [*khamaitupē*]).

963 For "the word *psŷkeîs*" read "the word *psûkhē̂* is".

980 *Gerōkhiā̄* is not an error; as A.C. Cassio, *SRCG* 1 (1998) 73-78 has brilliantly shown (cf. also M.G. Bonanno, *SRCG* 2 [1999] 63-64), it is a pun on *agerōkhiā̄* "pride, arrogance". I suspect that the pun was not an invention of Ar.'s but a standing anti-Spartan joke among Athenians, who believed (Dem. 20.107) that the members of the *gerousiā̄* were "masters of the masses": it would be piquantly amusing to hear on Spartan lips the derogatory name that Athenians had coined for a Spartan institution.

1083 F. García Romero, *CFC* 6 (1996) 102-3, suggests that the comparison is rather with the bulging abdomens of wrestlers due to training and rich diet (he points out that in ancient combat sports there were no weight limits); this makes better sense of the pun in 1085.

1092 R.L. Fowler, *EMC* 15 (1996) 245-9, criticizes (not without reason) those who claim, as I did in comm. here, that the play artificially ignores "the many alternative sexual outlets ... available to the Athenian husband". To most, he argues, the (expensive) alternatives were *not* in fact available (and, on slaves, cf. Xen. *Oec.* 10.12, which is in harmony with *Lys.*162-6). More importantly, if the play's basic assumption (that for most men, most of the time, fulfilling sex equalled consensual marital sex) were false, the play would not be funny but merely baffling (as if, to use Fowler's parallel, a present-day comedy were to picture the male world being forced to change its policies by a strike of prostitutes).

1094 For "faces and phalli" read "phalli": Thucydides' phrase *ta prosōpa*, which seems to mean "the faces", is an evasive euphemism meaning "the front parts". See I. Rodríguez Alfageme in F. De Martino and A.H. Sommerstein ed. *Studi sull'eufemismo* (Bari, 1999) 308-9.

1108-11 The proposal by J.W. White, to which Wilamowitz referred, was made in *HSCP* 17 (1906) 105.

*1126-7 having heard ... the talk of my father: the Euripidean Melanippe, contrariwise, claims to have acquired her wisdom from her *mother* (the prophetess Hippo, daughter of Cheiron); cf. Eur. fr. 484.1, and see L.K. Taaffe, *Aristophanes and Women* (London, 1993) 172 n.45 (who also acutely notes that the change is consistent with the increasing assimilation of Lysistrata to the – motherless – goddess Athena) and Mastromarco in López Eire ed. *Sociedad, política y literatura* 109.

1242 On ancient Greek bagpipes see now M.L. West, *Ancient Greek Music* (Oxford, 1992) 107-9. There is no other evidence that they existed before Hellenistic times, and West reasonably asks why, if the instrument here described is a bagpipe, "*phūsallis* [lit. something that can be expanded by puffing], which would denote the bag, is in the plural"; he does not, however, suggest any alternative identification for the instrument, and it is not implausible that an instrument consisting of several components should come to be known by the plural form of the name of its most prominent component. See also F.D. Harvey in C.A. Powell and S.J. Hodkinson ed. *The Shadow of Sparta* (London, 1994) 42.

1273-90 To the arguments I have adduced for holding that it is Lysistrata who speaks here, add that Hypothesis I explicitly says that "Lysistrata ... hands over the women to their respective menfolk to take away". There is no evidence that anyone in antiquity doubted that it was she who did so.

THESMOPHORIAZUSAE

Introductory Note

page

4   *that he was a hater and slanderer of women:* for "he" read "Euripides".

4   *his interest in current speculations:* "Sophocles seems to have made it a nearly unwavering principle to cloak words incorporating contemporary thought under a semi-transparent disguise ... [whereas] rhetoric in Euripides ... is presented dressed in almost the same clothing it wore outside the Theatre" (V. Bers in I. Worthington ed. *Persuasion: Greek Rhetoric in Action* [London, 1994] 181-2).

6 n.36   It has recently been shown that there are still further direct and indirect parodies of *Telephus* in *Thesm.*: see Addenda to comm. on 36ff. F. Jouan in P. Ghiron-Bistagne ed. *Thalie: Mélanges interdisciplinaires sur la comédie* (= *CGITA* 5 [1989]) 23, 27 anticipated my suggestion that *Telephus* had made a particularly strong impact on the child spectator Aristophanes, but added that this was not enough to account for his evident assumption that it would be very familiar to his audience.

8   *the basic paradox of acting:* the nature of role-playing, or acting, or impersonation, or *mimesis*, in *Thesm.* (and also in *Acharnians*) is illuminatingly discussed by I. Lada-Richards, *Arion* 5 (1997) 66-107, esp. 70-79.

10 n.56   On the paratragic techniques of *Thesm.* see M.G. Bonanno, *L'allusione necessaria* (Rome, 1990) 241-276; she too lays stress on the implicit claim of the superiority of comedy to tragedy, or (as she puts it, 276) of allopathic to homoeopathic catharsis!

Bibliography (including some additional pre-1994 items)

M.G. Bonanno, *L'allusione necessaria* (Rome, 1990) 241-276.

E. Bobrick, "Iphigeneia revisited: *Thesmophoriazusae* 1160-1225", *Arethusa* 24 (1991) 67-76.

J. Jouanna, "Structures scéniques et personnages: essai de comparaison entre les *Acharniens* et les *Thesmophories*", in P. Thiercy and M. Menu ed. *Aristophane: la langue, la scène, la cité* (Bari, 1997) 253-268.

E. Bobrick, "The tyranny of roles: playacting and privilege in Aristophanes' *Thesmophoriazusae*", in G.W. Dobrov ed. *The City as Comedy* (Chapel Hill NC, 1997) 177-197.

M.W. Habash, "The odd Thesmophoria of Aristophanes' *Thesmophoriazusae*", *GRBS* 38 (1997) 19-40.

A. Duncan, "Agathon, essentialism, and gender subversion in Aristophanes' *Thesmophoriazusae*", in S. Carlson and J. McGlew ed. *Performing the Politics of European Comic Drama* (Cedar Falls IA, 2000) 25-40.

Text and Translation (also critical apparatus, pp.139-156)[9]
line

40 Read συγκλῄσας.

71 After "because he's coming out" insert stage direction: [*He goes back inside.*]

102 (app.) For van Leeuwen read Hermann.

117-8 Read σεμνὸν (R) and ὄλβιόν τε (van Herwerden); the text I printed was ungrammatical.

276 (app.) For Fritzsche read Ellebodius.

282 (app.) For Hall & Geldart read Kaibel.

306 (app.) For Coulon read van Leeuwen.

312-3 (app.) For Hermann read Dindorf.

320 (app.) For Meineke read Hermann.

367 (app.) For Hermann read Bothe.

392 (app.) For Blaydes read Bothe.

395 For "bleachers" read "benches"; *ikria* can denote any flat wooden surface supported on vertical struts, and is therefore perfectly appropriate for the benches on which most spectators sat in Ar.'s time. It is doubtful whether dramatic performances had ever been staged in the Agora; references to *ikria* there either relate to, or derive from confusion with, stands set up for spectators watching the Panathenaic processions, and in Eratosthenes' reference to spectators watching from *ikria* "before the *theātron* was built", *theātron* probably denotes the stone auditorium built in the time of Lycurgus. See S. Scullion, *Three Studies in Athenian Dramaturgy* (Stuttgart, 1994) 52-65.

420 For τοῦτ' read ταῦτ' (R).

440 (app.) For Farreus read Zanetti.

495 (app.) For Bentley read Biset.

558 For τοῖς read ταῖς (R).

595 Read ἀγγελῶν.

602 For ἔχεις read ἔχῃς (R).

638 E. Degani, *Eikasmos* 7 (1996) 119-120 = A. López Eire ed. *Sociedad, política y literatura: comedia griega antigua* (Salamanca, 1997) 15-16, attractively proposes to give the first half of this line to "the Woman" (i.e. Critylla), repeating her instruction to Cleisthenes, and the second half ("You shameless scoundrel!") to Inlaw (cf. 611) protesting as he carries it out.

669 (app.) For Bergk read Beer.

736 Read μηχανώμεναι.

743 It may be preferable to understand *trikotylon* in the sense, attested by Hesychius, of "wine sold at three *kotylai* for an obol", the point being that this cheap wine was not very potent; trans. "Was it *vin ordinaire*, tell me, or how did you manage it?"

813 Read αὐθημερὸν.

879 (app.) For Gelenius read Grynaeus.

---

9   I am most grateful to two kind reviewers − S.D. Olson in *BMCR* 95.2.21 and C.F.L. Austin in *CR* 45 (1995) 431-2 − to one or both of whom are due most of the corrections in text and apparatus not otherwise attributed below.

955-6 Parker *Songs* 430 points out that my colometry (that of Dale) forces one to scan χεῖρα ῥυθμόν as –⏑– | – with two prosodic abnormalities; better take 955 as an aristophanean (ending with χεῖρα) and read in 956 ῥυθμὸν χορείας πᾶσ' ὕπαγε (Austin), an iambic dimeter.

968 (app.) For Bothe read Brunck.

981-2 For various reasons, the strongest of which is that no parallel can be found for the usage of ἔξαιρε that the text I print requires us to assume, A.F.H. Bierl, *Drama* 7 (1998) 27-47, argues that διπλῆν is an intrusive gloss and proposes <πόδας> instead (cf. Soph. *Ant.* 224, Eur. *Tro.* 325, 342, 545-7); if this is accepted, however, Ellebodius' χάριν in my view cannot be (Bierl's attempts to justify it are very forced) and we should read χάρᾳ χορείας, giving the sense "Raise your feet high and heartily in the joy of the dance!"

1027 (app.) For Sommerstein read Bergk. Colin Austin (ap. F. Lourenço, *Euphrosyne²* 28 [2000] 321-4) has suggested ἐφέστηκε <καί μ'> ὀλοὸν ἄφιλον ἐκρέμασεν.

1055 Read ἔπι.

1078 For με read μοι (R).

1109 (app.) For van Leeuwen read Kaibel.

1133 Read ἐπιτήκιζί (cf. apparatus).

1158 ἤλθετε (Hermann) eases the metrical analysis (see Parker, *Songs* 450-3), and it is hardly more difficult to posit two plurals being altered to duals than to posit one.

1158 (app.) For Wilamowitz read Blaydes.

1198 (app.) For Bothe read Biset.

1215 (app.) For Bergler read Brunck.

1216 (app.) For Enger read Blaydes.

Commentary

line

*5-21P. Mureddu, *Lexis* 9/10 (1992) 115-120, identifies the sources of some of the ideas here put in Euripides' mouth. The contrast between the senses of sight and hearing, and between their respective objects, appears to have been used by Gorgias to illustrate more than one argument (cf. [Arist.] *On Melissus, Xenophanes and Gorgias* 980b1-3; Sextus Empiricus, *Against the Mathematicians* 7.81), while the statement "in the beginning the Sky became a separate entity" (14) and the description of a sense-organ as a "funnel" and a "perforation" (18) come from Empedocles (respectively 31 A 49 and 31 B 84.12 D-K).

29   On the Agathon scene, especially the parodies, see now Kugelmeier 271-297.

*36-279 J. Jouanna in P. Thiercy and M. Menu ed. *Aristophane: la langue, la scène, la cité* (Bari, 1997) 253-268, shows that the whole episode of the approach to Agathon and its sequel is modelled on two scenes in *Acharnians* (the Country Dionysia scene, *Ach.* 239ff, and the approach to Euripides with the ensuing *Telephus* parody, *Ach* 395-597), but with additions and modifications which mostly have the effect of increasing the complexity of the action.

*133 I felt a tickle stealing right up my backside: implying that Agathon's lyrics are so seductive that they arouse pathic sexual desires even in so masculine a male as Inlaw.

140   I. Lada-Richards, *Initiating Dionysus* (Oxford, 1999) 36 n.69 disagrees with my comment that "a sword would be ... inappropriate for Dionysus" on the ground that it "ignores the wider cultural perspective afforded by Dionysiac iconography"; but while she shows that Dionysiac women (maenads, Bassarids) are often depicted in art carrying swords, she fails to show that *Dionysus himself* is so depicted.

161-2 For the pairing of Anacreon and Alcaeus cf. Ar. fr. 235.

232   C.W. Marshall, *G&R* 46 (1999) 201 n.52, points out that the Würzburg vase, which shows traces of stubble on Inlaw/Telephus's face, indicates that (as was possible, given that there was to be only one performance) the beard on the actor's mask was literally cut off, rather than being a detachable appendage.

312-330 M.W. Habash, *GRBS* 38 (1997) 27-28, notes that whereas the priestess had directed the women to pray to deities appropriate to the Thesmophoria, they actually pray to "important civic deities" with no mention of the Thesmophorian pair.

380   Mica is actually the third most important character in the drama, after Inlaw and Euripides; her role is valuably discussed by A.C. Clark, *Euripides in a Comic Mirror: The Tragodoumenai* (Diss. U. of N. Carolina 1998) 273-280.

401-4 Athenaeus 10.427e describes the custom: "they used to dedicate to their *dead* friends the *bits of food that fell from the table*, wherefore Euripides says about Stheneboia, *when she thinks that Bellerophon is dead*, [fr. 664]". My note should be corrected accordingly.

466-519 M.W. Habash, *Religious Aspects of Aristophanes' Acharnians, Thesmophoriazousae and Birds* (Diss. U. of Virginia 1994) 57 notes that Inlaw goes much further than Mica in "confessing" the criminality of women, especially in regard to adultery. Mica had alluded to this only indirectly ("we're not able to do *anything* now the way we used to before", 398-9, preceded and followed by references to husbands' suspicions of infidelity, and a mention of dogs kept "to frighten the wits out of seducers", 417): Inlaw avows "her" own guilt, and affirms that of others, in four explicit statements which take up nearly half "her" speech (476-501). Later "she" will go further still and cite two specific cases of murder (560-2), in both of which, as in so many murders in Euripidean and other tragedy, the victims are close family members.

547   The statement that Melanippe was raped rests on the sole evidence of Hyginus, who may be relying on *Melanippe the Captive* (he calls Melanippe, in the same sentence, "daughter of Desmontes", an obvious misunderstanding of the Greek play-title *Melanippē Desmōtis*). The surviving Hypothesis of *Melanippe the Wise* (most conveniently accessible in CCL 248-251), paraphrasing Melanippe's prologue-speech, uses the participle *migeisa* which normally implies consent; the reference to "a girl who had been raped" in Eur. fr. 485 concerns a hypothetical case and is anyway made by Melanippe herself, who is speaking in public (whereas the prologue-speech had been a monologue) and has every reason for wanting to put the most favourable construction on the behaviour of the twins' mother, just in case it is eventually discovered that *she* is their mother.

556, 557   Cf. Arist. *Top.* 145a22-25 which implies that a strigil could be used to draw off (*aruein*) liquids or grains, probably in the manner of a spoon; in my note on 557, "the curved strigil" should read "the concave blade of the strigil".

605   See Addenda to comm. on *Ach.* 88.

658 Regarding the reference to the Pnyx, it should be noted that the women's assembly is not presented in this play as a regular feature of the festival: the *probouleuma* of 372-9, ordering such an assembly to be held, implies that it would not have been held otherwise, and it is scheduled for the middle day of the Thesmophoria not because that was a customary day for a women's assembly but merely because it is "the day on which we have most free time". Hence J.J. Henderson, *Three Plays by Aristophanes: Staging Women* (New York and London, 1996) 93 is wrong to claim that "the play takes the matrons' assembly ... for granted, giving no hint that this was abnormal procedure", and to use this as an argument for placing the Thesmophorium on the Pnyx. Nor are such women's assemblies, in Ar., confined to the Thesmophoria; in *Eccl.* 18 we hear of a resolution passed (*edoxe*) by the women at the Scira.

*667 **is caught:** R reads μὴ λάθῃ "does not escape notice" (which is unmetrical), and Fritzsche conjectured με λάθῃ "escapes my notice"; since the latter reading has been defended by C. Prato, *QUCC* 58 (1998) 73, it perhaps needs to be pointed out that an offender who evades detection can neither pay a penalty (668) nor be made an example of (669-671, 673-7).

785-845 Several features of the chorus's defence of womankind in general, and their attack on a minority of bad women (exemplified by the mother of Hyperbolus) in particular, may be inspired by a speech in Euripides' *Melanippe the Captive* (Eur. fr. 660 Mette; see CCL pp.254-7); cf. Clark *Tragodoumenai* 216-227.

804 In fairness to Charminus it should be mentioned that he was outnumbered at Syme by perhaps three to one; but Athenians did not expect to lose naval battles under *any* circumstances.

840 See Addenda to comm. on *Ach.* 846.

986 For "*Peace* 383" read "*Peace* 381".

1056-97 A further reason for rejecting the view that Euripides impersonates Echo is that he otherwise takes only *male* roles in the re-enactments of his tragedies – just as at the start of the play he had had no thought of going to the Thesmophorium *himself* disguised as a woman, even though he would surely have made both a more committed and a more ingenious advocate for himself than any substitute could have been. Only when his tragic ploys fail does he become a woman, and then it is a *comic* woman (Artemisia).

1056-97 D. Gilula, *QSt* 44 (1996) 159-164, thinks that this scene, and in particular 1060-1, proves that Echo appeared on stage in Euripides' play; but her argument is based on a misinterpretation of 1060-1, which is spoken in the *persona* not of an actor but of Echo (as the feminine pronouns show). Echo did not need to be seen on stage in order for it to be true that she had "personally assisted Euripides in the competition".

*1133 **De foxy villain! de mongey drick 'e dried on me!:** it is likely that this mixed metaphor (a *fox* playing *monkey* tricks) would raise a good laugh. The Archer also makes here yet another gender blunder, treating *alōpēx* "fox" as masculine when in fact it was always grammatically feminine (regardless of the sex of the animal referred to); see A. López Eire, *La lengua coloquial de la comedia aristofánica* (Murcia, 1996) 155 n.312.

1198 Another possibility, favoured by Thiercy 1257, is that the Archer is promising "Artemisia" that she will receive her due *payment* later (for *komizesthai* = "receive a payment" cf. *Wasps* 690).

1218ff There is also another reminiscence of *Iphigeneia in Tauris* in this scene. E. Bobrick, *Arethusa* 24 (1991) 67-76, writing without knowledge of Hall's article, notes that the rescue of Inlaw by Artemisia in exchange for Fawn (Elaphion) recalls the rescue of Iphigeneia from the altar at Aulis by Artemis in exchange for a hind (*elaphos*), referred to in *IT* 28-29. She might have added that Thoas, whom Iphigeneia and the chorus deceive, is himself a Scythian (cf. the ancient *Hypothesis* to *IT* and Hdt. 4.99-100). Euripides is thus still using a device taken from one of his own recent plays; he no longer attempts, however, to involve Inlaw's guard in a theatrical fiction, but simply to deceive him — and it thus remains true that his technique is basically comic.

1231 The chorus's "function" here predominates over their "role", since while the singers' duty as a *dramatic chorus* is now done, as *women celebrating the Thesmophoria* they ought to remain where they are until the festival ends on the following day.

FROGS

Introduction

1 n.3   On Phrynichus' *Muses* see now F.D. Harvey in F.D. Harvey and J. Wilkins ed. *The Rivals of Aristophanes* (London/Swansea, 2000) 100-8.

5   *two possible developments:* another possibility was that Cyrus (or his father) might simply get tired of throwing good money after bad, if the Peloponnesian fleet continued to be unsuccessful (cf. p.7 note 32); hence the importance of concentrating all Athens' resources on the navy (see comm. on 1463-5) and, some thought, of inducing Alcibiades to return and command it (see comm. on 1422).

11   *Cratinus' Dionysalexandros:* the importance of this play as a model for *Frogs* is strongly (perhaps too strongly) emphasized by M. Farioli, *Aevum Antiquum* 7 (1994) 119-136, who suggests that the tribute to Cratinus in 357 shows Ar.'s own awareness of his debt.

11 n.52   A scholium to *Peace* 741 remarks that the "cowardly Dionysus" was as ubiquitous in comedy as the "hungry Heracles".

13   *the theme of the salvation of Athens:* the development of this theme, and Dionysus' development from self-centred hedonist to responsible citizen, is admirably sketched in I. Lada-Richards, *Initiating Dionysus* (Oxford, 1999) 216-230.

14   *the earliest sustained piece of literary criticism:* M. Cavalli in F. Conca ed. *Ricordando Raffaelle Cantarella* (Milan, 1999) 83-105 argues for a close relationship between the Aeschylus-Euripides contest and the *Contest of Homer and Hesiod*, which in its present form dates from about the time of Hadrian, but a version of which was known to Ar. (see comm. on *Peace* 1282-3). The same suggestion had already been made by N.J. Richardson, *CQ* 31 (1981) 2. If so (as noted by R.M. Rosen in a conference paper given at Leeds in November 2000), Ar. has effectively reversed the outcome of the contest, in which Hesiod triumphs because he sings of peaceful pursuits and Homer of war: in Ar. Aeschylus in the end triumphs because he encourages the Athenians to devote their resources to the war effort – not (I would add) that Ar. has lost his love of peace (cf. 714-7, 1532-3), but the maxim *si vis pacem, para bellum* is emphatically valid in the current situation.

15   *a responsibility to teach and advise his public:* E.R. Schwinge, in his valuable pamphlet *Griechische Tragödie und zeitgenössische Rezeption: Aristophanes und Gorgias* (Hamburg/Göttingen, 1997), assumes throughout, wrongly, that this is presented in *Frogs* as the *sole* function of tragic and other poetry; he shows, rightly, that if that were Ar.'s view it would be out of keeping with the evidence of tragedy itself, and that another view existed in the fifth century which stressed, as Aristotle did later, the *emotional* effects of tragedy, especially the (pleasurable) arousal of fear, pity and grief (see e.g. Gorgias, *Encomium of Helen* 8-10). The two views are not, of course, mutually exclusive; indeed Ar. shows himself well aware of the second (for Dionysus finds Euripidean drama intensely pleasurable, though he cannot explain why: 52-107, 1413), though the overall thrust of his play requires that the first be treated as the decisive criterion of a poet's merit.

18 n.86 See also E. Suárez de la Torre in A. López Eire ed. *Sociedad, política y literatura: comedia griega antigua* (Salamanca, 1997) 197-217, esp. 200-212.

Bibliography

Scholia. The older scholia to *Frogs* have now appeared as Pars III Fasciculus Ia of Koster's *Scholia in Aristophanem* (ed. M. Chantry [Groningen, 1999]). I have included below corrections to the apparatus where, but only where, improved information about the scholia has significantly affected the balance of evidence bearing on the constitution of the text. I have not in general cited mss. other than RVE except where they offer important new information; where they do, M is cited for preference.

Books and articles

N.J. Lowe, "Aristophanes' books", *Annals of Scholarship* 10 (1993) 63-83.

C.W. Marshall, "Amphibian ambiguities answered", *EMC* 40 (1996) 251-265.

P. von Möllendorff, "Αἰσχύλον δ' αἱρήσομαι: Der 'neue Aischylos' in den *Fröschen* des Aristophanes", *WJA* n.s. 21 (1996/7) 129-151.

E. Suárez de la Torre, "Las *Ranas* de Aristófanes y la religión de los atenienses", in A. López Eire ed. *Sociedad, política y literatura: comedia griega antigua* (Salamanca, 1997) 197-217.

E.R. Schwinge, *Griechische Tragödie und zeitgenössische Rezeption: Aristophanes und Gorgias* (Hamburg/Göttingen, 1997).

J.U. Schmidt, "Die Einheit der 'Frösche' des Aristophanes: Demokratische Erziehung und 'moderne' Dichtung in der Kritik", *WJA* 22 (1998) 73-100.

M. Cavalli, "Le *Rane* di Aristofane: modelli tradizionali dell'agone fra Eschilo ed Euripide", in F. Conca ed. *Ricordando Raffaelle Cantarella* (Milan, 1999) 83-105.

I. Lada-Richards, *Initiating Dionysus: Ritual and Theatre in Aristophanes' Frogs* (Oxford [sic], 1999).

M. Sonnino, "Le strategie militari di Pericle e le *Rane* di Aristofane (Aristoph. *Ran.* 1019-1025; 1435-1466)", *SRCG* 2 (1999) 65-97.

Note on the Text and Table of Sigla
page

30 *two ... papyrus fragments:* two further papyri were published by N. Gonis in *The Oxyrhynchus Papyri* LXVI (1999): Π79 (Oxyrhynchus Papyrus 4517; fourth century), containing 592-605 and 630-647, and Π80 (Oxyrhynchus Papyrus 4518; fifth century), containing 1244-8 and 1277-81.

31 U should be dated "late 13th": see Addenda to *Clouds* Table of Sigla.

Text and Translation

line

13 Read ποιήσω (see A.M. Bowie, *CR* 50 [2000] 272).

15 The apparatus entry on the scholia should read: Σᴱ records all the asterisked readings, Σᴿⱽ only σκεύη φέρ- and σκευηφορ-.

33 In apparatus, delete reference to ˡΣᴱ.

57 The true reading (in the form ἀπαπαί) should be credited to ᵞᵖΣᶿ, not to Fritzsche.

133 To witnesses for εἶναι add Photius; the scholia entry for this reading should be simply Σⱽᴱ.

216 For ἠνί" read ἦν.

229 Parker *Songs* 465 favours Hermann's conjecture ἔστερξαν <μὲν>, which gives the Frogs unbroken trochees throughout 228-234.

272 The first word of the line should be accented ἰαῦ.

320 For the reading Διαγόρας, the scholia entry should be ⁱΣᴿⱽᴱˡΣⱽᴱ, Aristarchus in Σⱽᴱ: for the reading δι' ἀγορᾶς, it should be ᵞᵖΕ, Apollodorus of Tarsus in Σⱽᴱ.

341 The scholia do not contain the words γὰρ ἥκεις τινάσσων, but they arguably (not certainly) *imply* this reading.

357 For the reading μηδὲ, the scholia entry should be ˡΣ(ii)ʸ: for the reading μήτε, it should be ˡΣ(i)ᴿⱽᴱ.

377 In apparatus, for "cf. Σᴱ" read "cf. Σⱽᴱ".

404 In apparatus, for ⁱΣᴿⱽᴱ read ⁱΣᴿⱽᴱ+λ

520 Before *To Dionysus*, insert *The Maid goes inside.*

526 In apparatus, for ˡΣⱽ read ˡΣⱽᴱ.

546 In apparatus, for Σᴿⱽᴱ read Σᴿ.

595 Π79 has κακβαληἰις, confirming the correctness of V's reading.

597 Π79 seems to have omitted στ(α)ι: the position of the surviving letters indicates that there would not have been enough space for this word.

599 Parker *Songs* 481 rightly adopts ὅδε (Blaydes) for ὅτι: a subject is needed, and ὅτι is not. Trans. "this fellow here will try and take ...".

600 Π79 has τουτ' ("that good thing"), but ταῦτ' ("this gear", viz. the Heracles costume) remains the preferable reading, since the hypothetical "good thing" has never been in Dionysus' possession and he could not therefore try and take it *back* (πάλιν).

641 Read ἀποδύεσθε.

645 To witnesses for (')παταξας, add ˡΣⱽᴱ: for (')παταξα σ', ˡΣᴹ. Π79 has]αc.

743 To witnesses for οἴμωζε, add ˡΣᴱᴹ.

788 For "and put" read "and he put"; see Addenda to Commentary ad loc.

800 For the reading πυκτα, the scholia entry should be ˡΣⱽ: for the reading πηκτα, it should be ˡΣᴱ.

818 The reading of ˡΣⱽᴱ (*sic*) is ἱππολόφων.

819 For the reading σκινδαλάμων vel sim., the scholia entry should be ⁱΣⱽ+λ ⁱΣᴿⱽᴱ 824; for the reading σκινδαλμῶν vel sim., it should be ⁱΣᴿᴱ+λ

925 For the reading μορμορ-, the scholia entry should be ˡΣᴹ (*not* ⁱΣᴿⱽᴱ).

970 In apparatus, the scholia entries should be: Κεῖος ᴬΣᵛ, Demetrius Ixion in Σᵛᴹ and Σ(i)ᴱ, Didymus in Σᴹ: Κῖος ᴬΣᴿ, Demetrius Ixion inΣᴿ and Σ(ii)ᴱ, Didymus in Σᴱ: Κῷος Aristarchus in Σᵛᴱ.

993 The true reading is also in ᴬΣᴱ.

1011 For Σᴿᵛᴱ read Σᵛᴱ.

1057 For the reading Παρνασσῶν, the scholia entry should be ᴵΣᴿ ᴬΣᴱ.

1066 The scholia imply that the verb is aorist, though it cannot be determined precisely what form the original commentator read; the surviving lemmata are present (-ειλλό- in R, -ιλλό- in VE).

1068 Actually it is Σᴿᵛᴹ that "know both readings": Σᴱ knows only παρά.

1180 To witnesses for ἀλλά μοῦστ' add ᴵΣᴹ.

1235 To witnesses for ἀπόδος add Σ(i)ᵛᴱ+λ: for ἀπόδου, ᴵΣ(ii)ᴿᵛᴱ.

1256 In apparatus, for Σᴿ read Σᴿᴱ.

1276 In apparatus, delete "Asclepiades in Σᵛᴱ": the scholium is so corrupt that we cannot determine what view Asclepiades took.

1335 Parker *Songs* 516 finds μελαίνας Νυκτὸς παῖδα to be "unmetrical", and reads with Dindorf Νυκτὸς παῖδα μελαίνας.

1505 In apparatus, for ᴬΣᵛ read ᴬΣᵛᴱ.

Commentary
line

13 See Addenda to comm. on *Clouds* 556.

*32 **picking up the *donkey* and carrying it:** a black-figure lekythos in the Louvre (CA 1730) shows a group (chorus?) of satyrs each carrying a mule on his back; see F. Lissarrague in M.L. Desclos ed. *Le rire des Grecs* (Grenoble, 2000) 114 and fig. 8.

62 To the comic references add Epicharmus fr. 21.

153 See Addenda to comm. on *Birds* 1372-1409.

323-353 This song is analysed by G. Mathews, *Maia* 49 (1997) 32-42.

366 Kugelmeier 240-2 brilliantly if audaciously suggests that the reference is to the (alleged) activities of Cinesias' *kakodaimonistai* club, which according to Lys. fr. 53 held its meetings *at the time of the new moon* — directly after (probably on the evening of) the last day of the month, on which offerings were made to Hecate; he might have compared Dem. 54.39 on Conon and the *ithyphalloi* who stole and ate the offerings (cf. *Wealth* 597), thus insulting Hecate and metaphorically defiling her shrines. More usually (e.g. E.R. Dodds, *The Greeks and the Irrational* [Berkeley, 1951] 200 n.61) the reference has been taken to be to a literal defilement of a Hecate-shrine by members of the club as an act of wilful *hybris* (for which cf. *Birds* 1054); this interpretation is supported by *Eccl.* 330, taken together with the statement of Lys. *loc.cit.* that Cinesias had committed "crimes against the gods which most people are ashamed even to mention but which you hear about from the comic poets year after year".

*423 **in the cemetery:** it is relevant that this is the kind of place (normally deserted) where prostitutes of the lowest grade (male or female) would go with their clients; see C.G. Brown, *Eikasmos* 8 (1997) 63, and Davidson 78-80 (citing Aeschines 1.80-85).

468 Lada-Richards *Initiating Dionysus* 176-7 notes that Heracles, both in art and in literature, specializes in seizing beasts with his hands; cf. Soph. *Trach.* 1089-1102 where he laments the ravaging of his "hands, back, breast and arms", which had defeated Cerberus and five other monsters or groups of monsters. See A. Schnapp in C. Bérard et al. ed. *Images et société en Grèce ancienne* (Lausanne, 1987) 123.

470-8 One line in this passage, 474 "will rend apart ... while thy lungs are gripped", does have an identifiable tragic source, Soph. *Trach.* 778 "an agonizing rending gripped his [Heracles'!] lungs"; while the combination of Echidna (473) and murry-eel (475) may derive from Aesch. *Cho.* 994 where Orestes thinks of them as possible analogues to the evil being that Clytaemestra was.

482 C.W. Marshall, *EMC* 42 (1999) 147, thinks that Dover and I were being over-literal here: a sponge is available, not because it was customary for travellers to carry one, but simply because one is needed for the ensuing business.

508 Does Xanthias, recalling what happened to Persephone herself, think it dangerous to eat in the underworld? See I. Rodríguez Alfageme in R.M. Aguilar et al. ed. Χάρις διδασκαλίας: *Homenaje a Luis Gil* (Madrid, 1994) 364-5. Heracles, we shall learn, had not been deterred by such considerations (551-8, 572-6); and at the end of the play Pluto will feast Dionysus and Aeschylus preparatory to sending them back to earth.

516 There is probably a reminiscence of Pherecrates fr. 113.29 where "girls ... just in the bloom of youth, and with their 'roses' trimmed" are said to pour the wine through funnels into diners' mouths at feasts *in the underworld*; see Rodríguez Alfageme *op.cit.* 365-6.

565 The particle *pou* perhaps implies rather that the speaker cannot imagine, seeing the unimpressive figure "Heracles" cuts now, why she should have been so frightened of him then (so van Leeuwen, Del Corno, Thiercy 1277).

*605-673 Lada-Richards *Initiating Dionysus* 315-9 compares this with the type of tragic scene (exemplified for us by Eur. *Ba.* 434-656, for Ar.'s audience probably by Aeschylus' plays about Pentheus and Lycurgus) in which Dionysus is maltreated or insulted; she notes that (i) whereas traditionally Dionysus miraculously escapes unhurt and smiling, here he is hurt and howls, despite (ii) having, contrary to his normal practice, explicitly identified himself (628-632) *before* being abused.

788-790 E.W. Handley, *AAH* 40 (2000) 153-4, points out that in 754-5 "the handshake and the first kiss are reciprocal", and suggests that this was a normal expectation and that accordingly, once it has been stated that Sophocles kissed Aeschylus, it will be assumed automatically that it was Aeschylus who then offered the other his hand. If this can be accepted, *ekeinos* in 790 can be Sophocles without difficulty.

886 I had taken a different, and better, view in *Aeschylean Tragedy* (Bari, 1996) 25-26: it is not at all unlikely that Aeschylus was indeed accused (perhaps for political reasons) of an offence against the Mysteries, but it is certain that if he was, he was acquitted, since conviction would inevitably have meant death.

940-4 After "dropsy" add "(cf. I. Rodríguez Alfageme in A. López Eire ed. *Sociedad, política y literatura: comedia griega antigua* [Salamanca, 1997] 165)".

943 N.J. Lowe, "Aristophanes' books", *Annals of Scholarship* 10 (1993) 63-83, traces, primarily from Ar., the development of a reading culture at Athens in the late fifth century, arguing that in *Frogs* tragedies are treated, for the first time, primarily as texts rather than as performances.

944   The absence of all reference to Cephisophon (or to any scandal involving Euripides' wife) in *Thesm.*, combined with the probable (though not certain) implication of 1048 below that the scandal was not (as in the later biographical tradition) the occasion for but *a punishment for* Euripides' allegedly misogynistic dramas, makes it likely that it broke between 410 and 408 (when it may have been alluded to in *Gerytades*, if Ar. fr. 596 comes from that play). If so, Euripides was presumably at that time married to a woman much younger than himself; in which case this marriage (i) must have been at least his second, and (ii) must have occurred later than spring 411, since Euripides could hardly have been accused in *Thesm.* 410-3 of discouraging old men from marrying young women if he had recently done so himself. Such a marriage, involving a well-known man who had written so much about wicked women, was almost bound to lead to scandalous rumours, particularly if there was in fact a personable young man who was a resident in, or a frequent visitor to, the marital home. That Cephisophon had had a hand in the composition of Euripides' lyrics (or perhaps rather of the music for them) may be perfectly true; dramatists had once always been their own composers, choreographers, directors and leading actors, but by 405 the last three functions were often (in the case of acting, always) performed for them by specialists, and with the increasing complexity and sophistication of music in the late fifth century it would not be surprising if some dramatists employed specialist musical composers too. The *Life of Euripides*, indeed, mentions the name of another alleged assistant to Euripides in this field, Timocrates of Argos (not otherwise known). I discuss this matter more fully in a paper forthcoming in a Festschrift for W.G. Arnott.

957   I should have added that "being in love" is anyway not something that one can be *taught* (Greek *erān*, unlike Latin *amare*, refers only to amatory *desire*, not to any steps one may take with a view to satisfying it).

983-8 Lada-Richards *Initiating Dionysus* 291-3 points out that this kind of detailed supervision of the household stores is a woman's job (cf. *Lys.* 495, *Eccl.* 211-2, *Lys.* 1.7, Pl. *Meno* 71e, Xen. *Oec.* 3.10-15, 7.3-10.13), and that there are other respects too in which Euripidean Man can be seen as somewhat feminized, e.g. his crafty use of words (957, 967-970, 1086), his physical unfitness (1087-98) and his wife's infidelity (1045-51).

*1005   **let your fountain spout:**   this type of language is frequently used in reference to poetic inspiration: cf. *Knights* 526ff (of Cratinus), Cratinus fr. 198, Pl. *Laws* 719c, and see Lada-Richards *Initiating Dionysus* 244.

*1032-5   **Orpheus ... Musaeus ... Hesiod ... Homer:**   these four are first named together, in the same order, by Hippias fr. 6 D-K.

1032   On Orphism and its relation to other religious and intellectual currents of archaic and classical times, see further R. Parker, "Early Orphism", in A. Powell ed. *The Greek World* (London, 1995) 483-510.

1076-7   On tacking see also now H.T. Wallinga, *Mnemosyne* 53 (2000) 431-447.

1081   Delete from "Ar. has thus converted ..." to end of note (cf. Addenda to comm. on *Thesm.* 547).

1244 The line was recycled by Critias in *Peirithous* (Critias fr.trag. 1.9).

1251-60   For the three successive pherecrateans of 1258-60 cf. (significantly?) Aesch. fr. 47a.818-820.

1266 Ephorus was a native not of the Italian Cyme/Cumae but of Cyme in Asia Minor.

1299-1300 Cf. Choerilus fr. 2 Bernabé, from his *Persica*: "Ah, happy was the servant *of the Muses* who was an expert in song in that old time, when the *meadow* was still virgin ground". Choerilus, who had been born in the first years of the fifth century (Suda χ595), was probably still alive in 406/5, since he spent some time in the retinue of Lysander (Plut. *Lys.* 18.7); he died at the court of Archelaus of Macedon (Suda *loc.cit.*) and therefore no later than 399. Sixty years earlier Pindar (*Olymp.* 9.26) had spoken of himself as "browsing in the garden of the Graces".

1301 For those who, like Dover and Kugelmeier 61, find Palmer's μέλι unacceptable (and I have some sympathy with Kugelmeier's view that it is "very artificial" to take the word as sarcastic), a simple solution (modifying a suggestion by van Leeuwen) is οὗτός δέ <γ'> ἀπὸ πάντων φέρει.

1309-28 There is a similar though much milder Euripidean lyric parody, also involving an apostrophe to arthropods (caterpillars in this case) and the trademark verb *helissein* (see comm. on 1314), in Strattis fr. 71.

1319 For "Archenomus" read "Archemorus".

1434 P. von Möllendorff, *WJA* n.s. 21 (1996/7) 134, sees this line as implying that Aeschylus speaks to the élite and Euripides to the masses — when what is wanted is a poet able to influence *all* classes of the community.

1435-66 Fresh attempts to solve this crux continue:

(a)   Von Möllendorff *op.cit.* 142-9 defends the transmitted text in its entirety, suggesting that 1437-41 is not to be taken as Euripides' answer to Dionysus' question, but as a preliminary demonstration of the absurdity of seeking a military solution to Athens' predicament, clearing the ground for the political recommendation that follows; but Euripides' words at 1442 represent a beginning, not a transition, and nothing in 1437-41 indicates that the lines are to be understood as merely a subsidiary part of Euripides' presentation (it would have taken only one word, μέν, to signal this).

(b)   Thiercy 1286-7 proposes the following arrangement: 1435-6; 1442; 1437-41; 1451-66; 1443-50 (with Aeschylus as interlocutor, Dionysus speaking 1449-50). This has several attractive features, but it produces an unlikely asyndeton at 1443 which can only be got rid of by arbitrary and inelegant emendation; it also makes Aeschylus give two pieces of advice to Euripides' one.

(c)   M. Sonnino, *SRCG* 2 (1999) 65-97, notes that 1442-50 differs stylistically from the rest of the passage (it has no resolved feet, and refers to the Athenians in the first person plural); he sees this as evidence that this is the section where Aeschylus speaks, but it could also be evidence that this was the section written for the second production. Sonnino's reconstruction is as follows:

First production: 1435-6, 1461-6 (Eur.), 1454-60 (Aesch.), 1442-50 (Aesch.)
Second production: same, but with 1463-6 replaced by 1437-41 + 1451-3.
This is unacceptable for reasons already discussed in my note (the late placement of 1442, and the impossibility of 1437-41 having been freshly written for a production in 404).

(d)   H. Kuch in J.A. López Férez ed. *Desde los poemas homéricos hasta la prosa griega del siglo IV d.C.* (Madrid, 1999) 183-200, accepting my reconstruction of the two versions of the passage, usefully points out (at 196-7) that there is a close structural parallel between 1437-41 and 1442-50. In each, Euripides' suggestion (1437-8 ~ 1443-4a) is not understood by Dionysus, who asks for clarification (1439 ~ 1444b-5) which

Euripides then provides; and in each, the suggestion and the clarification are both expressed as conditional protases.

1453 Alternatively, the main point of the line may lie in a secondary meaning of ὀξίδες: there may be an insinuation that Euripides' lyrics were often ὀξέα "acid, bitter, distasteful" (like those of Philocles, cf. *Wasps* 460-2 and references cited there) and that this was because they were really the work of Cephisophon (see on 944 above).

*1479 both of you: this, and *sphō* "you two" in the next line, imply, as Lada-Richards *Initiating Dionysus* 327 notes, that Pluto is treating Aeschylus, as well as Dionysus, as his equal; cf. comm. on 1517-8.

1480 Lada-Richards *Initiating Dionysus* 154-5 points out that *xenizein* "entertain" always refers to *official* hospitality given by a state to a distinguished visitor, normally at the Prytaneum (cf. 764); one may further note (i) that this helps explain *apoplein* "sail off" (which is how, in 406/5, all non-hostile visitors to Athens had to travel homewards) and secondly that it implies that Aeschylus is no longer a "citizen" of Hades (cf. comm. on 1517-8).

ECCLESIAZUSAE

page

13 *for the Guardians only:* Plato's society, therefore, while "communist" in a broad sense, is *not* "socialist" in the strict sense of providing for common ownership of the means of production; these will be in the hands of individual members of the lowest of his three social classes (who will, in effect, be taxed for the support of their rulers), and it is simply taken for granted that business life ("the things of the Agora") will proceed as it always has, subject to regulations whose nature is too obvious to need prescribing (*Rep.* 425c-e) and which are therefore presumably not envisaged as drastically novel. Praxagora's society, on the other hand, *is* socialist in this strict sense, envisaging as it does the communalization of *all* private property (598), including assets used in production such as land (597-8), slaves (cf. 593, 651), and equipment used in various stages of food preparation (730-741).

16 *Sparta provided precedents:* M.H. Dettenhofer, *Klio* 81 (1999) 95-111, stresses these parallels with Sparta (to which should be added points 4, 5 and 6 from the list I gave on p.14) and regards Spartan society as being the "elusive common source"; but she does not explain the origin of points 1, 2 and 7-11, which are common to Ar. and Plato and which in Sparta either did not exist or existed in a very much weaker form.

18 *real evils ... fantasy remedies:* cf. K.D. Koch, *Kritische Idee und komisches Thema* (Bremen, 1965).

21-22 *a scene ... in which female sexuality ran riot ... This is that scene:* but the riot is actually kept within remarkably narrow bounds. Although we have been led to expect that married women will behave like whores, we never actually see them doing so (the randy females of 877-1111 are three aged women and one unmarried teenager), and in the final scene the leading roles are played by the husband and the maidservant of Praxagora and it is totally forgotten that marriage and private property have been abolished; rather, the change from the old to the new society seems now to have consisted merely in the abolition of work (for men) and the introduction of free food and (for men, at least old men) free extra-marital sex with the wife's compliments.

28 *the action proceeds on an almost wholly secular level:* F.I. Zeitlin in S.D. Goldhill and R.G. Osborne ed. *Performance Culture and Athenian Democracy* (Cambridge, 1999) 167-197, likewise notes that the gods are absent from *Eccl.*; but she draws attention (181ff) to important connections between the play and the myth (Varro, cited by Augustine, *City of God* 18.9) of how male supremacy (together with marriage) was first established in the time of Cecrops, by Athena, as a paradoxical result of the contest between Athena and Poseidon in which the women, supporting Athena, had defeated the men by one vote. In *Eccl.*, for the first time since those days, the women again vote in the Assembly — and, without (because of the absence of?) divine intervention, reverse the outcome.

Bibliography

R. Bichler, *Von der Insel der Seligen zu Platons Staat: Geschichte der antiken Utopie* (Vienna, 1995) 85-110.

M.H. Dettenhofer, "Praxagoras Programm: Eine politische Deutung von Aristophanes' *Ekklesiazusai* als Beitrag zur inneren Geschichte Athens im 4. Jahrhundert v.Chr.", *Klio* 81 (1999) 95-111.

F.I. Zeitlin, "Aristophanes: the performance of utopia in the *Ecclesiazousae*", in S.D. Goldhill and R.G. Osborne ed. *Performance Culture and Athenian Democracy* (Cambridge, 1999) 167-197.

A.H. Sommerstein, "Nudity, obscenity and power: modes of female assertiveness in Aristophanes", in S. Carlson and J. McGlew ed. *Performing the Politics of European Comic Drama* (Cedar Falls IA, 2000).

S. Halliwell, "Aristophanic sex: the erotics of shamelessness", in M.C. Nussbaum and J. Sihvola ed. *The Night of Reason: Erotic Experience and Sexual Ethics in Ancient Greece and Rome* (Chicago, forthcoming).

Text and Translation
line

30   The chorus-leader, at least, must be carrying a lamp (cf. 27-28); so rightly M.C. English, *The Stage Properties of Aristophanic Comedy: A Descriptive Lexicon* (Diss. Boston U. 1999). 290. She must put it down during 268-278, and can then conveniently carry it off when the chorus leave (it is then still supposed to be dark).

265   Read εἰθισμέναι (misprint corrected by B. Pütz, *CR* 50 [2000] 272).

330   For σοι read σου (misprint corrected by Pütz *loc.cit.*)

686   For ἐλθεῖν read χωρεῖν (misprint corrected by Pütz *loc.cit.*)

721   Before this line insert Πρ. (omission corrected by S. Halliwell, *G&R* 46 [1999] 236).

810   Surely we should read, with Lenting, αὐταῖσιν (cf. 856)?

968   Add stage direction: [*The Girl withdraws from the window, as if about to come down.*]

1101   For "with a carbuncle on her cheek" read "with a leather bag under her chin". A. Lorenzoni, *Eikasmos* 8 (1997) 71-81, has given much the best explanation of this passage: she points out that a *lēkuthos* can be made of leather (see e.g. *IG* ii² 1533.33, Plut. *Sulla* 13.3, schol. Theocr. 2.156) and that this would be a very apt description of wrinkled, baggy skin (cf. Festus 318.23-24 Lindsay *scorteae ampullae vetustate rugosae* "leather flasks wrinkled with age") in the form e.g. of a double chin.

1105   For "(as may well be)" read "by any chance"; cf. Pl. *Tim.* 29c, and see P. McKechnie, *ZPE* 127 (1999) 160-1.

Commentary
line

1-18   On the role of lamps in women's life, see E. Parisinou, *G&R* 47 (2000) 19-43, esp. 19-22, 24-28.

102   The inscription of 374/3 (a law of which Agyrrhius is named as proposer) has now been published by R.S. Stroud, *The Athenian Grain-Tax Law of 374/3 B.C.* (Princeton, 1998), who gives (pp. 16-25) what is now the fullest discussion of Agyrrhius' career, with special emphasis on his connections with finance and business, in particular with the corn trade. The scholia here provide evidence for a second term as general (perhaps in 388/7) when Agyrrhius was based at Lemnos (this is the transmitted reading; "Lesbos" is not a variant, as Stroud 22 thinks, but a conjecture).

*186 whoever has received cash praises him (sc. Agyrrhius): as Stroud *op.cit.* 21 points out, there is a pun on *Agurrhios* and *argurion* "money"; if the actor was instructed to pronounce the word in an ambiguous manner, the line could actually be understood as "whoever has received something praises Agyrrhius to the skies". It very probably follows that Agyrrhius was actually nicknamed *Argurios* "Mr Cash".

446-9 Cf. also Eur. fr. 660.4-5 Mette (from *Melanippe the Captive*) which seems to refer to women's "unwitnessed contracts" which they "do not repudiate".

617 S. Halliwell, in an article to appear in M.C. Nussbaum and J. Sihvola ed. *The Night of Reason: Erotic Experience and Sexual Ethics in Ancient Greece and Rome* (Chicago, forthcoming), points out that "sitting" is what prostitutes do when waiting for clients: cf. Aeschines 1.74, 120; Pl. *Charm.* 163b; [Dem.] 59.67; Isaeus 6.19.

729/730 The evidence for *khorou* markings in *Wealth* is now considerably stronger; see comm. on *Wealth* 321/2, 958/9, 1096/7.

920 The reference to Pherecrates fr. 136 should be to Pherecrates fr. 159.

952-975 Halliwell *op.cit.* sees erotic mime as another possible model, referring to *P.Lit.Lond.* 50 and *POxy* 413, verso, cols. i-iii (both Hellenistic); cf. also J.N. Davidson in F.D. Harvey and J. Wilkins ed. *The Rivals of Aristophanes* (London/Swansea, 2000) 50-51.

987 There were actually *two* types of game played with *pettoi*, one being (like backgammon) a game of mixed skill and chance, the other a war-game of pure skill, whose most popular variety, *poleis*, seems to have most resembled draughts/checkers; see R.G. Austin, *Antiquity* 14 (1940) 257-271, and L. Kurke, *CP* 94 (1999) 247-267, esp. 255-8.

1026 For "that he knew nothing of the facts about which" read "that he could not affirm the truth of the facts to which". This procedure (1) is first mentioned in Isaeus 9, which cannot be earlier than 371, and it is unlikely to have existed before the introduction, in 378, of the rule whereby all depositions used in a trial had to be submitted in writing in advance; hence the reference here is almost certainly to procedure (2).

1106 W.J. Slater, *CQ* 49 (1999) 508-9, points out that "harbour" was a euphemism/metaphor for "brothel", comparing Eupolis fr. 55; Plautus, *Asinaria* 159, 241-2.

THE COMPLETE ARISTOPHANES

edited by Alan H. Sommerstein

1. ACHARNIANS

2. KNIGHTS

3. CLOUDS

4. WASPS

5. PEACE

6. BIRDS

7. LYSISTRATA

8. THESMOPHORIAZUSAE

9. FROGS

10. ECCLESIAZUSAE

11. WEALTH & Addenda to the previous volumes

Indexes *in preparation*

For full details of these and other volumes in the Aris & Phillips Classical Texts series, please write to the publishers or consult our website:

www.arisandphillips.com